The Penguin Book of
Irish Short Stories

EDITED BY
BENEDICT KIELY

PENGUIN BOOKS

PENGUIN BOOKS

Published by the Penguin Group
Penguin Books Ltd, 80 Strand, London WC2R ORL, England
Penguin Group (USA) Inc., 375 Hudson Street, New York, New York 10014, USA
Penguin Group (Canada), 90 Eglinton Avenue East, Suite 700, Toronto, Ontario, Canada M4P 2Y3
(a division of Pearson Penguin Canada Inc.)
Penguin Ireland, 25 St Stephen's Green, Dublin 2, Ireland (a division of Penguin Books Ltd)
Penguin Group (Australia), 250 Camberwell Road, Camberwell, Victoria 3124, Australia
(a division of Pearson Australia Group Pty Ltd)
Penguin Books India Pvt Ltd, 11 Community Centre, Panchsheel Park, New Delhi – 110 017, India
Penguin Group (NZ), 67 Apollo Drive, Rosedale, Auckland 0632, New Zealand
(a division of Pearson New Zealand Ltd)
Penguin Books (South Africa) (Pty) Ltd, 24 Sturdee Avenue, Rosebank,
Johannesburg 2196, South Africa

Penguin Books Ltd, Registered Offices: 80 Strand, London WC2R ORL, England

www.penguin.com

First published in Penguin Books 1981
Reissued in this edition 2011

2

This selection copyright © Penguin Books, 1981
Introduction copyright © Benedict Kiely, 1981
All rights reserved

This edition produced for The Book People Ltd,
Hall Wood Avenue, Haydock, St Helens WA11 9UL

The acknowledgements on pages 13 and 14 constitute an extension of this copyright page

Printed in Great Britain by Clays Ltd, St Ives plc

ISBN: 978-0-241-95545-1

www.greenpenguin.co.uk

CONTENTS

INTRODUCTION

Frank O'Connor, who had every right to speak on the matter, said that the Irish short story began with George Moore's collection, *The Untilled Field*. He meant the modern Irish short story and he knew as well as, or better than, anybody else that there had been short stories and long stories, and short stories that were parts of long stories, in Ireland and elsewhere since the word of King Goll, who later went crazy, was law from Ith to Emen. O'Connor in his later years superbly used radio and T.V. to offer his own stories not to the eye but to the ear, thereby going back to the method and style of any teller of folk-tales between the fire and the wall: a method and style in vogue in Gaelic places for longer than we know, and still surviving, and in full strength in the early 1940s when, in Rann na Feirsde in the Rosses of Donegal, I heard Johnny Shemisin tell the story of the cards of the gambler. In the same place my good friend Mici Sheain Neill had his own version of the story but, delighting in virtuosity, he can give you either version, faultlessly and from memory.

The classical saga literature overflows with delectable tales. My choice would have been the strange, colourful story of Iubadan the Dwarf, 'The Death of Fergus MacLeide', to be found most conveniently in that precious book, Cross and Slover's *Ancient Irish Tales*. But it is too long for inclusion, a complaint that will recur. Lady Gregory's retelling of another ancient tale in her Kiltartanese, or peasant, style seems a fair compromise between what was desirable and what was possible. Her Kiltartanese, indeed, has been much and wrongfully abused, for she did, at her best, make the saga literature available and eminently readable, and this fragment from the *Fiannaiocht*, the hero tales of Fionn and his men, can take its place anywhere as one of the most exquisitely true of all love stories.

The sagas survived; the current of the folk-tale ran underground into our own time. But Irish prose-fiction, properly so called and written in English (there were reasons that had nothing to do with literature why it was not being written in

Irish), begins with the start of the nineteenth century, with, to be exact, Maria Edgeworth's *Castle Rackrent* and, more importantly, William Carleton's *Traits and Stories of the Irish Peasantry*. The novel and the novella predominate during this period and I have picked, as carefully as I could, on three pieces that seem to me revelatory of the Irish mind of the era, and still valuable. I have passed over Charles Lever and Samuel Lover whose work is readily available elsewhere, and Crofton Croker who was a middling folklorist, and Sheridan Le Fanu who is off the main track and whose Gothic collection, *In A Glass Darkly*, is reasonably accessible.

The first of the three that I have selected is 'Wildgoose Lodge'. Although there are many lighter and happier moments in other works by Carleton, yet 'Wildgoose Lodge' may match with the mood and background of our times, even if that pitiable tragedy seems almost tolerable when compared with the current, continuing horror in the north-east of Ireland.

Stephen Gwynn is remembered now, if at all, as a biographer and as the traveller who wrote such a fine nostalgic book as *Highways and Byways in Donegal and Antrim*, but the strong story of his that I include does tell us a good deal about the Irish mind – then and now. Jane Barlow I might personally have preferred to Somerville and Ross, except that the Irish horse is a most important man, or woman, and must be allowed to speak, and no one ever helped him, or her, better to do so than those devoted female cousins.

But when all that is said, Frank O'Connor was right: God's plenty came after George Moore, but was influenced much less by him than by that other fringe people, the Russians. (Or is it that they only *used* to be considered a fringe people?) James Joyce said quite nastily that *Vain Fortune* was the best novel George Moore had written – nastily, because *Vain Fortune* was a novel about a failed artist. (The Irish, as the most honest of Englishmen said, are an honest people: they never speak well of each other.) And it is an embarrassing plenty for the anthologist who still has to move and breathe in a small country.

The fiction of George Moore that I would have preferred to include would be the odd, odd story of Albert Nobbs from

Celibate Lives, or any one of three that I can think of from *A Story-Teller's Holiday*. But 'Albert Nobbs' is too long, and to pick one out of *A Story-Teller's Holiday*, in which the episodes are indeed also lengthy, would be to damage a framework and a continuity.

W. B. Yeats said that what Chekhov had done for Russia, Frank O'Connor was doing for Ireland: a fair enough if facile comment. It does serve to point to the influence on O'Connor of the Russians, particularly Chekhov and Babel. They had their influence also on Sean O'Faolain, although he responded more vividly, it would seem to me, to the French: Maupassant, Daudet and that very-French Russian, Turgenev. O'Connor and Sean O'Faolain are two of the four pre-eminent names in the modern Irish short story. The other two are Mary Lavin and Liam O'Flaherty. And before O'Faolain and O'Connor, Daniel Corkery had been aware of the Russians and, before Corkery, that much-underestimated novelist, Patrick Augustine Sheehan – underestimated because, I feel, he was a Catholic priest and because also he had the misfortune to become a figure of national piety.

The names of those four masters of the *genre* and of the many others who have gathered around them over the last thirty or forty years do raise the oft-repeated (at least in Ireland) and rather wearying question: Do the Irish have, in relation to anybody else, any special capacity for the short story? O'Connor, perhaps, thought they had, and was prepared to argue that, while we were good at the short story, we were not any great shakes at the novel (see his book *The Lonely Voice*). This, against a lot of obviously contrary evidence. He even seemed to suggest that Mr Joyce may have lost his proper vocation when one particular short story got out of hand and ended up as a rather long novel. It is a theory that gains much from his eminent and mellifluous voice and that gains by being repeated, much as you make a book a bestseller by saying it is so; and some day a special sort of computer may satisfactorily work it out, by which time nobody may be interested any more in stories, short or long.

But the richness is there and that, as I have said, creates

its problems for the unfortunate anthologist. Space, unless you're in the Away Out There, is limited.

To use stories that have not been used in other anthologies, and only for that reason, is often to misrepresent the author and decrease the value of your own selection. In Tipperary they say that they don't have to pick a hurling team for the all-Ireland final, any fifteen young fellows from any crossroads will do; and with some poets and short-story writers one might almost pick blindfold: O'Faolain, O'Connor, Lavin, O'Flaherty. My selection, by the way, allows for two by O'Flaherty because, as may be seen, he more than any of the others writes of two worlds. But with other writers the choice is more limited, and there may even be men of one story as there are men of one poem. There is also a personal thing that neither the anthologist himself nor anybody else can account for.

For the anthologist, much more than the writer, is at the mercy of his critics, and few of them can be expected to agree totally with him, for one or more or many more good reasons. Worse still, he may even be at the mercy of his friends. The reader and purchaser of anthologies are at the mercy of the anthologist. So for all that is not here I apologize, first of all to myself since I have been the first to feel the deprivation. But for what is here it is not necessary to apologize: there isn't a story here that I wouldn't gladly read or re-read anywhere.

This being the case, I can now close my eyes and compile in my mind that other anthology, of those who are not here because, for example, their work is easily accessible elsewhere or because they are better known for work in other forms: neither of them very good reasons. The only sufficient reason is space, or rather the lack of it, a reason that, regrettably, has much influenced me. So, for my reader's guidance, I add here a formidable, wide and yet (particularly in as far as the younger writers now being published by David Marcus through the *Irish Press* and the *Poolbeg Press* are concerned) an incomplete list. To mention a few missing names: W. B. Yeats, James Stephens, Samuel Beckett, Lynn Doyle, Norah Hoult, Seamus O'Kelly (whose one masterpiece, *The Weaver's Grave*, is a short novel), Flann O'Brien, Brendan Behan, Joseph O'Connor,

Richard Power, Walter Macken, K. Arnold Price, Edward
Sheehy, Maurice Kennedy, John B. Keane, Kevin Casey, Maeve
Kelly, Desmond Hogan, Emma Cooke, Michael Curtin, Lucille
Redmond, Michael Coady, F. D. Sheridan, Maura Treacy, Kate
Cruise O'Brien and, perhaps, myself.

As in the case of F. D. Sheridan's 'Captives', Niall Quinn's
'Voyovic' and Anthony Glavin's 'One for Sorrow' appeared too
late for my purposes.

Irish language revivalists, among whom I may tentatively
include myself, may rightly object that no translations appear
here from modern Irish. Yet I feel that to include a few token
stories in translation would give a shabby idea of the quite
considerable achievement of writers in modern Irish. Better to
do a complete anthology and then translate it for the benefit
of those who are interested and who cannot read the stories
in the original. To print translations is, anyway, a poor way
to aid a language revival.

BENEDICT KIELY, 1981

The Daughter of King Under-Wave

LADY GREGORY

ONE snowy night of winter the Fianna were come into the house after their hunting. And about midnight they heard a knocking at the door, and there came in a woman very wild and ugly, and her hair hanging to her heels. She went to the place Finn was lying, and she asked him to let her in under the border of his covering. But when he saw her so strange and so ugly and so wild-looking he would not let her in. She gave a great cry then, and she went to where Oisin was, and asked him to let her shelter under the border of his covering. But Oisin refused her the same way. Then she gave another great scream, and she went over where Diarmuid was. 'Let me in,' she said, 'under the border of your covering.' Diarmuid looked at her, and he said: 'You are strange-looking and wild and ugly, and your hair is down to your heels. But come in for all that,' he said.

So she came in under the border of his covering.

'O Dairmuid,' she said then, 'I have been travelling over sea and ocean through the length of seven years, and in all that time I never got shelter any night till this night. And let me to the warmth of the fire now,' she said. So Diarmuid brought her over to the fire, and all the Fianna that were sitting there went away from it seeing her so ugly and so dreadful to look at. And she was not long at the fire when she said: 'Let me go under the warmth of the covering with you now.' 'It is asking too much you are,' said Diarmuid; 'first it was to come under the border you asked, and then to come to the fire, and now it is under the bed-covering with me you want to be. But for all that you may come,' he said.

So she came in under the covering, and he turned a fold of it between them. But it was not long till he looked at her, and what he saw was a beautiful young woman beside him, and she asleep. He called to the others then to come over, and he said: 'Is not this the most beautiful woman that ever was seen?' 'She is that,' they said, and they covered her up and did not awaken her.

But after a while she stirred, and she said: 'Are you awake, Diarmuid?' 'I am awake,' he said. 'Where would you like to see the best house built that ever was built?' she said. 'Up there on the hillside, if I had my choice,' said he, and with that he fell asleep.

And in the morning two men of the Fianna came in, and they said they were after seeing a great house up on the hill, where there was not a house before. 'Rise up, Diarmuid,' said the strange woman then; 'do not be lying there any longer, but go up to your house, and look out now and see it,' she said. So he looked out and he saw the great house that was ready, and he said: 'I will go to it, if you will come along with me.' 'I will do that,' she said, 'if you will make me a promise not to say to me three times what way I was when I came to you.' 'I will never say it to you for ever,' said Diarmuid.

They went up then to the house, and it was ready for them, with food and servants; and everything they could wish for they had it. They stopped there for three days, and when the three days were ended, she said: 'You are getting to be sorrowful because you are away from your comrades of the Fianna.' 'I am not sorrowful indeed,' said Diarmuid. 'It will be best for you to go to them; and your food and your drink will be no worse when you come back than they are now,' said she. 'Who will take care of my greyhound bitch and her three pups if I go?' said Diarmuid. 'There is no fear for them,' said she.

So when he heard that, he took leave of her and went back to the Fianna, and there was a great welcome before him. But for all that they were not well pleased but were someway envious, Diarmuid to have got that grand house and her love from the woman they themselves had turned away.

Now as to the woman, she was outside the house for a

while after Diarmuid going away, and she saw Finn, son of Cumhal, coming towards her, and she bade him welcome. 'You are vexed with me, Queen?' he said. 'I am not indeed,' she said; 'and come in now and take a drink of wine from me.' 'I will go in if I get my request,' said Finn. 'What request is there that you would not get?' said she. 'It is what I am asking, one of the pups of Diarmuid's greyhound bitch.' 'That is no great thing to ask,' she said; 'and whichever one you choose of them you may bring it away.'

So he got the pup, and he brought it away with him.

At the fall of night Diarmuid came back to the house, and the greyhound met him at the door and gave a yell when she saw him, and he looked for the pups, and one of them was gone. There was anger on him then, and he said to the woman: 'If you had brought to mind the way you were when I let you in, and your hair hanging, you would not have let the pup be brought away from me.' 'You ought not to say that, Diarmuid,' said she. 'I ask your pardon for saying it,' said Diarmuid. And they forgave one another, and he spent the night in the house.

On the morrow Diarmuid went back again to his comrades, and the woman stopped at the house, and after a while she saw Oisin coming towards her. She gave him a welcome, and asked him into the house, and he said he would come if he would get his request. And what he asked was another of the pups of the greyhound.

So she gave him that, and he went away bringing the pup with him. And when Diarmuid came back that night the greyhound met him, and she cried out twice. And he knew that another of the pups was gone, and he said to the greyhound, and the woman standing there: 'If she had remembered the way she was when she came to me, she would not have let the pup be brought away.'

The next day he went back again to the Fianna, and when he was gone, the woman saw Caoilte coming towards her, and he would not come in to take a drink from her till he had got the promise of one of the pups the same as the others.

And when Diarmuid came back that night the greyhound met him and gave three yells, the most terrible that ever were

heard. There was great anger on him then, when he saw all
the pups gone, and he said the third time: 'If this woman
remembered the way she was when I found her, and her hair
down to her heels, she would not have let the pup go.' 'O
Diarmuid, what is it you are after saying?' she said. He asked
forgiveness of her then, and he thought to go into the house,
but it was gone and the woman was gone on the moment, and
it was on the bare ground he awoke on the morrow. There
was great sorrow on him then, and he said he would search
in every place till he would find her again.

So he set out through the lonely valleys, and the first thing
he saw was the greyhound lying dead, and he put her on his
shoulder and would not leave her because of the love he had
for her. And after a while he met with a cowherd, and he
asked him did he see a woman going the way. 'I saw a woman
early in the morning of yesterday, and she walking hard,' said
the cowherd. 'What way was she going?' said Diarmuid. 'Down
that path below to the strand, and I saw her no more after
that,' he said.

So he followed the path she took down to the strand till he
could go no farther, and then he saw a ship, and he leaned on
the handle of his spear and made a light leap on to the ship,
and it went on till it came to land, and then he got out and
lay down on the side of a hill and fell asleep, and when he
awoke there was no ship to be seen. 'It is a pity for me to be
here,' he said, 'for I see no way of getting from it again.'

But after a while he saw a boat coming, and a man in the
boat rowing it, and he went down and got into the boat, and
brought the greyhound with him. And the boat went out over
the sea, and then down below it; and Diarmuid, when he went
down, found himself on a plain. And he went walking along
it, and it was not long before he met with a drop of blood. He
took it up and put it in a napkin. 'It is the greyhound lost
this,' he said. And after a while he met with another drop of
blood, and then with a third, and he put them in the napkin.
And after that again he saw a woman, and she gathering rushes
as if she had lost her wits.

He went towards her and asked her what news had she. 'I

cannot tell it till I gather the rushes,' she said. 'Be telling it while you are gathering them,' said Diarmuid. 'There is great haste on me,' she said. 'What is this place where we are?' said Diarmuid. 'It is Land-Under-Wave,' said she. 'And what use have you for the rushes when they are gathered?' 'The daughter of King Under-Wave is come home,' she said, 'and she was for seven years under enchantment, and there is sickness on her now, and all the physicians are gathered together and none of them can do her any good, and a bed of rushes is what she finds the wholesomest.' 'Will you show me where the king's daughter is?' said Diarmuid. 'I will do that,' said the woman; 'I will put you in the sheaf of rushes, and I will put the rushes under you and over you, and I will carry you to her on my back.' 'That is a thing you cannot do,' said Diarmuid. But she put the rushes about him, and lifted him on her back, and when she got to the room she let down the bundle. 'O come here to me,' said the daughter of King Under-Wave, and Diarmuid went over to her, and they took one another's hands, and were very joyful at that meeting. 'Three parts of my sickness is gone from me now,' she said then; 'but I am not well yet, and I never will be, for every time I thought of you, Diarmuid, on my journey, I lost a drop of blood of my heart.' 'I have got those three drops here in this napkin,' said Diarmuid, 'and take them now in a drink and you will be healed of your sickness.' 'They would do nothing for me,' she said, 'since I have not the one thing in the world that I want, and that is the thing I will never get,' she said. 'What thing is that?' said Diarmuid. 'It is the thing you will never get, nor any man in the world,' she said, 'for it is a long time they have failed to get it.' 'If it is in any place on the whole ridge of the world I will get it,' said Diarmuid. 'It is three draughts from the cup of the King of Magh an Ionganaidh, the Plain of Wonder,' she said, 'and no man ever got it or ever will get it.' 'Tell me where that cup is to be found,' said Diarmuid, 'for there are not as many men as will keep it from me on the whole ridge of the world.' 'That country is not far from the boundary of my father's country,' she said; 'but there is a little river between, and you would be sailing on that river in a ship, having the

wind behind it, for a year and a day before you would reach
to the Plain of Wonder.'

Diarmuid set out then, and he came to the little river, and
he was a good while walking beside it, and he saw no way
across it. But at last he saw a low-sized, reddish man that was
standing in the middle of the river. 'You are in straits, Diarmuid, grandson of Duibhne,' he said; 'and come here and put
your foot in the palm of my hand and I will bring you
through.' Diarmuid did as he bade him, and put his foot in
the red man's palm, and he brought him across the river. 'It is
going to the King of the Plain of Wonder you are,' he said,
'to bring away his cup from him; and I myself will go with you.'

They went on then till they came to the king's dun, and
Diarmuid called out that the cup should be sent out to him,
or else champions to fight with him should be sent out. It was
not the cup that was sent out, but twice eight hundred fighting
men; and in three hours there was not one of them left to
stand against him. Then twice nine hundred better fighters
again were sent out against him, and within four hours there
was not one of them left to stand against him. Then the king
himself came out, and he stood in the great door, and he said:
'Where did the man come from that has brought destruction on
the whole of my kingdom?' 'I will tell you that,' said he; 'I am
Diarmuid, a man of the Fianna of Ireland.' 'It is a pity you
have not sent a messenger telling me that,' said the king, 'and
I would not have spent my men upon you; for seven years
before you were born it was put in the prophecy that you
would come to destroy them. And what is it you are asking
now?' he said. 'It is the cup of healing from your own hand I
am asking,' said Diarmuid. 'No man ever got that cup from
me but yourself,' said the king, 'but it is easy for me to give
it to you, whether or not there is healing in it.'

Then the King of the Plain of Wonder gave Diarmuid the
cup, and they parted from one another; and Diarmuid went
on till he came to the river, and it was then he thought of the
red man, that he had given no thought to while he was at the
king's house. But he was there before him, and took his foot
in the palm of his hand and brought him over the river. 'I

know where it is you are going, Diarmuid,' he said then; 'it is
to heal the daughter of King Under-Wave that you have given
your love to. And it is to a well I give you the signs of you
should go,' he said, 'and bring a share of the water of that
well with you. And when you come where the woman is, it is
what you have to do, to put that water in the cup, and one of
the drops of blood in it, and she will drink it, and the same
with the second drop and the third, and her sickness will be
gone from her that time. But there is another thing will be
gone along with it,' he said, 'and that is the love you have for
her.'

'That will not go from me,' said Diarmuid. 'It will go from
you,' said the man; 'and it will be best for you to make no
secret of it, for she will know, and the king will know, that
you think no more of her then than of any other woman. And
King Under-Wave will come to you,' he said, 'and will offer you
great riches for healing his daughter. But take nothing from
him,' he said, 'but ask only a ship to bring you home again to
Ireland. And do you know who am I myself?' he said. 'I do
not know,' said Diarmuid. 'I am the messenger from beyond
the world,' he said; 'and I came to your help because your own
heart is hot to come to the help of another.'

So Diarmuid did as he bade him, and he brought the water
and the cup and the drops of blood to the woman, and she
drank them, and at the third draught she was healed. And no
sooner was she healed than the love he had for her was gone,
and he turned away from her. 'O Diarmuid,' she said, 'your love
is gone from me.' 'O, it is gone indeed,' said he.

Then there was music made in the whole place, and the
lamenting was stopped, because of the healing of the king's
daughter. And as to Diarmuid, he would take no reward and
he would not stop there, but he asked for a ship to bring him
home to Ireland, to Finn and the Fianna. And when he came
where they were, there was a joyful welcome before him.

The Cards of the Gambler

TRADITIONAL (JOHNNY SHEMISIN)

(translated by the Editor)

THE gambler, like the rest of his neighbours, had a hut of a house and a small bit of land. In spite of that he was pitifully poor. Wherever he went he'd have a pack of cards in his pocket. Whoever he met he'd coax him to gamble. He'd sit all night card-playing and lie all day asleep, and in that way his portion of land lay idle. While his neighbours were getting on in the world, he was going backwards.

He was gambling one night until he lost the last penny in his possession. He came home with the dawning of day and he was broken, bruised, and sorrowful, without money or the hope of money. Coming to the house, he found the neighbour women gathered in, dancing attendance on his wife, who was lying in danger of death. A young son had been born when he was card-playing away from his home.

The women asked the gambler to get the priest to baptize the child. He thought to himself that that was the least he could do, so off with him, and it wasn't long he was going until he saw a young man drawing towards him. By the shape of the young man he knew him for a stranger. He eyed him from the top of his head to the sole of his foot, and it seemed to him from the countenance and complexion of that young man that he had never seen anyone so handsome.

'You're going for the priest to baptize your child,' says the stranger.

'I am,' says the gambler, 'but how do you know where I am going or what is my business?'

'I am God,' said the stranger. 'Turn back and I will baptize your child.'

'I will not turn back,' said the gambler. 'If you're God you're not giving me a fair deal. When my neighbours are getting on in the world I'm going backwards, and on that account you'll have nothing to do with my child.'

He walked on, and it wasn't long until he saw another stranger drawing towards him. It was a big, long skeleton of a man, black-headed, with a sallow skin and a face like a corpse, just skin and bones. The gambler thought: 'There's little resemblance between yourself and God.' They saluted each other.

'You're going for the priest to baptize your child,' says the stranger.

'I am,' says the gambler. 'But I'd like to find out how you know where I'm going.'

'I am Death,' says the stranger. 'No person can come to the world or leave the world without my knowing. God met you before I met you and He offered to baptize your child. You should have accepted His offer. Turn back now and I'll be godfather to your child.'

The gambler and Death turned back until they came to the place where God was waiting for them. The three went to the gambler's house and God baptized the child and Death stood sponsor. Then God went away.

Says Death to the gambler: 'It wasn't right for you to let God leave you without asking a request from Him.'

The gambler went off after God, and when he came as far as Him, God asked him what he wanted.

'I am seeking a request from you,' says the gambler.

'What is the request?' says God.

'Give me victory in card-playing over the whole world,' says the gambler.

'You will get that,' says God.

The gambler, satisfied, turned towards home. Death met him on the way and asked him had he seen God.

'I saw God and I got my request,' says the gambler.

'What was that request?' says Death.

'A good request,' says the gambler; 'that I should have victory in card-playing over the whole world. And now I will win again as much money as I ever lost, and more besides.'

'It's a bad request,' says Death. 'Follow Him again and ask a good request from Him.'

The gambler set off again until he came as far as God, and he asked another request from Him.

'What is the request?' says God.

'Give me victory in healing over the whole world,' says the gambler.

'You will get that,' says God.

Joyfully the gambler returned, and when Death met him he told Death about the other request he'd been granted.

'It's a bad request,' says Death. 'Follow Him again and ask a good request from Him this time.'

The gambler went off again after God and asked Him for a third request.

'What is the request?' says God.

'Growing in my garden,' says the gambler, 'I have an apple-tree, and when I'm out card-playing by night the children of the neighbours steal the apples. I ask that if any person puts his hand on an apple his hand will stick to the apple and the apple to the tree until it is my will to set them free.'

'You will get the request,' says God.

Then the gambler went back to Death and said that he'd got a good request this time.

'What is it?' says Death.

'I won't tell anybody,' says the gambler.

'Fair enough,' says Death. 'You now have victory in healing over the whole world and that suits me poorly. I'll make a bargain with you about that request. When you go into a house in which a person is ailing, if I am sitting at the foot of the bed, heal him, but if I'm sitting at the head of the bed, let me have him – or I'll take yourself instead.'

'It's a bargain,' says the gambler.

Death went off about his business and the gambler went on card-playing, as he was accustomed. He won as much money as he had ever lost, and more besides, until in the end he could find nobody to play with him. Then he took to the doctoring.

He kept healing sick people until he had his riches made. His reputation went farther than his foot ever walked, and his fame was that he was the greatest doctor in the world.

There was a rich man living in Spain and he fell ill. The Spanish doctors attended him, but they weren't able to cure him. His relatives came and advised his wife to send for the gambler to attend her husband. They got ready a ship and a ship's crew and sailed for Ireland to bring the gambler over to Spain.

When the gambler entered the room where the sick man was lying, he found Death sitting at the head of the bed. Death scowled at the gambler and the gambler scowled back at Death.

'Can you heal my husband?' says the great lady.

'I cannot,' says the gambler.

' 'Tis a pity we sent to Ireland for you,' says she, 'if you came over only to put a scowl on you.'

She showed him a box filled with gold.

'If you heal him, I'll give you the contents of that box,' says she.

The gambler coveted the gold. He asked her to bring in four of the servant boys. When they came in he asked them to grip the four posts of the bed and to turn it around. They did that, and Death was left sitting at the foot of the bed. Then the gambler gave a healing herb to the sick man, and he rose up as sound and healthy as he had ever been.

The servants carried the box of gold to the ship for the gambler, but Death came after them on the road and gripped the gambler by the throat.

'O friend, for the sweet sake of Christ,' says the gambler, 'I implore you to allow me to return to Ireland to give the gold to my family and to make my will between them the way they will not be quarrelling on that account.'

'You can have what you implore,' says Death. 'But it won't be long until I'm with you again.'

The gambler sailed for Ireland with his portion of gold. The night he returned home he was talking and chatting about his adventures until the candle burned down to the last inch.

Then he carried the inch of candle to the bedside and he lay down. When he was stretched on the bed Death gripped him by the throat.

'O friend, for the sweet sake of Christ,' says the gambler, 'I haven't yet made my will. I ask you for a space of time until the inch of the candle is burnt.'

'You may have it,' says Death.

The gambler puffed at the candle and quenched the flame. 'That inch won't be burned for seven years,' says he.

'You tricked me,' says Death. 'But let it be so for seven years.'

Death didn't come back to the gambler until the seven years were spent. But no matter how long the day is, night comes at the end. A night at the end of the seven years when the gambler was lying on his bed, Death gripped him again by the throat.

'You must come with me now, gambler,' says he.

'O friend, for the sweet sake of Christ,' says the gambler, 'the thought sets me mad with the thirst. If you would pull an apple in my orchard and give it to me before you take me with you, perhaps it would ease that devouring thirst.'

Death went out to the apple-tree, but when he put his hand on an apple he stuck fast to it and the apple stuck fast to the tree. The gambler leaped out of his bed.

'You'll be there until I feel like releasing you,' says he.

'So that,' says Death, 'is the third request you got from God and kept a secret from me. Let me go now and I won't come near you until the end of another seven years.'

The gambler freed the hand of Death and didn't see him again for seven years. At the end of that time Death came, gripped his claw of a hand on the gambler's throat and gave him a good choking.

'O friend, for the sweet sake of Christ,' says the gambler, 'you're too hard on me. I ask only one other favour from you, and it isn't for life I'm asking. Allow me to say the Lord's Prayer – a thing I didn't say ever since I commenced the gambling.'

'You may have that favour,' says Death.

'Then I'll never say the prayer,' says the gambler.

'I see,' says Death, 'that you want to be alive after me and after the world.'

Death went away and seven years went round and the gambler was getting richer every day. He was one day walking out for pleasure when he saw a young boy sitting crying on the margin of the main road.

'What's wrong with you?' says the gambler.

'They won't let me go to Communion,' says he, 'because I don't know my prayers.'

'Why doesn't your father or mother teach you your prayers?'

'My father and my mother are dead and I am an orphan,' says the boy.

The gambler pitied him. 'I'll teach you your prayers,' says he.

He began on the Lord's Prayer and the boy recited it after him. When the prayer was said, Death stood up out of the shape of the boy and gripped the gambler by the throat.

'You'll trick me no longer,' says he – and he choked him dry.

The gambler took with him to hell his pack of cards. Himself and the devils were gambling until he didn't leave a square inch of hell in their possession. Then they banded together against him and banished him and his pack of cards.

The gambler went off until he came to the gates of heaven. But the gates were closed against him and he wouldn't be allowed to enter. He sat outside on a rock and began to play patience. Peter of the Keys took pity on him.

In the end Peter opened the gate and asked him in because of the pity he had shown to the orphan when he thought he didn't know his prayers. The gambler with a glad heart threw his cards from him and he walked in at the gates of heaven.

The cards of the gambler are spread on a rock at the gates of heaven from that day to this, and they may be seen by any person who goes that road.

Wildgoose Lodge

WILLIAM CARLETON

I HAD read the anonymous summons, but, from its general import, I believed it to be one of those special meetings convened for some purpose affecting the usual objects and proceedings of the body; at least, the terms in which it was conveyed to me had nothing extraordinary or mysterious in them beyond the simple fact that it was not to be a general but a select meeting. This mark of confidence flattered me, and I determined to attend punctually. I was, it is true, desired to keep the circumstance entirely to myself; but there was nothing startling in this, for I had often received summonses of a similar nature. I therefore resolved to attend, according to the letter of my instructions, 'on the next night, at the solemn hour of midnight, to deliberate and act upon such matters as should then and there be submitted to my consideration'. The morning after I received this message, I arose and resumed my usual occupations; but from whatever cause it may have proceeded, I felt a sense of approaching evil hang heavily upon me. The beats of my pulse were languid, and an indefinable feeling of anxiety pervaded my whole spirit; even my face was pale, and my eye so heavy that my father and brothers concluded me to be ill; an opinion which I thought at the time to be correct, for I felt exactly that kind of depression which precedes a severe fever. I could not understand what I experienced; nor can I yet, except by supposing that there is in human nature some mysterious faculty by which, in coming calamities, the dread of some fearful evil is anticipated, and that it is possible to catch a dark presentiment of the sensations which they subsequently produce. For my part, I can neither analyse nor define it; but on that day I knew it by painful experience, and so have a thousand others in similar circumstances.

It was about the middle of winter. The day was gloomy and tempestuous almost beyond any other I remember: dark clouds rolled over the hills about me, and a close, sleet-like rain fell in slanting drifts that chased each other rapidly towards the earth on the course of the blast. The outlying cattle sought the closest and calmest corners of the fields for shelter; the trees and young groves were tossed about, for the wind was so unusually high that it swept in hollow gusts through them with that hoarse murmur which deepens so powerfully on the mind the sense of dreariness and desolation.

As the shades of night fell, the storm, if possible, increased. The moon was half gone, and only a few stars were visible by glimpses, as a rush of wind left a temporary opening in the sky. I had determined, if the storm should not abate, to incur any penalty rather than attend the meeting; but the appointed hour was distant, and I resolved to be decided by the future state of the night.

Ten o'clock came, but still there was no change; eleven passed, and on opening the door to observe if there were any likelihood of its clearing up, a blast of wind, mingled with rain, nearly blew me off my feet. At length it was approaching to the hour of midnight; and on examining a third time, I found it had calmed a little, and no longer rained.

I instantly got my oak stick, muffled myself in my greatcoat, strapped my hat about my ears, and as the place of meeting was only a quarter of a mile distant, I presently set out.

The appearance of the heavens was lowering and angry, particularly in that point where the light of the moon fell against the clouds from a seeming chasm in them, through which alone she was visible. The edges of this chasm were faintly bronzed, but the dense body of the masses that hung piled on each side of her was black and impenetrable to sight. In no other point of the heavens was there any part of the sky visible – a deep veil of clouds overhung the horizon – yet was the light sufficient to give occasional glimpses of the rapid shifting which took place in this dark canopy, and of the

tempestuous agitation with which the midnight storm swept
to and fro beneath it.

At length I arrived at a long slated house situated in a
solitary part of the neighbourhood; a little below it ran a
small stream, which was now swollen above its banks, and
rushing with mimic roar over the flat meadows beside it. The
appearance of the bare slated building in such a night was
particularly sombre; and to those, like me, who knew the
purpose to which it was usually devoted, it was, or ought to
have been, peculiarly so. There it stood, silent and gloomy,
without any appearance of human life or enjoyment about or
within it. As I approached, the moon once more had broken
out of the clouds, and shone dimly upon the wet, glittering
slates and windows with a death-like lustre, that gradually
faded away as I left the point of observation and entered the
folding-door. It was the parish chapel.

The scene which presented itself here was in keeping not
only with the external appearance of the house, but with the
darkness, the storm, and the hour, which was now a little after
midnight. About eighty persons were sitting in dead silence
upon the circular steps of the altar. They did not seem to move;
and as I entered and advanced, the echo of my footsteps rang
through the building with a lonely distinctness, which added
to the solemnity and mystery of the circumstances about me.
The windows were secured with shutters on the inside; and
on the altar a candle was lighted, which burned dimly amid
the surrounding darkness, and lengthened the shadow of the
altar itself, and those of six or seven persons who stood on its
upper steps, until they mingled in the obscurity which shrouded
the lower end of the chapel. The faces of the men who sat on
the altar-steps were not distinctly visible, yet their prominent
and more characteristic features were in sufficient relief, and I
observed that some of the most malignant and reckless spirits
in the parish were assembled. In the eyes of those who stood
at the altar, and whom I knew to be invested with authority
over the others, I could perceive gleams of some latent and
ferocious purpose, kindled, as I soon observed, into a fiercer
expression of vengeance by the additional excitement of ardent

spirits, with which they had stimulated themselves to a point of determination that mocked at the apprehension of all future responsibility, either in this world or the next.

The welcome which I received on joining them was far different from the boisterous good-humour that used to mark our greetings on other occasions: just a nod of the head from this or that person, on the part of those who sat, with a *ghud dhemur tha thu?* in a suppressed voice, even below a common whisper; but from the standing group, who were evidently the projectors of the enterprise, I received a convulsive grasp of the hand, accompanied by a fierce and desperate look, that seemed to search my eye and countenance, to try if I were a person not likely to shrink from whatever they had resolved to execute. It is surprising to think of the powerful expression which a moment of intense interest or great danger is capable of giving to the eye, the features, and the slightest actions, especially in those whose station in society does not require them to constrain nature, by the force of social courtesies, into habits that conceal their natural emotions. None of the standing group spoke; but as each of them wrung my hand in silence, his eye was fixed on mine with an expression of drunken confidence and secrecy, and an insolent determination not to be gainsaid without peril. If looks could be translated with certainty, they seemed to say, 'We are bound upon a project of vengeance, and if you do not join us, remember that we can revenge.' Along with this grasp they did not forget to remind me of the common bond by which we were united, for each man gave me the secret grip of Ribbonism in a manner that made the joints of my fingers ache for some minutes afterwards.

There was one present, however – the highest in authority – whose actions and demeanour were calm and unexcited. He seemed to labour under no unusual influence whatever, but evinced a serenity so placid and philosophical that I attributed the silence of the sitting group, and the restraint which curbed in the outbreaking passions of those who stood, entirely to his presence. He was a schoolmaster, who taught his daily school in that chapel, and acted also, on Sunday, in the capacity of clerk to the priest – an excellent and amiable old man, who knew little of his illegal connections and atrocious conduct.

When the ceremonies of brotherly recognition and friendship were past, the captain (by which title I shall designate the last-mentioned person) stooped, and raising a jar of whiskey on the corner of the altar, held a wine-glass to its neck, which he filled, and, with a calm nod, handed it to me to drink. I shrunk back, with an instinctive horror at the profaneness of such an act, in the house, and on the altar, of God, and peremptorily refused to taste the proffered draught. He smiled mildly at what he considered my superstition, and added quietly, and in a low voice, 'You'll be wantin' it, I'm thinkin', afther the wettin' you got.'

'Wet or dry,' said I –

'Stop, man!' he replied, in the same tone; 'spake low. But why wouldn't you take the whiskey? Sure, there's as holy people to the fore as you; didn't they all take it? An' I wish we may never do worse nor dhrink a harmless glass o' whiskey to keep the cowld out, anyway.'

'Well,' said I, 'I'll jist trust to God and the consequences for the cowld, Paddy, *ma bouchal*; but a blessed dhrop of it won't be crossin' my lips, *avick*; so no more *gosther* about it – dhrink it yourself, if you like. Maybe you want it as much as I do; wherein I've the patthern of a good big coat upon me – so thick, your sowl, that if it was rainin' bullocks, a dhrop wouldn't get under the nap of it.'

He gave a calm but keen glance at me as I spoke.

'Well, Jim,' said he, 'it's a good comrade you've got for the weather that's in it; but, in the manetime, to set you a dacent patthern, I'll just take this myself;' saying which, with the jar still upon its side, and the forefinger of his left hand in its neck, he swallowed the spirits. 'It's the first I dhrank tonight,' he added; 'nor would I dhrink it now, only to show you that I've heart an' spirit to do the thing that we're all bound an' sworn to, when the proper time comes;' after which he laid down the glass, and turned up the jar, with much coolness, upon the altar.

During our conversation those who had been summoned to

this mysterious meeting were pouring in fast; and as each person approached the altar he received from one to two or three glasses of whiskey, according as he chose to limit himself; but, to do them justice, there were not a few of those present who, in spite of their own desire, and the captain's express invitation, refused to taste it in the house of God's worship. Such, however, as were scrupulous he afterwards recommended to take it on the outside of the chapel door, which they did, as by that means the sacrilege of the act was supposed to be evaded.

About one o'clock they were all assembled except six; at least, so the captain asserted, on looking at a written paper.

'Now, boys,' said he, in the same low voice, 'we are all present except the thraitors whose names I am goin' to read to you; not that we are to count thim thraitors till we know whether or not it was in their power to come. Anyhow, the night's terrible; but, boys, you're to know that neither fire, nor wather is to prevint yees when duly summoned to attind a meeting – particularly whin the summons is widout a name, as you have been told that there is always something of consequence to be done thin.'

He then read out the names of those who were absent, in order that the real cause of their absence might be ascertained, declaring that they would be dealt with accordingly. After this, with his usual caution, he shut and bolted the door, and having put the key in his pocket, ascended the steps of the altar, and for some time traversed the little platform from which the priest usually addresses the congregation.

Until this night I had never contemplated the man's countenance with any particular interest; but as he walked the platform I had an opportunity of observing him more closely. He was slight in person, apparently not thirty, and, on a first view, appeared to have nothing remarkable in his dress or features. I, however, was not the only person whose eyes were fixed upon him at that moment; in fact, every one present observed him with equal interest, for hitherto he had kept the object of the meeting perfectly secret, and of course we all felt anxious to know it. It was while he traversed the platform that I scrutinized his features with a hope, if possible, to glean from them some evidence of what was passing within him. I could, however, mark but little, and that little was at first rather from the intelligence which seemed to subsist between him and those whom I have already mentioned as standing against the altar, than from any indication of his own. Their gleaming eyes were fixed upon him with an intensity of savage and demon-like hope which blazed out in flashes of malignant triumph, as, upon turning, he threw a cool but rapid glance at them, to intimate the progress he was making in the subject to which he devoted the undivided energies of his mind. But in the course of his meditation I could observe, on one or two occasions, a dark shade come over his countenance that contracted his brow into a deep furrow, and it was then, for the first time, that I saw the Satanic expression of which his face, by a very slight motion of its muscles, was capable. His hands, during this silence, closed and opened convulsively; his eyes shot out two or three baleful glances, first to his confederates, and afterwards vacantly into the deep gloom of the lower part of the chapel; his teeth ground against each other like those of a man whose revenge burns to reach a distant enemy; and finally, after having wound himself up to a certain determination, his features relapsed into their original calm and undisturbed expression.

At this moment a loud laugh, having something supernatural in it, rang out wildly from the darkness of the chapel: he stopped, and putting his open hand over his brows, peered down into the gloom, and said calmly, in Irish, '*Bee dhu husth; ha nihl anam inh* – Hold your tongue; it is not yet the time.'

Every eye was now directed to the same spot, but in consequence of its distance from the dim light on the altar, none could perceive the person from whom the laugh proceeded. It was by this time near two o'clock in the morning.

He now stood for a few moments on the platform, and his chest heaved with a depth of anxiety equal to the difficulty of the design he wished to accomplish.

'Brothers,' said he – 'for we are all brothers – sworn upon all that's blessed an' holy to obey whatever them that's over us, manin' among ourselves, wishes us to do – are you now ready, in the name of God, upon whose althar I stand, to fulfil yer oaths?'

The words were scarcely uttered, when those who had stood beside the altar during the night sprang from their places, and descending its steps rapidly, turned round, and raising their arms, exclaimed, 'By all that's sacred an' holy, we're willin'!'

In the meantime, those who sat upon the steps of the altar instantly rose, and following the example of those who had just spoken, exclaimed after them, 'To be sure – by all that's sacred an' holy, we're willin'!'

'Now, boys,' said the captain, 'aren't yees big fools for your pains? An' one of yees doesn't know what I mane.'

'You're our captain,' said one of those who had stood at the altar, 'an' has yer ordhers from higher quarthers; of coorse, whatever ye command upon us we're bound to obey you in.'

'Well,' said he, smiling, 'I only wanted to thry yees; an' by the oath yees tuck, there's not a captain in the county has as good a right to be proud of his min as I have. Well, yees won't rue it, maybe, when the right time comes; and for that same rason every one of yees must have a glass from the jar – thim that won't dhrink it in the chapel can dhrink it widout; an' here goes to open the door for them.'

He then distributed another glass to every man who would accept it, and brought the jar afterwards to the chapel door, to satisfy the scruples of those who would not drink within. When this was performed, and all duly excited, he proceeded:

'Now, brothers, you are solemnly sworn to obey me, and I'm sure there's no thraithur here that ud parjure himself for a thrifle; but I'm sworn to obey them that's above me, manin' still among ourselves; an' to show you that I don't scruple to do it, here goes!'

He then turned round, and taking the Missal between his hands, placed it upon the altar. Hitherto every word was uttered in a low, precautionary tone; but on grasping the book, he again turned round, and looking upon his confederates with the same Satanic expression which marked his countenance before, exclaimed, in a voice of deep determination:

'By this sacred an' holy book of God, I will perform the action which we have met this night to accomplish, be that what it may; an' this I swear upon God's book an' God's althar!'

On concluding he struck the book violently with his open hand.

At this moment the candle which burned before him went suddenly out, and the chapel was wrapped in pitchy darkness; the sound as if of rushing wings fell upon our ears; and fifty voices dwelt upon the last words of his oath with wild and supernatural tones, that seemed to echo and to mock what he had sworn. There was a pause, and an exclamation of horror from all present; but the captain was too cool and steady to be disconcerted. He immediately groped about until he got the candle, and proceeding calmly to a remote corner of the chapel, took up a half-burned turf which lay there, and after some trouble, succeeded in lighting it again. He then explained what had taken place; which indeed was easily done, as the candle happened to be extinguished by a pigeon which sat directly above it. The chapel, I should have observed, was at this time, like many country chapels, unfinished inside, and the pigeons of a neighbouring dovecote had built nests among the rafters of the unceiled roof; which circumstance also explained the rushing of the wings, for the birds had been affrighted by the sudden loudness of the noise. The mocking voices were nothing but the echoes, rendered naturally more awful by the scene, the mysterious object of the meeting, and the solemn hour of the night.

When the candle was again lighted, and these startling circumstances accounted for, the persons whose vengeance had been deepening more and more during the night rushed to the altar in a body, where each, in a voice trembling with passionate eagerness, repeated the oath; and as every word was pronounced, the same echoes heightened the wildness of the horrible ceremony by their long and unearthly tones. The countenances of these human tigers were livid with suppressed rage; their knit brows, compressed lips, and kindled eyes fell under the dim light of the taper with an expression calculated to sicken any heart not absolutely diabolical.

As soon as this dreadful rite was completed, we were again startled by several loud bursts of laughter, which proceeded from the lower darkness of the chapel; and the captain, on hearing them, turned to the place, and reflecting for a moment, said in Irish, '*Gutsho nish, avohelhee* – Come hither now, boys.'

A rush immediately took place from the corner in which they had secreted themselves all the night; and seven men appeared, whom we instantly recognized as brothers and cousins of certain persons who had been convicted some time before for breaking into the house of an honest poor man in the neighbourhood, from whom, after having treated him with barbarous violence, they took away such firearms as he kept for his own protection.

It was evidently not the captain's intention to have produced these persons until the oath should have been generally taken; but the exulting mirth with which they enjoyed the success of his scheme betrayed them, and put him to the necessity of bringing them forward somewhat before the concerted moment.

The scene which now took place was beyond all power of description: peals of wild, fiend-like yells rang through the chapel, as the party which stood on the altar, and that which had crouched in the darkness, met; wringing of hands, leaping in triumph, striking of sticks and firearms against the ground and the altar itself, dancing and cracking of fingers, marked the triumph of some hellish determination. Even the captain for a time was unable to restrain their fury; but at length he mounted the platform before the altar once more, and, with a stamp of his foot, recalled their attention to himself and the matter in hand.

'Boys,' said he, 'enough of this, and too much; an' well for us it is that the chapel is in a lonely place, or our foolish noise might do us no good. Let thim that swore so manfully jist now stand a one side, till the rest kiss the book, one by one.'

The proceedings, however, had by this time taken too fearful a shape for even the captain to compel them to a blindfold oath. The first man he called flatly refused to answer until he should hear the nature of the service that was required. This was echoed by the remainder, who, taking courage from the firmness of this person, declared generally that until they first knew the business they were to execute none of them would take the oath. The captain's lip quivered slightly, and his brow again became knit with the same hellish expression which I have remarked gave him so much the appearance of an embodied fiend; but this speedily passed away, and was succeeded by a malignant sneer, in which lurked, if there ever did in a sneer, 'a laughing devil', calmly, determinedly atrocious.

'It wasn't worth yer whiles to refuse the oath,' said he mildly; 'for the truth is, I had next to nothing for yees to do. Not a hand, maybe, would have to rise; only jist to look on; an' if any resistance would be made, to show yourselves; yer numbers would soon make them see that resistance would be no use whatever in the present case. At all evints, the oath of secrecy must be taken, or woe be to him that will refuse that; he won't know the day, nor the hour, nor the minute when he'll be made a spatchcock ov.'

He then turned round, and placing his right hand on the Missal, swore, 'In the presence of God, and before His holy altar, that whatever might take place that night he would keep secret from man or mortal, except the priest, and that neither bribery, nor imprisonment, nor death would wring it from his heart.'

Having done this, he again struck the book violently, as if to confirm the energy with which he swore, and then calmly descending the steps, stood with a serene countenance, like a man conscious of having performed a good action. As this oath did not pledge those who refused to take the other to the perpetration of any specific crime, it was readily taken by all present. Preparations were then made to execute what was intended; the half-burned turf was placed in a little pot; another glass of whiskey was distributed; and the door being locked by the captain, who kept the key as parish clerk and master, the crowd departed silently from the chapel.

The moment those who lay in the darkness during the night made their appearance at the altar, we knew at once the persons we were to visit; for, as I said before, they were related to the miscreants whom one of those persons had convicted, in consequence of their midnight attack upon himself and his family. The captain's object in keeping them unseen was that those present, not being aware of the duty about to be imposed on them, might have less hesitation about swearing to its fulfilment. Our conjectures were correct, for on leaving the chapel we directed our steps to the house in which this devoted man resided.

The night was still stormy, but without rain; it was rather dark, too, though not so as to prevent us from seeing the clouds careering swiftly through the air. The dense curtain which had overhung and obscured the horizon was now broken, and large sections of the sky were clear, and thinly studded with stars that looked dim and watery, as did indeed the whole firmament; for in some places black clouds were still visible, threatening a continuance of tempestuous weather. The road appeared washed and gravelly; every dyke was full of yellow water, and every little rivulet and larger stream dashed its hoarse music in our ears; every blast, too, was cold, fierce, and wintry, sometimes driving us back to a standstill, and again, when a turn in the road would bring it in our backs, whirling us along for a few steps with involuntary rapidity. At length the fated dwelling became visible, and a short consultation was held in a sheltered place between the captain and the two parties who seemed so eager for its destruction. The firearms were now loaded, and their bayonets and short pikes, the latter shod and pointed with iron, were also got ready. The live coal which was brought in the small pot had become extinguished; but to remedy this, two or three persons from a remote part of the county entered a cabin on the wayside, and under pretence of lighting their own and their comrades' pipes, procured a coal of fire – for so they called a lighted turf. From the time we left the chapel until this moment a profound silence had been maintained; a circumstance which, when I considered the number of persons present, and the mysterious and dreaded object of their journey, had a most appalling effect upon my spirits.

At length we arrived within fifty perches of the house, walking in a compact body, and with as little noise as possible; but it seemed as if the very elements had conspired to frustrate our design, for on advancing within the shade of the farm-hedge, two or three persons found themselves up to the middle in water, and on stooping to ascertain more accurately the state of the place, we could see nothing but one immense sheet of it, spread like a lake over the meadows which surrounded the spot we wished to reach.

Fatal night! The very recollection of it, when associated with the fearful tempests of the elements, grows, if that were possible, yet more wild and revolting. Had we been engaged in any innocent or benevolent enterprise, there was something in our situation just then that had a touch of interest in it to a mind imbued with a relish for the savage beauties of nature. There we stood, about a hundred and thirty in number, our dark forms bent forward, peering into the dusky expanse of water, with its dim gleams of reflected light, broken by the weltering of the mimic waves into ten thousand fragments; whilst the few stars that overhung it in the firmament appeared to shoot through it in broken lines, and to be multiplied fifty-fold in the gloomy mirror on which we gazed.

Over us was a stormy sky, and around us a darkness through which we could only distinguish, in outline, the nearest objects, whilst the wind swept strongly and dismally upon us. When it was discovered that the common pathway to the house was inundated, we were about to abandon our object and return home. The captain, however, stooped down low for a moment, and almost closing his eyes, looked along the surface of the waters, and then raising himself very calmly, said, in his usual quiet tone, 'Yees needn't go back, boys; I've found a way; jist follow me.'

He immediately took a more circuitous direction, by which we reached a causeway that had been raised for the purpose of giving a free passage to and from the house during such inundations as the present. Along this we had advanced more than half way, when we discovered a breach in it, which, as afterwards appeared, had that night been made by the strength of the flood. This, by means of our sticks and pikes, we found to be about three feet deep and eight yards broad. Again we were at a loss how to proceed, when the fertile brain of the captain devised a method of crossing it.

'Boys,' said he, 'of coorse you've all played at leap-frog;
very well, strip and go in, a dozen of you, lean one upon the
back of another from this to the opposite bank, where one
must stand facing the outside man, both their shoulders agin
one another, that the outside man may be supported. Then
we can creep over you, an' a dacent bridge you'll be, anyway.'

This was the work of only a few minutes, and in less than
ten we were all safely over.

Merciful Heaven! how I sicken at the recollection of what
is to follow! On reaching the dry bank, we proceeded instantly,
and in profound silence, to the house. The captain divided us
into companies, and then assigned to each division its proper
station. The two parties who had been so vindictive all the
night he kept about himself; for of those who were present they
only were in his confidence, and knew his nefarious purpose –
their number was about fifteen. Having made these dispositions,
he, at the head of about five of them, approached the house
on the windy side, for the fiend possessed a coolness which
enabled him to seize upon every possible advantage. That he
had combustibles about him was evident, for in less than
fifteen minutes nearly one-half of the house was enveloped in
flames. On seeing this, the others rushed over to the spot where
he and his gang were standing, and remonstrated earnestly, but
in vain. The flames now burst forth with renewed violence,
and as they flung their strong light upon the faces of the
foremost group, I think hell itself could hardly present anything more Satanic than their countenances, now worked up
into a paroxysm of infernal triumph at their own revenge. The
captain's look had lost all its calmness, every feature started
out into distinct malignity; the curve in his brow was deep,
and ran up to the root of the hair, dividing his face into two
segments, that did not seem to have been designed for each
other. His lips were half open, and the corners of his mouth
a little brought back on each side, like those of a man expressing intense hatred and triumph over an enemy who is in the
death-struggle under his grasp. His eyes blazed from beneath
his knit eyebrows with a fire that seemed to be lighted up in
the infernal pit itself. It is unnecessary and only painful to

describe the rest of his gang. Demons might have been proud of such horrible visages as they exhibited; for they worked under all the power of hatred, revenge, and joy; and these passions blended into one terrible scowl, enough almost to blast any human eye that would venture to look upon it.

When the others attempted to intercede for the lives of the inmates, there were at least fifteen guns and pistols levelled at them.

'Another word,' said the captain, 'an' you're a corpse where you stand, or the first man who will dare to spake for them. No, no, it wasn't to spare them we came here. "No mercy" is the password for the night, an' by the sacred oath I swore beyant in the chapel, any one among yees that will attempt to show it will find none at my hand. Surround the house, boys, I tell ye, I hear them stirring. "No quarther – no mercy" is the ordher of the night.'

Such was his command over these misguided creatures, that in an instant there was a ring round the house to prevent the escape of the unhappy inmates, should the raging element give them time to attempt it; for none present durst withdraw themselves from the scene, not only from an apprehension of the captain's present vengeance or that of his gang, but because they knew that, even had they then escaped, an early and certain death awaited them from a quarter against which they had no means of defence. The hour now was about half past two o'clock. Scarcely had the last words escaped from the captain's lips, when one of the windows of the house was broken, and a human head, having the hair in a blaze, was descried, apparently a woman's, if one might judge by the profusion of burning tresses, and the softness of the tones, notwithstanding that it called, or rather shrieked, aloud for help and mercy. The only reply to this was the whoop from the captain and his gang of 'No mercy – no mercy!' and that instant the former and one of the latter rushed to the spot, and ere the action could be perceived, the head was transfixed with a bayonet and a pike, both having entered it together. The word mercy was divided in her mouth; a short silence ensued; the head hung down on the window, but was instantly tossed back into the flames!

This action occasioned a cry of horror from all present, except the gang and their leader, which startled and enraged the latter so much that he ran towards one of them, and had his bayonet, now reeking with the blood of its innocent victim, raised to plunge it in his body, when, dropping the point, he said in a piercing whisper that hissed in the ears of all, 'It's no use now, you know; if one's to hang, all will hang; so our safest way, you persave, is to lave none of them to tell the story. Ye may go now, if you wish; but it won't save a hair of your heads. You cowardly set! I knew if I had tould yees the sport, that none of yees, except my own boys, would come, so I jist played a thrick upon you; but remimber what you are sworn to, and stand to the oath ye tuck.'

Unhappily, notwithstanding the wetness of the preceding weather, the materials of the house were extremely combustible: the whole dwelling was now one body of glowing flame; yet the shouts and shrieks within rose awfully above its crackling, and the voice of the storm, for the wind once more blew in gusts and with great violence. The doors and windows were all torn open, and such of those within as had escaped the flames rushed towards them, for the purpose of further escape, and of claiming mercy at the hands of their destroyers; but whenever they appeared, the unearthly cry of 'No mercy' rung upon their ears for a moment, and for a moment only, for they were flung back at the points of the weapons which the demons had brought with them to make the work of vengeance more certain.

As yet there were many persons in the house whose cry for life was strong as despair, and who clung to it with all the awakened powers of reason and instinct. The ear of man could hear nothing so strongly calculated to stifle the demon of cruelty and revenge within him as the long and wailing shrieks which rose beyond the elements in tones that were carried off rapidly upon the blast, until they died away in the darkness that lay behind the surrounding hills. Had not the house been in a solitary situation, and the hour the dead of night, any person sleeping within a moderate distance must have heard them, for such a cry of sorrow rising into a yell of despair was almost sufficient to have awakened the dead. It was lost, however, upon the hearts and ears that heard it: to them – though, in justice be it said, to only comparatively a few of them – it was as delightful as the tones of soft and entrancing music.

The claims of the surviving sufferers were now modified: they supplicated merely to suffer death by the weapons of their enemies; they were willing to bear that, provided they should be allowed to escape from the flames; but no – the horrors of the conflagration were calmly and malignantly gloried in by their merciless assassins, who deliberately flung them back into all their tortures. In the course of a few minutes a man appeared upon the side-wall of the house, nearly naked; his figure, as he stood against the sky in horrible relief, was so finished a picture of woe-begone agony and supplication that it is yet as distinct in my memory as if I were again present at the scene. Every muscle, now in motion by the powerful agitation of his sufferings, stood out upon his limbs and neck, giving him an appearance of desperate strength, to which by this time he must have been wrought up; the perspiration poured from his frame, and the veins and arteries of his neck were inflated to a surprising thickness. Every moment he looked down into the flames which were rising to where he stood; and as he looked, the indescribable horror which flitted over his features might have worked upon the devil himself to relent. His words were few.

'My child,' said he, 'is still safe; she is an infant, a young crathur that never harmed you nor any one – she is still safe. Your mothers, your wives, have young innocent childher like it. Oh, spare her! – think for a moment that it's one of your own! – spare it, as you hope to meet a just God; or if you don't, in mercy shoot me first – put an end to me before I see her burned!'

The captain approached him coolly and deliberately. 'You'll prosecute no one now, you bloody informer,' said he; 'you'll convict no more boys for takin' an' ould gun an' pistol from you, or for givin' you a neighbourly knock or two into the bargain.'

Just then, from a window opposite him, proceeded the shrieks of a woman, who appeared at it with the infant in her arms.

She herself was almost scorched to death; but with the presence
of mind and humanity of her sex, she was about to put the
little babe out of the window. The captain noticed this, and
with characteristic atrocity, thrust, with a sharp bayonet, the
little innocent, along with the person who endeavoured to
rescue it, into the red flames, where they both perished.
This was the work of an instant. Again he approached the
man. 'Your child is a coal now,' said he, with deliberate
mockery; 'I pitched it in myself, on the point of this' – showing
the weapon – 'an' now is your turn' – saying which he clambered up, by the assistance of his gang, who stood with a
front of pikes and bayonets bristling to receive the wretched
man, should he attempt, in his despair, to throw himself from
the wall. The captain got up, and placing the point of his
bayonet against his shoulder, flung him into the fiery element
that raged behind him. He uttered one wild and terrific cry
as he fell back, and no more. After this, nothing was heard
but the crackling of the fire and the rushing of the blast: all
that had possessed life within were consumed, amounting either
to eleven or fifteen persons.

When this was accomplished, those who took an active part
in the murder stood for some time about the conflagration;
and as it threw its red light upon their fierce faces and rough
persons, soiled as they now were with smoke and black streaks
of ashes, the scene seemed to be changed to hell, the murderers
to spirits of the damned rejoicing over the arrival and the
torture of some guilty soul. The faces of those who kept aloof
from the slaughter were blanched to the whiteness of death;
some of them fainted, and others were in such agitation that
they were compelled to lean on their comrades. They became
actually powerless with horror. Yet to such a scene were they
brought by the pernicious influence of Ribbonism.

It was only when the last victim went down that the conflagration shot up into the air with most unbounded fury. The
house was large, deeply thatched, and well furnished; and the
broad red pyramid rose up with fearful magnificence towards
the sky. Abstractedly it had sublimity, but now it was associated with nothing in my mind but blood and terror. It was

not, however, without a purpose that the captain and his gang
stood to contemplate its effect. 'Boys,' said he, 'we had betther
be sartin that all's safe; who knows but there might be some
of the sarpents crouchin' under a hape o' rubbish, to come out
an' gibbet us tomorrow or next day; we had betther wait
awhile, anyhow, if it was only to see the blaze.'

Just then the flames rose majestically to a surprising height.
Our eyes followed their direction; and we perceived, for the
first time, that the dark clouds above, together with the intermediate air, appeared to reflect back, or rather to have caught,
the red hue of the fire. The hills and country about us appeared
with an alarming distinctness; but the most picturesque part
of it was the effect or reflection of the blaze on the floods that
spread over the surrounding plains. These, in fact, appeared
to be one broad mass of liquid copper; for the motion of the
breaking waters caught from the blaze of the high waving
column, as reflected in them, a glaring light, which eddied
and rose and fluctuated as if the flood itself had been a lake of
molten fire.

Fire, however, destroys rapidly. In a short time the flames
sank – became weak and flickering – by and by they shot out
only in fits – the crackling of the timbers died away – the surrounding darkness deepened – and, ere long, the faint light was
overpowered by the thick volumes of smoke that rose from the
ruins of the house and its murdered inhabitants.

'Now, boys,' said the captain, 'all is safe – we may go. Remember, every man of you, what you've sworn this night on the
book an' altar of God – not on a heretic Bible. If you perjure
yourselves, you may hang us; but let me tell you, for your
comfort, that if you do, there is them livin' that will take care
the lase of your own lives will be but short.'

After this we dispersed, every man to his own home.

Reader, not many months elapsed ere I saw the bodies of
this captain, whose name was Patrick Devaun, and all those
who were actively concerned in the perpetration of this deed
of horror, withering in the wind, where they hung gibbeted
near the scene of their nefarious villainy; and while I inwardly
thanked Heaven for my own narrow and almost undeserved
escape, I thought in my heart how seldom, even in this world,

justice fails to overtake the murderer, and to enforce the righteous judgement of God – that 'whoso sheddeth man's blood, by man shall his blood be shed.'

This tale of terror is, unfortunately, too true. The scene of hellish murder detailed in it lies at Wildgoose Lodge in the county of Louth, within about four miles of Carrickmacross, and nine of Dundalk. No such multitudinous murder has occurred, under similar circumstances, except the burning of the Sheas in the county of Tipperary. The name of the family burned in Wildgoose Lodge was Lynch. One of them had, shortly before this fatal night, prosecuted and convicted some of the neighbouring Ribbonmen, who visited him with severe marks of their displeasure in consequence of his having refused to enrol himself as a member of their body.

The language of the story is partly fictitious; but the facts are pretty closely such as were developed during the trial of the murderers. Both parties were Roman Catholics. There were, if the author mistake not, either twenty-five or twenty-eight of those who took an active part in the burning hanged and gibbeted in different parts of the county of Louth. Devaun, the ringleader, hung for some months in chains, within about a hundred yards of his own house, and about half a mile from Wildgoose Lodge. His mother could neither go into or out of her cabin without seeing his body swinging from the gibbet. Her usual exclamation on looking at him was, 'God be good to the sowl of my poor marthyr!' The peasantry, too, frequently exclaimed, on seeing him, 'Poor Paddy!' – a gloomy fact that speaks volumes.

EDITOR'S NOTE: Carleton added a further footnote. His shade may forgive me for dropping it. He walked through that country-side not long after the tragedy, and recalled it in this story and in an unfinished autobiography. Interested readers should consult 'Wildgoose Lodge: the Evidence and the Lore' by Professor Dan Casey of Oneonta, University of New York State, in the *County Louth Archaeological Journal*, Vol. XVIII, No. 2, 1974, and in the succeeding number.

St Brigid's Flood

STEPHEN GWYNN

Four or five men were gathered together that evening in Forsyth's rooms, talking the usual talk of anglers when they congregate – flies, bait, good days, bad days, droughts, and floods. Forsyth was just expressing his preference for the extreme type of flood river.

'A regular mountain stream, you know – no lake on it, no feeders to speak of, but just the scourings of the hills. When it comes down there's no need to bother about waiting till it clears; you watch till it stops rising, and then fish at once; and some time or other when you're on the water you're pretty sure to hit the psychological moment.'

'Yes; but how long does it last?' put in Legge.

'Oh, an hour, two hours, six hours. But it's amusing, any-how, to watch the water changing; it keeps up the interest – it's dramatic. I've seen a stream at Carrick get up five feet in the night, and go down to where it was in the forenoon.'

'If you come to that,' said Grayson, knocking his pipe on the mantelpiece, 'I've seen a flood get up about five feet in five minutes.'

Grayson was a man none of us had seen before. Forsyth had picked him up somewhere in Ireland. So, although what he said sounded pretty steep, none of us hooted.

'You mean a tide wave,' Legge suggested politely.

'Not in the least; just a flood out of the mountains like what Forsyth talks of. And if you like them dramatic, Forsyth, you'd have had your heart's content that time.'

'Well,' said Forsyth, 'I know they get the devil's own floods in the west of Ireland; but I don't see how that could have happened in the natural order of things.'

'I don't say that it did,' answered Grayson;
there were a good many people thought it didn't.
exactly as you say, that it was the devil's own p
to be quite accurate, the work of St Brigid, if you
her.'

'No,' said Forsyth; 'but expound.'

'Well,' said Grayson, as he filled his pipe and settled down
to narrative, 'I'm not strong on saints; but St Brigid has a lot
of sacred places all through Ireland, and just up near Killala
there's a well that she's supposed to have blessed. I was staying
on the other side of the country at a place called Teelin, in
the direction of Blacksod, where I had leave to fish the Bunlin
River. It was a pretty wild place, I tell you, in those days; for
the nearest rail was thirty miles off, and there weren't many of
the amenities of life at the inn. The fishing was no good
either, for the place was a regular nest of poachers, and they
had scooped out nearly every fish that was in the pools, so far
as I could hear or see. I would have chucked it, only for a
ruffian there that I made friends with – head and front of all
the poachers of the district, by his own story; but he gillied
for me in the daytime, and used to show me outlying streams
where I got some sport. And he swore to me by all his gods
that the weather was making up for a big flood, and then
there would be great fishing in the Bunlin. Besides, he was very
good company; so I stayed.

'I liked the people, too, and I had got pretty friendly with
them, though they didn't much care for strangers. You see,
the only strangers who ever came there were sporting tourists,
and interfered with peaceable poaching; there wasn't much
to bring anyone else. My word, but it was a desolate place!
Great brown moors sloping down off mountains that had no
particular shape, and running into great brown wastes of bog
that stretched out towards the sea. You hadn't even the comfort of looking out to the ocean horizon, for there is a kind of
low neck of land that runs between that country and the
Atlantic. So you saw nothing on earth but brown shapeless bog
and heather in all directions: just a little tillage along the
river of course, but practically a bare wilderness of bog. And
the valley of the river, so far as my fishing went, ran pretty

.aight east and west. It had no surprises or nooks or little prettinesses about it, but was just as broad and bare as a valley can be. Only at the boundary of my water it took a sharp turn, and the river was jammed up tight in a winding cleft. Dan, my poacher friend, was always talking to me about the splendid pool there was just above here; and one day when we were doing no good at all, I left him my rod – he was always mad keen to be fishing himself – and walked up to look at it.

'He said I couldn't miss it, and neither I could. When I got to the bridge – for I had struck back to the road – I could hear the rush of the little fall about fifty yards down, and I walked to it. The river came at an angle to the fall, and then it had a straight swift course of about a hundred yards in a deep confined channel. That day there was a lovely run at the head of it, but in any kind of flood the tail of the pool would be the chance. The place was a regular gorge. I walked down the right bank, which was just a handy height for fishing, but the other was a kind of cliff – you could see the track going up and down it like a sheep-run. At the end of the pool the sides of the gorge narrowed in again, so that I don't suppose the water was thirty feet across; but just there on the far side the cliff drew back from the bank, and right in by the river was a cottage, a good bit better-looking than most of them. I would have thought it must have belonged to a keeper, only that on my side there was a watcher's hut built of scraws of turf, and presumably put there to observe the man on the spot. I remember thinking as I looked at it that I wouldn't mind being the man on the spot, if I had a rod on the water, for the site was charming. The cottage was regularly in the arms of the hill; and it faced down the valley about south-west, with its gable-end to the river, protected from the westerly draught up the valley by a little knoll. He was probably a "well-doing" man, too, for just below this kind of gully the river curved to the right, and left a dozen acres or so of fairly level ground between it and the hills. All this was down in crops, cut up with stone walls, and there was only one other cottage near by – a much poorer one, too – so he probably held most of it. You see, I was taking stock of the place against the time when I should be a tenant.

'All the same, I should probably have forgotten most of these details; only, I fancy, one's memory is a sort of sensitive plate, which takes impressions, but they sink gradually in and fade into a blur unless something fixes them. Well, in this case I had the lines bitten in, pretty hard, just afterwards, in a way that stamped in my mind the position of that cottage, and the fact that the man had only one near neighbour. Just in the same way I am not likely to forget what otherwise would have faded away in a few days or weeks or months – the look of a fellow who came out of the cottage door and stared at me across the river – a big, burly, dark-complexioned ruffian. I said to myself at once: "That man's been in America." You know the type, Forsyth – rather aggressive. "I'm as good as you, anyway" – that sort of air. He was clean-shaven, too; that was another mark, for the men there all wear the beard, or else the old-fashioned scrap of whisker. Well, I went on downstream, and never gave him another thought; but the whole thing came back on me in a flash when I saw him again – lying quiet enough. That was when the first picture got bitten in and fixed.

'Just in the same way I shall always remember noticing an unusual feature in the landscape – a great massive outcrop of rock on the mountain side straight above the cottage. It broke the featureless character of the hills, and there was a big patch of that orange lichen on it that caught the sun finely, and it was good to look at. But especially I noticed it because it set me thinking of a man called Bowen, a sort of professor who used to fish with me, and do a lot of geologizing and botanizing on off-days. He would have been bound to invent some theory to explain why that great lump stayed there sticking out, while all the hill-slopes about were being pared off smooth. And afterwards, when the event happened, I wrote to him to come and look at geology in the making, but he was in the Andes or somewhere. Only, it wouldn't have done for him to theorize in Teelin about what happened. Everybody in Teelin is very clear that if the rock was there, it was put there with a purpose.

'However, of course, the day I was up there I was thinking
of nothing except that the pool was a splendid holding pool,
and that a man might possibly kill fish in it even in low water,
and that it probably wasn't swept out with nets, and probably
all mine were. At all events, Dan wasn't able to stir anything
in them, no more than I could. But he said the weather was
going to break, and he was right enough.

'It was the night before the 27th of August, when it broke
with a lot of thunder and rain, and in the morning it was
bright again; but the river was still rising, or anyhow not
falling. I went out and fished for a bit, waiting for the psychological moment that Forsyth talks about; but Dan said there
was more water to come and the fish wouldn't rise, though they
were up from the sea, for I saw them moving. By about four
o'clock it came on such a downpour as I hardly ever was out
in, and the day blackened and grew cold. You never saw
anything so forsaken as that valley looked in the drift of
water and smother of grey cloud. I went in, and while I was
changing it broke into thunder again – the kind of thunder
when you hear the sky torn across with a rip just over your
head, and the lightning makes you blink. In that kind of
storm human beings are just like animals, they always drift
together; and I was a human being, so I went downstairs into
the little shop. You know the kind of place – a clay floor between two counters: one counter is the bar, which is slopped
over with stale porter; the other is the shop, where they sell
damp matches, and envelopes gummed together, and tea and
biscuits, and every necessary of life in its least attractive form;
and the whole place reeks of porter and paraffin, and bacon,
and several other fragrances, and there is a window looking
to the street, hermetically closed.

'The entire household was there, of course. Michael Flynn,
the big chap who kept the hotel, was behind the bar. He wore
a Newgate fringe, not very much bristlier than his eyebrows;
his son was rummaging for something in a dark corner, and the
two girls were at the counter. Dan Keary was discoursing to
Flynn across the bar with a couple of other worthies, and
there was a woman sitting in the only chair, with her hands

crossed on a parcel in her lap and her head down. She had evidently come in from the country for shopping and been weather-bound, and at the first look I thought she was in a bad fright. Anyhow, she was perfectly silent, but her lips were moving all the time. The two girls were giggling rather nervously.

'I was feeling rather divided in my mind about this flood, for it seemed as if my luck was to come at the expense of a lot of poor people. I expected to hear talk of nothing but the desperate damage to the oats – which, of course, were being laid as flat as a board. But, to my surprise, the only thing that the men were discussing was the effect upon a sort of pious picnic – the excursion to a station at the Holy Well. "There was three carloads of them went through here this morning about eight o'clock," Michael Flynn said, "and one girl with a bad cough on her this while back." "Faith," said Dan, "maybe she would have been better in her bed a day like this." But Flynn was a very devout man, and he would not hear of this. "Well, now, I always heard it for a fact that there was never anyone yet that went to that Well in a right mind, and did what was set down for to be done, but they were the better of going – saving always," he said, looking sharp at the woman, who was sitting mumbling to herself, "that they would ask something not fit to be granted."

'I made a note, after my habit, to ask Dan for some explanation at a more convenient season. Just then, before any more could be said, we heard feet running down the road, the door was thrown open, and three men stepped in; the rain streaming off them made pools on the floor. The moment they spoke it was plain they belonged to another county, and I said to Dan, "Who are they?" "Three Highlanders out of Donegal working on a conthrack," he told me. The last of them to enter was one of the most powerful human beings I ever looked at – very tall and rather gaunt, with a small head and a jaw like a pike's; high cheekbones, forehead dinted in, and small deep-set eyes. In spite of its ruggedness, the face was pleasant though, a queer mixture of good-humour and possible ferocity. They stood there in a group dripping in the doorway, a little shy; and behind them was the strange unnatural darkness of the evening, darker than it would have been most days at eight o'clock.

' "God save us all, Neil," said Mick Flynn, speaking to the big man, "what kind of weather is that to be taking the road in? Is it from Mike O'Hanlon's you're coming?"

' "We thought it was quieter out of doors nor in," the man answered, with a twinkle in his eye. Then he caught sight of the woman sitting there, and turned away from Flynn. "That's a wild evening, Mrs O'Hea," he said.

'Obviously he didn't want to talk; but there was a quick-eyed little fellow with him who was ready enough and I saw Dan making up to him. "Was there any quarrel between yez and the O'Hanlons?"

' "There was quarrel enough, then, if Neil M'Nelis was as brave as he's big," the little man said, spitting viciously on the ground. "But he's that cautious like, he was afeard of killing Johnny O'Hanlon. Wasn't that what he told us, William?" he asked, turning to the other Donegal man.

'The big fellow interrupted before he could get an answer. "Bad luck to my tongue, then, if I told you what was not to be repeated, Ned M'Cormick. And if there was any trouble at all, wasn't it because you were for ever threeping it to Johnny O'Hanlon that I could beat him with a hand tied behind me? An' right well I know the kind of him, that if there was to be a fight, he's not the one that would quet it in a hurry. An' the drink was in him at the time he spoke."

' "Well, now," said Michael Flynn in his judicial way, "take my word for it, Neil, you done right. If it was in Mike O'Hanlon's house you were, and he seen any kind of fight and his brother getting worsted, he'd not stay looking."

' "An' if you beat the two of them," Dan Keary put in, "the O'Hanlons are a terrible strong clan, and they'd keep it up on you, as long as you were in this country."

' "Well," said the big man, "if Johnny O'Hanlon was looking help, he needn't go far to look it this day. There was half the O'Hanlons in the countryside in Mike's house before we quet."

' "Ay, troth," said Ned M'Cormick, "and great diversion with them. There was Mike himself and the wife and four childer: that's six; and there was Johnny O'Hanlon that came in middling cheerful from the station at Killala, and Black Peter Maloney with him, and his wife, that's Michael's sister: that's nine now. An' a couple more of them, cousins, John O'Hanlon and his wife, that came running in out of the rain from off the road. That's eleven.'

' "Ay," said the other Donegal man, "and the fiddler with them that was making down here for Teelin, against the fair. An' they had him up in the corner playin' for them to dance, before Johnny began to strip and square up at Neil thonder."

' "Lord save us! such a houseful," said Mick Flynn; "twelve of them, and the three of you."

' "Faith, there was one more, or the ninth part of one," said Ned M'Cormick. "For Michael had the tailor in with him making a new coat agin the fair." Then he turned to the woman that was sitting there, and he had a malicious look in his little eyes. I had noticed she had stopped mumbling to herself, and was listening very intently. The little fellow had noticed her too, but he made believe to be just catching sight of her.

' "Och, and is that yourself, Mrs O'Hea? Troth, then, Michael was talking of you; for he says to the tailor: 'God help you if the coat's not everything it ought to be. I'm for the fair at Teelin, and I'm bound to meet my sweetheart, Biddy O'Hea, and I'd like to be lookin' my best.' "

'She was an oldish woman, about fifty, I daresay, with a large, plain, round face; and her face itself didn't change much. But the whole of her body shook and bent together as she sat, and her fingers crisped themselves in a spasm of rage; and she spoke, but the words came so fast and broken that I couldn't hear what she was saying; only it was plain enough it wasn't sweet to hear.

'But M'Nelis took the little fellow by the shoulder and swung him round towards the door. "Bad luck to you for a spiteful wee divil!" said he. "Sure, Mrs O'Hea, don't mind his talk."

'But she got up and she gathered her shawl round herself

and her parcel, with hands still shaking violently and she began to speak, in the sing-song voice like a chant that Irish country people often fall into when they are in a passion.

' "'Twas on St Brigid's day I put my curse on Mike O'Hanlon and all that belongs to him and draws breath in his house. May the breath choke in their throats was the word I said, and I went to St Brigid's own water to say it! An' today there's a station at the Well, and the whole of the O'Hanlons is gathered under one roof, and them dancing and singing. An' my curse is on them an' them dancing and singing."

'There wasn't one of us that said a word, and for my own part I was what they call in my country "touched under". There's a lot of sound physiological observation in that phrase, if you think of it. She went across to the door, and just as she had it open, she turned and said to M'Nelis, "How many was in the O'Hanlon's house when you left it?" Then the door shut on her, and there was dead silence again, till one of the girls spoke with a frightened titter:

' "Lord save us! that's an awful woman."

' "She's a bloody witch," snapped out little M'Cormick, who had turned a sort of green.

' "Mind you, how quick she was to reckon out the thirteen," said Mick Flynn reflectively. 'Eleven O'Hanlons and the fiddler and the tailor. An' not one of us here or there noticed it."

' "Is it them notice it?" Dan struck in; "sure Michael would not value it a snuff of a candle if he knew. What does he care about the like of that? Just the very same as he cares about Biddy O'Hea and her curses. Hasn't he heard her curse him like that a hundher times? And doesn't he see her stand at the door of her cottage cursing him, and him going out in the morning and coming in at night?"

' "Well and well! Still and all, it's a wild evening, and I'm thinking, M'Nelis, maybe coming out of that was the best thing ever you did. Come now, boys, a glass of whiskey to put us in better heart."

'The thunder by that time was growling away in the distance, the rain had slackened a bit, and I was mighty curious about all this. What was even more important, I didn't want my gillie to go on the burst. So after one glass I hauled the reluctant Dan out with me to look at the river, knowing that if I got him as far as the bridge I could speed him on to Mrs Dan with some remnants of my half-crown in his pocket.

'The hotel stands where the main road up and down the valley is met at right angles by another making straight for the bridge, at which my fishing started. It was clearing a bit seawards, and the main rack of cloud came that way from the south-west. But up the valley, in among the hills, it looked wilder than ever; there was simply a black mass of vapour, twisted into queer shapes, apparently with a strong swirl from the east coming up against the general drift. Dan looked up at it.

' "Begor! Biddy O'Hea will get a cooling for her anger before she's gone far. Wouldn't you think the sky was going to fall? 'Twill be down on top of her before she gets to Dohoomiss Bridge."

' "Is it up there she lives?" I said.

' "You know the long pool you were looking at? Well, just a piece below that."

'I thought for a moment he meant the cottage I had my eye on, opposite the watcher's hut, and said so.

' "No, sir," said Dan, "that's where her enemy lives – O'Hanlon." Then I began to understand.

' "A big, black, clean-shaven fellow?" I said.

' "That's the very man. You seen him up there? Well, you might notice Biddy's cottage away back a bit in the hill. The way to it would be past O'Hanlon's; but he keeps a wicked dog there, and Biddy has a track now made for herself over the mountain. Och, yes," – for I asked him the obvious question – "but what can the craythur do? She's a widdy woman with a weak family of girls, an' she got bad usage from Mick O'Hanlon first and last."

'I asked him what they fell out about. "It was about some geese," said Dan, seeming to think that a final explanation. When I pressed for more details, it seemed that O'Hanlon said that she had stolen his and sold them, or she said that he had stolen hers – I forget which. Anyhow, Dan thought that the geese had been straying by the road and were just lifted by some of those fellows that go through driving big flocks of them to market. Then his cows got into her corn, and her cows got into his corn, and they accused one another of breaking down fences on purpose, and so it went on. I think maybe Dan was right, and there's no call to look for other reasons why those people should hate one another. In a town nobody has time to have enemies. It's only in the country that hatreds really ripen. You see a person going in and going out every day – he's part of the landscape almost – and every time you see him hate stirs in your belly. And you see few other people – hardly anyone else in a case like this. He fills the whole field of your vision. Then there are always these little incidents of geese, and gaps, and the like of that; and there's worse. His potatoes are growing near your potatoes, and his corn near your corn, and either you rejoice to see his doing worse, or you hate him like hell because his are doing better. That's the way you get a really fine well-rooted specimen of hate, that gets its nurture daily and grows like a tree. Love and hatred are both of them very much a matter of proximity, and your neighbour is twice as much your neighbour in the country.

'Still, everywhere in Arcadia you have these sort of feuds, and they aren't explosive. They simply blacken a nature slowly, they don't result in action. But in this case there was another feud which might very well have passed over, only that it underlay this hatred begotten of proximity, and was kept warm. There was a history commonplace enough, but dramatic in the ordinary way. I got it out of Dan by cross-questioning. This fellow Mike O'Hanlon was always what Dan called "a boyo": he was a poacher and a stiller of whiskey, of course, but Dan thought little of that. Only he broke the laws that these people respected as well as the laws they did not; he neglected his duty at confession, and he was pretty miscellaneous in his sweethearting. You know, of course, the peculiarity of Irish Catholics: they don't like sexual irregularity; and the wilder and more outlandish a place is in Ireland, the fewer illegitimate births there are. It may be temperament, tradition, training – I don't know which. But anyhow, the fact is certain. A man who runs loose is counted irreligious and disapproved of, and a woman who makes a slip might nearly as well hang herself at once. Well, in the course of his adventures Mike O'Hanlon came across Biddy O'Hea, who was then Biddy something else, and she was a woman of strong will and a violent temper, and she wanted to marry Mike. But she had no fortune, and anyhow very likely he had no notion of settling down. Perhaps she counted on that. But what she did was to marry a very old man who held this little farm up by the long pool. I couldn't get anything clear about dates; but there were children born, and after some time there was a fierce quarrel between Mike O'Hanlon and his father, and the priest was mixed up in it, and Mike went off to America. The pretext was some trouble about the seizure of a still, when the police were assaulted and one man badly hurt, and it was thought that Mike might be wanted. But Dan seemed to think that the reason why there was not the usual evidence forthcoming to establish Mike's alibi was that Mike's father and the priest wanted him out of the country.

'After a while old O'Hanlon died, and Mike came back to take up the farm, and, according to Dan, his morals were none the better. America is a questionable school, and there was a fellow out of a very lawless parish that I knew, who came back after a couple of years, saying he never seen wickedness right till he seen it in the streets of New York. The contact with civilization is not always a success for primitive natures. As Dan put it, there was no Christianity left in Mike O'Hanlon. Well, when he came back, Biddy O'Hea's old man was dead, and the priest himself tried to make up a marriage. But, as Dan said: "Faith, Michael was a good match now, and the wee house down by the pool was on the way to Biddy's, and there was a girl in it with a fortune of a hundher and fifty pound, and Mike carried his courting no farther nor that." So you may judge if the widow was kindly disposed to her neighbours when Mike settled in there. And I would say that in the slanging matches the geese and the gaps and the rest of it figured principally as a pretext.

'I don't know when the public quarrelling began or how long

it went on; the gatherings when it happened would only come once or twice a year. Only it became recognized that whenever Mike O'Hanlon and Biddy O'Hea met in a fair, there would always be this sort of encounter. And although O'Hanlon had the best of it for the rest of the year, and could always retort on her, and did, about her dirty little house and the weeds in her corn, and her starved-looking pony and so on, still, as Dan said, "she had the tongue of him", and public opinion was on her side. Well, I suppose the man wanted to silence her once and for all, and he didn't care how he did it, for, as I tell you, there was no Christianity in him. At all events the crisis came when they met in Teelin at a market, and Dan was there and went up to listen.

' "She joined on him at once," he said, "and maybe she didn't give him a dressing down. An' Mike stood there, with his back turned, letting on not to hear her, when all the while there was a ring of people round them the same as there would be round a fight. 'An',' says she at last, 'I wouldn't put clean pigs to sleep with that dirty ugly lump of a woman you have, and them little red leprechauns of childer.' An' at that Mike turned his head an' his shoulder and says: 'Well, there's two fine black-haired girls in your own house anyway, and proud I am of them; for it was little your ould crooked O'Hea had to do with the making of them.' An' then he turned on her and laughed in her face, wicked-like. 'Och, Biddy,' says he, 'don't be too hard on your old sweetheart.' And when she heard that she turned the colour of that stone," said Dan, striking on the bridge parapet, "and you would have thought she was going to drop; but faith, not she. She up with her hands like that to the sky, and she prayed God the words might choke in the throat of him. But you heard her cursing him herself, and I needn't be telling you the way of it. And sure it was no wonder she would be mad, for what person at all would put up with a thing like that cast up to them, let it be true or false – barring one that had no spirit at all in them?"

' "She doesn't want for spirit, anyhow, if she faced a storm like this," I said, looking up the valley. "They're getting it heavy up there. I suppose now she won't mind seeing her own crops go if his are washed out?"

'The whole head of the valley was lost in a black welter of cloud, as if a curtain was dropped between us and it. Dan took out his pipe and spat hard ...

' "She's a desperate woman that. What did she do but make the whole journey in her bare feet to the Holy Well, and she said a station backwards on him: ay, the whole of it, the five Paternosters and the five Hail Marys, and the prayer to Saint Brigid herself; every one of them backwards, beginning at the Amen, and praying that she might get the thing she desired, and that was the death by suffocating of Mike O'Hanlon and all his family."

'I remember the way Dan mouthed out the long words as if he enjoyed them, and I remember trying to say something in chaff about O'Hanlon's being in no danger of choking from drought, when Dan interrupted me. We were leaning both of us with our arms on the parapet of the bridge, looking up a long stretch they called the millpool, and watching the water automatically as it came tearing down – hardly discoloured at all, for there was no laboured land worth speaking of in the drainage. Suddenly Dan said to me in a puzzled way: "The water's falling."

'It sounded impossible; but sure enough, at the ford, about fifty yards up, the break of a stone was showing. I looked up at the valley: the sky was clearing, and for a minute I thought it had been only a local storm, and the upper water got none of it. But the river was running down now like the sand in an hour-glass – "Be damned to me if ever I see the like of that!" said Dan. Then he gave a shout: "Oh, merciful Jesus, look there!"

'There was no need for him to point up the stream, I tell you. A great yellow mass came round the corner up above, and broke into the millpool. It spread a bit then, but still it came on in a regular wall fully a foot high, and thick and muddy. Dan stood staring; but I caught hold of him: "Run, man! the bridge'll go." It didn't go, though; but I've often thought since that if it had we might as well have been on top of it as watching the flood from the roadway. I'll never forget the roar, ending in a sort of smack, as it came up against the masonry. There was a lot of stuff floating, of course; but only small things, till we saw a brownish mass coming down – it came at an awful pace. "Here's a hayrick," I said; but just as it reached the ford, I suppose, a rock met it and it wallowed right over. There wasn't the least doubt about it – it was half the thatch of a house. Well, I don't think I'm superstitious, but the only difference between Dan and me was that I said nothing and he spoke out. "As sure as death," he said, "it's O'Hanlon's. The whole of them's drownded."

'We started running back to the village, when a thought struck me. "Go you and give the alarm," I said; "I'm going up to Cudheen to see would there be any thing there."

'Cudheen was the name of a pool just above the millpool, and there was a tongue of gravel sticking out there; it was the sharpest bend on the river. I left Dan and ran across the fields; but when I got to the bank the stream had cut a new course for itself: the spit was gone, and instead of curving in by the left bank, it rushed straight down. Only it had gone down nearly as quick as it had risen, and on the gravel bank at my feet there was a man lying with only his legs in the water. It was O'Hanlon right enough.

'I dragged him high and dry. There was no use trying to do anything. In a minute Dan and three or four other fellows were up with me. "Lord save us!" was pretty much all they said. Then Dan spotted a thing I hadn't noticed. The coat was on the man, but twisted round the body, only one arm in the sleeve. And it was a half-made coat, just roughly stitched together.

' "Do you mind that?" Dan said. "He was just trying it on when the flood took him. Boys, but it must have been suddent."

'The more I thought of it, the less I could understand what had happened. I told them to take the body up to the roadside and into the village, and I started up the valley to see what had happened, on the off-chance of giving help. But I had no more doubt in my mind that Biddy O'Hea's curse had been fulfilled to the letter than any of the rest of them.

'I suppose it was about two miles up the road to the bridge, and we ran, or half ran, every step of the way. The rain was over, and it was clearer, if anything, than it had been; but still everything was that kind of blackish grey. About a mile up we took a short cut across a corner of hill, and as we got to the top of it, I saw a woman along the road on our left. In a little, when she noticed us running, she began to run too. It was Biddy O'Hea. By the time we had got a little farther a car passed us, lashing and galloping, with the priest and the doctor in it, and there was a stream of people all along the road behind us; but I could see the old woman coming along at a kind of shuffling trot in front of them. It was wonderful how she kept up.

'In another couple of minutes we turned the corner – Dan and I had caught hold of the back of the car, and were running with it – and then we saw what had happened. Biddy O'Hea's cottage was in sight plain enough; O'Hanlon's would be hidden by the ground in any case; but there was a long brown scar down the hillside just above it. Dan shouted in my ear – we were all too excited to speak quietly – "The Big rock's down on them." And sure enough, the boulder I had noticed sticking out was gone at last, as I suppose all the other boulders had gone century by century, down into the lowest level that the river course had scoured out.

'We crossed the bridge, still hanging to the car, and over the bank into the mountain, before the priest could get down; but the doctor, who was an active young chap, simply took a flying leap at the bank and was with us. The driver left the horse where he was, and ran too. But over the rough ground I couldn't keep up with Dan and the doctor, as they scrambled like goats among the heather, taking the angler's track along the river.

'There was a tearing great flood, of course, but nothing to account for washing out a house twenty feet up, till we got to the long pool. The water was back between the banks – it would generally be six or seven feet below them – but you could see it had been out till the gorge was filled like a bath. I could see nothing of O'Hanlon's house till I got right to the top of the last rise in the path, and there were Dan and the doctor looking down at it. The farther wall was standing and a bit of the near one, but the whole was heaped with clay and stuff. And right through the three gables of shed and cottage there was a monstrous savage gap, where the stone had bowled through as clean as a ball through a wicket. And there was the stone itself, fair in the throat of the stream at the very narrowest point. The water tore through in a sluice at each side of it, cutting in on the bank like a knife; while I was looking, a great piece of the far side fell with a plop.

'It was plain enough what had happened. A big rain-burst had detached the rock from its holding in the face of the hill; it had rolled down – and probably between the lash of the rain and the roar of the river at their doors the people in the house never even heard the sound of it. It had struck the wall and swept all before it; then lodging in the river-bed dammed up that terrible flood, and in a few seconds the whole place was awash. The little sort of lawn that the house stood in had been six or eight feet deep in water. Then the clay of the banks gave, and the river cut through, sucking out whatever floated, and tearing it along down to the sea. The whole place was as bare as your hand, only that, about the walls of the house, the loose earth that had been brought down with the falling stone was licked into smooth heaps. And when we came nearer we saw a man's boot sticking up through it.

'We fell to, tearing with our hands. But the clay was washed hard together. "Where'll we get spades?" I said. "Go up, Dan, to Biddy O'Hea's, and bring one down," said the priest. But you should have seen his face when he said it. Dan pretended not to hear him. Then the priest roared at him. "Ah, sure, what use?" Dan said sulkily. I caught hold of him, saying, "Come on, Dan." He went then; but there was no getting him to hurry. I ran on by myself. When I got to the house the door was shut and locked. I knocked first, then I kicked. There was the woman sitting by the fire; she never lifted her head. Two frightened-looking girls had let me in. I said, "Give me all the spades you have." They brought me a spade and a slane for turf-cutting, and I ran back. Dan was outside. "Was she in there?" he asked, with a face of terror. "Yes," I said – I was in no humour for talking – "go on with these," and I gave him the spades. He ran like a hare now, and I came on slower. By the time I got down there was a crowd about the place. When the clay was all turned over, they had got three bodies out, and a cat and two dogs and a pig. All O'Hanlon's livestock were out that evening, but nothing escaped that was under the roof. One man and a child were crushed right into the ground by the boulder. The man was Johnny O'Hanlon; and I saw big Neil M'Nelis, that he had wanted to fight, sobbing and crying over him, "Och, Johnny O'Hanlon, is that where you are now? You that was standing up to me that bold this day, and me as big again as you. It was the foul blow you met, Johnny." But little M'Cormick, the sharp-faced, red-headed little fellow, stood up there in the middle, and his eyes were as red as fire. "Boys," he said, "the rest of them's gone down the river. Where's the bloody witch that done this, till we send her after them?"

'It's a horrible thing to say; but when I thought of that old woman sitting crouched there by the fire, as if she was gloating over the defeat of her enemies, the man's words seemed natural. There wasn't much time to think, though. The priest was standing there, a big, red-faced, coarse-looking man as you could see. He took a step over, and he caught M'Cormick by the throat, and shook him like a rat. "Would you dare!" he said, "ye bad Christian! Would ye dare, then!" Then he threw the man from him, and he faced round, gathering the whole crowd in front of him with a sweep of his arm. Then he made the sign of the cross in the air, and raised one hand.

' "Go down on your knees, every one of you, and pray for the souls of them that God has cut off without warning in their sins."

'It was the strangest thing I ever saw, the change in him from a red-faced bully into the shepherd of his people. The fashion of his countenance changed, as the Bible says. And he prayed there standing over the dead bodies, while the men knelt round him in the twilight – rolling out the Latin words, that neither I nor they understood, in his great Connaught brogue. Then he stopped and spoke to them again. "Now you

will say one more Paternoster for the help of a soul that is
maybe in worse danger nor theirs, and in saying it you will
pray humbly to Almighty God that He may not bring down
upon your heads the fulfilment of your own evil desires. And
you will leave to the judgement of God the one that invoked
God's judgement."

'He began again in the broad Latin, kneeling himself, and
they said the prayer after him, sentence by sentence, kneeling
there on the wet sod. Then he stood up and shook himself.
"Away with you down the river, boys, and search every eddy
and backwater, and get nets and dredge the holes. There's ten
bodies needing Christian burial, and that's the last good turn
ever you'll do them."

'They broke up in a minute. The priest watched them
scatter, some going back to the bridge, some following down
the bank. Then he turned up the hill to the woman's house. I
know no more about it; but I couldn't understand the confidence with which he faced that job when he started up across
the heather at a slow pace, with his eyes fixed on the ground,
and reciting prayers to himself, for I could see his lips moving.
I have often speculated since on the scene there must have
been. However, as I have said, I know nothing of what happened; except that Biddy O'Hea was always a pattern Christian
from that day, and the neighbourhood regarded her with fear
certainly, but with a kind of veneration. They were vastly civil
to her, I need not tell you – and, what is more, to judge by
what I heard since, they are rather proud of her as a local
celebrity.

'The bodies were all recovered – most of them in the tide-
way. But we worked at the river all that night. I couldn't help
being grimly amused at the number of nets that were forthcoming in half an hour and the general handiness in working
them, and the promptitude and skill that was displayed in
getting out torches. I suppose there wasn't a man or boy but
had burned the water time and again. I tell you a queer thing,
though. There were over fifty salmon taken out that night as
they were working the nets – for there had been a tremendous
run of fish – but every one of them was put back.

'Oh no, it was no use to me; some other chaps did mighty well on the river before that flood had run down – one man got ten in a morning just above Dohoomiss. But I never threw a line. I didn't care to benefit by St Brigid's dispensations.'

Lisheen Races, Second-Hand

SOMERVILLE and ROSS

IT may or may not be agreeable to have attained the age of thirty-eight, but, judging from old photographs, the privilege of being nineteen has also its drawbacks. I turned over page after page of an ancient book in which were enshrined portraits of the friends of my youth, single, in David and Jonathan couples, and in groups in which I, as it seemed to my mature and possibly jaundiced perception, always contrived to look the most immeasurable young bounder of the lot. Our faces were fat, and yet I cannot remember ever having been considered fat in my life; we indulged in low-necked shirts, in 'Jemima' ties with diagonal stripes; we wore coats that seemed three sizes too small, and trousers that were three sizes too big; we also wore small whiskers.

I stopped at last at one of the David and Jonathan memorial portraits. Yes, here was the object of my researches; this stout and earnestly romantic youth was Leigh Kelway, and that fatuous and chubby young person seated on the arm of his chair was myself. Leigh Kelway was a young man ardently believed in by a large circle of admirers, headed by himself and seconded by me, and for some time after I had left Magdalen for Sandhurst I maintained a correspondence with him on large and abstract subjects. This phase of our friendship did not survive; I went soldiering to India, and Leigh Kelway took honours and moved suitably on into politics, as is the duty of an earnest young Radical with useful family connections and an independent income. Since then I had at intervals seen in the papers the name of the Honourable Basil Leigh Kelway mentioned as a speaker at elections, as a writer of thoughtful articles in the reviews, but we had never met, and nothing could have been less expected by me than the letter, written from Mrs Raverty's hotel, Skebawn, in which he told me he was making a tour in Ireland with Lord Waterbury, to whom he was private secretary. Lord Waterbury was at present having a few days' fishing near Killarney, and he himself, not being a fisherman, was collecting statistics for his chief on various points connected with the Liquor Question in Ireland. He had heard that I was in the neighbourhood, and was kind enough to add that it would give him much pleasure to meet me again.

With a stir of the old enthusiasm I wrote begging him to be my guest for as long as it suited him, and the following afternoon he arrived at Shreelane. The stout young friend of my youth had changed considerably. His important nose and slightly prominent teeth remained, but his wavy hair had withdrawn intellectually from his temples; his eyes had acquired a statesmanlike absence of expression, and his neck had grown long and bird-like. It was his first visit to Ireland, as he lost no time in telling me, and he and his chief had already collected much valuable information on the subject to which they had dedicated the Easter recess. He further informed me that he thought of popularizing the subject in a novel, and therefore intended to, as he put it, 'master the brogue' before his return.

During the next few days I did my best for Leigh Kelway. I turned him loose on Father Scanlan; I showed him Mohona, our champion village, that boasts fifteen public houses out of twenty buildings of sorts and a railway station; I took him to hear the prosecution of a publican for selling drink on a Sunday, which gave him an opportunity of studying perjury as a fine art, and of hearing a lady, on whom police suspicion justly rested, profoundly summed up by the sergeant as 'a woman who had th' appairance of having knocked at a back door'.

The net result of these experiences has not yet been given to the world by Leigh Kelway. For my own part, I had at the end of three days arrived at the conclusion that his society, when combined with a notebook and a thirst for statistics, was not what I used to find it at Oxford. I therefore welcomed a suggestion from Mr Flurry Knox that we should accompany

him to some typical country races, got up by the farmers at a
place called Lisheen, some twelve miles away. It was the worst
road in the district, the races of the most grossly unorthodox
character; in fact, it was the very place for Leigh Kelway to
collect impressions of Irish life, and in any case it was a blessed
opportunity of disposing of him for the day.

In my guest's attire next morning I discerned an unbending
from the role of cabinet minister towards that of sportsman;
the outlines of the notebook might be traced in his breast
pocket, but traversing it was the strap of a pair of field-glasses,
and his light grey suit was smart enough for Goodwood.

Flurry was to drive us to the races at one o'clock, and we
walked to Tory Cottage by the short cut over the hill, in the
sunny beauty of an April morning. Up to the present the weather
had kept me in a more or less apologetic condition; anyone
who has entertained a guest in the country knows the unjust
weight of responsibility that rests on the shoulders of the host
in the matter of climate, and Leigh Kelway, after two drench-
ings, had become sarcastically resigned to what I felt he regarded as my mismanagement.

Flurry took us into the house for a drink and a biscuit, to
keep us going, as he said, till 'we lifted some luncheon out of
the Castle Knox people at the races', and it was while we were
thus engaged that the first disaster of the' day occurred. The
dining-room door was open, so also was the window of the
little staircase just outside it, and through the window travelled
sounds that told of the close proximity of the stable-yard: the
clattering of hoofs on cobble-stones, and voices uplifted in loud
conversation. Suddenly from this region there arose a screech
of the laughter peculiar to kitchen flirtation, followed by the
clank of a bucket, the plunging of a horse, and then an uproar
of wheels and galloping hoofs. An instant afterwards Flurry's
chestnut cob, in a dogcart, dashed at full gallop into view, with
the reins streaming behind him, and two men in hot pursuit.
Almost before I had time to realize what had happened, Flurry
jumped through the half-opened window of the dining-room
like a clown in a pantomime, and joined in the chase; but the
cob was resolved to make the most of his chance, and went

away down the drive and out of sight at a pace that distanced everyone save the kennel terrier, who sped in shrieking ecstasy beside him.

'Oh merciful hour!' exclaimed a female voice behind me. Leigh Kelway and I were by this time watching the progress of events from the gravel, in company with the remainder of Flurry's household. 'The horse is desthroyed! Wasn't that the quare start he took! And all in the world I done was to slap a bucket of wather at Michael out the windy, and 'twas himself got it in place of Michael!'

'Ye'll never ate another bit, Bridgie Dunnigan,' replied the cook, with the exulting pessimism of her kind. 'The Master'll have your life!'

Both speakers shouted at the top of their voices, probably because in spirit they still followed afar the flight of the cob.

Leigh Kelway looked serious as we walked on down the drive. I almost dared to hope that a note on the degrading oppression of Irish retainers was shaping itself. Before we reached the bend of the drive the rescue party was returning with the fugitive, all, with the exception of the kennel terrier, looking extremely gloomy. The cob had been confronted by a wooden gate, which he had unhesitatingly taken in his stride, landing on his head on the farther side with the gate and the cart on top of him, and had arisen with a lame foreleg, a cut on his nose, and several other minor wounds.

'You'd think the brute had been fighting the cats, with all the scratches and scrapes he has on him!' said Flurry, casting a vengeful eye at Michael. 'And one shaft's broken and so is the dashboard. I haven't another horse in the place; they're all out at grass, and so there's an end of the races!'

We all three stood blankly on the hall-door steps and watched the wreck of the trap being trundled up the avenue.

'I'm very sorry you're done out of your sport,' said Flurry to Leigh Kelway, in tones of deplorable sincerity; 'perhaps as there's nothing else to do, you'd like to see the hounds ... ?'

I felt for Flurry, but of the two I felt more for Leigh Kelway as he accepted this alleviation. He disliked dogs, and held the newest views on sanitation, and I knew what Flurry's kennels could smell like. I was lighting a precautionary cigarette, when we caught sight of an old man riding up the drive. Flurry stopped short.

'Hold on a minute,' he said; 'here's an old chap that often brings me horses for the kennels; I must see what he wants.'

The man dismounted and approached Mr Knox, hat in hand, towing after him a gaunt and ancient black mare with a big knee.

'Well, Barrett,' began Flurry, surveying the mare with his hands in his pockets, 'I'm not giving the hounds meat this month, or only very little.'

'Ah, Master Flurry,' answered Barrett, 'it's you that's pleasant! Is it give the like o' this one for the dogs to ate! She's a vallyble strong young mare, no more than shixteen years of age, and ye'd sooner be lookin' at her goin' under a side-car than eatin' your dinner.'

'There isn't as much meat on her as'd fatten a jackdaw,' said Flurry, clinking the silver in his pockets as he searched for a matchbox. 'What are you asking for her?'

The old man drew cautiously up to him.

'Master Flurry,' he said solemnly, 'I'll sell her to *your* honour for five pounds, and she'll be worth ten after you give her a month's grass.'

Flurry lit his cigarette; then he said imperturbably, 'I'll give you seven shillings for her.'

Old Barrett put on his hat in silence, and in silence buttoned his coat and took hold of the stirrup leather. Flurry remained immovable.

'Master Flurry,' said old Barrett suddenly, with tears in his voice, 'you must make it eight, sir!'

'Michael!' called out Flurry with apparent irrelevance, 'run up to your father's and ask him would he lend me a loan of his side-car.'

Half an hour later we were, improbable as it may seem, on our way to Lisheen races. We were seated upon an outside-car of immemorial age, whose joints seemed to open and close again as it swung in and out of the ruts, whose tattered cushions stank of rats and mildew, whose wheels staggered and rocked like the legs of a drunken man. Between the shafts jogged the latest addition to the kennel larder, the eight-shilling mare. Flurry sat on one side, and kept her going at a rate of not less than four miles an hour; Leigh Kelway and I held on to the other.

'She'll get us as far as Lynch's anyway,' said Flurry, abandoning his first contention that she could do the whole distance, as he pulled her on to her legs after her fifteenth stumble, 'and he'll lend us some sort of a horse, if it was only a mule.'

'Do you notice that these cushions are very damp?' said Leigh Kelway to me in a hollow undertone.

'Small blame to them if they are!' replied Flurry. 'I've no doubt but they are out under the rain all day yesterday at Mrs Hurly's funeral.'

Leigh Kelway made no reply, but he took his notebook out of his pocket and sat on it.

We arrived at Lynch's at a little past three, and were there confronted by the next disappointment of this disastrous day. The door of Lynch's farmhouse was locked, and nothing replied to our knocking except a puppy, who barked hysterically from within.

'All gone to the races,' said Flurry philosophically, picking his way round the manure heap. 'No matter, here's the filly in the shed here. I know he's had her under a car.'

An agitating ten minutes ensued, during which Leigh Kelway and I got the eight-shilling mare out of the shafts and the harness, and Flurry, with our inefficient help, crammed the young mare into them. As Flurry had stated that she had been driven before, I was bound to believe him, but the difficulty of getting the bit into her mouth was remarkable, and so also was the crab-like manner in which she sidled out of the yard, with Flurry and myself at her head, and Leigh Kelway hanging on to the back of the car to keep it from jamming in the gateway.

'Sit up on the car now,' said Flurry when we got out on to the road; 'I'll lead her on a bit. She's been ploughed anyway; one side of her mouth's as tough as a gad!'

Leigh Kelway threw away the wisp of grass with which he had been cleaning his hands, and mopped his intellectual forehead; he was very silent. We both mounted the car, and Flurry, with the reins in his hand, walked beside the filly, who, with her tail clasped in, moved onward in a succession of short jerks.

'Oh, she's all right!' said Flurry, beginning to run, and dragging the filly into a trot; 'once she gets started ...' Here the filly spied a pig in a neighbouring field, and despite the fact that she had probably eaten out of the same trough with it, she gave a violent side-spring, and broke into a gallop.

'Now we're off!' shouted Flurry, making a jump at the car and clambering on; 'if the traces hold we'll do!'

The English language is powerless to suggest the view-halloo with which Mr Knox ended his speech, or to do more than indicate the rigid anxiety of Leigh Kelway's face as he regained his balance after the preliminary jerk and clutched the back rail. It must be said for Lynch's filly that she did not kick; she merely fled, like a dog with a kettle tied to its tail, from the pursuing rattle and jingle behind her, with the shafts buffeting her dusty sides as the car swung to and fro. Whenever she showed any signs of slackening, Flurry loosed another yell at her that renewed her panic, and thus we precariously covered another two or three miles of our journey.

Had it not been for a large stone lying on the road, and had the filly not chosen to swerve so as to bring the wheel on top of it, I dare say we might have got to the races; but by an unfortunate coincidence both these things occurred, and when we recovered from the consequent shock, the tyre of one of the wheels had come off, and was trundling with cumbrous gaiety into the ditch.

Flurry stopped the filly and began to laugh; Leigh Kelway said something startlingly unparliamentary under his breath.

'Well, it might be worse,' Flurry said consolingly as he lifted the tyre on to the car; 'we're not half a mile from a forge.'

We walked that half-mile in funereal procession behind the car; the glory had departed from the weather, and an ugly wall of cloud was rising up out of the west to meet the sun; the hills had darkened and lost colour, and the white bog cotton shivered in a cold wind that smelt of rain.

By a miracle the smith was not at the races, owing, as he

explained, to his having 'the toothaches', the two facts combined producing in him a morosity only equalled by that of Leigh Kelway. The smith's sole comment on the situation was to unharness the filly and drag her into the forge, where he tied her up. He then proceeded to whistle viciously on his fingers in the direction of a cottage, and to command, in tones of thunder, some unseen creature to bring over a couple of baskets of turf. The turf arrived in process of time, on a woman's back, and was arranged in a circle in a yard at the back of the forge. The tyre was bedded in it, and the turf was with difficulty kindled at different points.

'Ye'll not get to the races this day,' said the smith, yielding to a sardonic satisfaction; 'the turf's wet, and I haven't one to do a hand's turn for me.' He laid the wheel on the ground and lit his pipe.

Leigh Kelway looked pallidly about him over the spacious empty landscape of brown mountain slopes patched with golden furze and seamed with grey walls; I wondered if he were as hungry as I. We sat on stones opposite the smouldering ring of turf and smoked, and Flurry beguiled the smith into grim and calumnious confidences about every horse in the country. After about an hour, during which the turf went out three times, and the weather became more and more threatening, a girl with a red petticoat over her head appeared at the gate of the yard, and said to the smith:

'The horse is gone away from ye.'

'Where?' exclaimed Flurry, springing to his feet.

'I met him walking wesht the road there below, and when I thought to turn him he commenced to gallop.'

'Pulled her head out of the headstall,' said Flurry, after a rapid survey of the forge. 'She's near home by now.'

It was at this moment that the rain began; the situation could scarcely have been better stage-managed. After reviewing the position, Flurry and I decided that the only thing to do was to walk to a public house a couple of miles farther on, feed there if possible, hire a car, and go home.

It was an uphill walk, with mild, generous raindrops striking thicker and thicker on our faces; no one talked, and the grey clouds crowded up from behind the hills like billows of steam. Leigh Kelway bore it all with egregious resignation. I cannot pretend that I was at heart sympathetic, but by virtue of being his host I felt responsible for the breakdown, for his light suit, for everything, and divined his sentiment of horror at the first sight of the public house.

It was a long, low cottage, with a line of dripping elm trees overshadowing it; empty cars and carts round its door, and a babel from within, made it evident that the racegoers were pursuing a gradual homeward route. The shop was crammed with steaming countrymen, whose loud brawling voices, all talking together, roused my English friend to his first remark since we had left the forge.

'Surely, Yeates, we are not going into that place?' he said severely; 'those men are all drunk.'

'Ah, nothing to signify!' said Flurry, plunging in and driving his way through the throng like a plough. 'Here, Mary Kate!' he called to the girl behind the counter; 'tell your mother we want some tea and bread and butter in the room inside.'

The smell of bad tobacco and spilt porter was choking; we worked our way through it after him towards the end of the shop, intersecting at every hand discussions about the races.

'Tom was very nice. He spared his horse all along, and then he put into him –' 'Well, at Goggin's corner the third horse was before the second, but he was goin' wake in himself.' 'I tell ye the mare had the hind leg fasht in the fore.' 'Clancy was dipping in the saddle.' ' 'Twas a damn nice race whatever –'

We gained the inner room at last, a cheerless apartment, adorned with sacred pictures, a sewing-machine, and an array of supplementary tumblers and wineglasses; but, at all events, we had it so far to ourselves. At intervals during the next half-hour Mary Kate burst in with cups and plates, cast them on the table and disappeared, but of food there was no sign. After a further period of starvation and of listening to the noise in the shop, Flurry made a sortie, and, after lengthy and unknown adventures, reappeared, carrying a huge brown teapot and driving before him Mary Kate with the remainder of the repast. The bread tasted of mice, the butter of turf-smoke, the tea of brown paper, but we had got past the critical stage. I had entered upon my third round of bread and butter when the door was flung open, and my valued acquaintance, Slipper, slightly advanced in liquor, presented himself to our gaze. His bandy legs sprawled consequentially, his nose was redder than a coal of fire, his prominent eyes rolled crookedly upon us, and his left hand swept behind him the attempt of Mary Kate to frustrate his entrance.

'Good evening to my vinerable friend, Mr Flurry Knox!' he began, in the voice of a town crier, 'and to the Honourable Major Yeates, and the English gintleman!'

This impressive opening immediately attracted an audience from the shop, and the doorway filled with grinning faces as Slipper advanced farther into the room.

'Why weren't ye at the races, Mr Flurry?' he went on, his roving eye taking a grip of us all at the same time. 'Sure the Miss Bennetts and all the ladies was asking where were ye.'

'It'd take some time to tell them that,' said Flurry, with his mouth full; 'but what about the races, Slipper? Had you good sport?'

'Sport is it? Divil so pleasant an afternoon ever you seen,' replied Slipper. He leaned against a side table, and all the glasses on it jingled. 'Does your honour know O'Driscoll?' he went on irrelevantly. 'Sure you do. He was in your honour's stable. It's what we were all sayin'; it was a great pity your honour was not there, for the likin' you had to Driscoll.'

'That's thrue,' said a voice at the door.

'There wasn't one in the Barony but was gethered in it, through and fro,' continued Slipper, with a quelling glance at the interrupter; 'and there was tints for sellin' porther, and whiskey as pliable as new milk, and boys goin' round the tints outside, feeling for heads with the big ends of their blackthorns, and all kinds of recreations, and the Sons of Liberty's piffler and dhrum band from Skebawn; though faith! there was more of thim runnin' to look at the races than what was playin' in it; not to mention different occasions that the band-masther was atin' his lunch within in the whiskey tint.'

'But what about Driscoll?' said Flurry.

'Sure it's about him I'm tellin' ye,' replied Slipper, with the practised orator's watchful eye on his growing audience. ' 'Twas within in the same whiskey tint meself was, with the band-masther and a few of the lads, an' we buyin' a haporth o' crackers, when I seen me brave Driscoll landin' into the tint, and a pair o' thim long boots on him; him that hadn't a shoe nor a stocking to his foot when your honour had him picking grass out o' the stones behind in your yard. "Well," says I to meself, "we'll knock some spoort out of Driscoll!"

' "Come here to me, acushla!" says I to him; "I suppose it's some way wake in the legs y'are," says I, "an' the docthor put them on ye the way the people wouldn't thrample ye!"

' "May the divil choke ye!" says he, pleasant enough, but I knew by the blush he had he was vexed.

' "Then I suppose 'tis a left-tenant colonel y'are," says I; "yer mother must be proud out o' ye!" says I, "an' maybe ye'll lend her a loan o' thim waders when she's rinsin' yer bauneen in the river!" says I.

' "There'll be work out o' this!" says he, lookin' at me both sour and bitther.

' "Well indeed, I was thinkin' you were blue moulded for want of a batin'," says I. He was for fightin' us then, but afther we had him pacificated with about a quarther of a naggin o' sper-rits, he told us he was goin' ridin' in a race.

' "An' what'll ye ride?" says I.

' "Owld Bocock's mare," says he.

' "Knipes!" says I, sayin' a great curse; "is it that little stag-geen from the mountains; sure she's somethin' about the one age with meself," says I. "Many's the time Jamesy Geoghegan and meself used to be dhrivin' her to Macroom with pigs an' all soorts," says I; "an' is it leppin' stone walls ye want her to go now?"

' "Faith, there's walls and every vari'ty of obstackle in it," says he.

' "It'll be the best o' your play, so," says I, "to leg it away home out o' this."

' "An' who'll ride her, so?" says he.

' "Let the divil ride her," says I.'

Leigh Kelway, who had been leaning back seemingly half asleep, obeyed the hypnotism of Slipper's gaze, and opened his eyes.

'That was now all the conversation that passed between himself and meself,' resumed Slipper, 'and there was no great delay afther that till they said there was a race startin' and the dickens a one at all was goin' to ride only two, Driscoll and one Clancy. With that then I seen Mr Kinahane, the Petty Sessions clerk, goin' round clearin' the coorse, an' I gethered a few o' the neighbours, an' we walked the fields hither and over till we seen the most of the' obstackles.

' "Stand aisy now by the plantation," says I; "if they get to come as far as this, believe me ye'll see spoort," says I, "an' 'twill be a convanient spot to encourage the mare if she's anyway wake in herself," says I, cuttin' somethin' about five foot of an ash sapling out o' the plantation.

' "That's yer sort!" says owld Bocock, that was travellin' the racecoorse, peggin' a bit o' paper down with a thorn in front of every lep, the way Driscoll'd know the handiest place to face her at it.

'Well, I hadn't barely thrimmed the ash plant –'

'Have you any jam, Mary Kate?' interrupted Flurry, whose meal had been in no way interfered with by either the story or the highly-scented crowd who had come to listen to it.

'We have no jam, only thraycle, sir,' replied the invisible Mary Kate.

'I hadn't the switch barely thrimmed,' repeated Slipper firmly, 'when I heard the people screechin', an' I seen Driscoll an' Clancy comin' on, leppin' all before them, an' owld Bocock's mare bellusin' an' powdherin' along, an' bedad! whatever obstackle wouldn't throw *her* down, faith, she'd throw *it* down, an' there's the thraffic they had in it.

' "I declare to me sowl," says I, "if they continue on this way there's a great chance some one o' thim'll win," says I.

' "Ye lie!" says the bandmasther, bein' a thrifle fulsome after his luncheon.

' "I do not," says I, "in regard to seein' how soople them two boys is. Ye might observe," says I, "that if they have no convanient way to sit on the saddle, they'll ride the neck o' the horse till such time as they gets an occasion to lave it," says I.

'"Arrah, shut yer mouth!" says the bandmasther; "they're puckin' out this way now, an' may the divil admire me!" says he, "but Clancy has the other bet out, and the divil such leatherin' and beltin' of owld Bocock's mare ever you seen as what's in it!" says he.

'Well, when I seen them comin' to me, and Driscoll about the length of the plantation behind Clancy, I let a couple of bawls.

'"Skelp her, ye big brute!" says I. "What good's in ye that ye aren't able to skelp her?"'

The yell and the histrionic flourish of his stick with which Slipper delivered this incident brought down the house. Leigh Kelway was sufficiently moved to ask me in an undertone if 'skelp' was a local term.

'Well, Mr Flurry, and gintlemen,' recommenced Slipper, 'I declare to ye when owld Bocock's mare heard thim roars she sthretched out her neck like a gandher, and when she passed me out she give me a couple of grunts, and looked at me as ugly as a Christian.

'"Hah!" says I, givin' her a couple o' dhraws o' th' ash plant across the butt o' the tail, the way I wouldn't blind her; "I'll make ye grunt!" says I, "I'll nourish ye!"

'I knew well she was very frightful of th' ash plant since the winter Tommeen Sullivan had her under a side-car. But now, in place of havin' any obligations to me, ye'd be surprised if ye heard the blaspheemious expressions of that young boy that was ridin' her; and whether it was over-anxious he was, turnin' around the way I'd hear him cursin', or whether it was some slither or slide came to owld Bocock's mare, I dunno, but she was bet up agin the last obstacle but two, and before ye could say "Schnipes", she was standin' on her two ears beyond in th' other field! I declare to ye, on the vartue of me oath, she stood that way till she reconnoithered what side would Driscoll fall, an' she turned about then and rolled on him as cosy as if he was meadow grass!'

Slipper stopped short; the people in the doorway groaned appreciatively; Mary Kate murmured, 'The Lord save us!'

'The blood was dhruv out through his nose and ears,' continued Slipper, with a voice that indicated the cream of the narration, 'and you'd hear his bones crackin' on the ground! You'd have pitied the poor boy.'

'Good heavens!' said Leigh Kelway, sitting up very straight in his chair.

'Was he hurt, Slipper?' asked Flurry casually.

'Hurt is it?' echoed Slipper in high scorn; 'killed on the spot!' He paused to relish the effect of the denouement on Leigh Kelway. 'Oh, divil so pleasant an afthernoon ever you seen; and indeed, Mr Flurry, it's what we were all sayin', it was a great pity your honour was not there for the likin' you had for Driscoll.'

As he spoke the last word there was an outburst of singing and cheering from a car-load of people who had just pulled up at the door. Flurry listened, leaned back in his chair, and began to laugh.

'It scarcely strikes one as a comic incident,' said Leigh Kelway, very coldly to me; 'in fact, it seems to me that the police ought –'

'Show me Slipper!' bawled a voice in the shop; 'show me that dirty little undherlooper till I have his blood! Hadn't I the race won only for he souring the mare on me! What's that you say? I tell ye he did! He left seven slaps on her with the handle of a hayrake –'

There was in the room in which we were sitting a second door, leading to the back yard, a door consecrated to the unobtrusive visit of so-called 'Sunday travellers'. Through it Slipper faded away like a dream, and, simultaneously, a tall young man, with a face like a red-hot potato tied up in a bandage, squeezed his way from the shop into the room.

'Well, Driscoll,' said Flurry, 'since it wasn't the teeth of the rake he left on the mare, you needn't be talking!'

Leigh Kelway looked from one to the other with a wilder expression in his eye than I had thought it capable of. I read in it a resolve to abandon Ireland to her fate.

At eight o'clock we were still waiting for the car that we had been assured should be ours directly it returned from the races.

At half past eight we had adopted the only possible course that
remained, and had accepted the offers of lifts on the laden cars
that were returning to Skebawn, and I presently was gratified
by the spectacle of my friend Leigh Kelway wedged between a
roulette table and its proprietor on one side of a car, with Driscoll and Slipper, mysteriously reconciled and excessively drunk,
seated, locked in each other's arms, on the other. Flurry and I,
somewhat similarly placed, followed on two other cars. I was
scarcely surprised when I was informed that the melancholy
white animal in the shafts of the leading car was Owld Bocock's
much-enduring steeplechaser.

The night was very dark and stormy, and it is almost super-
fluous to say that no one carried lamps; the rain poured upon
us, and through wind and wet Owld Bocock's mare set the pace
at a rate that showed she knew from bitter experience what was
expected from her by gentlemen who had spent the evening in
a public house; behind her the other two tired horses followed
closely, incited to emulation by shouting, singing, and a liberal
allowance of whip. We were a good ten miles from Skebawn, and
never had the road seemed so long. For mile after mile the
half-seen low walls slid past us, with occasional plunges into
caverns of darkness under trees. Sometimes from a wayside cabin
a dog would dash out to bark at us as we rattled by; sometimes
our cavalcade swung aside to pass, with yells and counter-yells,
crawling carts filled with other belated race-goers.

I was nearly wet through, even though I received considerable
shelter from a Skebawn publican, who slept heavily and irre-
pressibly on my shoulder. Driscoll, on the leading car, had struck
up an approximation to the 'Wearing of the Green', when a
wavering star appeared on the road ahead of us. It grew
momently larger; it came towards us apace. Flurry, on the car
behind me, shouted suddenly:

'That's the mail-car, with one of the lamps out! Tell those
fellows ahead to look out!'

But the warning fell on deaf ears.

> *'When laws can change the blades of grass*
> *From growing as they grow —'*

howled five discordant voices, oblivious of the towering proximity of the star.

A Bianconi mail-car is nearly three times the size of an
ordinary outside-car, and when on a dark night it advances,
Cyclops-like, with but one eye, it is difficult for even a sober
driver to calculate its bulk. Above the sounds of melody there
arose the thunder of heavy wheels, the splashing trample of
three big horses, then a crash and a turmoil of shouts. Our cars
pulled up just in time, and I tore myself from the embrace of
my publican to go to Leigh Kelway's assistance.

The wing of the Bianconi had caught the wing of the smaller
car, flinging Owld Bocock's mare on her side and throwing
her freight headlong on top of her, the heap being surmounted
by the roulette table. The driver of the mail-car unshipped his
solitary lamp and turned it on the disaster. I saw that Flurry
had already got hold of Leigh Kelway by the heels, and was
dragging him from under the others. He struggled up hatless,
muddy and gasping, with Driscoll hanging on by his neck,
still singing the 'Wearing of the Green'.

A voice from the mail-car said incredulously, *'Leigh Kelway!'*
A spectacled face glared down upon him from under the dripping spikes of an umbrella.

It was the Right Honourable the Earl of Waterbury, Leigh
Kelway's chief, returning from his fishing excursion.

Meanwhile Slipper, in the ditch, did not cease to announce
that 'Divil so pleasant an afthernoon ever ye seen as what was
in it!'

Home Sickness

GEORGE MOORE

He told the doctor he was due in the bar-room at eight o'clock in the morning; the bar-room was in a slum in the Bowery; and he had only been able to keep himself in health by getting up at five o'clock and going for long walks in the Central Park.

'A sea-voyage is what you want,' said the doctor. 'Why not go to Ireland for two or three months? You will come back a new man.'

'I'd like to see Ireland again.'

And he began to wonder how the people at home were getting on. The doctor was right. He thanked him, and three weeks after he landed in Cork.

As he sat in the railway-carriage he recalled his native village, built among the rocks of the large headland stretching out into the winding lake. He could see the houses and the streets, and the fields of the tenants, and the Georgian mansion and the owners of it; he and they had been boys together before he went to America. He remembered the villagers going every morning to the big house to work in the stables, in the garden, in the fields – mowing, reaping, digging, and Michael Malia building a wall; it was all as clear as if it were yesterday, yet he had been thirteen years in America; and when the train stopped at the station, the first thing he did was to look round for any changes that might have come into it. It was the same blue limestone station as it was thirteen years ago, with the same five long miles between it and Duncannon. He had once walked these miles gaily, in little over an hour, carrying a heavy bundle on a stick, but he did not feel strong enough for the walk today, though the evening tempted him to try it. A car was waiting at the station, and the boy, discerning from his accent and his dress that Bryden had come from America, plied him with questions, which Bryden answered rapidly, for he wanted to hear who were still living in the village, and if there was a house in which he could get a clean lodging. The best house in the village, he was told, was Mike Scully's, who had been away in a situation for many years, as a coachman in the King's County, but had come back and built a fine house with a concrete floor. The boy could recommend the loft, he had slept in it himself, and Mike would be glad to take in a lodger, he had no doubt. Bryden remembered that Mike had been in a situation at the big house. He had intended to be a jockey, but had suddenly shot up into a fine tall man, and had become a coachman instead; and Bryden tried to recall his face, but could only remember a straight nose and a somewhat dusky complexion.

So Mike had come back from King's County, and had built himself a house, had married – there were children for sure running about; while he, Bryden, had gone to America, but he had come back; perhaps he, too, would build a house in Duncannon, and – his reverie was suddenly interrupted by the carman.

'There's Mike Scully,' he said, pointing with his whip, and Bryden saw a tall, finely built, middle-aged man coming through the gates, who looked astonished when he was accosted, for he had forgotten Bryden even more completely than Bryden had forgotten him; and many aunts and uncles were mentioned before he began to understand.

'You've grown into a fine man, James,' he said, looking at Bryden's great width of chest. 'But you're thin in the cheeks, and you're very sallow in the cheeks too.'

'I haven't been very well lately – that is one of the reasons I've come back; but I want to see you all again.'

'And thousand welcome you are.'

Bryden paid the carman, and wished him 'God-speed'. They divided the luggage, Mike carrying the bag and Bryden the bundle, and they walked round the lake, for the townland was at the back of the domain; and while walking he remembered the woods thick and well forested; now they were wind-worn, the drains were choked, and the bridge leading across the lake inlet was falling away. Their way led between long fields where herds of cattle were grazing, the road was broken – Bryden wondered how the villagers drove their carts over it, and Mike told him that the landlord could not keep it in repair, and he would not allow it to be kept in repair out of the rates, for then it would be a public road, and he did not think there should be a public road through his property.

At the end of many fields they came to the village, and it looked a desolate place, even on this fine evening, and Bryden remarked that the county did not seem to be as much lived in as it used to be. It was at once strange and familiar to see the chickens in the kitchen; and, wishing to re-knit himself to the old customs, he begged of Mrs Scully not to drive them out, saying they reminded him of old times.

'And why wouldn't they?' Mike answered, 'he being one of ourselves bred and born in Duncannon, and his father before him.'

'Now, is it truth ye are telling me?' and she gave him her hand, after wiping it on her apron, saying he was heartily welcome, only she was afraid he wouldn't care to sleep in a loft.

'Why wouldn't I sleep in a loft, a dry loft! You're thinking a good deal of America over here,' he said, 'but I reckon it isn't all you think it. Here you work when you like and you sit down when you like; but when you've had a touch of blood-poisoning as I had, and when you have seen young people walking with a stick, you think that there is something to be said for old Ireland.'

'You'll take a sup of milk, won't you? You must be dry,' said Mrs Scully.

And when he had drunk the milk, Mike asked him if he would like to go inside or if he would like to go for a walk.

'Maybe resting you'd like to be.'

And they went into the cabin and started to talk about the wages a man could get in America, and the long hours of work.

And after Bryden had told Mike everything about America that he thought of interest, he asked Mike about Ireland. But Mike did not seem to be able to tell him much. They were all very poor – poorer, perhaps, than when he left them.

'I don't think anyone except myself has a five-pound note to his name.'

Bryden hoped he felt sufficiently sorry for Mike. But after all, Mike's life and prospects mattered little to him. He had come back in search of health, and he felt better already; the milk had done him good, and the bacon and the cabbage in the pot sent forth a savoury odour. The Scullys were very kind, they pressed him to make a good meal; a few weeks of country air and food, they said, would give him back the health he had lost in the Bowery; and when Bryden said he was longing for a smoke, Mike said there was no better sign than that. During his long illness he had never wanted to smoke, and he was a confirmed smoker.

It was comfortable to sit by the mild peat fire watching the smoke of their pipes drifting up the chimney, and all Bryden wanted was to be left alone; he did not want to hear of anyone's misfortunes, but about nine o'clock a number of villagers came in, and Bryden remembered one or two of them – he used to know them very well when he was a boy; their talk was as depressing as their appearance, and he could feel no interest whatever in them. He was not moved when he heard that Higgins the stonemason was dead; he was not affected when he heard that Mary Kelly, who used to go to do the laundry at the Big House, had married; he was only interested when he heard she had gone to America. No, he had not met her there; America is a big place. Then one of the peasants asked him if he remembered Patsy Carabine, who used to do the gardening at the Big House. Yes, he remembered Patsy well. He had not been able to do any work on account of his arm; his house had fallen in; he had given up his holding and gone into the poorhouse. All this was very sad, and to avoid hearing any further unpleasantness, Bryden began to tell them about America. And they sat round listening to him; but all the talking was on his side; he wearied of it; and looking round the group he recognized a ragged hunchback with grey hair; twenty years ago he was a young hunchback and, turning to him, Bryden asked him if he were doing well with his five acres.

'Ah, not much. This has been a poor season. The potatoes failed; they were watery – there is no diet in them.'

These peasants were all agreed that they could make nothing out of their farms. Their regret was that they had not gone to America when they were young; and after striving to take an interest in the fact that O'Connor had lost a mare and a foal worth forty pounds, Bryden began to wish himself back in the slum. And when they left the house he wondered if every evening would be like the present one. Mike piled fresh sods on the fire, and he hoped it would show enough light in the loft for Bryden to undress himself by.

The cackling of some geese in the street kept him awake, and he seemed to realize suddenly how lonely the country was, and he foresaw mile after mile of scanty fields stretching all round the lake with one little town in the far corner. A dog howled in the distance, and the fields and the boreens between him and the dog appeared as in a crystal. He could hear Michael breathing by his wife's side in the kitchen, and he could barely resist the impulse to run out of the house, and he might have yielded to it, but he wasn't sure that he mightn't awaken Mike as he came down the ladder. His terror increased, and he drew the blanket over his head. He fell asleep and awoke and fell asleep again, and lying on his back he dreamed of the men he had seen sitting round the fireside that evening, like spectres they seemed to him in his dream. He seemed to have been asleep only a few minutes when he heard Mike calling him. He had come half-way up the ladder, and was telling him that breakfast was ready.

'What kind of a breakfast will he give me?' Bryden asked himself as he pulled on his clothes. There were tea and hot griddle cakes for breakfast, and there were fresh eggs; there was sunlight in the kitchen, and he liked to hear Mike tell of the work he was going to be at in the farm – one of about fifteen acres, at least ten of it was grass; he grew an acre of potatoes, and some corn, and some turnips for his sheep. He had a nice bit of meadow, and he took down his scythe, and as he put the whetstone in his belt Bryden noticed a second scythe, and he asked Mike if he should go down with him and help him to finish the field.

'It's a long time since you've done any mowing, and it's heavier work than you think for. You'd better go for a walk by the lake.' Seeing that Bryden looked a little disappointed he added, 'If you like you can come up in the afternoon and help me to turn the grass over.' Bryden said he would, and the morning passed pleasantly by the lake shore – a delicious breeze rustled in the trees, and the reeds were talking together, and the ducks were talking in the reeds; a cloud blotted out the sunlight, and the cloud passed and the sun shone, and the reed cast its shadow again in the still water; there was a lapping always about the shingle; the magic of returning health was sufficient distraction for the convalescent; he lay with his eyes fixed upon the castles, dreaming of the men that had manned the battlements; whenever a peasant driving a cart or an ass or an old woman with a bundle of sticks on her back went by, Bryden kept them in chat, and he soon knew the village by heart. One day the landlord from the Georgian mansion set on the pleasant green hill came along, his retriever at his heels, and stopped, surprised at finding somebody whom he didn't know on his property. 'What, James Bryden!' he said. And the story was told again how ill health had overtaken him at last, and he had come home to Duncannon to recover. The two walked as far as the pine-wood, talking of the county, what it had been, the ruin it was slipping into, and as they parted Bryden asked for the loan of a boat.

'Of course, of course!' the landlord answered, and Bryden rowed about the islands every morning; and resting upon his oars looked at the old castles, remembering the prehistoric raiders that the landlord had told him about. He came across the stones to which the lake-dwellers had tied their boats, and these signs of ancient Ireland were pleasing to Bryden in his present mood.

As well as the great lake there was a smaller lake in the bog where the villagers cut their turf. This lake was famous for its pike, and the landlord allowed Bryden to fish there, and one evening when he was looking for a frog with which to bait his line he met Margaret Dirken driving home the cows for the milking. Margaret was the herdsman's daughter, and lived in a cottage near the Big House; but she came up to the village whenever there was a dance, and Bryden had found himself opposite to her in the reels. But until this evening he had had little opportunity of speaking to her, and he was glad to speak to someone, for the evening was lonely, and they stood talking together.

'You're getting your health again,' she said, 'and will be leaving us soon.'

'I'm in no hurry.'

'You're grand people over there; I hear a man is paid four dollars a day for his work.'

'And how much,' said James, 'has he to pay for his food and for his clothes?'

Her cheeks were bright and her teeth small, white and beautifully even; and a woman's soul looked at Bryden out of her soft Irish eyes. He was troubled and turned aside, and catching sight of a frog looking at him out of a tuft of grass, he said:

'I have been looking for a frog to put upon my pike line.'

The frog jumped right and left, and nearly escaped in some bushes, but he caught it and returned with it in his hand.

'It is just the kind of frog a pike will like,' he said. 'Look at its great white belly and its bright yellow back.'

And without more ado he pushed the wire to which the hook was fastened through the frog's fresh body, and dragging it through the mouth he passed the hooks through the hind-legs and tied the line to the end of the wire.

'I think,' said Margaret, 'I must be looking after my cows; it's time I got them home.'

'Won't you come down to the lake while I set my line?'

She thought for a moment and said:

'No, I'll see you from here.'

He went down to the reedy tarn, and at his approach several snipe got up, and they flew above his head uttering sharp cries.

His fishing-rod was a long hazel-stick, and he threw the frog as far as he could in the lake. In doing this he roused some wild ducks; a mallard and two ducks got up, and they flew towards the larger lake in a line with an old castle; and they had not disappeared from view when Bryden came towards her, and he and she drove the cows home together that evening.

They had not met very often when she said: 'James, you had better not come here so often calling to me.'

'Don't you wish me to come?'

'Yes, I wish you to come well enough, but keeping company isn't the custom of the country, and I don't want to be talked about.'

'Are you afraid the priest would speak against us from the altar?'

'He has spoken against keeping company, but it is not so much what the priest says, for there is no harm in talking.'

'But if you're going to be married, there is no harm in walking out together.'

'Well, not so much, but marriages are made differently in these parts; there isn't much courting here.'

And next day it was known in the village that James was going to marry Margaret Dirken.

His desire to excel the boys in dancing had caused a stir of gaiety in the parish, and for some time past there had been dancing in every house where there was a floor fit to dance upon; and if the cottager had no money to pay for a barrel of beer, James Bryden, who had money, sent him a barrel, so that Margaret might get her dance. She told him that they sometimes crossed over into another parish where the priest was not so averse to dancing, and James wondered. And next morning at Mass he wondered at their simple fervour. Some of them held their hands above their head as they prayed, and all this was very new and very old to James Bryden. But the obedience of these people to their priest surprised him. When he was a lad they had not been so obedient, or he had forgotten their obedience; and he listened in mixed anger and wonderment to the priest, who was scolding his parishioners, speaking to them by name, saying that he had heard there was dancing going on in their homes. Worse than that, he said he had seen boys and girls loitering about the road, and the talk that went on was of one kind – love. He said that newspapers containing love stories were finding their way into the people's houses, stories about love, in which there was nothing elevating or ennobling. The people listened, accepting the priest's opinion without question. And their pathetic submission was the submission of a primitive people clinging to religious authority, and Bryden contrasted the weakness and incompetence of the people about him with the modern restlessness and cold energy of the people he left behind him.

One evening, as they were dancing, a knock came to the door, and the piper stopped playing, and the dancers whispered:

'Someone has told on us: it is the priest.'

And the awe-stricken villagers crowded round the cottage fire, afraid to open the door. But the priest said that if they didn't open the door he would put his shoulder to it and force it open. Bryden went towards the door, saying he would allow no one to threaten him, priest or no priest, but Margaret caught his arm and told him that if he said anything to the priest, the priest would speak against them from the altar, and they would be shunned by the neighbours.

'I've heard of your goings-on,' he said, 'of your beer-drinking and dancing. I'll not have it in my parish. If you want that sort of thing you had better go to America.'

'If that is intended for me, sir, I'll go back tomorrow. Margaret can follow.'

'It isn't the dancing, it's the drinking I'm opposed to,' said the priest, turning to Bryden.

'Well, no one has drunk too much, sir,' said Bryden.

'But you'll sit here drinking all night,' and the priest's eyes went to the corner where the women had gathered, and Bryden felt that the priest looked on the women as more dangerous than the porter. 'It's after midnight,' he said, taking out his watch.

By Bryden's watch it was only half past eleven, and while they were arguing about the time, Mrs Scully offered Bryden's umbrella to the priest, for in his hurry to stop the dancing the priest had gone out without his; and, as if to show Bryden that he bore him no ill will, the priest accepted the loan of the umbrella, for he was thinking of the big marriage fee that Bryden would pay him.

'I shall be badly off for the umbrella tomorrow,' Bryden said, as soon as the priest was out of the house. He was going with his father-in-law to a fair. His father-in-law was learning him how to buy and sell cattle. The country was mending, and a man might become rich in Ireland if he only had a little capital. Margaret had an uncle on the other side of the lake who would give twenty pounds, and her father would give another twenty pounds. Bryden had saved two hundred pounds. Never in the village of Duncannon had a young couple begun life with so much prospect of success, and some time after Christmas was spoken of as the best time for the marriage; James Bryden said that he would not be able to get his money out of America before the spring. The delay seemed to vex him, and he seemed anxious to be married, until one day he received a letter from America, from a man who had served in the bar with him. This friend wrote to ask Bryden if he were coming back. The letter was no more than a passing wish to see Bryden again. Yet Bryden stood looking at it, and everyone wondered what could be in the letter. It seemed momentous, and they hardly believed him when he said it was from a friend who wanted to know if his health were better. He tried to forget the letter, and he looked at the worn fields, divided by walls of loose stones, and a great longing came upon him.

The smell of the Bowery slum had come across the Atlantic, and had found him out in his western headland; and one night he awoke from a dream in which he was hurling some drunken customer through the open doors into the darkness. He had seen his friend in his white duck jacket throwing drink from glass into glass amid the din of voices and strange accents; he had heard the clang of money as it was swept into the till, and his sense sickened for the bar-room. But how should he tell Margaret Dirken that he could not marry her? She had built her life upon this marriage. He could not tell her that he would not marry her ... yet he must go. He felt as if he were being hunted; the thought that he must tell Margaret that he could

not marry her hunted him day after day as a weasel hunts a
rabbit. Again and again he went to meet her with the intention
of telling her that he did not love her, that their lives were
not for one another, that it had all been a mistake, and that
happily he had found out it was a mistake soon enough. But
Margaret, as if she guessed what he was about to speak of, threw
her arms about him and begged him to say he loved her, and
that they would be married at once. He agreed that he loved
her, and that they would be married at once. But he had not
left her many minutes before the feeling came upon him that
he could not marry her – that he must go away. The smell of
the bar-room hunted him down. Was it for the sake of the
money that he might make there that he wished to go back? No,
it was not the money. What then? His eyes fell on the bleak
country, on the little fields divided by bleak walls; he remembered the pathetic ignorance of the people, and it was these
things that he could not endure. It was the priest who came to
forbid the dancing. Yes, it was the priest. As he stood looking
at the line of the hills, the bar-room seemed by him. He heard
the politicians, and the excitement of politics was in his blood
again. He must go away from this place – he must get back to
the bar-room. Looking up, he saw the scanty orchard, and he
hated the spare road that led to the village, and he hated the
little hill at the top of which the village began, and he hated
more than all other places the house where he was to live with
Margaret Dirken – if he married her. He could see it from where
he stood – by the edge of the lake, with twenty acres of pasture
land about it, for the landlord had given up part of his demesne
land to them.

He caught sight of Margaret, and he called her to come
through the stile.

'I have just had a letter from America.'

'About the money?'

'Yes, about the money. But I shall have to go over there.'

He stood looking at her, wondering what to say; and she
guessed that he would tell her that he must go to America before
they were married.

'Do you mean, James, you will have to go at once?'

'Yes,' he said, 'at once. But I shall come back in time to be married in August. It will only mean delaying our marriage a month.'

They walked on a little way talking, and every step he took James felt that he was a step nearer the Bowery slum. And when they came to the gate Bryden said:

'I must walk on or I shall miss the train.'

'But,' she said, 'you are not going now – you are not going today?'

'Yes, this morning. It is seven miles. I shall have to hurry not to miss the train.'

And then she asked him if he would ever come back.

'Yes,' he said, 'I am coming back.'

'If you are coming back, James, why don't you let me go with you?'

'You couldn't walk fast enough. We should miss the train.'

'One moment, James. Don't make me suffer; tell me the truth. You are not coming back. Your clothes – where shall I send them?'

He hurried away, hoping he would come back. He tried to think that he liked the country he was leaving, that it would be better to have a farmhouse and live there with Margaret Dirken than to serve drinks behind a counter in the Bowery. He did not think he was telling her a lie when he said he was coming back. Her offer to forward his clothes touched his heart, and at the end of the road he stood and asked himself if he should go back to her. He would miss the train if he waited another minute, and he ran on. And he would have missed the train if he had not met a car. Once he was on the car he felt himself safe – the country was already behind him. The train and the boat at Cork were mere formulae; he was already in America.

And when the tall skyscraper stuck up beyond the harbour, he felt the thrill of home that he had not found in his native village and wondered how it was that the smell of the bar seemed more natural than the smell of fields, and the roar of crowds more welcome than the silence of the lake's edge. He entered into negotiations for the purchase of the bar-room. He took a wife, she bore him sons and daughters, the bar-room prospered, property came and went; he grew old, his wife died, he retired from business, and reached the age when a man begins to feel there are not many years in front of him, and that all he has had to do in life has been done. His children married, lonesomeness began to creep about him in the evening, and when he looked into the firelight, a vague tender reverie floated up, and Margaret's soft eyes and name vivified the dusk. His wife and children passed out of mind, and it seemed to him that a memory was the only real thing he possessed, and the desire to see Margaret again grew intense. But she was an old woman, she had married, maybe she was dead. Well, he would like to be buried in the village where he was born.

There is an unchanging, silent life within every man that none knows but himself, and his unchanging silent life was his memory of Margaret Dirken. The bar-room was forgotten and all that concerned it, and the things he saw most clearly were the green hillside, and the bog lake and the rushes about it, and the greater lake in the distance, and behind it the blue line of wandering hills.

The Ploughing of Leaca-na-Naomh

DANIEL CORKERY

WITH which shall I begin – man or place? Perhaps I had better first tell of the man; of him the incident left so withered that no sooner had I laid eyes on him than I said: Here is one whose blood at some terrible moment of his life stood still, stood still and never afterwards regained its quiet, old-time ebb-and-flow. A word or two then about the place – a sculped-out shell in the Kerry mountains, an evil-looking place, green-glaring like a sea when a storm had passed. To connect man and place together, even as they worked one with the other to bring the tragedy about, ought not then to be so difficult.

I had gone into those desolate treeless hills searching after the traces of an old-time Gaelic family that once were lords of them. But in this mountainy glen I forgot my purpose almost as soon as I entered it.

In that round-ended valley – they call such a valley a coom – there was but one farmhouse, and Considine was the name of the householder – Shawn Considine, the man whose features were white with despair; his haggard appearance reminded me of what one so often sees in war-ravaged Munster – a ruined castle-wall hanging out above the woods, a grey spectre. He made me welcome, speaking slowly, as if he was not used to such amenities. At once I began to explain my quest. I soon stumbled; I felt that his thoughts were far away. I started again. A daughter of his looked at me – Nora was her name – looked at me with meaning; I could not read her look aright. Hap-hazardly I went through old family names and recalled old world incidents; but with no more success. He then made to speak; I could catch only broken phrases, repeated again and

again. 'In the presence of God.' 'In the Kingdom of God.' 'All
gone for ever.' 'Let them rest in peace' (I translate from the
Irish). Others too there were of which I could make nothing.
Suddenly I went silent. His eyes had begun to change. They
were not becoming fiery or angry – that would have emboldened
me, I would have blown on his anger; a little passion, even an
outburst of bitter temper would have troubled me but little if
in its sudden revelation I came on some new fact or even a new
name in the broken story of that ruined family. But no; not
fiery but cold and terror-stricken were his eyes becoming. Fear
was rising in them like dank water. I withdrew my gaze, and
his daughter ventured on speech:

'If you speak of the cattle, noble person, or of the land, or
of the new laws, my father will converse with you; but he is
dark about what happened long ago.' Her eyes were even more
earnest than her tongue – they implored the pity of silence.

So much for the man. A word now about the place where his
large but neglected farmhouse stood against a bluff of rock.
To enter that evil-looking green-mountained glen was like
entering the jaws of some slimy, cold-blooded animal. You felt
yourself leaving the sun, you shrunk together, you hunched
yourself as if to bear an ugly pressure. In the far-back part of
it was what is called in the Irish language a *leaca* – a slope of
land, a lift of land, a bracket of land jutting out from the side
of a mountain. This leaca, which the daughter explained was
called Leaca-na-Naomh – the Leaca of the Saints – was very
remarkable. It shone like a gem. It held the sunshine as a field
holds its crop of golden wheat. On three sides it was pedestalled
by the sheerest rock. On the fourth side it curved up to join
the parent mountain-flank. Huge and high it was, yet height
and size took some time to estimate, for there were mountains
all around it. When you had been looking at it for some time
you said aloud: 'That leaca is high!' When you had stared for
a longer time you said: 'That leaca is immensely high – and
huge!' Still the most remarkable thing about it was the way it
held the sunshine. When all the valley had gone into the gloom
of twilight – and this happened in the early afternoon – the
leaca was still at mid-day. When the valley was dark with night

and the lamps had been long alight in the farmhouse, the leaca
had still the red gleam of sunset on it. It hung above the misty
valley like a velarium – as they used to call that awning-cloth
which hung above the emperor's seat in the amphitheatre.

'What is it called, do you say?' I asked again.

'Leaca-na-Naomh,' she replied.

'Saints used to live on it?'

'The hermits,' she answered, and sighed deeply.

Her trouble told me that that leaca had to do with the fear
that was burrowing like a mole in her father's heart. I would
test it. Soon afterwards the old man came by, his eyes on the
ground, his lips moving.

'That leaca,' I said, 'what do you call it?'

He looked up with a startled expression. He was very white;
he couldn't abide my steady gaze.

'Nora,' he cried, raising his voice suddenly and angrily, 'cas
isteach iad, cas isteach iad!' He almost roared at the gentle
girl.

'Turn in – what?' I said, roughly; 'the cattle are in long ago.'

' 'Tis right they should,' he answered, leaving me.

Yes, this leaca and this man had between them moulded out
a tragedy, as between two hands.

Though the sun had gone I still sat staring at it. It was far
off, but whatever light remained in the sky had gathered to it.
I was wondering at its clear definition among all the vague and
misty mountain-shapes when a voice quivering with age, high
and untuneful, addressed me:

' 'Twould be right for you to see it when there's snow on it.'

'Ah!'

' 'Tis blinding!' The voice had changed so much as his inner
vision strengthened that I gazed up quickly at him. He was a
very old man, somewhat fairy-like in appearance, but he had
the eyes of a boy. These eyes told me he was one who had lived
imaginatively. Therefore I almost gripped him lest he should
escape; from him would I learn of Leaca-na-Naomh. Shall I
speak of him as a vassal of the house, or as a tatter of the
family, or as a spall of the rough landscape? He was native to
all three. His homespun was patched with patches as large and

as straight-cut as those you'd see on a fisherman's sail. He was,
clothes and all, the same colour as the aged lichen of the rocks;
but his eyes were as fresh as dew.

Gripping him, as I have said, I searched his face, as one
searches a poem for a hidden meaning.

'When did it happen, this dreadful thing?' I said.

He was taken off his guard. I could imagine, I could almost
feel his mind struggling, summoning up an energy sufficient to
express his idea of how as well as when the thing happened.
At last he spoke deliberately.

'When the master' – I knew he meant the householder – 'was
at his best, his swiftest and strongest in health, in riches, in
force and spirit.' He hammered every word.

'Ah!' I said; and I noticed the night had begun to thicken,
fitly I thought, for my mind was already making mad leaps
into the darkness of conjecture. He began to speak a more
simple language.

'In those days he was without burden or ailment – unless
maybe every little biteen of land between the rocks that he
had not as yet brought under the plough was a burden. This,
that, yonder, all those fine fields that have gone back again
into heather and furze, it was he made them. There's sweat in
them! But while he bent over them in the little dark days of
November, dropping his sweat, he would raise up his eyes and
fix them on the leaca. *That* would be worth all of them, and
worth more than double all of them if it was brought under the
plough.'

'And why not?' I said.

'Plough the bed of the saints?'

'I had forgotten.'

'You are not a Gael of the Gaels maybe?'

'I had forgotten; continue; it grows chilly.'

'He had a serving man; he was a fool; they were common
in the country then; they had not been as yet herded into
asylums. He was a fool; but a true Gael. That he never forgot
except once.'

'Continue.'

'He had also a sire horse. Griosach he called him, he was so
strong, so high and princely.'

'A plough horse?'

'He had never been harnessed. He was the master's pride and boast. The people gathered on the hillside when he rode him to Mass. You looked at the master; you looked at the horse; the horse knew the hillsides were looking at him. He made music with his hoofs, he kept his eyes to himself, he was so proud.'

'What of the fool?'

'Have I spoken of the fool?'

'Yes, a true Gael.'

' 'Tis true, that word. He was as strong as Griosach. He was what no one else was: he was a match for Griosach. The master petted the horse. The horse petted the master. Both of them knew they went well together. But Griosach the sire horse feared Liam Ruadh the fool; and Liam Ruadh the fool feared Griosach the sire horse. For neither had as yet found out that he was stronger than the other. They would play together like two strong boys, equally matched in strength and daring. They would wrestle and throw each other. Then they would leave off; and begin again when they had recovered their breath.'

'Yes,' I said, 'the master, the horse Griosach, the fool Liam – now, the Leaca, the Leaca.'

'I have brought in the Leaca. It will come in again – now! The master was one day standing at a gap for a long time; there was no one near him. Liam Ruadh came near him. "It is not lucky to be silent as that," he said. The master raised his head and answered:

' "The Leaca for wheat."

'The fool nearly fell down in a sprawling heap. No one had ever heard of anything like that.

' "No," he said like a child.

' "The Leaca for wheat," the master said again, as if there was someone inside him speaking.

'The fool was getting hot and angry. "The Leaca for prayer!" he said.

' "The Leaca for wheat," said the master, a third time.

'When the fool heard him he gathered himself up and roared – a loud "O-oh!" It went around the hills like sudden thunder; in the little breath he had left he said: "The Leaca for prayer!"

'The master went away from him; who could tell what might have happened?

'The next day the fool was washing a sheep's diseased foot – he had the struggling animal held firm in his arms when the master slipped behind him and whispered in his ear:

' "The Leaca for wheat."

'Before the fool could free the animal the master was gone. He was a wild, swift man that day. He laughed. It was that self-same night he went into the shed where Liam slept and stood a moment looking at the large face of the fool working in his dreams. He watched him like that a minute. Then he flashed the lantern quite close into the fool's eyes so as to dazzle him, and he cried out harshly, "The Leaca for wheat," making his voice appear far off, like a trumpet call, and before the fool could understand where he was, or whether he was asleep or awake, the light was gone and the master was gone.

'Day after day the master put the same thought into the fool's ear. And Liam was becoming sullen and dark. Then one night long after we were all in our sleep we heard a wild crash.

'The fool had gone to the master's room. He found the door bolted. He put his shoulder to it. The door went in about the room, and the arch above it fell in pieces around the fool's head – all in the still night.

' "Who's there? What is it?" cried the master, starting up in his bed.

' "Griosach for the plough!" said the fool.

'No one could think of Griosach being hitched to a plough. The master gave him no answer. He lay down in his bed and covered his face. The fool went back to his straw. Whenever the master now said, "The Leaca for wheat," the fool would answer, "Griosach for the plough."

'The tree turns the wind aside, yet the wind at last twists the tree. Like wind and tree master and fool played against each other, until at last they each of them had spent their force.

' "I will take Griosach and Niamh and plough the leaca," said the fool; it was a hard November day.

' "As you wish," said the master. Many a storm finished with a little sob of wind. Their voices were now like a little wind.

'The next night a pair of smiths were brought into the coom

all the way from Aunascawl. The day after that the mountains were ringing with their blows as the ploughing gear was over-hauled. Without rest or laughter or chatter the work went on, for Liam was at their shoulders, and he hardly gave them time to wipe their sweaty hair. One began to sing " 'Tis my grief on Monday now", but Liam struck him one blow and stretched him. He returned to his work quiet enough after that. We saw the fool's anger rising. We made way for him; and he was going back and forth the whole day long; in the evening his mouth began to froth and his tongue to blab. We drew away from him; wondering what he was thinking of. The master himself began to grow timid; he hadn't a word in him; but he kept looking up at us from under his brow as if he feared we would turn against him. Sure we wouldn't; wasn't he our master – even what he did?

'When the smiths had mounted their horses that night to return to Aunascawl, one of them stooped down to the master's ear and whispered: "Watch him, he's in a fever."

' "Who?"

' "The fool." That was a true word.

'Some of us rode down with the smiths to the mouth of the pass, and as we did so, snow began to fall silently and thickly. We were glad; we thought it might put back the dreadful business of the ploughing. When we returned towards the house we were talking. But a boy checked us.

' "Whisht!" he said.

'We listened. We crept beneath the thatch of the stables. Within we heard the fool talking to the horses. We knew he was putting his arms around their necks. When he came out, he was quiet and happy-looking. We crouched aside to let him pass. Then we told the master.

' "Go to your beds," he said, coldly enough.

'We played no cards that night; we sang no songs; we thought it too long until we were in our dark beds. The last thing we thought of was the snow falling, falling, falling on Leaca-na-Naomh and on all the mountains. There was not a stir or a sigh in the house. Everyone feared to hear his own bed creak. And at last we slept.

'What awoke me? I could hear voices whispering. There was

fright in them. Before I could distinguish one word from another I felt my neck creeping. I shook myself. I leaped up. I looked out. The light was blinding. The moon was shining on the slope of new snow. There was none falling now; a light thin wind was blowing out of the lovely stars.

'Beneath my window I saw five persons standing in a little group, all clutching one shoulder like people standing in a flooded river. They were very still; they would not move even when they whispered. As I wondered to see them so fearfully clutching one another, a voice spoke in my room:

' "For God's sake, Stephen, get ready and come down."

' "Man, what's the matter with ye?"

' "For God's sake come down."

' "Tell me, tell me!"

' "How can I? Come down!"

'I tried to be calm; I went out and made for that little group, putting my hand against my eyes, the new snow was so blinding.

' "Where's the master?" I said.

' "There!" They did not seem to care whether or not I looked at the master.

'He was a little apart; he was clutching a jut of rock as if the land was slipping from his feet. His cowardice made me afraid. I was hard put to control my breath.

' "What are ye, are ye all staring at?" I said.

' "Leaca na —" the voice seemed to come from over a mile away, yet it was the man beside me had spoken.

'I looked. The leaca was a dazzling blaze, it was true, but I had often before seen it as bright and wonderful. I was puzzled.

' "Is it the leaca ye're all staring —" I began; but several of them silently lifted up a hand and pointed towards it. I could have stared at them instead; whether or not it was the white moonlight that was on them, they looked like men half-frozen, too chilled to speak. But I looked where those outstretched hands silently bade me. Then I, too, was struck dumb, and became one of that icy group, for I saw a little white cloud moving across the leaca, a feathery cloud, and from the heart of it there came every now and then a little flash of fire, a spark.

Sometimes, too, the little cloud would grow thin, as if it was scattering away, at which times it was a moving shadow we saw. As I blinked at it, I felt my hand groping about to catch something, to catch someone, to make sure of myself; for the appearance of everything, the whiteness, the stillness, and then that moving cloud whiter than anything else, whiter than anything in the world, and so like an angel's wing moving along the leaca, frightened me until I felt like fainting away. To make things worse, straight from the little cloud came down a whisper, a long, thin, clear, silvery cry: "Griosach! Ho-o-o-oh! Ho-o-o-oh!", a ploughing cry. We did not move; we kept our silence: everyone knew that that cry was going through everyone else as through himself, a lash of coldness. Then I understood why the master was hanging on to a rock; he must have heard the cry before anyone else. It was terrible, made so thin and silvery by the distance; and yet it was a cry of joy – the fool had conquered Griosach!

'I do not know what wild thoughts had begun to come into my head when one man in the group gasped out, "Now!" and then another, and yet another. Their voices were breath, not sound. Then they all said "Ah!" and I understood the fear that had moved their tongues. I saw the little cloud pause a moment on the edge of the leaca, almost hang over the edge, and then begin to draw back from it. The fool had turned his team on the verge and was now ploughing up against the hill.

' "O-o-h," said the master, in the first moment of relief; it was more like a cry of agony. He looked round at us with ghastly eyes; and our eyeballs turned towards his, just as cold and fixed. Again that silvery cry floated down to us: "Griosach! Ho-o-o-oh!" And again the lash of coldness passed through every one of us. The cry began to come more frequently, more triumphantly, for now again the little cloud was ploughing down the slope, and its pace had quickened. It was making once more for that edge beneath which was a sheer fall of hundreds of feet.

'Behind us, suddenly, from the direction of the thatched stables came a loud and high whinny – a call to a mate. It was so unexpected, and we were all so rapt up in what was before our eyes, that it shook us, making us spring from one another. I was the first to recover.

' "My God," I said, "that's Niamh, that's Niamh!"

'The whinny came again; it was Niamh surely.

' "What is he ploughing with, then? What has he with Griosach?"

'A man came running from the stables; he was trying to cry out; he could hardly be heard:

' "Griosach and Lugh! Griosach and Lugh!"

'Lugh was another sire horse; and the two sires would eat each other; they always had ill-will for each other. The master was staring at us.

' " 'Tisn't Lugh?" he said, with a gurgle in his voice.

'No one would answer him. We were thinking if the mare's cry reached the sires their anger would blaze up and no one could hold them; but why should Liam have yoked such a team?

' "Hush! hush!" said a woman's voice.

'We at once heard a new cry; it came down from the leaca: "Griosach, back! Back!" It was almost inaudible, but we could feel the swiftness and terror in it. "Back! Back!" came down again. "Back, Griosach, back!"

' "They're fighting, they're fighting – the sires!" one of our horse-boys yelled out – the first sound above a breath that had come from any of us, for he was fonder of Lugh than of the favourite Griosach, and had forgotten everything else. And we saw that the little cloud was almost at a standstill, yet that it was disturbed; sparks were flying from it; and we heard little clanking sounds, very faint, coming from it. They might mean great leaps and rearings.

'Suddenly we saw the master spring from that rock to which he had been clinging as limp as a leaf in autumn, spring from it with great life and roar up towards the leaca:

' "Liam, Liam! Liam Ruadh!" He turned to us, "Shout, boys, and break his fever," he cried. "Shout, shout!"

'We were glad of that.

' "Liam! Liam! Liam Ruadh!" we roared.

' "My God! My God!" we heard as we finished. It was the master's voice; he then fell down. At once we raised our voices again; it would keep us from seeing or hearing what was happening on the leaca.

'"Liam! Liam! Liam Ruadh!"

'There was wild confusion.

'"Liam! Liam! Liam! Ruadh! Ruadh! Ruadh!" the mountains were singing back to us, making the confusion worse. We were twisted about – one man staring at the ground, one at the rock in front of his face, another at the sky high over the leaca, and one had his hand stretched out like a signpost on a hilltop; I remember him best; none of us were looking at the leaca itself. But we were listening and listening and at last they died, the echoes, and there was a cold silence, cold, cold. Then we heard old Diarmuid's passionless voice begin to pray:

'"Abhaile ar an sioruidheacht go raibh a anam." "At home in Eternity may his soul –" We turned round, one by one, without speaking a word, and stared at the leaca. It was bare! The little cloud was still in the air – a white dust, ascending. Along the leaca we saw two thin shadowy lines – they looked as if they had been drawn in very watery ink on its dazzling surface. Of horses, plough, and fool there wasn't a trace. They had gone over the edge while we roared.

'Noble person, as they went over I'm sure Liam Ruadh had one fist at Lugh's bridle, and the other at Griosach's, and that he was swinging high in the air between them. Our roaring didn't break his fever, say that it didn't, noble person? But don't question the master about it. I have told you all!'

'I will leave this place tonight,' I said.

'It is late, noble person.'

'I will leave it now; bring me my horse.'

That is why I made no further inquiries in that valley as to the fate of that old Gaelic family that were once lords of those hills. I gave up the quest. Sometimes a thought comes to me that Liam Ruadh might have been the last of an immemorial line, no scion of which, if God had left him his senses, would have ploughed the Leaca of the Saints; no, not even if it were to save him from begging at fairs and in public houses.

Grace

JAMES JOYCE

Two gentlemen who were in the lavatory at the time tried to lift him up: but he was quite helpless. He lay curled up at the foot of the stairs down which he had fallen. They succeeded in turning him over. His hat had rolled a few yards away and his clothes were smeared with the filth and ooze of the floor on which he had lain, face downwards. His eyes were closed and he breathed with a grunting noise. A thin stream of blood trickled from the corner of his mouth.

These two gentlemen and one of the curates carried him up the stairs and laid him down again on the floor of the bar. In two minutes he was surrounded by a ring of men. The manager of the bar asked everyone who he was and who was with him. No one knew who he was, but one of the curates said he had served the gentleman with a small rum.

'Was he by himself?' asked the manager.

'No, sir. There was two gentlemen with him.'

'And where are they?'

No one knew; a voice said:

'Give him air. He's fainted.'

The ring of onlookers distended and closed again elastically. A dark medal of blood had formed itself near the man's head on the tessellated floor. The manager, alarmed by the grey pallor of the man's face, sent for a policeman.

His collar was unfastened and his necktie undone. He opened his eyes for an instant, sighed and closed them again. One of the gentlemen who had carried him upstairs held a dinged silk hat in his hand. The manager asked repeatedly did no one know who the injured man was or where had his friends gone.

The door of the bar opened and an immense constable entered. A crowd which had followed him down the laneway collected outside the door, struggling to look in through the glass panels.

The manager at once began to narrate what he knew. The constable, a young man with thick immobile features, listened. He moved his head slowly to right and left and from the manager to the person on the floor, as if he feared to be the victim of some delusion. Then he drew off his glove, produced a small book from his waist, licked the lead of his pencil and made ready to indite. He asked in a suspicious provincial accent:

'Who is the man? What's his name and address?'

A young man in a cycling-suit cleared his way through the ring of bystanders. He knelt down promptly beside the injured man and called for water. The constable knelt down also to help. The young man washed the blood from the injured man's mouth and then called for some brandy. The constable repeated the order in an authoritative voice until a curate came running with the glass. The brandy was forced down the man's throat. In a few seconds he opened his eyes and looked about him. He looked at the circle of faces and then, understanding, strove to rise to his feet.

'You're all right now?' asked the young man in the cycling-suit.

'Sha, 's nothing,' said the injured man, trying to stand up.

He was helped to his feet. The manager said something about a hospital and some of the bystanders gave advice. The battered silk hat was placed on the man's head. The constable asked:

'Where do you live?'

The man, without answering, began to twirl the ends of his moustache. He made light of his accident. It was nothing, he said: only a little accident. He spoke very thickly.

'Where do you live?' repeated the constable.

The man said they were to get a cab for him. While the point was being debated a tall agile gentleman of fair complexion, wearing a long yellow ulster, came from the far end of the bar. Seeing the spectacle, he called out:

'Hallo, Tom, old man! What's the trouble?'

'Sha, 's nothing,' said the man.

The newcomer surveyed the deplorable figure before him and then turned to the constable, saying:

'It's all right, constable. I'll see him home.'

The constable touched his helmet and answered:

'All right, Mr Power!'

'Come now, Tom,' said Mr Power, taking his friend by the arm. 'No bones broken. What? Can you walk?'

The young man in the cycling-suit took the man by the other arm and the crowd divided.

'How did you get yourself into this mess?' asked Mr Power.

'The gentleman fell down the stairs,' said the young man.

'I' 'ery 'uch o'liged to you, sir,' said the injured man.

'Not at all.'

' 'an't we have a little ... ?'

'Not now. Not now.'

The three men left the bar and the crowd sifted through the doors into the laneway. The manager brought the constable to the stairs to inspect the scene of the accident. They agreed that the gentleman must have missed his footing. The customers returned to the counter, and a curate set about removing the traces of blood from the floor.

When they came out into Grafton Street, Mr Power whistled for an outsider. The injured man said again as well as he could:

'I' 'ery 'uch o'liged to you, sir. I hope we'll 'eet again. 'y na'e is Kernan.'

The shock and the incipient pain had partly sobered him.

'Don't mention it,' said the young man.

They shook hands. Mr Kernan was hoisted on to the car and, while Mr Power was giving directions to the carman, he expressed his gratitude to the young man and regretted that they could not have a little drink together.

'Another time,' said the young man.

The car drove off towards Westmoreland Street. As it passed the Ballast Office the clock showed half past nine. A keen east wind hit them, blowing from the mouth of the river. Mr Kernan was huddled together with cold. His friend asked him to tell how the accident had happened.

'I 'an't 'an,' he answered, ''y 'ongue is hurt.'

'Show.'

The other leaned over the wheel of the car and peered into
Mr Kernan's mouth but he could not see. He struck a match
and, sheltering it in the shell of his hands, peered again into
the mouth which Mr Kernan opened obediently. The swaying
movement of the car brought the match to and from the
opened mouth. The lower teeth and gums were covered with
clotted blood and a minute piece of the tongue seemed to
have been bitten off. The match was blown out.

'That's ugly,' said Mr Power.

'Sha, 's nothing,' said Mr Kernan, closing his mouth and
pulling the collar of his filthy coat across his neck.

Mr Kernan was a commercial traveller of the old school
which believed in the dignity of its calling. He had never been
seen in the city without a silk hat of some decency and a pair
of gaiters. By grace of these two articles of clothing, he said,
a man could always pass muster. He carried on the tradition
of his Napoleon, the great Blackwhite, whose memory he
evoked at times by legend and mimicry. Modern business
methods had spared him only so far as to allow him a little
office in Crowe Street, on the window blind of which was
written the name of his firm with the address – London, E.C.
On the mantelpiece of this little office a little leaden battalion
of canisters was drawn up and on the table before the window
stood four or five china bowls which were usually half full of a
black liquid. From these bowls Mr Kernan tasted tea. He took
a mouthful, drew it up, saturated his palate with it and then
spat it forth into the grate. Then he paused to judge.

Mr Power, a much younger man, was employed in the
Royal Irish Constabulary Office in Dublin Castle. The arc of
his social rise intersected the arc of his friend's decline, but
Mr Kernan's decline was mitigated by the fact that certain of
those friends who had known him at his highest point of
success still esteemed him as a character. Mr Power was one
of these friends. His inexplicable debts were a byword in his
circle; he was a debonair young man.

The car halted before a small house on the Glasnevin road
and Mr Kernan was helped into the house. His wife put him

to bed, while Mr Power sat downstairs in the kitchen asking the children where they went to school and what book they were in. The children – two girls and a boy, conscious of their father's helplessness and of their mother's absence, began some horseplay with him. He was surprised at their manners and at their accents, and his brow grew thoughtful. After a while Mrs Kernan entered the kitchen, exclaiming:

'Such a sight! Oh, he'll do for himself one day and that's the holy alls of it. He's been drinking since Friday.'

Mr Power was careful to explain to her that he was not responsible, that he had come on the scene by the merest accident. Mrs Kernan, remembering Mr Power's good offices during domestic quarrels, as well as many small, but opportune loans, said:

'O, you needn't tell me that, Mr Power. I know you're a friend of his, not like some of the others he does be with. They're all right so long as he has money in his pocket to keep him out from his wife and family. Nice friends! Who was he with tonight, I'd like to know?'

Mr Power shook his head but said nothing.

'I'm so sorry,' she continued, 'that I've nothing in the house to offer you. But if you wait a minute I'll send round to Fogarty's, at the corner.'

Mr Power stood up.

'We were waiting for him to come home with the money. He never seems to think he has a home at all.'

'O, now, Mrs Kernan,' said Mr Power, 'we'll make him turn over a new leaf. I'll talk to Martin. He's the man. We'll come here one of these nights and talk it over.'

She saw him to the door. The carman was stamping up and down the footpath, and swinging his arms to warm himself.

'It's very kind of you to bring him home,' she said.

'Not at all,' said Mr Power.

He got up on the car. As it drove off he raised his hat to her gaily.

'We'll make a new man of him,' he said. 'Good night, Mrs Kernan.'

*

Mrs Kernan's puzzled eyes watched the car till it was out of sight. Then she withdrew them, went into the house and emptied her husband's pockets.

She was an active, practical woman of middle age. Not long before she had celebrated her silver wedding and renewed her intimacy with her husband by waltzing with him to Mr Power's accompaniment. In her days of courtship, Mr Kernan had seemed to her a not ungallant figure: and she still hurried to the chapel door whenever a wedding was reported and, seeing the bridal pair, recalled with vivid pleasure how she had passed out of the Star of the Sea Church in Sandymount, leaning on the arm of a jovial well-fed man, who was dressed smartly in a frock-coat and lavender trousers and carried a silk hat gracefully balanced upon his other arm. After three weeks she had found a wife's life irksome and, later on, when she was beginning to find it unbearable, she had become a mother. The part of mother presented to her no insuperable difficulties and for twenty-five years she had kept house shrewdly for her husband. Her two eldest sons were launched. One was in a draper's shop in Glasgow and the other was clerk to a tea-merchant in Belfast. They were good sons, wrote regularly and sometimes sent home money. The other children were still at school.

Mr Kernan sent a letter to his office next day and remained in bed. She made beef-tea for him and scolded him roundly. She accepted his frequent intemperance as part of the climate, healed him dutifully whenever he was sick and always tried to make him eat a breakfast. There were worse husbands. He had never been violent since the boys had grown up, and she knew that he would walk to the end of Thomas Street and back again to book even a small order.

Two nights after, his friends came to see him. She brought them up to his bedroom, the air of which was impregnated with a personal odour, and gave them chairs at the fire. Mr Kernan's tongue, the occasional stinging pain of which had made him somewhat irritable during the day, became more polite. He sat propped up in the bed by pillows and the little colour in his puffy cheeks made them resemble warm cinders.

He apologized to his guests for the disorder of the room, but at the same time looked at them a little proudly, with a veteran's pride.

He was quite unconscious that he was the victim of a plot which his friends, Mr Cunningham, Mr M'Coy and Mr Power had disclosed to Mrs Kernan in the parlour. The idea had been Mr Power's, but its development was entrusted to Mr Cunningham. Mr Kernan came of Protestant stock and, though he had been converted to the Catholic faith at the time of his marriage, he had not been in the pale of the Church for twenty years. He was fond, moreover, of giving side-thrusts at Catholicism.

Mr Cunningham was the very man for such a case. He was an elder colleague of Mr Power. His own domestic life was not very happy. People had great sympathy with him, for it was known that he had married an unpresentable woman who was an incurable drunkard. He had set up house for her six times; and each time she had pawned the furniture on him.

Every one had respect for poor Martin Cunningham. He was a thoroughly sensible man, influential and intelligent. His blade of human knowledge, natural astuteness particularized by long association with cases in the police courts, had been tempered by brief immersions in the waters of general philosophy. He was well informed. His friends bowed to his opinions and considered that his face was like Shakespeare's.

When the plot had been disclosed to her, Mrs Kernan had said:

'I leave it all in your hands, Mr Cunningham.'

After a quarter of a century of married life, she had very few illusions left. Religion for her was a habit, and she suspected that a man of her husband's age would not change greatly before death. She was tempted to see a curious appropriateness in his accident and, but that she did not wish to seem bloody-minded, she would have told the gentlemen that Mr Kernan's tongue would not suffer by being shortened. However, Mr Cunningham was a capable man; and religion was religion. The scheme might do good and, at least, it could do no harm. Her beliefs were not extravagant. She believed steadily in the Sacred Heart as the most generally useful of all

Catholic devotions and approved of the sacraments. Her faith was bounded by her kitchen, but, if she was put to it, she could believe also in the banshee and in the Holy Ghost.

The gentlemen began to talk of the accident. Mr Cunningham said that he had once known a similar case. A man of seventy had bitten off a piece of his tongue during an epileptic fit and the tongue had filled in again, so that no one could see a trace of the bite.

'Well, I'm not seventy,' said the invalid.

'God forbid,' said Mr Cunningham.

'It doesn't pain you now?' asked Mr M'Coy.

Mr M'Coy had been at one time a tenor of some reputation. His wife, who had been a soprano, still taught young children to play the piano at low terms. His line of life had not been the shortest distance between two points and for short periods he had been driven to live by his wits. He had been a clerk in the Midland Railway, a canvasser for advertisements for *The Irish Times* and for *The Freeman's Journal*, a town traveller for a coal firm on commission, a private inquiry agent, a clerk in the office of the Sub-Sheriff, and he had recently become secretary to the City Coroner. His new office made him professionally interested in Mr Kernan's case.

'Pain? Not much,' answered Mr Kernan. 'But it's so sickening. I feel as if I wanted to retch off.'

'That's the booze,' said Mr Cunningham firmly.

'No,' said Mr Kernan. 'I think I caught cold on the car. There's something keeps coming into my throat, phlegm or –'

'Mucus,' said Mr M'Coy.

'It keeps coming like from down in my throat; sickening thing.'

'Yes, yes,' said Mr M'Coy, 'that's the thorax.'

He looked at Mr Cunningham and Mr Power at the same time with an air of challenge. Mr Cunningham nodded his head rapidly and Mr Power said:

'Ah, well, all's well that ends well.'

'I'm very much obliged to you, old man,' said the invalid.

Mr Power waved his hand.

'Those other two fellows I was with –'

'Who were you with?' asked Mr Cunningham.

'A chap. I don't know his name. Damn it now, what's his name? Little chap with sandy hair ...'

'And who else?'

'Harford.'

'Hm,' said Mr Cunningham.

When Mr Cunningham made that remark, people were silent. It was known that the speaker had secret sources of information. In this case the monosyllable had a moral intention. Mr Harford sometimes formed one of a little detachment which left the city shortly after noon on Sunday with the purpose of arriving as soon as possible at some public-house on the outskirts of the city where its members duly qualified themselves as *bona-fide* travellers. But his fellow-travellers had never consented to overlook his origin. He had begun life as an obscure financier by lending small sums of money to workmen at usurious interest. Later on he had become the partner of a very fat, short gentleman, Mr Goldberg, in the Liffey Loan Bank. Though he had never embraced more than the Jewish ethical code, his fellow-Catholics, whenever they had smarted in person or by proxy under his exactions, spoke of him bitterly as an Irish Jew and an illiterate, and saw divine disapproval of usury made manifest through the person of his idiot son. At other times they remembered his good points.

'I wonder where did he go to,' said Mr Kernan.

He wished the details of the incident to remain vague. He wished his friends to think there had been some mistake, that Mr Harford and he had missed each other. His friends, who knew quite well Mr Harford's manners in drinking, were silent. Mr Power said again:

'All's well that ends well.'

Mr Kernan changed the subject at once.

'That was a decent young chap, that medical fellow,' he said. 'Only for him —'

'O, only for him,' said Mr Power, 'it might have been a case of seven days, without the option of a fine.'

'Yes, yes,' said Mr Kernan, trying to remember. 'I remember now there was a policeman. Decent young fellow, he seemed. How did it happen at all?'

'It happened that you were peloothered, Tom,' said Mr Cunningham gravely.

'True bill,' said Mr Kernan, equally gravely.

'I suppose you squared the constable, Jack,' said Mr M'Coy.

Mr Power did not relish the use of his Christian name. He was not straight-laced, but he could not forget that Mr M'Coy had recently made a crusade in search of valises and portmanteaus to enable Mrs M'Coy to fulfil imaginary engagements in the country. More than he resented the fact that he had been victimized, he resented such low-playing of the game. He answered the question, therefore, as if Mr Kernan had asked it.

The narrative made Mr Kernan indignant. He was keenly conscious of his citizenship, wished to live with his city on terms mutually honourable and resented any affront put upon him by those whom he called country bumpkins.

'Is this what we pay rates for?' he asked. 'To feed and clothe these ignorant bostooms ... and they're nothing else.'

Mr Cunningham laughed. He was a Castle official only during office hours.

'How could they be anything else, Tom?' he said.

He assumed a thick, provincial accent and said in a tone of command:

'65, catch your cabbage!'

Everyone laughed. Mr M'Coy, who wanted to enter the conversation by any door, pretended that he had never heard the story. Mr Cunningham said:

'It is supposed – they say, you know – to take place in the depot where they get these thundering big country fellows, omadhauns, you know, to drill. The sergeant makes them stand in a row against the wall and hold up their plates.' He illustrated the story by grotesque gestures.

'At dinner, you know. Then he has a bloody big bowl of cabbage before him on the table and a bloody big spoon like a shovel. He takes up a wad of cabbage on the spoon and pegs it across the room and the poor devils have to try and catch it on their plates: 65, *catch your cabbage.*'

Everyone laughed again: but Mr Kernan was somewhat indignant still. He talked of writing a letter to the papers.

'These yahoos coming up here,' he said, 'think they can boss the people. I needn't tell you, Martin, what kind of men they are.'

Mr Cunningham gave a qualified assent.

'It's like everything else in this world,' he said. 'You get some bad ones and you get some good ones.'

'O yes, you get some good ones, I admit,' said Mr Kernan, satisfied.

'It's better to have nothing to say to them,' said Mr M'Coy. 'That's my opinion!'

Mrs Kernan entered the room and, placing a tray on the table, said:

'Help yourselves, gentlemen.'

Mr Power stood up to officiate, offering her his chair. She declined it, saying she was ironing downstairs, and, after having exchanged a nod with Mr Cunningham behind Mr Power's back, prepared to leave the room. Her husband called out to her:

'And have you nothing for me, duckie?'

'O, you! The back of my hand to you!' said Mrs Kernan tartly.

Her husband called after her:

'Nothing for poor little hubby!'

He assumed such a comical face and voice that the distribution of the bottles of stout took place amid general merriment.

The gentlemen drank from their glasses, set the glasses again on the table and paused. Then Mr Cunningham turned towards Mr Power and said casually:

'On Thursday night, you said, Jack?'

'Thursday, yes,' said Mr Power.

'Righto!' said Mr Cunningham promptly.

'We can meet in M'Auley's,' said Mr M'Coy. 'That'll be the most convenient place.'

'But we mustn't be late,' said Mr Power earnestly, 'because it is sure to be crammed to the doors.'

'We can meet at half-seven,' said Mr M'Coy.

'Righto!' said Mr Cunningham.

'Half-seven at M'Auley's be it!'

There was a short silence. Mr Kernan waited to see whether he would be taken into his friends' confidence. Then he asked:

'What's in the wind?'

'O, it's nothing,' said Mr Cunningham. 'It's only a little matter that we're arranging about for Thursday.'

'The opera, is it?' said Mr Kernan.

'No, no,' said Mr Cunningham in an evasive tone, 'it's just a little ... spiritual matter.'

'O,' said Mr Kernan.

There was silence again. Then Mr Power said, point-blank:

'To tell you the truth, Tom, we're going to make a retreat.'

'Yes, that's it,' said Mr Cunningham, 'Jack and I and M'Coy here – we're all going to wash the pot.'

He uttered the metaphor with a certain homely energy and, encouraged by his own voice, proceeded:

'You see, we may as well all admit we're a nice collection of scoundrels, one and all. I say, one and all,' he added with gruff charity and turning to Mr Power. 'Own up now!'

'I own up,' said Mr Power.

'And I own up,' said Mr M'Coy.

'So we're going to wash the pot together,' said Mr Cunningham.

A thought seemed to strike him. He turned suddenly to the invalid and said:

'D'ye know what, Tom, has just occurred to me? You might join in and we'd have a four-handed reel.'

'Good idea,' said Mr Power. 'The four of us together.'

Mr Kernan was silent. The proposal conveyed very little meaning to his mind, but, understanding that some spiritual agencies were about to concern themselves on his behalf, he thought he owed it to his dignity to show a stiff neck. He took no part in the conversation for a long while, but listened, with an air of calm enmity, while his friends discussed the Jesuits.

'I haven't such a bad opinion of the Jesuits,' he said, intervening at length. 'They're an educated order. I believe they mean well, too.'

'They're the grandest order in the Church, Tom,' said Mr

Cunningham, with enthusiasm. 'The General of the Jesuits stands next to the Pope.'

'There's no mistake about it,' said Mr M'Coy, 'if you want a thing well done and no flies about, you go to a Jesuit. They're the boyos have influence. I'll tell you a case in point . . .'

'The Jesuits are a fine body of men,' said Mr Power.

'It's a curious thing,' said Mr Cunningham, 'about the Jesuit Order. Every other order of the Church had to be reformed at some time or other, but the Jesuit Order was never once reformed. It never fell away.'

'Is that so?' asked Mr M'Coy.

'That's a fact,' said Mr Cunningham. 'That's history.'

'Look at their church, too,' said Mr Power. 'Look at the congregation they have.'

'The Jesuits cater for the upper classes,' said Mr M'Coy.

'Of course,' said Mr Power.

'Yes,' said Mr Kernan. 'That's why I have a feeling for them. It's some of those secular priests, ignorant, bumptious –'

'They're all good men,' said Mr Cunningham, 'each in his own way. The Irish priesthood is honoured all the world over.'

'O yes,' said Mr Power.

'Not like some of the other priesthoods on the Continent,' said Mr M'Coy, 'unworthy of the name.'

'Perhaps you're right,' said Mr Kernan, relenting.

'Of course I'm right,' said Mr Cunningham. 'I haven't been in the world all this time and seen most sides of it without being a judge of character.'

The gentlemen drank again, one following another's example. Mr Kernan seemed to be weighing something in his mind. He was impressed. He had a high opinion of Mr Cunningham as a judge of character and as a reader of faces. He asked for particulars.

'O, it's just a retreat, you know,' said Mr Cunningham. 'Father Purdon is giving it. It's for businessmen, you know.'

'He won't be too hard on us, Tom,' said Mr Power persuasively.

'Father Purdon? Father Purdon?' said the invalid.

'O, you must know him, Tom,' said Mr Cunningham, stoutly. 'Fine, jolly fellow! He's a man of the world like ourselves.'

'Ah ... yes. I think I know him. Rather red face; tall.'

'That's the man.'

'And tell me, Martin ... Is he a good preacher?'

'Munno ... It's not exactly a sermon, you know. It's just a kind of a friendly talk, you know, in a common-sense way.'

Mr Kernan deliberated. Mr M'Coy said:

'Father Tom Burke, that was the boy!'

'O, Father Tom Burke,' said Mr Cunningham, 'that was a born orator. Did you ever hear him, Tom?'

'Did I ever hear him!' said the invalid, nettled. 'Rather! I heard him ...'

'And yet they say he wasn't much of a theologian,' said Mr Cunningham.

'Is that so?' said Mr M'Coy.

'O, of course, nothing wrong, you know. Only sometimes, they say, he didn't preach what was quite orthodox.'

'Ah! ... he was a splendid man,' said Mr M'Coy.

'I heard him once,' Mr Kernan continued. 'I forget the subject of his discourse now. Crofton and I were in the back of the ... pit, you know ... the –'

'The body,' said Mr Cunningham.

'Yes, in the back near the door. I forget now what ... O yes, it was on the Pope, the late Pope. I remember it well. Upon my word it was magnificent, the style of the oratory. And his voice! God! hadn't he a voice! *The Prisoner of the Vatican*, he called him. I remember Crofton saying to me when we came out –'

'But he's an Orangeman, Crofton, isn't he?' said Mr Power.

' 'Course he is,' said Mr Kernan, 'and a damned decent Orangeman, too. We went into Butler's in Moore Street – faith, I was genuinely moved, tell you the God's truth – and I remember well his very words. *Kernan*, he said, *we worship at different altars*, he said, *but our belief is the same*. Struck me as very well put.'

'There's a good deal in that,' said Mr Power. 'There used always be crowds of Protestants in the chapel where Father Tom was preaching.'

'There's not much difference between us,' said Mr M'Coy. 'We both believe in –'

He hesitated for a moment.

'. . . in the Redeemer. Only they don't believe in the Pope and in the mother of God.'

'But, of course,' said Mr Cunningham quietly and effectively, 'our religion is *the* religion, the old, original faith.'

'Not a doubt of it,' said Mr Kernan warmly.

Mrs Kernan came to the door of the bedroom and announced: 'Here's a visitor for you!'

'Who is it?'

'Mr Fogarty.'

'O, come in! come in!'

A pale, oval face came forward into the light. The arch of its fair trailing moustache was repeated in the fair eyebrows looped above pleasantly astonished eyes. Mr Fogarty was a modest grocer. He had failed in business in a licensed house in the city because his financial condition had constrained him to tie himself to second-class distillers and brewers. He had opened a small shop on Glasnevin Road where, he flattered himself, his manners would ingratiate him with the housewives of the district. He bore himself with a certain grace, complimented little children and spoke with a neat enunciation. He was not without culture.

Mr Fogarty brought a gift with him, a half-pint of special whiskey. He inquired politely for Mr Kernan, placed his gift on the table and sat down with the company on equal terms. Mr Kernan appreciated the gift all the more since he was aware that there was a small account for groceries unsettled between him and Mr Fogarty. He said:

'I wouldn't doubt you, old man. Open that, Jack, will you?'

Mr Power again officiated. Glasses were rinsed and five small measures of whiskey were poured out. This new influence enlivened the conversation. Mr Fogarty, sitting on a small area of the chair, was specially interested.

'Pope Leo XIII,' said Mr Cunningham, 'was one of the lights of the age. His great idea, you know, was the union of the Latin and Greek Churches. That was the aim of his life.'

'I often heard he was one of the most intellectual men in Europe,' said Mr Power. 'I mean, apart from his being Pope.'

'So he was,' said Mr Cunningham, 'if not *the* most so. His motto, you know, as Pope, was *Lux upon Lux – Light upon Light*.'

'No, no,' said Mr Fogarty eagerly. 'I think you're wrong there. It was *Lux in Tenebris*, I think – *Light in Darkness*.'

'O yes,' said Mr M'Coy, '*Tenebrae*.'

'Allow me,' said Mr Cunningham positively, 'it was *Lux upon Lux*. And Pius IX his predecessor's motto was *Crux upon Crux* – that is, *Cross upon Cross* – to show the difference between their two pontificates.'

The inference was allowed. Mr Cunningham continued.

'Pope Leo, you know, was a great scholar and a poet.'

'He had a strong face,' said Mr Kernan.

'Yes,' said Mr Cunningham. 'He wrote Latin poetry.'

'Is that so?' said Mr Fogarty.

Mr M'Coy tasted his whiskey contentedly and shook his head with a double intention, saying:

'That's no joke, I can tell you.'

'We didn't learn that, Tom,' said Mr Power, following Mr M'Coy's example, 'when we went to the penny-a-week school.'

'There was many a good man went to the penny-a-week school with a sod of turf under his oxter,' said Mr Kernan sententiously. 'The old system was the best: plain honest education. None of your modern trumpery ...'

'Quite right,' said Mr Power.

'No superfluities,' said Mr Fogarty.

He enunciated the word and then drank gravely.

'I remember reading,' said Mr Cunningham, 'that one of Pope Leo's poems was on the invention of the photograph – in Latin, of course.'

'On the photograph!' exclaimed Mr Kernan.

'Yes,' said Mr Cunningham.

He also drank from his glass.

'Well, you know,' said Mr M'Coy, 'isn't the photograph wonderful when you come to think of it?'

'O, of course,' said Mr Power, 'great minds can see things.'

'As the poet says: *Great minds are very near to madness*,' said Mr Fogarty.

Mr Kernan seemed to be troubled in mind. He made an

effort to recall the Protestant theology on some thorny points and in the end addressed Mr Cunningham.

'Tell me, Martin,' he said. 'Weren't some of the popes – of course, not our present man, or his predecessor, but some of the old popes – not exactly ... you know ... up to the knocker?'

There was a silence. Mr Cunningham said:

'O, of course, there were some bad lots ... But the astonishing thing is this. Not one of them, not the biggest drunkard, not the most ... out-and-out ruffian, not one of them ever preached *ex cathedra* a word of false doctrine. Now isn't that an astonishing thing?'

'That is,' said Mr Kernan.

'Yes, because when the Pope speaks *ex cathedra*,' Mr Fogarty explained, 'he is infallible.'

'Yes,' said Mr Cunningham.

'O, I know about the infallibility of the Pope. I remember I was younger then ... Or was it that –?'

Mr Fogarty interrupted. He took up the bottle and helped the others to a little more. Mr M'Coy, seeing that there was not enough to go round, pleaded that he had not finished his first measure. The others accepted under protest. The light music of whiskey falling into glasses made an agreeable interlude.

'What's that you were saying, Tom?' asked Mr M'Coy.

'Papal infallibility,' said Mr Cunningham, 'that was the greatest scene in the whole history of the Church.'

'How was that, Martin?' asked Mr Power.

Mr Cunningham held up two thick fingers.

'In the sacred college, you know, of cardinals and archbishops and bishops there were two men who held out against it while the others were all for it. The whole conclave except these two was unanimous. No! They wouldn't have it!'

'Ha!' said Mr M'Coy.

'And they were a German cardinal by the name of Dolling ... or Dowling ... or –'

'Dowling was no German, and that's a sure five,' said Mr Power, laughing.

'Well, this great German cardinal, whatever his name was, was one; and the other was John MacHale.'

'What?' cried Mr Kernan. 'Is it John of Tuam?'

'Are you sure of that now?' asked Mr Fogarty dubiously. 'I thought it was some Italian or American.'

'John of Tuam,' repeated Mr Cunningham, 'was the man.'

He drank and the other gentlemen followed his lead. Then he resumed:

'There they were at it, all the cardinals and bishops and archbishops from all ends of the earth and these two fighting dog and devil until at last the Pope himself stood up and declared infallibility a dogma of the Church *ex cathedra*. On the very moment John MacHale, who had been arguing and arguing against it, stood up and shouted out with the voice of a lion: *"Credo!"*'

'*I believe!*' said Mr Fogarty.

'*Credo!*' said Mr Cunningham. 'That showed the faith he had. He submitted the moment the Pope spoke.'

'And what about Dowling?' asked Mr M'Coy.

'The German cardinal wouldn't submit. He left the Church.'

Mr Cunningham's words had built up the vast image of the Church in the minds of his hearers. His deep, raucous voice had thrilled them as it uttered the word of belief and submission. When Mrs Kernan came into the room, drying her hands, she came into a solemn company. She did not disturb the silence, but leaned over the rail at the foot of the bed.

'I once saw John MacHale,' said Mr Kernan, 'and I'll never forget it as long as I live.'

He turned towards his wife to be confirmed.

'I often told you that?'

Mrs Kernan nodded.

'It was at the unveiling of Sir John Gray's statue. Edmund Dwyer Gray was speaking, blathering away, and here was this old fellow, crabbed-looking old chap, looking at him from under his bushy eyebrows.'

Mr Kernan knitted his brows and, lowering his head like an angry bull, glared at his wife.

'God!' he exclaimed, resuming his natural face, 'I never saw such an eye in a man's head. It was as much as to say: *I have you properly taped, my lad*. He had an eye like a hawk.'

'None of the Grays was any good,' said Mr Power.

There was a pause again. Mr Power turned to Mrs Kernan and said with abrupt joviality:

'Well, Mrs Kernan, we're going to make your man here a good holy pious and God-fearing Roman Catholic.'

He swept his arm round the company inclusively.

'We're all going to make a retreat together and confess our sins — and God knows we want it badly.'

'I don't mind,' said Mr Kernan, smiling a little nervously.

Mrs Kernan thought it would be wiser to conceal her satisfaction. So she said:

'I pity the poor priest that has to listen to your tale.'

Mr Kernan's expression changed.

'If he doesn't like it,' he said bluntly, 'he can ... do the other thing. I'll just tell him my little tale of woe. I'm not such a bad fellow —'

Mr Cunningham intervened promptly.

'We'll all renounce the devil,' he said, 'together, not forgetting his works and pomps.'

'Get behind me, Satan!' said Mr Fogarty, laughing and looking at the others.

Mr Power said nothing. He felt completely out-generalled. But a pleased expression flickered across his face.

'All we have to do,' said Mr Cunningham, 'is to stand up with lighted candles in our hands and renew our baptismal vows.'

'O, don't forget the candle, Tom,' said Mr M'Coy, 'whatever you do.'

'What?' said Mr Kernan. 'Must I have a candle?'

'O yes,' said Mr Cunningham.

'No, damn it all,' said Mr Kernan sensibly, 'I draw the line there. I'll do the job right enough. I'll do the retreat business and confession, and ... all that business. But ... no candles! No, damn it all, I bar the candles!'

He shook his head with farcical gravity.

'Listen to that!' said his wife.

'I bar the candles,' said Mr Kernan, conscious of having created an effect on his audience and continuing to shake his head to and fro. 'I bar the magic-lantern business.'

Everyone laughed heartily.

'There's a nice Catholic for you!' said his wife.

'No candles!' repeated Mr Kernan obdurately. 'That's off!'

The transept of the Jesuit Church in Gardiner Street was almost full; and still at every moment gentlemen entered from the side door and, directed by the lay-brother, walked on tiptoe along the aisles until they found seating accommodation. The gentlemen were all well dressed and orderly. The light of the lamps of the church fell upon an assembly of black clothes and white collars, relieved here and there by tweeds, on dark mottled pillars of green marble and on lugubrious canvases. The gentlemen sat in the benches, having hitched their trousers slightly above their knees and laid their hats in security. They sat well back and gazed formally at the distant speck of red light which was suspended before the high altar.

In one of the benches near the pulpit sat Mr Cunningham and Mr Kernan. In the bench behind sat Mr M'Coy alone: and in the bench behind him sat Mr Power and Mr Fogarty. Mr M'Coy had tried unsuccessfully to find a place in the bench with the others, and, when the party had settled down in the form of a quincunx he had tried unsuccessfully to make comic remarks. As these had not been well received, he had desisted. Even he was sensible of the decorous atmosphere and even he began to respond to the religious stimulus. In a whisper, Mr Cunningham drew Mr Kernan's attention to Mr Harford, the moneylender, who sat some distance off, and to Mr Fanning, the registration agent and mayor-maker of the city, who was sitting immediately under the pulpit beside one of the newly elected councillors of the ward. To the right sat old Michael Grimes, the owner of three pawnbroker's shops, and Dan Hogan's nephew, who was up for the job in the Town Clerk's office. Farther in front sat Mr Hendrick, the chief reporter of *The Freeman's Journal*, and poor O'Carroll, an old friend of Mr Kernan's, who had been at one time a considerable commercial figure. Gradually, as he recognized familiar faces, Mr Kernan began to feel more at home. His hat, which had been rehabilitated by his wife, rested upon his knees. Once or twice he pulled down his cuffs with one hand while he held the brim of his hat lightly, but firmly, with the other hand.

A powerful-looking figure, the upper part of which was draped with a white surplice, was observed to be struggling up into the pulpit. Simultaneously the congregation unsettled, produced handkerchiefs and knelt upon them with care. Mr Kernan followed the general example. The priest's figure now stood upright in the pulpit, two-thirds of its bulk, crowned by a massive red face, appearing above the balustrade.

Father Purdon knelt down, turned towards the red speck of light and, covering his face with his hands, prayed. After an interval, he uncovered his face and rose. The congregation rose also and settled again on its benches. Mr Kernan restored his hat to its original position on his knee and presented an attentive face to the preacher. The preacher turned back each wide sleeve of his surplice with an elaborate large gesture and slowly surveyed the array of faces. Then he said:

'For the children of this world are wiser in their generation than the children of light. Wherefore make unto yourselves friends out of the mammon of iniquity so that when you die they may receive you into everlasting dwellings.'

Father Purdon developed the text with resonant assurance. It was one of the most difficult texts in all the Scriptures, he said, to interpret properly. It was a text which might seem to the casual observer at variance with the lofty morality elsewhere preached by Jesus Christ. But, he told his hearers, the text had seemed to him specially adapted for the guidance of those whose lot it was to lead the life of the world and who yet wished to lead that life not in the manner of wordlings. It was a text for business men and professional men. Jesus Christ, with His divine understanding of every cranny of our human nature, understood that all men were not called to the religious life, that by far the vast majority were forced to live in the world, and, to a certain extent, for the world: and in this sentence He designed to give them a word of counsel, setting before them as exemplars in the religious life those very worshippers of Mammon who were of all men the least solicitous in matters religious.

He told his hearers that he was there that evening for no terrifying, no extravagant purpose; but as a man of the world speaking to his fellow-men. He came to speak to business men and he would speak to them in a businesslike way. If he might use the metaphor, he said, he was their spiritual accountant; and he wished each and every one of his hearers to open his books, the books of his spiritual life, and see if they tallied accurately with conscience.

Jesus Christ was not a hard taskmaster. He understood our little failings, understood the weakness of our poor fallen nature, understood the temptations of this life. We might have had, we all had from time to time, our temptations: we might have, we all had, our failings. But one thing only, he said, he would ask of his hearers. And that was: to be straight and manly with God. If their accounts tallied in every point to say:

'Well, I have verified my accounts. I find all well.'

But if, as might happen, there were some discrepancies, to admit the truth, to be frank and say like a man:

'Well, I have looked into my accounts. I find this wrong and this wrong. But, with God's grace, I will rectify this and this. I will set right my accounts.'

The Tent

LIAM O'FLAHERTY

A SUDDEN squall struck the tent. White glittering hailstones struck the shabby canvas with a wild noise. The tent shook and swayed slightly forward, dangling its tattered flaps. The pole creaked as it strained. A rent appeared near the top of the pole like a silver seam in the canvas. Water immediately trickled through the seam, making a dark blob.

A tinker and his two wives were sitting on a heap of straw in the tent, looking out through the entrance at the wild moor that stretched in front of it, with a snowcapped mountain peak rising like the tip of a cone over the ridge of the moor about two miles away. The three of them were smoking cigarettes in silence. It was evening, and they had pitched their tent for the night in a gravel pit on the side of the mountain road crossing from one glen to another. Their donkey was tethered to the cart beside the tent.

When the squall came the tinker sat up with a start and looked at the pole. He stared at the seam in the canvas for several moments and then he nudged the two women and pointed upwards with a jerk of his nose. The women looked but nobody spoke. After a minute or so the tinker sighed and struggled to his feet.

'I'll throw a few sacks over the top,' he said.

He picked up two brown sacks from the heap of blankets and clothes that were drying beside the brazier in the entrance and went out. The women never spoke, but kept on smoking. The tinker kicked the donkey out of his way. The beast had stuck his hind quarters into the entrance of the tent as far as possible, in order to get the heat from the wood burning in the brazier.

The donkey shrank away sideways still chewing a wisp of the hay which the tinker had stolen from a haggard the other side of the mountain. The tinker scrambled up the bank against which the tent was pitched. The bank was covered with rank grass into which yesterday's snow had melted in muddy cakes.

The top of the tent was only about eighteen inches above the bank. Beyond the bank there was a narrow rough road, with a thick copse of pine trees on the far side, within the wired fence of a demesne, but the force of the squall was so great that it swept through the trees and struck the top of the tent as violently as if it were standing exposed on the open moor. The tinker had to lean against the wind to prevent himself being carried away. He looked into the wind with wide-open nostrils.

'It can't last,' he said, throwing the two sacks over the tent, where there was a rent in the canvas. He then took a big needle from his jacket and put a few stitches in them.

He was about to jump down from the bank when somebody hailed him from the road. He looked up and saw a man approaching, with his head thrust forward against the wind. The tinker scowled and shrugged his shoulders. He waited until the man came up to him.

The stranger was a tall, sturdily built man, with a long face and firm jaws and great sombre dark eyes, a fighter's face. When he reached the tinker he stood erect with his feet together and his hands by his sides like a soldier. He was fairly well dressed, his face was clean and well shaved, and his hands were clean. There was a blue figure of something or other tattooed on the back of his right hand. He looked at the tinker frankly with his sombre dark eyes. Neither spoke for several moments.

'Good evening,' the stranger said.

The tinker nodded without speaking. He was looking the stranger up and down, as if he were slightly afraid of this big, sturdy man, who was almost like a policeman or a soldier or somebody in authority. He looked at the man's boots especially. In spite of the muck of the roads, the melted snow and the hailstones, they were still fairly clean, and looked as if they were constantly polished.

'Travellin'?' he said at length.

'Eh,' said the stranger, almost aggressively. 'Oh! Yes, I'm lookin' for somewhere to shelter for the night.'

The stranger glanced at the tent slowly and then looked back to the tinker again.

'Goin' far?' said the tinker.

'Don't know,' said the stranger angrily. Then he almost shouted: 'I have no bloody place to go to ... only the bloody roads.'

'All right, brother,' said the tinker, 'come on.'

He nodded towards the tent and jumped down into the pit. The stranger followed him, stepping carefully down to avoid soiling his clothes.

When he entered the tent after the tinker and saw the women, he immediately took off his cap and said: 'Good evening.' The two women took their cigarettes from their mouths, smiled and nodded their heads.

The stranger looked about him cautiously and then sat down on a box to the side of the door near the brazier. He put his hands to the blaze and rubbed them. Almost immediately a slight steam rose from his clothes. The tinker handed him a cigarette, murmuring: 'Smoke?'

The stranger accepted the cigarette, lit it, and then looked at them. None of them were looking at him, so he sized them up carefully, looking at each suspiciously with his sombre dark eyes. The tinker was sitting on a box opposite him, leaning languidly backwards from his hips, a slim, tall, graceful man, with a beautiful head poised gracefully on a brown neck, and great black lashes falling down over his half-closed eyes, just like a woman. A womanish-looking fellow, with that sensuous grace in the languid pose of his body which is found only among aristocrats and people who belong to a very small work-less class, cut off from the mass of society, yet living at their expense. A young fellow, with proud, contemptuous, closed lips and an arrogant expression in his slightly expanded nostrils. A silent fellow, blowing out cigarette smoke through his nostrils and gazing dreamily into the blaze of the wood fire. The two women were just like him in texture, both of them slatterns, dirty and unkempt, but with the same proud, arrogant, contemptuous look in their beautiful brown faces. One was dark-haired and black-eyed. She had a rather hard expression in her face and seemed very alert. The other woman was golden-haired, with a very small head and finely developed jaw, that stuck out level with her forehead. She was surpassingly beautiful, in spite of her ragged clothes and the foul condition of her hair, which was piled on her tiny skull in knotted heaps, uncombed. The perfect symmetry and delicacy of her limbs, her bust and her long throat that had tiny freckles in the white skin, made the stranger feel afraid of her, of her beauty and her presence in the tent.

'Tinkers,' he said to himself. 'Awful bloody people.'

Then he turned to the tinker.

'Got any grub in the place ... eh ... mate?' he said brusquely, his thick lips rapping out every word firmly, like one accustomed to command inferiors. He hesitated before he added the word 'mate', obviously disinclined to put himself on a level of human intercourse with the tinker.

The tinker nodded and turned to the dark-haired woman.

'Might as well have supper now, Kitty,' he said softly.

The dark-haired woman rose immediately, and taking a blackened can that was full of water, she put it on the brazier. The stranger watched her. Then he addressed the tinker again.

'This is a hell of a way to be, eh?' he said. 'Stuck out on a mountain. Thought I'd make Roundwood tonight. How many miles is it from here?'

'Ten,' said the tinker.

'Good God!' said the stranger.

Then he laughed, and putting his hand in his breast pocket, he pulled out a half-pint bottle of whiskey.

'That is all I got left,' he said, looking at the bottle.

The tinker immediately opened his eyes wide when he saw the bottle. The golden-haired woman sat up and looked at the stranger eagerly, opening her brown eyes wide and rolling her tongue in her cheek. The dark-haired woman, rummaging in a box, also turned around to look. The stranger winked an eye and smiled.

'Always welcome,' he said. 'Eh? My curse on it, anyway. Anybody got a corkscrew?'

The tinker took a knife from his pocket, pulled out a corkscrew from its side and handed it to the man. The man opened the bottle.

'Here,' he said, handing the bottle to the tinker. 'Pass it round. I suppose the women'll have a drop.'

The tinker took the bottle and whispered to the dark-haired woman. She began to pass him mugs from the box.

'Funny thing,' said the stranger, 'when a man is broke and hungry, he can get whiskey but he can't get grub. Met a man this morning in Dublin and he knew bloody well I was broke, but instead of asking me to have a meal, or giving me some money, he gave me that. I had it with me all along the road and I never opened it.'

He threw the end of his cigarette out the entrance.

'Been drinkin' for three weeks, curse it,' he said.

'Are ye belonging to these parts?' murmured the tinker, pouring out the whiskey into the tin mugs.

'What's that?' said the man, again speaking angrily, as if he resented the question. Then he added: 'No. Never been here in me life before. Question of goin' into the workhouse or takin' to the roads. Got a job in Dublin yesterday. The men downed tools when they found I wasn't a member of the union. Thanks. Here's luck.'

'Good health, sir,' the women said.

The tinker nodded his head only, as he put his own mug to his lips and tasted it. The stranger drained his at a gulp.

'Ha,' he said. 'Drink up, girls. It's good stuff.'

He winked at them. They smiled and sipped their whiskey.

'My name is Carney,' said the stranger to the tinker. 'What do they call you?'

'Byrne,' said the tinker. 'Joe Byrne.'

'Hm! Byrne,' said Carney. 'Wicklow's full o' Byrnes. Tinker, I suppose?'

'Yes,' murmured the tinker, blowing a cloud of cigarette smoke through his puckered lips. Carney shrugged his shoulders.

'Might as well,' he said. 'One thing is as good as another Look at me. Sergeant-major in the army two months ago. Now I'm tramping the roads. That's boiling.'

The dark-haired woman took the can off the fire. The other woman tossed off the remains of her whiskey and got to her feet to help with the meal. Carney shifted his box back farther out of the way and watched the golden-haired woman eagerly. When she moved about, her figure was so tall that she had to stoop low in order to avoid the roof of the tent. She must have been six feet in height, and she wore high-heeled shoes which made her look taller.

'There is a woman for ye,' thought Carney. 'Must be a gentleman's daughter. Lots o' these shots out of a gun in the county Wicklow. Half the population is illegitimate. Awful moody people, these tinkers. I suppose the two of them belong to this Joe. More like a woman than a man. Suppose he never did a stroke of work in his life.'

There was cold rabbit for supper, with tea and bread and butter. It was excellent tea, and it tasted all the sweeter on account of the storm outside which was still raging. Sitting around the brazier they could see the hailstones driving through a grey mist, sweeping the bleak black moor, and the cone-shaped peak of the mountain in the distance, with a whirling cloud of snow around it. The sky was rent here and there with a blue patch, showing through the blackness.

They ate the meal in silence. Then the women cleared it away. They didn't wash the mugs or plates, but put everything away, probably until morning. They sat down again after drawing out the straw, bed-shape, and putting the clothes on it that had been drying near the brazier. They all seemed to be in a good humour now with the whiskey and the food. Even the tinker's face had grown soft, and he kept puckering up his lips in a smile. He passed around cigarettes.

'Might as well finish that bottle,' said Carney. 'Bother the mugs. We can drink outa the neck.'

'Tastes sweeter that way,' said the golden-haired woman, laughing thickly, as if she were slightly drunk. At the same time she looked at Carney with her lips open.

Carney winked at her. The tinker noticed the wink and the girl's smile. His face clouded and he closed his lips very tightly. Carney took a deep draught and passed him the bottle. The tinker nodded his head, took the bottle and put it to his lips.

'I'll have a stretch,' said Carney. 'I'm done in. Twenty miles since morning. Eh?'

He threw himself down on the clothes beside the yellow-haired woman. She smiled and looked at the tinker. The tinker paused with the bottle to his lips and looked at her through almost closed eyes savagely. He took the bottle from his lips and bared his white teeth. The golden-haired woman shrugged her shoulders and pouted. The dark-haired woman laughed aloud, stretched back with one arm under her head and the other stretched out towards the tinker.

'Sht,' she whistled through her teeth. 'Pass it along, Joe.'

He handed her the bottle slowly, and as he gave it to her she clutched his hand and tried to pull him to her. But he tore his hand away, got up and walked out of the tent rapidly.

Carney had noticed nothing of this. He was lying close to the woman by his side. He could feel the softness of her beautiful body and the slight undulation of her soft side as she breathed. He became overpowered with desire for her and closed his eyes, as if to shut out the consciousness of the world and of the other people in the tent. Reaching down he seized her hand and pressed it. She answered the pressure. At the same time she turned to her companion and whispered:

'Where's he gone?'

'I dunno. Ran out.'

'What about?'

'Phst.'

'Give us a drop.'

'Here ye are.'

Carney heard the whispering, but he took no notice of it. He heard the golden-haired one drinking and then drawing a deep breath.

'Finished,' she said, throwing the bottle to the floor. Then she laughed softly.

'I'm going out to see where he's gone,' whispered the dark-haired one. She rose and passed out of the tent. Carney immediately turned around and tried to embrace the woman by his side. But she bared her teeth in a savage grin and pinioned his arms with a single movement.

'Didn't think I was strong,' she said, putting her face close to his and grinning at him.

He looked at her seriously, surprised and still more excited.

'What ye goin' to do in Roundwood?' she said.

'Lookin' for a job,' he muttered thickly.

She smiled and rolled her tongue in her cheek.

'Stay here,' she said.

He licked his lip and winked his right eye. 'With you?'

She nodded.

'What about him?' he said, nodding towards the door.

She laughed silently. 'Are ye afraid of Joe?'

He did not reply, but, making a sudden movement, he seized her around the body and pressed her to him. She did not resist, but began to laugh, and bared her teeth as she laughed. He tried to kiss her mouth but she threw back her head and he kissed her cheek several times.

Then suddenly there was a hissing noise at the door. Carney sat up with a start. The tinker was standing in the entrance, stooping low, with his mouth open and his jaw twisted to the right, his two hands hanging loosely by his sides, with the fingers twitching. The dark-haired woman was standing behind him, peering over his shoulder. She was smiling.

Carney got to his feet, took a pace forward, and squared himself. He did not speak. The golden-headed woman uttered a loud peal of laughter, and, stretching out her arms, she lay flat on the bed, giggling.

'Come out here,' hissed the tinker.

He stepped back. Carney shouted and rushed at him, jumping the brazier. The tinker stepped aside and struck Carney a terrible blow on the jaw as he passed him. Carney staggered against the bank and fell in a heap. The tinker jumped on him like a cat, striking him with his hands and feet all together. Carney roared; 'Let me up, let me up. Fair play.' But the tinker kept on beating him until at last he lay motionless at the bottom of the pit.

'Ha,' said the tinker.

Then he picked up the prone body, as lightly as if it were an empty sack, and threw it to the top of the bank. 'Be off, you –' he hissed.

Carney struggled to his feet on the top of the bank and looked at the three of them. They were all standing now in front of the tent, the two women grinning, the tinker scowling. Then he staggered on to the road, with his hands to his head.

'Good-bye, dearie,' cried the golden-headed one.

Then she screamed. Carney looked behind and saw the tinker carrying her into the tent in his arms.

'God Almighty!' cried Carney, crossing himself.

Then he trudged away fearfully through the storm towards Roundwood.

'God Almighty!' he cried at every two yards. 'God Almighty!'

The Conger Eel

LIAM O'FLAHERTY

HE was eight feet long. At the centre of his back he was two feet in circumference. Slipping sinuously along the bottom of the sea at a gigantic pace, his black, mysterious body glistened and twirled like a wisp in a foaming cataract. His little eyes, stationed wide apart in his flat-boned, broad skull, searched the ocean for food. He coursed ravenously for miles along the base of the range of cliffs. He searched fruitlessly, except for three baby pollocks which he swallowed in one mouthful without arresting his progress. He was very hungry.

Then he turned by a sharp promontory and entered a cliff-bound harbour where the sea was dark and silent, shaded by the concave cliffs. Savagely he looked ahead into the dark waters. Then instantaneously he flicked his tail, rippling his body like a twisted screw, and shot forward. His long, thin, single whisker, hanging from his lower snout like a label tag, jerked back under his belly. His glassy eyes rested ferociously on minute white spots that scurried about in the sea a long distance ahead. The conger eel had sighted his prey. There was a school of mackerel a mile away.

He came upon them headlong, in a flash. He rose out of the deep from beneath their white bellies, and gripped one mackerel in his wide-open jaws ere his snout met the surface. Then, as if in a swoon, his body went limp, and tumbling over and over, convulsing like a crushed worm, he sank lower and lower until at last he had swallowed the fish. Then immediately he straightened out and flicked his tail, ready to pursue his prey afresh.

The school of mackerel, when the dread monster had appeared among them, were swimming just beneath the surface of

the sea. When the eel rushed up they had hurled themselves
clean out of the water with the sound of innumerable grains of
sand being shaken in an immense sieve. The thousand blue and
white bodies flashed and shimmered in the sun for three
moments, and then they disappeared, leaving a large patch of
the dark water convulsing turbulently. Ten thousand little fins
cut the surface of the sea as the mackerel set off in headlong
flight. Their white bellies were no longer visible. They plunged
down into the depths of the sea, where their blue-black sides
and backs, the colour of the sea, hid them from their enemy.
The eel surged about in immense figures of eight; but he had
lost them.

Half hungry, half satisfied, he roamed about for half an
hour, a demented giant of the deep, travelling restlessly at an
incredible speed. Then at last his little eyes again sighted his
prey. Little white spots again hung like faded drops of brine
in the sea ahead of him. He rushed thither. He opened his jaws
as the spots assumed shape, and they loomed up close to his
eyes. But just as he attempted to gobble the nearest one, he
felt a savage impact. Then something hard and yet intangible
pressed against his head and then down along his back. He
leaped and turned somersault. The hard, gripping material
completely enveloped him. He was in a net. While on all sides
of him mackerel wriggled gasping in the meshes.

The eel paused for two seconds amazed and terrified. Then
all around him he saw a web of black strands hanging miraculously in the water, everywhere, while mackerel with heaving
gills stood rigid in the web, some with their tails and heads both
caught and their bodies curved in an arch, others encompassed
many times in the uneven folds, others girdled firmly below the
gills with a single black thread. Glittering, they eddied back
and forth with the stream of the sea, a mass of fish being
strangled in the deep.

Then the eel began to struggle fiercely to escape. He hurtled
hither and thither, swinging his long slippery body backwards
and forwards, ripping with his snout, surging forward suddenly
at full speed, churning the water. He ripped and tore the net,
cutting great long gashes in it. But the more he cut and ripped

the more deeply enmeshed did he become. He did not release himself, but he released some of the mackerel. They fell from the torn meshes, stiff and crippled, downwards, sinking like dead things. Then suddenly one after another they seemed to wake from sleep, shook their tails, and darted away, while the giant eel was gathering coil upon coil of the net about his slippery body. Then, at last, exhausted and half strangled, he lay still, heaving.

Presently he felt himself being hauled up in the net. The net crowded around him more, so that the little gleaming mackerel, imprisoned with him, rubbed his sides and lay soft and flabby against him, all hauled up in the net with him. He lay still. He reached the surface and gasped, but he made no movement. Then he was hauled heavily into a boat, and fell with a thud into the bottom.

The two fishermen in the boat began to curse violently when they saw the monstrous eel that had torn their net and ruined their catch of mackerel. The old man on the oars in the bow called out: 'Free him and kill him, the whore.' The young man who was hauling in the net looked in terror at the slippery monster that lay between his feet, with its little eyes looking up cunningly, as if it were human. He almost trembled as he picked up the net and began to undo the coils. 'Slash it with your knife,' yelled the old man, 'before he does more harm.' The young man picked up his knife from the gunwale where it was stuck, and cut the net, freeing the eel. The eel with a sudden and amazing movement, glided up the bottom of the boat, so that he stretched full length.

Then he doubled back, rocking the boat as he beat the sides with his whirling tail, his belly flopping in the water that lay in the bottom. The two men screamed, both crying: 'Kill him, or he'll drown us.' 'Strike him on the nable.' They both reached for the short, thick stick that hung from a peg amidships. The young man grabbed it, bent down, and struck at the eel. 'Hit him on the nable!' cried the old man; 'catch him, catch him, and turn him over.'

They both bent down, pawing at the eel, cursing and panting, while the boat rocked ominously and the huge conger eel glided around and around at an amazing speed. Their hands clawed his sides, slipping over them like skates on ice. They gripped him with their knees, they stood on him, they tried to lie on him, but in their confusion they could not catch him.

Then at last the young man lifted him in his arms, holding him in the middle, gripping him as if he were trying to crush him to death. He staggered upwards. 'Now strike him on the nable!' he yelled to the old man. But suddenly he staggered backwards. The boat rocked. He dropped the eel with an oath, reaching out with his hands to steady himself. The eel's head fell over the canted gunwale. His snout dipped into the sea. With an immense shiver, he glided away, straight down, down to the depths, down like an arrow, until he reached the dark, weed-covered rocks at the bottom.

Then stretching out to his full length he coursed in a wide arc to his enormous lair, far away in the silent depths.

Lovers of the Lake

SEAN O'FAOLAIN

'THEY might wear whites,' she had said, as she stood sipping her tea and looking down at the suburban tennis players in the square. And then, turning her head in that swift movement that always reminded him of a jackdaw: 'By the way, Bobby, will you drive me up to Lough Derg next week?'

He replied amiably from the lazy deeps of her armchair.

'Certainly! What part? Killaloe? But is there a good hotel there?'

'I mean the other Lough Derg. I want to do the pilgrimage.'

For a second he looked at her in surprise and then burst into laughter; then he looked at her peeringly.

'Jenny! Are you serious?'

'Of course.'

'Do you mean that place with the island where they go around on their bare feet on sharp stones, and starve for days, and sit up all night ologroaning and ologoaning?' He got out of the chair, went over to the cigarette box on the bookshelves, and, with his back to her, said coldly, 'Are you going religious on me?'

She walked over to him swiftly, turned him about, smiled her smile that was whiter than the whites of her eyes, and lowered her head appealingly on one side. When this produced no effect she said:

'Bobby! I'm always praising you to my friends as a man who takes things as they come. So few men do. Never looking beyond the day. Doing things on the spur of the moment. It's why I like you so much. Other men are always weighing up, and considering and arguing. I've built you up as a sort of magnificent, wild, brainless tomcat. Are you going to let me down now?'

After a while he had looked at his watch and said:

'All right, then. I'll try and fix up a few days free next week. I must drop into the hospital now. But I warn you, Jenny, I've noticed this Holy Joe streak in you before. You'll do it once too often.'

She patted his cheek, kissed him sedately, said, 'You are a good boy,' and saw him out with a loving smile.

They enjoyed that swift morning drive to the Shannon's shore. He suspected nothing when she refused to join him in a drink at Carrick. Leaning on the counter they had joked with the barmaid like any husband and wife off on a motoring holiday. As they rolled smoothly around the northern shore of Lough Gill, he had suddenly felt so happy that he had stroked her purple glove and winked at her. The lough was vacant under the midday sun, its vast expanse of stillness broken only by a jumping fish or by its eyelash fringe of reeds. He did not suspect anything when she sent him off to lunch by himself in Sligo, saying that she had to visit an old nun she knew in the convent. So far the journey had been to him no more than one of her caprices; until a yellow signpost marked 'TO BUNDORAN' made them aware that her destination and their parting was near, for she said:

'What are you proposing to do until Wednesday?'

'I hadn't given it a thought.'

'Don't go off and forget all about me, darling. You know you're to pick me up on Wednesday about midday?'

After a silence he grumbled:

'You're making me feel a hell of a bastard, Jenny.'

'Why on earth?'

'All this penitential stuff is because of me, isn't it?'

'Don't be silly. It's just something I thought up all by myself out of my own clever little head.'

He drove on for several miles without speaking. She looked sideways, with amusement, at his ruddy, healthy, hockey-player face glimmering under the peak of his checked cap. The brushes at his temples were getting white. Everything about him bespoke the distinguished Dublin surgeon on holiday: his pale-green shirt, his darker-green tie, his double-breasted waistcoat, his driving gloves with the palms made of woven cord. She looked pensively towards the sea. He growled:

'I may as well tell you this much, Jenny: if you were my wife, I wouldn't stand for any of this nonsense.'

So their minds had travelled to the same thought? But if she were his wife, the question would never have arisen. She knew by the sudden rise of speed that he was in one of his tempers, so that when he pulled in to the grass verge, switched off, and turned towards her she was not taken by surprise. A seagull moaned high overhead. She lifted her grey eyes to his, and smiled, waiting for the attack.

'Jenny, would you mind telling me exactly what all this is about? I mean, why are you doing this fal-lal at this particular time?'

'I always wanted to do this pilgrimage. So it naturally follows that I would do it sometime, doesn't it?'

'Perhaps. But why, for instance, this month and not last month?'

'The island wasn't open to pilgrims last month.'

'Why didn't you go last year instead of this year?'

'You know we went to Austria last year.'

'Why not the year before last?'

'I don't know. And stop bullying me. It is just a thing that everybody wants to do sometime. It is a special sort of Irish thing, like Lourdes, or Fatima, or Lisieux. Everybody who knows about it feels drawn to it. If you were a practising Catholic you'd understand.'

'I understand quite well,' he snapped. 'I know perfectly well that people go on pilgrimages all over the world. Spain. France. Mexico. I shouldn't be surprised if they go on them in Russia. What I am asking you is what has cropped up to produce this extra-special performance just *now*?'

'And I tell you I don't know. The impulse came over me suddenly last Sunday looking at those boys and girls playing tennis. For no reason. It just came. I said to myself, "All right, go now!" I felt that if I didn't do it on the impulse, I'd never do it at all. Are you asking me for a rational explanation? I haven't got one. I'm not clever and intelligent like you, darling.'

'You're as clever as a bag of cats.'

She laughed at him.

'I do love you, Bobby, when you are cross. Like a small boy.'

'Why didn't you ask George to drive you?'

She sat up straight.

'I don't want my husband to know anything whatever about this. Please don't mention a word of it to him.'

He grinned at his small victory, considered the scythe of her jawbone, looked at the shining darkness of her hair, and re-started the car.

'All the same,' he said after a mile, 'there must be some reason. Or call it a cause if you don't like the word reason. And I'd give a lot to know what it is.'

After another mile:

'Of course, I might as well be talking to that old dolmen over there as be asking a woman why she does anything. And if she knew she wouldn't tell you.'

After another mile:

'Mind you, I believe all this is just a symptom of something else. Never forget, my girl, that I'm a doctor. I'm trained to interpret symptoms. If a woman comes to me with a pain ...'

'Oh, yes, if a woman comes to Surgeon Robert James Flannery with a pain he says to her, "Never mind, that's only a pain." My God! If a woman has a pain she has a bloody pain!'

He said quietly:

'Have you a pain?'

'Oh, do shut up! The only pain I have is in my tummy. I'm ravenous.'

'I'm sorry. Didn't they give you a good lunch at the convent?'

'I took no lunch; you have to arrive at the island fasting. That's the rule.'

'Do you mean to say you've had nothing at all to eat since breakfast?'

'I had no breakfast.'

'What will you get to eat when you arrive on the island?'

'Nothing. Or next to nothing. Everybody has to fast on the island the whole time. Sometime before night I might get a cup of black tea, or hot water with pepper and salt in it. I believe it's one of their lighthearted jokes to call it soup.'

Their speed shot up at once to sixty-five. He drove through Bundoran's siesta hour like the chariot of the Apocalypse. Nearing Ballyshannon they slowed down to a pleasant, humming fifty.

'Jenny!'

'Yes?'

'Are you tired of me?'

'Is this more of you and your symptoms?'

He stopped the car again.

'Please answer my question.'

She laid her purple-gloved hand on his clenched fist.

'Look, darling! We've known one another for six years. You know that like any good little Catholic girl I go to my duties every Easter and every Christmas. Once or twice I've told you so. You've growled and grumbled a bit, but you never made any fuss about it. What are you suddenly worrying about now?'

'Because all that was just routine. Like the French or the Italians. Good Lord, I'm not bigoted. There's no harm in going to church now and again. I do it myself on state occasions, or if I'm staying in some house where they'd be upset if I didn't. But this sort of lunacy isn't routine!'

She slewed her head swiftly away from his angry eyes. A child in a pink pinafore with shoulder frills was driving two black cows through a gap.

'It was never routine. It's the one thing I have to hang on to in an otherwise meaningless existence. No children. A husband I'm not in love with. And I can't marry you.'

She slewed back to him. He slewed away to look up the long empty road before them. He slewed back; he made as if to speak; he slewed away impatiently again.

'No?' she interpreted. 'It isn't any use, is it? It's my problem, not yours. Or if it is yours, you've solved it long ago by saying it's all a lot of damned nonsense.'

'And how have you solved it?' he asked sardonically.

'Have you any cause to complain of how I've solved it? Oh, I'm not defending myself. I'm a fraud, I'm a crook, I admit it. You are more honest than I am. You don't believe in anything. But it's the truth that all I have is you and ...'

'And what?'

'It sounds so blasphemous I can't say it.'

'Say it!'

'All I have is you, and God.'

He took out his cigarette case and took one. She took one. When he lit hers their eyes met. He said, very softly, looking up the empty road:

'Poor Jenny! I wish you'd talked like this to me before. It is, after all, as you say, your own affair. But what I can't get over is that this thing you're doing is so utterly extravagant. To go off to an island, in the middle of a lake, in the mountains, with a lot of Crawthumpers of every age and sex, and no sex, and peel off your stockings and your shoes and go limping about on your bare feet on a lot of sharp stones, and kneel in the mud, psalming and beating your breast like a criminal, and drink nothing for three days but salt water ... it's not like you. It's a side of you I've never known before. The only possible explanation for it must be that something is happening inside you that I've never seen happen before!'

She spread her hands in despair. He chucked away his cigarette and restarted the car. They drove on in silence. A mist began to speckle the windscreen. They turned off the main road into sunless hills, all brown as hay. The next time he glanced at her she was making up her face; her mouth rolling the lipstick into her lips; her eyes rolling around the mirror. He said:

'You're going to have a nice picnic if the weather breaks.'

She glanced out apprehensively.

'It won't be fun.'

A sudden flog of rain lashed into the windscreen. The sky had turned its bucket upside down. He said:

'Even if it's raining, do you still have to keep walking around on those damn stones?'

'Yes.'

'You'll get double pneumonia.'

'Don't worry, darling. It's called Saint Patrick's Purgatory. He will look after me.'

That remark started a squabble that lasted until they drew up beside the lake. Other cars stood about like stranded boats. Other pilgrims stood by the boat slip, waiting for the ferry, their backs hunched to the wind, their clothes ruffled like the fur of cattle. She looked out across the lough at the creeping worms of foam.

He looked about him sullenly at the waiting pilgrims, a green bus, two taxiloads of people waiting for the rain to stop. They were not his kind of people at all, and he said so.

'That,' she smiled, 'is what comes of being a surgeon. You don't meet people, you meet organs. Didn't you once tell me that when you are operating you never look at the patient's face?'

He grunted. Confused and hairy-looking clouds combed themselves on the ridges of the hills. The lake was crumpled and grey except for those yellow worms of foam blown across it in parallel lines. To the south a cold patch of light made it all look far more dreary. She stared out towards the island and said:

'It's not at all like what I expected.'

'And what the hell did you expect? Capri?'

'I thought of an old island, with old grey ruins, and old holly trees and rhododendrons down to the water, a place where old monks would live.'

They saw tall buildings like modern hotels rising by the island's shore, an octagonal basilica big enough for a city, four or five bare, slated houses, a long shed like a ballroom. There was one tree. Another bus drew up beside them and people peered out through the wiped glass.

'Oh, God!' she groaned. 'I hope this isn't going to be like Lourdes.'

'And what, pray, is wrong with Lourdes when it's at home?'

'Commercialized. I simply can't believe that this island was the most famous pilgrimage of the Middle Ages. On the rim of the known world. It must have been like going off to

Jerusalem or coming home brown from the sun with a cockle in your hat from Galilee.'

He put on a vulgar Yukon voice:

'Thar's gold somewhere in them thar hills. It looks to me like a damn good financial proposition for somebody.'

She glared at him. The downpour had slackened. Soon it almost ceased. Gurgles of streams. A sound of pervasive drip. From the back seat she took a small red canvas bag marked TWA.

'You will collect me on Wednesday about noon, won't you?'

He looked at her grimly. She looked every one of her forty-one years. The skin of her neck was corrugated. In five years' time she would begin to have jowls.

'Have a good time,' he said, and slammed in the gears, and drove away.

The big, lumbering ferryboat was approaching, its prow slapping the corrugated waves. There were three men to each oar. It began to spit rain again. With about a hundred and fifty men and women, of every age and, so far as she could see, of every class, she clambered aboard. They pushed out and slowly they made the crossing, huddling together from the wind and rain. The boat nosed into its cleft and unloaded. She had a sensation of dark water, wet cement, houses, and a great number of people; and that she would have given gold for a cup of hot tea. Beyond the four or five whitewashed houses – she guessed that they had been the only buildings on the island before trains and buses made the pilgrimage popular – and beyond the cement paths, she came on the remains of the natural island: a knoll, some warm grass, the tree, and the roots of the old hermit's cells across whose teeth of stone barefooted pilgrims were already treading on one another's heels. Most of these bare-footed people wore mackintoshes. They not only stumbled on one another's heels, they kneeled on one another's toes and tails; for the island was crowded – she thought there must be nearly two thousand people on it. They were packed between the two modern hostels and the big church. She saw a priest in sou'wester and gum boots. A nun waiting for the new arrivals at the door of the women's hostel took her name and address, and gave her the number of her cubicle. She went upstairs to it, laid her red bag on the cot, sat beside it, unfastened her garters, took off her shoes, unpeeled her nylons, and without transition became yet another anonymous pilgrim. As she went out among the pilgrims already praying in the rain, she felt only a sense of shame as if she were specially singled out under the microscope of the sky. The wet ground was cold.

A fat old woman in black, rich-breasted, grey-haired, took her kindly by the arm and said in a warm, Kerry voice: 'You're shivering, you poor creature! Hould hard now. Sure, when we have the first station done they'll be giving us the ould cup of black tay.'

And laughed at the folly of this longing for the tea. She winced when she stepped on the gritty concrete of the terrace surrounding the basilica, built out on piles over the lake. A young man smiled sympathetically, seeing that she was a delicate subject for the rigours before her: he was dressed like a clerk, with three pens in his breast pocket, and he wore a Total Abstinence badge.

'Saint's Island they call it,' he smiled. 'Some people think it should be called Divil's Island.'

She disliked his kindness – she had never in her life asked for pity from anybody, but she soon found that the island floated on kindness. Everything and everybody about her seemed to say, 'We are all sinners here, wretched creatures barely worthy of mercy.' She felt the abasement of the doomed. She was among people who had surrendered all personal identity, all pride. It was like being in a concentration camp.

The fat old Kerrywoman was explaining to her what the routine was, and as she listened she realized how long her stay would really be. In prospect it had seemed so short: come on Monday afternoon, leave on Wednesday at noon; it had seemed no more than one complete day and two bits of nights. She had not foreseen that immediately after arriving she must remain out of doors until the darkness fell, walking the rounds of the stones, praying, kneeling, for about five hours. And

even then she would get no respite, for she must stay awake
all night praying in the basilica. It was then that she would
begin the second long day, as long and slow as the night; and
on the third day she would still be walking those rounds until
midday. She would be without food, even when she would have
left the island, until the midnight of that third day.

'Yerrah, but sure,' the old woman cackled happily, 'they say
that fasting is good for the stomach.'

She began to think of 'they'. They had thought all this up.
They had seen how much could be done with simple prayers.
For when she began to tot up the number of paternosters and
Aves that she must say, she had to stop at the two thousandth.
And these reiterated prayers must be said while walking on the
stones, or kneeling in the mud, or standing upright with her
two arms extended. This was the posture she disliked most.
Every time she came to do it, her face to the lake, her arms
spread, the queue listening to her renouncing her sins, she had
to force herself to the posture and the words. The first time
she did it, with the mist blowing into her eyes, her arms out
like a crucifix, her lips said the words but her heart cursed
herself for coming so unprepared, for coming at all. Before she
had completed her first circuit – four times around each one
of six cells – one ankle and one toe were bleeding. She was
then permitted to ask for the cup of black tea. She received
it sullenly, as a prisoner might receive his bread and
water.

She wished after that first circuit to start again and complete a second – the six cells, and the seven other ordeals at
other points of the island – and so be done for the day. But she
found that 'they' had invented something else: she must merge
with the whole anonymous mass of pilgrims for mass prayer
in the church.

A slur of wet feet; patter of rain on leaded windows; smells
of bog water and damp clothing; the thousand voices responding to the incantations. At her right a young girl of about
seventeen was uttering heartfelt responses. On her left an old
man in his sixties gave them out loudly. On all sides, before
her, behind her, the same passionate exchange of energy, while

all she felt was a crust hardening about her heart, and she thought, in despair, 'I have no more feeling than a stone!' And she thought, looking about her, that tonight this vigil would go on for hour after hour until the dark, leaded windows coloured again in the morning light. She leaned her face in her palms and whispered, 'O God, please let me out of myself!' The waves of voices beat and rumbled in her ears as in an empty shell.

She was carried out on the general sliding whispering of the bare feet into the last gleamings of the daylight to begin her second circuit. In the porch she cowered back from the rain. It was settling into a filthy night. She was thrust forward by the crowd, flowed with its force to the iron cross by the shingle's edge. She took her place in the queue and then with the night wind pasting her hair across her face she raised her arms and once again renounced the world, the flesh, and the Devil. She did four circles of the church on the gritty concrete. She circled the first cell's stones. She completed the second circle. Her prayers were become numb by now. She stumbled, muttering them, up and down the third steeply sloped cell, or bed. She was a drowned cat and one knee was bleeding. At the fourth cell she saw him.

He was standing about six yards away looking at her. He wore a white raincoat buttoned tight about his throat. His feet were bare. His hair was streaked down his forehead as if he had been swimming. She stumbled towards him and dragged him by the arm down to the edge of the boat slip.

'What are you doing here?' she cried furiously. 'Why did you follow me?'

He looked down at her calmly:

'Why shouldn't I be here?'

'Because you don't believe in it! You've just followed me to sneer at me, to mock at me! Or from sheer vulgar curiosity!'

'No,' he said, without raising his voice. 'I've come to see just what it is that you believe in. I want to know all about you. I want to know why you came here. I don't want you to do anything or have anything that I can't do or can't know. And as for believing – we all believe in something.'

Dusk was closing in on the island and the lake. She had to peer into his face to catch his expression.

'But I've known you for years and you've never shown any sign of believing in anything but microscopes and microbes and symptoms. It's absurd, you couldn't be serious about anything like this. I'm beginning to hate you!'

'Are you?' he said so softly that she had to lean near him to hear him over the slapping of the waves against the boat slip. A slow rift in the clouds let down a star; by its light she saw his smile.

'Yes!' she cried, so loudly that he swept out a hand and gripped her by the arm. Then he took her other arm and said gently:

'I don't think you should have come here, Jenny. You're only tearing yourself to bits. There are some places where some people should never go, things some people should never try to do – however good they may be for others. I know why you came here. You feel you ought to get rid of me, but you haven't the guts to do it, so you come up here into the mountains to get your druids to work it by magic. All right! I'm going to ask them to help you.'

He laughed and let her go, giving her a slight impulse away from him.

'Ask? You will *ask*? Do you mean to tell me that you have said as much as one single, solitary prayer on this island?'

'Yes,' he said casually, 'I have.'

She scorned him.

'Are you trying to tell me, Bobby, that you are doing this pilgrimage?'

'I haven't fasted. I didn't know about that. And, anyway, I probably won't. I've got my pockets stuffed with two pounds of the best chocolates I could buy in Bundoran. I don't suppose I'll even stay up all night like the rest of you. The place is so crowded that I don't suppose anybody will notice me if I curl up in some corner of the boathouse. I heard somebody saying that people had to sleep there last night. But you never know – I might – I just might stay awake. If I do, it will remind me of going to midnight Mass with my father when I was a kid. Or going to retreats, when we used all hold up a lighted candle and renounce the Devil.

'It was a queer sensation standing there by the lake and saying those words all over again. Do you know, I thought I'd completely forgotten them!'

'The next thing you're going to say is that you believe in the Devil! You fraud!'

'Oh, there's no trouble about believing in that old gentleman. There isn't a doctor in the world who doesn't, though he will give him another name. And on a wet night, in a place like this, you could believe in a lot of things. No, my girl, what I find it hard to believe in is the flesh and the world. They are good things. Do you think I'm ever going to believe that your body and my body are evil? And you don't either! And you are certainly never going to renounce the world, because you are tied to it hand and foot!'

'That's not true!'

His voice cut her like a whip:

'Then why do you go on living with your husband?'

She stammered feebly. He cut at her again:

'You do it because he's rich, and you like comfort, and you like being a "somebody".'

With a switch of her head she brushed past him. She did not see him again that night.

The night world turned imperceptibly. In the church, for hour after hour, the voices obstinately beat back the responses. She sank under the hum of the prayer wheel, the lust for sleep, her own despairs. Was he among the crowd? Or asleep in a corner of the boatshed? She saw his flatly domed fingers, a surgeon's hand, so strong, so sensitive. She gasped at the sensual image she had evoked.

The moon touched a black window with colour. After an age it had stolen to another. Heads drooped. Neighbours poked one another awake with a smile. Many of them had risen from the benches in order to keep themselves awake and were circling the aisles in a loose procession of slurring feet, responding as they moved. Exhaustion began to work on her mind. Objects began to disconnect, become isolated each within its own outline – now it was the pulpit, now a statue, now a crucifix. Each object took on the vividness of a hallucination. The crucifix detached itself from the wall and leaned towards her, and for a long while she saw nothing but the heavy pendant body, the staring eyes, so that when the old man at her side let his head sink over on her shoulder and then woke up with a start, she felt him no more than if they were two fishes touching in the sea. Bit by bit the incantations drew her in; sounds came from her mouth; prayers flowed between her and those troubled eyes that fixed hers. She swam into an ecstasy as rare as one of those perfect dances of her youth when she used to swing in a whirl of music, a swirl of bodies, a circling of lights, floated out of her mortal frame, alone in the arms that embraced her.

Suddenly it all exploded. One of the four respites of the night had halted the prayers. The massed pilgrims relaxed. She looked blearily about her, no longer disjunct. Her guts rumbled. She looked at the old man beside her. She smiled at him and he at her.

'My poor old knees are crucified,' he grinned.

'You should have the skirts,' she grinned back.

They were all going out to stretch in the cool, and now dry, air, or to snatch a smoke. The amber windows of the church shivered in a pool of water. A hearty-voiced young woman leaning on the balustrade lit a match for her. The match hissed into the invisible lake lapping below.

'The ould fag,' said the young woman, dragging deep on her cigarette, 'is a great comfort. 'Tis as good as a man.'

'I wonder,' she said, 'what would Saint Patrick think if he saw women smoking on his island?'

'He'd beat the living lights out of the lot of us.'

She laughed aloud. She must tell him that ... She began to wander through the dark crowds in search of him. He had said something that wasn't true and she would answer him. She went through the crowds down to the boat slip. He was standing there, looking out into the dark as if he had not stirred since she saw him there before midnight. For a moment she regarded him, frightened by the force of the love that gushed into her. Then she approached him.

'Well, Mr Worldly Wiseman? Enjoying your boathouse bed?'

'I'm doing the vigil,' he said smugly.

'You sound almighty pleased with yourself.'

He spoke eagerly now:

'Jenny, we mustn't quarrel. We must understand one another. And understand this place. I'm just beginning to. An island. In a remote lake. Among the mountains. Night-time. No sleep. Hunger. The conditions of the desert. I was right in what I said to you. Can't you see how the old hermits who used to live here could swim off into a trance in which nothing existed but themselves and their visions? I told you a man can renounce what he calls the Devil, but not the flesh, not the world. They thought, like you, that they could throw away the flesh and the world, but they were using the flesh to achieve one of the rarest experiences in the world! Don't you see it?'

'Experiences! The next thing you'll be talking about is symptoms.'

'Well, surely, you must have observed?' He peered at the luminous dial of his watch. 'I should say that about four o'clock we will probably begin to experience a definite sense of dissociation. After that a positive alienation ...'

She turned furiously from him. She came back to say:

'I would much prefer, Bobby, if you would have the decency to go away in the morning. I can find my own way home. I hope we don't meet again on this island. Or out of it!'

'The magic working?' he laughed.

After that she made a deliberate effort of the mind to mean and to feel every separate word of the prayers – which is a great foolishness since prayers are not poems to be read or even understood; they are an instinct; to dance would be as wise. She thought that if she could not feel what she said, how could she mean it, and so she tried to savour every word, and, from trying to mean each word, lagged behind the rest, sank into herself, and ceased to pray. After the second respite she prayed only to keep awake. As the first cold pallor of morning came into the windows, her heart rose again. But the eastern hills are high here and the morning holds off stubbornly. It is the worst hour of the vigil, when the body ebbs, the prayers sink to a drone, and the night seems to have begun all over again.

At the last respite she emerged to see pale tents of blue on the hills. The slow cumulus clouds cast a sheen on the water. There is no sound. No birds sing. At this hour the pilgrims are too awed or too exhausted to speak, so that the island reverts to its ancient silence in spite of the crowds.

By the end of the last bout she was calm like the morning lake. She longed for the cup of black tea. She was unaware of her companions. She did not think of him. She was unaware of herself. She no more thought of God than a slave thinks of his master, and after she had drunk her tea she sat in the morning sun outside the women's hostel like an old blind woman who has nothing in life to wait for but sleep.

The long day expired as dimly as the vapour rising from the water. The heat became morbid. One is said to be free on this second day to converse, to think, to write, to read, to do anything at all that one pleases except the one thing everybody wants to do – to sleep. She did nothing but watch the clouds, or listen to the gentle muttering of the lake. Before noon she heard some departing pilgrims singing a hymn as the great ferryboats pushed off. She heard their voices without longing; she did not even desire food. When she met him she was without rancour.

'Still here?' she said, and when he nodded: 'Sleepy?'

'Sleepy.'

'Too many chocolates, probably.'

'I didn't eat them. I took them out of my pockets one by one as I leaned over the balustrade, and guessed what centre each had – coffee, marshmallow, nut, toffee, cream – and dropped it in with a little splash to the holy fishes.'

She looked up at him gravely.

'Are you really trying to join in this pilgrimage?'

'Botching it. I'm behindhand with my rounds. I have to do five circuits between today and tomorrow. I may never get them done. Still, something is better than nothing.'

'You dear fool!'

If he had not walked away then, she would have had to; such a gush of affection came over her at the thought of what he was doing, and why he was doing it – stupidly, just like a man; sceptically, just like a man; not admitting it to himself, just like a man; for all sorts of damn-fool rational reasons, just like a man; and not at all for the only reason that she knew was his real reason: because she was doing it, which meant that he loved her. She sat back, and closed her eyes, and the tears of chagrin oozed between her lids as she felt her womb stir with desire of him.

When they met again it was late afternoon.

'Done four rounds,' he said so cheerfully that he maddened her.

'It's not golf, Bobby, damn you!'

'I should jolly well think not. I may tell you my feet are in such a condition I won't be able to play golf for a week. Look!'

She did not look. She took his arm and led him to the quietest corner she could find.

'Bobby, I am going to confess something to you. I've been thinking about it all day trying to get it clear. I know now why I came here. I came because I know inside me that some day our apple will have to fall off the tree. I'm forty. You are nearly fifty. It will have to happen. I came here because I thought it right to admit that some day, if it has to be, I am willing to give you up.'

He began to shake all over with laughter.

'What the hell are you laughing at?' she moaned.

'When women begin to reason! Listen, wasn't there a chap some time who said, "O God, please make me chaste, but not just yet"?'

'What I am saying is "now", if it has to be, if it can be, if I can make it be. I suppose,' she said wildly, 'I'm really asking for a miracle, that my husband would die, or that you'd die, or something like that that would make it all come right!'

He burst into such a peal of laughter that she looked around her apprehensively. A few people near them also happened to be laughing over something and looked at them indulgently.

'Do you realize, Bobby, that when I go to confession here I will have to tell all about us, and I will have to promise to give you up?'

'Yes, darling, and you won't mean a single word of it.'

'But I always mean it!'

He stared at her as if he was pushing curtains aside in her.

'Always? Do you mean you've been saying it for six years?'

'I mean it when I say it. Then I get weak. I can't help it, Bobby. You know that!' She saw the contempt in his eyes and began to talk rapidly, twisting her marriage ring madly around her finger. He kept staring into her eyes like a man staring down the long perspective of a railway line waiting for the engine to appear. 'So you see why there wasn't any sense in asking me yesterday why I come now and not at some other time, because with me there isn't any other time, it's always *now*, I meet you *now*, and I love you *now*, and I think it's not right *now*, and then I think, "No, not *now*", and then I say I'll give you up *now*, and I mean it every time until we meet again, and it begins all over again, and there's never any end to it until some day I can say, "Yes, I used to know him once, but not *now*", and then it will be a *now* where there won't be any other *now* any more because there'll be nothing to live for.'

The tears were leaking down her face. He sighed:

'Dear me! You have got yourself into a mess, haven't you?'

'O God, the promises and the promises! I wish the world would end tonight and we'd both die together!'

He gave her his big damp handkerchief. She wiped her eyes and blew her nose and said:

'You don't mean to go to confession, do you?'

He chuckled sourly.

'And promise? I must go and finish a round of pious golf.

I'm afraid, old girl, you just want to get me into the same
mess as yourself. No, thank you. You must solve your own
problems in your own way, and I in mine.'

That was the last time she spoke to him that day.

She went back to the balustrade where she had smoked with
the hearty girl in the early hours of the morning. She was
there again. She wore a scarlet beret. She was smoking again.
She began to talk, and the talk flowed from her without stop.
She had fine broad shoulders, a big mobile mouth, and a pair
of wild goat's eyes. After a while it became clear that the
woman was beside herself with terror. She suddenly let it all
out in a gush of exhaled smoke.

'Do you know why I'm hanging around here? Because I
ought to go into confession and I'm in dread of it. He'll tear
me alive. He'll murdher me. It's not easy for a girl like me, I
can promise you!'

'You must have terrible sins to tell?' she smiled comfortingly.

'He'll slaughter me, I'm telling you.'

'What is it? Boys?'

The two goat's eyes dilated with fear and joy. Her hands
shook like a drunkard's.

'I can't keep away from them. I wish to God I never came
here.'

'But how silly! It's only a human thing. I'm sure half the
people here have the same tale to tell. It's an old story, child,
the priests are sick of hearing it.'

'Oh, don't be talking! Let me alone! I'm criminal, I tell
yeh! And there are things you can't explain to a priest. My
God, you can hardly explain 'em to a doctor!'

'You're married?' – looking at her ring.

'Poor Tom! I have him wore out. He took me to a doctor
one time to know would anything cure me. The old foolah took
me temperature and gave me a book like a bus guide about
when it's safe and when it isn't safe to make love, the ould
eedjut! I was pregnant again before Christmas. Six years married and I have six kids; nobody could stand that gait o' going.
And I'm only twenty-four. Am I to have a baby every year of

my life? I'd give me right hand this minute for a double whiskey.'

'Look, you poor child! We are all in the same old ferryboat here. What about me?'

'You?'

'It's not men with me, it's worse.'

'Worse? In God's name, what's worse than men?'

The girl looked all over her, followed her arm down to her hand, to her third finger.

'One man.'

The tawny eyes swivelled back to her face and immediately understood.

'Are you very fond of him?' she asked gently, and taking the unspoken answer said, still more pityingly, 'You can't give him up?'

'It's six years now and I haven't been able to give him up.'

The girl's eyes roved sadly over the lake as if she were surveying a lake of human unhappiness. Then she threw her butt into the water and her red beret disappeared into the maw of the church porch.

She saw him twice before the dusk thickened and the day grew cold again with the early sunset. He was sitting directly opposite her before the men's hostel, smoking, staring at the ground between his legs. They sat facing one another. They were separated by their identities, joined by their love. She glimpsed him only once after that, at the hour when the sky and the hills merge, an outline passing across the lake. Soon after she had permission to go to her cubicle. Immediately she lay down she spiralled to the bottom of a deep lake of sleep.

She awoke refreshed and unburthened. She had received the island's gift: its sense of remoteness from the world, almost a sensation of the world's death. It is the source of the island's kindness. Nobody is just matter, poor to be exploited by rich, weak to be exploited by the strong; in mutual generosity each recognizes the other only as a form of soul; it is a brief, harsh Utopia of equality in nakedness. The bare feet are a symbol of that nakedness unknown in the world they have left.

The happiness to which she awoke was dimmed a little by a conversation she had with an Englishman over breakfast – the usual black tea and a piece of oaten bread. He was a city man who had arrived the day before, been up all night while she slept. He had not yet shaved; he was about sixty-two or -three; small and tubby, his eyes perpetually wide and unfocusing behind pince-nez glasses.

'That's right,' he said, answering her question. 'I'm from England. Liverpool. I cross by the night boat and get here the next afternoon. Quite convenient, really. I've come here every year for the last twenty-two years, apart from the war years. I come on account of my wife.'

'Is she ill?'

'She died twenty-two years ago. No, it's not what you might think – I'm not praying for her. She was a good woman, but, well, you see, I wasn't very kind to her. I don't mean I quarrelled with her, or drank, or was unfaithful. I never gambled. I've never smoked in my life.' His hands made a faint movement that was meant to express a whole life, all the confusion and trouble of his soul. 'It's just that I wasn't kind. I didn't make her happy.'

'Isn't that,' she said, to comfort him, 'a very private feeling? I mean, it's not in the Ten Commandments that thou shalt make thy wife happy.'

He did not smile. He made the same faint movement with his fingers.

'Oh, I don't know! What's love if it doesn't do that? I mean to say, it is something godly to love another human being, isn't it? I mean, what does "godly" mean if it doesn't mean giving up everything for another? It isn't human to love, you know. It's foolish, it's a folly, a divine folly. It's beyond all reason, all limits. I didn't rise to it,' he concluded sadly.

She looked at him, and thought, 'A little fat man, a clerk in some Liverpool office all his life, married to some mousey little woman, thinking about love as if he were some sort of Greek mystic.'

'It's often,' she said lamely, 'more difficult to love one's husband, or one's wife, as the case may be, than to love one's neighbour.'

'Oh, much!' he agreed without a smile. 'Much! Much more difficult!'

At which she was overcome by the thought that inside ourselves we have no room without a secret door; no solid self that has not a ghost inside it trying to escape. If I leave Bobby I still have George. If I leave George I still have myself, and whatever I find in myself. She patted the little man's hand and left him, fearing that if she let him talk on, even his one little piece of sincerity would prove to be a fantasy, and in the room that he had found behind his own room she would open other doors leading to other obsessions. He had told her something true about her own imperfection, and about the nature of love, and she wanted to share it while it was still true. But she could not find him, and there was still one more circuit to do before the ferryboat left. She did meet Goat's Eyes. The girl clutched her with tears magnifying her yellow-and-green irises and gasped joyously:

'I found a lamb of a priest. A saint anointed! He was as gentle! "What's your husband earning?" says he. "Four pounds ten a week, Father," says I. "And six children?" says he. "You poor woman," says he, "you don't need to come here at all. Your Purgatory is at home." He laid all the blame on poor Tom. And, God forgive me, I let him do it. "Bring him here to me," says he, "and I'll cool him for you." God bless the poor innocent priest, I wish I knew as little about marriage as he does. But –' and here she broke into a wail – 'sure he has me ruined altogether now. He's after making me so fond of poor Tommy I think I'll never get home soon enough to go to bed with him.' And in a vast flood of tears of joy, of relief, and of fresh misery: 'I wish I was a bloomin' nun!'

It was not until they were all waiting at the ferryboat that she saw him. She managed to sit beside him in the boat. He touched her hand and winked. She smiled back at him. The bugler blew his bugle. A tardy traveller came racing out of the men's hostel. The boatload cheered him, the bugler helped him aboard with a joke about people who can't be persuaded to stop praying, and there was a general chaff about people who have a lot to pray about, and then somebody raised the parting hymn, and the rowers began to push the heavy oars, and singing they were slowly rowed across the summer lake back to the world.

They were driving back out of the hills by the road they had come, both silent. At last she could hold in her question no longer:

'Did you go, Bobby?'

Meaning: had he, after all his years of silence, of rebellion, of disbelief, made his peace with God at the price of a compact against her. He replied gently:

'Did I probe your secrets all these years?'

She took the rebuke humbly, and for several miles they drove on in silence. They were close, their shoulders touched, but between them there stood that impenetrable wall of identity that segregates every human being in a private world of self. Feeling it she realized at last that it is only in places like the lake-island that the barriers of self break down. The tubby little clerk from Liverpool had been right. Only when love desires nothing but renunciation, total surrender, does self surpass self. Everybody who ever entered the island left the world of self behind for a few hours, exchanged it for what the little man had called a divine folly. It was possible only for a few hours – unless one had the courage, or the folly, to renounce the world altogether. Then another thought came to her. In the world there might also be escape from the world.

'Do you think, Bobby, that when people are in love they can give up everything for one another?'

'No,' he said flatly. 'Except perhaps in the first raptures?'

'If I had a child I think I could sacrifice anything for it. Even my life.'

'Yes,' he agreed. 'It has been known to happen.'

And she looked at him sadly, knowing that they would never be able to marry, and even if she did that she would never have children. And yet, if they could have married, there was a lake ...

'Do you know what I'm planning at this moment?' he asked breezily.

She asked without interest what it was.

'Well, I'm simply planning the meal we're going to eat tonight in Galway, at midnight.'

'At midnight? Then we're going on with this pilgrimage? Are we?'

'Don't *you* want to? It was your idea in the beginning.'

'All right. And what are we going to do until midnight? I've never known time to be so long.'

'I'm going to spend the day fishing behind Glencar. That will kill the hungry day. After that, until midnight, we'll take the longest possible road around Connemara. Then would you have any objections to mountain trout cooked in milk, stuffed roast kid with fresh peas and spuds in their jackets, apple pie and whipped cream, with a cool Pouilly-Fuissé, a cosy 1929 claret, West of Ireland Pont l'Évêque, finishing up with Gaelic coffee and two Otards? Much more in your line, if I know anything about you, than your silly old black tea and hot salt water.'

'I admit I like the things of the flesh.'

'You live for them!'

He had said it so gently, so affectionately that, half in dismay, half with amusement, she could not help remembering Goat's Eyes, racing home as fast as the bus would carry her to make love to her Tommy. After that they hardly spoke at all, and then only of casual things such as a castle beside the road, the sun on the edging sea, a tinker's caravan, an opening view. It was early afternoon as they entered the deep valley at Glencar and he probed in second gear for an attractive length of stream, found one and started eagerly to put his rod together. He began to walk up against the dazzling bubble of water and within an hour was out of sight. She stretched herself out on a rug on the bank and fell sound asleep.

It was nearly four o'clock before she woke up, stiff and thirsty. She drank from a pool in the stream, and for an hour she sat alone by the pool, looking into its peat-brown depth, as vacantly contented as a tinker's wife to live for the moment, to let time wind and unwind everything. It was five o'clock before she saw him approaching, plodding in his flopping waders, with four trout on a rush stalk. He threw the fish at her feet and himself beside them.

'I nearly ate them raw,' he said.

'Let's cook them and eat them,' she said fiercely.

He looked at her for a moment, then got up and began to gather dry twigs, found Monday's newspaper in the car – it looked like a paper of years ago – and started the fire. She watched while he fed it. When it was big enough in its fall to have made a hot bed of embers he roasted two of the trout across the hook of his gaff, and she smelled the crisping flesh and sighed. At last he laid them, browned and crackly, on the grass by her hand. She took one by its crusted tail, smelt it, looked at him, and slung it furiously into the heart of the fire. He gave a sniff-laugh and did the same with his.

'Copy-cat!' she said.

'Let's get the hell out of here,' he said, jumping up. 'Carry the kit, will you?'

She rose, collected the gear, and followed him saying:

'I feel like an Arab wife. "Carry the pack. Go here. Go there."'

They climbed out of the glens on to the flat moorland of the Easky peninsula where the evening light was a cold ochre gleaming across green bogland that was streaked with all the weedy colours of a strand at ebb. At Ballina she suggested that they should have tea.

'It will be a pleasant change of diet!' he said.

When they had found a café and she was ordering the tea he said to the waitress:

'And bring lots of hot buttered toast.'

'This,' she said, as she poured out the tea and held up the milk jug questioningly, 'is a new technique of seduction. Milk?'

'Are you having milk?'

'No.'

'No, then.'

'Some nice hot buttered toast?'

'Are you having toast?' he demanded.

'Why the bloody hell should it be up to me to decide?'

'I asked you a polite question,' he said rudely.

'No.'

'No!'

They looked at one another as they sipped the black tea like two people who are falling head over heels into hatred of one another.

'Could you possibly tell me,' he said presently, 'why I bother my head with a fool of a woman like you?'

'I can only suppose, Bobby, that it is because we are in love with one another.'

'I can only suppose so,' he growled. 'Let's get·on!'

They took the longest way round he could find on the map, west into County Mayo, across between the lakes at Pontoon, over the level bogland to Castlebar. Here the mountains walled in the bogland plain with cobalt air – in the fading light the land was losing all solidity. Clouds like soapsuds rose and rose over the edges of the mountains until they glowed as if there was a fire of embers behind the blue ranges. In Castlebar he pulled up by the post office and telephoned to the hotel at Salthill for dinner and two rooms. When he came out he saw a poster in a shop window and said:

'Why don't we go to the pictures? It will kill a couple of hours.'

'By rights,' she said, 'you ought to be driving me home to Dublin.'

'If you wish me to, I will.'

'Would you if I asked you?'

'Do you want me to?'

'I suppose it's rather late now, isn't it?'

'Not at all. Fast going we could be there about one o'clock. Shall we?'

'It wouldn't help. George is away. I'd have to bring you in and give you something to eat, and ... Let's go to the blasted movies!'

The film was *Charley's Aunt*. They watched its slapstick gloomily. When they came out, after nine o'clock, there was still a vestigial light in the sky. They drove on and on, westward still, prolonging the light, prolonging the drive, holding off the night's decision. Before Killary they paused at a black-faced lake, got out, and stood beside its quarried beauty. Nothing along its stony beach but a few wind-torn rushes.

'I could eat you,' he said.

She replied that only lovers and cannibals talk like that.

They dawdled past the long fiord of Killary where young people on holiday sat outside the hotel, their drinks on the trestled tables. In Clifden the street was empty, people already climbing to bed, as the lights in the upper windows showed. They branched off on the long coastal road where the sparse whitewashed cottages were whiter than the foam of waves that barely suggested sea. At another darker strand they halted, but now they saw no foam at all and divined the sea only by its invisible whispering, or when a star touched a wave. Midnight was now only an hour away.

Their headlights sent rocks and rabbits into movement. The heather streamed past them like kangaroos. It was well past eleven as they poured along the lonely land by Galway Bay. Neither of them had spoken for an hour. As they drove into Salthill there was nobody abroad. Galway was dark. Only the porch light of the hotel showed that it was alive. When he turned off the engine, the only sound at first was the crinkle of contracting metal as the engine began to cool. Then to their right they heard the lisping bay. The panel button lit the dashboard clock.

'A quarter to,' he said, leaning back. She neither spoke nor stirred. 'Jenny!' he said sharply.

She turned her head slowly and by the dashboard light he saw her white smile.

'Yes, darling?'

'Worn out?' he asked, and patted her knee.

She vibrated her whole body so that the seat shook, and stretched her arms about her head, and lowering them let her head fall on his shoulder, and sighed happily, and said:

'What I want is a good long drink of anything on earth except tea.'

*

These homing twelve-o'clockers from Lough Derg are well known in every hotel all over the west of Ireland. Revelry is the reward of penance. The porter welcomed them as if they were heroes returned from a war. As he led them to their rooms he praised them, he sympathized with them, he patted them up and he patted them down, he assured them that the ritual grill was at that moment sizzling over the fire, he proffered them hot baths, and he told them where to discover the bar. 'Ye will discover it ...' was his phrase. The wording was exact, for the bar's gaiety was muffled by dim lighting, drawn blinds, locked doors. In the overheated room he took off his jacket and unloosed his tie. They had to win a corner of the counter, and his order was for two highballs with ice in them. Within two minutes they were at home with the crowd. The island might never have existed if the barmaid, who knew where they had come from, had not laughed: 'I suppose ye'll ate like lions?'

After supper they relished the bar once more, sipping slowly now, so refreshed that they could have started on the road again without distaste or regret. As they sipped they gradually became aware of a soft strumming and drumming near at hand, and were told that there was a dance on in the hotel next door. He raised his eyebrows to her. She laughed and nodded.

They gave it up at three o'clock and walked out into the warm-cool of the early summer morning. Gently tipsy, gently tired, they walked to the little promenade. They leaned on the railing and he put his arm about her waist, and she put hers around his, and they gazed at the moon silently raking its path across the sea towards Aran. They had come, she knew, to the decisive moment. He said:

'They have a fine night for it tonight on the island.'

'A better night than we had,' she said tremulously.

After another spell of wave fall and silence he said:

'Do you know what I'm thinking, Jenny? I'm thinking that I wouldn't mind going back there again next year. Maybe I might do it properly the next time?'

'The next time?' she whispered, and all her body began to dissolve and, closing her eyes, she leaned against him. He, too, closed his eyes, and all his body became as rigid as a steel girder that flutters in a storm. Slowly they opened their love-drunk eyes, and stood looking long over the brightness and blackness of the sea. Then, gently, ever so gently, with a gentleness that terrified her, he said:

'Shall we go in, my sweet?'

She did not stir. She did not speak. Slowly turning to him she lifted her eyes to him pleadingly.

'No, Bobby, please, not yet.'

'Not yet?'

'Not tonight!'

He looked down at her, and drew his arms about her. They kissed passionately. She knew what that kiss implied. Their mouths parted. Hand in hand they walked slowly back to the hotel, to their separate rooms.

The Luceys

FRANK O'CONNOR

It's extraordinary, the bitterness there can be in a town like ours between two people of the same family. More particularly between two people of the same family. I suppose living more or less in public as we do we are either killed or cured by it, and the same communal sense that will make a man be battered into a reconciliation he doesn't feel gives added importance to whatever quarrel he thinks must not be composed. God knows, most of the time you'd be more sorry for a man like that than anything else.

The Luceys were like that. There were two brothers, Tom and Ben, and there must have been a time when the likeness between them was greater than the difference, but that was long before most of us knew them. Tom was the elder; he came in for the drapery shop. Ben had to have a job made for him on the County Council. This was the first difference and it grew and grew. Both were men of intelligence and education but Tom took it more seriously. As Ben said with a grin, he could damn well afford to with the business behind him.

It was an old-fashioned shop which prided itself on only stocking the best, and though the prices were high and Tom in his irascible opinionated way refused to abate them — he said haggling was degrading! — a lot of farmers' wives would still go nowhere else. Ben listened to his brother's high notions with his eyes twinkling, rather as he read the books which came his way, with profound respect and the feeling that this would all be grand for some other place, but was entirely inapplicable to the affairs of the County Council. God alone would ever be able to disentangle these, and meanwhile the only course open to a prudent man was to keep his mind to himself. If Tom didn't like the way the County Council was run, neither did Ben, but that was the way things were, and it rather amused him to rub it in to his virtuous brother.

Tom and Ben were both married. Tom's boy, Peter, was the great friend of his cousin, Charlie – called 'Charliss' by his Uncle Tom. They were nice boys; Peter a fat, heavy, handsome lad who blushed whenever a stranger spoke to him, and Charles with a broad face that never blushed at anything. The two families were always friendly; the mothers liked to get together over a glass of port wine and discuss the fundamental things that made the Lucey brothers not two inexplicable characters but two aspects of one inexplicable family character; the brothers enjoyed their regular chats about the way the world was going, for intelligent men are rare and each appreciated the other's shrewdness.

Only young Charlie was occasionally mystified by his Uncle Tom; he hated calling for Peter unless he was sure his uncle was out, for otherwise he might be sent into the front room to talk to him. The front room alone was enough to upset any high-spirited lad, with its thick carpet, mahogany sideboard, ornamental clock, and gilt mirror with cupids. The red curtains alone would depress you, and as well as these there was a glass-fronted mahogany bookcase the length of one wall, with books in sets, too big for anyone only a priest to read: *The History of Ireland*, *The History of the Popes*, *The Roman Empire*, *The Life of Johnson*, and *The Cabinet of Literature*. It gave Charlie the same sort of shivers as the priest's front room. His uncle suited it, a small, frail man, dressed in clerical black with a long pinched yellow face, tight lips, a narrow skull going bald up the brow, and a pair of tin specs.

All conversations with his uncle tended to stick in Charlie's mind for the simple but alarming reason that he never understood what the hell they were about, but one conversation in particular haunted him for years as showing the dangerous state of lunacy to which a man could be reduced by reading old books. Charlie was no fool, far from it; but low cunning and the most genuine benevolence were mixed in him in almost equal parts, producing a blend that was not without charm but gave no room for subtlety or irony.

'Good afternoon, Charliss,' said his uncle after Charlie had tied what he called 'the ould pup' to the leg of the hallstand. 'How are you?'

'All right,' Charlie said guardedly. (He hated being called Charliss; it made him sound such a sissy.)

'Take a seat, Charliss,' said his uncle benevolently. 'Peter will be down in a minute.'

'I won't,' said Charlie. 'I'd be afraid of the ould pup.'

'The expression, Charliss,' said his uncle in that rasping little voice of his, 'sounds like a contradiction in terms, but, not being familiar with dogs, I presume 'tis correct.'

'Ah, 'tis,' said Charlie, just to put the old man's mind at rest.

'And how is your father, Charliss?'

'His ould belly is bad again,' said Charlie. 'He'd be all right only the ould belly plays hell with him.'

'I'm sorry to hear it,' his uncle said gravely. 'And tell me, Charliss,' he added, cocking his head on one side like a bird, 'what is he saying about me now?'

This was one of the dirtiest of his Uncle Tom's tricks, assuming that Charlie's father was saying things about him, which to give Ben his due, he usually was. But on the other hand, he was admitted to be one of the smartest men in town, so he was entitled to do so, while everyone without exception appeared to agree that his uncle had a slate loose. Charlie looked at him cautiously, low cunning struggling with benevolence in him, for his uncle though queer was open-handed, and you wouldn't want to offend him. Benevolence won.

'He's saying if you don't mind yourself you'll end up in the poorhouse,' he said with some notion that if only his uncle knew the things people said about him he might mend his ways.

'Your father is right as always, Charliss,' said his uncle, rising and standing on the hearth with his hands behind his back and his little legs well apart. 'Your father is perfectly right. There are two main classes of people, Charliss — those who gravitate towards the poorhouse and those who gravitate towards the gaol ... Do you know what "gravitate" means, Charliss?'

'I do not,' said Charlie without undue depression. It struck him as being an unlikely sort of word.

' "Gravitate", Charliss, means "tend" or "incline". Don't tell me you don't know what they mean!'

'I don't,' said Charlie.

'Well, do you know what this is?' his uncle asked smilingly as he held up a coin.

'I do,' said Charlie, humouring him as he saw that the conversation was at last getting somewhere. 'A tanner.'

'I am not familiar with the expression, Charliss,' his uncle said tartly and Charlie knew, whatever he'd said out of the way, his uncle was so irritated that he was liable to put the tanner back. 'We'll call it sixpence. Your eyes, I notice, gravitate towards the sixpence' (Charlie was so shocked that his eyes instantly gravitated towards his uncle) 'and in the same way, people gravitate, or turn naturally, towards the gaol or poorhouse. Only a small number of either group reach their destination, though – which might be just as well for myself and your father,' he added in a low impressive voice, swaying forward and tightening his lips. 'Do you understand a word I'm saying, Charliss?' he added with a charming smile.

'I do not,' said Charlie.

'Good man! Good man!' his uncle said approvingly. 'I admire an honest and manly spirit in anybody. Don't forget your sixpence, Charliss.'

And as he went off with Peter, Charlie scowled and muttered savagely under his breath: 'Mod! Mod! Mod! The bleddy mon is mod!'

When the boys grew up, Peter trained for a solicitor while Charlie, one of a large family, followed his father into the County Council. He grew up a very handsome fellow with a square, solemn, dark-skinned face, a thick red lower lip, and a mass of curly black hair. He was reputed to be a great man with greyhounds and girls and about as dependable with one as with the others. His enemies called him 'a crooked bloody bastard' and his father, a shrewd man, noted with alarm that Charlie thought him simple-minded.

The two boys continued the best of friends, though Peter, with an office in Asragh, moved in circles where Charlie felt himself lost; professional men whose status was calculated on their furniture and food and wine. Charlie thought that sort of entertainment a great pity. A man could have all the fun he wanted out of life without wasting his time on expensive and unsatisfactory meals and carrying on polite conversation while you dodged between bloody little tables that were always falling over, but Charlie, who was a modest lad, admired the way Peter never knocked anything over and never said: 'Chrisht!' Wine, coffee-cups, and talk about old books came as easy to him as talk about a dog or a horse.

Charlie was thunderstruck when the news came to him that Peter was in trouble. He heard it first from Mackesy the detective, whom he hailed outside the courthouse. (Charlie was like his father in that; he couldn't let a man go by without a greeting.)

'Hullo, Matt,' he shouted gaily from the courthouse steps. 'Is it myself or my father you're after?'

'I'll let ye off for today,' said Mackesy, making a garden seat of the crossbar of his bicycle. Then he lowered his voice so that it didn't travel farther than Charlie. 'I wouldn't mind having a word with a relative of yours, though.'

'A what, Matt?' Charlie asked, skipping down the steps on the scent of news. (He was like his father in that, too.) 'You don't mean one of the Luceys is after forgetting himself?'

'Then you didn't hear about Peter?'

'Peter! Peter in trouble! You're not serious, Matt?'

'There's a lot of his clients would be glad if I wasn't, Cha,' Mackesy said grimly. 'I thought you'd know about it as ye were such pals.'

'But we are, man, we are,' Charlie insisted. 'Sure, wasn't I at the dogs with him – when was it? – last Thursday? I never noticed a bloody thing, though, now you mention it, he was lashing pound notes on that Cloonbullogue dog. I told him the Dalys could never train a dog.'

Charlie left Mackesy, his mind in a whirl. He tore through the cashier's office. His father was sitting at his desk, signing paying-orders. He was wearing a grey tweed cap, a grey tweed suit, and a brown cardigan. He was a stocky, powerfully built man with a great expanse of chest, a plump, dark, hairy face, long quizzical eyes that tended to close in slits; hair in his nose, hair in his ears; hair on his high cheekbones that made them like small cabbage-patches.

He made no comment on Charlie's news, but stroked his chin and looked worried. Then Charlie shot out to see his uncle. Quill, the assistant, was serving in the shop and Charlie stumped in behind the counter to the fitting-room. His uncle had been looking out the back, all crumpled up. When Charlie came in he pulled himself erect with fictitious jauntiness. With his old black coat and wrinkled yellow face he had begun to look like an old rabbi.

'What's this I hear about Peter?' began Charlie, who was never one to be ceremonious.

'Bad news travels fast, Charlie,' said his uncle in his dry little voice, clamping his lips so tightly that the wrinkles ran up his cheeks from the corners of his mouth. He was so upset that he forgot even to say 'Charliss'.

'Have you any notion how much it is?' asked Charlie.

'I have not, Charlie,' Tom said bitterly. 'I need hardly say my son did not take me into his confidence about the extent of his robberies.'

'And what are you going to do?'

'What can I do?' The lines of pain belied the harsh little staccato that broke up every sentence into disjointed phrases as if it were a political speech. 'You saw yourself, Charliss, the way I reared that boy. You saw the education I gave him. I gave him the thing I was denied myself, Charliss. I gave him an honourable profession. And now for the first time in my life I am ashamed to show my face in my own shop. What can I do?'

'Ah, now, ah, now, Uncle Tom, we know all that,' Charlie said truculently, 'but that's not going to get us anywhere. What can we do now?'

'Is it true that Peter took money that was entrusted to him?' Tom asked oratorically.

'To be sure he did,' replied Charlie without the thrill of horror which his uncle seemed to expect. 'I do it myself every month, only I put it back.'

'And is it true he ran away from his punishment instead of standing his ground like a man?' asked Tom, paying no attention to him.

'What the hell else would he do?' asked Charlie, who entirely failed to appreciate the spiritual beauty of atonement. 'Begod, if I had two years' hard labour facing me, you wouldn't see my heels for dust.'

'I dare say you think I'm old-fashioned, Charliss,' said his uncle, 'but that's not the way I was reared, nor the way my son was reared.'

'And that's where the ferryboat left ye,' snorted Charlie. 'Now that sort of thing may be all very well, Uncle Tom, but 'tis no use taking it to the fair. Peter made some mistake, the way we all make mistakes, but instead of coming to me or some other friend, he lost his nerve and started gambling. Chrisht, didn't I see it happen to better men? You don't know how much it is?'

'No, Charliss, I don't.'

'Do you know where he is, even?'

'His mother knows.'

'I'll talk to my old fellow. We might be able to do something. If the bloody fool might have told me on Thursday instead of backing that Cloonbullogue dog!'

Charlie returned to the office to find his father sitting at his desk with his hands joined and his pipe in his mouth, staring nervously at the door.

'Well?'

'We'll go over to Asragh and talk to Toolan of the Guards ourselves,' said Charlie. 'I want to find out how much he let himself in for. We might even get a look at the books.'

'Can't his father do it?' Ben asked gloomily.

'Do you think he'd understand them?'

'Well, he was always fond of literature,' Ben said shortly.

'God help him,' said Charlie. 'He has enough of it now.'

' 'Tis all his own conceit,' Ben said angrily, striding up and down the office with his hands in his trouser pockets. 'He was always good at criticizing other people. Even when you got in here it was all influence. Of course, he'd never use influence. Now he wants us to use it.'

'That's all very well,' Charlie said reasonably, 'but this is no time for raking up old scores.'

'Who's raking up old scores?' his father shouted angrily.

'That's right,' Charlie said approvingly. 'Would you like me to open the door so that you can be heard all over the office?'

'No one is going to hear me at all,' his father said in a more reasonable tone – Charlie had a way of puncturing him. 'And I'm not raking up any old scores. I'm only saying now what I always said. The boy was ruined.'

'He'll be ruined with a vengeance unless we do something quick,' said Charlie. 'Are you coming to Asragh with me?'

'I am not.'

'Why?'

'Because I don't want to be mixed up in it at all. That's why. I never liked anything to do with money. I saw too much of it. I'm only speaking for your good. A man done out of his money is a mad dog. You won't get any thanks for it, and anything that goes wrong, you'll get the blame.'

Nothing Charlie could say would move his father, and Charlie was shrewd enough to know that everything his father said was right. Tom wasn't to be trusted in the delicate negotiations that would be needed to get Peter out of the hole; the word here, the threat there; all the complicated machinery of family pressure. And alone he knew he was powerless. Despondently he went and told his uncle and Tom received the news with resignation, almost without understanding.

But a week later Ben came back to the office deeply disturbed. He closed the door carefully behind him and leaned across the desk to Charlie, his face drawn. For a moment he couldn't speak.

'What ails you?' Charlie asked with no great warmth.

'Your uncle passed me just now in the Main Street,' whispered his father.

Charlie wasn't greatly put out. All of his life he had been made a party to the little jabs and asides of father and uncle, and he did not realize what it meant to a man like his father, friendly and popular, this public rebuke.

'That so?' he asked without surprise. 'What did you do to him?'

'I thought you might know that,' his father said, looking at him with a troubled air from under the peak of his cap.

'Unless 'twas something you said about Peter?' suggested Charlie.

'It might, it might,' his father agreed doubtfully. 'You didn't – ah – repeat anything I said to you?'

'What a bloody fool you think I am!' Charlie said indignantly. 'And indeed I thought you had more sense. What did you say?'

'Oh, nothing. Nothing only what I said to you,' replied his father and went to the window to look out. He leaned on the sill and then tapped nervously on the frame. He was haunted by all the casual remarks he had made or might have made over a drink with an acquaintance – remarks that were no different from those he and Tom had been passing about one another all their lives. 'I shouldn't have said anything at all, of course, but I had no notion 'twould go back.'

'I'm surprised at my uncle,' said Charlie. 'Usually he cares little enough what anyone says of him.'

But even Charlie, who had moments when he almost understood his peppery little uncle, had no notion of the hopes he had raised and which his more calculating father had dashed. Tom Lucey's mind was in a rut, a rut of complacency, for the idealist too has his complacency and can be aware of it. There are moments when he would be glad to walk through any mud, but he no longer knows the way; he needs to be led; he cannot degrade himself even when he is most ready to do so. Tom was ready to beg favours from a thief. Peter had joined the Air Force under an assumed name, and this was the bitterest blow of all to him, the extinction of the name. He was something of an amateur genealogist, and had managed to convince himself, God knows how, that his family was somehow related to the Gloucestershire Lucỹs. This was already a sort of death.

The other death didn't take long in coming. Charlie, in the way he had, got wind of it first, and, having sent his father to break the news to Min, he went off himself to tell his uncle. It was a fine spring morning. The shop was empty but for his uncle, standing with his back to the counter studying the shelves.

'Good morning, Charliss,' he crackled over his shoulder. 'What's the best news?'

'Bad, I'm afraid, Uncle Tom,' Charlie replied, leaning across the counter to him.

'Something about Peter, I dare say?' his uncle asked casually, but Charlie noticed how, caught unawares, he had failed to say 'my son', as he had taken to doing.

'Just so.'

'Dead, I suppose?'

'Dead, Uncle Tom.'

'I was expecting something of the sort,' said his uncle. 'May the Almighty God have mercy on his soul! ... Con!' he called at the back of the shop while he changed his coat. 'You'd better close up the shop. You'll find the crepe on the top shelf and the mourning-cards in my desk.'

'Who is it, Mr Lucey?' asked Con Quill. ' 'Tisn't Peter?'

' 'Tis, Con, 'tis, I'm sorry to say,' and Tom came out briskly with his umbrella over his arm. As they went down the street two people stopped them: the news was already round.

Charlie, who had to see about the arrangements for the funeral, left his uncle outside the house and so had no chance of averting the scene that took place inside. Not that he would have had much chance of doing so. His father had found Min in a state of collapse. Ben was the last man in the world to look after a woman, but he did manage to get her a pillow, put her legs on a chair and cover her with a rug, which was more than Charlie would have given him credit for. Min smelt of brandy. Then Ben strode up and down the

darkened room with his hands in his pockets and his cap over
his eyes, talking about the horrors of airplane travel. He knew
he was no fit company for a woman of sensibility like Min, and
he almost welcomed Tom's arrival.

'That's terrible news, Tom,' he said.

'Oh, God help us!' cried Min. 'They said he disgraced us,
but he didn't disgrace us long.'

'I'd sooner 'twas one of my own, Tom,' Ben said excitedly.
'As God is listening to me I would. I'd still have a couple left,
but he was all ye had.'

He held out his hand to Tom. Tom looked at it, then at him,
and then deliberately put his own hands behind his back.

'Aren't you going to shake hands with me, Tom?' Ben asked
appealingly.

'No, Ben,' Tom said grimly. 'I am not.'

'Oh, Tom Lucey!' moaned Min with her crucified smile.
'Over your son's dead body!'

Ben looked at his brother in chagrin and dropped his hand.
For a moment it looked as though he might strike him. He
was a volatile, hot-tempered man.

'That wasn't what I expected from you, Tom,' he said, making
a mighty effort to control himself.

'Ben,' said his brother, squaring his frail little shoulders,
'you disrespected my son while he was alive. Now that he's
dead I'd thank you to leave him alone.'

'I disrespected him?' Ben exclaimed indignantly. 'I did nothing of the sort. I said things I shouldn't have said. I was upset.
You know the sort I am. You were upset yourself and I dare say
you said things you regret.'

' 'Tisn't alike, Ben,' Tom said in a rasping, opinionated tone.
'I said them because I loved the boy. You said them because you
hated him.'

'I hated him?' Ben repeated incredulously. 'Peter? Are you
out of your mind?'

'You said he changed his name because it wasn't grand enough
for him,' Tom said, clutching the lapels of his coat and stepping from one foot to another. 'Why did you say such a mean,
mocking, cowardly thing about the boy when he was in trouble?'

'All right, all right,' snapped Ben. 'I admit I was wrong to say it. There were a lot of things you said about my family, but I'm not throwing them back at you.'

'You said you wouldn't cross the road to help him,' said Tom. Again he primmed up the corners of his mouth and lowered his head. 'And why, Ben? I'll tell you why. Because you were jealous of him.'

'I was jealous of him?' Ben repeated. It seemed to him that he was talking to a different man, discussing a different life, as though the whole of his nature was being turned inside out.

'You were jealous of him, Ben. You were jealous because he had the upbringing and education your own sons lacked. And I'm not saying that to disparage your sons. Far from it. But you begrudged my son his advantages.'

'Never!' shouted Ben in a fury.

'And I was harsh with him,' Tom said, taking another nervous step foward while his neat waspish little voice grew harder, 'I was harsh with him and you were jealous of him, and when his hour of trouble came he had no one to turn to. Now, Ben, the least you can do is to spare us your commiserations.'

'Oh, wisha, don't mind him, Ben,' moaned Min. 'Sure, everyone knows you never begrudged my poor child anything. The man isn't in his right mind.'

'I know that, Min,' Ben said, trying hard to keep his temper. 'I know he's upset. Only for that he'd never say what he did say – or believe it.'

'We'll see, Ben, we'll see,' said Tom grimly.

That was how the row between the Luceys began, and it continued like that for years. Charlie married and had children of his own. He always remained friendly with his uncle and visited him regularly; sat in the stuffy front room with him and listened with frowning gravity to Tom's views, and no more than in his childhood understood what the old man was talking about. All he gathered was that none of the political parties had any principle and the country was in a bad way due to the inroads of the uneducated and ill-bred. Tom looked more and more like a rabbi. As is the way of men of character in provincial towns, he tended more and more to become a collection of mannerisms, a caricature of himself. His academic jokes on his simple customers became more elaborate; so elaborate, in fact, that in time he gave up trying to explain them and was content to be set down as merely queer. In a way it made things easier for Ben; he was able to treat the breach with Tom as another example of his brother's cantankerousness, and spoke of it with amusement and good nature.

Then he fell ill. Charlie's cares were redoubled. Ben was the world's worst patient. He was dying and didn't know it, wouldn't go to hospital, and broke the heart of his wife and daughter. He was awake at six, knocking peremptorily for his cup of tea; then waited impatiently for the paper and the post. 'What the hell is keeping Mick Duggan? That fellow spends half his time gossiping along the road. Half past nine and no post!' After that the day was a blank to him until evening when a couple of County Council chaps dropped in to keep him company and tell him what was afoot in the courthouse. There was nothing in the long low room, plastered with blue and green flowered wallpaper, but a bedside table, a press, and three or four holy pictures, and Ben's mind was not on these but on the world outside – feet passing and repassing on errands which he would never be told about. It broke his heart. He couldn't believe he was as bad as people tried to make out; sometimes it was the doctor he blamed, sometimes the chemist who wasn't careful enough of the bottles and pills he made up – Ben could remember some shocking cases. He lay in bed doing involved calculations about his pension.

Charlie came every evening to sit with him. Though his father didn't say much about Tom, Charlie knew the row was always there in the back of his mind. It left Ben bewildered, a man without bitterness. And Charlie knew he came in for some of the blame. It was the illness all over again: someone must be slipping up somewhere; the right word hadn't been dropped in the right quarter or a wrong one had been dropped instead. Charlie, being so thick with Tom, must somehow be to blame. Ben did not understand the inevitable. One night it came out.

'You weren't at your uncle's?' Ben asked.

'I was,' Charlie said with a nod. 'I dropped in on the way up.'

'He wasn't asking about me?' Ben asked, looking at him out of the corner of his eye.

'Oh, he was,' Charlie said with a shocked air. 'Give the man his due, he always does that. That's one reason I try to drop in every day. He likes to know.'

But he knew this was not the question his father wanted answered. That question was: 'Did you say the right words? Did you make me out the feeble figure you should have made me out, or did you say the wrong thing, letting him know I was better?' These things had to be managed. In Charlie's place Ben would have managed it splendidly.

'He didn't say anything about dropping up?' Ben asked with affected lightness.

'No,' Charlie said with assumed thoughtfulness. 'I don't remember.'

'There's blackness for you!' his father said with sudden bitterness. It came as a shock to Charlie; for it was the first time he had heard his father speak like that, from the heart, and he knew the end must be near.

'God knows,' Charlie said, tapping one heel nervously, 'he's a queer man. A queer bloody man!'

'Tell me, Charlie,' his father insisted, 'wouldn't you say it to him? 'Tisn't right and you know 'tisn't right.'

' 'Tisn't,' said Charlie, tearing at his hair, 'but to tell you the God's truth I'd sooner not talk to him.'

'Yes,' his father added in disappointment. 'I see it mightn't do for you.'

Charlie realized that his father was thinking of the shop, which would now come to him. He got up and stood against the fireplace, a fat, handsome, moody man.

'That has nothing to do with it,' he said. 'If he gave me cause I'd throw his bloody old shop in his face in the morning. I don't want anything from him. 'Tis just that I don't seem to be able to talk to him. I'll send Paddy down tonight and let him ask him.'

'Do, do,' his father said with a knowing nod. 'That's the

very thing you'll do. And tell Julie to bring me up a drop of whiskey and a couple of glasses. You'll have a drop yourself?'

'I won't.'

'You will, you will. Julie will bring it up.'

Charlie went to his brother's house and asked him to call on Tom and tell him how near the end was Paddy was a gentle, good-natured boy with something of Charlie's benevolence and none of his guile.

'I will to be sure,' he said. 'But why don't you tell him? Sure, he thinks the world of you.'

'I'll tell you why, Paddy,' Charlie whispered with his hand on his brother's sleeve. 'Because if he refused me I might do him some injury.'

'But you don't think he will?' Paddy asked in bewilderment.

'I don't think at all, Paddy,' Charlie said broodingly. 'I know.'

He knew all right. When he called on his way home the next afternoon his mother and sister were waiting for him, hysterical with excitement. Paddy had met with a cold refusal. Their hysteria was infectious. He understood now why he had caught people glancing at him curiously in the street. It was being argued out in every pub, what Charlie Lucey ought to do. People couldn't mind their own bloody business. He rapped out an oath at the two women and took the stairs three at a time. His father was lying with his back to the window. The whiskey was still there as Charlie had seen it the previous evening. It tore at his heart more than the sight of his father's despair.

'You're not feeling too good?' he said gruffly.

'I'm not, I'm not,' Ben said, lifting the sheet from his face. 'Paddy didn't bring a reply to that message?' he added questioningly.

'Do you tell me so?' Charlie replied, trying to sound shocked.

'Paddy was always a bad man to send on a message,' his father said despondently, turning himself painfully in the bed, but still not looking at Charlie. 'Of course, he hasn't the sense. Tell me, Charlie,' he added in a feeble voice, 'weren't you there when I was talking about Peter?'

'About Peter?' Charlie exclaimed in surprise.

'You were, you were,' his father insisted, looking at the window. 'Sure, 'twas from you I heard it. You wanted to go to Asragh to look at the books, and I told you if anything went wrong you'd get the blame. Isn't that all I said?'

Charlie had to readjust his mind before he realized that his father had been going over it all again in the long hours of loneliness and pain, trying to see where he had gone wrong. It seemed to make him even more remote. Charlie didn't remember what his father had said; he doubted if his uncle remembered.

'I might have passed some joke about it,' his father said, 'but sure I was always joking him and he was always joking me. What the hell more was there in it?'

'Oh, a chance remark!' agreed Charlie.

'Now, the way I look at that,' his father said, seeking his eyes for the first time, 'someone was out to make mischief. This town is full of people like that. If you went and told him, he'd believe you.'

'I will, I will,' Charlie said, sick with disgust. 'I'll see him myself today.'

He left the house, cursing his uncle for a brutal egotist. He felt the growing hysteria of the town concentrating on himself and knew that at last it had got inside him. His sisters and brothers, the people in the little shops along the street, expected him to bring his uncle to book, and failing that, to have done with him. This was the moment when people had to take their side once and for all. And he knew he was only too capable of taking sides.

Min opened the door to him, her red-rimmed eyes dirty with tears and the smell of brandy on her breath. She was near hysterics, too.

'What way is he, Charlie?' she wailed.

'Bad enough, Aunt Min,' he said as he wiped his boots and went past her. 'He won't last the night.'

At the sound of his voice his uncle had opened the sitting-room door and now he came out and drew Charlie in by the hand. Min followed. His uncle didn't release his hand, and betrayed his nervousness only by the way his frail fingers played over Charlie's hand, like a woman's.

'I'm sorry to hear it, Charliss,' he said.

'Sure, of course you are, Uncle Tom,' said Charlie, and at the first words the feeling of hysteria within him dissolved and left only a feeling of immense understanding and pity. 'You know what brought me?'

His uncle dropped his hand.

'I do, Charliss,' he said and drew himself erect. They were neither of them men to beat about the bush.

'You'll come and see the last of him,' Charlie said, not even making the question.

'Charliss,' Tom said with that queer tightening at the corners of his mouth, 'I was never one to hedge or procrastinate. I will not come.'

He almost hissed the final words. Min broke into a loud wail.

'Talk to him, Charlie, do! I'm sick and tired of it. We can never show our faces in the town again.'

'And I need hardly say, Charliss,' his uncle continued with an air of triumph that was almost evil, 'that that doesn't trouble me.'

'I know,' Charlie said earnestly, still keeping his eyes on the withered old face with the narrow-winged, almost transparent nose. 'And you know that I never interfered between ye. Whatever disagreements ye had, I never took my father's side against you. And 'twasn't for what I might get out of you.'

In his excitement his uncle grinned, a grin that wasn't natural, and that combined in a strange way affection and arrogance, the arrogance of the idealist who doesn't realize how easily he can be fooled.

'I never thought it, boy,' he said, raising his voice. 'Not for an instant. Nor 'twasn't in you.'

'And you know too you did this once before and you regretted it.'

'Bitterly! Bitterly!'

'And you're going to make the same mistake with your brother that you made with your son?'

'I'm not forgetting that either, Charliss,' said Tom. 'It wasn't today nor yesterday I thought of it.'

'And it isn't as if you didn't care for him,' Charlie went on remorselessly. 'It isn't as if you had no heart for him. You know he's lying up there waiting for you. He sent for you last night and you never came. He had the bottle of whiskey and the two glasses by the bed. All he wants is for you to say you forgive him ... Jesus Christ, man,' he shouted with all the violence in him roused, 'never mind what you're doing to him. Do you know what you're doing to yourself?'

'I know, Charliss,' his uncle said in a cold, excited voice. 'I know that too. And 'tisn't as you say that I have no heart for him. God knows it isn't that I don't forgive him. I forgave him long years ago for what he said about – one that was very dear to me. But I swore that day, Charliss, that never the longest day I lived would I take your father's hand in friendship, and if God was to strike me dead at this very moment for my presumption I'd say the same. You know me, Charliss,' he added, gripping the lapels of his coat. 'I never broke my word yet to God or man. I won't do it now.'

'Oh, how can you say it?' cried Min. 'Even the wild beasts have more nature.'

'Some other time I'll ask you to forgive me,' added Tom, ignoring her.

'You need never do that, Uncle Tom,' Charlie said with great simplicity and humbleness. ' 'Tis yourself you'll have to forgive.'

At the door he stopped. He had a feeling that if he turned he would see Peter standing behind him. He knew his uncle's barren pride was all he could now offer to the shadow of his son, and that it was his dead cousin who stood between them. For a moment he felt like turning and appealing to Peter. But he was never much given to the supernatural. The real world was trouble enough for him, and he went slowly homeward, praying that he might see the blinds drawn before him.

The Cat Jumps

ELIZABETH BOWEN

AFTER the Bentley murder, Rose Hill stood empty two years. Lawns mounted to meadows; white paint peeled from the balconies; the sun, looking more constantly, less fearfully, in than sightseers' eyes through the naked windows, bleached the floral wallpapers. The week after the execution Harold Bentley's legatees had placed the house on the books of the principal agents, London and local. But though sunny, up to date, and convenient, though so delightfully situate over the Thames valley (above flood level), within easy reach of a golf-course, Rose Hill, while frequently viewed, remained unpurchased. Dreadful associations apart, the privacy of the place had been violated; with its terraced garden, lily-pond and pergola cheerfully rose-encrusted, the public had been made too familiar. On the domestic scene, too many eyes had burnt the impress of their horror. Moreover, that pearly bathroom, that bedroom with wide outlook over a loop of the Thames ... 'The Rose Hill Horror': headlines flashed up at the very sound of the name. 'Oh, *no*, dear!' many wives had exclaimed, drawing their husbands hurriedly from the gate. 'Come away!' they had urged, crumpling the agent's order to view as though the house were advancing upon them. And husbands came away – with a backward glance at the garage. Funny to think a chap who was hanged had kept his car there.

The Harold Wrights, however, were not deterred. They had light, bright, shadowless, thoroughly disinfected minds. They believed that they disbelieved in most things but were unprejudiced; they enjoyed frank discussions. They dreaded nothing but inhibitions: they had no inhibitions. They were pious agnostics, earnest for social reform; they explained everything to their children, and were annoyed to find their children could not sleep at nights because they thought there was a complex under the bed. They knew all crime to be pathological, and read their murders only in scientific books. They had vita glass put into all their windows. No family, in fact, could have been more unlike the mistaken Harold Bentleys.

Rose Hill, from the first glance, suited the Wrights admirably. They were in search of a cheerful weekend house with a nice atmosphere, where their friends could join them for frank discussions, and their own and their friends' children 'run wild' during the summer months. Harold Wright, who had a good head, got the agent to knock six hundred off the quoted price of the house. 'That unfortunate affair,' he murmured. Jocelyn commended his inspiration. Otherwise, they did not give the Bentleys another thought.

The Wrights had the floral wallpapers all stripped off and the walls cream-washed; they removed some disagreeably thick pink shades from the electricity and had the paint renewed inside and out. (The front of the house was bracketed over with balconies, like an over-mantel.) Their bedroom mantelpiece, stained by the late Mrs Bentley's cosmetics, had to be scrubbed with chemicals. Also, they had removed from the rock-garden Mrs Bentley's little dog's memorial tablet, with a quotation on it from *Indian Love Lyrics*. Jocelyn Wright, looking into the unfortunate bath – *the* bath, so square and opulent, with its surround of nacreous tiles – said, laughing lightly, she supposed anyone *else* would have had that bath changed. 'Not that that would be possible,' she added; 'the bath's built in ... I've always wanted a built-in bath.'

Harold and Jocelyn turned from the bath to look down at the cheerful river shimmering under a spring haze. All the way down the slope cherry-trees were in blossom. Life should be simplified for the Wrights; they were fortunate in their mentality.

After an experimental weekend, without guests or children, only one thing troubled them: a resolute stuffiness, upstairs and down – due, presumably, to the house's having been so long shut up – a smell of unsavoury habitation, of rich cigarette-smoke stale in the folds of unaired curtains, of scent spilled on unbrushed carpets; an alcoholic smell – persistent in their perhaps too sensitive nostrils after days of airing, doors and windows open, in rooms drenched thoroughly with sun and wind. They told each other it came from the parquet; they didn't like it, somehow. They had the parquet taken up – at great expense – and put down plain oak floors.

In their practical way, the Wrights now set out to expel, live out, live down, almost (had the word had place in their vocabulary) to 'lay' the Bentleys. Deferred by trouble over the parquet, their occupation of Rose Hill (which should have dated from mid April) did not begin till the end of May. Throughout a week, Jocelyn had motored from town daily, so that the final installation of themselves and the children was able to coincide with their first weekend party – they asked down five of their friends to warm the house.

That first Friday, everything was auspicious; afternoon sky blue as the garden irises; later, a full moon pendent over the river; a night so warm that, after midnight, their enlightened friends, in pyjamas, could run on the blanched lawns in a state of high though rational excitement. Jane, Jacob, and Janet, their admirably spaced-out children, kept awake by the moonlight, hailed their elders out of the nursery skylight. Jocelyn waved to them; they never had been repressed.

The girl Muriel Barker was found looking up the terraces at the house a shade doubtfully. 'You know,' she said, 'I do rather wonder they don't feel ... *sometimes* ... you know what I mean?'

'No,' replied her companion, a young scientist.

Muriel sighed. 'No one would mind if it had been just a short sharp shooting. But it was so ... prolonged. It went on all over the house. Do you remember?' she said timidly.

'No,' replied Mr Cartaret. 'It didn't interest me.'

'Oh, nor me either!' agreed Muriel quickly, but added: 'How he must have hated her ...'

The scientist, sleepy, yawned frankly and referred her to Krafft-Ebing. But Muriel went to bed with *Alice in Wonder-*

land; she went to sleep with the lights on. She was not, as Jocelyn realized later, the sort of girl to have asked at all.

Next morning was overcast; in the afternoon it rained, suddenly and heavily – interrupting, for some, tennis, for others, a pleasant discussion, in a punt, on marriage under the Soviets. Defeated, they all rushed in. Jocelyn went round from room to room, shutting tightly the rain-lashed casements along the front of the house. These continued to rattle; the balconies creaked. An early dusk set in; an oppressive, almost visible moisture, up from the darkening river, pressed on the panes like a presence and slid through the house. The party gathered in the library, round an expansive but thinly burning fire. Harold circulated photographs of modern architecture; they discussed these tendencies. Then Mrs Monkhouse, sniffing, exclaimed: 'Who uses "Trèfle Incarnat"?'

'Now, *who* ever would –' her hostess began scornfully. Then from the hall came a howl, a scuffle, a thin shriek. They sat too still; in the dusky library Mr Cartaret laughed out loud. Harold Wright, indignantly throwing open the door, revealed Jane and Jacob rolling at the foot of the stairs, biting each other, their faces dark with uninhibited passion. Bumping alternate heads against the foot of the banisters, they shrieked in concert.

'Extraordinary,' said Harold; 'they've never done that before. They have always understood each other so well.'

'I wouldn't do that,' advised Jocelyn, raising her voice slightly; 'you'll hurt your teeth. Other teeth won't grow at once, you know.'

'You should let them find that out for themselves,' disapproved Edward Cartaret, taking up the *New Statesman*. Harold, in perplexity, shut the door on his children, who soon stunned each other to silence.

Meanwhile, Sara and Talbot Monkhouse, Muriel Barker and Theodora Smith had drawn together over the fire in a tight little knot. Their voices twanged with excitement. By that shock, just now, something seemed to have been released. Even Cartaret gave them half his attention. They were discussing *crime passionnel*.

'Of course, if that's what they really *want* to discuss ...'

thought Jocelyn. But it did seem unfortunate. Partly from an innocent desire to annoy her visitors, partly because the room felt awful – you would have thought fifty people had been there for a week – she went across and opened one of the windows, admitting a pounce of damp wind. They all turned, startled, to hear rain crash on the lead of an upstairs balcony. Muriel's voice was left in forlorn solo: 'Dragged herself ... whining "Harold" ...'

Harold Wright looked remarkably conscious. Jocelyn said brightly, 'Whatever *are* you talking about?' But, unfortunately, Harold, on almost the same breath, suggested: 'Let's leave that family alone, shall we?' Their friends all felt they might not be asked again. Though they did feel, plaintively, that they had been being natural. However, they disowned Muriel, who, getting up abruptly, said she thought she'd like to go for a walk in the rain before dinner. Nobody accompanied her.

Later, overtaking Mrs Monkhouse on the stairs, Muriel confided: absolutely, she could not stand Edward Cartaret. She could hardly bear to be in the room with him. He seemed so ... cruel. Cold-blooded? No, she meant cruel. Sara Monkhouse, going into Jocelyn's room for a chat (at her entrance Jocelyn started violently), told Jocelyn that Muriel could not stand Edward, could hardly bear to be in a room with him. 'Pity,' said Jocelyn. 'I had thought they might do for each other.' Jocelyn and Sara agreed that Muriel was unrealized: what she ought to have was a baby. But when Sara, dressing, told Talbot Monkhouse that Muriel could not stand Edward, and Talbot said Muriel was unrealized, Sara was furious. The Monkhouses, who never did quarrel, quarrelled bitterly, and were late for dinner. They would have been later if the meal itself had not been delayed by an outburst of sex-antagonism between the nice Jacksons, a couple imported from London to run the house. Mrs Jackson, putting everything in the oven, had locked herself into her room.

'Curious,' said Harold; 'the Jacksons' relations to each other always seemed so modern. They have the most intelligent discussions.'

Theodora said she had been re-reading Shakespeare – this

brought them point-blank up against *Othello*. Harold, with Titanic force, wrenched round the conversation to relativity: about this no one seemed to have anything to say but Edward Cartaret. And Muriel, who by some mischance had again been placed beside him, sat deathly, turning down her dark-rimmed eyes. In fact, on the intelligent sharp-featured faces all round the table something – perhaps simply a clearness – seemed to be lacking, as though these were wax faces for one fatal instant exposed to a furnace. Voices came out from some dark interiority; in each conversational interchange a mutual vote of no confidence was implicit. You would have said that each personality had been attacked by some kind of decomposition.

'No moon tonight,' complained Sara Monkhouse. Never mind, they would have a cosy evening; they would play paper games, Jocelyn promised.

'If you can see,' said Harold. 'Something seems to be going wrong with the light.'

Did Harold think so? They had all noticed the light seemed to be losing quality, as though a film, smoke-like, were creeping over the bulbs. The light, thinning, darkening, seemed to contract round each lamp into a blurred aura. They had noticed, but, each with a proper dread of his own subjectivity, had not spoken.

'Funny stuff,' Harold said, 'electricity.'

Mr Cartaret could not agree with him.

Though it was late, though they yawned and would not play paper games, they were reluctant to go to bed. You would have supposed a delightful evening. Jocelyn was not gratified.

The library stools, rugs, and divans were strewn with Krafft-Ebing, Freud, Forel, Weiniger, and the heterosexual volume of Havelock Ellis. (Harold had thought it right to instal his reference library; his friends hated to discuss without basis.) The volumes were pressed open with paper-knives and small pieces of modern statuary; stooping from one to another, purposeful as a bee, Edward Cartaret read extracts aloud to Harold, to Talbot Monkhouse, and to Theodora Smith, who stitched *gros point* with resolution. At the far end of the library, under a sallow drip from a group of electric candles,

Mrs Monkhouse and Miss Barker shared an ottoman, spines pressed rigid against the wall. Tensely one spoke, one listened.

'And these,' thought Jocelyn, leaning back with her eyes shut between the two groups, 'are the friends I liked to have in my life. Pellucid, sane ...'

It was remarkable how much Muriel knew. Sara, very much shocked, edged up till their thighs touched. You would have thought the Harold Bentleys had been Muriel's relatives. Surely, Sara attempted, in one's large, bright world one did not think of these things? Practically, they did not exist! Surely Muriel should not ... But Muriel looked at her strangely.

'Did you know,' she said, 'that one of Mrs Bentley's hands was found in the library?'

Sara, smiling a little awkwardly, licked her lip. 'Oh,' she said.

'But the fingers were in the dining-room. He began there.'

'Why isn't he in Broadmoor?'

'That defence failed. He didn't really subscribe to it. He said having done what he wanted was worth anything.'

'Oh!'

'Yes, he was nearly lynched ... She dragged herself upstairs. She couldn't lock any doors – naturally. One maid – her maid – got shut into the house with them: he'd sent all the others away. For a long time everything seemed so quiet: the maid crept out and saw Harold Bentley sitting half way up-stairs, finishing a cigarette. All the lights were full on. He nodded to her and dropped the cigarette through the banisters. Then she saw the ... the state of the hall. He went upstairs after Mrs Bentley, saying: "Lucinda!" He looked into room after room, whistling; then he said *"Here we are"*, and shut a door after him.

'The maid fainted. When she came to, it was still going on, upstairs ... Harold Bentley had locked all the garden doors; there were locks even on the French windows. The maid couldn't get out. Everything she touched was ... sticky. At last she broke a pane and got through. As she ran down the garden – the lights were on all over the house – she saw Harold Bentley moving about in the bathroom. She fell right over the edge of a terrace and one of the tradesmen picked her up next day.

'Doesn't it seem odd, Sara, to think of Jocelyn in that bath?'

Finishing her recital, Muriel turned on Sara an ecstatic and brooding look that made her almost beautiful. Sara fumbled with a cigarette; match after match failed her. 'Muriel, *you* ought to see a specialist.'

Muriel held out her hand for a cigarette. 'He put her heart in her hat-box. He said it belonged in there.'

'You had no right to come here. It was most unfair on Jocelyn. Most ... indelicate.'

Muriel, to whom the word was, properly, unfamiliar, eyed incredulously Sara's lips.

'How dared you come?'

'I thought I might like it. I thought I ought to fulfil myself. I'd never had any experience of these things.'

'Muriel ...'

'Besides, I wanted to meet Edward Cartaret. Several people said we were made for each other. Now, of course, I shall never marry. Look what comes of it ... I must say, Sara, I wouldn't be you or Jocelyn. Shut up all night with a man all alone – I don't know how you dare sleep. I've arranged to sleep with Theodora, and we shall barricade the door. I noticed something about Edward Cartaret the moment I arrived: a kind of insane glitter. He is utterly pathological. He's got instruments in his room, in that black bag. Yes, I looked. Did you notice the way he went on and on about cutting up that cat, and the way Talbot and Harold listened?'

Sara, looking furtively round the room, saw Mr Cartaret making passes over the head of Theodora Smith with a paper-knife. Both appeared to laugh heartily, but in silence.

'Here we are,' said Harold, showing his teeth, smiling.

He stood over Muriel with a syphon in one hand, glass in the other.

At this point Jocelyn, rising, said she, for one, intended to go to bed.

Jocelyn's bedroom curtains swelled a little over the noisy window. The room was stuffy and – insupportable, so that she did not know where to turn. The house, fingered outwardly by the wind that dragged unceasingly past the walls, was, within, a solid silence: silence heavy as flesh. Jocelyn dropped her wrap to the floor, then watched how its feathered edges crept a little. A draught came in, under her bathroom door.

Jocelyn turned away in despair and hostility from the strained, pale woman looking at her from her oblong glass. She said aloud, 'There *is* no fear'; then, within herself, heard this taken up: 'But the death fear, that one is not there to relate! If the spirit, dismembered in agony, dies before the body! If the spirit, in the whole knowledge of its dissolution, drags from chamber to chamber, drops from plane to plane of awareness (as from knife to knife down an oubliette), shedding, receiving, agony! Till, long afterwards, death, with its little pain, is established in the indifferent body.' There was no comfort: death (now at every turn and instant claiming her) was, in its every possible manifestation, violent death: ultimately, she was to be given up to terror.

Undressing, shocked by the iteration of her reflected movements, she flung a towel over the glass. With what desperate eyes of appeal, at Sara's door, she and Sara had looked at each other, clung with their looks – and parted. She could have sworn she heard Sara's bolt slide softly to. But what then, subsequently, of Talbot? And what – she eyed her own bolt, so bright (and, for the late Mrs Bentley, so ineffective) – what of Harold?

'It's atavistic!' she said aloud, in the dark-lit room, and kicking her slippers away, got into bed. She took *Erewhon* from the rack, but lay rigid, listening. As though snatched by a movement, the towel slipped from the mirror beyond her bedend. She faced the two eyes of an animal in extremity, eyes black, mindless. The clock struck two: she had been waiting an hour.

On the floor, her feathered wrap shivered again all over. She heard the other door of the bathroom very stealthily open, then shut. Harold moved in softly, heavily, knocked against the side of the bath, and stood still. He was quietly whistling.

'Why didn't I understand? He must always have hated me. It's tonight he's been waiting for ... *He wanted this house.* His look, as we went upstairs ...'

She shrieked 'Harold!'

Harold, so softly whistling, remained behind the imperturbable door, remained quite still ... 'He's *listening* for me ...' One pinpoint of hope at the tunnel-end: to get to Sara, to Theodora, to Muriel. Unmasked, incautious, with a long tearing sound of displaced air, Jocelyn leapt from the bed to the door.

But her door had been locked from the outside.

With a strange rueful smile, like an actress, Jocelyn, skirting the foot of the two beds, approached the door of the bathroom. 'At least I have still ... my feet.' For for some time the heavy body of Mrs Bentley, tenacious of life, had been dragging itself from room to room. *'Harold!'* she said to the silence, face close to the door.

The door opened on Harold, looking more dreadfully at her than she had imagined. With a quick, vague movement he roused himself from his meditation. Therein he had assumed the entire burden of Harold Bentley. Forces he did not know of assembling darkly, he had faced for untold ages the imperturbable door to his wife's room. She would be there, densely, smotheringly there. She lay like a great cat, always, over the mouth of his life.

The Harolds, superimposed on each other, stood searching the bedroom strangely. Taking a step forward, shutting the door behind them:

'Here we are,' said Harold.

Jocelyn went down heavily. Harold watched.

Harold Wright was appalled. Jocelyn had fainted: Jocelyn never had fainted before. He shook, he fanned, he applied restoratives. His perplexed thoughts fled to Sara – oh, Sara certainly. 'Hi!' he cried, 'Sara!' and successively fled from each to each of the locked doors. There was no way out.

Across the passage a door throbbed to the maniac drumming of Sara Monkhouse. She had been locked in. For Talbot, agonized with solicitude, it was equally impossible to emerge from his dressing-room. Further down the passage, Edward Cartaret, interested by this nocturnal manifestation, wrenched and rattled his door-handle in vain.

Muriel, on her silent way through the house to Theodora's

bedroom, had turned all the keys on the outside, impartially. She did not know which door might be Edward Cartaret's. Muriel was a woman who took no chances.

A Memory

MARY LAVIN

JAMES did all right for a man on his own. An old woman from the village came in for a few hours a day and gave him a hot meal before she went home. She also got ready an evening meal needing only to be heated up. As well, she put his breakfast egg in a saucepan of water beside the paraffin stove, with a box of matches beside it in case he mislaid his own. She took care of all but one of the menial jobs of living. The one she couldn't do for him was one James hated most – cleaning out ashes from the grate in his study and lighting up the new fire for the day.

James was an early riser and firmly believed in giving the best of his brain to his work. So, the minute he was dressed he went out to the kitchen and lit the stove under the coffee pot. Then he got the ash bucket and went at the grate. When the ashes were out the rest wasn't too bad. There was kindling in the hot press and the old woman left a few split logs for getting up a quick blaze. He had the room well warmed by the time he had eaten his breakfast. His main objection to doing the grate was that he got his suit covered with ashes. He knew he ought to wear tweeds now that he was living full time at the cottage, but he stuck obstinately to his dark suit and white collar, feeling as committed to this attire as to his single state. Both were part and parcel of his academic dedication. His work filled his life as it filled his day. He seldom had occasion to go up to the University. When he went up it was to see Myra, and then only on impulse if for some reason work went against him. This did happen periodically in spite of his devotion to it. Without warning a day would come when he'd wake up in a queer, un-settled mood that would send him prowling around the cottage, lighting up cigarette after cigarette and looking out of the window until he'd have to face the fact that he was not going to do a stroke. Inevitably the afternoon would see him with his hat and coat on, going down the road to catch the bus for Dublin – and an evening with Myra.

This morning he was in fine fettle though, when he dug the shovel into the mound of grey ash. But he was annoyed to see a volley of sparks go up the black chimney. The hearth would be hot, and the paper would catch fire before he'd have time to build his little pyre. There was more kindling in the kitchen press, but he'd have felt guilty using more than the allotted amount, thinking of the poor old creature wielding that heavy axe. He really ought to split those logs himself.

When he first got the cottage, he used to enjoy that kind of thing. But after he'd been made a research professor and able to live down there all year round, he came to have less and less zest for manual work. He sort of lost the knack of it. Ah well, his energies were totally expended in mental work. It would not be surprising if muscularly he got a bit soft.

James got up off his knees and brushed himself down. The fire was taking hold. The nimble flames played in and out through the dead twigs as sunlight must once have done when the sap was green. Standing watching them, James flexed his fingers. He wouldn't like to think he was no longer fit. Could his increasing aversion to physical labour be a sign of decreasing vigour? He frowned. He would not consider himself a vain man, it was simply that he'd got used to the look of himself; was accustomed to his slight, spare figure. But surely by mental activity he burned up as much fuel as any navvy or stevedore? Lunatics never had to worry about exercise either! Who ever saw a corpulent madman? He smiled. He must remember to tell that to Myra. Her laugh was always so quick and responsive although, even if a second or two later, she might seize on some inherently serious point in what had at first amused her. It was Myra who had first drawn his attention to this curious transference – this drawing off of energies – from the body to the brain. She herself had lost a lot of the skill in her fingers. When she was younger – or so she claimed – she'd been quite a good cook, and could sew, and that kind of thing, although frankly James couldn't imagine her being much good about the house. But when she gave up teaching and went into free-lance translation, her work began to make heavy demands on her, and she too, like him, lost all inclination for physical chores. Now – or so she said – she could not bake a cake to save her life. As for sewing – well here again frankly – to him the sight of a needle in her hand would be ludicrous. In fact he knew – they both knew – that when they first met, it was her lack of domesticity that had been the essence of her appeal for him. For a woman, it was quite remarkable how strong was the intellectual climate of thought in which she lived. She had concocted a sort of cocoon of thought and wrapped herself up in it. One became aware of it immediately one stepped inside her little flat. There was another thing! The way she used the word flat to designate what was really a charming little mews house. It was behind one of the Georgian squares, and it had a beautiful little garden at the back and courtyard in front. He hadn't been calling there for very long until he understood why she referred to it as her flat. It was a word that did not have unpleasant connotations of domesticity.

Her little place had a marvellously masculine air, and yet, miraculously, Myra herself remained very feminine. She was, of course, a pretty woman, although she hated him to say this – and she didn't smoke, or drink more than a dutiful pre-dinner sherry with him, which she often forgot to finish. And there was a nice scent from her clothes, a scent at times quite disturbing. It often bothered him, and was occasionally the cause of giving her the victory in one of the really brilliant arguments that erupted so spontaneously the moment he stepped inside the door.

Yes, it was hard to believe Myra could ever have been a home-body. But if she said it was so, then it *was* so. Truth could have been her second name. With regard to her domestic failure, she had recently told him a most amusing story. He couldn't recall the actual incident, but it had certainly cor-roborated her theory of the transference of skill. It was – she said – as if part of her had become palsied, although at the

time her choice of that word had made him wince, it was so
altogether unsuitable to a woman like her, now obviously in
her real prime. He'd pulled her up on that. Verbal exactitude
was something they both knew to be of the utmost importance,
although admittedly rarer to find in a woman than a man.

'It is a quality I'd never have looked to find in a woman,
Myra,' he'd said to her on one of his first visits to the flat –
perhaps his very first.

He never forgot her answer.

'It's not something I'd ever expect a man to look for in a
woman,' she said. 'Thank you, James, for not jumping to the
conclusion that I could not possibly possess it.'

Yes – that must have been on his first visit because he'd
been startled by such quick-fire volley in reply to what had
been only a casual compliment. No wonder their friendship got
off to a flying start!

Thinking of the solid phalanx of years that had been built
up since that evening, James felt a glow of satisfaction, and
for a moment he didn't realize that the fire he was supposed to
be tending had got off to a good start, and part at least of his
sense of well-being was coming from its warmth stealing over
him.

The flames were going up the chimney with soft nervous
rushes and the edges of the logs were decked with small sharp
flames, like the teeth of a saw. He could safely leave it now
and have breakfast. But just then he did remember what it was
Myra had been good at when she was young. Embroidery!
She had once made herself an evening dress with the bodice
embroidered all over in beads. And she'd worn it. So it must
have been well made. Even his sister Kay, who disliked Myra,
had to concede she dressed well. Yes, she must indeed have been
fairly good at sewing in her young days. Yet one day recently
when she ripped her skirt in the National Library she hadn't
been able to mend it.

'It wasn't funny, James,' she chided when he laughed. 'The
whole front pleat was ripped. I had to borrow a needle and
thread from the lavatory attendant. Fortunately I had plenty
of time – so when I'd taken it off and sewed it up I decided to

give it a professional touch – a finish – with a tailor's arrow. It took time but it was well done and the lavatory attendant was very impressed when I held the skirt up! But next minute when I tried to step into it I found I'd sewn the back to the front. I'd formed a sort of gusset. Can you picture it. I'd turned it into trousers!'

Poor Myra! He laughed still more.

'I tell you, it's not funny, James. And it's the same with cooking. I used at least to be able to boil an egg, whereas now –' she shrugged her shoulders. 'You know how useless I am in the kitchen.'

She had certainly never attempted to cook a meal for him. They always went out to eat. There was a small café near the flat and they ate there. Or at least they did at the start. But when one evening they decided they didn't really want to go out – perhaps he'd had a headache, or perhaps it was a really wet night, but anyway, whatever it was, Myra made no effort to – as she put it – slop up some unappetizing smather. Instead she lifted the phone, and got on to the proprietor of their little café and – as she put it – administered such a dose of coaxyorum – she really had very amusing ways of expressing herself – that he sent round two trays of food. Two trays, mind you. That was so like her – so quick, so clever. And tactful, too. That night marked a new stage in their relationship.

They'd been seeing a lot of each other by then. He'd been calling to the flat pretty frequently and when they went out for a meal, although the little café was always nearly empty, he had naturally paid the bill each time.

'We couldn't go on like that though, James!' she'd said firmly when he'd tried to pay for the trays of food that night. And she did finally succeed in making him see that if he were to come to the flat as often as she hoped he would – and as he himself certainly hoped – it would put her under too great an obligation to have him pay for the food every time.

'Another woman would be able to run up some tasty little dish that wouldn't cost tuppence,' she said, 'but' – she made a face – 'that's out. All the same I can't let you put me under too great a compliment to you. Not every time.'

In the end they'd settled on a good compromise. They each paid for a tray.

He had had misgivings, but she rid him of them.

'What would you eat if I wasn't here, Myra?' he'd asked.

'I wouldn't have *cooked* anything, that's certain,' she said, and he didn't pursue the topic, permitting himself just one other brief inquiry.

'What do other people do, I wonder?'

This Myra dismissed with a deprecating laugh.

'I'm afraid I don't know,' she said. 'Or care! Do you?'

'Oh Myra!' In that moment he felt she elevated them both to such pure heights of integrity. 'You know I don't,' he said, and he'd laid his hand over hers as she sat beside him on the sofa.

'That makes two of us!' she said, and she drew a deep breath of contentment.

It was a rich moment. It was probably at that moment he first realized the uniquely undemanding quality of her feeling for him.

But now James saw that the fire was blazing madly. He had to put on another log or it would burn out too fast. He threw on a log and was about to leave the study when, as he passed his desk, a nervous impulse made him look to see that his papers were not disarranged, although there was no one to disturb them.

The papers, of course, were as he had left them. But then the same diabolical nervousness made him go over and pick up the manuscript. Why? He couldn't explain, except that he'd worked late the previous night and, when he did that, he was always idiotically nervous next day, as if he half expected to find the words had been mysteriously erased during the night. That had happened once! He'd got up one morning as usual, full of eagerness to take up where he thought he'd left off, only to find he'd stopped in the middle of a sentence – had gone to bed defeated, leaving a most involved and complicated sentence unfinished. He'd only dreamed that he'd finished it off.

This morning, thank heavens, it was no dream. He'd finished the sentence – the whole chapter. It was the last chapter too.

A little rephrasing, perhaps some rewording, and the whole thing would be ready for the typist.

Standing in the warm study with the pages of his manuscript in his hand, James was further warmed by a self-congratulatory glow. This was the most ambitious thing he'd attempted so far – it was no less than an effort to trace the creative process itself back, as it were, to its source-bed. How glad he was that he'd stuck at it last night. He'd paid heavily for it by tossing around in the sheets until nearly morning. But it was worth it. His intuitions had never yielded up their meanings so fast or so easily. But suddenly his nervousness returned. He hoped to God his writing wasn't illegible? No. It was readable. And although his eye did not immediately pick up any of the particularly lucid – even felicitous – phrases that he vaguely remembered having hit upon, he'd come on them later when he was re-reading more carefully.

Pleased, James was putting down the manuscript, but on an impulse he took up the last section again. He'd bring it out to the kitchen and begin his re-reading of it while he was having his breakfast, something he never did, having a horror of food-stains on paper. It might, as it were, recharge his batteries, because in spite of his satisfaction with the way the work was going, he had to admit to a certain amount of physical lethargy, due to having gone to bed so late.

It was probably wiser in the long run to do like Myra and confine oneself to a fixed amount of work per day. Nothing would induce Myra to go beyond her predetermined limit of two thousand words a day. Even when things were going well! It was when they were going well that paradoxically she often stopped work. Really her method of working amazed him. When she encountered difficulty she went doggedly on, worrying at a word like a dog with a bone – as she put it – in order, she explained, to avoid carrying over her frustration with it to the next day. On the other hand, when things were going well and her mind was leaping forward like a flat stone skimming the surface of a lake (her image, again not his, but good, good), *then* sometimes she stopped.

'Because then, James, I have a residue of enthusiasm to start

me off next day! I'm not really a dedicated scholar like you –
I need stimulus.'

She had a point. But her method wouldn't work for him. It
would be mental suicide for him to tear himself away when he
was excited. It was only when things got sticky he stopped:
when an idea sort of seized up in his mind and he couldn't go
on.

There was nothing sticky about last night though. Last night
his brain buzzed with ideas. Yet now, sitting down to his egg,
the page in his hand seemed oddly dull – a great hunk of
abstraction. He took the top off the egg before reading on.
But after a few paragraphs he looked at the numbering of the
pages. Had the pages got mixed up? Here was a sentence that
seemed to be in the wrong place. The whole passage made no
impact. And what was this? He'd come on a line that was
meaningless, absolutely meaningless – gibberish. With a sickening feeling James put down the manuscript and took a gulp of
coffee. Then, by concentrating hard, he could perceive – could
at least form a vague idea of – what he'd been trying to get at
in this clumsy passage. At one point, indeed, he had more or less
got it, but the chapter as a whole –? He sat there stunned.

What had happened? Could it be that what he'd taken for
creative intensity had been only nervous exhaustion? Was
that it? Was Myra right? Should he have stopped earlier? Out
of the question. In the excited state he'd been in, he wouldn't
have slept a wink at all – even in the early hours. And what else
could he have done but go to bed? A walk, perhaps? At that
time of night? On a country road in the pitch dark? It was all
very well for Myra – the city streets were full of people at all
hours, brightly lit, and safe underfoot.

Anyway, Myra probably did most of her work in the morning. He didn't really know for sure of course, except that whenever he turned up at the flat there was never any sign of papers
about the place. The thought of that neat and orderly flat
made him look around the cottage and suddenly he felt depressed. The old woman did her best, but she wasn't up to
very much. The place could do with a rub of paint, the woodwork
at least, but he certainly wasn't going to do it. He wouldn't be

able. James frowned again. Why was his mind harping on this theme of fitness? He straightened up as if in protest at some accusation, but almost at once he slumped down, not caring.

He got exercise enough on the days he went to Dublin. First the walk to the bus. Then the walk at the other end, because no matter what the weather, he always walked from the bus to the flat. It was a good distance too, but it prolonged his anticipation of the evening ahead.

Ah well! He wouldn't be going today. That was certain. He gathered up his pages. He'd have to slog at this thing till he got it right. He swallowed down the last of his coffee. Back to work.

The fire at any rate was going well. It was roaring up the chimney. The sun, too, was pouring into the room. Away across the river in a far field cattle were lying down: a sign of good weather it was said.

Hastily, James stepped back from the window and sat down at his desk. It augured badly for his work when he was aware of the weather. Normally he couldn't have told if the day was wet or fine.

That was the odd thing about Dublin. There the weather did matter. There he was aware of every fickle change in the sky, especially on a day like today that began with rain and later gave way to sunshine. The changes came so quick in the city. They took one by surprise, although one was alerted by a thousand small signs, whereas the sodden fields were slow to recover after the smallest shower. In Dublin the instant there was a break in the clouds, the pavements gave back an answering glint. And after that came a strange white light mingling water and sun, a light that could be perceived in the reflections underfoot without raising one's eyes to the sky at all. And how fast then the paving stones dried out into pale patches. Like stepping stones, these patches acted strangely on him, putting a skip into his otherwise sober step!

Talk of the poetry of Spring. The earth's rebirth! Where was it more intoxicating than in the city, the cheeky city birds filling the air with song, and green buds breaking out on branches so black with grime it was as if iron bars had sprouted.

Thinking of the city streets, his feet ached to be pacing them. James glanced out again at the fields with hatred.

Damn, damn, damn. The damage was done. He'd let himself get unsettled. It would be Dublin for him today. He looked at the clock. He might even go on the early bus. Only what would he do up there all day? His interest in Dublin had dwindled to its core, and the core was Myra.

All the same, he decided to go on the early bus. 'Come on, James! Be a gay dog for once. Get the early bus. You'll find plenty to do. The bookshops! The National Library! Maybe a film? Come on. You're going whether you like it or not, old fellow.'

Catching up the poker, James turned the blazing logs over to smother their flames. A pity he'd lit the fire, or rather it was a pity it couldn't be kept in till he got back. It would be nice to return to a warm house. But old Mrs Nully had a mortal dread of the cottage taking fire in his absence. James smiled thinking how she had recently asked why he didn't install central heating. In a three-roomed cottage! Now where on earth had she got that notion he wondered, as he closed the door and put the key under the mat for her. Then, as he strode off down to the road, he remembered that a son of hers had been taken on as houseman in Asigh House, and the son's wife gave a hand there at weekends. The old woman had probably been shown over the house by them before the Balfes moved into it.

The Balfes! James was nearly at the road, and involuntarily he glanced back across the river to where a fringe of fir trees in the distance marked out the small estate of Asigh. Strange to think – laughable really – that Emmy, who once had filled every cranny of his mind, should only come to mind now in a train of thought that had its starting point in a plumbing appliance!

Here James called himself to order. It was a gross exaggeration to have said – even to himself – that Emmy had ever entirely filled his mind. He'd only known her for a year, and that was the year he finished his Ph.D. He submitted the thesis at the end of the year, and his marks, plus the winning of

the travelling scholarship, surely spoke for a certain detachment
of mind even when he was most obsessed by her?

He glanced back again at the fir trees. Emmy only stood
out in his life because of the violence of his feeling for her.
It was something he had never permitted himself before; and
never would again. When the affair ended, it ended as completely as if she had been a little skiff upon a swiftly flowing
river, which, when he'd cut the painter, was carried instantly
away. For a time he'd had no way of knowing whether it had
capsized or foundered. As it happened, Emmy had righted herself and come to no harm.

Again James had to call himself to order. How cruel he
made himself seem by that metaphor. Yet for years that was
how he'd felt obliged to put it to himself. That was how he'd
put it to Myra when he first told her about Emmy. But Myra
was quick to defend him, quick to see, and quick to show him
how he had acted in self-defence. His career would have been
wrecked, because, of course, with a girl like Emmy marriage
would have become inescapable. And, of course, then as now,
marriage for him was out. It was never really in the picture.

Later, after Myra appeared on the scene, he came to believe
that a man and woman could enter into a marriage of minds.

'But when one is young, James,' Myra said, 'one can't be
expected to be both wise and foolish at the same time.'

A good saying. He'd noticed, and appreciated, the little sigh
with which she accompanied her words, as if she didn't just
feel *for* him but *with* him. Then she asked the question that
a man might have asked.

'She married eventually I take it, this Emmy?'

'Oh good lord, yes.' How happy he was to be able to answer
in the affirmative. If Emmy had not married, it would have
worried him all his life. But she did. And, all things considered,
surprisingly soon.

'Young enough to have a family?' Myra probed, but kindly,
kindly. He nodded. 'I take it,' she said then, more easily, 'I
take it she married that student who –'

James interrupted '– the one she was knocking around with
when I first noticed her?'

'Yes, the one that was wrestling with that window when you had to step down from the rostrum and yank it open yourself?'

Really, Myra was unique. Her grasp of the smallest details of that incident, even then so far back in time, was very gratifying.

He had been conducting a tutorial and the lecture room got so stuffy he'd asked if someone would open a window. But when a big burly fellow – the footballer-type – tried with no success, James strode down the classroom himself, irritably, because he half thought the fellow might be having him on to create a diversion. And when he had to lean in across a student whose chair was right under the window, he was hardly aware it was a girl, as he exerted all his strength to bring down the heavy sash. Only when the sash came down and the fresh air rushed in overhead did he find he was looking straight into the eyes of a girl – Emmy.

That was all. But during the rest of the class their eyes kept meeting. And the next day it was the same. Then he began to notice her everywhere, in the corridors, in the Main Hall, and once across the Aula Maxima at an inaugural ceremony. And she'd seen him too. He knew it. But for a long time, several weeks, there was nothing between them except this game of catch-catch with their eyes. And always, no matter how far apart they were, it was as if they had touched.

James soon found himself trembling all over when her eyes touched him. Then one day in the library she passed by his desk and he saw that a paper in her hand was shaking as if there was a breeze in the air. But there was no breeze. Still, deliberately he delayed the moment of speaking to her because there was a kind of joy in waiting. And funnily enough when they did finally speak, neither of them could afterwards remember what their first spoken words had been. They had already said so much with their eyes.

Myra's comment on this, though, was very shrewd. 'You had probably said all there was to say, James.' Again she gave that small sigh of hers that seemed to put things in proportion: to place him, and Emmy too, on the map of disenchantment where all mankind, it seems, must sojourn for a time. And indeed it

was sad to think that out of the hundreds of hours that he
and Emmy had spent together, wandering along the damp
paths of Stephen's Green, sitting in little cafés, and standing
under the lamps of Leeson Street where he was in lodgings, he
could recall nothing of what was said. 'You probably spent
most evenings trying out ideas for your thesis on her, poor
girl.' Myra had a dry humour at times, but he had to acknow-
ledge it was likely enough, although, if so, Emmy used to
listen as if she were drinking in every word.

When he'd got down at last to the actual writing of the
thesis, they did not meet so often. In fact he could never quite
remember their last meeting either; not even what they had
said to each other at parting. Of course long before that they
must have faced up to his situation. He'd been pretty sure
of getting the travelling scholarship, so it must have been an
understood thing that he'd be going away for at least two years.
And in the end, he left a month sooner than he'd intended.
They never actually did say goodbye. He'd gone without seeing
her – just left a note at her digs. And for a while he wasn't even
sure if she'd got it. She'd got it all right. She wrote and thanked
him. How that smarted! *Thanked* him for breaking it off with
her. Years later, telling Myra, he still felt the sting of that.

Myra was marvellous though.

'Hurt pride, my dear James, nothing more. Don't let it spoil
what is probably the sweetest thing in life – for all of us, men
or women – our first, shy, timid love.' There was a tenderness
in her voice. Was she remembering some girlish experience of
her own? The pang of jealousy that went through him showed
how little Emmy had come to mean to him.

Myra put him at ease.

'We all go through it, James: it's only puppy love.'

'Puppy love! I was twenty-six, Myra!'

'Dear, dear James.' She smiled. 'Don't get huffy. I know quite
well what age you were. You were completing your Ph.D., and
you were old enough to conduct tutorials. You were not at the
top of the tree, but you had begun the ascent!'

It was so exactly how he'd seen himself in those days, that he
laughed. And with that laugh the pain went out of the past.

'Dear James,' she said again, 'anyone who knows you – and loves you,' she added quickly, because they tried never to skirt away from that word love, although they gave it a connotation all their own – 'anyone who loves you, James, would know that even then, where women were concerned, you'd be nothing but a lanky, bashful boy. Wait a minute!' She sprang up from the sofa. 'I'll show you what I mean.' She took down the studio photograph she'd made him get taken the day of his honorary doctorate. 'Here!' She shoved the silver frame into his hands, and, going into the room where she slept, she came back with another photograph. 'You didn't know I had this one?' He saw with some chagrin that it was a blow-up from a group photograph taken on the steps of his old school at the end of his last year. 'See!' she said. 'It's the same face in both, the same ascetical features, the same look of dedication.' Then she pressed the frame, face inward, against her breast. 'Oh James, I bet Emmy was the first girl you ever looked at! My dear, it was not so much the girl as the experience itself that bowled you over.'

Emmy was not the first girl he'd looked at. In those days he was always looking at girls, but looking at them from an unbridgeable distance. When he looked at Emmy, the space between them seemed to be instantly obliterated. Emmy had felt the same. That day in class her mind had been a million miles away. She was trying to make up her mind about getting engaged to the big burly fellow, the one who couldn't open the window; James could not remember his name, but he was a type that could be attractive to women. The fellow was pestering her to marry him, and the attentions of a fellow like that could have been very flattering to a girl like Emmy. She was so young. Yet, after she met him it was as if a fiery circle had been blazed around them, allowing no way out for either until he, James, in the end had to close his eyes and break through, not caring about the pain as long as he got outside again.

Because Myra was right. Marriage would have put an end to his academic career. For a man like him it would have been suffocating.

'Even now!' Myra said, and there was a humorous expression

on her face, because of course, in their own way, he and Myra *were* married. Then, in a businesslike way, as if she were filling a form for filing away, she asked him another question. 'What family did they have?'

'She had five or six children, I think, although she must have been about thirty by the time she married,' James couldn't help throwing his eyes up to heaven at the thought of such a household. Myra too raised her eyebrows.

'You're joking?' she said. 'Good old Balfe!' But James was staring at her, hardly able to credit she had picked up Emmy's married name. He himself had hardly registered it the first time *he'd* heard it, so that when last summer Asigh House had been bought by people named Balfe, it simply hadn't occurred to him that it could have been Emmy and her husband until one day on the road a car passed him and the woman beside the driver reminded him oddly of her. The woman in the car was softer and plumper and her hair was looser and more untidy – well, fluffier anyway – than Emmy's used to be, or so he thought until suddenly he realized it *was* her. Emmy! She didn't recognize him though. But then she wasn't looking his way. She was looking out over the countryside through which she was passing. It was only when the car turned left at the cross-road the thought hit him, that she had married a man named Balfe, and that Balfe was the name of the people who'd bought Asigh. It was a shock. Not only because of past associations, but more because he had never expected any invasion of his privacy down here. It was his retreat, from everything and everyone. Myra – even Myra – had never been down there. She was too sensible to suggest such a thing. And he wouldn't want her to come either.

Once when he'd fallen ill, he'd lost his head and sent her a telegram, but even then she'd exercised extreme discrimination. She dispatched a nurse to take care of him, arranging with the woman to phone her each evening from the village. Without once coming down, she had overseen his illness – which fortunately was not of long duration. She had of course ascertained to her satisfaction that his condition was not serious. The main thing was that she had set a firm precedent for them both. It was different when he was convalescing. Then she insisted that he come up to town and stay in a small hotel near the flat, taking his evening meal with her, as on ordinary visits except – James smiled – except that she sent a taxi to fetch him and carry him back, although the distance involved was negligible, only a block or two.

Remembering her concern for him on that occasion, James told himself that he could never thank her enough. He resolved to let her see he did not take her goodness for granted. Few women could be as self-effacing.

Yet, in all fairness to Emmy, she had certainly effaced herself fast. One might say drastically. After that one note of thanks – it jarred again that she had put it like that – he had never once heard or seen her until that day she passed him here on the road in her car. So much for his fears for his privacy. Unfounded! For days he'd half expected a courtesy call from them, but after a time he began to wonder if they were aware at all that he lived in the neighbourhood? After all, their property was three or four miles away, and the river ran between. It was just possible Emmy knew nothing of his existence. Yet somehow he doubted it. As the crow flies he was less than two miles away. He could see their wood. And was it likely the local people would have made no mention of him? No, it was hard to escape the conclusion that Emmy might be avoiding him. Although Myra – who was never afraid of the truth – had not hesitated to say that Emmy might have forgotten him altogether!

'Somehow I find that hard to believe, Myra,' he'd said, although, after he'd made the break, there had been nothing. Nothing, nothing, nothing.

But Myra was relentless.

'You may not like to believe it, James, but it could be true all the same,' she said. Then she tried to take the hurt out of her words by confessing that she herself found it dispiriting to think a relationship that had gone so deep could be erased completely. 'I myself can't bear to think she did not recognize you that day she passed you on the road. *She* may have changed, **you** said she'd got stouter' – that wasn't the word he'd used, but he'd let it pass – 'whereas you, James, can hardly have changed at all, in essentials I mean. Your figure must be the same as when you were a young man. I can't bear to think she didn't even *know* you.'

'She wasn't looking straight at me, Myra.'

'No matter! You'd think there'd have been some telepathy between you; some force that would *make* her turn. Oh, I can't bear it!'

She was so earnest he had to laugh.

'It is a good job she didn't see me,' he said. Emmy being nothing to him then, it was just as well there should be no threat to his peace and quiet.

Such peace; such quiet. James looked around at the sleepy countryside. The bus was very late though! What was keeping it?

Ah, here it came. Signalling to the driver, James stepped up quickly on to the running-board, so the man had hardly to do more than go down into first gear before starting off again. In spite of how few passengers there were, the windows were fogged up, and James had to clear a space on the glass with his hand to see out. It was always a pleasant run through the rich Meath fields, but soon the unruly countryside gave way to neatly squared-off fields with pens and wooden palings, where cattle were put in for the night before being driven to the slaughterhouse.

James shuddered. He was no countryman. Not by nature anyway. He valued the country solely for the protection it gave him from people. When he lived in Dublin he used to work in the National Library, but as he got older he began to feel that in the eyes of the students and the desk-messengers he could have appeared eccentric. Not objectionably so, just rustling his papers too much, and clearing his throat too loudly; that kind of thing. He'd have been the first to find that annoying in others when he was young. The cottage was much better. It also served to put that little bit of distance between him and Myra which they both agreed was essential.

'If I lived in Dublin, I'd be here at the flat every night of the week,' he'd once said to her. 'I'm better off down there – I suppose – stuck in the mud!'

That was an inaccurate – an unfair – description of his little retreat, but the words had come involuntarily to his lips, which showed how he felt about the country in general. The city streets of Dublin were so full of life, and the people were so dapper and alert compared with the slow-moving country people. Every time he went up there he felt like an old fogy – that was until he got to Myra's, because Myra immediately gave him back a sense of being alive. Mentally at least, Myra made him feel more alive than twenty men.

The bus had now reached O'Connell Bridge, where James usually descended, so he got out. He ought to have got out sooner and walked along the Quays. One could kill a whole morning looking over the book barrows. Now he would have to walk back to them.

Perhaps he ought not to have come on the early bus? It might not be so easy to pass the time. And after browsing to his heart's content and leaning for a while looking over the parapet on to the Liffey, it was still only a little after one o'clock when he strolled back to the centre of the city. He'd have to eat something and that would use up another hour or more. He'd buy a paper and sit on over his coffee.

James hadn't bargained on the lunchtime crowds though. All the popular places were crowded, and in a few of the better places, one look inside was enough to send him off! These places too were invaded by the lunchtime hordes, and the menu would cater for these barbarians. If there should by chance happen to be a continental dish on the menu – a goulash or a pasta – it would nauseate him to see the little clerks attacking it with knife and fork as if it was a mutton chop.

At this late hour, how about missing out on lunch altogether? It never hurt to skip a meal, although, mind you, he was peckish. How about a film? He hadn't been in a cinema for years. And just then, as if to settle the matter, James saw he was passing a cinema. It was exceptionally small for a city cinema, but without another thought he bolted inside.

Once inside, he regretted that he hadn't checked the time of the showings. He didn't fancy sitting through a newsreel, to say nothing of a cartoon. He had come in just in the middle of a particularly silly cartoon. He sat in the dark fuming. To think he'd let himself in for this stuff. It was at least a quarter of an hour before he realized with rage that he must have strayed into one of the new-fangled newsreel cinemas about which Myra had told him. For another minute he sat staring at the screen, trying to credit the mentality of people who voluntarily subjected themselves to this kind of stuff. He was about to leave and make for the street when without warning his eyes closed. He didn't know for how long he had dozed off, but on waking he was really ravenous. But wouldn't it be crazy to eat at this hour and spoil his appetite for the meal with Myra? He could, he supposed, go around to the flat earlier – now – immediately? Why wait any longer? But he didn't know at what hour Myra herself got there. All he knew was that she was always there after seven, the time he normally arrived.

But wasn't it remarkable, now he came to think of it, that she *was* always there when he called. Very occasionally at the start she had let drop dates on which she had to go to some meeting or other, and he'd made a mental note of them, but as time went on she gave up these time-wasting occupations. There had been one or two occasions she had been going out, but had cancelled her arrangements immediately he came on the scene. He had protested of course, but lamely, because quite frankly it would have been frightfully disappointing to have come so far and found she really had to go out.

Good God – supposing that were to happen now? James was so scared at the possibility of such a catastrophe he determined to lose no more time but get around there quick. Just in case. He stepped out briskly.

The lane at the back of Fitzwilliam Square, where Myra had her mews, was by day a hive of small enterprises. A smell of cellulosing and sounds of welding filled the air. In one court-yard there was a little fellow who dealt in scrap-iron and he made a great din. But by early evening, the big gates closed on these businesses, the high walls made the lane a very private place, and the mews-dwellers were disturbed by no sound harsher than the late song of the birds nesting in the trees of the doctors' gardens.

Walking down the lane and listening to those sleepy bird-

notes gave James greater pleasure than walking on any country
road. His feet echoed so loudly in the stillness that sometimes
before he rapped on her gate at all, Myra would come running
out across the courtyard to admit him. A good thing that!
Because otherwise he'd have had to rap with his bare knuckles:
Myra had no knocker.

'You know I don't encourage callers, James,' she'd said once,
smiling. 'Few people ferret me out here – except you; and of
course, the tradesmen. And I know their step too! It's nearly as
quiet here as in your cottage.'

'Quiet?' He'd raised his eyebrows. 'Listen to those birds; I
never heard such a din!'

Liking a compliment to be oblique, she'd squeezed his arm
as she drew him inside.

This evening, however, James was less than halfway down
the lane when at the other end he saw Myra appear at the
wicket gate. If she hadn't been bareheaded, he'd have thought
she was going out!

'Myra?' he called in some dismay.

She laughed as she came to meet him. 'I heard your footsteps,' she said. 'I told you! I always do.'

'From this distance?'

She took his arm and smiled up at him. 'That's nothing!
It's a wonder I don't hear you walking down the country road
to get the bus.' She matched her step with his. Normally he
hated to be linked, but with Myra it seemed to denote equality,
not dependence. Suddenly she unlinked her arm. 'Well, I may
as well confess something,' she said more seriously. 'This evening I was listening for you. I was expecting you.'

They had reached the big wooden gate of the mews and
James, glancing in through the open wicket across the court-
yard, was startled to see, through the enormous window by
which she had replaced the doors of the coach-house, that the
little table at which they ate was indeed set up, and with places
laid for two! She wasn't joking, then. An unpleasant thought
crossed his mind – was she expecting someone else? But reading
his mind, Myra shook her head.

'Only you, James.'

'I don't understand –'

'Neither do I!' she said quickly. 'I *was* expecting you though. And I ordered our trays!' Here she wrinkled her nose in a funny way she had. 'I made the order a bit more conservative than usual. No prawns!' He understood at once. He loved prawns. 'So you see,' she continued, 'if my oracle failed and you didn't come, the food would do for sandwiches tomorrow. As you know, I'm no use at hotting up left-overs. It smacks too much of –'

He knew. He knew.

'Too wifey,' he smiled. And she smiled. This was the word they'd earmarked to describe a certain type of woman they both abhorred.

'You could always have fed the prawns to the cat next door,' James said. 'Whenever I'm coming he's sitting on the wall smacking his lips.'

'But James,' she said, and suddenly she stopped smiling, 'he doesn't know when you're coming – any more than me!'

'Touché,' James admitted to being caught out there. He wasn't really good at smart remarks. 'Ah well, it's a lucky cat who knows there's an even chance of a few prawns once or twice a month. That's more than most cats can count on.' Bending his head, he followed her in through the wicket. 'Some cats have to put up with a steady diet of shepherd's pie and meat loaf.'

They were inside now, and he sank down on the sofa. Myra, who was still standing, shuddered.

'What would I do if you were the kind of man who *did* like shepherd's pie?' she said. 'I'm sure there are such men.' But she couldn't keep up the silly chaff. 'I think maybe I'd love you enough to try and make it –' she laughed '– if I could. I don't honestly think I'd be able. The main thing is that you are *not* that type. Let's stop fooling. Here, allow me to give you a kiss of gratitude – for being you.'

Lightly she laid her cheek against his, while he for his part took her hand and stroked it.

It was one of the more exquisite pleasures she gave him, the touch of her cool skin. His own hands had a tendency to

get hot although he constantly wiped them with his handkerchief. He had always preferred being too cold to being too hot.
Once or twice when he had a headache – which was not often –
Myra had only to place her hand on his forehead for an instant
and the throbbing ceased. This evening he didn't have a headache, but all the same he liked the feel of her hand on his
face.

'Do that again,' he said.

'How about fixing the drinks first?' she said.

That was his job. But he did not want to release her hand,
and he made no attempt to stand up. Unfortunately just then
there was a rap on the gate.

'Oh bother,' he said.

'It's only the Catering Service,' Myra said, and for a minute
he didn't get the joke. Myra laughed then and he noticed she
meant the grubby little pot-boy who brought the trays around
from the café.

'Let me get them,' he said, but she had jumped up and in a
minute she was back with them.

'I must tell you,' she said. 'You know the man who owns the
café? Well, he gave me such a dressing-down this morning
when I was ordering these.' James raised his eyebrows as he
held open the door of the kitchenette to let her through. 'Just
bring in the warming plate, will you please, James,' she said
interrupting herself. 'I'll pop the plates on it for a second while
we have our little drink.' She glanced at her watch. 'Oh, it's
quite early still.' She looked back at him. 'But you were a
little later than usual, I think, weren't you?'

'I don't think so,' he said vaguely, as he fitted the plug of
the food-warmer into the socket. 'If anything, I think I was a
bit earlier. But I could be wrong. When one has time to kill,
it's odd how often one ends up being late in the end!'

'Time to kill?'

She looked puzzled. Then she seemed to understand. 'Oh
James. You make me tired. You're so punctilious. Haven't I
told you a thousand times that you don't have to be polite with
me? If your bus got in early you should have come straight to
the flat! Killing time indeed! Standing on ceremony, eh?'

He handed her her drink.

'You were telling me something about the proprietor of the café – that he was unpleasant about something? You weren't serious?'

'Oh that! Of course not.'

Yet for some reason he was uneasy. 'Tell me,' he said authoritatively.

Naturally, she complied. 'He was really very nice,' she said. 'He intended phoning me. He just wanted to say there was no need to wash the plates before sending them back. I'm to hand them to the messenger in the morning just as they are – and not *attempt* to wash them.' Knowing how fastidious she was, James was about to pooh-pooh the suggestion, but she forestalled him. 'I can wrap them up in the napkins, and then I won't be affronted by the sight. And I need feel under no compliment to the café – it's in their own interests as much as in mine. They have a big washing-machine – I've seen it – with a special compartment like a dentist's sterilization cabinet, and of course they couldn't be sure that a customer would wash them properly. You can imagine the cat's lick some women would give them!'

James could well imagine it. He shuddered. Myra might hate housework, but anything she undertook she did to perfection. Unexpectedly she held out her glass.

'Let's have another drink,' she said. They seldom took more than one. 'Sit down,' she commanded. 'Let's be devils for once.' This time, though, she sat on the sofa and swung her feet up on it, so he had to sit in the chair opposite. 'There's nothing that makes the ankles ache like thinking too hard,' she said.

James didn't really understand what she meant, but he laughed happily.

'Seriously!' she said. 'I am feeling tired this evening. I'm so glad you came. I think maybe I worked extra hard this morning because I was looking forward to seeing you later. Oh, I'm so glad you came, James. I would have been bitterly disappointed if you hadn't showed up.'

James felt a return of his earlier uneasiness.

'I'm afraid that premonition of yours is more than I can

understand,' he said, but he spoke patiently, because she was
not a woman who had to be humoured. 'As a matter of fact I
never had less intention of coming to town. I'd already lit the
fire in my study when I suddenly took the notion. I had to put
the fire out!'

At that, Myra left down her glass and swung her feet back on
to the floor.

'What time did you leave?' she asked, and an unusually crisp
note in her voice took him unawares.

'I thought I told you,' he said apologetically, although there
was nothing for which to apologize. 'I came on the morning
bus.'

'Oh!' It was only one word, but it fell oddly on his ears. She
reached for her drink again then, and swallowed it down.
Somehow that too bothered him. 'Is that what you meant by
having to kill time?' she asked.

'Well –' he began, not quite knowing what to say. He took
up his own drink and let it down fairly fast for him.

'Oh, don't bother to explain,' she said. 'I think you will
agree, though, it would have been a nice gesture to have lifted
a phone and let me know you were in town and coming here
tonight.'

'But –'

'No buts about it. You knew I'd be here waiting whether you
came or not. Isn't that it?'

'Myra!'

He hardly recognized her in this new mood. Fortunately
the next moment she was her old self again.

'Oh James, forgive me. It's just that you've *no* idea – simply
no idea – how much it meant to me tonight to know in advance –' she stopped and carefully corrected herself '– to have
had that curious feeling – call it instinct if you like – that you
were coming. It made such a difference to my whole day. But
now –' her face clouded over '– to think that instead of just
having had a hunch about it, I could have known for certain.
Oh, if only you'd been more thoughtful, James.' Sitting up
straighter, she looked him squarely in the eye. 'Or were you
going somewhere else and changed your mind?'

What a foolish question.

'As if I ever go anywhere else!'

Her face brightened a bit at that, but not much.

'You'll hardly believe it,' she said after a minute, 'but I could have forgiven you more easily if you had been going somewhere else and coming here *was* an afterthought. It would have excused you more.'

Excused? What was all this about? He must have looked absolutely bewildered, because she pulled herself up.

'Oh James, please don't mind me.' She leant forward and laid a hand on his knee. 'Your visits give me such joy – I don't need to tell you that – I ought to be content with what I have. Not knowing in advance is one of the little deprivations that I just have to put up with, I suppose.'

But now James was beginning to object strongly to the way she was putting everything. He stood up. As if his doing so unnerved her, she stood up too.

'It may seem a small thing to ask from you, James, but I repeat what I said – you could have phoned me.' Then, as if that wasn't bad enough, she put it into the future tense. 'If you would only try, once in a while, to give me a ring, even from the bus depot, so I could –'

'Could what?' James couldn't help the coldness in his voice although, considering the food that was ready on the food-warmer, his question, he knew, was ungenerous. On the other hand, he felt it was absolutely necessary to keep himself detached, if the evening was not to be spoiled. He forced himself to speak sternly. 'Much as I enjoy our little meals together, it's not for the food I come here, Myra. You must know that.' He very, very nearly added that in any case he paid for his own tray, but when he looked at her he saw she had read those unsaid words from his eyes. He reddened. There was an awkward silence. Yet when she spoke, she ignored everything he had said. She harked back to what she herself had said.

'Wouldn't it be a very small sacrifice to make, James, when one thinks of all the sacrifices I've made for you? And over so many years?' Her words, which to him were exasperating beyond belief, seemed to drown her in a torrent of self-pity. 'So many, many years,' she whispered.

It was only ten.

'You'd think it was a lifetime,' he said irritably. Her face flushed.

'What is a lifetime, James?' she asked, and when he made no reply she helped him out. 'Remember it is not the same for a woman as for a man. *You* may think of yourself as a young blade, but I ...'

She faltered again, as well she might, and bit her lip. She wasn't going to cry, was she? James was appalled. Nothing had ever before happened that could conceivably have given rise to tears, but it was an unspoken law with them that a woman should never shed tears in public. Not just unspoken either. On one occasion years ago, she herself had been quite explicit about it.

'We do cry sometimes, we women, poor weaklings that we are. But I hope I would never be foolish enough to cry in the presence of a man. And to do so to you of all people, James, would be despicable.' At the time he'd wondered why she singled him out. Did she think him more sensitive than most? He'd been about to ask when she'd given one of her witty twists to things. 'If I did, I'd have you snivelling too in no time,' she said.

Yet here she was now, for no reason at all, on the brink of tears, and apparently making no effort to fight them back.

Myra was making no effort to stem her tears because she did not know she was crying. She really did despise tears. But now it seemed to her that perhaps she'd been wrong in always hiding her feelings. Other women had the courage to cry. Even in public too. She'd seen them at parties. And recently she'd seen a woman walking along the street in broad daylight with tears running down her cheeks, not bothering to wipe them away. Thinking of such women, she wondered if she perhaps had sort of – she paused to find the right word – sort of denatured herself for James?

Denatured: it was an excellent word. She'd have liked to use it then and there, but she had just enough sense left to keep it to herself for the moment. Some other time, when they were talking about someone else, she would bring it out and impress him. She must not forget the word.

When Myra's thoughts returned to James she felt calmer about him. He was not unkind. He was not cruel – the opposite in fact. What had gone wrong this evening was more her fault than his. When they'd first met she had sensed deep down in him a capacity for the normal feelings of friendship and love. Yet throughout the years she had consistently deflected his feelings away from herself and consistently encouraged him to seal them off. Tonight it seemed that his emotional capacity was completely dried up. Despair overcame her. She'd never change him now. He was fixed in his faults, cemented into his barren way of life. Tears gushed into her eyes again, but this time she leant her head back quickly to try and prevent them rolling down; but they brimmed over and splashed down on her hands.

'Oh James, I'm sorry,' she whispered, but she saw her apology was useless: the damage was done. Then her heart hardened. What harm? She wasn't really sorry. Not for him anyway. Oh, not for him. It was for herself she was sorry.

Grasping at a straw, she then tried to tell herself nothing was ever too late. Perhaps tonight some lucky star had stood still in the sky over her head and forced her to be true to herself for once. James would see the real woman for a change. Oh, surely he would. And surely he would come over and put his arm around her. He would; he would. She waited.

When he did not move, and did not utter a single word, she had to look up.

'Oh no!' she cried. For what she saw in his eyes was ice. 'Oh James, have you no heart? What you have done to me is unspeakable! Yet you can't even pity me!'

James spoke at last. 'And what, Myra, what may I ask have I done to you?'

'You have –' She stopped, and for one second she thought she'd have control enough to bite back the word, but she hadn't. 'You have denatured me,' she said.

Oh God, what had she done *now*? Clapping her hands over her mouth too late, she wondered if she could pretend to some other meaning in the words. Instead, others words gushed out, words worse and more hideous. Hearing them, she herself

could not understand where they came from. It was as if, out of
the corners of the room, she was being prompted by voices of
all the women in the world who'd ever been let down, or fancied
themselves badly treated. The room vibrated with their whispers. Go on, they prompted. Tell him what you think of him.
Don't let him get away with it. He has got off long enough. To
stop the voices she stuck her fingers into her ears, but the voices
only got louder. She had to shout them down. She saw James's
lips were moving, trying to say something, but she could not
hear him with all the shouting. When she finally caught a word
or two of what he said, she herself stopped trying to penetrate
the noise. Silence fell. She saw James go limp with relief.

'What did you say? I – I didn't hear you,' she gulped.

'I said that if that's the way you feel, Myra, there's nothing
for me to do but to leave.'

She stared at him. He was going over to the clothes' rack
and was taking down his coat. What had got into them? How
had they become involved in this vulgar scene? She had to
stop him. If he went away like this, would he ever come back?
A man of his disposition? Could she take him back? Neither of
them was of a kind to gloss over things and leave them unexplained, knowing that unexplained they could erupt again –
and again. Something had been brought to light that could
never be forced back underground. Better all the same to let
their happiness dry up if it must, than be blasted out of existence like this in one evening. Throwing out her arms, she ran
blindly towards him.

'James, I implore you. James! James! Don't let this happen
to us.' She tried to enclose him with her arms, but somehow he
evaded her and reached to take his gloves from the lid of the
gramophone. Next thing she knew he'd be at the door.

'Do you realize what you're doing?' She pushed past him
and ran to the door, pressing her back against it and throwing
out her arms to either side. It was an outrageous gesture of
crucifixion, and she knew she was acting out of character.
She was making another and more frightful mistake. 'If you
walk out this door, you'll never come through it again,
James.'

All he did was try to push her to one side, not roughly, but not gently.

'James! Look at me!'

But what he said then was so humiliating she wanted to die.

'I am looking, Myra,' he said.

There seemed nothing left to do but hit him. She thumped at his chest with her closed fists. That made him stand back all right. She had achieved that at least! If she was not going to get a chance to undo the harm she'd done, then she'd go the whole hog and let him think the worst of her. She was ashamed to think she had been about to renege on herself. She flung out her arms again, not hysterically this time, but with passion, real, real passion. Let him see what he was up against. But whatever he thought, James said nothing. And he'd have to be the one to speak first. Myra couldn't trust herself any more.

In the end, she did have to speak. 'Say something, James,' she pleaded.

'All right,' he said then. 'Be so kind, Myra, as to tell me what you think you're gaining by this performance?' he nodded at her outstretched arms. 'This nailing of yourself to the door like a stoat!'

The look in his eyes was ugly. She let her arms fall at once and, running back to the sofa, flung herself face down upon it, screaming and kicking her feet.

She didn't even hear the door bang after him, or the gate slam.

Outside in the air, James regretted that he had not shut the door more gently, but after the coarse and brutal words he had just used it was inconsistent to worry about the small niceties of the miserable business. His ugly words echoed in his mind, and he felt defiled by them. He had an impulse to go back and apologize, if only for his language. Nothing justified that kind of thing from a man. He actually raised his hand to rap on the gate, but he let it fall, overcome by a stronger impulse – to make good his escape. But as he hurried up the lane, his unuttered words too seemed base and unworthy – a mean-minded figure of speech – that could only be condoned by the

fact that he had been so grievously provoked, and by the overwhelming desire that had been engendered in him to get out
in the air. If Myra had not stood aside and let him pass, he'd
have used brute force. All the same, nothing justified the inference that he was imprisoned. Never, never had she done anything to hold him. Never had he been made captive except
perhaps by the pull of her mind upon his mind. He'd always
been free to come or go as he chose. If in the flat they had
become somewhat closed-in of late, it was from expediency –
from not wanting to run into stupid people. If they had gone
out to restaurants or cafés nowadays, some fool would be sure
to blunder over and join them, reducing their evening to the
series of banalities that passed for conversation with most people.
No, no, the flat was never a prison. Never. It was their nest. And
now he'd fallen out of the nest. Or worse still, been pushed out.
All of a sudden James felt frightened. Was it possible she had
meant what she said? Could it be that he would never again be
able to go back there? Nonsense. She was hysterical.

He stood for a minute considering again whether he should
not perhaps go back? Not that he'd relish it. But perhaps he
ought to do so – in the interests of the future. No, he decided.
Better give her time to calm down. Another evening would
be preferable. If necessary, he'd be prepared to come up again
tomorrow evening. Or later this same evening? That would be
more sensible. He looked back. She must be in a bad state when
she hadn't run out after him. Normally she'd come to the gate
and stay standing in the lane until he was out of sight. Even
in the rain.

James shook his head. What a pity. If she'd come to the gate,
he could have raised his hands or something, given some sign –
the merest indication would be enough – of his forgiveness.
He could have let her see he bore no rancour. But the gesture
would not want to be ambiguous. Not a wave; that would be
over-cordial, and he didn't want her stumbling up the lane
after him. No more fireworks, thank you! But it would not
want to appear final either. A raised hand would have been the
best he could do at that time. He was going to walk on again
when it occurred to him that if he'd gone back he need not

have gone inside. Just a few words at the gate; but on the whole it was probably better to wait till she'd calmed down. Then he could safely take some of the blame, and help her to save face. Fortunately he did not have the vanity that, in another man, might make such a course impossible. It was good for the soul sometimes to assume blame – even wrongly. James immediately felt better, less bottled up. He walked on. But he could not rid his thoughts of the ugly business. He ought to have known that no woman on earth but was capable, at some time or another, of a lapse like Myra's. And Myra, of course, was a woman. How lacking he'd been in foresight. He'd have to go more carefully with her in future. Next time they met, although he would not try to exonerate himself from the part he'd played in the regrettable scene, at the same time it would not be right to rob her of the therapeutic effects of taking her share of the blame. He felt sure that, being fair-minded people, both of them, they would properly apportion all blame.

Anyway, he resolved to put the whole thing out of his mind until after he'd eaten. To think he'd eaten nothing since morning! After he'd had some food he'd be better able to handle the situation.

James had reached the other end of the lane now and gone out under the arch into Baggot Street again. Where would he eat? He'd better head towards the centre of the city. It ought not to be as difficult as it had been at midday, although an evening meal in town could be quite expensive. He didn't want a gala-type dinner, but not some awful slop either that would sicken him. He was feeling bad. The tension had upset his stomach and he was not sure whether he was experiencing hunger pangs or physical pain. Damn Myra. If she'd been spoiling for a fight, why the devil hadn't she waited till after their meal? She'd say this was more of his male selfishness, but if they had eaten they'd have been better balanced and might not have had a row at all. What a distasteful word – the word row! Yet, that's what it was – a common row. James came to a stand again. He wouldn't think twice of marching back and banging on the gate and telling her to stop her nonsense and put the food on the table. She was probably heartbroken. But if that was the case, she'd have come to the door with her face flushed and her hair in disorder. Sobered by such a distasteful picture, he walked on. He could not possibly subject her to humiliation like that. It would be his duty to protect her from exposing herself further. Perhaps he'd write her a note and post it in the late-fee box at the G.P.O. before he got the bus for home. She'd have it first thing in the morning, and after a good night's sleep she might be better able to take what he had to say. He began to compose the letter.

'*Dear Myra –*' But he'd skip the beginning: that might be sticky. He'd have to give that careful thought. The rest was easy. Bits and pieces of sentences came readily to his mind – '*We must see to it that, like the accord that has always existed between us, discord too, if it should arise, must be –*'

That was the note to sound. He was beginning to feel his old self again. He probably ought to make reference to their next meeting. Not too soon – this to strike a cautionary note – but it might not be wise to let too much time pass either –

'*because, Myra, the most precious element of our friendship –*'

No, that didn't sound right. After tonight's scene, friendship didn't appear quite the right word. A new colouring had been given to their relationship by their tiff. But here James cursed under his breath. Tiff. Such a word! What next? Where were these trite words coming from? She'd rattled him all right. Damn it. Oh damn it.

James abandoned the letter for a moment when he realized he had been plunging along without regard to where he was headed. Where would he eat? There used to be a nice quiet little place in Molesworth Street, nearly opposite the National Library. It was always very crowded, but with quite acceptable sorts from the library or the Arts School. He made off down Kildare Street.

When James reached the café in Molesworth Street, however, and saw the padlock on the area railings, he belatedly remembered it was just a coffee-shop, run by voluntary aid for some charitable organization, and only open mornings. He stood, stupidly staring at the padlock. Where would he go now? He didn't feel like traipsing all over the city. Hadn't there been talk some time ago about starting a canteen in the National Library! Had that got under way? He looked across the street. An old gentleman was waddling in the Library gate with his briefcase under his arm. James strode after him.

But just as he'd got to the entrance, the blasted porter slammed the big iron gate – almost in his face. He might have had his nose broken.

'Sorry, sir. The Library is closed. Summer holidays, sir.'

'But you just let in someone! I saw that man –'

James glared after the old man who was now ambling up the steps to the reading room.

'The gentleman had a pass, sir,' the porter said. 'There's a skeleton staff on duty in the stacks, and the Director always gives out a few permits to people doing important research.' The fellow was more civil now. 'It's only fair, sir. It wouldn't do, sir, would it, to refuse people whose work is –' But here he looked closer at James and, recognizing him, his civility changed into servility. 'I beg your pardon, Professor,' he said. 'I didn't recognize you, sir. I would have thought you'd have applied for a permit. Oh dear, oh dear!' The man actually wrung his hands. 'If it was even yesterday, I could have got hold of the Director on the phone, but he's gone away – out of the country too, I understand.'

'Oh, that's all right,' James said, somewhat mollified by being recognized and remembered. He was sorry that he, in turn, could not recall the porter's name. 'That's all right,' he repeated. 'I wasn't going to use the Library anyway. I thought they might have opened that canteen they were talking about some time back –?'

'Canteen, sir? When was that?' The fellow had clearly never heard of the project. He was looking at James as if he was Lazarus come out of the tomb.

'No matter. Good evening!' James said curtly, and he walked away. Then, although he had never before in his life succumbed to the temptation of talking to himself, now, because it was so important, he put himself a question out loud.

'Have I lost touch with Dublin?' he asked. And he had to

answer simply and honestly, 'I have.' He should have known the Library was always closed this month. If only there was a friend on whom he could call. But he'd lost touch with his friends too.

He looked around. There used to be a few eating-places in this vicinity, or rather he could have sworn there were. It hardly seemed possible they were *all* closed down. Where on earth did people eat in Dublin nowadays? They surely didn't go to the hotels? In his day the small hotels were always given over at night to political rallies or football clubs. And the big hotels were out of the question. Not that he'd look into the cost at this stage. He stopped. If it was anywhere near time for his bus, he wouldn't think twice of going straight back without eating at all.

It was all very well for Myra. She ate hardly anything anyway. He often felt that, as far as food went, their meal together meant nothing to her. Setting up that damned unsteady card-table, and laying out those silly plates of hers shaped like vine leaves and too small to hold enough for a bird. They reminded him of when his sisters used to make him play babby-house.

Passing Trinity College, James saw there was still two hours to go before his bus, but it was just on the hour. There might be a bus going to Cavan? The Cavan bus passed through Garlow Cross, only a few miles from the cottage. How about taking that? He'd taken it once years ago, and, although he was younger and fitter in those days, he was tempted to do it. His stomach was so empty it was almost caving in, but he doubted if he could eat anything now. He felt sickish. He might feel better after sitting in the bus. And better anything than hanging about the city.

At that moment on Aston Quay James saw the Cavan bus. It was filling up with passengers, and the conductor and driver, leaning on the parapet of the Liffey, were taking a last smoke. James was about to dash across the street, but first he dashed into a sweet shop to buy a bar of chocolate, or an apple. The sensation in his insides was like something gnawing at his guts. He got an apple and a bar of chocolate as well, but he nearly missed the bus. Very nearly. The driver was at the wheel and the engine was running. James had to put on a sprint to get across the street, and even then the driver was pulling on the big steering-wheel and swivelling the huge wheels outward into the traffic before putting the bus in motion. James jumped on the step.

'Dangerous that, sir,' said the young conductor.

'You hadn't begun to move!' James replied testily, while he stood on the platform getting his breath back.

'Could have jerked forward, sir. Just as you were stepping up!'

'You think a toss would finish me off, eh?' James said. He meant the words to be ironical, but his voice hadn't been light-hearted enough to carry off the joke.

The conductor didn't smile. 'Never does any of us any good, sir, at any age.'

James looked at him with hatred. The fellow was thin and spectacled. Probably the over-conscientious sort. Feeling no inclination to make small talk, he lurched into the body of the bus and sat down on the nearest seat. He was certainly glad to be off his feet. He hadn't noticed until now how they ached. Such a day. Little did he think setting off that it would be a case of About Turn and Quick March.

James slumped down in his seat, but when he felt the bulge of the apple in his pocket he brightened up, and was about to take it out when he was overcome by a curious awkwardness with regard to the conductor. Instead, keeping his hand buried in his pocket, he broke off a piece of the chocolate and surreptitiously put it into his mouth. He would nearly have been too tired to chew the apple. He settled back on the seat and tried to doze. But now Myra's words kept coming back. They were repeating on him, like indigestion.

To think she should taunt him with how long they'd known each other. Wasn't it a good thing they'd been able to put up with each other for so long? What else but time had cemented their relationship? As she herself had once put it, very aptly, they'd invested a lot in each other. Well, as far as he was concerned she could have counted on *her* investment to the end.

Wasn't it their credo that it didn't take marriage lines to bind
together people of their intregity? He had not told her, not in
so many words – from delicacy – but he had made provision
for her in his will. He'd been rather proud of the way he'd
worded the bequest too, putting in a few lines of appreciation
that were, he thought, gracefully but, more important, tactfully
expressed.

Oh, why had she doubted him? Few wives could be as sure
of their husbands as she of him – but he had to amend this –
as she *ought* to be, because clearly she had set no value on his
loyalty. What was that she'd said about the deprivations she'd
suffered? *'One of the many deprivations!'* Those might not have
been her exact words, but that was more or less what she'd
implied. What had come over her? He shook his head. Had
they not agreed that theirs was the perfect solution for facing
the drearier years of ageing and decay? That dreary time was
not imminent, of course, but alas it would inevitably come.
The process of ageing was not attractive, and they both agreed
that if they were continually together – well, really married
for instance – the afflictions of age would be doubled for them.
On the other hand, with the system they'd worked out, neither
saw anything but what was best, and best preserved, in the
other. As the grosser aspects of age became discernible, if they
could not conceal them from themselves, at least they could
conceal them from each other. To put it flatly, if they had
been married a dozen times over, that would still be the way
he'd want things to be at the end. It was disillusioning now to
find she had not seen eye to eye with him on this. Worse still,
she'd gone along with him and paid lip-service to his ideals
while underneath she must all the time have dissented.

Suddenly James sat bolt upright. That word she used: deprivation. She couldn't have meant that he'd done her out of
children? What a thought! Surely it was unlikely that she
could have had a child even when they first met? What age
was she then? Well, perhaps not too old, but surely to God she
was at an age when she couldn't have fancied putting herself
in *that* condition? And what about all the cautions that were
given now on the danger of late conception? How would *she*

like to be saddled with a retarded child? Why, it was her who first told him about recent medical findings! And – wait a minute – that was early in their acquaintance too, if he remembered rightly. He could recall certain particulars of the conversation. They had been discussing her work, and the demands it made on her. She was, of course, aware from the first that *he* never wanted children, that he abhorred the thought of a houseful of brats, crawling everywhere, and dribbling and spitting out food. They overran a place. As for the smell of wet diapers about a house, it nauseated him. She'd pulled him up on that, though.

'Not soiled diapers, James. The most slovenly woman in the world has more self-respect than to leave dirty diapers lying about. But I grant you there often is a certain odour – I've found it myself at times in the homes of my friends, and it has surprised me, I must say – but it comes from *clean* diapers hanging about to air. At worst it's the smell of steam. They have to be boiled you know.' She made a face. 'I agree with you, though. It's not my favourite brand of perfume.'

Those were her very words. If he were to be put in the dock at this moment, he could swear to it. Did that sound like a woman who wanted a family? Yet tonight she had insinuated – James was so furious he clenched his hands and dug his feet into the floorboards as if the bus were about to hurtle over the edge of an abyss and he could put a brake on it.

Then he thought of something else: something his sister Kay had said.

It was the time Myra had had to go into hospital for a few weeks. Nothing serious, she'd said. Nothing to worry about, or so she'd told him. Just a routine tidying up job that most people – presumably she meant women – thought advisable. Naturally he'd encouraged her to get it over and done with: not to put it on the long finger. The shocking thing was how badly it had shaken her. He was appalled at how frightful she'd looked for months afterwards. Finally the doctors ordered her to take a good holiday, although it hadn't been long since her summer holidays. She hadn't gone away in the summer, except for one long weekend in London, but she'd packed up her work

and he'd gone up more often. But the doctor was insistent that
this time she was to go away. Oddly enough, her going away
had hit him harder than her going into hospital. If they could
have gone away together, it would have been different. That, of
course, was impossible. There was no longer a spot on the globe
where one mightn't run the risk of bumping into some busybody
from Dublin.

'What will I do while you're away?' he'd asked.

'Why don't you come up here as usual,' she suggested, 'except
you need order only one tray.'

But she overestimated the charm of the flat for its own sake.
And he told her so.

'Nonsense,' she said. 'Men are like cats and dogs: it's their
habitat they value, not the occupants.'

'I'll tell you what I'll do,' he said finally. 'I'll come up the
day you're coming back and I'll have a fire lit – how about
that?'

'Oh James, you are a dear. It would make me so glad to be
coming back.'

'I should hope you'd be glad to be coming back anyway?'

'Oh yes, but you must admit it would be extra special to be
coming back to find you here – in our little nest.'

There! James slapped his knee. *That* was where he'd got the
word nest. He had to hand it to her; she was very ingenious
in avoiding the word 'home'. She was at her best when it came
to these small subtleties other people overlooked. And the day
she was due back he had fully intended to be in the flat before
her, were it not for a chance encounter with his sister Kay and
a remark of hers that upset him.

Kay knew all about Myra. Whether she approved of her or
not James did not know: Kay and himself were too much
alike to embarrass each other by confidences. That was why
he found what she said that day so extraordinary.

'Very sensible of her to go away,' Kay had said; 'otherwise
it takes a long time, I believe, to recover from that beastly business.' Beastly business? What did she mean? Unlike herself,
Kay had gone on and on. 'Much messier than childbirth I
understand. Also, I've heard, James, that it's worse for an un-

married woman –' she paused '– I mean a childless woman.'
Then feeling – as well she might – that she'd overstepped herself, she looked at her watch. 'I'll have to fly,' she said. And
perhaps to try and excuse her indiscretion, she resorted to
something else that was rare for Kay – banality. 'It's sort of the
end of the road for them, I suppose,' she said, before she hurried
away leaving him confused and dismayed.

He had never bothered to ask Myra what her operation had
been. He didn't see that it concerned him. At any age there
were certain danger zones for a woman, that had to be kept
under observation. But what if it had been a hysterectomy! Was
that any business of his? Medically speaking, it wasn't all
that different from any other -ectomy – tonsillectomy, appen-
dectomy. What was so beastly about it? If it came to that, the
most frightful mess of all was getting one's antrums cleaned out.
He knew all about *that*. Anyway, the whole business was outside his province. Or at least he had thought so then.

Then, then, then. But now, now it was as if he'd been asked
to stand up and testify to something. It was most unfair. Myra
herself had never arraigned him. Neither before nor after.
Admittedly he had not given her much encouragement. But he
could have sworn that she herself hadn't given a damn at the
time. Ah, but – and this was the rub – the whole business could
have bred resentment, could have rankled within her and gone
foetid. Considered in this new light, the taunts she had flung at
him tonight could no longer be put down to hysteria and
written off – something long-festering had suppurated. He put
his hand to his head. Dear God, to think she had allowed him
to bask all those years in a fool's paradise!

He closed his eyes. Thank heavens he hadn't demeaned himself by going back to try and patch things up. He'd left the
way open, should he decide to sever the bond completely. Perhaps he ought to sever it, if only on the principle that, if a person
once tells you a lie, that puts an end to truth between you forever. A lie always made him feel positively sick. And God
knows he felt sick enough as it was. There was a definite burning sensation now in his chest as well as his stomach. He looked
around the steamy bus. Could it be the fumes of the engine

that were affecting him? He'd have liked to go and stand on the platform to get some fresh air, but he hated to make himself noticeable, although the bus was now nearly empty. He stole a look at the other passengers to see if anyone was watching him. He might have been muttering to himself, or making peculiar faces. Just to see if anyone would notice, he stealthily, but deliberately, made a face into the window, on which the steam acted like a backing of mercury. And sure enough, the damn conductor was looking straight at him. James felt he had to give the fellow a propitiating grin, which the impudent fellow took advantage of immediately.

'Not yet, sir,' he said. 'I'll tell you when you're there!'

Officious again. Well, smart as he was, he didn't know his countryside. Clearing a space on the foggy glass, James looked out. It was getting dark outside now, but the shape of the trees could still be seen against the last light in the west. The conductor was wrong! They *were* there! He jumped to his feet.

'Not yet, sir,' the blasted fellow called out again, and loudly this time for all to hear.

Ignoring him, James staggered down the bus to the boarding-platform, where, without waiting for the conductor to do it, he defiantly hit the bell to bring the bus to a stop. The fellow merely shrugged his shoulders. James threw an angry glance at him and then, although the bus had not quite stopped, deliberately and only taking care to face the way the bus was travelling so that if he did fall it would be less dangerous, he jumped off.

Luckily he did not fall. He felt a bit shaken; as he regained his balance precariously on the dark road, he was glad to think he had spiked that conductor. He could tell he had by the smart way the fellow hit the bell again and set the bus once more in motion, and that, for all his solicitude on the Quays, he'd hardly have noticed if one had fallen on one's face on the road; or cared.

And Myra? If Myra were to read a report of the accident in the newspaper tomorrow, how would *she* feel? More interesting still – what would she tell her friends? Secretive as their relationship was supposed to be, James couldn't help wondering if she might not have let the truth leak out to some people. Indeed, this suspicion had lurked in his mind for some time, but he only fully faced it now.

What about those phone calls she sometimes got? Those times when she felt it necessary to plug out the phone and carry it into her bedroom? Or else talk in a lowered voice, very different from the normal way in which she'd call out 'wrong number' and bang down the receiver? Now that he thought about it, the worst give-away was when she'd let the phone ring and ring without answering it at all. It nearly drove him mad listening to that ringing.

'What will they think, Myra?' he'd cry. When she used to say the caller would think she was out, he nearly went demented altogether at her lack of logic.

'They wouldn't keep on ringing if they didn't suspect you were here,' he exploded once.

Ah! The insidiousness of her answer hadn't fully registered at the time. *Now* it did though.

'Oh, they'll understand.' That was what she'd said.

Understand what? He could only suppose she had given her friends some garbled explanation of things.

'Oh damn her! Damn her!' he said out loud again. There was no reason now why he shouldn't talk out loud or shout if he liked here on the lonely country road. 'Damn, damn,' he shouted. 'Damn, damn, damn!'

Immediately James felt uncomfortable. What if there was someone listening? A few yards ahead, to the left, there was a lighted window. But suddenly he was alerted to something odd. There should not be a light on the left. The shop at the cross-roads should be on the other side. He looked around. Could that rotten little conductor have been right? Had he got off too soon. Perhaps that was why the fellow had hit that bell so smartly? To give him no time to discover his mistake?

For clearly he *had* made a mistake, and a bloody great one. He peered into the darkness. But the night was too black, he could see nothing. He had no choice but to walk on.

By the time James had passed the cottage with the lighted window, his eyes were getting more used to the dark. All the same, when a rick of hay reared up to one side of the road it might have been a mountain! Where was he at all? And a few seconds later when unexpectedly the moon slipped out from behind the clouds and glinted on the tin roof of a shed in the distance, it might have been the sheen of a lake for all he recognized of his whereabouts. Just then, however, he caught sight of the red tail-light of the bus again. It had only disappeared because the bus had dipped into a valley. It was now climbing out of the dip again, and going up a steep hill. Ah! he knew that hill. He wasn't as far off his track as he thought. Only a quarter of a mile or so, but he shook his head. In his present state that was about enough to finish him. Still, things could have been worse.

Meanwhile a wisp of vapoury cloud had come between the moon and the earth, and in a few minutes it was followed by a great black bank of cloud. Only for a thin green streak in the west it would have been pitch dark again. This streak shed no light on his way, but it acted on James like a sign, an omen.

He passed the hayrick. He passed the tin shed. But now another mass of blackness rose up to the left and came between him and the sky. It even hid the green streak this time, though he was able to tell by a sudden resinous scent in the air and a curious warmth that the road was passing through a small wood. His spirits rose at once. These were trees he could see from his cottage. Immediately, his mistake less disastrous, the distance lessened. If only that conductor could know how quickly he had got his bearings! The impudent fellow probably thought he'd left him properly stranded. And, perhaps as much to spite the impudent fellow as anything else, at that instant a daring thought entered his mind and he gave it heed. What if he were to cut diagonally across this wood? It could save him half a mile. It would actually be putting his mistake to work for him.

'What about it, James? Come on. Be a sport,' he jovially exhorted himself.

And seeing that his green banner was again faintly discernible through the dark trees, he called on it to be his lodestar, and scrambled up on the grass bank that separated the road from the wood.

James was in the wood before it came home to him that of course this must be Asigh wood – it must belong to the Balfes! No matter. Why should he let that bother him? The wood was nowhere near their house as far as he remembered its position by daylight. It was composed mostly of neglected, self-seeded trees, more scrub than timber – almost waste ground – ground that had probably deteriorated into commonage.

As he advanced into the little copse – wood was too grand a designation for it – James saw it was not as dense as it seemed from the road, or else at this point there was a pathway through it. Probably it was a short-cut well known to the locals, because, even in the dark, he thought he saw sodden cigarette packets on the ground, and there were toffee wrappers and orange peels lodged in the bushes. Good signs.

Further in, however, his path was unexpectedly blocked by a fallen tree. It must have been a long time lying on the ground because, when he put his hand on it to climb over, it was wet and slimy. He quickly withdrew his hand in disgust. He'd have to make his way round it.

The path was not very well defined on the other side of the log. It looked as if people did not after all penetrate this far. The litter at the edge of the wood had probably been left by children! Or by lovers who only wanted to get out of sight of the road? Deeper in, the scrub was thicker, and in one place he mistook a strand of briar for barbed wire, it was so tough and hard to cut through. You'd need wire clippers!

James stopped. Was it foolhardy to go on? He'd already ripped the sleeve of his suit. However, the pain in his stomach gave him his answer. Nothing that would get him home quicker was foolish.

'Onward, James,' he said wearily.

And then, damn it, he came to another fallen tree. Again he had to work his way around it. Mind you, he hadn't counted on this kind of thing. The upper branches of this tree spread out over an incredibly wide area. From having to look down, instead of up, he found that – momentarily of course – he'd lost his sense of direction. Fortunately, through the trees, he could take direction from his green banner. Fixing on it, he forged ahead.

But now there were new hazards. At least twice, tree stumps nearly tripped him, and there were now dried ruts that must have been made by timber lorries at some distant date. Lucky he didn't sprain his ankle. He took out his handkerchief and wiped his forehead. At this rate he wouldn't make very quick progress. He was beginning to ache in every limb, and when he drew a breath, a sharp pain ran through him. The pains in his stomach were indistinguishable now from all the other pains in his body. It was like the way a toothache could turn the whole of one's face into one great ache. The thought of turning back plagued him too at every step. Stubbornly, though, he resisted the thought of turning. To go on could hardly be much worse than to go back through those briars?

A second later James got a fall, a nasty fall. Without warning, a crater opened up in front of him and he went head-first into it. Another fallen tree, blown over in a storm evidently, because the great root that had been ripped out of the ground had taken clay and all with it, leaving this gaping black hole. Oh God! He picked himself up and mopped his forehead with his sleeves.

This time he had to make a wide detour. Luckily after that the wood seemed to be thinning out. He was able to walk a bit faster, and so it seemed reasonable to deduce that he might be getting near to the road at the other end. His relief was so great that perhaps that was why he did not pause to take his bearings again, and when he did look up he was shocked to see the green streak in the sky was gone. Or had it? He swung around. No, it was there, but it seemed to have veered around and was now behind him. Did that mean he was going in the wrong direction? Appalled, he leant back against a tree. His legs were giving way under him. He would not be able to go another step without a rest. And now a new pain had struck him between the shoulders. He felt around with his foot in the darkness looking for somewhere to sit, but all he could feel were wads of soggy leaves from summers dead and gone.

Perhaps it was just as well – if he sat down he might not be able to get up again. Then the matter was taken out of his hands. He was attacked by a fit of dizziness, and his head began to reel. To save himself from falling he dropped down on one knee and braced himself with the palms of his hands against the ground. Bad as he was, the irony of his posture struck him – the sprinter, tensed for the starter's pistol! Afraid of cramp he cautiously got to his feet. And he thought of the times when, as a youngster playing hide-and-seek, a rag would be tied over his eyes and he would be spun around like a top, so that when the blindfold was removed he wouldn't know which way to run.

Ah, there was the green light! But how it had narrowed! It was only a thin line now. Still, James lurched towards it. The bushes had got dense again and he was throwing himself against them, as against a crashing wave, while they for their part seemed to thrust him back. Coming to a really thick clump, he gathered up enough strength to hurl himself against it, only to find that he went through it as if it was a bank of fog, and sprawled out into another clearing.

Was it the road at last? No. It would have been lighter overhead. Instead a solid mass of blackness towered over him, high as the sky. Were it not for his lifeline of light, he would have despaired. As if it too might quench, he feverishly fastened his eyes on it. It was not a single line any more. There were three or four lines. Oh God, no? It was a window, a window with a green blind drawn down, that let out only the outline of its light. A house? Oh God, not Balfe's? In absolute panic James turned, and with the vigour of frenzy crashed back through the undergrowth in the way he had come. This time the bushes gave way freely before him, but the silence that had pressed so dank upon him was shattered at every step and he was betrayed by the snapping and breaking of twigs. When a briar caught on his sleeve it gave out a deafening rasp. Pricks from a gorse bush bit into his flesh like sparks of fire, but worse still was the prickly heat of shame that ran over his whole body.

'Damn, damn, damn,' he cried, not caring suddenly what noise he made. Why had he run like that – like a madman – using up his last store of strength? What did he care about anyone or anything if only he could get out of this place? What if it was Balfe's? It was hardly the house. Probably an outbuilding. Or the quarters of a hired hand. Why hadn't he called out?

Sweat was breaking out all over him now, and he had to exert a superhuman strength not to let himself fall spent on the ground, because if he did he'd stay there. He wouldn't be able to get up. To rest for a minute he dropped on one knee again. The pose of the athlete again! Oh, it was a pity Myra couldn't see him, he thought bitterly, but then for a moment he had a crazy feeling that the pose was for real. He found himself tensing the muscles of his face, as if at any minute a real shot would blast off and he would spring up and dash madly down a grassy sprint-track.

It was then that a new, a terrible, an utterly unendurable pain exploded in his chest.

'God, God!' he cried. His hands under him were riveted to the ground. Had he been standing he would have been thrown. 'What is the matter with me?' he cried. And the question rang out over all the wood. Then, as another spasm went through him, other questions were torn from him. Was it a heart attack? A stroke? In abject terror, not daring to stir, he stayed crouched. 'Ah, Ah, Ahh ...' The pain again. The pain, the pain, the pain.

'Am I dying?' he gasped, but this time it was the pain that answered, and answered so strangely James didn't understand, because it did what he did not think possible: it catapulted him to his feet, and filled him with a strength that never, never in his life had he possessed. It ran through him like a bar of iron – a staunchion that held his ribs together. He was turned into a man of iron! If he raised his arms now and thrashed about, whole trees would give way before him, and their branches, brittle as glass, would clatter to the ground. 'See Myra! See!' he cried out. So he had lost his vigour? He'd show her! But he had taken his eyes off the light. Where was it? Had it gone out? 'I told you not to go out,' he yelled at it, and lifting his iron feet he went crashing towards where he had seen it last.

But the next minute he knew there was something wrong. Against his face he felt something wet and cold, and he was almost overpowered by the smell of rank earth and rotting leaves. If he'd fallen, he hadn't felt the fall. Was he numbed?

James raised his head. He'd have to get help. But when he tried to cry out, no sound came.

The light? Where was it? 'Oh, don't go out,' he pleaded to it, as if it was the light of life itself, and to propitiate it he gave it a name. 'Don't go out, Emmy,' he prayed. Then came the last and most anguished question of all. Was he raving? No, no. It was only a window. But in his head there seemed to be a dialogue of two voices, his own and another that answered derisively, 'What window?' James tried to explain that it was the window in the classroom. Hadn't he opened it when the big footballer wasn't able to pull down the sash, but he, James, had leant across the desk and brought it down with one strong pull. But where was the rush of sweet summer air? There was only a deathly chill. And where was Emmy?

Then, with a last desperate effort, James tried to stop his mind from stumbling and tried to fasten it on Myra. Where was *she*? She wouldn't have failed him. But she *had* failed him. Both of them had failed him. Under a weight of bitterness too great to be borne, his face was pressed into the wet leaves and, when he gulped for breath, the rotted leaves were sucked into his mouth.

The Game Cock

MICHAEL McLAVERTY

When I was young we came to Belfast and my father kept a game cock and a few hens. At the back of the street was waste ground where the fowl could scrape, and my father built a shed for them in the yard and sawed a hole in the back door so that they could hop in and out as they took the notion. In the mornings our cock was always first out on the waste ground.

We called him Dick, but he was none of your ordinary cocks, for he had a pedigree as long as your arm, and his grandfather and grandmother were of Indian breed. He was lovely to look at, with his long yellow legs, black glossy feathers in his chest and tail, and reddish streaky neck. In the long summer evenings my father would watch him for hours, smiling at the way he tore the clayey ground with his claws, coming on a large earwig, and calling the hens to share it. But one day when somebody landed him with a stone, my father grew so sad that he couldn't take his supper.

We had bought him from Jimmy Reilly, the blind man, and many an evening he came to handle him. I would be doing my school exercise at the kitchen table, my father, in his shirt sleeves, reading the paper. A knock would come to the door, and with great expectancy in his voice my father'd say, 'That's the men now. Let them in, son.'

And when I opened the door I'd say, 'Mind the step!' and in would shuffle wee Johnny Moore leading the blind man. They'd sit on the sofa: Jimmy Reilly, hat on head, and two fists clasped round the shank of the walking-stick between his legs; and Johnny Moore with a stinking clay pipe in his mouth.

As soon as they started the talk I'd put down my pen and listen to them.

'Sit up to the fire, men, and get a bit of the heat.'

'That's a snorer of a fire you've on, Mick,' would come from the blind man.

'What kind of coals is them?' says Johnny Moore, for he had my father pestered with questions.

'The best English; them's none of your Scotch slates!'

And what's the price of them a ton?'

'They cost a good penny,' my father would answer crossly.

'And where do you get them?'

The blind man's stick would rattle on the kitchen tiles and he'd push out his lower lip, stroke his beard and shout, 'They're good coals, anyway, no matter where they're got.' And then add in his slow natural voice, 'How's the cock, Mick?'

'He's in fine fettle, Jimmy. He's jumping out of his pelt.' And he'd tell how the comb was reddening and how he had chased Maguire's dunghill of a rooster from about the place. And the blind man would smile and say, 'That's the stuff! He'll soon have the walk to himself; other cocks would annoy him.'

With a lighted candle I would be sent out to the yard to lift Dick off his roost. The roosts were so low that the cock wouldn't bruise his feet when flying to the ground. He'd blink his eyes and cluck-cluck in his throat when I'd bring him into the gaslight and hand him to the blind man.

Jimmy fondled him like a woman fondling a cat. He gently stroked the neck and tail, and then stretched out one wing and then the other. 'He's in great condition. We could cut his comb and wattles any time and have him ready for Easter.' And he'd put him down on the tiles and listen to the scrape of his claws. Then he'd feel the muscles on the thighs, and stick out his beard with joy. 'There's no coldness about that fella, Mick. He has shoulders on him as broad as a bulldog. Aw, my lovely fella,' feeling the limber of him as his claws pranced on the tiles. 'He'll do us credit. A hould ye he'll win a main.'

My father would stuff his hands in his pockets and rise off his heels, 'And you think he's doing well, Jimmy?'

'Hould yer tongue, man; I wish I was half as fit,' Jimmy would answer, his sightless eyes raised to the ceiling.

And one evening as they talked like this about the cock and forthcoming fights, Johnny Moore sneaked across to the table and gave me sums out of his head: A ropemaker made a rope for his marrying daughter, and in the rope he made twenty knots and in each knot he put a purse, and in each purse he put seven threepenny bits and nine halfpennies. How much of a dowry did the daughter get?

I couldn't get the answer and he took his pipe from his mouth and laughed loudly. 'The scholars, nowadays, have soft brains. You can't do it with your pencil and paper and an old man like me can do it in my head.'

My face burned as I said, 'But we don't learn them kind of sums.' He laughed so much that I was glad when it was time for him to lead the blind man home.

A few evenings afterwards they were back again; the blind man with special scissors to cut Dick's comb and wattles. Jimmy handed the scissors to my father, then he held the cock, his forefinger in its mouth and his thumb at the back of its head.

'Now, Mick,' said he, 'try and cut it in one stroke.'

When my sisters saw the chips of comb snipped off with the scissors and the blood falling on the tiles they began to cry, 'That's a sin, father! That's a sin!'

'Tush, tush,' said my father, and the blood on his sleeves. 'He doesn't feel it. It's like getting your hair cut. Isn't that right, Jimmy?'

'That's right; just like getting your toe-nails cut.'

But when Dick clucked and shook his head with pain, my sisters cried louder and were sent out to play, and I went into the scullery to gather cobwebs to stop the bleeding.

In a few days the blood had hardened and Dick was his old self again. The men came nearly every night and talked about the cock fights to be held near Toome at Easter. They made plans for Dick's training and arranged how he was to be fed.

About a fortnight before the fights my father got a long box and nailed loose sacking over the front to keep it in darkness.

Dick was put into this and his feathers and tail were clipped. For the first two days he got no feed so as to keep his weight down. Then we gave him hard-boiled eggs, but they didn't agree with him and made him scour. The blind man recommended a strict diet of barley and barley water. 'That's the stuff to keep his nerves strong and his blood up. A hould you it'll not scour him.'

Every morning we took him from his dark box and gave him a few runs up and down the yard. Johnny Moore had made a red flannel bag stuffed with straw, and Dick sparred at this daily, and when he had finished, my father would lift him in his arms, stroke him gently, and sponge the feet and head. Day by day the cock grew peevish, and once when he nebbed at me I gave him a clout that brought my father running to the yard.

The night before the fights the steel spurs were tied on him to see how he would look in the pit. 'Ah, Jimmy, if you could see him,' said my father to the blind man. 'He's the picture of health.'

The blind man fingered his beard and putting a hand in his pocket, took out a few pound notes and spat on them for luck. 'Put that on him tomorrow. There's not another cock this side of the Bann nor in all County Derry that could touch him.' Even Johnny Moore risked a few shillings, and the next morning before five o'clock my father wakened me to go to Toome.

It was Easter Monday and there were no trains running early so we set off to walk to the Northern Counties Railway to catch the half-six train. The cock was in a potato bag under my arm, and I got orders not to squeeze him, while my father carried the overcoats and a gladstone filled with things for my granny, who lived near the place where the cocks were to fight.

The streets were deserted, and our feet echoed in the chill air. Down the Falls Road we hurried. The shop-blinds were pulled down, the tram lines shining, and no smoke coming from the chimneys. At the Public Baths my father looked at his watch and then stood out in the road to see the exact time by the Baths' clock.

'Boys-a-boys, my watch is slow. We'll need to hurry.' In the excitement the cock got his neb out and pecked at me. I dropped the bag, and out jumped the cock and raced across the tram lines, the two of us after him.

'Don't excite him, son. Take him gently.' We tried to corner him in a doorway, my father with his hand outstretched calling in his sweetest way, 'Dick, Dick, Dicky.' But as soon as he stooped to lift him, the cock dived between his legs, and raced up North Howard Street, and stood contemplating a dark-green public lavatory.

'Whisht,' said my father, holding my arm as I went to go forward. 'Whisht! If he goes in there we'll nab him.'

The cock stood, head erect, and looked up and down the bare street. Then he scraped each side of his bill on the step of the lavatory and crowed into the morning.

'Man, but that's the brazen tinker of a cock for you,' said my father, looking at his watch. And then, as if Dick were entering the hen-shed, in he walked, and in after him tiptoed my father, and out by the roofless top flew the cock with a few feathers falling from him.

I swished him off the top and he flew for all he was worth over the tram lines, down Alma Street and up on a yard wall.

'We'll be late for the train if we don't catch him quick, and maybe have the peelers down on us before we know where we are.'

Up on the wall I was heaved and sat with legs astride. The cock walked away from me, and a dog in the yard yelped and jumped up the back door.

'I'm afraid, Da, I'm afraid.'

'Come down out of that and don't whinge there.'

A baby started to cry and a man looked out of a window and shouted, 'What the hell's wrong?'

'We're after a cock,' replied my father apologetically.

The man continued to lean out of the window in his shirt, and a woman yelled from the same room, 'Throw a bucket of water round them, Andy. A nice time of the morning to be chasing a bloody rooster.'

Here and there a back door opened and barefooted men in

their shirts and trousers came into the entry. They all chased after Dick.

'Ah, easy, easy,' said my father to a man who was swiping at Dick savagely with a yard-brush. 'Don't hit him with that.'

By this time the cock had walked half way down the entry, still keeping to the top of yard walls. Women shouted and dogs barked, and all the time I could hear my father saying, 'If we don't catch him quick we'll miss the train.'

'Aw,' said one man, looking at the scaldy appearance of the cock. 'Sure he's not worth botherin' about. There's not as much on him as'd set a rat-trap.'

My father kept silent about Dick's pedigree for he didn't want anyone to know about the cockfights, and maybe have the police after us.

We had now reached the end of the entry and Dick flew off the wall and under a little handcart that stood in a corner. Five men bunched in after him, and screeching and scolding the cock was handed to my father.

'I can feel his heart going like a traction engine,' he said, when we were on the road again. 'He'll be bate. The blind man's money and everybody's money will be lost. Lost!'

We broke into a trot, I carrying the gladstone, and my father the cock and the overcoats. Along York Street we raced, gazing up at the big clocks and watching the hands approach half-six. Sweat broke out on us and a stitch came in my side, but I said nothing as I lagged along trying to keep pace.

We ran into the station and were just into the carriage when out went the train.

'Aw-aw-aw,' said my father, sighing out all his breath in one puff. 'I'm done. Punctured! That's a nice start for an Easter Monday!'

He took off his hard hat and pulled out a handkerchief. His bald head was speckled with sweat and the hat had made a red groove on his brow. He puffed and ah-ee-d so many times I thought he'd faint, and I sat with my heart thumping, my shirt clammy with sweat, waiting with fear for what he'd say. But he didn't scold me.

'It was my own fault,' he said. 'I should have tied a bit of string round the neck of the bag. He'll be bate! He'll be bate!'

He took the spurs from his pocket and pulled the corks off the steel points. 'I might as well strap them on a jackdaw as put them on Dick this day, for he'll be tore asunder after that performance.'

As the train raced into the country we saw the land covered with a thin mist, and ploughed fields with shining furrows. The cold morning air came into the carriage; it was lovely and fresh. My father's breathing became quieter, and he even pointed out farms that would make great 'walks' for cocks. It was going to be a grand day: a foggy sun was bursting through, and crows flew around trees that were laden with their nests.

Dick was taken from the bag and petted; and then my father stretched himself out on the seat and fell asleep. I watched the telegraph wires rising and falling, and kept a lookout for the strange birds that were cut out in the hedge near Doagh.

When we came to Toome my father tied the neck of the bag with a handkerchief and sent me on in front for fear the police might suspect something. The one-streeted village was shady and cool, the sun skimming the house-tops. Pieces of straw littered the roads, and a few hens stood at the closed barrack door, their droppings on the doorstep.

We passed quickly through the silent village and turned on to the long country road that led to my granny's. Behind us the train rumbled and whistled over the bridge; and then across the still country came the dull cheer of the Bann waterfall and the wind astir in the leafing branches. Once my father told me to sit and rest myself while he crossed a few fields to a white cottage. It wasn't long until he was back again. 'I've got the stuff in my pocket that'll make him gallop. The boys in Lough Beg made a run of poteen for Easter.'

When we reached my granny's she was standing at the door, a string garter fallen round her ankle, and a basin in her hand; near her my uncle's bicycle was turned upside down and he was mending a puncture. They had a great welcome for us and smiled when my father put the poteen on the table. He took tumblers from the dresser, filled one for my granny, and in another he softened a few pieces of bread for the cock.

My granny sat at the fire and at every sip she sighed and held the glass up to the light. 'Poor fellas, but they run great risks to make that. None of your ould treacle about the Lough Beg stuff ... made from the best of barley.'

As she sipped it she talked to me about my school, and the little sense my father had in his head to be bothering himself about game cocks and maybe land himself in jail; and when the car came up for him she went to the door and waved him off. 'Mind the peelers,' she shouted. 'Ye'd never know where they'd be sniffing around.'

During the day I played about the house and tormented the tethered goat, making her rise on her hind legs. I went to the well at the foot of the field and carried a bucket of water to my granny, and she said I was a big, strong man. Later my uncle brought me through the tumbled demesne wall and showed me where he had slaughtered a few trees for the fire. I talked to him about Dick and I asked him why he didn't keep game cocks. He laughed at me and said, 'I wouldn't have them about the place. They destroy the hens and make them as wild as the rooks.' I didn't talk any more about game cocks, but all the time we walked to the Big House I thought about Dick and wondered would he win his fights. The Big House was in ruins, crows were nesting in the chimneys, and the lake was covered with rushes and green scum. When I asked my uncle where were all the ladies and gentlemen and the gamekeeper, he spat through the naked windows and replied, 'They took the land from the people and God cursed them.'

When we came back my granny was standing at the door looking up and down the road wondering what was keeping my father. A few fellows coming from the cockfights passed on bicycles, and soon my father arrived. He was in great form, his face red, and his navy-blue trousers covered with clay.

The cock's comb was scratched with blood, his feathers streaky, and his eyes half shut. He was left in the byre until the tea was over. While my father was taking the tea he got up from the table and stood in the middle of the floor telling how Dick had won his fights. 'Five battles he won and gave away weight twice.'

'Take your tea, Mick, and you can tell us after,' my granny said, her hands in her sleeves, and her feet tapping the hearth.

He would eat for a few minutes and he'd be up again. 'Be the holy frost if you'd seen him tumbling the big Pyle cock from Derry, it'd have done yer heart good. I never seen the like of it. Aw, he's a great battler. And look at the morning he put in on them yard walls ... up and down a dozen streets he went, running and flying and crowing. And then to win his fights. Wait till Jimmy Reilly hears about this and the nice nest egg I have for him. The poteen was great stuff. A great warrior!' And he smiled in recollection.

I was glad when he was ready for home and gladder still when we were in the train where I made the wheels rumble and chant: *They took the land from the people ... God cursed them.*

It was dark when we reached Belfast and I carried Dick in the potato bag. We got into a tram at the station; the lights were lit and we sat downstairs. The people were staring at my father, at the clabber on his boots and the wrinkles on his trousers. But he paid no heed to them. In the plate glass opposite I could see our reflections; my father was smiling with his lips together, and I knew he was thinking of the cock.

'He's very quiet, Da,' I whispered. 'The fightin' has fairly knocked the capers out of him.'

'Aw, son, he's a great warrior,' and he put his hand in his pocket and slipped me a half-crown. 'I'll get his photo took as soon as he's his old self again.'

I held the money tightly in my hand, and all the way home I rejoiced that Johnny Moore wasn't with us, for he would have set me a problem about a half-crown.

In the kitchen I left my bag on the floor and sat on the sofa, dead tired. My father got down the olive oil to rub on Dick's legs, but when he opened the bag the cock never stirred. He took him out gently and raised his head, but it fell forward limply, and from the open mouth blood dripped to the floor.

'God-a-God, he's dead!' said my father, stretching out one of the wings. He held up the cock's head in the gaslight and looked at him. Then he put him on the table without a word and sat on a chair. For awhile I said nothing, and then I asked quietly, 'What'll you do with him, Da?'

He turned and looked at the cock, stretched out on the table. 'Poor Dick!' he said. And I felt a lump rise in my throat.

Then he got up from the chair. 'What'll I do with him! What'll I do with him! I'll get him stuffed! That's what I'll do with him!'

The American Apples

SEAMUS DE FAOITE

THE only plants she had grown before were geraniums. They blossomed for her the way cats purr for spinsters. I can't recall the names of the varieties but I remember the blossoms: the one that was a crimson stray – away from elegance and somehow a stranger to all but herself in the place, the pinks with a blush that set with the sun on the youth of our grandmothers, the purples, the red that was a rose without smell and the white that smelled like a veil away for years in lavender. I know with what prim docility they grew for her in greying earth in sweet-tins brought from shops to the sills of the rooms in New Lane where we lived.

As an altar boy I went often on to the High Altar of the Cathedral when the priest away below in the pulpit droned the last prayers of Holy Hour. I would fit the long lighted taper into the brass tube on the cone cowl of the extinguisher and light the hundreds of candles, from the Tabernacle all the way down red-carpeted steps to the patterned tiles of the Sanctuary. Every cluster of candles I lit raised a richness of flowers out of stained-glassed dusk. Flowers from the hot-houses of the earl and the agent and the manager and the doctor; in root and on stem they were there in their thousands, smelling like cool incense, but never was there a geranium in the lot that was better than my mother's.

Even that the sweet-tins had discreet burial there in urns of beaten brass and bronze, I used to recognize her few flowers when my butterfly flame hovered over them, holding their own with the best.

So when the old man laughed on the day of the apples, I let

laughter alone while she prised the pips from the hearts with her nail: no hard task because the brother and I had gnawed our way to the core. They were sleek, cider-wry yellow apples, freckled where they had out-bowed leaf shade on the branch.

She was sitting on the edge of the chair near the hearth. The hat she had bought, after fourteen years in Boston, to her wedding, flaunted the wear and tear in fur felt with one defiant feather. The black nap of the coat that travelled with it wore a silver clip in the right lapel for the same reason. The ten years since she was twenty-five showed in her heart-shaped face only in a slight slackness of flesh below her chin.

The brother sat cross-legged on the floor looking up at her. I too sat on the floor between a basket of groceries and two heads of cabbage. The old man stood over us, hat at angle, thumb hooked to the watch pocket of his waistcoat.

While she had shopped he was detailed to have an eye on the brother and me in that one of two rooms near the slates of a two-storey tenement, and his ear had been at full cock for her step on the cobbles. Tap-a-tap-tap she came, eighteen to the dozen down the lane, in the hall and up the stairs. He drew on his hat, poked for pipe and plug, and felt for coin in pants pockets, but by then she was in at the door. One in each hand she held the apples, the basket on her arm and the cabbages cuddled by her elbows.

'Look what I got for the boys,' she said, a bit breathless, her eyes making more of the gift than was usual.

'Apples!'

'More, boys!'

'What, woman?' asked the father.

'American apples!' she said.

'Only that you told us, they could be out of Pat Carty's sour half-acre in Ballydribeen,' the old man joked.

'Here Michael, here Kevin,' she said, and then put her load on the floor.

'Eat them,' she urged, before we had a tooth in them.

'God, I thought we were to have them under a glass globe with a lamp burning in worship of their highnesses,' the old man said.

'I'm not rushing ye, boys,' she told us, 'but I'm going to keep the seeds and save them till 'tis spring again. I'll save the seeds.'

'And save your soul,' mocked the old man.

'If saving seeds would save a soul I'd have to rob an orchard for yours.'

'A Boston orchard.'

'One tree out of a Boston orchard would do.'

'No, woman, mine is one Irish soul that's not for sale in American dollars.'

'I brought my soul home with me, and some dollars too,' she snapped.

When she held the seeds in her palm the old man laughed. Moving to the door, he ballad-sang:

> 'The Yanks are coming,
> You can hear them humming
> Over there . . .'

She pretended not to hear as she put the seeds in an envelope and put the envelope between the Sacred Heart picture and the warmth of the hob.

'Over there. Neither here nor there,' mocked the old man in the doorway.

'When spring comes we'll see,' she called after him as he went to slake a summer thirst.

The lane gave spring no easy coming amongst us. Flowering weeds had laboured birth in old mortar along old walls. Grass stems over-reached in lankness so that bright green tips might show between and above the slug-backed cobbles. House-bound old people had to wait for their cage-bound birds to sing again before they could be sure that they had weathered another winter. But ahead of weed and grass and finch song, she took the seeds from hob-warmth. Next morning she took a distemper tin with her to her usual first Mass at the Friary. Coming home, she reached through the Friary railings for fists of earth from a flower-bed. Then on she came with another tinful of monastery garden for her sills.

She waited until the hour between the father's going to work and ours to school before she brought tin and seeds together on the sill. School bags on hip, the brother and I watched her prod four holes in the earth with one of the old man's chisels and drop a seed into each hole.

A murmur of mist soothered on the lane. Rain beads roped and broke along the rusty shute above the open window.

'A wonderful day to plant seeds, but bad for the pay-packet if it gets any more rainy, so you don't know where you are,' she told us. 'A stone set in damp, sweats for years after, whereas a seed set in mist is set in growth, they say. Ye remember ye said the apples were nice tasted?' We said we did.

'Were they really sweet?'

'Sweet with a tang.'

'And juicy?'

'Oh, yes.'

'Remember how they looked myself. Yellowy-goldy and marked like blackbirds' eggs. Maybe from these four seeds four trees of them will grow. The ways of God are wonderful.' She looked from the tins to us and back to the tins again. 'I wonder are they that wonderful?' Then, wide-eyed, she looked at me and said: 'Oh, God forgive me.'

'We can say a prayer,' Kevin encouraged in all earnestness and her laughter raced up and down and up its scale. Then, suddenly serious herself, she said: 'School now; off to school; school is important.'

'I wonder do I know about that looney Cromwell's killings all over the country?' Kevin asked, scratching behind an ear.

'We can say a prayer,' she mimicked, laughing again. 'But you do, Kevin,' she added, all concern.

But Kevin's sleepy-headed solemnity was too much for her. Her laughter followed us down the stairs. When we reached the lane her serious face was waiting over the sill of flowers for us.

'Kevin, Cromwell happened in sixteen-something. He was a bad man, but the strange thing was that when he had slaught-ered hundreds of people he – '

'I know,' Kevin interrupted. He gave her one of his slow-fashion grins. 'He said a prayer.'

The three of us laughed that time. Then Kevin butted his

thick thatch into the mist with the two steps he always held ahead of me. I listened to her laughter gentling over the planted seeds and wondered idly whether a thing would grow from them.

I don't think she wondered though. So far as I know she never wondered where her gift for growing things came from. She was bred of a lane like our lane, daughter of a stone-mason, married to a stone-mason bred of a lane that like ours was wrought of stone, paved with stone that let nothing of root thrive on it but lichen and moss and nothing between but the weed and the striplet of grass. In fact our lane's very bareness may have been a reason why she wanted us out of it, but certain it is that she wanted Kevin and me to stay longer in school than our kind, to have Boston at home, no less, and she had an idea that a lane was a bad start for that.

Two years from the morning of the seeds she had us a walk distant from town in a stone house that had two cat-swings of flower pot in front, a crusty quarter-acre of one-time common-age to pass for garden at the back. How that came about is another story. But in the way the peacock-feather and the silver clip had more to be defiant about everyday.

But a bank manager had been persuaded that a meagre-enough warren of dollars would bed and breed issue with docile rows of shillings kidnapped on the roll from a four-pound pay-packet to butcher, baker, grocer, tailor and the old man's pocket on Saturday pay-day, when there was pay. Urban coun-cillors were persuaded that the manager was persuaded that the old man was convinced that the age of miracles was not dead.

The old man argued, angered, mocked and then laughed the way he did about the seeds. But it was on the night that we left the lane for the house in the country that he had reason to remember the seeds again.

Daylight for the flitting would be merciless on the few sticks of furniture, she thought, and her hopes were answered by an October night without moon or stars. In a rumble of iron-shod wheels Mick Breen's dray lantern rocked down the lane like a buoy-light in an inshore harbour. The shoes of his Clydesdale chipped flint sparks big as match-spurts off the cobbles. The

old man's face loomed bronze-like in the museum half-glow
of the lantern before Mick knew who he had and where he was.

She helped the lantern with her hob-lamp in the doorway
while the old man gave Mick a hand. The old man held the
lamp while she fetched the geraniums tin by tin for careful
placing in a packing case at the back of the dray. When the
last geranium was in place and she faced for the house he asked
her: 'What now?'

'You'll see,' she told him.

Mick put me sitting on a folded sack under a sleek slope of
the horse's rump and put the lantern in my grip. 'The heat of
it will keep you warm,' he told me. He himself sat opposite,
with Kevin in the old man's timber armchair, in line with the
horse's tail, between us. With her footsteps in the hall came
the old man's question:

'And what the hell might they be, woman?'

'Two Boston apple trees to save your soul.'

'Well, I'll be damned.'

'Not if you don't decide to leave us before these two little
plants that grew are trees.'

'Put them in the ould box with the flowers.'

'Indeed I will not.'

'Then what'll you do, woman?'

'Why, carry them myself, of course.'

'Not with me, you won't.'

'Then I'll have to walk alone.'

'You damn well will.'

She was standing in the doorway with the tins held against
her body. He was facing her with the hob-lamp still lighting
in his hand.

'It will be a poor journey to the new house if I have to
walk alone to it,' she said.

'Then dump the ould weeds out of my sight,' he said.

'They're not weeds. They're only stems with a few leaves now
but they'll be trees one day.'

'All right, put 'em in the box.'

'No,' she insisted, and as if to ease over the firm finality of
the word she added: 'They had the courage to grow in the old

house so 'twould be a shame if anything happened them before
they saw the new house.'

'Their ould lad saw the new world, isn't that enough?' he
jibed, but you could tell that he was near the end of patience.
Her answer did not help either.

'They're going to a new world now. I'm taking them there
myself.'

'What!' he cried, and on the word she tried a pleasantry.

'A wonder the lamp wouldn't help you to see light.'

She could hardly have said a more unsuitable thing. Suddenly made aware of the lamp he saw how ridiculous he looked.

'To hell with the light,' he cried, swinging the lamp arm
violently. The lamp arced over the dray and quenched in a
globe-burst against the blank wall opposite. The horse heaved
forward. The dray rattled my teeth together. I had a glimpse
of the mother following on with the tins before I had to look
ahead for balance on the jigging perch. Sound of the wheels
must have been listened for by the neighbours. Door after door
to lane's end opened. Families called out of kitchen glow of
light and warmth 'God go with ye, good luck, safe home!'

When I could venture to look back I saw her and the old
man walking together through doorway light. She was bowing
and smiling like a celebrity on parade. He was carrying the
seedlings in their tins.

On more and roomier sills of windows more generous with
light she tended her tin-can garden throughout the winter,
but I think that from Christmas onward she watched through
the windows for the spring. Back of the house she saw fields
swell in a green wave to foam along the skyline into firs. The
air was full of free birds' wings. The air itself felt free, it
seemed to have hinted to her about spring even before the
trees or the fields or the birds showed awareness of it. Anyhow
she was out one morning in the back plot with a digging fork
where a skim of frost tinselled in sun that had only lit to
boast about.

Again it was in that hour between the old man's departure
for work and ours for school. Small-spare in the quarter-acre
she picked at the hard earth like a robin at a crust in the
school yard. Her palms let down her will-power in that first

day but she had done enough for the old man to notice the
bird scratch on the alligator hide of our domain. He was
always suspicious of her motives in these displays of industry,
especially in departments where he felt she must have known
how futile her own attempts must be. He never could decide
how much honest effort went into the work and how much was
stage-setting for intimidation to stalk on and leer up at his
place in the gods.

To be on the safe side he staged a show of his own: champ-
ing, tossing his head at the roof, roaring murder to the rafters,
then blaspheming his way to a door-bang exit for the fork
to the toolshed to dig between dinner and dark of that evening
– and every evening after he pick-axed and forked in that plot
till the crows flapped home to their rookery-ring of beeches.
So when spring came down the hill of fields she was there in
the torn earth, intimidating with a young tree in each hand,
the empty distemper tins beside the cast-off work-boots of the
old man.

I can't recall how many springs went by before the men of
the house realized that the way of God with trees was wonderful after all. She had known before us that her forlorn-looking
hopes had bole and branch and leaf. Her worry had been that
never in any spring had the trees held blossoms and never in
autumn were there apples to pick. Every spring she had watched,
but for every summer there was only leaf for every autumn to
wither.

Her garden otherwise was all that a garden should be.
Cabbages, carrots, parsnips, radishes, rhubarb, thyme; currants
like drops of claret and sherry and currants black as pitch
blobs; gooseberries green and bitter, gooseberries red and
amber and kind; raspberries, strawberries, melons and parsley
thronged from the earth to her. All of them travelled with
her in baskets to market to keep the shillings rolling dollar-
wards in the bank for the house. The shilling that came home
with her travelled back on other days to pay for each term
of mine as a day-boy in the town's seminary and out of town
once a week to Kevin, who had got a scholarship to a college
a train-day journey up country.

Hardly a root stirred in the earth without her knowing. Cat-like she watched for weeds and pounced on them, bearing them away by the apronful to dump under the privet hedge where cats slumbered with one eye awake for other quarry. With the slumbering cats' quietness of pleasure she saw the colour of the crops richen between soil and stalk and stem and leaf. But always, I think, there was one dreaming eye on the apple trees, and year by year the dream was chilling in it.

Then one Saturday afternoon, when the garden was prostrate in autumnal dying and the trees humped in a tattered shroud of withering, the old man stood at the kitchen back window looking out at them, kindling his pipe, smoke oozing about the hat he had on for the road to a pub with pay-day substance. Without moving his gaze from the garden he said: 'I see the Yanks are yet to come?'

The flat-iron slowed to a stop on his shirt for Mass in the morning. Still looking at the kitchen table top she said with careful carelessness: 'I know that well.'

'I wonder is it how the haggart isn't grand enough for 'em?'

'The trees weren't too grand to grow in it.'

'Like hens without eggs, only we could eat the hens.'

'And use the trees for firing,' she countered.

'Green burning,' he gave back, going to the front door. 'Is there anything you want from town?'

'You home early and sober,' she told him.

He laughed and closed the door. She finished her ironing without a word, cleared the table and then went to look out the window. I was greasing the leather of a football boot out of washboard curl and stiffness.

'I wonder why the trees don't bear fruit, Michael?' she asked me without turning.

'I don't know,' I said.

With that the old man returned to the doorway.

'Do you know where Tommy Cronin lives, Mick? I couldn't know his pub because he never takes a wet, but you knock around with his son?'

He went when I told him where Tommy lived. I wondered at his closing the door as if there was a child to wake with the sound of the lock. But in the feel of the silence he left after him

I knew why. She was at the core of it, and my gaze was drawn
by it to her. Her stillness might have had no breathing in it, so
still she stood, yet the silence it summoned to her had unease.
Hers was the blank back of a woman in a moment when she
relinquishes yet another illusion to leak away from her in
tears. When she turned there were no tears but I caught her
unawares by the look I had not time to take away from her.
She winced at it, recovered instantly, but what she meant for a
smile of not-caring ended in one of never-mind.

Without a word she went through the pantry into the yard. I
heard her poking in the toolshed. I took a turn at the window
myself, in time to see her walk up the centre path of the
garden towards the apple trees, standing together in an oval
green patch half-way up. Her hands were held in front of her.
Her back had lost anonymity now, as when the belief relinquished makes room for a belief less easy to give home to. She
looked who she was, but not quite what she had been, somehow.

When she was some paces from the oval she paused for an
instant, then she walked on purposefully and went sidewise on
her knees beside the right-hand tree. With a sweep she rasped
the teeth of a saw through tender bark to blossom-white pith
of the young tree and sawed till the shock head bowed inch
by inch, to collapse in a sigh of near-spent leaves on to the
ground. When she stepped over the stump towards the comrade tree I felt I should persuade her to stop, without quite
knowing why. I was in the act of moving when she paused in
the act of kneeling. She straightened slowly and looked intently
from the lowest to the highest branch of that remaining tree.
Then she let the saw fall from her hand, stood on for another
moment and walked back quickly towards the house.

I schooled my impulse to look up from the boots when she
arrived in the kitchen. Between the laying of a saucer and a
cup she paused.

'I cut one of the trees, Michael,' she said. Before I could
comment she ran on with 'I was going to cut the other but I felt
that the patch would be bare without something in it.' She
paused again, the pause of an instant, then she added:
'Wouldn't that be the thing?'

'Just so,' I said, without any inflection whatever.

There was a longer pause then, as if my saying of my say left the situation wholly hers again.

'What would you like for tea, Michael?' she asked me suddenly, and I felt as if she were home from a journey.

That evening, on plea of a football club meeting, I got away to a fourpenny hop in the Old Town Hall. The evening felt as if winter was near enough to have chilled it with the breath of cold that I could feel at the open neck of my shirt. I had gone several hundred yards when I heard her calling my name. When I turned she was running towards me with my mackintosh. The manner of her running made me see how worn-out-of-time she was going. The heart shape of her face was that of an old heart now and in the folds of loose flesh under her chin I could see the pulse-beats of an old heart floundering in her breathlessness.

'Those meeting rooms are draughty, Michael, and there is quite a cold out this evening. Better wear your coat.'

I was about to refuse it when I remembered I had in mind to lure a harpie from the dance and that the coat would be handy. I took the coat.

'Goodbye now, Michael,' she said as if we had not met for a year and would not meet again for another.

On her way back to the house she paused to wave to me but after the second occasion I looked back no more.

The harpie delayed me longer than I bargained for, and I walked home under a mooned midnight, bright as a wan-gone noon. The key was in the front-door lock and I let myself into the hall without a sound. My hand was on the kitchen light-switch when I saw her shape between me and the smouldering fire.

I switched on the light. With what had been a rich blue dressing-gown, gold roped on the edges – the last remaining item of her American trousseau – now gone to fadedness, she sat slippered in the old man's armchair in front of the fire. She turned to look at me intently, her hair hanging loose about her face from a shoe-string on her nape.

'Michael, this is no hour for a seminary boy to come home. What would the priests say if they knew of it?'

'The meeting was heated and lasted longer than anyone thought,' I lied.

'Besides, 'tis after twelve and you can't have supper, going to Communion in the morning.'

'I'm not hungry,' I said.

'And your father has not come home yet. Drinking money that we could do with to hold house and home where he is the only wage-earner, while I run myself to rags to keep up appearances in ye. 'Tis at the point now that one week of idleness for him and disaster faces all my hopes.'

The banging of the front gate and a lurched step signalled the old man's coming in his cups. Slurring of footsoles on concrete told of effort to find balance before facing the four steps and the pathway to the door.

'Come quickly. Leave the light on or he'll brain himself. If he finds you here there'll be questions about where you were.'

She pulled me by the arm after her up the stairs. We were hardly on the landing before he fell in at the door. She held me until he had picked himself up, telling himself to steady up, let there be no panic, woman and children first and God for us all. Without question of the light in the kitchen he side-stepped into it in a half keel-over that ended in the slap of his palm against the hob to keep from falling again. When the chair-joints screeched under his sudden weight she relaxed her grip on my wrist. She firmed it again in reassurance, put a finger to her lips and tip-toed to her room. I followed suit to mine.

Moonlight through the open window had transformed it into a place of grace like a mendicant's cell. A moth fluttering upstream towards the moon's face was ivory white as a prayer of grace under way might be. When I thought of the harpie, the thought felt like a stain, but I brought it with me to the ivory moth in the moonlight and looked out the window. I felt I was fighting that pure fierce light with my life for re-possession of a room that had been mine, and that the harpie was merely a spectator at the struggle, leer-luring with her eyes for my eyes under a loop of her oil-heavy hair. Moonlight was focused direct upon the earth, with such intensity that the butt of the cut tree showed like a bleached wound in the withered garden.

A chair crashed in the kitchen and the old man's unsteady steps sounded through the pantry. The back door banged open. The steps stumbled across the yard and presently I could see him hatless at the garden gate. Up the centre path he went, his head huddled in his left shoulder-blade, his left hand straight out, like a punch-drunk has-been of the ring reliving in perpetuity the moment before the final crash to canvas. When he was four paces from the trees he stopped in his tracks. After a long pause the outstretched hand counted one-two, one-two where the comrade trees should have been; then one, and one again it counted, then it wove a nought over the fallen tree. He was talking aloud but I could not hear what he was saying.

He blundered up to the rooted tree and gripped a branch. Holding on with one hand he groped in his pocket with the other. What he removed from the pocket was recognizable when the two hands came to play on it and a blade flashed for an instant in the moonlight. His pocket-knife. Head down he butted through the lower branches of the tree to the bole. Then round the bole slowly, carefully he groped, his right hand obviously working on it all the time.

When he had come full circle he shadow-boxed down the garden to the house again, face swollen, eyes glazed, to make the punch-drunk likeness nearer true than ever. Through the house he barged without closing a door; up the stairs and into their room.

'What the hell happened up there?' he shouted in the room doorway.

'Up where?' she asked, coolly and firm.

'Woman, I said!!'

'What now?'

'That tree!'

'Oh, I cut it down with the saw.'

'What did you do that for?'

'Why shouldn't I?'

'Why should you?'

'Up to now 'twas you supplied all the reasons for that. The Yanks are coming. Dump the old weeds. A hen without eggs.'

That last gave him pause. Sufficient for her to run in explanation: 'Trees without fruit have no place in that garden. Fruit would sell and we need all we can sell with our purse the way it is and our commitments the way they are.'

'Was that what you were thinking when you saved the seeds and planted 'em?'

'Times have changed.'

'And who the hell changed 'em?'

'I did. And 'tis up to me to see to it, as far as I can, that the change is for the better.'

'By God, 'tis mighty practical you got of a sudden.'

'I'm practical now, yes.'

'Full-blown practical.'

'Yes, I have to be.'

'Then why didn't you cut down the second tree?'

After a pause she said: 'Come to bed and don't disgrace us with that shouting.'

'I'll shout all I like, when I like, how I like and where I like.'

'Come to bed.'

'Listen, woman,' he shouted, 'leave that second tree.'

I lay on the bed for a while, hearing his voice drone on in querulousness, then drowsiness, then it was lost into silence and snoring. I went down to close the doors. At the back door, curiosity got the better of me and I went up the garden to the apple tree. A band of bark was cut with surprising neatness from the bole at the point where he had used the knife. I wondered why. Then I remembered that the Tommy Cronin he had inquired about last evening was by way of being a gardener.

From that I guessed correctly that, by what seemed to me like rule of thumb, he had performed a grafting operation on the barren tree. I never told him I knew about it. She neither knew nor noticed that it had been done.

She had other things to occupy her mind. Christmas ended the best of winter in beginning a period of idleness for the old man. She dreaded idleness for many reasons, he for one special reason, his inability to live without working. Signing at the Labour Exchange hurt his dignity in craft and taking the

palmful of silver every Friday seemed to him like cadging,
doing Judas on his principles.

He would return from signing with a paper in his pocket and
read slowly through patched-up spectacles, rising to pace the
kitchen, window to window, when his eyes got tired of a
combination of bad glasses and unlovely print.

Noticeable in particular was the restlessness of his squat
strong hands. Again and again he would anchor them with
his thumbs to his leather belt but always they broke free to
poke for a pipe he could not light that often on short tobacco,
to grope in trousers pocket for coin that was not there, to
punish each other's leathern palms with prominent knuckles
or plunder a matchbox for stems to chew to ease his craving
for tobacco. His hands seemed to live a life of their own in a
period like that. They were of him but not quite with him,
like gun-dogs fidgeting about the master's heels on a day when
hills held promise for the hunt.

She made much to-do with little and less to do with. She
whipped lean meals to lively meal-times with rush and bustle
in the making. Her bustle irritated him because he was missing
the customary pint off the neck of the bottle before drawing his
chair to table. His careful pacing between the windows irritated
her because it seemed to knell the futility of her make-believe
when the meals were met by hunger. They snapped at each
other when their minds met, then they stood on opposite
sides of a palpable silence. Buff bank envelopes cut with elegant
edge to the heart of the matter at intervals. Then the wedding-
present silver and the mantel clock and her American gold
watch travelled with her to the pawn shop. In the lane she
would have had her dollars to draw on. In crop-time she would
have had baskets for market. Now there was an arid garden
and in the centre a barren tree.

Until spring. Spring's first flowering showed on her geraniums.
Tending them eased odd hours for her between house chores
and questing visits to chapel. Spring brought the fork to the
old man's hands and they drove it into the earth, with a will
for the job that in time of craft they had done with contumely.
Spring brought sun to the sills, song to the silence, growth
to the soil and leaves to the apple tree.

Spring brought her into the garden to plant while he prepared the ground ahead of her. In the first days she looked at the leafing tree when she entered the garden. She did that every day, until the third or fourth day after leafing was complete, and the tree looked as if it had given all it could to the year and was content. I can say that with certainty because, in guise of study at the window of my room, I brooded on how I was going to ease over to her the fact that I was not going on for the priesthood; my reason for going to the seminary in the first place and her strongest wish.

I was at the window on the morning that the tree had blossom for the sun, a white froth of blossom broken by the leaves so it looked like the lace on a surplice, a garland for a bride, a quilt for a marriage bed.

The old man had seen it first because he was in the garden before I came to the window. She came into the garden with an apron of seed potatoes, dragging the loose boots. Propped by the handle of the spade in his armpit the old man watched her as she moved along the drill spacing the seed, her cloth-bound head bowing towards the tree. Seeing me at the window the old man nodded at the tree and beckoned me down. When I arrived in the garden her unconsciously ceremonial, ritual-like bows in the spacing of the seed had brought her blue-clothed head under the white blossom. She put seed in the last place, put her hands on the small of her back to help her straighten. Her head touched a branch of blossom as it raised, then the branch flicked before her like a wand and she was looking at the transformed tree. Her body tensed. She stood staring at the tree without expression for several seconds. Then 'Oh, oh, oh,' she whispered. Then hardly above a whisper, 'Oh, oh, oh God, isn't it lovely!'

Her face broke on all its lines into a smile. Her eyes brightened slowly from glow to real brightness. The left-over potato seed dropped on her boots and she was walking into the tree. She walked right on into the bole. She cupped her palms about the slim stem.

'Michael, Dad! Look at my tree, look at my tree!' she called.

'The Yanks are here at last,' said the old man.

'Oh, God, isn't it lovely?' she cried.

With a smile she emerged out of the tree looking straight at the old man.

'Now didn't I tell you I would have a fruiting tree,' she said.

He said: 'Wonders will never cease,' then he began to smooth the earth over the drill of new-set potato seed. Before she could turn her smile towards me I walked down the garden, away from both of them.

First Conjugation

JULIA O'FAOLAIN

SHE was from Cremona: a patrician creature in her forties, who had followed her refugee husband to our town and taught Italian in our local university. Her colleagues here were peasants' grandsons abandoned by ambition at the top of Ireland's academic tree. Noncoms in an army with nowhere to go, they treated their meek students with weary irony. Among them, the signora's presence was like moonlight in a well. Each glimpse of her was tonic in that tight, cast-concrete arena where the inner walls were painted a washable urine-green.

She alone supplied the hyper-vividness I had expected from college and did so in the first few weeks. In their academic gowns, other teachers became moulting crows or funeral mutes. She wore hers like a ball-dress and her green-shadowed Parmigianino neck rose thrillingly from between its gathered billows. Her hair circled her head with the austere vigour of black mountain-streams. Her body moved like channelled water and she had a higher charge of life than anyone I had ever seen.

Her controlled vibrancy enthralled me, as did an aloof pity for our simplicity, and the prodigality with which, perhaps for her private amusement, she proposed considerations too fine for our grasp. Had I been a male student I would have been in love with her.

As it was, her beauty set standards towards which, despairingly, I aspired. At night in bed I thought of her, sometimes making up stories in which I won her esteem, sometimes letting myself become her and move through marvellous though

shadowy adventures. At sixteen I was pursuing my waking
dreams with flagging zest. I longed for something actual to
happen and was beginning to think of men. To reconcile my
yearnings, I, as the signora, fancied I was courted by a man.
'Oh thou,' he whispered, 'art wondrous as the evening air/
In wanton Arethusa's azure arms ...' Who was he? It was hard
to give him a face, for I did not know any worthy men. Only
students who, if they were not clerics, were pimply, or had
necks like plucked quails, or faces, as my friend Ita put it,
'like babies' bottoms': a sexual disgrace to any girl they might
approach. Not that they approached Ita or me. Or rather, only
Nick Lucy did, whose sad puffy face appeared with inappro-
priate suddenness in my dream, staring with his hang-dog
look at me-the-signora just as he stared at me-myself every
morning in the coffee shop.

Clot! Squirt! How *dare* he disturb my private fancies! I
hated him! Maybe he was thinking of me? Telepathically
bullying me into thinking of *him*? At the thought that no one
but Nick Lucy would do the like I bit the pillow with rage.

'Hold on to Nick,' Ita had recommended that morning
when he'd gone to buy us both some doughnuts. 'He'll be
useful!'

'He's awful-looking!'

'They all are,' said Ita looking round the coffee shop. 'We've
no choice.'

'Mike McGillacuddy isn't so bad,' I argued. 'You wouldn't
go round with him if he looked like Nick!'

'Mike's ghastly really,' said Ita; 'he's stuck on himself! But
he has VV.'

'What's that?'

'Vehicular value: VV! It means he has a car. A fellow with
a car can take you places where you meet other fellows. If you
stay home, you never meet any. No fear of *them* coming looking for us!'

'Well, Nick has no VV – car.'

'One car's enough,' Ita said. 'But we need a man each. Don't
you see! Any sort of stooge will do so long as we can go
to a dance with him or into a pub. Girls can't go into pubs alone
and *that's* where you meet men. When we meet some attractive

ones, we can drop the stooges. So my sister says. She says Irish fellows don't *like* girls,' Ita explained patiently, 'so it has to be a tough chase with no holds barred.'

Ita's sister was four years older than we and engaged, so she, I supposed, must know. I agreed to put up with Nick.

'Though,' I said, 'he gives me the creeps.'

He did. In the last few months my body had become an Aeolian harp, resonant to the slightest breath. If I stirred the down on my arms or the nape of my neck with a pencil tip, pleasure rippled up my spine. When Nick Lucy picked books from my desk, the brush of his sleeve against my cheek had the toad pressure of jellied frogspawn.

'Put down those books, Lucy! I don't want you carrying my books!'

'O.K., O.K., spitfire!' he said and went off, sauntering and hurt, for he was as moody and torn by yens as myself.

'She's awful to me,' he said to Ita.

'Ah,' Ita said as people do, 'she likes you really.'

I didn't. I was embarrassed by him: a pasty drip whose plight, however, upset me. For I knew he dreamed of me as I did of Signora Perruzzi and that I had 'led him on'. I knew a gawky face was not the emanation of a gawky soul, but that handsome was as handsome did. Or I tried to know. Yes! Yes! But the leaven of my sensuality was stuck deep in the dough of snobbery. I couldn't *make* myself like him, could I? The man who would set my veins foaming was going to have to be spiffing to look at, dream-standard, unlike poor Nick whose plainness seemed somehow contagious.

'Don't follow me to Italian class,' I told him.

I could be kind to him at coffee or, better still, in the leaf-screened alleys of the college grounds where he amused me with stories of his country childhood; but I dreaded being seen with him by the signora. Nick's niceness was not of the sort that met the eye, and I imagined *her* eye as more exacting than my own. Her high-arched brows looked ironic, and I could not imagine her tall neck flexing in pity. Or didn't want to imagine it.

To show he wouldn't be bullied, Nick followed me to Italian class anyhow, and sat in the back row drawing my profile.

I ignored him. It was 'conversation' where the signora gave
of her best. She must have been dazzling in the Fascist *salons*
of ten years before. Now she exercised her high-powered
weapons on three seminarists, four nuns, a few flat-vowelled
peasants from the midlands, and myself. I strained towards her.
Why had she had to leave Italy? Why wound up in this
provincial stopping-place from which we all – even the four
blue nuns bound eventually to nurse Florentine aristocrats and
Prato businessmen – intended to progress? What war crimes
were hers that she taught here for a pittance, wasting her corus-
cations in this pee-green room, under the bare electric light
bulb and the painted-over crucifix on the wall? (A Radical
professor had insisted on having all crucifixes in the classrooms
painted over and now, it was rumoured, objected on political
grounds to the signora's being on the staff. The pale patch
hung behind her like a reproof.)

'In our patriotic time in Italy,' the signora sighed, 'we used
the *voi* not the *Lei*. It is nearer the ancient Roman *tu*.'

She laughed an opulent laugh. Unnecessarily lavish, its
throatiness evoked the pile of deep carpets and the fur of
snuggly coats in a Lombard winter. She was a gay, not a pitiful,
exile. 'The Romans,' she said sweetly, 'were democratic. The
Lei was a subservient Spanish importation.'

Nick, whose father had been in the British army, muttered
in the back row.

I turned round. 'Shut up!' I whispered.

When I looked back up, the signora's eyes were on me. She
frowned. Then her lips formed a brief, tight smile.

'I see,' she cried sprightly. 'You are impatient for conversation! Well, *I* shall converse and you may note my phrases,
since your Italian is perhaps not up to replying. What,' she
murmured dreamily, 'shall we discuss? I have it: love. Love is
the great Italian subject. Or so,' she mocked, 'foreigners think.
Who care for it perhaps more than Italians themselves. Well, we
have the verb *amare*, first conjugation, regular. *Io amo*, I love.
Tu ami' – she beamed her attention at a point in the back
row, and I stirred apprehensively – 'you love. *Tu ami la ragazza*'
– unbelievably, she was addressing herself to Nick – 'you love

the girl,' she told him. '*Egli ama*, he loves.' She turned to the others, and nodded so unmistakably, first in Nick's direction and then in mine, that even the blue nuns giggled and stared from him to me. 'He loves the girl,' said the cruel signora. Oh belle dame sans merci! Dry-mouthed, I listened in horror. She was more beautiful than ever. And bad! Just as I had supposed! But why with me? Why? 'He comes to class because he loves the girl. *Ella ama*, or *essa*, or we may say *lei ama*,' said Signora Perruzzi with maddening sloth, 'may all mean – for Italian is a rich language – she loves.'

I felt as though she were putting worms on me, as though she were stripping and streaking me with filth. 'If she couples me with him again ... If she says ...' I could not think what she might say next. Had she X-ray eyes? Did she know I had worshipped her? Was this her way of refusing my devotion? I felt the paralysing embarrassment, the shame I used to feel as a child when I was dreaming out loud and suddenly suspected that my brother had crept under my bed to surprise and deride me. The agony of those few seconds while I used to grope for the electric light switch returned, now realized and suffocating. 'I'll get up,' I thought weakly, 'I'll walk out.' It was Nick I loathed even while the signora tormented me. 'He's enjoying this,' I thought with ferocious injustice, 'he's happy at being connected with me.' *Odiare*, to hate, supplied my grammar: First Conjugation, regular.

' "Does she love him?" ' pronounced the signora, 'may be rendered in Italian without any inversion: *Lei lo ama?*' She stared at me. '*Lo ama?*' she repeated inquiringly, 'which may also mean "do *you* love him?" Do you?' she asked me. 'Do you?'

I picked up my books and left the room.

As I passed the four nuns, their sleek, blue-veiled heads bent low over the verbs of the First Conjugation.

That's all: a child's humiliation. Even as 'my most embarrassing moment', it would hardly rate in competition with men who lost their trunks on the beach or girls surprised in haircurlers by their suitors. Signora Perruzzi, if she remembered

her own teens, may have felt a tiny twinge of compunction.
But more likely not. How could she know on what tumid, thin-
skinned areas she had trodden, or that for me the offence was
absolute?

I, absorbed in the symmetrics of my own taboos, was just
as unaware of her – the real signora. And when I hurt her, it
was not a planned *quid pro quo*, but the random flailing
movement of a creature uncertain of its own location.

In the next few weeks she tried to win me round, inviting
me to her flat where she had little Italian evenings with fried
polenta and great moments from Italian opera on records.
Before the pivotal conversation class (B.C.), nothing would have
given me more joy. Now I refused. Her verve, I fancy, flagged
a little under my disdain. She could *have* her flat-vowelled
midlanders, seminarists and nuns. I stayed aloof. I did agree
to do a paper on D'Annunzio for the Modern Language
Society, but only to deride the poet of 'our patriotic time in
Italy'. She gave me good marks. She had not noticed my
idolizing of herself and did not seem to care when I attacked
her idol.

And then our worlds impinged.

A bachelor friend of my parents begged me to come and
make sandwiches for an adult party he was giving and, as a
reward, invited me to stay. It was a musical party to celebrate
the arrival in our town of a well-known pianist, and among
the guests was Signor Perruzzi, my signora's husband. She
herself did not come.

He couldn't have been more than half her height.

'Are you sure,' I asked my host, 'that that's he?'

'Yes,' he said, 'that's Signor Perruzzi.'

He was a fat blackbird of a fellow from Rome with all his
weight tilted forward, so that his evening tails rose a little on
his behind, as though he were constantly considering leaning
over to kiss someone's hand. He had a lively blackberry eye,
a wet mouth and warm jolly contours to a face which didn't
have a single hollow in it. He was altogether astonishingly unlike
his wife, and kept flinging little candied cherries into his mouth
which puffed his cheeks out so that he looked like Tweedledum.

And yet it was he, our host told me, who was the cause of their exile. He had been an ardent Fascist, had composed hymns and marching tunes for Mussolini, and had even committed imprudences during the days of the Badoglio government.

'Not only political, rather scabrous I gather. Something to do with assaulting a minor,' said the host and then, having looked at me, clearly decided to get off that tack. 'He can't go back,' he told me. 'And he can't get work. He was a well-known conductor, you know, but there's a ban against him. His anti-semitism ...'

'And she?' I asked, thinking of her green-tinged skin, her fine, violent face.

'Oh, she's just a housewife. Nobody has anything against *her*. She adores him and puts up with a lot. He's a bastard to her,' said the host and moved off to welcome someone new.

I was carrying a tray of sandwiches and moved towards Signor Perruzzi. Would he have one, I asked in careful Italian. He swung round. His hands revolved like a conjuror's. Words flowed with the rush of an open faucet. He was common, a stage Italian, a charm-vendor. He dished out technicolour, cream-topped compliments with the familiar phony friendliness of his Irish equivalent. I didn't need to know Rome to know *him*.

'*Ma guarda, guarda che bella signorina!*'

He lengthened the i-i-i of signorina as the Irish uncle-type would have done with that of cailín. ('Isn't she a gorgeous little cailín antirely!')

'And you know Italian? You are studying with my wife? Are all her students as pretty as you? No wonder she keeps them hidden!'

The tone was the same but the look in his fruity eyes was not. Unblinking, cat-like, they changed quality, seemed to change substance as they stared into mine. There was a shameless, peeled excitement in them which I had never seen, never imagined, and which contrasted disquietingly with the platitudes which emerged soothingly from his soft lips. 'Is she a good teacher?' he asked. The eyes were black basalt. 'She'll give you a Lombard accent! You should come and have lessons with me. I talk the best Italian. *Lingua toscana in bocca romana!* Do you know what that means? The Tuscan tongue in a Roman mouth!' His own tongue travelled the damp surface of his lips. Suddenly he leaned, almost toppled, towards me. He was smaller than I was – how much smaller than she? *'Conosce l'amore?'* he asked. 'Do you know love?' I stared at him. What could he mean? One *felt* love. How could one *know* it? And why was he asking *me* such a thing? Remembering how the signora had conjugated the verb to love, I blushed.

He did not smile as an Irishman might. His spearing gaze and my giggle were interrupted by our host who said that my father was leaving and that I should get my coat. I went, but on my way back passed Signor Perruzzi again. 'Going so soon?' he asked. 'Little girls have to get their beauty sleep!' His tone was light and I felt let down as though he had reneged on a promise. But at the door he was there again. 'When?' he whispered swiftly, for my father had already gone out to the lift.

'When what?'

'Our conversation lesson?'

'Oh,' I said, 'that was a joke, wasn't it?' and ran out to the landing. 'Goodbye,' I called. 'Give my regards to your wife.' As the lift went down I saw him turn. He was a fat little man.

I thought of him as I sat in Italian class, where the signora now seemed less marvellous to me. Coldly, I noted the wrinkles at the corners of her eyes. The poetry she liked to quote seemed soppy.

> 'Ecco settembre,' she read, 'O amore mio triste, sogneremo.
> In questo ciel l'estremo sogno si dileguerà.
> D'un pensoso dolore, settembre il ciel riempie,
> Gli languon sulle tempie, le rose dell'està.'

Was *he* her *amore triste*? What had our host meant by his being a bastard to her? Perruzzi's eyes came back to me when I closed my own, imperiously. Black, I thought, like beetles. Round and black like fresh excrement of goats. But that did not send them away.

Then one morning I took a book the signora had lent me
and went around to their flat. It was a Saturday and I thought
she might be out shopping as my mother often was on Saturday
mornings. Signor Perruzzi opened the door.

'Ah,' he said. 'The little signorina!'

Even in my flat-heeled shoes I was taller than he, but I
knew he had said 'little' to reassure me and exorcize something
imminent and furtive in the air.

'I brought back the signora's book,' I said and stood there.

He took it. 'Will you have a coffee?'

'If you're having some,' I said, 'thank you.' And I followed
him into the signora's kitchen.

It was an Irish kitchen, rented, with only a few foreign
touches: a half-moon-shaped meat-chopper, a coffee machine.
Signor Perruzzi reached up to the shelf for this. His hand
brushed my neck and I trembled. *'Piccola!'* He relinquished
the gadget on its shelf, took hold of my shoulders and, pulling
them downwards, kissed my neck which he could just reach.
He seized my two weakly struggling hands. *'Bambina,'* he
whispered and, squashing one hand into his tightly encased
stomach, started pushing it determinedly downwards. I jerked
it away, then, as he grabbed me, braced my knee against his
thigh and, freeing myself with a wrench, fell backwards to
collide with someone who had just opened the back door. It
was the signora who was arriving, loaded with parcels.

She gave a little scream: 'Eugenio!' then picked up her
fallen groceries and put them on the table.

I tried to stand up but my ankle was hurt and shot sharp
pains up my leg when I tried to lean on it. I had to sit on a
chair, massaging myself and waiting while Signor and Signora
Perruzzi quarrelled in rapid Italian. He screamed and she spoke
with calm, cold clarity so that anything I did understand
came from her. 'Ah no,' she kept saying, 'not again, not any
more!' And then: 'I'd rather leave right now!' And later:
'Scandal, I can't stand scandal! This one's only sixteen!' Neither
of them paid any attention to me and I had time to make two
or three more attempts to stand up and go, but each time my leg
collapsed under me and I had to sit back on the chair. It was

so dreadful to have to sit there listening that the pain was almost a relief. When finally Signor Perruzzi, after a particularly shrill crescendo of shouting, paused, bowed to me and walked with slow dignity out the inner door, I began to wonder whether the signora might not assault me physically. Guilt is an isolating feeling and I felt no pity for either of the Perruzzis. Not even wonder at myself. All I wanted was to get home as quickly as possible and forget.

'Are you hurt?' the signora asked quietly. She was probably as eager to get rid of me as I was to go. 'It's probably just a sprain. Lean on my shoulder. See if you can hop as far as the car and I'll give you a lift home.'

We did as she said and she drove me home without saying anything more. I kept looking out the window on my side and only once, when a van braked suddenly on the other side and gave me an excuse, did I glance at her face. It was expressionless but, from close up, the wrinkles were encroaching tendrils of shadow on the apricot lightness.

'This is our gate,' I said. 'Thank you for the lift. I think I can get out myself.' I didn't want her meeting my parents.

She faced me. 'I have to ask you something. It's important to me. You're old enough to understand . . .' Suddenly her lips were puckering. The Signora Perruzzi had begun to cry.

Ashamed for both of us, holding my hands tightly in my lap, I waited; I would not have known how to help her if I had still loved her and I did not love her.

'Did he,' she asked, 'did my husband ask you to come to the flat this morning? Did he tell you *I* would be there?'

I looked at her.

'Did he *ask* you to come?' she repeated a little sharply.

I hesitated and then: 'Yes,' I told her, 'yes, he did. He was most insistent,' I said, 'actually. I'm sorry about everything, Signora Perruzzi. Goodbye.'

I hopped out of the car by myself in spite of the pain and dragged myself inside our gate. When I heard the car drive off I called to the maid to come and help me.

'I fell,' I told her, 'getting off the bus.'

*

It was April, almost the end of the academic year. With the excuse of my ankle I was able to stay home and avoid going to any more Italian classes. In June we had exams. It was during the luncheon break, one examination day, that I ran into Signor Perruzzi in the college grounds. He was feeding the ducks with a little boy of about five, and I would have sneaked by behind their backs but that he caught sight of me and called: 'Signorina!'

'Hullo,' I said, gave him a great gush of a smile and rushed on.

But he ran after me. 'Signorina, wait! I have been wanting to ask ...' He was trotting to keep up with me, dragging the child by the hand, so I had to stop.

'Please,' I begged, 'can't we forget ...'

'No, no!' Signor Perruzzi's eyes leaped in all directions. He was no longer bouncy but deflated. Muddy, semi-circular shadows furrowed the flesh at the corners of his eyes and mouth. When he turned round to the child, he took the opportunity of checking up on the alley behind us. 'My son,' he explained. 'Say hullo,' he told the child but turned away from him at once. 'My wife has got the wrong impression,' he told me. 'It is most unfortunate. For reasons you can't know ...' he spoke rapidly and with a vague urgency. 'Most grave. For me. I must ask you to help me ...' His eyes shifted. 'You remember the last time ... we met? It was merely a moment of tenderness,' said Signor Perruzzi, while the child pulled out of his arm. 'An impulse. If *you* could tell my wife that. Tell her,' he begged, 'that it was not premeditated ...'

At that moment I saw the signora herself. 'Mama!' yelled the child, running towards her. The signora opened her arms to sweep it up and the black bat-wings of her B.A. gown closed vengefully around it. She strode towards us. Pitiful and repellent, the wrinkles in her face moved in the sun like the long-jointed legs of agonizing insects. Both she and her husband looked old to me.

'So,' she said in English, 'you continue to make appointments! My God, Eugenio, I cannot sleep, cannot work with worrying about a fresh scandal. If you would even pick on adults ...'

'Maria, I swear,' said her husband. 'There was no appointment. I just met the signorina by chance, two minutes ago. Ask her, I have never given her an appointment. *Ask* her!'

'I asked her the last time,' the signora retorted sourly, 'and she told me then that you *had* made an appointment to meet behind my back! And *you swore* then that there had been no appointment! Eugenio, it is too much ...'

This time, unhampered by any twisted ankle, I fled. As I went I could hear the ebb and suspiration of their voices incomprehensibly wrangling. Bitter, painful and obscure, the sounds pursued me across the garden.

I felt guilt of course, remorse which I buried as fast and deeply as I could. What, I argued with myself, could I do anyway? Even if I were to retract my lie, tell the signora that her husband had *not* invited me to their flat that morning or arranged to meet me in the college gardens, she would not believe me. Would she? Besides, wasn't he clearly a bad hat? A weak, lecherous, morally soft creature? I flailed in him my own uncertain shames. She would be well rid of him.

It was October and the start of a new academic year when I heard that she had returned with the child to Italy. She was looking for an annulment, it was thought, and he was hanging round town living on expedients. Eventually, I caught sight of him in the street, looking no longer like a blackbird but like a mournful thrush in a tweed coat which someone must have given him, for its padded shoulders drooped half-way to his elbow. He did not see me and I cannot remember if I spared him a passing regret.

I had given up Italian and was busy competing with Ita for the attentions of Nick Lucy who had become muscular, tanned and worldly during a summer in the south of France. If we ever did mention Signora Perruzzi after that, it was to laugh – happily – at the way she had made fun of us during conversation class.

Fairyland

PATRICK KAVANAGH

THOUGH the fairies had many strongholds in South Monaghan only once did I stumble into Fairyland. It was an Irish ass – that wisest of beasts – that led me out of it.

My mother wanted to visit a friend who lived beyond the Hill of Mullacrew. We got the loan of an ass and cart and one fine Sunday morning in summer set off. I was driving, and on the wrong side of the seat-board, too. Every time I lifted the stick to beat the ass I tilted my mother's hat. She said I was a bad driver. I should have sat on the right-hand side so as to give my whip-hand free play. The ass knew I was an amateur and took full advantage of it. I suppose he laughed.

'You'll destroy my good hat,' my mother said.

'That saves my poor back,' was probably what the ass was thinking.

We progressed fairly well on the outward journey. The road was dry. There was a fresh breeze blowing in from the Irish Sea. We met people going to Mass. Once or twice the ass shied at scraps of wind-blown newspaper. My mother gripped the side-board.

We arrived and saw my mother's friend. At the end of our stay it began to rain. We looked up at the sky and decided that the shower would blow off. The ass brayed. The rain held off till we were a mile on our way home and then it came down. Luckily we had a winnowing sheet in the cart. The winnowing sheet was for putting over the cart to shade it from the sun – the sun would loosen the shoeing on the wheels; it served as a rain-proof now. It was pouring when we passed over the Hill of Mullacrew. I saw the old fair-green through the holes in the winnowing sheet.

The ass made poor progress over the muddied roads.

The Hill of Mullacrew was a bald common without a tree or landmark on its crown. A flock of wild scraggy goats were carrying out manoeuvres on the Hill.

Around the Hill's base there stood half a dozen houses and the relics of oul' dacency in the form of two public houses.

Outside one of the pubs, we saw a man moping in the rain.

'Did ye see any bobbies?' he asked us. We said we didn't.

This man was on guard while the non-bona-fides quenched their Sunday thirst.

The roads around Mullacrew were a tangled skein; they were laid down by random and led everywhere and nowhere. My mother knew these roads well and we managed to pick our way till we came to the town of Louth. The town of Louth had seen better days. At one time all roads led there. One crooked street comprised the town.

All roads surely led to it and as far as we could make out none led from it. My mother knew the town well; she had lived there for a year and normally would have been a good guide through the maze of roads.

We encouraged the ass to take the most likely road. He grumbled a little. When we had gone down the road a half-mile or so my mother noticed it strange. It was still pouring rain. My mother inquired of a man standing on his doorway if we were on the right road for Inniskeen.

'Aw me poor woman,' he said, 'this road leads to the Mill o' Louth.'

He directed us to go back.

'The first turn on yer right after ye pass Watty Gernon's,' he said.

We turned the ass round. My mother knew Watty Gernon's house. We found a turning and took that way. The ass didn't seem too pleased. When we had gone a bit that road we came to a locked gate: the road was a cul-de-sac. Back again we went. We came to a blacksmith's forge. Around the anvil were a crowd of young men playing cards. We inquired the way to the town of Louth. My mother said to the men that if she got back to Louth she would be able to find the right road. The men in the forge were not of one mind.

'The best thing to do, woman,' one said, 'is to turn to yer left at Duffy's Cross.'

'No, that's an out-of-the-way road,' another contradicted. 'Go straight the way yer goin' and take the second turn to yer left.'

Several others gave this opinion, and surely this multitude of counsellors darkened wisdom. We travelled on. In about half an hour we came to the forge again; the blacksmith was standing in the door.

'In the Name of God, are ye here again?' he said.

'Indeed we are,' my mother said.

All that evening we drove around the wet roads. The poor ass was tired and as heartbroken as ourselves.

At one point the road was flooded; the ass refused to ford it and we were compelled to turn back.

'If we could only get back to Louth I'd be able to find the road,' my mother kept saying. But we couldn't get back to Louth.

We were in Fairyland, and it was a wet day.

Everything seemed strange. The folk we saw were not ordinary mortals.

I suggested letting the ass go what way he liked. I had often heard of people gone astray following the instinct in the shape of an ass after human reason had failed.

My mother agreed. There was nothing else for it. We gave the ass his head. I let the reins slack and the ass with his head bowed plodded along we knew not in what direction.

'This is Ballykelly,' my mother exclaimed shortly afterwards.

We were relieved. We were in our own familiar country.

When we got home father and all the household were watching at the gate.

'We had our eyes out on pot-sticks,' they said. 'Where were ye?'

'In Fairyland,' I answered.

Some days later I told the story to John Cassidy.

'Why didn't ye turn yer coats?' he said.

When old George heard the tale he felt like Saint Thomas when that Doubter who didn't doubt (Dostoevski was right, Saint Thomas believed all along) put his fingers into the wounds of Our Lord.

'Paddy,' George stared at me, 'ye were with the Wee Fellas.'

'Only for the ass we'd never escape,' I said.

'Indeed you would not,' he supported; 'sure the ass is a blessed animal.'

'They Also Serve . . .'

MERVYN WALL

ONE afternoon a middle-aged man walked up to the gateway of Dublin Castle. He had such a smart way of walking and held himself so upright that the policeman on duty had touched his helmet respectfully before he noticed the little man's outmoded and shabby clothes. Mr Carmody coughed nervously before he spoke.

'I beg your pardon. Is this Dublin Castle?'

The policeman stared down at him as if suspicious of a joke. 'Yes,' he admitted, 'it is.'

'I have an appointment with Mr Watkins,' Mr Carmody explained. 'Perhaps you would be so kind as to tell me where I would find him.'

The policeman looked him up and down and replied sternly:

'There are seven departments of government in the Castle and a staff of over two thousand.'

Mr Carmody shifted nervously.

'He's in the Department of Fisheries.'

The policeman moved two paces and stood with his arm stretched out like a signpost.

'Go down there,' he said, 'across the Lower Yard, round by the Chapel Royal, and when you come up against a blank wall, turn to the left.'

Mr Carmody began to thank him, but the policeman went on without heeding him.

'The Department of Fisheries is moving out today to another building, but you may get the man you're looking for if he hasn't left.'

Mr Carmody thanked him again, crooked his umbrella on

his arm and walked through the gates. He crossed the Lower Castle Yard, glancing up at the black battlements of the Wardrobe Tower. He turned the corner by the Chapel Royal, gazing with admiration at the Latin inscription over the doorway. He did exactly as the policeman had told him, and in a few minutes he came to a group standing round a door. Officials were hurrying in and out giving directions to some workmen who were loading filing boxes and bundles of papers on to a van. Mr Carmody went up to some young men who stood with waterproof coats folded over their arms.

'I beg your pardon,' he said, 'could you tell me if this is the Department of Fisheries?'

'Yes,' answered one, 'but we're moving out today to make room for Internal Affairs. Were you looking for anyone in particular?'

'I have an appointment with Mr Watkins,' explained Mr Carmody.

'I don't know that he hasn't left. Try the second floor, turn to the right, and when you come to a fire extinguisher it's the third door on the left.'

Mr Carmody thanked him and went in. He mounted two flights of stairs and, turning to the right, found himself on a landing from which he could see quite a number of fire extinguishers. He was standing in a narrow passage summoning up courage to enter one of the rooms when a door suddenly opened and out came a heavy table and pinned him to the opposite wall. From the other end of the table a workman's red face gazed across at him in astonishment. When Mr Carmody was released he thanked the workman and knocked at the first door he came to. A voice said: 'Come in,' and Mr Carmody hastily took off his bowler hat and entered. An elderly man was sitting at a table writing.

'Hello,' he said, 'have you come to move the safe?'

Mr Carmody said he had come to see Mr Watkins.

'I don't know that Watkins is in the building,' replied the elderly man. 'You see, we're vacating these offices. Is there anything I can do?'

Mr Carmody coughed with some embarrassment. 'Well, it

was about a post,' he said. 'I have been looking for a job for some time past, and someone, a friend of mine, spoke to Mr Watkins, who wrote to me to call and see him.'

The elderly man looked at him severely.

'You can't get into the Civil Service that way,' he said. 'You must pass a qualifying examination and receive a certificate of appointment from the Minister. Besides, I doubt if Mr Watkins – he holds a comparatively junior position.'

'It wasn't a post in the Civil Service,' Mr Carmody put in hurriedly. 'I thought he might know of something outside in the city. I thought he'd be able to give me some advice as to how I should proceed.'

The elderly man looked at Mr Carmody for a moment.

'How old are you?' he asked.

'Forty-two.'

The elderly man seemed to become suddenly embarrassed.

'You'd better wait for Mr Watkins,' he said.

He led the way to the door. Mr Carmody took his umbrella and followed. The elderly man tried to bring Mr Carmody up another flight of stairs, but he was prevented by two diminutive workmen who had got into difficulties with a large filing press at a place where the banisters curved.

'They're moving furniture,' said the elderly man. 'It's hardly safe to be out in the corridors.'

Mr Carmody agreed with him.

'You'd better wait in here,' the elderly man said, leading the way to a room at the end of the passage. 'I'll send in Watkins when he turns up.'

Mr Carmody thanked him and took the liberty of sitting down on the edge of a chair.

The room was small and ugly. There was a calendar on the wall with the day's date, 27th January 1922. The only furniture was the chair on which he was sitting; and a table littered with papers. Among them was a file of about forty typed pages of foolscap fixed together with a brass fastener. Mr Carmody blew off the dust and read: 'Suggested Scheme for the Industrial Development of the Ballinacorrig Oyster Beds.' He turned the first page and began to read with mild interest.

An hour passed. He suddenly realized that everything was very quiet. He could no longer hear the workmen in the passages. He tiptoed to the door, opened it and put out his head. For some time he heard nothing, then he became aware of approaching footsteps, and a young man turned the corner and came down the passage reading a sheet of paper as he walked, so that he did not see Mr Carmody until he was close by.

'Hello,' he said in a surprised voice when he saw Mr Carmody's head. 'Are you waiting for someone?'

Mr Carmody told him about his appointment.

'The Department of Fisheries has moved out,' said the young man, 'but, of course, if you have an appointment with someone, no doubt he'll turn up.'

He was a friendly young fellow with ginger hair, and he seemed to have time on his hands for he offered Mr Carmody a cigarette and loitered round the room talking for a bit.

'I'm from Internal Affairs,' he explained. 'We'll be moving in this evening, and they sent me on in advance with a list of the rooms we're to occupy. That's in case the Department of Arts and Crafts tries to grab any of our rooms. They're in the same building, you see. They're extending, too. They're getting some of these rooms Fisheries were in.'

'I didn't know two Government departments were ever housed in the same building,' said Mr Carmody.

'Oh, Lord, yes,' replied the young man, 'often. Just according as there's accommodation. In this building Arts and Crafts were all mixed up with Fisheries, one room one department, the next room the other department. They'll be all mixed up with us now.'

'A very remarkable system,' said Mr Carmody.

'Ah,' declared the ginger-headed young man, 'what does it matter? We get to know our own rooms quick enough, and a stranger has only to inquire.'

'A country's Civil Service is a wonderful organization,' said Mr Carmody.

'Ay,' grinned the young man. 'You see, it's only a few weeks since the Irish Government took over from the British. That's why all this changing of buildings is going on. And there have been practically no hitches. The Civil Service isn't really such a funny institution as people make out. It's slow in its movements, but it's sure.' He went to the window. 'I think I hear the Board of Works men arriving with the furniture. I wonder is this room of yours on my list.' He opened the door. 'Number 107. No. Arts and Crafts must be coming in here.'

'I hope Mr Watkins hasn't forgotten that he made an appointment with me,' said Mr Carmody, 'I'm sure I've been waiting over an hour.'

The young man hesitated at the door. 'He may have been delayed, there's so much confusion today on account of the staff moving out. Might be worth your while waiting for a bit, that's if you're not in a hurry anywhere.'

Mr Carmody assured him that he wasn't in a particular hurry anywhere and that he'd wait for another while.

'Goodbye now,' said the ginger-headed young man, and he went out.

Mr Carmody sat down again and, resting his head between his hands, went on with his reading. He was re-perusing Section 23, which was not at all clear, when the trampling of feet and an occasional crash informed him that Government furniture was once more being moved. He continued to read until the sounds of activity came to the corridor outside. He listened for a while, and then as he was getting anxious lest Mr Watkins had indeed forgotten him, he went over again and opened the door. Workmen were moving tables into the room next to his. An official stood alongside with a piece of paper and a red pencil in his hand. A workman came down the passage carrying a pile of papers.

'Arts and Crafts stuff,' he said.

'Right,' said the official. 'Bring them in.'

'What about the end room?' asked another. 'Is there anything to go in there?'

The official read the number over Mr Carmody's head, 107, and he consulted his list. 'No, we're not getting 107. Internal Affairs must be moving in there.'

'That's all, then?' asked the first workman.

'That's all,' said the official, and without as much as a glance at Mr Carmody they all went down the corridor.

For a few minutes he stood in the doorway, then he stepped

back into the room. 'That's queer,' he said to himself, 'this room is not on the Internal Affairs list and not on the Arts and Crafts list, and each of them thinks it belongs to the other department.'

He sat thinking what a great organization the Civil Service of a country was, and yet how easily a mistake like that could be made. Then he sat for a long time watching the light fade out of the sky above the roof of a tenement house in Ship Street. It was growing late in the afternoon, the room was no longer light, soon it would be half dark. He knew suddenly that Mr Watkins must have forgotten the appointment and that the right thing for him to do was to go away and call tomorrow at the new offices, wherever they were; but he found he was unwilling to go. His heart sickened when he thought of having to go out again into the chill fog of the city. He thought of the misery of his position, the heart-breaking search for a job, any job at all, and the interviews with successful patronizing men, which were such a hurt to his shyness and his pride.

Christ Church Cathedral bell sounded its warning notes, and then it slowly struck the hour. Four o'clock. He remembered his miserable lodgings where there was no fire and where the rent was not paid. He thought of the misery of having to go on living at all. 'I'll stay till five when they all go,' he said to himself; 'at least there are hot pipes here and the room is warm.' He got up and groped for the electric light switch. He took off his overcoat and hung it behind the door. Then he seated himself at the table again with his head in his hands and forced himself to go on with his reading.

Half past four had struck when he was surprised by a quick step in the passage and a knock at the door. A young man came in.

'Good evening,' he said briskly, laying on the table what seemed to be a list of names. 'I hardly know where I am with all this moving about of staff. What's your name, please?'

Mr Carmody told him, and the young man added the name quickly to the list.

'I'll be round on the thirty-first about eleven,' he said. 'You'll be here about that time I suppose?'

'Here?' said Mr Carmody.

'Yes, at eleven on Friday, the thirty-first. In this room.'

'Oh, you're from Mr Watkins?'

'No,' replied the young man, looking puzzled, 'from Mr O'Brien.'

'Oh,' said Mr Carmody, not understanding a word.

'I'll always be here at eleven,' said the young man. 'Good evening,' and he went out briskly, leaving Mr Carmody gaping after him in astonishment.

On Friday at eleven o'clock Mr Carmody sat in the room at the end of the corridor waiting for the young man to arrive. He did not understand why he was to be there, but he believed it was all connected in some way with the original appointment made by Mr Watkins. The room was unchanged, the table was still littered with abandoned papers. At five past eleven the young man came in, brisk as before, with a bundle of paper slips in his hand.

'Good morning,' he said. 'Awful work we have over in Finance, what with the change of Government and the staffs moving all round the city. Your name is –?'

'Carmody,' said the other, wondering what was going to happen next.

'Benedict Carmody,' said the young man selecting a slip of paper from his bundle and laying it on the table. 'I'll be here at the same time on the last day of next month. Good morning.'

When the door closed Mr Carmody gazed with amazement at the slip of paper. It was headed 'Department of Internal Affairs Vote' and it was a cheque for thirty pounds.

Mr Carmody has now been in occupation of the little room for seventeen years. He comes in every morning about a quarter to eleven and reads the newspaper, then he looks at the ceiling and smokes cigarettes through a long holder until lunchtime. He meditates at times on the vastness of a country's Civil Service and says to himself that it isn't such a funny institution as people make out. The 'Suggested Scheme for the Industrial Development of the Ballinacorrig Oyster Beds' lies permanently on the table before him, lest by not appearing to be at work he should give scandal to anyone who may come into his room by mistake. He is very rarely disturbed, however, since in his second year he wrote 'Private' on a sheet of paper and pasted it on the door. He feels himself perfectly secure, as the officials of each department no doubt imagine he belongs to the other one whenever they chance to see him in the passages, that is if they think about him at all.

In the afternoons he usually goes for a stroll through the streets or sits in one of the city parks until the evening editions of the newspapers come out. Sometimes he takes a week's or a fortnight's holiday, but he is always careful to be back on the last day of the month to receive a brisk young man with a bundle of cheques.

He has six years to run before he reaches the retiring age. He is beginning to worry about whether they will give him a pension.

A Meeting in Middle Age

WILLIAM TREVOR

'I AM Mrs da Tanka,' said Mrs da Tanka. 'Are you Mr Mileson?' The man nodded, and they walked together the length of the platform, seeking a compartment that might offer them a welcome, or failing that, and they knew the more likely, simple privacy. They carried each a small suitcase, Mrs da Tanka's of white leather or some material manufactured to resemble it, Mr Mileson's battered and black. They did not speak as they marched purposefully: they were strangers one to another, and in the noise and the bustle, examining the lighted windows of the carriages, there was little that might constructively be said.

'A ninety-nine years' lease,' Mr Mileson's father had said, 'taken out in 1862 by my grandfather, whom of course you never knew. Expiring in your lifetime, I fear. Yet you will by then be in a sound position to accept the misfortune. To renew what has come to an end; to keep the property in the family.' The property was an expression that glorified. The house was small and useful, one of a row, one of a kind easily found; but the lease when the time came was not renewable – which released Mr Mileson of a problem. Bachelor, childless, the end of the line, what use was a house to him for a further ninety-nine years?

Mrs da Tanka, sitting opposite him, drew a magazine from an assortment she carried. Then, checking herself, said: 'We could talk. Or do you prefer to conduct the business in silence?' She was a woman who filled, but did not overflow from, a fair-sized, elegant, quite expensive tweed suit. Her hair, which was grey, did not appear so; it was tightly held to her head, a reddish gold colour. Born into another class she would have been a chirpy woman; she guarded against her chirpiness, she disliked the quality in her. There was often laughter in her eyes, and as often as she felt it there she killed it by the severity of her manner.

'You must not feel embarrassment,' Mrs da Tanka said. 'We are beyond the age of giving in to awkwardness in a situation. You surely agree?'

Mr Mileson did not know. He did not know how or what he should feel. Analysing his feelings he could come to no conclusion. He supposed he was excited but it was more difficult than it seemed to track down the emotions. He was unable, therefore, to answer Mrs da Tanka. So he just smiled.

Mrs da Tanka, who had once been Mrs Horace Spire and was not likely to forget it, considered those days. It was a logical thing for her to do, for they were days that had come to an end as these present days were coming to an end. Termination was on her mind: to escape from Mrs da Tanka into Mrs Spire was a way of softening the worry that was with her now, and a way of seeing it in proportion to a lifetime.

'If that is what you want,' Horace had said, 'then by all means have it. Who shall do the dirty work – you or I?' This was his reply to her request for a divorce. In fact, at the time of speaking, the dirty work as he called it was already done: by both of them.

'It is a shock for me,' Horace had continued. 'I thought we could jangle along for many a day. Are you seriously involved elsewhere?'

In fact she was not, but finding herself involved at all reflected the inadequacy of her married life and revealed a vacuum that once had been love.

'We are better apart,' she had said. 'It is bad to get used to the habit of being together. We must take our chances while we may, while there is still time.'

In the railway carriage she recalled the conversation with vividness, especially that last sentence, most especially the last five words of it. The chance she had taken was da Tanka, eight years ago. 'My God,' she said aloud, 'what a pompous bastard he turned out to be.'

Mr Mileson had a couple of those weekly publications for which there is no accurate term in the language: a touch of a single colour on the front – floppy, half-intellectual things, somewhere between a journal and a magazine. While she had her honest mags. *Harper's. Vogue.* Shiny and smart and rather silly. Or so thought Mr Mileson. He had opened them at dentists' and doctors', leafed his way through the ridiculous advertisements and aptly titled model girls, unreal girls in unreal poses, devoid it seemed of sex, and half the time of life. So that was the kind of woman she was.

'Who?' said Mr Mileson.

'Oh, who else, good heavens! Da Tanka I mean.'

Eight years of da Tanka's broad back, so fat it might have been padded beneath the skin. He had often presented it to her; he was that kind of man. Busy, he claimed; preoccupied.

'I shall be telling you about da Tanka,' she said. 'There are interesting facets to the man; though God knows, he is scarcely interesting in himself.'

It was a worry, in any case, owning a house. Seeing to the roof; noticing the paint cracking on the outside, and thinking about damp in mysterious places. Better off he was, in the room in Swiss Cottage; cosier in winter. They'd pulled down the old house by now, with all the others in the road. Flats were there instead: bulking up to the sky, with a million or so windows. All the gardens were gone, all the gnomes and the Snow White dwarfs, all the winter bulbs and the little paths of crazy paving; the bird-baths and bird-boxes and bird-tables; the miniature sandpits, and the metal edging, ornate, for flower-beds.

'We must move with the times,' said Mrs da Tanka, and he realized that he had been speaking to her; or speaking aloud and projecting the remarks in her direction since she was there.

His mother had made the rockery. Aubretia and sarsaparilla and pinks and Christmas roses. Her brother, his uncle Edward, bearded and queer, brought seaside stones in his motor car. His father had shrugged his distaste for the project, as indeed for all projects of this nature, seeing the removal of stones from the seashore as being in some way disgraceful, even dishonest. Behind the rockery there were loganberries: thick, coarse, inedible fruit, never fully ripe. But nobody, certainly not Mr Mileson, had had the heart to pull away the bushes.

'Weeks would pass,' said Mrs da Tanka, 'without the exchange of a single significant sentence. We lived in the same house, ate the same meals, drove out in the same car, and all he would ever say was: "It is time the central heating was on." Or: "These windscreen-wipers aren't working." '

Mr Mileson didn't know whether she was talking about Mr da Tanka or Mr Spire. They seemed like the same man to him: shadowy, silent fellows who over the years had shared this woman with the well-tended hands.

'He will be wearing city clothes,' her friend had said, 'grey or nondescript. He is like anyone else except for his hat, which is big and black and eccentric.' An odd thing about him, the hat: like a wild oat almost.

There he had been, by the tobacco kiosk, punctual and expectant; gaunt of face, thin, fiftyish; with the old-fashioned hat and the weekly papers that somehow matched it, but did not match him.

'Now would you blame me, Mr Mileson? Would you blame me for seeking freedom from such a man?'

The hat lay now on the luggage-rack with his carefully folded overcoat. A lot of his head was bald, whitish and tender like good dripping. His eyes were sad, like those of a retriever puppy she had known in her childhood. Men are often like dogs, she thought; women more akin to cats. The train moved smoothly, with rhythm, through the night. She thought of da Tanka and Horace Spire, wondering where Spire was now. Opposite her, he thought about the ninety-nine-year lease and the two plates, one from last night's supper, the other from breakfast, that he had left unwashed in the room at Swiss Cottage.

'This seems your kind of place,' Mr Mileson said, surveying the hotel from its ornate hall.

'Gin and lemon, gin and lemon,' said Mrs da Tanka, matching the words with action: striding to the bar.

Mr Mileson had rum, feeling it a more suitable drink though he could not think why. 'My father drank rum with milk in it. An odd concoction.'

'Frightful, it sounds. Da Tanka is a whiskey man. My previous liked stout. Well, well, so here we are.'

Mr Mileson looked at her. 'Dinner is next on the agenda.'

But Mrs da Tanka was not to be moved. They sat while she drank many measures of the drink; and when they rose to demand dinner they discovered that the restaurant was closed and were ushered to a grill-room.

'You organized that badly, Mr Mileson.'

'I organized nothing. I know the rules of these places. I repeated them to you. You gave me no chance to organize.'

'A chop and an egg or something. Da Tanka at least could have got us soup.'

In 1931 Mr Mileson had committed fornication with the maid in his parents' house. It was the only occasion, and he was glad that adultery was not expected of him with Mrs da Tanka. In it she would be more experienced than he, and he did not relish the implication. The grill-room was lush and vulgar. 'This seems your kind of place,' Mr Mileson repeated rudely.

'At least it is warm. And the lights don't glare. Why not order some wine?'

Her husband must remain innocent. He was a person of importance, in the public eye. Mr Mileson's friend had repeated it, the friend who knew Mrs da Tanka's solicitor. All expenses paid, the friend had said, and a little fee as well. Nowadays Mr Mileson could do with little fees. And though at the time he had rejected the suggestion downright, he had later seen that friend – acquaintance really – in the pub he went to at half past twelve on Sundays, and had agreed to take part in the drama. It wasn't just the little fee; there was something rather like prestige in the thing; his name as co-respondent – now *there* was something you'd never have guessed! The hotel bill to find its way to Mrs da Tanka's husband who would pass it to his solicitor. Breakfast in bed, and remember the face of the maid who brought it. Pass the time of day with her, and make sure she remembered yours. Oh very nice, the man in the pub said, very nice Mrs da Tanka was – or so he was led to believe. He batted his eyes at Mr Mileson; but Mr Mileson said it didn't matter, surely, about Mrs da Tanka's niceness. He knew his duties: there was nothing personal about them. He'd do it himself, the man in the pub explained, only he'd never be able to keep his hands off an attractive middle-aged woman. That was the trouble about finding someone for the job.

'I've had a hard life,' Mrs da Tanka confided. 'Tonight I need your sympathy, Mr Mileson. Tell me I have your sympathy.' Her face and neck had reddened: chirpiness was breaking through.

In the house, in a cupboard beneath the stairs, he had kept his gardening boots. Big, heavy army boots, once his father's. He had worn them at weekends, poking about in the garden.

'The lease came to an end two years ago,' he told Mrs da Tanka. 'There I was with all that stuff, all my gardening tools, and the furniture and bric-à-brac of three generations to dispose of. I can tell you it wasn't easy to know what to throw away.'

'Mr Mileson, I don't like that waiter.'

Mr Mileson cut his steak with care: a three-cornered piece, neat and succulent. He loaded mushroom and mustard on it, added a sliver of potato and carried the lot to his mouth. He masticated and drank some wine.

'Do you know the waiter?'

Mrs da Tanka laughed unpleasantly; like ice cracking. 'Why should I know the waiter? I do not generally know waiters. Do you know the waiter?'

'I ask because you claim to dislike him.'

'May I not dislike him without an intimate knowledge of the man?'

'You may do as you please. It struck me as a premature decision, that is all.'

'What decision? What is premature? What are you talking about? Are you drunk?'

'The decision to dislike the waiter I thought to be premature. I do not know about being drunk. Probably I am a little. One has to keep one's spirits up.'

'Have you ever thought of wearing an eye-patch, Mr Mileson? I think it would suit you. You need distinction. Have you led an empty life? You give the impression of an empty life.'

'My life has been as many other lives. Empty of some things, full of others. I am in possession of all my sight, though. My eyes are real. Neither is a pretence. I see no call for an eye-patch.'

'It strikes me you see no call for anything. You have never lived, Mr Mileson.'

'I do not understand that.'

'Order us more wine.'

Mr Mileson indicated with his hand and the waiter approached. 'Some other waiter, please,' Mrs da Tanka cried. 'May we be served by another waiter?'

'Madam?' said the waiter.

'We do not take to you. Will you send another man to our table?'

'I am the only waiter on duty, madam.'

'It's quite all right,' said Mr Mileson.

'It's not quite all right. I will not have this man at our table, opening and dispensing wine.'

'Then we must go without.'

'I am the only waiter on duty, madam.'

'There are other employees of the hotel. Send us a porter or the girl at the reception.'

'It is not their duty, madam –'

'Oh nonsense, nonsense. Bring us the wine, man, and have no more to-do.'

Unruffled, the waiter moved away. Mrs da Tanka hummed a popular tune.

'Are you married, Mr Mileson? Have you in the past been married?'

'No, never married.'

'I have been married twice. I am married now. I am throwing the dice for the last time. God knows how I shall find myself. You are helping to shape my destiny. What a fuss that waiter made about the wine!'

'That is a little unfair. It was you, you know –'

'Behave like a gentleman, can't you? Be on my side since you are with me. Why must you turn on me? Have I harmed you?'

'No, no. I was merely establishing the truth.'

'Here is the man again with the wine. He is like a bird. Do you think he has wings strapped down beneath his waiter's clothes? You are like a bird,' she repeated, examining the waiter's face. 'Has some fowl played a part in your ancestry?'

'I think not, madam.'

'Though you cannot be sure. How can you be sure? How can you say you think not when you know nothing about it?'

The waiter poured the wine in silence. He was not embarrassed, Mr Mileson noted; not even angry.

'Bring coffee,' Mrs da Tanka said.

'Madam.'

'How servile waiters are! How I hate servility, Mr Mileson! I could not marry a servile man. I could not marry that waiter, not for all the tea in China.'

'I did not imagine you could. The waiter does not seem your sort.'

'He is your sort. You like him, I think. Shall I leave you to converse with him?'

'Really! What would I say to him? I know nothing about the waiter except what he is in a professional sense. I do not wish to know. It is not my habit to go about consorting with waiters after they have waited on me.'

'I am not to know that. I am not to know what your sort is, or what your personal and private habits are. How could I know? We have only just met.'

'You are clouding the issue.'

'You are as pompous as da Tanka. Da Tanka would say issue and clouding.'

'What your husband would say is no concern of mine.'

'You are meant to be my lover, Mr Mileson. Can't you act it a bit? My husband must concern you dearly. You must wish to tear him limb from limb. Do you wish it?'

'I have never met the man. I know nothing of him.'

'Well then, pretend. Pretend for the waiter's sake. Say something violent in the waiter's hearing. Break an oath. Blaspheme. Bang your fist on the table.'

'I was not told I should have to behave like that. It is against my nature.'

'What is your nature?'

'I'm shy and self-effacing.'

'You are an enemy to me. I don't understand your sort. You have not got on in the world. You take on commissions like this. Where is your self-respect?'

'Elsewhere in my character.'

'You have no personality.'

'That is a cliché. It means nothing.'

'Sweet nothings for lovers, Mr Mileson! Remember that.'

They left the grill-room and mounted the stairs in silence. In their bedroom Mrs da Tanka unpacked a dressing-gown. 'I shall undress in the bathroom. I shall be absent a matter of ten minutes.'

Mr Mileson slipped from his clothes into pyjamas. He brushed his teeth at the wash-basin, cleaned his nails and splashed a little water on his face. When Mrs da Tanka returned he was in bed.

To Mr Mileson she seemed a trifle bigger without her day-time clothes. He remembered corsets and other containing garments. He did not remark upon it.

Mrs da Tanka turned out the light and they lay without touching between the cold sheets of the double bed.

He would leave little behind, he thought. He would die and there would be the things in the room, rather a number of useless things with sentimental value only. Ornaments and ferns. Reproductions of paintings. A set of eggs, birds' eggs he had collected as a boy. They would pile all the junk together and probably try to burn it. Then perhaps they would light a couple of those fumigating candles in the room, because other people are insulting when other people die.

'Why did you not get married?' Mrs da Tanka said.

'Because I do not greatly care for women.' He said it, throwing caution to the winds, waiting for her attack.

'Are you a homosexual?'

The word shocked him. 'Of course I'm not.'

'I only asked. They go in for this kind of thing.'

'That does not make me one.'

'I often thought Horace Spire was more that way than any other. For all the attention he paid to me.'

As a child she had lived in Shropshire. In those days she loved the country, though without knowing, or wishing to know, the names of flowers or plants or trees. People said she looked like Alice in Wonderland.

'Have you ever been to Shropshire, Mr Mileson?'

'No. I am very much a Londoner. I lived in the same house all my life. Now the house is no longer there. Flats replace it. I live in Swiss Cottage.'

'I thought you might. I thought you might live in Swiss Cottage.'

'Now and again I miss the garden. As a child I collected birds' eggs on the common. I have kept them all these years.'

She had kept nothing. She cut the past off every so often, remembering it when she cared to, without the aid of physical evidence.

'The hard facts of life have taken their toll of me,' said Mrs da Tanka. 'I met them first at twenty. They have been my companions since.'

'It was a hard fact the lease coming to an end. It was hard to take at the time. I did not accept it until it was well upon me. Only the spring before I had planted new delphiniums.'

'My father told me to marry a good man. To be happy and have children. Then he died. I did none of those things. I do not know why except that I did not care to. Then old Horry Spire put his arm around me and there we were. Life is as you make it, I suppose. I was thinking of homosexual in relation to that waiter you were interested in downstairs.'

'I was not interested in the waiter. He was hard done by, by you, I thought. There was no more to it than that.'

Mrs da Tanka smoked and Mr Mileson was nervous; about the situation in general, about the glow of the cigarette in the darkness. What if the woman dropped off to sleep? He had heard of fires started by careless smoking. What if in her confusion she crushed the cigarette against some part of his body? Sleep was impossible: one cannot sleep with the thought of waking up in a furnace, with the bells of fire brigades clanging a death knell.

'I will not sleep tonight,' said Mrs da Tanka, a statement which frightened Mr Mileson further. For all the dark hours the awful woman would be there, twitching and puffing beside him. *I am mad. I am out of my mind to have brought this upon myself.* He heard the words. He saw them on paper written in his handwriting. He saw them typed, and repeated again as on a telegram. The letters jolted and lost their order. The words were confused, skulking behind a fog. 'I am mad,' Mr Mileson said, to establish the thought completely, to bring it into the open. It was a habit of his; for a moment he had forgotten the reason for the thought, thinking himself alone.

'Are you telling me now you are mad?' asked Mrs da Tanka, alarmed. 'Gracious, are you worse than a homo? Are you some sexual pervert? Is that what you are doing here? Certainly that was not my plan, I do assure you. You have nothing to gain from me, Mr Mileson. If there is trouble I shall ring the bell.'

'I am mad to be here. I am mad to have agreed to all this. What came over me I do not know. I have only just realized the folly of the thing.'

'Arise then, dear Mileson, and break your agreement, your promise and your undertaking. You are an adult man, you may dress and walk from the room.'

They were all the same, she concluded: except that while others had some passing superficial recommendation, this one it seemed had none. There was something that made her sick about the thought of the stringy limbs that were stretched out beside her. What lengths a woman will go to to rid herself of a horror like da Tanka!

He had imagined it would be a simple thing. It had sounded like a simple thing: a good thing rather than a bad one. A good turn for a lady in need. That was as he had seen it. With the little fee already in his possession.

Mrs da Tanka lit another cigarette and threw the match on the floor.

'What kind of a life have you had? You had not the nerve for marriage. Nor the brains for success. The truth is you might not have lived.' She laughed in the darkness, determined to hurt him as he had hurt her in his implication that being with her was an act of madness.

Mr Mileson had not before done a thing like this. Never before had he not weighed the pros and cons and seen that danger was absent from an undertaking. The thought of it all made him sweat. He saw in the future further deeds: worse deeds, crimes and irresponsibilities.

Mrs da Tanka laughed again. But she was thinking of something else.

'You have never slept with a woman, is that it? Ah, you poor thing! What a lot you have not had the courage for!' The bed heaved with the raucous noise that was her laughter, and the bright spark of her cigarette bobbed about in the air.

She laughed, quietly now and silently, hating him as she hated da Tanka and had hated Horace Spire. Why could he not be some young man, beautiful and nicely-mannered and gay? Surely a young man would have come with her? Surely there was one amongst all the millions who would have done the chore with relish, or at least with charm?

'You are as God made you,' said Mr Mileson. 'You cannot help your shortcomings, though one would think you might by now have recognized them. To others you may be all sorts of things. To me you are a frightful woman.'

'Would you not stretch out a hand to the frightful woman? Is there no temptation for the woman's flesh? Are you a eunuch, Mr Mileson?'

'I have had the women I wanted. I am doing you a favour. Hearing of your predicament and pressed to help you, I agreed in a moment of generosity. Stranger though you were, I did not say no.'

'That does not make you a gentleman.'

'And I do not claim it does. I am gentleman enough without it.'

'You are nothing without it. This is your sole experience.

In all your clerkly subservience you have not paused to live. You
know I am right, and as for being a gentleman – well, you are
of the lower middle classes. There has never been an English
gentleman born of the lower middle classes.'

She was trying to remember what she looked like; what
her face was like, how the wrinkles were spread, how old she
looked and what she might pass for in a crowd. Would men
not be cagey now and think that she must be difficult in her
ways to have parted twice from husbands? Was there a third
time coming up? Third time lucky, she thought. Who would
have her, though, except some loveless Mileson?

'You have had no better life than I,' said Mr Mileson. 'You
are no more happy now. You have failed, and it is cruel to
laugh at you.'

They talked and the hatred grew between them.

'In my childhood young men flocked about me, at dances
in Shropshire that my father gave to celebrate my beauty.
Had the fashion been duels, duels there would have been.
Men killed and maimed for life, carrying a lock of my hair on
their breast.'

'You are a creature now, with your face and your fingernails. Mutton dressed as lamb, Mrs da Tanka!'

Beyond the curtained windows the light of dawn broke into
the night. A glimpse of it crept into the room, noticed and
welcomed by its occupants.

'You should write your memoirs, Mr Mileson. To have seen
the changes in your time and never to know a thing about
them! You are like an occasional table. Or a coat-rack in the
hall of a boarding-house. Who shall mourn at your grave, Mr
Mileson?'

He felt her eyes upon him; and the mockery of the words
sank into his heart with intended precision. He turned to her
and touched her, his hands groping about her shoulders. He
had meant to grasp her neck, to feel the muscles struggle
beneath his fingers, to terrify the life out of her. But she,
thinking the gesture was the beginning of an embrace, pushed
him away, swearing at him and laughing. Surprised by the
misunderstanding, he left her alone.

*

The train was slow. The stations crawled by, similar and ugly. She fixed her glance on him, her eyes sharpened; cold and powerful.

She had won the battle, though technically the victory was his. Long before the time arranged for their breakfast Mr Mileson had leaped from bed. He dressed and breakfasted alone in the dining-room. Shortly afterwards, after sending to the bedroom for his suitcase, he left the hotel, informing the receptionist that the lady would pay the bill. Which in time she had done, and afterwards pursued him to the train, where now, to disconcert him, she sat in the facing seat of an empty compartment.

'Well,' said Mrs da Tanka, 'you have shot your bolt. You have taken the only miserable action you could. You have put the frightful woman in her place. Have we a right,' she added, 'to expect anything better of the English lower classes?'

Mr Mileson had foolishly left his weekly magazines and the daily paper at the hotel. He was obliged to sit barefaced before her, pretending to observe the drifting landscape. In spite of everything, guilt gnawed him a bit. When he was back in his room he would borrow the vacuum cleaner and give it a good going over: the exercise would calm him. A glass of beer in the pub before lunch; lunch in the A B C; perhaps an afternoon cinema. It was Saturday today: this, more or less, was how he usually spent Saturday. Probably from lack of sleep he would doze off in the cinema. People would nudge him to draw attention to his snoring; that had happened before, and was not pleasant.

'To give you birth,' she said, 'your mother had long hours of pain. Have you thought of that, Mr Mileson? Have you thought of that poor woman crying out, clenching her hands and twisting the sheets? Was it worth it, Mr Mileson? You tell me now, was it worth it?'

He could leave the compartment and sit with other people. But that would be too great a satisfaction for Mrs da Tanka. She would laugh loudly at his going, might even pursue him to mock in public.

'What you say about me, Mrs da Tanka, can equally be said of you.'

'Are we two peas in a pod? It's an explosive pod in that case.'

'I did not imply that. I would not wish to find myself sharing a pod with you.'

'Yet you shared a bed. And were not man enough to stick to your word. You are a worthless coward, Mr Mileson. I expect you know it.'

'I know myself, which is more than can be said in your case. Do you not think occasionally to see yourself as others see you? An ageing woman, faded and ugly, dubious in morals and personal habits. What misery you must have caused those husbands!'

'They married me, and got good value. You know that, yet dare not admit it.'

'I will scarcely lose sleep worrying the matter out.'

It was a cold morning, sunny with a clear sky. Passengers stepping from the train at the intermediate stations, muffled up against the temperature, finding it too much after the warm fug within. Women with baskets. Youths. Men with children, with dogs collected from the guard's van.

Da Tanka, she had heard, was living with another woman. Yet he refused to admit being the guilty party. It would not do for someone like da Tanka to be a public adulterer. So he had said. Pompously. Crossly. Horace Spire, to give him his due, hadn't given a damn one way or the other.

'When you die, Mr Mileson, have you a preference for the flowers on your coffin? It is a question I ask because I might send you off a wreath. That lonely wreath. From ugly, frightful Mrs da Tanka.'

'What?' said Mr Mileson, and she repeated the question.

'Oh well – cow-parsley, I suppose.' He said it, taken off his guard by the image she created; because it was an image he often saw and thought about. Hearse and coffin and he within. It would not be like that probably. Anticipation was not in Mr Mileson's life. Remembering, looking back, considering events and emotions that had been at the time mundane perhaps – this kind of thing was more to his liking. For by hindsight there was pleasure in the stream of time. He could not establish his funeral in his mind; he tried often but ended up always with a funeral he had known: a repetition of his parents' passing and the accompanying convention.

'Cow-parsley?' said Mrs da Tanka. Why did the man say cow-parsley? Why not roses or lilies or something in a pot? There had been cow-parsley in Shropshire; cow-parsley on the verges of dusty lanes; cow-parsley in hot fields buzzing with bees; great white swards rolling down to the river. She had sat among it on a picnic with dolls. She had lain on it, laughing at the beautiful anaemic blue of the sky. She had walked through it by night, loving it.

'Why did you say cow-parsley?'

He did not know, except that once on a rare family outing to the country he had seen it and remembered it. Yet in his garden he had grown delphiniums and wallflowers and asters and sweet-peas.

She could smell it again: a smell that was almost nothing: fields and the heat of the sun on her face, laziness and summer. There was a red door somewhere, faded and blistered, and she sat against it, crouched on a warm step, a child dressed in the fashion of the time.

'Why did you say cow-parsley?'

He remembered, that day, asking the name of the white powdery growth. He had picked some and carried it home; and had often since thought of it, though he had not come across a field of cow-parsley for years.

She tried to speak again, but after the night there were no words she could find that would fit. The silence stuck between them, and Mr Mileson knew by instinct all that it contained. She saw an image of herself and him, strolling together from the hotel, in this same sunshine, at this very moment, lingering on the pavement to decide their direction and agreeing to walk to the promenade. She mouthed and grimaced and the sweat broke on her body, and she looked at him once and saw words die on his lips, lost in his suspicion of her.

The train stopped for the last time. Doors banged; the

throng of people passed them by on the platform outside. They collected their belongings and left the train together. A porter, interested in her legs, watched them walk down the platform. They passed through the barrier and parted, moving in their particular directions. She to her new flat where milk and mail, she hoped, awaited her. He to his room; to the two unwashed plates on the draining board and the forks with egg on the prongs; and the little fee propped up on the mantelpiece, a pink cheque for five pounds, peeping out from behind a china cat.

Desert Island

TERENCE DE VERE WHITE

THE Barclays bought Grangemore to house their famous collection. It was the largest mansion in that part of the country, and on this particular afternoon in June the guests were so numerous that it was impossible to get through the hall. I was standing on the lawn, wondering how our host would bear up under the strain. He must have been suffering agonies of apprehension about his precious things at the mercy of this throng.

'Funny thing about Barclay,' my companion said, as another car drew up at the door, 'he hasn't a friend in the world.'

As a caption under a drawing of the milling crowd it would have been worthy of the *New Yorker*; but it was not said for fun, nor was it malicious. The Barclays always struck me, for all the entertaining that they did, as essentially a lonely pair. They filled the house at weekends with English friends, who regarded them, I often thought, as if they were Robinson Crusoes; and when they came back and found me on the guest list again I was given the sort of attention appropriate to Man Friday.

And that exactly was the sort of role I played at Grangemore. Mrs Barclay, whom, after a time, I was invited to call 'Helen', never went to any trouble to disguise the fact that in England I could hardly have expected to find myself at their board. 'You are the only Irish person we know,' she used to say; and always added 'except Michael, of course.' Michael trained their three racehorses, and he was made a very special fuss of. I had no cause for complaint. In course of time I became quite the Mayor of the Palace. There were occasions when the guests were particularly uninteresting, when Helen would say, 'You show them around.'

Faces fell at this. To begin with, not everyone wants to behave as if he were in a museum when visiting a private house, especially after dinner. And being given no choice in the matter and left to the care of another guest – and one of no importance – did nothing to sweeten the circumstances. It was usually a grim-faced group that I conducted round the reception rooms. Occasionally a guest would rebel and refuse to move. So far from annoying the hosts, this was always well received and produced an approximation to hilarity on several occasions. The Barclays, you see, were merely doing their duty. It gave them no pleasure to send parties of inspection round their premises; but they felt obliged to. It relieved their sense of guilt for being so rich. And they could think of nothing else for their guests to do. When the tours of inspection were over – having sat down to dinner at eight and with the prospect of a longish drive for anyone who had to return to Dublin – there was very little time for more than a nightcap before the party broke up. By then a fearful solemnity had set in, and parting was on all sides a blessed relief.

I could never think of the Barclays apart from their possessions; not only because I met them always in their own house, but because the subject of conversation seldom travelled far away from objects of art. And all through dinner one knew that it was only the prelude to that inevitable inspection and the enlightened comments worn out by over-use.

Among his books in the library he had built on as an extension to the mansion, Humphrey was livelier than in the house proper. This was natural enough: he had collected them himself, and he knew a great deal about bindings. Every sale catalogue came to him. He had someone to buy for him in the principal capitals. I hesitate to guess what he must have spent on his hobby, but as he got the best advice it was really a gilt-edged investment. Not that he looked on it in that way. He had the pure passion of a collector. His pale eyes lit up when he told us about a rare bible on papyrus that he had run to earth with the directors of all the great libraries in the

world on his heels. The inside of the books did not interest
him. It was the covers he cared for. I always picture the
Barclays surrounded by copies of *Vogue* and the expensive art
magazines, with the latest novel beside them. When they
were alone they played patience, if he wasn't looking through
book catalogues or studying *Apollo* and the *Connoisseur*.

The origin of our friendship was a lucky guess on my part.
I arrived at the house with a group of earnest people whom
the Barclays had permitted to visit the collection. They had
greeted us wanly in the hall, then he took one group to the
library and Mrs Barclay led another round the treasures in
the house. My companions were not acquitting themselves
very well; our guide, no doubt, described them to herself as
'very Irish'. One in particular was making a show of herself,
regarding it as a point of national pride to dispute every attribution. I could have kicked her. It was bad manners, even
if she had the knowledge, which she hadn't. Hers was the
impregnable front of complacent ignorance; but she was not
going to allow an English woman to get away with the idea
that she had anything that could not be bettered in the
national collections.

'That's a nice little Teniers you have,' this importunate
woman said when we entered a closet off the drawing-rooms.
For once she felt sure of an attribution; and pride mellowed
her for the moment. I knew a little about Dutch painting, and
I was sufficiently irritated by her manners throughout the
afternoon to contradict. 'A Brouwer, I should have thought.'

'You are quite right,' Mrs Barclay turned to me gratefully.
'My husband's uncle bought it from Duveen. He said at the
time it was the best Brouwer outside Holland.'

My companion made a face, expressing her unconcern for
a mere slip of the tongue of no more significance than
Duveen (whoever he was). The incident served a useful purpose.
It shut her up; she went round doggedly and silently after
that, as if she were making an inventory of national
grievances.

But when we gathered in the hall to make our farewells —
no refreshment was provided — Mr Barclay took me aside. 'I

hear you recognized the Brouwer,' he said. 'Everyone calls it a
Teniers. It's such a relief to meet anyone who appreciates our
few things.'

I met them again somewhere and she came up to me at once,
recalling the incident. I began to think of it as my signature
tune. Soon after that I received an invitation to dine. Some of
the guests were from England and were staying in the house.
They had the air of knowing their hosts only slightly better
than the local visitors, who did not know them at all. We had
all been collected in a haphazard way; but everyone had a
reason for being present – being the head of this or of that;
a representative figure – I was unique in being of no significance
whatever. I was surprised to find myself beside my hostess at
dinner. She talked away in a flutteringly confidential manner
of the troubles of transplantation, the difficulty of getting
servants, the worry of leaving the precious things. In London
they had a flat, and a villa in Provence. It was the devil to get
servants in France, she told me. I listened sympathetically. In
comparison to hers, my life seemed to be singularly free of
care. One of their horses had gone lame on the eve of a race.
Another had failed to justify the enormous sum they paid for
it. The National Gallery in London wanted to borrow their
Fra Angelico; it was difficult to refuse; but the wall would look
sad without it. A restorer was coming from Italy to deal with
the flaking paint in the Tintoretto. This meant that they
would have to retrench this year in some of their expenses. And
Humphrey had his eye on a Chaucer.

I made appropriately sympathetic noises. It was the only
demand the conversation made on me. 'You work in Dublin?'
was the extent of her curiosity about my – admittedly – not
very eventful life. I assumed they were childless. There seemed
in all their apartments no room for one. What would a child
do in such a house? But I was wrong.

'It's such a bore that Julia doesn't hunt – she lost her
nerve – and there is literally nothing else to do here in the
winter,' she said, adding, 'Julia is our daughter.'

'Could you not stay here in the summer and spend the
winter in London?'

'We don't like leaving the collection for so long. We always spend Easter in France and Christmas in London, but except to fly over when we have dentists to see and that sort of thing, we have decided that we are better off here. I love Ireland,' she added rather surprisingly. 'The people are so friendly. I mean the working-class people. But we don't seem to be able to get to know anyone else – as friends, I mean. There seems to be an unbridgeable gap. I can't quite describe it exactly. As if we spoke a different language. That is why we were so delighted to meet you.'

All I had done was to recognize the Brouwer, and it aston-ished me to find that it had made such an impression, and could possibly be the basis of a friendship. But it was. I found myself so frequently at the Barclays' parties that I lost count. Each was exactly like the other, and the conversation on every occasion was almost identical. At some stage or other during the evening Mrs Barclay would say to me of some acquain-tance, 'He is Irish, but not what *you* would call Irish.' It was an unintended snub. I came to look forward to it, and had bets about it with myself. Sometimes there were among the guests from England people who answered to this description. One was called Pat, and another was a major in the Irish Guards, but certainly nobody would suspect either of any Irish connection, without being told.

The Barclays never said anything amusing; and that might explain why they built up a character as a humourist for me. If I had gained admission to their friendship by an appearance of expertise, I held my place as a court jester. It was no strain. There was no competition. Anything more recondite than a reference to the weather was greeted with a smirk from him and a peal of laughter from her. 'It's the way you put things,' she said. 'You must meet' – referring to some celebrity – 'he'd adore you.'

I acquired another function. I became a social register for the local scene. Helen (we had come to that) rang me up at least once a week to inquire about some new acquaintance. The Barclays seemed to have no faculty themselves to deter-mine what people were like. It was as though they had come to live in the jungle or the further reaches of Mongolia. 'They seemed nice. Tell me about them.'

At first I was flattered, and then I began to despise myself and disliked my role. I was being a social quisling. It came to an end without my having shown the courage to resign. I failed to get briefs at the bar, and took a job in a lawyer's office in Canada. I sent a card to the Barclays at Christmas but got none in return, and felt a little hurt. I didn't look them up when I came back to Ireland on annual leave; but one day I walked into Julia in Dublin. She was in black, and I hesitated to inquire for her parents. She was, as always, direct.

'Mummy died on Wednesday. I was away. It was very sudden.'

I said what one says. Julia made it easy. I only once saw her express any emotion, and so far as appearances went now, she was perfectly calm. I inquired after her father. He must be distraught, I said.

'He's all right.'

'I don't suppose he wants to see anyone at the moment.'

'I'm sure he would like to see you. He's on his own. But I'd ring up if I were you. He hates droppers-in.'

It was as encouraging as Julia could be. I decided to telephone. They had been kind to me in their way; and I had been a little sad as well as piqued to find that out of sight I was also out of mind. Perhaps I was to blame. I should have written. They got millions of Christmas cards. Mine had probably gone unnoticed.

Humphrey greeted me on the telephone as if I had never been away. 'I knew you would be upset,' he said. 'I'm all alone. Come down tonight and have a chop with me.'

Of all the evenings I had spent there I enjoyed that one most. We sat at a small table in the library. He talked away about his books. He was on the track of the Chaucer again. It was touch and go. He never mentioned Helen. I asked about Julia. Would she live with him? I was curious to know if there were any prospects of her marrying, but if there were I suppose he would not have told me.

'She won't leave London,' he said.

I hoped she was well. In spite of her grief, I thought she
looked as pretty as ever when I met her, I said. I remembered
that Humphrey always talked about Julia as if she were a
beauty. It was somehow endearing. She was, for her mother's
daughter, surprisingly plain.

'Even now,' he smiled wanly, 'I can't make out why she
isn't married,' he said.

I was a very young man when the Barclays took me up, and
averagely susceptible. There was only one likeness of Julia in
their house, a painting done by somebody who did everybody's child that year. It hung in a little room they called their
'den', Julia at the age of six — a mass of yellow hair in a
primrose dress, nursing a cat. One could just make out the
suggestion of features under the hair. A clever formula; I
wondered if the artist employed it when the children were
pretty. But I only thought of that after I met Julia. Her absence, casual references to her doings — she moved from one
exotic spot to another — and her father's way of referring to
her built up an image in my mind that gave the evening she
was going to appear an excitement that her parents' parties
never aroused in me.

She ought to have been outstandingly pretty. Helen was
like a Gainsborough, and Humphrey was so elegant that he
conveyed an impression of being much better looking than
in fact he was. My disappointment when I saw Julia was of the
kind I experienced when I saw the Mona Lisa for the first
time. In that case I had been brought up on reproductions and
should have known what to expect; but Pater's prose had
bitten deep, and I expected to be overcome when I saw the
original. I wasn't.

I hope I didn't show my disappointment on this occasion.
What made it more poignant was her marked resemblance to
both the parents. She was too tall. Then, her father was tall.
Her eyes were large and blue — as her mother's were — but
the mother's sparkled like frost; her daughter's were frozen
over. Her hair was pepper colour now and worn long. She had a
trick of moving it from one side of her face to the other when
she was talking as if it had some function that had gone out

of order. Her clothes were very expensive, but somehow wrong. They might have been selected by her father, not for her, but for his idea of her.

I thought that he doted on his daughter; but when she was present neither of the parents took any notice of her. She had her silent place among the guests, the usual visitors from England, and the Irish contingent – the Director of this, the President of that – gallantly pretending to be friends. There was never anybody of her own age, which I guessed to be about twenty.

I was right. She had a coming-out party the next year; it was in London, and I was not invited. The Barclays kept their worlds apart. That summer they had a house-party for the Horse Show; for once it included young people. I met them on the Sunday after the week's diversions. They seemed – perhaps I was prejudiced – rather a colourless lot. They had paired off, but nobody seemed to belong to Julia. The week of dances had done nothing for her, except to make her sleepy. She yawned quite a lot.

I always found her very difficult to talk to, and although we were much more of an age, I was not enlisted for her entertainment, but remained exclusively a friend of the parents. It would have caused me chagrin had I had any romantic feelings; but I had none and preferred the status I was accorded.

In any event, the Horse Show apart, no effort seemed to be made to entertain for Julia. One assumed that her social life took place in London, where, if she met the Irish, they were, in Helen's phrase, 'Not what you would call Irish'.

One morning Helen rang me up. Julia, she explained, had been invited to a hunt ball and told to bring a partner. A suitable one had been found in London and was to have been flown in; but, at the last moment, he had failed. Would I help out? It was very short notice. She asked me to do it for her. She couldn't have been nicer about it. I had to accept, but I did not look forward to the evening. And in proof it was worse than I feared. I called for Julia and we drove thirty miles to one house where we had dinner and then twenty miles to another where the dance took place.

It might have been pleasant to assume the role of cavalier

for a change, and I was prepared to play up if Julia, for her part, made the smallest effort. But she threw cold water on any charade of that description from the start. It was a bore for me, she said. It must be. She had been looking forward to Charley's coming. They had been seeing quite a lot of one another, but he had started to take someone else out – a Chinese girl – and his sudden attack of flu was a diplomatic excuse. She knew it. Most of her friends bored her, but Charley had been different. He could do things like playing the guitar. He was also a good mimic. She was sorry she couldn't attempt to imitate him. She had protested when she heard that her mother had invited me to fill the gap. It would have been much better to have called the evening off. She disliked the people we were going to dine with particularly and she hated dances at any time. After that she lapsed into silence, interrupted once when she asked if I had a cigarette about me. She had forgotten to bring her own. She was forbidden to smoke, I remembered.

We arrived at a crowded house where nobody seemed to know anyone, and dinner arrived on the table as if by a miracle. I said as much, and thought how Helen would have laughed and drawn attention to another pearl of wit. Julia made an expression of mild disgust.

'Something hot at last,' I said when the champagne arrived. A joke of Disraeli's that had proved useful on similar occasions in the past. It fell flat; so, it happened, did the wine.

After dinner a move was made towards the cars, and I found myself driving Julia and another couple who flirted in the back and ignored us.

I never danced very well, and Julia asked me why I had never learnt to at our first attempt. 'I think we had better sit down,' she said, after the second circuit. The evening dragged on. Once or twice she was claimed from me, usually by older men whom I had met with her parents. It was quite a surprise when a youth with a very red face and an obviously borrowed evening suit came up and asked awkwardly if she would dance with him. He looked like a farm-hand, and I half expected Julia to refuse; but, on the contrary, she jumped up at once. I caught a glimpse of them whirling round. Her face was flushed, her eyes were approximately gay. I lost sight of her after that until five o'clock, when I was aroused from sleep in a chair in the bar by a touch on my shoulder.

'We're going home,' Julia said.

In the car, she stared straight before her and never turned her head towards me, so that I could only catch a vague impression of her face in the windscreen. But even from that reflection I saw that she had become transformed. There was a hard brightness about her as if she was drugged.

She never stopped talking, in a low excited voice. I wondered if she had been drinking; it was hard to believe that dancing, or even flirting, with that gauche youth could have worked such a metamorphosis.

She never referred to him or to the dance or seemed to be warmed by any aftermath of pleasure. Her talk was bitter – and incessant.

She described the boredom of her life, the dullness of her parents, their selfishness. She hated antiques and paintings, ancient or modern, and silver and ivories and rare books. She hated art and she hated artists. She enjoyed the cinema; she worshipped Elvis Presley. He might be getting on, but he was still divine. She found her parents' friends intolerable. Pansies, for the most part. If she could have her way she would burn the house down and see its contents go up in smoke with a cheer.

I let her go on, except when she attacked her parents. I said they had been very good to me.

'They hate the Irish,' she said. 'They despise them. They left England because they thought it was breaking up. They don't really care for anyone very much. Humphrey prefers his bindings to anyone on earth. And Helen thinks about nothing except her appearance. She spends hours on it every day. Hours. How old do you think she is?'

I preferred not to guess.

'I'll tell you. She will be sixty next birthday. I know. They were married ten years before I arrived. I was an accident. The worst accident they ever had except the day the butler put his foot through a Ming vase. Humphrey hit him and had to pay through the nose when he sued for assault. I got hysteria, I laughed so much. The parents sent me away for three months. Humphrey began to go grey after that. He's seventy. Did you know?'

She said 'seventy' with a venom that made me start; she must have remarked it, because she stopped abruptly, and never opened her mouth until we arrived at her house. She opened the door, yawning; the light was on in the hall.

'Do you know the way to your room?'

I said I did and found when I got upstairs that I had spoken the truth. There was a bust of Socrates on the landing and I remembered that my door was on the far side of it.

I was curious to see whether Julia's outburst and unwelcome confidences would change our relations in any way. These things, as a rule, create a secret understanding, or she might regret her loss of self-control and hate me in consequence. But I was unaware of any alteration in her manner towards me; when I came to dinner again I got the usual welcomes, the synthetically effusive ones from the parents; from Julia a nod and a stare.

Helen died as I said; and I went back to Canada. For various reasons I did not come to Ireland again for holidays, and I never heard a word about the Barclays until one day I saw in a newspaper that Humphrey was dead. His age was given as seventy-three − so Julia was right! − and the paragraph said that his collection had been left to the Irish Government. That was as it should be if Julia hated it. There would be more than enough money to keep her in comfort. And I hoped that now at last she would feel free to live as she wanted to. A vivid recollection of the strange night at the ball came back to me. The only time I had ever seen Julia look animated, when she was dancing with a farm-hand. Perhaps she had married him already, or would now, and grow fat and comfortable, surrounded by pigs, and little fat philistines of children. Free from parents and possessions at last. I wrote her a letter of sympathy, but remembering that nocturnal confidence I was not fulsome. But I said, and I wanted to say, that her father had always treated me hospitably and kindly. She sent no reply.

Ten years later in a Dublin hotel I saw a notice advertising the Barclay Museum – open to the public every afternoon except Monday. As I had nothing to do and a car was at my disposal I decided to indulge a nostalgic urge. I always regret these impulses. As Dr Johnson said, it is a melancholy form of pleasure.

Nothing had changed very much at Grangemore; but now there was a turnstile in the doorway. The house was obviously a tourist attraction; there were several buses in waiting outside; and there was a handful of people in the hall. Suddenly I regretted my visit. We should bury certain parts of the past, and this, for me, was one of them. But, having come so far – thirty miles – it was easier to go on. I paid six shillings, but refused to buy a catalogue; after all, I was practically qualified to act as a guide to the establishment.

There was a group of Americans in the hall, talking very loudly. They wanted a guide, it seemed, and I very nearly offered my services. Fortunately I held my tongue, for at that moment a party which had been touring the house debouched into the hall again.

The next conducted tour would be at four, I heard the porter say. The Americans obediently formed a queue. The guide turned away, to rest I suppose until the time came to lead the next party round. I caught a glimpse of her. 'Julia,' I cried. She stopped to see who had called her name. But as I crossed the hall she gave no sign of recognition. She had changed very little, and I would have known her anywhere. I knew I had put on weight and shed some hair, but had I become totally unrecognizable?

'Have you forgotten me?'

She remembered then. I asked her how she was. She said she was quite well. I asked her where she was living. 'Here,' she said. 'What are you doing now?' she inquired, after a pause. I was still in Canada, I explained. 'I was in Dublin for a few days and wanted to recall the pleasant times I had in this wonderful house.'

She let the remark pass, and nothing came to mind to add to it.

'If you will forgive me,' she said, 'I must bring the next lot round.'

She didn't wait for my reply, but stepped into the hall and shouted, 'This way, please.'

It didn't sound like Julia's voice, as I remembered it; but then, I had not heard it very often. Nor was it like her mother's, which had the tinkle of small glass. And this had a different kind of hardness. Then I remembered Humphrey hailing a taxi. She had her father's voice. It was something else he had left her.

Meles Vulgaris

PATRICK BOYLE

'What are you reading, darling?'

Her voice was muffled by the turtle-necked sweater out of which she was struggling.

He pulled the bedclothes further up his chest, adjusted the pillow and turned a page.

'Come again?'

'There wasn't a cheep –' her chin emerged '– out of you –' the sweater was peeled from her rolled-back ears '– all evening. It must be –' a last effort and she was free '– a powerful book.'

'Uh-huh.'

She pitched the sweater on to a chair seat, shook out her wiry black hair and examined herself critically in the mirror.

'Sitting hunched up over an old book since tea-time,' she told the frowning sun-tanned reflection, 'without a word to say for yourself.' Eyes – sloe-black, deep-set, heavy-lidded – gazed back at her appraisingly. 'You know, darling, it's lonely all day in the house by yourself.' With tentative fingertips, she smoothed out the crow's feet. 'No one to talk to till you're home for the weekends.' Her gaze slid over the tiny frightening folds and wrinkles of the neck and sought comfort in the firm brown flesh of arms and shoulders. The mirrored face smiled ruefully. 'It's a wonder I don't start talking to myself.'

'Uh-huh.' With finger and thumb, he rasped gently the lifted ready-to-be-turned leaf.

She swung round.

'I believe you weren't listening to a word I said.'

'Sorry, honey. I wasn't paying attention.'

She reached out a hand. Curious.

'What's it about, anyway?'

He handed her the book.

'*The Badger*.' She leafed the pages rapidly. 'It looks like some sort of text book.'

'So it is.'

Frowning, she studied the stylized animal on the jacket.

'Why the sudden interest in badgers?' she asked.

'I saw it –' he nodded towards the book '– displayed in a bookshop window.'

'But what on earth induced you to buy it?'

'A sudden impulse. It reminded me of that holiday we had in the Blue Stack mountains. When we saw the badger fight.'

Her face lit up.

'But that was years ago.'

He rolled over on his side, tucked the bedclothes in round his shoulders and burrowed into the pillow.

'Oh,' he mumbled, 'I remember it – remember it right well.'

He yawned.

'The book tells you how the little fellows tick.'

The common badger – meles vulgaris – a genus of burrowing carnivores, is found in hilly or wooded districts in almost every part of the country. More common in the West than in the East.

Sunday morning after Mass. Around the church gate the usual crowd of men standing about in groups, talking football, greyhounds, hangovers, weather. From the outskirts Micky Hogan beckoning. Moving away from the crowd before he spoke.

'Are you for the match the day?'

'I don't know. Why?'

'They're drawing a badger up at Johnny John's.'

'D'you tell me! What dogs have they got? Mind you, it's not everyone will chance getting his dog mauled or maybe killed by a brock.'

'Hawker Downey is bringing along that treacherous whelp of a Kerry Blue of his. A right mauling might put manners on it.'

'Any other?'

'They have another Kerry Blue lined up. A good one.'

'Whose?'

'The curate's. The boys are going to whip it when he's gone to the match.'

'Och, go to God. There'll be the queer rumpus when he finds out.'

'The dog'll be at the gate to meet him when he gets back from the game. It might be a wee scratch or two the worse for the trip but sure the silly brute is always in trouble. You should take the car and we'll head into the Blue Stacks. It'll be right gas.'

'How did they catch the badger?'

'D'you mind the Johnny Johns complaining about the fox slaughtering their fowl?'

'Aye.'

'Well, they found pad marks yesterday morning outside the hen house. The tracks led to a badger's earth not a stone's throw from the house. The nest was dug up, the sow and the three cubs killed and Mister Brock himself is for the high jump this afternoon.'

The badger is a member of the order Carnivora and has large teeth but, contrary to popular belief, it does not prey on poultry and young lambs. It feeds on insects, small mammals, molluscs and earthworms, supplemented by vegetable material such as fruit, nuts and grass.

Still riffling the pages of the book, she stared blindly at the unfamiliar photographs. Tenderness welled up inside her, tearing at throat and eyes. Perhaps he too was thinking of their first holiday together after they were married. When he had taken the firm's car and they had driven into the foothills of Croaghgorm to his Aunt Ellen's tiny farmhouse. There was no money to go any place else. But who cared? They had spent three weeks there, coddled and fussed over by Aunt Ellen.

They had moved round together in a daze. Drunk with love. Shouting their crazy enchantment at the echoing hills. Bound together with such hunger for each other that the warmth left the blazing summer sun if they moved apart.

For those three weeks they had only one body between them – a parched thirsty body that soaked up happiness like a sponge. It was on the last day of that unforgettable holiday that they brought Micky with them to the badger fight in the Blue Stacks.

The baiting had already started when the car bumped and slithered up the last stretch of track and into Johnny John's yard. A crowd of mountain men stood around watching Hawker Downey – a fussy wee know-all – trying to coax, drag, push his stupid gulpin of a dog into an overturned barrel. Each time he got the Kerry Blue's forequarters inside the barrel, the dog would wriggle free, dashing around among the onlookers, wagging its stumpy tail.

The crowd hooted and jeered.

'Put your shoulder to him, Downey.'

'Take away the cowardly cur.'

'Give the curate's dog a trial.'

'Crawl into the barrel yourself, Hawker.'

Downey was nettled. He got the dog by the scruff of the neck and the skin of the hump and fairly hurled it into the barrel.

'Sic him, Garry!' he urged. 'Sic the brock!'

Never did dog react quicker. It bounced back out of the barrel, shot between Downey's splayed legs and never cried halt till it reached the safety of the dunghill, where it ploutered about in the soggy muck, wagging a doubtful, disillusioned tail. Whistles, threats, curses, wouldn't shift it.

There was nothing for it but to try out the curate's dog. Much against his will Micky Hogan, who sometimes exercised the dog for Father Bradley, was prevailed on to handle it.

'I'll gamble the curate will blame me for this day's work, if he gets to hear of it. So keep your traps shut. All of you,' he said.

The Kerry Blue trotted at his heels to the barrel mouth. He patted its flank.

'In you go, champ,' he said.

The dog moved in willingly enough. For as long as it took Micky to straighten up, take a cigarette butt from behind his ear and light it, the dog stayed stiff-legged, tail quivering, before it backed out slowly. Once clear of the barrel it stopped, shaking its head violently.

Micky grabbed it. Examined the muzzle.

'Not a scratch,' he announced. 'There's only one remedy for this disease. The toe of me boot.'

'You may give over, Hogan,' a querulous voice called. It was the old fellow himself, Johnny John. He was standing at the kitchen door, watching the proceedings with a sardonic smile. 'I told the young fellows to get fox-terriers. But of course they knew better. Those dogs you've got aren't worth a curse. They'll never face the barrel.'

'For why?'

'The smell of the brock has them stomached.'

One of the characteristics of the badger is the possession of musk- or stink-glands. These anal glands are used as a result of fear or excitement. The recognition of danger will stimulate secretion and trigger off the defence mechanism.

A hand ruffled his hair.

'Unhook me, will you, honey.'

Reaching up a hand towards the voice, he pawed the air blindly.

'Come on, lazy-bones,' she urged. 'I can't get this wretched thing off.'

His eyes opened to black bra straps biting into sun-browned skin. As he fumbled with the hooks, buried deep in flesh, she chattered on:

'How's that for a tan? I was the whole week stretched out on the lawn. Sun-bathing. We get so little sun it would be a shame not to make the most of this hot spell. God knows, it's hard enough to get a decent tan up. Olive oil helps, of course. But then you must be careful not to fall asleep or you'll get fried. Properly fried.'

The loosened bra fell away. With outstretched arms she spun around.

'Becoming, isn't it?'

The brown body appeared to be encompassed by a monstrous pair of white plastic goggles out of which glared two angry bulging bloodshot eyes.

His flesh crept with embarrassment.

'Most exotic,' he said.

She flushed with pleasure.

'You really think so?'

He yawned wide and loud.

'Sure.'

His head dropped back on the pillow.

It was decided to let the dogs attack in the open where the rank smell would be dispersed. The crowd scattered back from the barrel. The two dogs were leashed.

One of the young Johnny Johns gripped the bottom of the barrel. Tilted it. Slowly. To knee level. Scrabbling noises. Higher still. More scrabbling noises. Up to hip level. Silence.

'He's lodged, boy,' called Johnny John. 'You may shake him out of it.'

The young fellow shook the barrel. Cautiously. Nothing happened. Harder this time. Still no result.

'You'll get no windfalls that way,' someone shouted.

'Slew the barrel round, Peter,' the old man ordered.

A murmur of appreciation went round.

'Sound man.'

'The old dog for the hard road.'

'It takes yourself Johnny.'

Slowly Peter swung the barrel on its base. The crowd began to close in. The old man moved out from the porch. One of the dogs whimpered.

At the quarter turn the badger came slithering out, still clawing wildly for purchase.

It crouched, facing its tormentors, the grey-black hair on its body bristling like a hedgehog, its black and white head flat to the ground. Although it remained motionless, its whole body, from snout to stumpy tail seethed with controlled energy.

This fierce smothered tension dominated the crowd with a

threatening fist. No one moved. Peter still held up the tilted
barrel. Hogan's smoked-down butt scorched the palm of his
hand unheeded. Halted in mid-stride Johnny John waited, ash-
plant poised.

Again a dog whimpered.

The crouching badger leaped forward. It picked no gap in
the ranks of its enemies. It hurled itself at them and they broke
before it. Shouting and cursing: shouldering, elbowing, pushing each other, in their anxiety to get out of the path of this
savage creature running amuck; they backed away.

Through this opening dashed the badger. Ahead lay freedom.
A length of laneway, a thick hedge, a familiar track reeking
with the smell of its kind, the safety – somewhere – of an un-
ravaged set.

There was one enemy left. Johnny John.

Wily and tough as the brock itself, he had moved out towards the yard gate and now, with stamping feet and flailing
ash-plant, he headed the badger back towards the closed and
bolted outhouses.

Baffled, uncertain, the badger slowed down, scuttling along
with a lurching, waddling gait. The length of the outhouses it
ran, seeking shelter – scurrying, hesitating, scurrying again –
like a businessman hunting for a seat in a crowded train.

*The feet of the badger are plantigrade: the animal walks on
the flat of its feet, including the heel, in contrast to the
Ungulates, which walk on their toes.*

He clung doggedly to his share of the bedclothes as she
plunged into bed, wriggling and threshing around, till she was
coiled up under the glow of the bed light, an open magazine
held between pillow and bedclothes.

The glossy leaves crackled imposingly as she flicked them
over, seeing not mink-coated figures, luscious dishes of food,
enormous luxury automobiles, but grim, hungry, plush-covered
hills.

'Why don't we go back there again?' she said. 'Sometime.'

'Where?' His voice was muffled by the pillow.

'Croaghgorm.'

The bed springs creaked as he shifted peevishly.

'What would we be going there for? Aunt Ellen's dead.'

'We could stay some place else. A farm-house in the hills.'

Again he shifted. Rolling over on his back. To the ceiling he spoke – patiently, reasonably, wearily.

'Look, Sheila. In a cottage in Croaghgorm you would last exactly one night. No hot water. No foam rubber mattress. No thick pile carpets. No radiogram. Above all nothing to do. Except you tramp the mountains, helping them to herd sheep.'

Her heart contracted as she felt the spring of the moss under her bare feet, the cool squelch of mud oozing between her toes.

'Or sit in the house all day blinded by a smoking turf fire.'

She drew in her breath, sniffing the acrid, heady, wholly delicious, fragrance of burning turf: watched with sleepy eyes the flames die down as the brown ash formed; heard the tired sigh as the burnt-out sods collapsed.

'Not forgetting the peaceful night's rest you'll have with sheep dogs barking, cattle bawling and roosters crowing their heads off at day-break.'

She rolled over facing him.

'We must go, dear. Some time. If it's only for the day.'

'All right. All right.'

He pulled the bedclothes over his head.

The badger disappeared into the opening between two out-houses.

'He's got away.'

'Why didn't you mill him, Johnny?'

'Loose the dogs.'

The old man pranced about in the gap, waving the stick.

'He picked the baiting-pitch himself,' he said, as the crowd gathered in the opening. 'And a better choice he couldn't have made if he'd searched all Ireland.'

It was a cul-de-sac. The gable ends of two outhouses – one of concrete, the other galvanized iron – a few yards apart, linked by a man-high stone wall.

Around these confines the badger sniffed, scratching the

ground here and there with a tentative forepaw. Where the zinc shed met the wall, it started digging.

By the time the decision had been reached to send in Hawker's dog first, the badger had rooted out a hole large enough to warrant the use of its hind paws. With these it scattered back the uprooted clay into an ever-rising parapet. When the Kerry Blue came charging in, the badger wheeled around, keeping to the shelter of its burrow, to face its assailant, teeth bared in a silent snarl.

It crouched motionless but for the grinning muzzle that swung from side to side parrying the probing onslaughts of the dog. This swaying exotically striped head, slender, graceful, compact with fierce vigilance seemed to repudiate the huddled body, craven, lumpish, dingy, belonging surely to a different and inferior species.

The dog pounced. It grabbed the badger at the back of the head where the long grey body-hairs begin. Secure from the snapping jaws by this shrewd grip, it whipped up the striped head, shook it violently and slammed it back to the ground. It pinned down the badger's head, pressing it into the loose clay whilst it gnawed and grunted, grunted and gnawed, shifting its grip deeper and deeper through the thick hair, as if it sought to sink its teeth into solid flesh.

Always it was thwarted. Choked by the mass of coarse wiry hair, it was forced to loosen its hold, gulping in a quick mouthful of air before it pounced again.

The badger crouched supine, muzzle buried in the clay. Waiting.

At last the gasping dog released its hold. For one vulnerable second it loomed over its enemy, its slavering jaws content to threaten. In that second the badger struck.

The striped head reared up. Snapping jaws closed on a dangling ear. A yelp. Frenzied scuffling as the growling dog sought to free itself. A wild howl. The badger, still gripping the torn ear, had lashed out with one of its forefeet, raking the dog's muzzle – once, twice – with its long gouging claws before the poor brute broke free. Bleeding from lacerated ear and jowl, it backed away yapping.

Johnny John struck the ground with his stick.

'You may take the cowardly brute to hell out of that,' he said.
'A Kerry Blue's no use to fight once it starts giving tongue.'

Downey grabbed his dog and lugged it away. The badger
went back to its burrowing. Micky Hogan started to un-
leash the second dog, now trembling and straining at the
lead.

'You mightn't bother your barney, Hogan,' said Johnny
John. 'That dog'll never best a brock. Didn't I tell it was a
soople, snapping animal you wanted. Not a big lazy get the like
of thon, that'll fall asleep on the grip.'

Micky looked up.

'I'm surprised at you, Johnny,' he said. 'Have you no respect
for the cloth?' He stooped over the dog. 'Go in there, Father
Fergus, and show this anti-clerical gentleman how you handle
a heretic.' He released the dog. 'Off you go, chum.'

The dog advanced cautiously. Every few paces it paused,
straddle-legged, watchful, snarling muzzle out-thrust, its gaze
fastened on the badger, now faced round awaiting its attacker.
It advanced to within arm's length of the striped muzzle before
it came to a halt, crouched on stiffened forefeet. It growled
softly, continuously – a growl so far back in its throat that it
sounded like a harmless gentle purr.

The badger held its ground, beady eyes bright, alert, muzzle
cocked, lips drawn back in its soundless snarl.

The two animals crouched, locked into stasis by the hate and
fear that glared back at them from alien eyes. So long did they
remain poised that a shout went up when the tension was broken
at last by the pouncing dog.

'He's nailed him!'

'Good on you, Fergus!'

'Hold tight to him!'

Johnny John said quietly:

'There'll be trouble when he loosens yon grip.'

The dog had gripped the badger by the snout and was tugging
it from its burrow into open ground. The badger with splayed
feet, resisted. It was of no avail. Heaving and jerking, the Kerry
Blue drew the badger inch by struggling inch over the clay
parapet until it had the thirty-pound carcase out on level

ground. At this moment the dog's hindfeet lost their purchase on the moiled ground.

The sudden skid loosened the hold of the dog's jaws. It was the badger's chance. Teeth crunched. A yelp of pain from the dog. The badger's clumsy body came to life – squirming, wriggling, jerking. At last it was free. Snout torn and bleeding. One eye damaged. Dragged from its sheltering burrow. But free.

It began to sidle towards the uprooted trench. The dog blocked its path, menacing the badger with bared and bloody teeth.

'The brock has relieved the poor bugger of half his bucking tongue,' someone said in an awe-stricken voice.

'What did I tell you?' said Johnny John.

This time there was no preliminary sparring. The dog closed in at once, only manoeuvring so that his attack came from the badger's rear, safe from the deadly teeth and claws. Like a boxer using his reach, the dog took advantage of longer legs and greater agility. It leapt around the badger, darting out and in, feinting to charge until it lured its enemy into position. Then it pounced.

Sometimes it succeeded in straddling the badger, flattening it on the ground, where it could tear and maul the defenceless animal's head. But not for long. The badger would break free, roll over on its back and rip with lethal claws the dog's unprotected belly.

Slow, ungainly, its heavy stumpy-legged body unsuited to swift exchanges, the badger was content to remain on the defensive. But always it was dangerous. Let the Kerry Blue fail to duck away quick enough after releasing its grip and another gash was added to its scored and bleeding body.

Except for the scuffle of paws on the trampled clay, the panting of the dog as it sparred for an opening, an occasional grunt from either animal, the struggle was fought out with quiet decorum. Indeed for long stretches there was complete silence as the two animals lay locked together, jerking spasmodically as the dog strove to deepen its grip or the badger to free itself.

If both had not been so mired and bloody – the badger's slender elegant head being so plastered with blood and clay that the parti-coloured striping could no longer be discerned – they could have been tricking together harmlessly. Or dozing in the sun. Or even coupling.

It was evident that the strain of continual attack was wearying the dog. Its movements were now clumsy, sluggish: its lithe evasions slowing down. At last the inevitable happened.

The Kerry Blue came charging in obliquely. Swerved to escape the grinning expectant muzzle. A moment of teetering indecision. A shout from the crowd.

'The brock has got him!'

'It'll tear the throat out of him!'

'Maybe we should separate them, lads?'

'Throw Downey's craven cur in on top of them.'

Hawker called:

'Will I let Garry have another go at him, Johnny?'

The old man squirted a jet of tobacco-juice towards the straining dog. Said he:

'Damn the differ it'll make. The brock is the boss. He'll beat the two of them.'

Hawker loosed the dog.

'Sic him!' he said. 'Sic the bastard!'

The dog went in, running low to the ground, watching its comrade back away, dragging after it the badger, in a frantic effort to break the throttling hold. Ignoring threats, jeers and pleadings, it waited its opportunity. An unexpected jerk put the badger's legs sprawling. The wary dog pounced, grabbing the badger by a hind leg. Tugging at its hold, it swung the badger off the ground till it dangled belly up, its teeth still sunk in its enemy's throat.

Before the badger could right itself, the dog slammed the helpless body down on its back and, shifting its hold, bit deeply into the tender flesh of the groin.

So swiftly did the badger release its grip and lash out with scourging claws at the already lacerated muzzle of its new assailant that the agonized yapping of both dogs – the throttled and the mauled – broke out simultaneously. Still yapping, they fled to either side of the enclosure where they wheeled round, barking and growling. They were in poor shape. Bloody. Mangled. Shivering with fright.

'That burrowing bastard has made a slaughter-house job of them,' said Micky Hogan.

Johnny John spat, a quick explosive spurt. He said:

'Didn't I warn you the brock would master the pair of them? Better if you call in your wretched curs before he drives them ahead of him into the village.'

The badger had limped back into the scooped out trench. It commenced digging again. With its forepaws only. Soon its claws could be heard rasping on the cement foundation of the shed. It stopped. Changed position and burrowed again till once more stopped by the cement. Twice more it tried, before it started on the galvanized iron. Inserting a paw under the bottom of the sheeting, it commenced to tear at it, tearing and tugging until at last it managed to secure a purchase for its jaws.

'In the name of God,' someone said, with a nervous laugh, 'does it mean to pull the building over its head like Samson?'

The badger was worrying at the metal sheeting – tugging, snapping, gnawing – its body coiling and uncoiling, as it strove to chew or tear its way to freedom.

'You'd think it was crunching biscuits,' one of the young Johnny Johns said. 'With jaws the like of yon, it'd chew itself out of Sing Sing.'

The badger has extremely powerful jaws. A peculiar feature of the lower jaw is that it locks in a transverse elongated socket in such a complete manner that it will not dislocate: if it comes away at all the skull will be fractured.

An elbow jogged him.

'Are you asleep?'

'Eugh! ... Eh? ... Aye!' A long sighing breath. Part moan, part fretful wail.

'Come off it, Brer Fox. You're codding nobody. Lying awake brooding on the silly old badgers you were reading about all evening.'

She ran a teasing finger down the bones of his spine.

'Wha's-a matter? Whdja-want?'

'Oh, nothing. I thought you were asleep.'

'Darling, I've had a long, hard day. I'm jaded out. Beat to the ropes. Let's go to sleep, what d'you say?'

He clutched the bedclothes. Huddled down lower in the bed. Breathed loudly, steadily, through his nose.

The men were debating the fate of the badger.

'Destroy the brute. That's the only thing to be done.'

'Look at the shape it's left the dogs.'

'What'll the curate say when he sees the cut of Fergus?'

'Small odds about those whining hoors,' said Johnny John. 'Didn't the brock lather the daylights out of the pair of them? We'd be poor sports to slaughter it after that.'

'Let it go,' he urged.

'So that it can raid more hen-houses?'

'Or spread ruin round the district with its burrowing?'

'Aye! Or maybe start attacking the young lambs?'

Johnny John was overborne.

'All right,' he said. 'Fetch out a mattock.'

It was decided that Clarke, the village butcher, would dispatch the badger. Mattock at the ready, he moved in towards the gnawing animal. A few paces from the burrow he halted as the badger swung round to face him. Three cautious steps brought him within striking distance of the snarling muzzle. He hefted the mattock. Balanced it carefully, judging his target. Brought the blade smashing down square on the badger's poll, driving its head deep into the clay. A neat professional stroke.

The butcher stood over the motionless body, leaning on the shaft of the mattock. He was about to turn away, satisfied with a job well done, when the badger stirred. Raised its bloodied muzzle from the clay. Struggled erect.

Again Clarke chopped the heavy-bladed weapon down on the badger's skull, crushing the mangled head to the ground. Slowly, painfully, the snarling muzzle was raised in defiance.

Twice more the butcher swung down the mattock before Johnny John's shouts penetrated his shocked bewilderment.

'In God's name, give over, Butcher. You'll never do away with the brute that way.'

The old man rushed into the enclosure.

'Gimme that tool, man,' he said, grabbing the mattock. 'You'll take the edge off the blade. D'you not know that a brock's skull will stand up to a charge of buckshot?'

A feature of the badger is the extraordinary growth of the interparietal ridge of bone on the dorsal surface of the skull in the mid line. This ridge is half an inch deep in places and serves to protect the main surface of the skull from blows delivered directly from above, though its prime purpose is for the attachment of the powerful jaw muscles.

'Tell me,' she murmured, her breath fanning his ear, 'what attraction a badger has got that the rest of us lack?'

She had rolled over, cuddling herself against his back.

'Can't you let a fellow sleep?' He edged away unobtrusively.

'What has it got?' she insisted, snuggling closer.

'It's got courage. Courage. Tenacity. Fortitude.'

'Where do the rest of us come in?' Her hand burrowed into the jacket of his pyjamas. 'Wouldn't we all act the same way with our back to the wall? Courage and ferocity!' She sniffed. 'There's more to it than that. Surely?' Her fingers drummed an urgent message on his chest. 'You'd never ask someone to take second place to a stupid old badger.' A warm leg slid over his own. 'Would you, darling?'

'Sheila ... please!'

He shook himself free. Reached up and switched off the light. Fists clenched, eyes squeezed shut – he lay, trying to ignore the reproach in her rigid outstretched body. When at last her breathing had steadied to the rhythm of sleep, he tugged the bedclothes back over himself, relaxed and opened his eyes to the dark.

Queer, he thought, how she had got to the core of things. Unwittingly. For surely, without tenacity, courage and ferocity were futile.

The courage of the badger is legendary. A shy, inoffensive animal, with no natural enemies, it will yet, if cornered, ex-

hibit a ferocity noteworthy in a creature of such small dimen-
sions. It is utterly fearless. Whether bird, beast or reptile: the
forces of nature or the savagery of man – nothing can daunt
it.

Johnny John was standing an arm's length from the badger.
'There's only one way to kill a brock,' he said, over his
shoulder.

He raised the mattock. 'A clout on the muzzle.'

He swung down the blade.

At the same instant the badger charged. The squelch of the
blade on the animal's back and the cry of dismay from the old
man came together.

'So help me God,' he wailed. 'I didn't mean to do it.'

He dropped the mattock. With horror-stricken gaze he
watched the badger. Hindquarters flattened to the ground,
grinning muzzle still lifted in challenge, it continued towards
him, dragging its helpless body forward on stubborn forepaws.

'A wee tap on the nose. As God is my judge, that's what I
tried to do,' Johnny John pleaded.

'Come away out of that, Da, or it'll maybe maul you,' one of
the boys called out.

The mattock lay across the badger's path. An unsurmountable
barrier to the crippled beast. Feebly it pawed at the heavy implement striving to push or pull it aside. Without success. At
last, the infuriated animal sank its teeth in the wooden shaft,
lifting the handle clear of the ground. Unable to drag itself
further forward, it lay stretched out, eyes glaring madly ahead,
clenched jaws holding aloft the murderous weapon. The matted,
filthy, blood-stained animal had already the ugly anonymous
appearance of death.

The old man was near to tears. In his distress he shuffled a
few steps to either side, beating the fist of one hand into the
palm of the other.

'Where's my stick?' he muttered. 'Where the hell's my stick?'

He shook his fist at the watching crowd.

'It's all your fault, you ignorant pack of hallions. Didn't I
pray and plead with you to let the brock go? Now look what
you've done.'

He moved back towards them, changing direction aimlessly, his gaze scanning the ground.

'Where did I drop my stick? It must be someplace hereabouts.'

He looked up.

'Let none of you ever boast of this day's work. It was pure butchery, that's what it was. A cowardly bit of blackguardism. There's more spunk in the brock than in the whole bloody issue of you.'

He halted.

'Will some of you find me stick ... or some other implement ...' He looked back over his shoulder, as though fearful of being overheard. 'Till I put an end to its ... Oh, Mother of God!'

The badger had released its grip on the mattock. It rolled over on its back. Screaming.

It kept screaming – a loud sustained yell of defiance that not even the onslaught of death could subdue to a whimper: that ceased abruptly only with the slack-jaw and the glazing eye.

There are many conflicting theories regarding the significance of the badger's peculiar yell. Some naturalists believe it to have sexual origins: others that it has some connection with the death or funeral rites of this strange animal. All are agreed on the blood-curdling quality of the cry.

Lying wide-eyed and sleepless, he tried to close his ears to the appalling sound. It was no use. The voice of the dying badger refused to be silenced.

For all these years it had resounded in his memory with the urgency of a trumpet call – the wild defiant shout of an animal ringed about with enemies. He had thought to cast himself in this heroic mould. To be a maverick. Forever in the ranks of the embattled minority. Instead there had been a slow erosion of ideals, a cowardly retreat from one decent belief after another until at last he found himself in the ranks of the majority. The ring of craven curs that hemmed in and crushed the unruly, those few who dared cry: *'Non serviam!'*

The badger cry was now a pitiful sound. A shrill squeal of protest. The rage tinged with terror: the defiance with despair. The cry of something crushed, defeated, abandoned.

Desolation – a grey waste of futility and failure – engulfed him. His skin crawled. His limbs cringed in revulsion at the extent of his betrayal. Shivering, he eased over towards the warmth beside him. At once the rhythm of her breathing changed. She was awake. Had been all along. Lying there. Listening. Waiting to smother him with forgiveness. To hell with that for a caper. There was no absolution needed in this case.

The springs creaked as he shifted back, dragging the bed-clothes with him. It would be the price of her if she got her death of cold. The answer to her prayer. He coiled himself up, tucking in round his neck the bedclothes stretched between them.

Hardly was he settled down for sleep than the tranquil breathing became intolerable. He could envisage the patient, anguished, uncomplaining eyes of a holy picture staring into the darkness. Nursing its bitter wounds. God knows, you'd find it hard not to pity her.

He turned towards her.

'Sheila,' he whispered.

Once more the tiny catch in her breathing.

Gently he stroked the tense stubborn body, feeling it yield to his touch. She rolled over. Facing him.

'What's wrong?' she murmured.

Disconcerted, he stammered.

'Are ... are ... are you awake?'

She snuggled closer.

Feebly he grappled with her questing hand, warm and sticky with sweat. Lips fastened on his. Murmured:

'You *do* ... want me ... don't you?'

She buried her face in his neck.

'Grrr!' she growled happily. 'It's good to know I'm still on the wanted list.'

Acting out the familiar prologue, he held her in his arms, seeing only a mangled body mired and misshaped, bloodied muzzle grinning senselessly at a senseless sky: hearing only the scream of agony that death alone could arrest.

A feeling of loneliness swept over him. A bitter hopeless

loneliness that he knew to be surrender. The sin of Judas. The ultimate and unforgivable catastrophe.

He shivered.

'Darling!' Hoarse, breathless, she clutched at him with avid, furious hands. 'Oh, darling! Darling!'

Ballintierna in the Morning

BRYAN MACMAHON

ONE clear cold morning in November two young men boarded a south-bound train in Kingsbridge Station, Dublin. Both were bareheaded and wore shabby tweed overcoats. That they were fitters was a fact indicated by a black timber attaché case which one of the men was carrying; there were also tell-tale smudges of grease on their cuffs and on the edges of their overcoat pockets. Their names were Bernie Byrne and Arthur Lowe: they were being sent by their firm to repair the boiler of a country Creamery in County Kildare.

Byrne was an albino; his complexion was over-fresh and his eyes were the eyes of a tamed white rodent. His hair was cut short to avoid attracting undue attention, but the irrepressible pink of his body had bubbled up through his scalp. His expression had a disconcerting trick of trading idiocy for sagacity at the most unexpected moments. Arthur Lowe's face gave promise of being cadaverous before he was twenty-five. He had a facial tic. He was so sallow that one could not imagine his intestines to be other than grey rubber tubes. His humour, of which he was extremely niggardly, was slow, droll and deliberate. His dyspepsia, already chronic, had made him a person subject to sudden bouts of unreasoning irritation.

During the journey down – a bare hour's run – they remained standing in the corridor with their elbows resting on the horizontal guard-bar of a window. Since they were young, they resented the fact that they were wearing their working clothes while travelling – this was the reason that they did not enter a compartment. The corridor was ammoniac and stale and had little to offer them except the beginnings of train-queasiness. Despite this they found the ride slightly exhilarating, and it was with an unmistakable, if indeed somewhat subdued, sense of adventure that they looked out into the widening day. People passing to the lavatory crushed by them with barely articulated apologies. The young men gave room with excessive readiness as if to compensate with manners what they lacked in clothes. Looking downwards at an angle of forty-five degrees Byrne saw in the compartment behind him a sickish girl of four or five who was mouthing biscuits. The compartment was crowded; at a station he heard a stout woman praise the virtues of Aylesbury ducks. Some time afterwards he heard a voice from the other side of the compartment begin: 'There's nothing on earth the matter with my husband, but ...'

The men alighted at a small station in County Kildare. An impish boy of twelve with a red head and a freckled face met them. That he was a playboy was instantly obvious. His face cracked up with contagious glee as he asked:

'Are ye the men to mend the Creamery?'

'We are!'

The albino was laughing. The boy's face set for a moment as he examined Byrne's face and eyes. The albino resented the examination.

'The manager says I'm to show ye the way. If ye like, I'll get the case sent up in a Creamery car and ye can take the short-cut across the bog?'

'Across the bog?'

'Aye!'

'That'll suit me fine,' said Byrne.

The boy roared at the porter who, on closer inspection, proved also to have a red head and was obviously a brother of the guide: 'Hey, Mick, send that up in the next car!'

When they came out of the station they saw the trees. From an old oak depended the tattered remnants of summer finery now eked out in ragged brown bunting; a mendicant beech held out in emaciated hands the last of its unspent coppers; the furze was flecked with in-between-season gold. Beneath the trees they saw the bogland. As they approached it they lost interest in the trees and were taken with the as yet finite landscape. Following the boy they crossed the fence between the trees and were then on the floor of the bog.

Before them a turf bank reared itself in a great black rectangular box with planed-away corners. Drawing near they saw that, close to the surface, this rampart had crazied into fissures that had oozed irregularly shaped knobs of semi-dried peat. Clean rushes in tight clumps sprang from the chocolate-coloured ground. Bog-holes were filled with ink or quicksilver according to the light's quirk. A not repulsive odour of old sulphur came up out of the mould underfoot.

Their guide was agility itself. He sprang to a step in the black bog-wall, gained purchase and leaped up. The two young men followed. Then they saw the countryside in its entirety. It had all the variety of a display of tweeds in a shop window. Under their feet it was prune and orange and vermilion, with sometimes a lichen blazing up in a brilliant green. The leathery heather swished hungrily around their boots. The large white bones of fallen and stripped trees were flung here and there in the canyons of the cutaway. The sun had bleached them and the wind had antlered them. Two or three newly erected labourers' cottages were placed around the periphery of the bog: what with their red roofs, green doors, white walls and tarred plinths they had a wholly fictitious prettiness. A disconsolate black cow moved dully beside each of these dwellings. The sky was a wash of grey clouds. On the near horizon they saw the scarlet and white hulk of the Creamery. Beyond it were the crisp orthodox hills of the Irish skyline.

The men strode along, singularly braced by the morning air. To breathe it was in itself an adventure. Since the ground underfoot was reasonably dry they had the sensation of walking on eiderdowns. On their left they saw a hollow square carpeted with *fionnán* as white as wood fibre. It was growing in great tufts which were heavily matted in one another. The hollow seemed as snug as the bottom of a delf-crate. Their guide dropped into this hollow, at the same time signalling to the men not to make unnecessary noise. Byrne and Lowe followed warily. The youngster had his hands extended with the palms turned backwards. He was tiptoeing forward, his pert head turning this way and that. Suddenly he stood stock-still and the wings of his nostrils widened. His eyes were fixed on a tuft of grass before him. Seeing him standing thus the two men halted. Then the boy threw himself forward on the ground. Lying prone he scrambled into a ball, bringing his knees up to him and clawing at his belly. The men heard a squeal coming from beneath the boy. For all the world it sounded like the complaint of an injured infant.

'I have him! I have him! I so-hoed the hare!' The youngster's voice was blotched with an excitement which immediately communicated itself to the men who began to laugh and query eagerly. Lowe's tic began to beat furiously. Meanwhile the little actor was making the most of his moment on the stage. He rolled over to his knees, thence to his feet, all the while clutching something in the pit of his stomach. Then the men saw the elongated whitish body trimmed with red-brown fur. They saw the cut and curve of the great hind legs, the squashed ears and the huge protuberant eyes. Carefully the boy gathered the animal together, all the while keeping the hind legs under firm control.

All three grew strangely intimate after sharing this experience together. With a nod of his head the boy indicated the hare's form in the grass. The albino immediately crouched and bared the snug little arch. They all saw where the bones of the hare's buttocks had bared the dark clay. Byrne and Lowe in turn placed the backs of their hands on the floor of the form and remarked that it was still warm. As they stood up, each man shrank and shrank in imagination until he was a hare in the form peering out at the world through the tangled stems of the grasses.

Then Bernie Byrne asked: 'Hey! what are you going to do with him?'

This was a question the boy had not asked himself previously. He took refuge in a laughing vagueness. But the actor in him suddenly provided the answer.

'I don't know ... unless I kill him!'

'Will you give him to me?' asked the albino.

'Alive?'

'Yes, alive!'

'Sure I'll give him to you. I'll put him in a bag above at the Creamery and you can take him with you.'

Arthur Lowe had recovered his moroseness. 'What do you want him for?'

'I don't know ... I'll do something with him.' Byrne smiled and grew remote. This withdrawal irked Lowe who said, 'Come on or we'll never get this job done.'

It was night when they returned to the city. A frosty river-wind caused them to shudder as they emerged from the station. Arthur Lowe was carrying the timber case; Byrne had the hare in a bag. They took a bus to O'Connell Bridge.

Looking up the great thoroughfare, Byrne suddenly discovered that he had been granted the power to view his city with novel eyes. For one thing the balusters of the bridge were now wondrously white. The diffused light in the street was almost as impalpable as floating powder: it hung in a layer perhaps twenty feet in height and then it fined upwards into the windless city rigging. Over this was the unremembered night sky. Dan O'Connell himself and his satellites in bronze had all fused to form a drowsy octopus; Nelson was a cold hero on an eminence waiting to be quickened by a brilliant anecdote. The trams were lively enough, but they had gone to great pains to conceal their pattering feet. To the left and right Neon displayed its inability to form a right angle. Now and again a ragamuffin wind, shot with gaseous green slime, clambered up the ladders in the river walls and shrugged its facile way in and out of the arcades and the ice-cream parlours. The curves of the lamp-standards interpreted benevolence in terms of cement.

The people, too, had altered. In a remote nook in the street, cerulean lanterns were busy transforming the passers-by into death's heads. The theatre queues were composed of sexless, friendless, kinless persons who had voluntarily assembled thus in batches to make it easy for them to be gathered to God. The managements of the eating-houses had scraped circles or triangles or squares or lunes in the frosted rear glass of their windows through which the prudent could observe the imprudent eating lime-green hens. Objects in breeches and skirts trod on the grey-green cellar lights and applauded themselves for their intrepidity. A girl with her partner passed by hurriedly; a shell-pink dance·frock was showing below her dark coat. Suddenly she leaned forward and, egging her face onwards to a gambler's vivacity, said sweetly, 'But Joseph ...' Two workmen passed by; one of them was saying vehemently and gutturally, 'Play yer cards, I said, play yer cards.'

The albino had halted by the O'Connell Monument. His eyes were luminous in the dark.

'Hey!' called Lowe. 'Whatta yeh doin'?'

Byrne did not answer. He stepped softly in under the statue where it was semi-dark. He ripped the slip-knot on the sack's mouth, caught the sack by the bottom, and spilled the hare out on the ground. The animal was cramped: he gave three sorry hops, then crouched against the base of the statue. Above him Octopus O'Connell gave no indication of ambling.

(A hare is composed of three delightful ovals with swivels at the neck and loins. First there is the great oval of the body, balanced above and below by the smaller ovals of the head and hind quarters. The oval of the hind quarters is fragmentary but may be indicated satisfactorily enough by a simple illustration. The flexible ears are propellers, the tail a rudder. After that it is a question of power propelling a mechanism that is in perfect equipoise.

But wherever the power of the animal is generated, it finds expression in the spatulate hind legs which have the gift of spurning the world. Spurning the world – that's the secret out! That is what makes the hare so surpassingly gallant and his beholders so chagrined and superstitious.)

Sallowface was very quiet as he watched the albino. The tic flicked in his morose features. His face cleared as he gradually acquitted his companion of blackguardism. Byrne had begun to smile curiously; he crouched with legs set well apart. His two palms began to aim the hare towards the lighted street. The animal moved in the desired direction but, as yet, his gait consisted of despicable lopes. There was no indication that he could be so transcendently swift. Suddenly he stopped and began to cosy himself on a tram-track. Then he looked like an illustration of a hare in a child's picture-book. A breath of

river-wind came upon him and eddied his fur; this wind also
edged the albino's anger. He stripped his teeth and shouted,
'Yeh-Yeh-Yeh!' He raced his heavy boots and cried 'Hulla-hulla-
hulla!' as he slipped his imaginary hounds. The somnolent hare
became suddenly charged with action. First he sprang erect
until he was a vibrant red loop laced with white shadow. His
ears were tuned to the street. Then he began to pelt up mid-road.
All the while the maniacal teeth of the albino were volleying
'Yeh-Yeh-Yeh!' behind him.

At first the hare's passing occasioned little comment. The
people continued to stilt along or stand in lacklustre lumps.
Then someone began to cry out 'The Hare! The Hare!'

(You have seen the breeze impishly test the flexibility of a
barley field; you have seen a child's hand ruffle the tassels of a
countrywoman's shawl; you have seen a window-wind bring to
life the dead hair of a deskful of schoolgirls.)

'The Hare! The Hare!'

Passion sprang up in the people as if it were a Jack-in-the-
Box. The alert among the six thousand persons began to gesticu-
late and run. 'The Hare! The Hare!' they shouted. The street
rocked in its own uproar. The rushing, roaring people miraculously had sons and sisters and friends.

'The Hare! The Hare!'

Meanwhile the animate talisman darted here and there, setting his red torch to the golden thatch of the street. Now and
again he stopped abruptly. When he did so, no part of the
street was hidden from his exophthalmic-goitrous eyes. His
ability to stop was amazing. There was no doubt whatsoever
that he was terrified, yet his body was incapable of demonstrat-
ing dread and thus his terror masqueraded as alertness. He
seemed to be aware that the milling people were roaring for his
blood. And the people? They continued to demonstrate that
mankind is a huge wind-rocked stone balanced on a cliff-face.
Either that or (absurdity of absurdities) the greyhound is present
in everyone, together with the bittern, the plaice, and the ele-
phant.

Then the blazing galleon of a tram bore down upon the
animal. He lost the sense of his exits. He raced towards the

lighted street wall which miraculously opened before him in
the form of an entrance to a subterranean barber's shop. He
sped downwards, breaking the many parallel gleams of the
metal stair-treads.

The barbers stood in reverent ranks attending to the customers. With long cool hops the hare passed through and went
in the half-open doorway of an inner store-room which was
roofed at its farthest end by opaque cellar-lights. The room
had a repulsive smell compounded of superannuated combs and
hair-oil in semi-rusty tins. Along one wall was a long bench. The
hare lay down beneath it.

The crowd from the street surged down the stairway. They
were a shade intimidated when they saw the hieratic gestures
of the barbers. The head barber came forward – he also owned
the premises – and began to shepherd the intruders with his
scissors and comb. His name was Richard Collis and he had the
urbanity that has come to be associated with commercial com-
petence. The man had a skull the shape of an inflated pig-
bladder; his complexion, though a trifle over-scarlet, was
undoubtedly first class. The points of his moustache were his
twin-treasures and compensated in some measure for a childless marriage. His thinning hair was as a large cross placed on
his bare shoulders. With every step he took towards the intruders he filched the significance from their entrance and made
it appear a vulgar brawl.

'It's a hare, mister.'

'A hare's after coming into your shop.'

They took refuge in defeated laughter and the inevitable
puns.

Richard Collis brought the full searchlight of his suavity to
bear on the crowd on the stairway. Those nearest him were
light-blinded by its rays. But his rear was unguarded: he felt
the nick-snip of the many scissors die down behind him and
whenever a snip did come it seemed as if one of the younger
barbers were cocking a snook at his poll. He turned to his staff
and rebuked them with a glance. The music of scissors and
razor began again, but at a much slower tempo. Turning once
more, he found the people at the head of the stairway quite

merry and mutinous. It took all his charm and tact to expel them without appearing undignified.

Then a young barber pointed and said: 'He's gone into the room, sir.'

Richard Collis asked his customer to hold him excused. He entered the store-room, switched on the light and closed the door softly behind him. He saw the hare beneath the bench – a brown huddle which had achieved an unmistakable domesticity. The animal's panting was difficult to apprehend. Step by step the barber stole nearer. The hare swivelled his head but did not move away. Richard Collis got down on his knees. The hare watched him, first with friendliness, then with apathy. There came a sudden lull in the minor thunder of boots on the cellar lights. The barber stayed thus watching the hare for an appreciable while.

Then Richard Collis's countenance sagged, spruced, then sagged irretrievably. The skin of his face, as yet under some small control, proved to be covering a volatile squirming flesh. Unsuspected nerves jerked in patches like wind-flaws on still water. His tongue had ballooned and was filling his mouth. His lower lip essayed speech a few times before it succeeded.

'Wisha, God be with you, Ballintierna in the morning!'

He continued to kneel thus in trance while high in his mind the years clinked by like silver beads. Gradually his face grew less ruined. At last the renewed thunder of the boots on the cellar-glass aroused him. Then he arose and returned to his shop, closing the door reverently behind him.

Lebensraum

AIDAN HIGGINS

FRAULEIN SEVI KLEIN left Germany in the spring of her thirty-ninth year; travelling alone from Cologne to Ostend, she crossed the Channel, and from Folkestone to London found herself in the company of sober British citizens. She took a reserved seat facing the engine on the London train, her feet on the carriage floor as settled as ball-and-claw furniture, both fierce-looking and 'arranged' after the manner of such extremities, curving downwards towards a relentless grip. Her hips and spine conveyed the same impression, but reinforced, becoming the down-turned head of a dumb creature with muzzle lowered as though drinking; her eyelids seemed an intolerable weight. Her knees were pressed modestly together; she had hands of remarkable beauty and dressed in a manner suitable for someone possibly ten years younger. At Victoria Station she hired a cab, read out the name of a Kensington hotel from her pocket-book and was driven there with a moderate amount of luggage strapped into the boot. This was in the summer of 1947.

Sevi Klein walked the streets with the rolling gait of a sailor. In the National Gallery she stood minute below the paintings of Veronese, marvelling at his immense hot-faced women. Here she had met her match, for she was a lady herself down to the cockpit, but below that a snake chitterling or a chitterling snake.

Inevitably she walked into trouble at night on the Bayswater Road. The whores told her exactly what she could do with herself in Cockney and French, a dark one pouring baleful abuse into one ear, brandishing a copy of the Sierra Leone *Observer*. She said:

'*Vergiss es,*' thinking she preferred the Brinkgasse. Several times she was accosted by late gentlemen passing in Palace

Avenue, until she took to scaling the fence into Kensington Gardens. She sat on the cement edge of the Round Pond with both feet submerged, the red glow of her cigarette reflected in the water between her legs; leaning forward until the monotonous passage of in-going and out-going traffic on Bayswater Road became dulled and remote. After a while she heard only the wind in the trees and the stirrings of the geese across from her. At last she threw away her cigarette and sat in the water, hearing nothing.

Her flat was a dark place into which an uncertain sun never entered, but in summer loitered for a couple of hours on the balcony before creeping away. She opened the full-length windows to sit drinking coffee in the sun, dropping her ash through the iron grid, staring into the chestnut tree opposite. On odd Sundays the terrace resounded to the deafening strains of an itinerant drum-and-accordion band.

The whores continued to be suspicious of her. A freelance who lived in the basement next door had noticed her nocturnal habits and irregular hours of business and passed on the information. She roamed the streets with an air free yet constrained, like a castaway. Growing attached to Kensington Gardens she liked to spend whole days there in summer dressed as briefly as decency would permit, sitting on a deck-chair under the hawthorns. She read constantly and brought out a covered basket of sandwiches and cold beer. She enjoyed drinking but missed the bitter Kölsch beer of 'Vater Rhein'.

In dull weather the Gardens were deserted at evening save for old women exercising dogs. Then she went sauntering down the avenues of trees beyond the equestrian statue, heading for the Serpentine, a small figure silhouetted for an instant where the lanes ran together, dwindling, shapeless, then blotted out. Her favourite pub was the Queensway Underground. An already strong thirst was improved every time she passed the entrance and caught the dead air carried up by the lift. Then the gates crashed to on another lift full of pale commuters – the light vanishing as the contraption sank from sight.

One evening in June of that year she had drunk a little too much again and was flushed and talkative; meeting her reflection in one of the mirrors behind the bar, she knew it. The mirrors created an hexagonal smoke-filled confusion, and in these the patrons would sometimes encounter unexpectedly their own befuddled stares directed back at them from unlikely angles between shining tunnels of bottles. There upon the reflection of her own features another's strange features sank. A question was directed at her. Looking up she came face to face with a Mr Michael Alpin, late of Dublin, the doubtful product of Jesuit casuistry and the Law School. As far as the eye could see the patrons, with downcast eyes, were drinking their anxious beer. On one side a drunk repeated:

'Fizzillogical ... (inaudible) ... Swizzer-land ... Yesh, Shir,' and a sober one said over and over again: 'Really I don't know whether to buy that house or not ... now really I don't.' An elderly gentleman who had blown his nose too hard had to leave his drink and retire bleeding to the toilets. But Michael Alpin looked down into the small crucified face under the love-locks with the accumulated arrogance of a man who had made cuckolds (this was far from being the case, for he had emerged out of a past barren as Crusoe's as far as passionate attachments went). Would she care to join him in a drink? Would she? Nothing daunted, she gave him one quick look and said:

'Very well, thank you. I think I could.'

With some such preliminaries their life together had begun: in smoke, uproar and the sight of blood as if in the midst of a bombardment – to the skirl of a barrel-organ in the street outside and the look of incomprehension on his face (for he knew not a word of the language), while she chattered away in German.

They left arm-in-arm at closing time. He informed her that he had thrown up his profession and gone to seek his fortune on the continent of Europe. Morose and unsettled, he wore the air of a conspirator passing through enemy territory at night (although everything about him suggested furtive though arrested flight – a figure of doom superimposed on the landscape in dramatic photogravure). Plunged in a gloom out of which no succour could hope to lift him, Alpin the versatile Bachelor of Arts was twelve years her junior.

They set up house together in Newton Road, Paddington.

Her forthright manner both perturbed and enchanted him. He himself had attempted to expand his hopes by the guarded necessity of having innumerable alternatives and had almost succeeded in abolishing them altogether. In the following summer they crossed to Dublin. They were seen at the Horse Show where Sevi's curious manner of dressing was noticed by the press, her photograph appearing in the next morning's newspaper over the caption: 'Miss S. Klein, a visitor from Cologne, photographed in the jumping enclosure yesterday.' After that they moved to a hotel twenty miles down the coast, driving through the pass one evening in a hired car, hoisting their baggage on to the Grand Hotel counter and signing their false names with a flourish: 'Mr and Mrs Abraham Siebrito, Cascia House, Swiss Cottage, London N.W.3.' There they came together at last steadfast as man and wife, though he was almost young enough to be her own long-lost son, and no marriage lines had ever been cried over them.

They lay together at night listening to the freight trains pulling through the tunnels, exchanging confidences. She spoke of a wet night at Enschede on the German–Dutch border. Woken in the early hours of the morning by bicycle bells and noises from the drunks in the lane behind the hotel, she had heard a monstrous voice roar with a blare almost of ordnance, and in English:

'Run! Run! Run from me! ... But do not run in a circle!' He mentioned a Negro whom he had observed buying a newspaper outside the *S-Bahn* in Berlin, and how the action of selecting money from a reefer-jacket, dropping it into the vendor's box, taking a newspaper, thrusting it under his arm and entering the station, was performed to a rhythm almost ballad-like – a flowing series of poetic actions, he said, as appropriate as the equivalent in an uncorrupted community, performed with the 'rightness' of hundreds of years of repetition behind it; the same economical gestures he had seen put to another use on Inishere when the islandmen were launching the currachs. Into a mechanical and self-conscious milieu the Negro had introduced something as natural and unexpected as the village pumps encountered among the chromium and neon signs on the *Kurfürstendamm*.

'But why not?' she said. 'After all, the Negro has been a city man since the invention of printing.'

'But not as a free man, Sevi,' he said. 'Not free.'

'Free?' said Sevi faintly. '*Herr Gott!* Who's free?'

Then she slept with her knees drawn up, drawing on oxygen as the dying draw on air. From such deep sleeps, recurring over and over again, light as sediment, heavy as evidence, she was not so much woken up as retrieved. He did not attempt to touch her, for there were depths into which he did not care to penetrate. Apprehensive of a bitterness and venom half-perceived or guessed at beyond her habitual kindness, beyond her ability to be hurt, while he himself was attempting the impossible – to hold such contradictory elements together in his love. Every day he feared he would lose her, and every night he feared he was going to bed alone, seeing her bound so: the distress of a frontier people obliged to present their backs to grievance and opposition. About her hung an air of demolition; taking herself so much for granted, she seemed immune to her own destruction. Her presence admitted no other alternative; she could only be relieved when she was let go. Since he held the scales in his hand, perhaps he felt also that she was disappointed in him. Looking for an arena where she could be put away, she had not found it in his cold bed. Even though his love was offered *in extremis*. Even though he was himself invaded and all his neutrality violated.

She went for long walks alone; returning late at night, re-entering the sleeping village, coming to the hotel where her lover lay sleeping. As she ascended the stairs, the building seemed to shake, so that he awoke to become the unborn child in her womb, and the whole resounding house her stomach. She stood outside the door listening before taking the handle in her hands and tearing it open. He started up in bed. Standing with the light behind her she hissed into the dark bedroom:

'*Michael, bist du aufgewacht? ... Ich bin zurück gekommen.*'

Sevi chain-smoked everywhere, taking volumes of Proust into dinner, dining on prawns. Rain kept them indoors for days on end, arguing on the stairs; she went out only to exercise her dachshund, Rosa Flugel, or to attend Mass. She came down to dinner in a housecoat of faded blue denim such as greengrocers favour, ate rapidly, reading from a book propped up before her, arranging prune-stones in an absent manner on the cloth. He loved and desired her, incapable of the most rudimentary caution. He felt a tension in her which would not permit her to age – holding her years like a pendant about a no-longer-young neck. Thus she came to invoke for him the incautious women of the eighteenth century, talented yet promiscuous, half whore, half wife. Thinking of Sevi he remembered Madame de Warens, and made himself participator in what he had lost. When he touched her flesh, it seemed infested with another life. Sevi too was a woman never at rest, so that intimacy with her seemed hardly possible; she had travelled all her life and would probably continue to do so until the day of her death – his own intervention swept aside; so that she would always be out of reach. If sleep and death, as we are told, bestow on us a 'guilty immunity', then travel does too, for the traveller is perpetually in the wrong context; and she was such a traveller. Sevi Klein belonged by right to that unfortunate line of women found in history (and almost extinct in their own time) which its progress, in an unreasonable search for attitudes, abuses; at least there was a certain melancholy in her eye which suggested she was part of such an abuse. 'Unrelated' in the way that the sentiment 'Pray for the Donor' in churches is unrelated to the disorder of death itself and to the imminent horrors of the *Ewigkeit*, or to any condition such sentiments affected to cover, one waited in vain for the 'real' Sevi to appear. She smiled no reassuring modern smile, but now and then produced a rare and archaic one of her own, a smirk that unpeopled the world. Sometimes the expressions so calmly uttered by her in the English tongue contained inaccuracies open to the widest interpretation; and towards these breaches in the walls of common usage his fears were constantly running, without, however, ever being able to close the gap. An act of revenge for her threatened to be a clumsy and unusually indelicate operation. Sooner or later in all her own undertakings wild flaws appeared, disorderly and complete. Gored by the Bull of Roman Catholicism, she had once made a pilgrimage to the Holy City, where an ardent male citizen had attempted to assault her indecently in a prominent position on Sancta Scala, in the course of Passion Week ceremonies.

She had only to think, 'Now I have something extraordinary in my hands', for the object, no matter what it was, to collapse on her. She said:

'In Paris it was like this – I thought that I was going to faint outside the Musée Grevin. The brightness of the streets had made me dizzy. I tried to ask for a glass of water in a shop there, but I couldn't make myself understood; they gave me a box of matches instead. Every day I passed that place they came out to laugh at me.'

No, she knew nothing of the larger resources and confounding quality of female tears, and thus could sneer in character:

'Verliebte lieben es, in Gewahrsam genommen zu werden.' Of her no timid lover need ask, beg:

'Am I debauching you, or are you debauching me?' because as a young girl she had already spared him that embarrassment. 'Wir glauben nicht an die Legende von uns selbst weil sie im Entstehen ist ...'

Justice hardly seemed to apply to her, her own nature not being porous enough, or lacking the space, the safe margin, for a change of heart, or for forgiveness.

From the beginning their relationship had proceeded erratically in a series of uncalculated rejections. She could be relied upon to say:

'Look, I haven't changed' – as if this justified her as a 'woman in love' instead of condemning her as an out-and-out imposter. It was as though she must live a little ahead of herself, in the condition of having to be continually roused out of her absence. It was true also that Sevi still escaped him. Another damp morning would begin, day breaking wretchedly, and without many preliminaries she would stand before the window, looking out on the sodden and discoloured earth, thinking her own thoughts. Both beaches lay deserted; gulls were collected over them, veering about, crying. The scavengers were collecting muck on the foreshore where Sevi had bathed naked. Her impatient form, damp hair and piteous skin! That part of me that is not me, in the person of another. There in a dream he had embraced her.

She crept back into bed beside him without a word and soon was asleep again. As he too began to sleep he was advancing into her, and advancing was troubled by a dream.

In the dream – in the dream! Hastening along the road among a crowd of pilgrims – never fast enough! Dreaming, he heard real cries coming from the rear, and blows. The pilgrims were taking to the ditches. He flung himself in among them and found his hands fastened on a woman's skirts. He was a child. Someone was passing, but it was forbidden to look. The pilgrimage to the queen was interrupted because she was coming in person on the road, hell for leather among her entourage. Power was passing, shaking the air. From the ditches on either side the bolder spirits were peering, whispering. He uncovered his head and looked.

At the level of his eyes and striding away from him down the crown of the road, he saw a heavily built woman dressed in a transparent raincoat worn open like a cloak, above it a bald pate. In the ditches they were whispering in astonishment among themselves. Then the dream carried him abruptly forward into the town.

In the last part of the dream all were dispersing from the town rapidly, as though threatened. He found himself, adult now, hurrying out hand-in-hand with a girl who was unknown to him. The town was under shell-fire but the queen and her court had to remain behind. In great fear for himself, he felt the ground shift under his feet and his heart race as though to outstrip the danger. But the first shell was already airborne. He sensed it coming through the clouds of dust raised ahead of him by the feet of the pilgrims. It exploded up ahead in the crowd. He plunged on – almost racing now – hoping that the next would pass over his head. The smoke of the first explosion came drifting back, and as he went forward into it he sensed, low and directed, the dropping trajectory of the second. Then he saw it. Silently, almost casually, a white object was lobbing towards him, gathering speed as it turned down. Too late already he flung up his arms. The shell crashed through the

walls of his chest, firing itself point-blank into his soft un-
militant heart. Localized and unhinged, his last soundless yell
went up. A blinding detonation followed, casting him out of
sleep.

He awoke trembling in the grey light. Beside him Sevi huddled lifeless. He touched her; she groaned once and turned
over. Incurable, incurable! So it would continue until all the
charts of the body were stowed away, the record of its blood
and its thinking completed, and the light of the eyes extinguished. He felt then as he or another might feel at the hour
of death, when the loathing borne by the suffering flesh goes
out like a sigh to the objects the dying person stares at, and
all the refuse collected together by that person in a lifetime is
brought up to date, stamped with a formal seal (corruption
itself) and made part of the universal collection; so that the
disgust with the Self, total and languishing no more, is trans-
mitted to inanimate objects – sinless as well as free in space and
time – and the dead person freed at last from the responsibility
of feeling.

The coast road entered the hills beyond Shanganagh, climbing in the half-dark between cedar and eucalyptus. In the light
again, houses appeared, designed like citadels and displaying
Italian names. Built into the granite above the beach, they
gazed without expression over the bay. The beach resembled
a sand quarry converging on a sea. Semi-naked bathers descended wooden steps on its blind side, going down and shutting
from sight the mock-Italian frontage, balconies and awnings,
the chorus of eucalyptus trees.

They came on the coast train in the season, appearing first
on the horizon in the most purposeful and heroic shapes, the
women numerous and always protesting. Crowds of them lay
on the shore all day in extraordinary attitudes of repose, while
from above more and more were descending with the measured
tramp of the damned. No wind disturbed the incoming sea or
the prostrate people, and in the glare all that could be delinea-
ted was destroyed. Shore and sea merged, dog and clown were
swallowed up in inextinguishable fire. On the high stanchions of

the Tea-Rooms the bearded John Player sailor was burning, remote and lugubrious in hammered tin.

So the days drew out, tides entering and leaving, the heat continuing, the floating bodies aimless and inert on the water. Time appeared as a heavy hand giving or taking their life away, falling anyway, impartially on sand, on feeble walls, on tired summer trappings. And the smoke going straight up from the stands; and the children crying (a sound blood-dimmed and heavy to the ear, as though conducted there not by the air itself but by brass or copper); and the damp elders prone everywhere. For Saturday had come again and Saturday's tired population was at the sea.

All who arrived at the beach from sloblands and city – the deposed Kings and Queens of Torrent Hill, the bands of nuns released for the day from *L'ordre des Ombres*, the Old Oak Infant Orphanage, the hooligans from Zoar Street – came shaken with a suspended summer lust, to hold a commemorative service on the summer passing and the free days. Submitting to chance freedom but performing the act diffidently and as though enacting a scene obviously 'beyond' them. A company coming down resigned, without too much enthusiasm and without too much style, into the Promised Land. The bulk, unconcerned with fair play, knowing in its bones the awfulness of any dealing, lay claim to their territory as graveyards lay claim to the dead. So these citizens were to claim this beach, lying there like an army fallen amidst its baggage; ground mollifying them, taking them into its secret at last, completing them. Admitting at the same time that under the name of 'Hospitality' is concealed various disorders; heavy bodies saying in effect:

'*This is our ground; let us exploit it*' (the resources of a spirit seldom fired, conceiving only this drear Heaven of abject claims). So they descended in an uneven line all through summer, no individual shape an heroic shape any longer, but all the shape of the common plural.

One evening a member of the *lazzaroni* appeared on the beach. Destitute and unwhole, escaped from the tenements, he had made his way out of the station, dressed in an ancient overcoat which reached below the knees, found the steps, and arrived. The bay water was dead calm; an odour of eucalyptus hung in the air. The young ladies who had come from the hill convent were just collecting themselves together, preparing to leave. He had watched them from his perch, unseen and pawing himself doubtfully, without ever taking his eyes away. Spread below him he saw an intoxication of green uniforms and then a flurry of undressing, and then bare flesh, then girls shouting and swimming, and now dressed again and going. While the face hung above them, chalk-white where paralysis had killed it, the bleak jaw-line and the bared teeth presented as component sections of the human skull, the profound bone base of all emotion glaring back its final indifference. The freak face stared down, motionless and cold, negligent as features gouged in putty, with a stare which took in the area and then destroyed it – the observer himself lost somewhere between unrelated head and unrelated body. Confronted with this, all would be left in doubt, waiting for the final kindness to put it right or the final unkindness to annihilate it. The bay water remained calm; smoke rose blue into the air from the cooking stands; the nuns, careening themselves at a decent remove, were showing an emancipated leg on the Feast-day of St James the Greater.

Nuns apart, the people were to become aware of him as they might have become aware of the stench, the effluvium, which surrounds and yet contains discarded and putrefying matter. Not deformed in any striking manner, there remained something foul about his person, an uncertain wavering line drawing him down and compelling him to be recognized. They were looking at an imbecile, one of themselves, a person loose and lost, a young fellow in his mid-twenties – a 'fact' in the way a multiple exposure in photography is a fact, something irregular yet perfect, perfect yet a mechanical abuse of itself. Beyond that he was nothing, could be nothing, for there was nothing left over, no place where they, weeping with solicitude, could put their hands and say, 'This at least is ours'. He was like something they could not recollect. He was a disturbance in their minds. The normally healthy, when their health breaks down, speak of being 'in poor shape'; but he, who had seldom been healthy and never been normal, was poor shape incarnate. He was the Single One, a neuter.

A tenement child had lured him to ground level with her sly eyes, with a movement of her head which was partly a deliberate soliciting and partly that dumb invitation we tender a beast. He crept out after her, the child turning and grinning, spilling water from her shining can. So he found himself among the people at last.

He began wandering about, head shaking and feet uncertain – a nameless fear. A tall and disjointed figure fashioned by all manner of winds, whose every movement was apprehensive, trailing his wake of misery behind. His stare lacked momentum, falling short of the object before he could 'take it in', painfully slow hands closing on the dog's head after the animal had moved, closing on air. His touch was more an experiment than an act of possession. The eyes he turned on them were dark and liquid, barbicans in his shattered face, guarded and half-closed like the identical crenels of a tower: that old and wary perspective of eyes behind which the senses stood armed and uneasy – a minute suspicious stir in the wall's face. None could pity or deplore or 'place' him because he could not be found, could not find himself, lost and swallowed up by a continual and forbidding silence. No way remained open to remind him of a former disturbance which he could have gone back to and reclaimed – as a dog draws back its fangs from the security of the kennel, so this creature was drawing back from the appropriating touch on the arm which would identify him as a poor blind man. His feet were the first to despair, dragging the shadow, shadow in its turn flinching from the outstretched 'charitable' hand. He was struck at such a pitch of intensity that he had to be heard to the end.

Those who were leaving made to pass him, but in their embarrassment wheeled round to face him, at a loss and unhappy, clutching at their possessions and saying to their children: 'Come along now ... oh, now come along!' not even knowing where to look any more. Then he covered his face, churning in the sand, cancelling himself with his own hand. The shadows on the cabins were locked together for an instant and then wrenched apart. They did not wish to see him or be witness to this distress, for among them he was an effigy and a blasphemy, something beyond the charity of God or man. Perishing so in his own presence, he seemed to be devouring himself. Existing outside perspective, he could not be considered as an equivalent to themselves.

Thrown out of order and at a loss, the herd was in full retreat, their dreadful faces turned about, their mouths wailing soundlessly. And then nothing. Silence fell. He went alone through it, ignored. Their silence, no longer a retreat, became an intermission – a trying situation out of which all hoped presently to advance, voluble and unrepentant, back into the good life out of which all had been cast. Presented with this figure of doom their Christian feelings had fled. Here was no blind man, only one who did not care to remember; this patient brought no dreams to the session.

And so, little by little, life returned and darkness fell. All the living were out and about as though nothing had happened, blown hither and thither by the high winds of commiseration, holding aloft their stupendous banners, being obliging, running messages (their obligations running before, to rob them), being spiteful. Spiteful!

Hin-und her-gerissen! ... Schweinfieber! Save the patronage of their kind names. They went down blind into the dark pool, the shadows falling everywhere and the ending never likely. They went down. Dark clouds were forming overhead. Look here! Look there! Unkind life is roaring by in its topmost branches.

The late summer when he had watched that had gone for good. Now it was winter: late evening-time in an Irish October. The short winter day was drawing to an end. He sat on the sea-wall and watched her tramping along the bluff, heralded by piteous cries from some climbing goats. She came trailing into sight after a while, crossing below, bare-footed, trailed by her low German hound; she resembled a person who never intended to come back. He watched her, a dark blur by the water's edge, her shoulders were moving. He leant forward (could she be crying?) and saw she was writing with a stick on the sand, the palimpsest. *'Das ist des Pudels,'* she wrote, and below that one word, *'Kern'*, in a crabbed backhand. That was that. The tired eye had begun to close; soon they could go their various ways. It was not as if light had been drained from the sand but as if darkness had been poured into it. Now almost invisible, he sat aloft so that Sevi came for the last time, walking slowly against the sea and against the last light, penetrating him as an oar breaks water. But not stopping, retreating, descending stairs of sand, going out slowly followed by the dog. He watched her evaporating, crawling into her background, not declining it, deliberately seeking it, lurching away from him to stumble into a new medium (a way she had), beating down the foreshore like a lighter going aground. Her hair undone went streaming back from her head; for an instant longer she remained in sight, contracting and expanding in the gloom, and then was gone.

The tide rose now until it covered the entire shore. Shallow yet purposeful water embraced the extremity of the seawall. Invisible gulls were complaining, worrying, somewhere over its dark unpeaceful depths. Anxiously the pier lights waved a mile to the south – a remote outfall of light more dingy than the sky, now dropping, now drowned in intervening wave. Michael Alpin walked out of the dark construction of the wall, broken here and there by heavy seas. He stood over her scrawlings, her last abuse. Unbuttoning himself he took his stance staring out to sea, his lust or love in the end reduced to this. Retreating to the wall he laid his face against its intolerable surface of freezing stone. As he began to go down, the false surf light and the remote light along the pier, diminishing, swung away.

There is no commencement or halfway to that fall: only its continuing.

Return of the Boy

MICHAEL J. MURPHY

I WONDER was I wise in letting old Felim go back to that pub: for my own peace of mind more than his. It won't bother him any more; but I'll neither know nor be satisfied until I've completed the venture as I promised. Because, platitudinous or not, few of us know ourselves as adequately as we think – or should.

One of my weak spots I know to be a nagging, obstinate, obsessional quirk of conscience. And knowing it I should never have promised Felim I would go back some day. Now I'll have to go back to that pub in the lonely hills of Co. Down, one side of Banbridge in the North of Ireland, 'The Bann' to us in South Armagh: back to make an outrageous toast, loud and declamatory, as Felim would have made it.

The pub, mercifully, may now be closed. More than likely it's a jazzed-up chromium 'Inn' with a sign in garish illumination at night; with barmen wearing crested jackets and epaulettes; or with satiny American sleeve-waistcoats and arm-bands. Even if they don't throw me out it would be almost blasphemy to make the toast Felim requested against a background of perpetual Pop from in-built loud-speakers.

Unless of course the bar-room remains as it was: stone-flagged floor, open fire and long wooden stools, and pints of stout served in thick fluted glasses, so that thirsty locals with a first drink 'drive the stout below the chapel windows': the sort of bar-room, against carpeted lounges, that locals have come to title in sardonic, resentful guffaws as 'The Eejits' Ward'.

They had a folk saying in our part of South Armagh about going back – or not going back; I can't remember which. But

maybe a man has to go back if only to find out why he
shouldn't have gone – or why he should: as old Felim certainly
found out that time we went back to The Bann where he'd
been a hired servant as a barefooted boy of ten years of age.
Or did he find out?

I wish I could recall that vernacular saying; but idiomatic
sayings and half-doors and the custom of the Hiring Fairs all
seem to have gone out together. Few in our parish at Slieve
Gullion remember the old sayings; certainly not the saying
they made about Felim himself.

It was a bitter saying better forgotten. If people wanted to
spike an impulsive promise, or belittle any emotional threat,
they'd say with sarcasm: 'Suppin' scaldin' broth with the point
of an awl – the way Felim A'Heer went back to The Bann.'

They said it even after he had gone back; for no one except
his daughter-in-law and myself ever knew he had – not even
his son Joe. Like myself, Felim must have remembered his
threat mouthed through porter at the dances held to celebrate
the return of hired servants from their six months' terms down
around The Bann: dances held on kitchen floors; himself with
the old men around the fireside recalling their own gruelling
days as servants in the same Black North among Orange
Protestant Masters. At every dance Felim would make his threat.
He would go back: back to The Bann some fine November day
when the crop had been happed and saved; when he had a
decent stitch to his back; one shilling not having to break its
neck overtaking the other in his pocket; back down to the
place he'd been hired in at ten years of age; back to hammer
the Orange soul-case out of the Protestant hide of the gett who
had been his master, a proper old rip by the name of William
Andrew McAlecson ...

He had been saying that every May and November for years,
but had never ventured further than the town of Newry in
Co. Down to sell a beast or make a market. And so they had
inevitably tagged that saying about scalding broth on the point
of an awl to his name when the occasion of emotional threat or
promise called for it.

Only for his son Joe he might never have gone back. Joe was

an only child and at the time doing well as a navvy-ganger with an excavation company in England; Joe's wife and two young children remained at home with Felim on the ten acres of moory mountain land; as well of course as Felim's wife, who was bed-fast. When she died I knew Joe meant to change things and had been biding his time. He planned to close the house, let the land and bring the whole family including Felim to England.

But after the funeral Felim was stunned. For three days he sat at the fan-bellows idly turning the wheel and watching the fire, always wearing his long, old, heavy overcoat. He continually smoked his cutty clay with its notched tin lid. He spoke to no one, not even the children he worshipped. Felim was tall and gaunt with deep-sunk grey eyes in a narrow head, and he seemed to shrink. On the third day, Joe announced that he was leaving for England and would return in a month to bring the whole family, including Felim, back to England.

Felim roused like a scalded wolfhound that had been dozing Go to England among the strangers, was it? What would happen the likes of him at his time o' day in a mad country like England? – What would happen the land?

Land ... Land? Joe had countered; land that wouldn't physic a snipe: half the fields no different than graveyards except that the stones had no names cut on them: land of that sort could go to hell as far as he was concerned ...

I tried to intervene; so did Joe's wife, a stranger to South Armagh. Felim growled like a beagle; and before we could stop Joe, he had said it:

'You'll neither lead nor drive an' never have. Never would. You'll go nowhere. "Suppin' scaldin' broth with the point of an awl –"'

'Joe –?'

'"The way Felim A'Heer went back to The Bann ..."'

Felim couldn't have heard the saying until then; but he knew what it meant and how it had been coined. He seemed to stagger up to the room to his bed.

.Joe regretted his outburst and told me so as we left that evening from Newry railway station (gone now too). I was with him as far as Portadown; here I changed for Omagh on my way to the Sperrin Mountains in Co. Tyrone where I was collecting folklore at the time; he went on to Belfast on his way to England. About noon the next day I had a wire from Joe's wife: Felim was missing and would I return. I did so at once. We searched everywhere and in every pub for miles around; he had been in a few but had left. Towards midnight of the second day police found him one side of Camlough Lough half-immersed in a disused flax-dam beside an old road, trapped by a net of briars over the water and weeds. The briars probably saved his life, but he was horribly torn around the face. The police said he appeared to be somewhat delirious, saying something about going back somewhere ...

We got him home and attended to. I heard nothing more until the day before a November market in Newry. Could I, his daughter-in-law wrote, be in Newry when the banks opened? Felim was determined to pay the rent himself and insisted on going alone. He was, she said, much drawn in on himself of late, speaking little. She even wondered if it might be a wise turn to bring him back to The Bann and set his mind at rest. It might settle and satisfy him. Rather than leave him alone she had refused to join Joe in England. The children doted on him. She'd never do a day's good if anything else happened to him ...

I went to Newry. The morning broke calmly out of a November fog, and by the time I got there the worn November sun was fingering scrolls of ear-plug cloud out of the folds of the hills around the town. Opposite a bank I saw Felim. He was along with a few men dressed in sober country clothes like himself. They all seemed to be fascinated by the great brass knob on the door of the bank, watching it even when they exchanged a few words among one another.

When the bank door opened they crossed the street in fits and starts like men going apprehensively to a court-house or gaol. I watched Felim go in; watched him come out. In the doorway of the bank he lit his cutty clay pipe. He blew out a great cloud of smoke. I knew the other men would do the same: a votive incense to a deep-rooted notion of land freedom still haunted by fugitive memories of landlords, bailiffs and eviction.

When I bumped into him at a corner, as if by accident, his grey eyes stirred and then glared into mine. He didn't offer to shake hands and at once I got uneasy.

Before I could make a mock exclamation he says:

'Thon daughter-in-law of mine? She wrote somethin'?'

I denied it black and blue, aware that the shrewd eyes were fixed on me. I swore I had heard of an old folk storyteller somewhere near The Bann and was on my way to hunt for him. I even invented a name for the man; said I would have to inquire for him in pubs along the way. Certainly in the pubs since forges were closing then for good.

'You'll never make a good liar,' he says, and added: 'but before you make a bigger liar of yourself, the wisest thing for us to do is to go in somewhere ourselves.' And he set off ahead of me, his long coat flapping to his swinging gait.

In the bar over the second half-one of whiskey, his morose mood began to break up. He muttered laments for his dead wife. Next he berated the world, then his son Joe. No nature in the young people any more. But he rhapsodized over his two grandchildren – healthy as trouts – his hand was on my shoulder by then – he'd give his heart's blood for any of them. And the daughter-in-law was as good as gold – and then he began to roar for the barman to fill up our drinks. I protested but he slapped the counter and cried:

'Hell roast me skin, aren't we out? An' when a fella's out let him *be* out!'

A little plump man on a stool beside us may have thought we were getting rowdy, for he slid off. Just then Felim whirled from the bar calling for the bowsey of a barman and bumped into the little man, who excused himself and stepped round Felim. Felim grabbed him, apologized himself and asked him to wait for a drink. The little man thanked him and said he couldn't; he had to catch a bus to Banbridge. And he trundled off.

Felim stood staring at the door for a moment. Then he whirled to me. The barman had meanwhile appeared and was waiting.

'When a fella's out,' Felim cried, 'let a fella be out. Are you game?'

'Game ball,' I cried, hoping to match his humour.

'No sooner said than done. Come on.'

I caught a glimpse of the barman twitching up nostrils and shoulders in the same movement as we left. The bus for Banbridge stood with engine running just along the main street.

Beside me in the side-seat of the Banbridge bus he was in great form.

'Did I ever tell you,' he began, pawing the clay pipe from under his huge moustache, 'how I come walkin' out of The Bann after me hirin' term in borrowed boots?' He had, but I didn't say so. A few heads tentatively half-turned towards us. The little plump man sat in the seat immediately in front, his back to us. 'Me father,' says Felim – and he touched his cap in respect – 'I hope the man's happy in Heaven – me father walked the whole road down one Sunday to The Bann where I was hired with an old half-done pair of boots for me. An ould pair of elastic-sided woman's boots borrowed off a neighbour at home. But at a penny a week, mind you. An old hag of a woman they called Sadie the Cailleach – "Cailleach" means "hag". Isn't that right?'

I assured him he was right; up the bus the heads turned sufficiently to enable me to see smirks being exchanged. Felim hadn't noticed.

'Sadie the Cailleach,' he goes on. 'She's dead an' rotten this years on top of years above in Dromintee graveyard – may Heaven be all their bed.' And again touched his cap.

He was going to continue when the conductor moved to take our fares. Felim stayed my hand and hauled out a fistful of silver. Then he was stumped: he didn't know where we were going. Neither did I. Suddenly he remembered and, once more, heads turned and faces smirked, for he shouted the name like a slogan of freedom or triumph:

'The road to McAlecson's shop an' pub! This side of the forge!'

At that the conductor was stumped and looked for assistance to me. But the little man in the seat before us half-turned and said over his shoulder knowingly that it was a 'wheen o' years since there was a forge there'. He told the conductor where he thought we wanted to get off. I hadn't a chance to note how the other passengers accepted this event.

Felim paid, and then leaned towards the plump little man and asked him if he knew McAlecson's.

'Only the old doll in the pub,' he replied, without turning full to face Felim. 'You might say I didn't.'

'You missed nothin'.' And Felim was already jabbing the little man's shoulder with the stem of his pipe. 'That old doll would be the stuck-up damsel used to help in the pub, I'd say. I'll say this for her though – she used to sneak out the bottle of stout for me to carry to the fella of McAlecson's who was in bad health – with the weakness you understand – consumption. What they call TB the day.'

The little man was trying to whistle.

'He was put sleepin' on the loft with me – for company. Coughin' his heart's blood out many a night. An' him heart-afeared of the rats,' Felim guffawed. The little man was chewing his lip. The heads turned again but the smirks had frozen. 'I used to chase the rats for him with Sadie the Cailleach's bleddy ould elastic-sided boots – fire them at the rats. As for William Andrew McAlecson himself I hope he's in hell – a thief with as much nature in his Orange heart as a stickin' bull, as black as the ...'

Felim's voice switched off like the fading drone of a siren. The little man had begun to whistle loudly, looking up at one side of the roof of the bus, then the other, in uneasy disassociation. Felim himself hadn't noticed, but had at least realized that he wasn't at an old-time Hiring Dance fireside, saying his piece as he had always done. He fidgeted. I couldn't think of anything to say. He began to ransack his pockets. I asked him what he was looking for.

'The flamin' pipe,' he whispered, as morosely as ever.

I told him the pipe was in his mouth.

Houses flashed by, aloof, spaced, lonely; a lake with a cranog island; guttery straw-strewn yards with moping cattle. Felim growled: 'A lonely ould sort of a country like I thought it was. But changed. This is a fool's errand we're on. I'm surprised you let me.'

The landscape was lonelier still when we left the bus, although cars sped up and down the main highway and stirred the fallen leaves. Somewhere among the hillocks of land a threshing-mill was at work; the drum of the mill moaned and soughed as it gulped sheaves of oats; it might have been making its own lament for the dying year. The only soul in sight was a road surfaceman shovelling a drain along a road to our right.

Felim turned up the road. Screened by tall hawthorns red with haw we found the pub. It looked as if a high wind had rattled it. The door was closed and every window but one and a kitchen window was shuttered and all had iron bars. There was a signboard, but the blubberings of ancient paint had spat away the name.

As I knocked on the door I heard Felim groan like an ailing animal. I knocked again and heard him swear; but it was his son Joe he was cursing. He was muttering something about getting to hell away from the place when surprisingly the door opened slowly and a little woman with hair as white as fine teased new rope let us in. She closed the door on our heels as if to keep out the whimper of the leaves drifting in hosts like lost hungry elves over the cobbles. The woman led us to a room; it was the room with the unshuttered window. A fire had been set in a huge open grate but not lighted.

I ordered whiskey and she left us silently, not having said a word. Felim was moaning again. To lift his mind I asked him if the room had been a shop or a bar-room, for great hooks coated in whitewash hung from ceiling beams. But he didn't seem to care or want to talk; just glared at me and up at the ceiling, then down at the stone-flagged floor.

The woman came back as silently as she had left. We took the drinks from her hands. I had the correct sum in coins ready and these she dropped casually into some pocket in her dress. Still without speaking she crossed to the window and stood looking out. Looking at her, Felim let a groan which echoed as if the room were a vault. It was as cold as a vault too.

I didn't know what to say. The woman stood at the window

as vague as a cobweb against the wan light outside. She was
dressed entirely in black, right to the neck where a ruffle-like
collar pushed against her hair. I wondered if she was listening,
hoping we would speak. Or was she looking at something?

But there was nothing to see, only the road, the leaves,
silently now, drifting, a bare hedge shivering in the winds, and
beyond it a field of potatoes yet to be dug, the drills of dead
stalks bleached and as withered as her own hair. Once, an
amber light fondled the stalks, then withdrew – snail-horn
quick – as if from a touch as cold as death.

I pretended to study the old hooks in the ceiling; to study
an old faded print of a calendar; to finger the notches in the
stools along the wall stained and smoothed by generations of
trouser-seats in hard corduroy. Behind me I heard Felim burst
a sigh in his groaning way, like a saturated cow. He said as if
speaking thought aloud:

'Well man aye elastics ...'

'You mean Sadie the Cailleach's elastics?' I said.

'An' if I did?'

'Shouldn't we see the loft you slept in? Where you fired
Sadie's elastics at the rats?'

He swirled his drink and prepared to let it down. 'We
better,' he said resignedly, 'be makin' our road short back
home be Newry.'

'But you always said –'

'Never mind what the hell I said. I can mind thon loft too
bleddy well – especially the night thon fella died on me –
choked in his own blood.'

There was a movement at the window – a cobweb stirring in
a draught – and the woman was suddenly gone. His graphic
memory was perhaps too vivid for her. Yet at the door she
appeared to pause, then went on, silent as ever in her sandals.
Felim had been watching her too.

'We can't leave now without orderin' another round. When
you get it, lower it quick till we get to hell outa here. We
should never have come.' There was something I should say
but couldn't think of it. He went on gratingly, watching the
window: 'A black, cold lonely country an' always was. Not a

bleddy mountain in sight. No houses. Ask them for a drink in my time an' they handed you a tin an' pointed to a pump. Wouldn't give you the black of their nail ...'

The woman returned almost unnoticed: she was carrying two full glasses of whiskey. She gave one to me because I was nearest, the other to Felim. He gaped at the drink, then at the woman.

'I was goin' to order a half-one, mam, not a full glass, but seein' as it's here ... And he took the glass in one hand and with the other reached into his pocket.

She held his hand in the pocket through the cloth. The amber light was back outside, and against the window I couldn't see her face. But I heard her voice, low and trembling.

'Keep your money in your pocket. That drink's on me. For Sadie the Cailleach's elastic boots.'

Without another word she turned and went back to the window, again looking out.

A passing car blasted sound like blasphemy into the room. It faded in a drone. The leaves stirred and whirled in concert, silently. Felim seemed to wait for the woman to speak. She remained silent. He said huskily:

'How – do you mean, mam?'

'Don't think it ill-bred of me,' she replied, the words spoken to the window, 'but you have an up-the-country tongue: where the hired servant boys came from. You would be the boy with Sadie the Cailleach's elastic-sided boots.'

Felim didn't answer; but I watched his glass tilt until the whiskey began to drip, then spill. With her back to us the woman went on:

'Your master William Andrew was my uncle. He lived beyond his hundredth year and had a clear mind almost to the last.' She spoke as if saying something she had to say so that she could forget it for ever. 'He had scores of boys he could never remember. But he never forgot the boy with Sadie the Cailleach's elastics.'

'You mean he – minded me a boy here?'

'Because of the elastics. It amused him.' You felt she was trying desperately to smile. Then she said:

' "Cailleach" is your old Gaelic word for hag, I believe.'

'Old woman,' I put in gently, quickly.

'Hag I was told.' Edged with sharp authority she dismissed me; I took the hint and stayed quiet. Felim was gaping at her back. Her voice softened as she said: 'That young man you saw die on the loft – he was my brother.'

'Lord rest him,' Felim whispered, instinctively, instantly raising his hand to his cap in the traditional touch of respect, but suddenly cutting short the gesture: as if he had been about to raise his cap to a strange Catholic Chapel only to be told it was a Protestant Church.

'He never forgot you – my uncle I mean.' She seemed actually to chuckle. 'Never. Neither did I, but – we won't go in to that now.' And this time she chuckled outright and turned to face us though remaining at the window. 'I'm the last of the McAlecsons – the name I mean. I have a cousin who runs the place – she's in The Bann on business or she'd – we should have the fire lit, I know. But we rarely have anyone until night-time now.'

'An' I mind the rows of carts outside there –'

She cut him off abruptly: 'All gone now.' Maybe she was wise not to want to remember. 'All gone. All changed.'

'The world's changed.' Felim's voice boomed in the room. 'An' the people changed with them.'

'Drink that up,' she said quickly. 'Then you must have tea with me.'

We both protested; Felim was gesturing as well. Too much bother. Hadn't we whiskey? More than good enough. Anyway he wanted to see the old loft up the road. Was it there? She nodded, merely blinking at him, but shrewdly. He would call on his way back – Felim swore he would call. In between he was gulping the whiskey. I thought I knew what was in his mind and said nothing; for I was watching the woman, believing I knew what went on in her mind as well. She was watching him now intently. She watched him finish his drink – gulp, cough, splutter – then look for a place except the stool to set down his glass. She seemed as if about to step forward to take it from him, then held back, folded one hand over the

other and blinked again. Her eyes were close and red-rimmed.
And then she slowly turned back to look out the window.

Suddenly, silently as ever, she turned to go. Felim almost
loped after her. She opened the door and let us out. Once outside she closed the door on the whimpering scurry of the in-
rushing leaves.

From the doorstep Felim strode out ahead of me, back down
the road towards the main highway. I let him go. Suddenly he
yanked off his cap. The wind tweaked at his scant hair and I
saw his shoulders shake; the cap he held to his face. He
roughly drew it on again, striding ahead until he came abreast
of the surfaceman shovelling in the roadside drain. Again he
whipped off his cap, stopped, wheeled about, seemed to see me
for the first time, and turned back to the surfaceman. He took
out half-a-crown and speech rushed from him as he said to the
man:

'I want you to give a message to the old woman back in the
pub there.'

The man, crouched over his shovel, knew we had just left,
and though he barely paused in his work the halt revealed his
justifiable suspicion. He said at length:

'Is it old Sadie you mean?'

I repeated her name. I'm sure Felim kept repeating it in his
mind too; for now his own face was as stunned-looking as the
surfaceman's was stiff with suspicion. Under his breath he
said to the man:

'Aye, then ... to old Sadie. Tell her the boy with Sadie the
Cailleach's elastics hadn't –'

'Sowl an' I'll not,' the man cut in. He went on working with
pointed determination. 'An old uncle, if you must know, put
that nickname on Sadie ages ago an' she never took well till it.
She took law of a man once over that nickname ...'

'Do you tell me that?' Felim said, as if a deep secret of
existence had been revealed to him for the first time. He
straightened. Then he burst into great guffaws of laughter
which startled me as well as the surfaceman who, with shovel-
shaft resting on a knee, was staring up at him. He went on
laughing into the wind. The leaves seemed to caper to his

mood. I mused on the delicate, fragile, even madly ironic supports that can sustain the memory of a human relationship
over the decades: the image of a pair of old boots forming
such a link was at once farcical and frightening. That's why
Felim's laughter had startled me.

I saw him press the coin into the surfaceman's hand.

'Never mind about Sadie the Cailleach, then.' He paused.
'Just tell old Sadie that ... McAlecson's up-the-country boy
with the ould boots hadn't the heart to go back. Can you mind
to tell her that?'

'Wi' pleasure man,' said the surfaceman, spitting on the
coin before he put it in his waistcoat pocket.

We had twenty minutes to wait on a bus back to Newry, but
Felim didn't speak; indeed he stood apart with his back to me
as if to stall any intention to talk. He almost flung himself
into the bus. But once seated, we both turned as if moved by the
same thought and looked back through the window.

Haws on the roadside hedges made crimson blurs. Leaves
swirled in our wake like outsize burnished chaff. I remembered
the sound of that threshing-mill ... and saw a road running
back imponderably into Time, powered by the endless irony of
living that reminded me of the endless pulley-belt on that
threshing-mill, linking engine to mill, memory to man and
woman; the sound of that drum lamenting for man and land
and blighted love and inherited bigotry and beliefs; and yet
that sound at the same time fulfilling the promise of Harvest!
Of life.

In Newry Felim refused to take a drink. He even insisted
on seeing me to the railway station on my way back to The
Sperrins in Co. Tyrone; he had time on his hands. He was
tongue-tied. His eyes were misty. Not once did he refer to my
mythical storyteller, a lie I'd forgotten about by then myself.
When the train pulled in, he took my hand in both his own
and squeezed hard. His eyes were now moist. I knew it wasn't
altogether because he was parting with me.

'If we had our lives to live over again – Ah, but sure, what's
the good of talkin'?' He stared with his moist eyes unasham-
edly for a long time into mine. 'I want you to promise' – he

was finding difficulty in speaking – 'Promise you'll go back one day. It looked mean the way I run out. But I had to. I had to.'

I said I believed the old woman would have understood.

'Just the same,' he went on, 'I want you to promise. You'll be near the place – you're all over the country. Your hand an' word to God?' I promised. 'I want you to go in an' drink a health to her – we clean forgot to drink her health. Tell her why. Above all, anyway, go back: go back even if she's not there an' drink my health an' your own to Sadie the Cailleach. When I think that an ould pair of elastic-sided boots ... Ah, what's the use o' talkin'? What's a man to say?'

The train came in then and drowned whatever else he had hoped to say. And quickly he squeezed a pound note into my fist and was away before I could protest. Without gesture of any kind he staggered through passengers joining the train and was gone.

I next heard about him from his daughter-in-law; she was in England by then with her family and Joe – and Felim. I wrote to him but he didn't reply. I wasn't too disappointed – he was never much of a hand with the pen; but I believed he had other reasons for keeping silent.

Last week his own granddaughter wrote to tell me about his death and burial in an English grave in the Midlands. The young hand had the impersonal tone of the modern young blood and seemed to be awfully amused in writing an awfully funny thing: that before his death the old man raved for two whole days about an old pair of elastic-sided boots! Exclamation mark and all.

I replied, but ignored her remarks on the boots.

Now I suppose I will have to go back to that pub near The Bann. I want to go back anyway. One should go back sometimes, as I think tradition told us. The old woman will be dead of course. Some relation will have taken the place over – perhaps that young cousin she mentioned. Married now no doubt. If there is an 'Eejits' Ward' of a bar – and even if there isn't – it tempts some odd quirk of humour or cussedness to imagine the reaction when – aloud of course – I give my toast to 'Sadie the Cailleach's ould elastic-sided boots'.

Someone in the pub may have heard of the nickname, perhaps from the old woman, or from someone in the area; they may even resent it as the woman had, except to ourselves. And they may not have heard: total recall is no longer a necessity for the folk mind. They may indulgently think me funny, or mad, or unsuitably bucolic for the trendy drinkers of today entrenched in new patterns of suspect belief more ignorant in superstition than the old.

I won't be content with delivering the toast; I may even declaim it tauntingly. Then I'll go on to propound the ludicrous supports which tenuously sustain and preserve a human relationship arrested in memory where none was thought to exist. I'll talk of the implied denunciation of partisan emotions. At that they will become convinced I'm about to talk sectarian politics and will certainly throw me out.

I've been thrown out of pubs for less worthy reasons. The very thought of it makes me more than a little drunk already. What the hell: when a fella's out – let him *be* out!

The Eagles and the Trumpets

JAMES PLUNKETT

WHEN the girl crossed from the library, the square was bathed in August sunshine. The folk from the outlying areas who had left their horses and carts tethered about the patriotic monument in the centre were still in the shops, and the old trees which lined either side emphasized the stillness of the morning. She went down a corridor in the Commercial Hotel and turned left into the bar. She hardly noticed its quaintness, the odd layout of the table, its leather chairs in angles and corners, the long low window which looked out on the dairy yard at the back. After six years in the town she was only aware of its limitations. But the commercial traveller startled her. She had not expected to find anyone there so early. He raised his eyes and when he had stared at her gloomily for a moment, he asked, 'Looking for Cissy?'

One of the things she had never got used to was this easy familiarity of the country town. But she accepted it. One either accepted or became a crank.

'No,' she answered, 'Miss O'Halloran.'

'You won't see her,' he said. 'It's the first Friday. She goes to the altar and has her breakfast late.' He had a glass of whiskey in front of him and a bottle of Bass. He gulped half the whiskey and then added, 'I'll ring the bell for you.'

'Thank you.'

His greyish face with its protruding upper lip was vaguely familiar. Probably she had passed him many times in her six years without paying much attention. Now she merely wondered about his black tie. She heard the bell ringing remotely and after a moment Cissy appeared. The girl said:

'I really wanted Miss O'Halloran. It's a room for a gentleman tonight.' She hesitated. Then reluctantly she added, 'Mr Sweeney.' As she had expected, Cissy betrayed immediate curiosity.

'Not Mr Sweeney that stayed here last autumn?'

'Yes. He hopes to get in on the afternoon bus.'

Cissy said she would ask Miss O'Halloran. When she had gone to inquire, the girl turned her back on the traveller and pretended interest in an advertisement for whiskey which featured two dogs, one with a pheasant in its mouth. The voice from behind her asked:

'Boy-friend?'

She had expected something like that. Without turning she said, 'You're very curious.'

'Sorry. I didn't mean that. I don't give a damn. Do you drink?'

'No, thank you.'

'I was going to offer you something better than a drink. Good advice.' The girl stiffened. She was the town librarian, not a chambermaid. Then she relaxed and almost smiled.

'If you ever do,' the voice added sadly, 'don't mix the grain with the grape. That's what happened to me last night.'

Cissy returned and said Mr Sweeney could have room seven. Miss O'Halloran was delighted. Mr Sweeney had been such a nice young man. Her eye caught the traveller and she frowned.

'Mr Cassidy,' she said pertly, 'Miss O'Halloran says your breakfast's ready.'

The traveller looked at her with distaste. He finished his whiskey and indicated with a nod of his head the glass of Bass which he had taken in his hand.

'Tell Miss O'Halloran I'm having my breakfast,' he said. But Cissy was admiring the new dress.

'You certainly look pretty,' she said enviously.

'Prettiest girl in town,' the traveller added for emphasis.

The girl flushed. Cissy winked and said, 'Last night he told me I was.'

'Did I?' the traveller said, finishing his Bass with a grimace of disgust. 'I must have been drunk.'

*

On the first Friday of every month, precisely at 11.45, the chief clerk put on his bowler hat, hung his umbrella on his arm and left to spend the rest of the day inspecting the firm's branch office. It was one of the few habits of the chief clerk which the office staff approved. It meant that for the rest of the evening they could do more or less as they pleased. Sweeney, who had been watching the monthly ceremony from the public counter with unusual interest, turned around to find Higgins at his elbow.

'You're wanted,' he was told.

'Who?'

'Our mutual musketeer – Ellis. He's in his office.'

That was a joke. It meant Ellis was in the storeroom at the top of the building. Part of the duties assigned to Ellis was the filing away of forms and documents. The firm kept them for twenty-five years, after which they were burned. Ellis spent interminable periods in the storeroom, away from supervision and interference. It was a much-coveted position. Sweeney, disturbed in his day-dreaming, frowned at Higgins and said:

'Why the hell can't he come down and see me?' It was his habit to grumble. He hated the stairs up to the storeroom and he hated the storeroom. He disliked most of the staff, especially the few who were attending night-school classes for accountancy and secretarial management in order to get on in the job. Put into the firm at nineteen years of age because it was a good, safe, comfortable job, with a pension scheme and adequate indemnity against absences due to ill-health, he realized now at twenty-six that there was no indemnity against the boredom, no contributory scheme which would save his manhood from rotting silently inside him among the ledgers and the comptometer machines. From nine to five he decayed among the serried desks with their paper baskets and their telephones, and from five onwards there was the picture house, occasional women, and drink when there was money for it.

The storeroom was a sort of paper tomb, with tiers of forms and documents in dusty bundles, which exhaled a musty odour. He found Ellis making tea. A paper-covered book had been flung to one side. On the cover he could make out the words

Selected Poems, but not whose they were. He was handed a cup of tea with a chocolate biscuit in the saucer.

'Sit down,' Ellis commanded.

Sweeney, surprised at the luxury of the chocolate biscuit, held it up and inspected it with raised eyebrows.

Ellis offered milk and sugar.

'I pinched them out of Miss Bouncing's drawers,' he said deliberately.

Sweeney, secure in the knowledge that the chief clerk was already on his way across town, munched the biscuit contentedly and looked down into the street. It was filled with sunshine. Almost level with his eyes, the coloured flags on the roof of a cinema lay limp and unmoving, while down below three charwomen were scrubbing the entrance steps. He took another biscuit and heard Ellis saying conversationally, 'I suppose you're looking forward to your weekend in the country.'

The question dovetailed unnoticed in Sweeney's thought.

'I've been wanting to get back there since last autumn. I told you there was a girl ...'

'With curly eyes and bright blue hair.'

'Never mind her eyes and her hair. I've tried to get down to see her twice, but it didn't come off. The first time you and I drank the money — the time Dacey got married. The second, I didn't get it saved in time. But I'm going today. I've just drawn the six quid out of Miss Bouncing's holiday club.'

'What bus are you getting?'

'The half-past-two. His nibs has gone off so I can slip out.'

'I see,' Ellis said pensively.

'I want you to sign me out at five.'

They had done things like that for one another before. Turning to face him, Ellis said, 'Is there a later bus?'

'Yes. At half past eight. But why?'

'It's ... well, it's a favour,' Ellis said uncertainly. With sinking heart Sweeney guessed at what was coming.

'Go on,' he invited reluctantly.

'I'm in trouble,' Ellis said. 'The old man was away this past two weeks and I hocked his typewriter. Now the sister's phoned me to tip me off he's coming home at half past two.

They only got word after breakfast. If I don't slip out and re-deem it there'll be stinking murder. You know the set-up at home.'

Sweeney did. He was aware that the Ellis household had its complications.

'I can give it back to you at six o'clock,' Ellis prompted.

'Did you try Higgins?' Sweeney suggested hopefully.

'He hasn't got it. He told me not to ask you but I'm desperate. There's none of the others I can ask.'

'How much do you need?'

'Four quid would do me – I have two.'

Sweeney took the four pound notes from his wallet and handed them over. They were fresh and stiff. Miss Bouncing had been to the bank. Ellis took them and said:

'You'll get this back. Honest. Byrne of the Prudential is to meet me in Slattery's at six. He owes me a fiver.'

Still looking at the limp flags on the opposite roof, Sweeney suggested, 'Supposing he doesn't turn up.'

'Don't worry,' Ellis answered him. 'He will. He promised me on his bended knees.'

After a pause he diffidently added, 'I'm eternally grateful ...'

Sweeney saw the weekend he had been aching for receding like most of his other dreams into a realm of tantalizing un-certainty.

'Forget it,' he said.

Sweeney, who was standing at the public counter, looked up at the clock and found it was half past two. Behind him many of the desks were empty. Some were at lunch, others were tak-ing advantage of the chief clerk's absence. It only meant that telephones were left to ring longer than usual. To his right, defying the grime and the odd angles of the windows, a streak of sunlight slanted across the office and lit up about two square feet of the counter. Sweeney stretched his hand towards it and saw the sandy hairs on the back leap suddenly into gleaming points. He withdrew it shyly, hoping nobody had seen him. Then he forgot the office and thought instead of the country town, the square with its patriotic statue, the trees which lined it, the girl he had met on that autumn day while he was

walking along through the woods. Sweeney had very little
time for romantic notions about love and women. Seven years
knocking about with Ellis and Higgins had convinced him that
Romance, like good luck, was on the side of the rich. It preferred to ride around in motor-cars and flourished most where
the drinks were short and expensive. But meeting this strange
girl among the trees had disturbed him. Groping automatically
for the plausible excuse, he had walked towards her with a
pleasurable feeling of alertness and wariness.

'This path,' he said to her, 'does it lead me back to the
town?' and waited with anxiety for the effect. He saw her
assessing him quickly. Then she smiled.

'It does,' she said, 'provided you walk in the right direction.'

He pretended surprise. Then after a moment's hesitation he
asked if he might walk back with her. He was staying in the
town, he explained, and was still finding his way about. As
they walked together he found out she was the town librarian,
and later, when they had met two or three times and accepted
one another, that she was bored to death with the town. He
told her about being dissatisfied too, about the office and its
futility, about having too little money. One evening when they
were leaning across a bridge some distance from the town, it
seemed appropriate to talk rather solemnly about life. The
wind rippled the brown water which reflected the fading
colours of the sky. He said:

'I think I could be happy here. It's slow and quiet. You
don't break your neck getting somewhere and then sit down
to read the paper when you've got there. You don't have
twenty or thirty people ahead of you every morning and evening – all queuing to sign a clock.'

'You can be happy anywhere or bored anywhere. It depends
on knowing what you want.'

'That's it,' he said. 'But how do you find out? I never have.
I only know what I don't want.'

'Money – perhaps?'

'Not money really. Although it has its points. It doesn't
make life any bigger though, does it? I mean, look at most of
the people who have it.'

'Dignity?' she suggested quietly.

The word startled him. He looked at her and found she was quite serious. He wondered if one searched hard enough, could something be found to be dignified about. He smiled.

'Do you mean an umbrella and a bowler hat?'

He knew that was not what she meant at all, but he wanted her to say more.

'No,' she said, 'I mean to have a conviction about something. About the work you do or the life you lead.'

'Have you?' he asked.

She was gazing very solemnly at the water, the breeze now and then lifting back the hair from her face.

'No,' she murmured. She said it almost to herself. He slipped his arm about her. When she made no resistance he kissed her.

'I'm wondering why I didn't do that before,' he said when they were finished.

'Do you ... usually?' she asked.

He said earnestly, 'For a moment I was afraid.'

'Of me?'

'No. Afraid of spoiling everything. Have I?'

She smiled at him and shook her head.

At five they closed their ledgers and pushed in the buttons which locked the filing cabinets. One after the other they signed the clock which automatically stamped the time when they pulled the handle. The street outside was hardly less airless than the office, the pavements threw back the dust-smelling August heat. Sweeney, waiting for Higgins and Ellis at the first corner, felt the sun drawing a circle of sweat about his shirt collar and thought wistfully of green fields and roadside pubs. By now the half-past-two bus would have finished its journey. The other two joined him and they walked together by the river wall, picking their way through the evening crowds. The tea-hour rush was beginning. Sweeney found the heat and the noise of buses intolerable. A girl in a light cotton frock with long hair and prominent breasts brushed close to them. Higgins whistled and said earnestly, 'Honest to God, chaps. It's not fair. Not on a hot evening.'

'They're rubber,' Ellis offered with contempt.

'Rubber be damned.'

'It's fact,' Ellis insisted. 'I know her. She hangs them up on the bedpost at night.'

They talked knowledgeably and argumentatively about falsies until they reached Slattery's lounge. Then, while Ellis began to tell them in detail how he had smuggled the typewriter back into his father's study, Sweeney sat back with relief and tasted his whiskey. A drink was always welcome after a day in the office; even to hold the glass in his hand and lie back against his chair gave him a feeling of escape. Hope was never quite dead if he had money enough for that. But this evening it wasn't quite the same. He had hoped to have his first drink in some city pub on his way to the bus, a quick drink while he changed one of his new pound notes and savoured the adventure of the journey before him, a long ride with money in his pocket along green, hedged roads, broken by pleasant half-hours in occasional country pubs. When Higgins and Ellis had bought their rounds he called again. Whenever the door of the lounge opened he looked up hopefully. At last he indicated the clock and said to Ellis, 'Your friend should be here.'

'Don't worry,' Ellis assured him, 'he's all right. He'll turn up.' Then he lifted his drink and added, 'Well – here's to the country.'

'The country,' Higgins sighed. 'Tomorrow to fresh fiends and pastors new.'

'I hope so,' Sweeney said. He contrived to say it as though it didn't really matter, but watching Ellis and Higgins he saw they were both getting uneasy. In an effort to keep things moving Higgins asked, 'What sort of a place is it?'

'A square with a statue in it and trees,' Sweeney said. 'A hotel that's fairly reasonable. Free fishing if you get on the right side of the guards. You wouldn't think much of it.'

'No sea – no nice girls in bathing dresses. No big hotel with its own band.'

'Samuel Higgins,' Ellis commented. 'The Man Who Broke the Bank at Monte Carlo.'

'I like a holiday to be a real holiday,' Higgins said stoutly. 'Stay up all night and sleep all day. I like sophistication, nice girls and smart hotels. Soft lights and glamour and sin. Lovely sin. It's worth saving for.'

'We must write it across the doorway of the office,' Sweeney said.

'What?'

'Sin Is Worth Saving For.'

It had occurred to him that it was what half of them did. They cut down on cigarettes and scrounged a few pounds for their Post Office Savings account or Miss Bouncing's Holiday Club so that they could spend a fortnight of the year in search of what they enthusiastically looked upon as sin. For him sin abounded in the dusty places of the office, in his sweat of fear when the morning clock told him he was late again, in the obsequious answer to the official question, in the impulse which reduced him to pawing the hot and willing typist who passed him on the deserted stairs.

'I don't have to save for sin,' he commented finally.

'Oh – I know,' Higgins said, misunderstanding him. 'The tennis club is all right. So are the golf links on Bank Holiday. But it's nicer where you're not known.'

'View three,' Ellis interjected. 'Higgins the Hen Butcher.'

'Last year there was a terrific woman who got soft on me because I told her I was a commercial pilot. The rest of the chaps backed me up by calling me Captain Higgins. I could have had anything I wanted.'

'Didn't you?'

'Well,' Higgins said, in a tone which suggested it was a bit early in the night for the intimate details. 'More or less.' Then they consulted the clock again.

'It doesn't look as though our friend is coming,' Sweeney said.

'We'll give him till seven,' Ellis said. 'Then we'll try for him in Mulligan's or round in the Stag's Head.'

The girl watched the arrival of the bus from the entrance to the hotel. As the first passenger stepped off she smiled and

moved forward. She hovered uncertainly. Some men went past
her into the bar of the Commercial, the conductor took luggage from the top, the driver stepped down from his cabin
and lit a cigarette. Townspeople came forward too, some with
parcels to be delivered to the next town, some to take parcels
sent to them from the city. He was not among the passengers
who remained. The girl, aware of her new summer frock, her
long white gloves, the unnecessary handbag, stepped back
against the wall and bumped into the traveller.

'No boy-friend,' he said.

She noticed he had shaved. His eyes were no longer bloodshot. But the sun emphasized the grey colour of his face with
its sad wrinkles and its protruding upper lip. As the crowd
dispersed he leaned up against the wall beside her.

'I had a sleep,' he said. 'Nothing like sleep. It knits up the
ravelled sleeve of care. Who said that, I wonder?'

'Shakespeare,' she said.

'Of course,' he said, 'I might have guessed it was Shakespeare.'

'He said a lot of things.'

'More than his prayers,' the traveller conceded. Then he
looked up at the sun and winced.

'God's sunlight,' he said unhappily. 'It hurts me.'

'Why don't you go in out of it?' she suggested coldly.

'I've orders to collect. I'm two days behind. Do you like the
sun?'

'It depends.'

'Depends with me, too. Depends on the night before. Mostly
I like the shade. It's cool and it's easy on the eyes. Sleep and
the shade. Did Shakespeare say anything about that I wonder?'

'Not anything that occurs to me.' She wished to God he
would go away.

'He should, then,' the traveller insisted. 'What's Shakespeare
for, if he didn't say anything about sleep and the shade?'

At another time she might have been sorry for him, for his
protruding lip, his ashen face, the remote landscape of sorrow
which lay behind his slow eyes. But she had her own disappointment. She wanted to go into some quiet place and weep.
The sun was too strong and the noise of the awakened square

too unsettling. 'Let's talk about Shakespeare some other time,' she suggested. He smiled sadly at the note of dismissal.

'It's a date,' he said. She saw him shuffling away under the cool trees.

When they left Slattery's they tried Mulligan's and in the Stag's Head Higgins said he could eat a farmer's arse, so they had sandwiches. The others had ham and beef, but Sweeney took egg because it was Friday. There was a dogged streak of religion in him which was scrupulous about things like that. Even in his worst bouts of despair he still could observe the prescribed forms. They were precarious footholds which he hesitated to destroy and by which he might eventually drag himself out of the pit. After the Stag's Head Ellis thought of the Oval.

'It's one of his houses,' he said. 'We should have tried it before. What's the next bus?'

'Half eight.'

'Is it the last?'

'The last and ultimate bus. Aston's Quay at half past eight. Let's forget about it.'

'It's only eight o'clock. We might make it.'

'You're spoiling my drink.'

'You're spoiling mine too,' Higgins said, 'all this fluting around.'

'You see. You're spoiling Higgins' drink too.'

'But I feel a louser about this.'

'Good,' Higgins said pleasantly. 'Ellis discovers the truth about himself.'

'Shut up,' Ellis said.

He dragged them across the city again.

The evening was cooler. Over the western reaches of the Liffey, barred clouds made the sky alternate with streaks of blue and gold. Steeples and tall houses staggered upwards and caught the glowing colours. There was no sign of Byrne in the Oval. They had a drink while the clock moved round until it was twenty minutes to nine.

'I shouldn't have asked you,' Ellis said with genuine remorse.

'That's what I told you,' Higgins said. 'I told you not to ask him.'

'Byrne is an arch louser,' Ellis said bitterly. 'I never thought he'd let me down.'

'You should know Byrne by now,' Higgins said. 'He has medals for it.'

'But I was in trouble. And you both know the set-up at home. Christ, if the old man found out about the typewriter . . .'

'Look,' Sweeney said, 'the bus is gone. If I don't mind, why should you? Go and buy me a drink.' But they found they hadn't enough money left between them, so they went around to the Scotch House where Higgins knew the manager and could borrow a pound.

Near the end of his holiday he had taken her to a big hotel at a seaside resort. It was twenty miles by road from the little town, but a world away in its sophistication. They both cycled. Dinner was late and the management liked to encourage dress. A long drive led up to the imposing entrance. They came to it cool and fresh from the sea, their wet swimming togs knotted about the handlebars. It was growing twilight and he could still remember the rustle of piled leaves under the wheels of their bicycles. A long stone balustrade rose from the gravelled terrace. There was an imposing ponderousness of stone and high turrets.

'Glenawling Castle,' he said admiringly. She let her eyes travel from the large and shiny cars to the flag-mast some hundreds of feet up in the dusky air.

'Comrade Sweeney,' she breathed, 'cast your sweaty night-cap in the air.'

They walked on a thick carpet across a foyer which smelled of rich cigar smoke. Dinner was a long, solemn ritual. They had two half-bottles of wine, white for her, red for himself. When he had poured she looked at both gleaming glasses and said happily:

'Isn't it beautiful? I mean the colours.' He found her more astoundingly beautiful than either the gleaming red or the white.

'You are,' he said. 'Good God, you are.'

She laughed happily at his intensity. At tables about them young people were in the minority. Glenawling Castle catered to a notable extent for the more elevated members of the hierarchy, Monsignors and Bishops who took a little time off from the affairs of the Church to play sober games of golf and drink discreet glasses of brandy. There were elderly businessmen with their wives, occasional and devastatingly bored daughters.

After dinner they walked in the grounds. The light had faded from the sky above them, but far out to sea an afterglow remained. From the terrace they heard the sound of breakers on the beach below and could smell the strong autumn smell of the sea. They listened for some time. He took her hand and said: 'Happy?'

She nodded and squeezed his fingers lightly.

'Are you?'

'No,' he said. 'I'm sad.'

'Why sad?'

'For the old Bishops and the Monsignors and the business-men with their bridge-playing wives.'

They both laughed. Then she shivered suddenly in the cool breeze and they went inside again to explore further. They investigated a room in which elderly men played billiards in their shirt sleeves, and another in which the elderly women sat at cards. In a large lounge old ladies knitted, while in deep chairs an occasional Bishop read somnolently from a priestly book. Feeling young and a little bit out of place, they went into the bar which adjoined the ballroom. There were younger people here. He called for drinks and asked her why she frowned.

'This is expensive for you,' she said. She took a pound note from her bag and left it on the table.

'Let's spend this on the drinks,' she suggested.

'All of it?'

She nodded gravely. He grinned suddenly and gave it to the attendant.

'Pin that on your chest,' he said, 'and clock up the damage until it's gone.'

The attendant looked hard at the note. His disapproval was silent but unmistakable.

'It's a good one,' Sweeney assured him. 'I made it myself.'

They alternated between the ballroom and the bar. In the bar she laughed a lot at the things he said, but in the ballroom they danced more or less silently. They were dancing when he first acknowledged the thought which had been hovering between them.

'I've only two days left.'

'One, darling.'

'Tomorrow and Saturday.'

'It's tomorrow already,' she said, looking at her watch. Now that it was said, it was unavoidably necessary to talk about it.

'It's only about two hours by bus,' he said. 'I can get down to see you sometimes. There'll be weekends.'

'You won't though,' she said sadly.

'Who's going to stop me?'

'You think you will now, but you won't. A holiday is a holiday. It comes to an end and you go home and then you forget.'

They walked through the foyer which was deserted now. The elderly ladies had retired to bed, and so had the somnolent churchmen with their priestly books.

'I won't forget,' he said when they were once again on the terrace. 'I want you too much.'

The leaves rustled again under their wheels, the autumn air raced past their faces coldly.

'That's what I mean,' she said simply. 'It's bad wanting anything too much.' Her voice came anonymously from the darkness beside him.

'Why?' he asked.

Their cycle lamps were two bars of light in a vast tunnel of darkness. Sometimes a hedge gleamed green in the light or a tree arched over them with mighty and gesticulating limbs.

'Because you never get it,' she answered solemnly.

*

Sweeney, looking through the smoke from Higgins and Ellis to the heavily built man whom he did not like, frowned and tried to remember what public house he was in. They had been in so many and had drunk so much. He was at that stage of drunkenness where his thoughts required an immense tug of his will to keep them concentrated. Whenever he succumbed to the temptation to close his eyes, he saw them wandering and grazing at a remote distance from him, small white sheep in a landscape of black hills and valleys. The evening had been a pursuit of something which he felt now he would never catch up with, a succession of calls on some mysterious person who had always left a minute before. It had been of some importance, whatever he had been chasing, but for the moment he had forgotten why. Taking the heavily built man whom he didn't like as a focal point, he gradually pieced together the surroundings until they assumed a vague familiarity and then a positive identity. It was the Crystal. He relaxed, but not too much, for fear of the woolly annihilation that might follow, and found Higgins and the heavily built man swopping stories. He remembered that they had been swopping stories for a long time. The heavily built man was a friend of Higgins. He had an advertising agency and talked about the golf club and poker and his new car. He had two daughters – clever as hell. He knew the Variety Girls and had a fund of smutty stories. He told them several times they must come and meet the boys. 'Let's leave this hole,' he said several times, 'and I'll run you out to the golf club. No bother.' But someone began a new story. And besides, Sweeney didn't want to go. Every time he looked at the man with his neat suit and his moustache, his expensively fancy waistcoat, with the pin in his tie, he was tempted to get up and walk away. But for Higgins' sake he remained and listened. Higgins was telling a story about a commercial traveller who married a hotel-keeper's daughter in a small country town. The traveller had a protruding upper lip while the daughter, Higgins said, had a protruding lower lip. Like this, Higgins said. Then he said, look here, he couldn't tell the story if they wouldn't pay attention to him.

'This'll be good, boys,' the man said, 'this will be rich. I think I know this one. Go on.'

But Higgins said, hell no, they must look at his face. It was a story and they had to watch his face or they'd miss the point.

'Christ no,' Ellis said, 'not your face.'

Sweeney silently echoed the remark, not because he really objected to Higgins's face but because it was difficult to focus it in one piece.

Well, Higgins said, they could all sugar off, he was going to tell the story and shag the lot of them.

'Now, then,' the man said, 'we're all friends here. No unpleasantness and no bickering, what?'

'Well,' Higgins continued, 'the father of the bride had a mouth which twisted to the left and the mother's mouth, funny enough, twisted to the right. So on the bridal night the pair went to bed in the hotel which, of course, was a very small place, and when the time came to get down to a certain important carry-on, the nature of which would readily suggest itself to the assembled company – no need to elaborate – the commercial traveller tried to blow out the candle. He held it level with his mouth but, of course, on account of the protruding upper lip his breath went down in the direction of his chin and the candle remained lit.' Higgins stuck out his lip and demonstrated for their benefit the traveller's peculiar difficulty.

' "Alice," said the traveller to his bride. "I'll have to ask you to do this." So her nibs had a go and, of course, with the protruding lower lip, her breath went up towards her nose, and lo and behold the candle was still lighting.' Again Higgins demonstrated. ' "There's nothing for it, John, but call my father," says she. So the oul' fella is summoned and he has a go. But with his lips twisted to the left the breath goes back over his shoulder and the candle is still lighting away. "Dammit, this has me bet," says the father. "I'll have to call your mother," and after a passable delay the oul' wan appears on the scene, but, of course, the same thing happens, her breath goes out over her right shoulder this time, and there the four of them stand in their nightshirts looking at the candle and won-

dering what the hell will they do next. So they send out for the schoolmaster, and the schoolmaster comes in and they explain their difficulty and ask him for his assistance and "certainly," he says, "it's a great pleasure." And with that he wets his finger and thumb and pinches the wick and, of course, the candle goes out.' Higgins wet his finger and thumb and demonstrated on an imaginary candle. 'Then the father looks at the other three and shakes his head. "Begod," says he, "did youse ever see the likes of that; isn't education a wonderful thing?"'
The heavily built man guffawed and asserted immediately that he could cap that. It was a story about a commercial traveller too. But as he was about to start they began to call closing-time, and he said again that they must all come out to the golf club and meet the boys.

'Really,' he said, 'you'll enjoy the boys. I'll run you out in the car.'

'Who's game?' Higgins asked.

Ellis looked at Sweeney and waited. Sweeney looked at the heavily built man and decided he didn't dislike him after all. He hated him.

'Not me,' he said, 'I don't want any shagging golf clubs.'

'I don't care for your friend's tone,' the man began, his face reddening.

'And I don't like new cars,' Sweeney interrupted, rising to his feet.

'Look here,' the heavily built man said threateningly. Ellis and Higgins asked the stout man not to mind him.

'Especially new cars driven by fat bastards with fancy waistcoats,' Sweeney insisted. He saw Ellis and Higgins moving in between him and the other man. They looked surprised and that annoyed him further. But to hit him, he would have had to push his way through them and it would take so much effort that he decided it was hardly worth it after all. So he changed his mind. But he turned around as he went out.

'With fancy pins in their ties,' he concluded. People moved out of his way.

They picked him up twenty minutes later at the corner. He was gazing into the window of a tobacconist shop. He was

wondering now why he had behaved like that. He had a desire
to lean his forehead against the glass. It looked so cool. There
was a lonely ache inside him. He barely looked round at them.

'You got back quick,' Sweeney said.

'Oh, cut it out,' Ellis said, 'you know we wouldn't go without you.'

'I hate fat bastards with fancy pins,' Sweeney explained. But
he was beginning to feel it was a bit inadequate.

'After all,' Higgins said, 'he was a friend of mine. You might
have thought of that.'

'Sugar you and your friends.'

Higgins flushed and said, 'Thanks, I'll remember that.'

Pain gathered like a ball inside Sweeney and he said with
intensity, 'You can remember what you sugaring well like.'

'Look,' Ellis said, 'cut it out – the pair of you.'

'He insulted my friend.'

'View four,' Ellis said, 'Higgins the Imperious.'

'And I'll be obliged if you'll cut out this View two View
three View four stuff ...'

'Come on,' Ellis said wearily, 'kiss and make up. What we
all need is another drink.'

It seemed a sensible suggestion. They addressed themselves to
the delicate business of figuring out the most likely speakeasy.

The last bus stayed for twenty minutes or so and then chug-
ged out towards remoter hamlets and lonelier roads, leaving the
square full of shadows in the August evening, dark under the
trees, grey in the open spaces about the statue. The air felt
thick and warm, the darkness of the sky was relieved here and
there with yellow and green patches. To the girl there was a
strange finality about the departure of the bus, as though all
the inhabitants had boarded it on some impulse which would
leave the square empty for ever. She decided to have coffee,
not in the Commercial where Cissy was bound to ask questions,
but in the more formal- atmosphere of the Imperial. She had
hoped to be alone, and frowned when she met the traveller in
the hallway. He said:

'Well, well. Now we can have our chat about Shakespeare.'

She noticed something she had not observed earlier – a small piece of newspaper stuck on the side of his cheek where he had cut himself shaving. For some reason it made her want to laugh. She could see too that he was quite prepared to be re-buffed and guessed his philosophy about such things. Resig-nation and defeat were his familiars.

'I see you've changed your location,' she said, in a voice which indicated how little it mattered.

'So have you.'

'I was going to have coffee.'

'We can't talk Shakespeare over coffee,' he invited. 'Have a drink with me instead.'

'I wonder should I. I really don't know you,' she answered coolly.

'If it comes to that,' he said philosophically, 'who does?'

They went into the lounge. The lounge in the Imperial paid attention to contemporary ideas. There were tubular tables and chairs, a half moon of a bar with tube lighting which provided plenty of colour but not enough light. The drink was a little dearer, the beer, on such evenings in August, a little too warm. He raised his glass to her.

'I'm sorry about the boy-friend,' he said. She put down her glass deliberately.

'I'd rather you didn't say things like that,' she said. 'It's not particularly entertaining. I'm not Cissy from the Commercial, you know.'

'Sorry,' he said repentantly, 'I meant no harm. It was just for talk's sake.'

'Then let's talk about you. Did you pick up your two days' orders?'

'No,' he said sadly, 'I'm afraid I didn't. I'm afraid I'm not much of a commercial traveller. I'm really a potter.'

'Potter?'

'Yes. I potter around from this place to that.'

She noticed the heavy upper lip quivering and gathered that he was laughing. Then he said :

'That's a little joke I've used hundreds of times. It amuses me because I made it up myself.'

'Do you often do that?'

'I try, but I'm not much good at it. I thought of that one, God knows how many years ago, when things began to slip and I was in bed in the dark in some little room in some cheap hotel. Do you ever feel frightened in a strange room?'

'I'm not often in strange rooms.'

'I am. All my life I've been. When I put out the light I can never remember where the door is. I suppose that's what makes me a pretty poor specimen of a traveller.'

'So you thought of a joke?'

'Yes.'

'But why?'

'It helps. Sometimes when you feel like that, a joke has more comfort than a prayer.'

She saw what he meant and felt some surprise.

'Well,' she prompted. 'Why do you travel?'

'It was my father's profession too. He was one of the old stock. A bit stiff and ceremonious. And respected, of course. In those days they didn't have to shoot a line. They had dignity. First they left their umbrella and hat in the hallstand. Then there was some polite conversation. A piece of information from the city. A glass of sherry and a biscuit. Now you've got to talk like hell and drive like hell. I suppose he trained me the wrong way.'

He indicated her glass.

'You'll have another?' he asked.

She looked again at his face and made her decision. She was not quite sure what it would involve, but she knew it was necessary to her to see it out.

'I think I will,' she said.

He asked her if she liked her work, but she was not anxious to discuss herself at all. She admitted she was bored. After their third drink he asked her if she would care to drive out with him to Glenawling Castle. There were not likely to be people there who knew them and, besides, there would be dancing. She hesitated.

'I know what you're thinking,' he said, 'but you needn't worry. I'm no he-man.' She thought it funny that that was not what had occurred to her at all. Then he smiled and added:

'With this lip of mine I don't get much opportunity to practise.'

They got into the car which took them up the hill from the square and over the stone bridge with its brown stream. The traveller looked around at her.

'You're a pretty girl,' he said warmly, 'prettiest I've met.'

She said coolly, 'Prettier than your wife?'

'My wife is dead.'

She glanced involuntarily at the black tie.

'Yes,' he said, 'a month ago.' He waited. 'Does that shock you?' he asked.

'I'm afraid it does.'

'It needn't,' he said. 'We were married for eighteen years, and for fifteen of that she was in a lunatic asylum. I didn't visit her this past eight or nine years. They said it was better. I haven't danced for years either. Do you think I shouldn't?'

'No,' she said after a pause. 'I think it might do you good. You might get over being afraid of strange rooms.'

'At forty-five?' he asked quietly.

His question kept the girl silent. She looked out at the light racing along the hedges, the gleaming leaves, the arching of trees.

They eventually got into Annie's place. It was one of a row of tall and tottering Georgian houses. Ellis knew the right knock and was regarded with professional affection by the ex-boxer who kept the door. They went in the dark up a rickety stair to a room which was full of cigarette smoke. They had to drink out of cups, since the girls and not the liquor were the nominal attraction. There was some vague tradition that Annie was entitled to serve meals too, but to ask for one was to run the risk of being thrown out by the ex-boxer. The smell of the whiskey in his cup made Sweeney shiver. He had had whiskey early in the evening and after it plenty of beer. Experience had taught him that taking whiskey at this stage was a grave mistake. But no long drinks were available and one had to drink. Ellis noted his silence.

'How are you feeling?' he asked with friendly solicitude.

'Like the Chinese maiden?' Higgins suggested amiably and tickled the plump girl who was sitting on his knee.

'No,' Sweeney said, 'like the cockle man.'

'I know,' Higgins said, 'like the cockle man when the tide came in. We all appreciate the position of that most unfortunate gentlemen.' He tickled the plump girl again. 'Don't we, Maisie?'

Maisie, who belonged to the establishment, giggled.

'You're a terrible hard root,' she said admiringly.

There were about a dozen customers in the place. One group had unearthed an old-fashioned gramophone complete with sound horn and were trying out the records. They quarrelled about whose turn it was to wind it and laughed uproariously at the thin nasal voices and the age of the records. Sweeney was noted to be morose and again Ellis had an attack of conscience.

'I feel a louser,' Ellis said.

'Look,' Sweeney said. 'I told you to forget it.'

'Only for me you could be down the country by now.'

'Only for me you could be out at the golf club,' Sweeney said. 'Drinking with the best spivs in the country. You might even have got in the way of marrying one of their daughters.'

The gramophone was asking a trumpeter what he was sounding now.

'God,' Maisie said, 'my grandfather used to sing that. At a party or when he'd a few jars aboard. I can just see him.'

'My God. Where?' Higgins asked in mock alarm.

'In my head – Smarty,' Maisie said. 'I can see him as if it was yesterday. Trumpet-eer what are yew sounding now – Is it the cawl I'm seeking?'

They looked in amazement at Maisie, who had burst so suddenly into song. She stopped just as suddenly and gave a sigh of warm and genuine affection. 'It has hairs on it right enough – that thing,' she commented.

'What thing?' Higgins inquired salaciously and was rewarded with another giggle and a playful slap from Maisie.

'Maisie darling,' Ellis appealed, 'will you take Higgins away to some quiet place?'

'Yes,' Sweeney said. 'Bury his head in your bosom.'

Maisie laughed and said to Higgins, 'Come on, sweetheart. I want to ask them to put that thing on the gramophone again.' As they went away the thought struck Sweeney that Mary Magdalene might have looked and talked like that, and he remembered something which Ellis had quoted to him earlier in the week. He waited for a lull among the gramophone-playing group and leaned forward. He said, groping vaguely:

'Last week you quoted me something, a thing about the baptism of Christ ... I mean a poem about a painting of the baptism of Christ ... do you remember what I mean?'

'I think I do,' Ellis said. Then quickly and without punctuation he began to rattle off a verse. 'A painter of the Umbrian School Designed upon a gesso ground The nimbus of the baptized God The wilderness is cracked and browned.'

'That's it,' Sweeney said. 'Go on.'

Ellis looked surprised. But when he found Sweeney was not trying to make a fool of him, he clasped the cup tightly with both hands and leaned across the table. He moved it rhythmically in a small wet circle and repeated the previous verse. Then he continued with half-closed eyes.

> 'But through the waters pale and thin
> Still shine the unoffending feet ...'

'The unoffending feet,' Sweeney repeated, almost to himself. 'That's what I wanted. Christ — that's beautiful.'

But the gramophone rasped out again and the moment of quietness and awareness inside him was shattered to bits. Higgins came with three cups which he left down with a bang on the table.

'Refreshment,' he said. 'Annie's own. At much personal inconvenience.'

Sweeney looked up at him. He had been on the point of touching something and it had been knocked violently away from him. That always happened. The cups and the dirty tables, the people drunk about the gramophone, the girls and the cigarette smoke and the laughter seemed to twist and tangle themselves into a spinning globe which shot forward and shattered about him. A new record whirled raspingly on the gramophone for a moment before a tinny voice gave out the next song.

> *Have you got another girl at home like Susie,*
> *Just another little girl upon the family tree?*
> *If you've got another girl at home like Susie ...*

But the voice suddenly lost heartiness and pitch and dwindled into a lugubrious grovelling in the bass.

'Somebody wind the bloody thing,' Ellis screamed. Somebody did so without bothering to lift off the pick-up arm. The voice was propelled into a nerve-jarring ascent from chaos to pitch and brightness. Once again the composite globe spun towards him. Sweeney held his head in his hands and groaned. When he closed his eyes he was locked in a smelling cellar with vermin and excrement on the floor, a cellar in which he groped and slithered. Nausea tautened his stomach and sent the saliva churning in his mouth. He rose unsteadily.

'What is it?' Ellis asked.

'Sick,' he mumbled. 'Filthy sick.'

They left Higgins behind and went down into the street. Tenements with wide-open doors yawned a decayed and malodorous breath, and around the corner the river between grimy walls was burdened with the incoming tide. Sweeney leaned over the wall.

'Go ahead,' Ellis said.

'I can't.'

'Stick your fingers down your throat.'

Sweeney did so and puked. He trembled. Another spasm gripped him. Ellis, who was holding him, saw a gull swimming over to investigate this new offering.

'It's an ill wind ...' he said aloud.

'What's that?' Sweeney asked miserably, his elbows still on the wall, his forehead cupped in his hands.

'Nothing,' Ellis said. He smiled quietly and looked up at the moon.

*

'Do you mind if I ask you something?' the girl said. 'It's about your wife.'

'Fire ahead,' the traveller said gently.

They stood on the terrace in front of the hotel. Below them the sea was calm and motionless, but from behind them, where the large and illuminated windows broke the blackened brick of the castle, the sounds of the band came thinly.

'You haven't seen her for eight or nine years.'

'Fifteen,' the traveller corrected. 'You needn't count the few visits between.'

The girl formulated her next question carefully.

'When you married her,' the girl asked, 'did you love her?' The traveller's face was still moist after the dancing. She saw the small drops of sweat on his forehead while he frowned at the effort to recall the emotion of eighteen years before.

'I don't know,' he answered finally. 'It's funny. I can't exactly remember.'

The girl looked down at the pebbles. She poked them gently with her shoe.

'I see,' she said softly.

He took her hand. Then they both stood silently and watched the moon.

It rode in brilliance through the August sky. It glinted on the pebbled terrace. It stole through curtain chinks into the bedrooms of the sleeping Monsignors and Bishops, it lay in brilliant barrenness on the pillows of stiff elderly ladies who had no longer anything to dream about. Sweeney, recovering, found Ellis still gazing up at it, and joined him. It was high and radiant in the clear windy spaces of the sky. It was round and pure and white.

'Corpus Domini Nostri,' Sweeney murmured.

Ellis straightened and dropped his cigarette end into the water below.

'Like an aspirin,' he said, 'like a bloody big aspirin.'

Mr Sing My Heart's Delight

BRIAN FRIEL

ON the first day of every new year, I made the forty-five-mile journey by train, mail car, and foot across County Donegal to my granny's house which sat at the top of a cliff above the raging Atlantic at the very end of the parish of Mullaghduff. This annual visit, lasting from January until the nights began to shorten sometime in March, was made primarily for Granny's benefit: during those months Grandfather went across to Scotland to earn enough money to tide them over the rest of the year. But it suited me admirably too: I missed school for three months, I got away from strict parents and bothersome brothers and sisters, all younger than I, and in Granny's house I was cock-of-the-walk and everything I did was right.

The house consisted of one room in which Granny and Grandfather lived and slept. It was a large room lit by a small window and a door which could be left open for the greater part of the day because it faced east and the winds usually blew from the west. There were three chairs, a table, a bed in the corner, a dresser, and an open hearth-fire over which stretched the mantelpiece, the focal point of the room. In such bare surroundings, that mantelpiece held a rich array. A china dog stood guard at each end and between them there was a shining silver alarm clock, two vases, a brass elf holding a cracked thermometer whose mercury had long since been spilled, a golden picture frame enclosing a coloured photograph of a racehorse, and the shells of three sea urchins, sitting on three matchboxes covered with red crepe paper. Every year I went there, I had to have each of those pieces handed down to me for examination and appraisal and my pleasure in them made them even more precious to Granny.

She herself was a small, plump woman who must have been petite and very pretty. She was always dressed in black – boots, woollen stockings, overall – a dark, inelegant black, turning grey with too much washing and too much exposure to the weather. But above the neck, she was a surprise of strong colour: white hair, sea-blue eyes, and a quick, fresh face, tanned deep with sun. When something delighted her, she had a habit of wagging her head rapidly from side to side like a precocious child with ringlets and, although she was over sixty then, she behaved like a woman half that age. Indeed, when I felt tired or lazy and she would challenge me to race her to the byre or dare me to go beyond her along the rocks at low water, I used to tell her that she was 'nothing but a giddy, featherheaded old woman', repeating what I had heard my mother say of her so often.

Even on the best day in summer, Mullaghduff is a desolate place. The land is rocky, barren, uneven, covered by a brown heather that never blooms and hacked into a crazy jigsaw by hundreds of tiny rivulets no more than a foot wide which seemed to flow in as many different directions and yet cunningly avoid crossing one another. Granny's house lay at the most inaccessible end of this vast waste, three miles from the nearest road. It was a strange place to make a home but Grandfather was a dour, silent man and he probably felt that by marrying the girl of seventeen who had an infant daughter but no father to claim it, he had shown sufficient charity: the least she could do was accept the terms of his proposal. Or perhaps he was jealous of her vivacity and attractiveness and thought that the wide Atlantic behind her and a three-mile stretch of moor before her would be good deterrents to a roaming spirit. Whatever his motives, he succeeded in cutting her off so completely from the world that at the time of her death, shortly after my thirteenth birthday, the longest journey she had ever made was to the town of Strabane, fifty-two miles away, and that journey she had made the month before her marriage to fix up legal documents in connection with her baby, my mother.

She and I had riotous times together. We laughed with one

another and at one another. (A constant source of fun was Granny's English. Gaelic was her first tongue and she never felt at ease in English which she shouted and spat out as if it were getting in her way.) We used to sit up until near midnight, chatting and gossiping, and then instead of going to bed, perhaps decide suddenly to feast ourselves on herring fried in butter or on sand eels roasted on the red coals or on a wild duck that was for the next day's dinner. Or we would huddle round the fire and I would read to her stories from my school reading-book – she could neither read nor write. She would listen avidly to these, her face keen with interest, not missing a word, making me go back over a paragraph which she did not fully understand or halting me with a question about some detail in the story.

'Were you in a bus ever? A real bus – for people?'

'Once.'

'What was it like, what? Was it bad on the stomach, was it?'

Or after reading, she herself would retell the story to me ('Just to see did I understand it right') especially if it was a tale about the daring of the lighthouse-keeper's daughter or a cameo biography of someone like Madam Curie or Florence Nightingale. And then the greed for knowledge about the outside world would fall away as quickly from her and she would jump to her feet and say, 'Christ, son, we near forgot!' She used this swear word without any suggestion of profanity and because, I believe now, she rarely heard the conversation of women of her own time. 'If we run to the lower rocks, we'll see the Norwegian fishing boats going round the point. Hurry, son, hurry! They're a sight on a good night. Hurry!'

Out there on the rump of Mullaghduff she had no ready-made entertainments to amuse me, but she thought nothing of her own discomfort to make my stay with her more interesting. We often rose before dawn to see wild geese spearing through the icy air high above the ocean. Or we sat for hours at a stretch on the flat rocks below her house to get a glimpse of sharks encircling an oily patch that betrayed a shoal of mackerel and then attacking it. Or we waded knee-deep in water at the shallow strand and felt the terrible thrill of fluke wriggling beneath our bare feet, closed our eyes and plunged our hands down to lift them out. I know now that all these little expeditions were thought up to amuse me but I am also certain that, once we had embarked on them, Granny enjoyed them every bit as much as I did.

'Christ, it's a calf I have under my foot and not a fluke at all!' she would squeal with nervous delight, her blue eyes radiant with joy. 'Come here, son! Come here and steady the arm of me!'

Or if we were standing on top of the hump of ground behind her house to get a good view of a passing transatlantic liner, all sequins of lights, she would fill it for me with a passenger list of gay, carefree people: 'Lords and ladies,' she would say. 'The men of them handsome and straight as heroes and the women of them in bright silks down to their toes and all of them laughing and dancing and drinking wine and singing. Christ, son, but they're a happy old cargo!'

There was a February gale blowing in from the sea the evening the packman battled his way up to us. I watched him through the kitchen window, a shrub in the middle of the bog, only it was bending against the wind. Then it grew to a man and then a man with a cardboard case half as big as himself. When he was a stone's throw from the door, I saw that he was coloured. In those days, packmen were fairly common in remote areas. They went from house to house with their packs or cases of clothes and socks and bed linens and table cloths and gaudy knick-knacks and if a customer had no money for the goods chosen, the packmen were usually willing to settle for the value in poultry or fish. They had the name of being sharp dealers, dishonest even.

The sight of this packman put the fear of God in me because mother had taught us to be wary of all packmen and I had never seen a coloured man before in my life. I led Granny to the window and peeped out from behind her.

'Will he attack us?' I whimpered.

'Christ and if he does, he'll meet his match in this house!' she said bravely and threw open the door. 'Come in, lad,' she roared into the storm. 'Come in and rest yourself, for no goat could have made the climb up here today but a fool like yourself.'

He backed into the kitchen, dragging his huge case after him. He dropped into a chair at the door and his head fell back to a resting position against the wall. His breath came in quick, short gasps and he made no effort to speak, he was so exhausted.

I took a step closer to him to examine him. He was a young man, no more than twenty, with a smooth, hazel skin that was a tight fit for his face. The crown of his head was swathed in a snow-white turban, wound round like a bandage. His shoulders were narrow, his body puny, his trousers frayed and wet from the long grass, and his feet as small as my younger sister's. Then I saw his hands. They were fine and delicate and the fingers tipped with pink nails as polished as fresh seaweed. On the third finger of his left hand was a ring. It was a gold ring, wrought in imitation of a snake which held between its mouth and tail a damson-coloured stone. As I watched it, the colour became vaporous, like smoke in a bottle, and seemed to writhe languidly in a coiling movement. Now it was purple, now rose, now black, now blood-red, now blue, now the colour of sloes in the August sun. I was still gazing at its miracles when the packman slid to his knees on the ground and began reciting in a low, droning voice, 'I sell beau-ti-ful things, good lady; everything to adorn your beau-ti-ful home. What is it you buy? Leenens, silks, sheets, beau-ti-ful pictures for your walls, beau-ti-ful cardigans for the lady. What is it you buy?'

As he spoke, he opened his case and removed all its contents, painting the floor with yellows and greens and whites and blues. He did not offer any one item but displayed everything as if for his own gratification – and no wonder, for he owned all the riches of the earth.

'You buy, good lady? What is it you buy?' he intoned without interest, without enthusiasm, but by rote, because he was tired beyond caring. His eyes never left the ground and his hands spread the splashes of colour out and around him until he was an island in a lake of brightness.

For a moment, Granny said nothing. She was dazzled by the packman's wares and at the same time she was trying desperately not to miss whatever it was he was saying and his accent was difficult for her. When at last words came to her, they broke from her in a sort of cry.

'Aw, Christ, sweet Christ, look at them! Look at them! Aw, God, what is there like them things!' Then rapidly to me, 'What is he saying, son, what? Tell me what it is he's saying.' Then to the packman, 'Mister, I don't speak English too good, mister. Aw, Christ, mister, but they're grand treasures, mister, grand.'

She dropped to the floor beside him and stretched her hands out as if in benediction over the goods. Then her arms went gently down and the tips of her fingers brushed over the surfaces of the garments. She went silent with awe and her mouth opened. Only her eyes were quick with ecstasy.

'Try them on, good lady. Sample what I have to sell.'

She turned to me to confirm that she had heard correctly.

'Put on the things you like,' I said. 'Go ahead.'

She looked at the packman, searching his face to see was he in earnest, fearful in case he was not.

'I have no money, Mister Packman. No money.'

As if she had not spoken, the packman went on rearranging his colours and did not look up. Only routine was carrying him through.

'Try them on. They are beau-ti-ful. All.'

She hesitated momentarily, poised over the limitless choice.

'Go on,' I said impatiently. 'Hurry up.'

'Everything for the good lady and for her home,' mumbled the packman to the ground. 'Sample what I have to sell.'

She swooped on them as if she were going to devour them. Her fingers found a scarlet blouse which she snatched up and held against her chest. She looked down at it, looked to us for approbation, held it under her chin and smoothed it out against her, while her other hand went instinctively to her hair which she gathered back from her face. Then she was absolutely still, waiting for our verdict.

'Beau-ti-ful,' mumbled the packman automatically.

'Beautiful,' I said, anxious to have everything sampled and done with.

'Beautiful,' echoed Granny, softly, slowly, as if she were using the word for the first time.

Then suddenly she was on her feet, towering above us and leaping around the kitchen floor in a wild, mocking dance. 'Christ!' she squealed. 'Youse would have me as silly in the head as the two of youse are. Look at me! Look at me! Fit for a palace I am, in all my grandeur!'

Then she cut loose altogether. She flung the blouse to the floor and seized a yellow mohair stole which she draped around her shoulders and paraded up and down the floor in time to her own singing. Then she tried on a green hat and then white gloves and then a blue cardigan and then a multicoloured apron, all the time singing or dancing or waving her arms, all the time shaking her head like mad, delighted, embarrassed, drunk with pleasure, completely carried away.

Before she had gone through half of the garments, the years put an end to her antics and she flung herself exhausted on top of the bed and let herself go limp. 'Now, mister, you can take the bloody load away,' she panted, 'for I have no money to buy anything.'

Again the packman did not hear her but shuffled his goods with weary patience and said in his dressy way, 'This you like, good lady.' He touched a pair of brass candlesticks. 'Beau-ti-ful. Very cheap. Very, very cheap.' Granny waved her hands in dismissal.

'No money, Mister. No money.'

'Or you like this, good lady, this beau-ti-ful picture of the Holy Divine Redeemer. Also very cheap to you, good lady.'

She closed her eyes and shook her head and waited for her energy to return.

'A lovely thing this, kind lady.' His hand happened on a tiny box covered with imitation leather. Inside lay half a dozen apostle spoons. 'These I sell by large numbers. Everybody loved them. I cannot get them enough,' he said without conviction. 'The box to you, good lady, for half price.'

'Shut up!' she snapped with sudden venom, springing up to

a sitting position on the bed and scattering the languor that had emanated from the dealer. 'Shut up, Packman! We are poor people here! We have nothing! Shut up!'

The packman's head sank lower to the ground and he began gathering his goods in to him. It was dark now and he fumbled with the catch on his case.

She regretted her outburst at once because she hopped off the bed and began building up the peat fire. 'You'll eat with us, Packman; there'll be hunger on you. We can offer you ...' She paused and swung round to me. 'Christ, son, we'll roast the grouse that was to be Sunday's dinner! That's what we'll do. Grouse and praties and butter and buttermilk and soda farls – a feast, by Christ, a feast!' She turned to the packman. 'Can your stomach hold a feast, Packman?'

'Anything, good lady. Anything.'

'A feast it'll be then,' she pronounced. 'A feast and be damned to Sunday.'

She rolled up her sleeves and began setting the table. The packman closed his case and went to a corner where he merged with the dark.

'Tell me, Packman,' she called to him from her work. 'What do they call you, what?'

'Singh,' he said.

'What?'

'Singh,' he repeated.

'Man, but that's a strange name. Sing. Sing,' she said, feeling the sound on her tongue. 'I'll tell you what I'll call you, Packman,' she went on, 'I'll call you Mr Sing My Heart's Delight! That's what I'll call you – a good, big mouthful. Mr Sing My Heart's Delight!'

'Yes,' he said submissively.

'Now, Mr Sing My Heart's Delight, let the sleep come over you for an hour and when I give you the call, there'll be a feast and a festival before your eyes. Close your eyes and sleep, you poor, battered man, you.'

He closed his eyes obediently and within five minutes his head had fallen on his chest.

We ate by the light of an oil lamp, Granny at the bottom

of the table, me in the middle, and the packman in the place
of honour at the top. It must have been a month since he had
a square meal because he bolted his food ravenously and did
not lift his eyes until his plate was cleaned. Then he sat back
in his seat and smiled at us for the first time. He looked boyish
now that he was sated.

'Thank you, good lady,' he said. 'A beau-ti-ful meal.'

'You're welcome,' she said. 'May none of us ever want.' She
held the bone of the grouse's leg between her fingers and drew
patterns on her plate, her head to one side.

'Where do you come from, Mr Sing My Heart's Delight?'
Her tone suggested she was beginning a series of questions.

'The Punjab,' he said.

'And where might that be?'

'India, good lady.'

'India,' she repeated. 'Tell me, is India a hot country, is it?'

'Very warm. Very warm and very poor.'

'Very poor,' she said quietly, adding the detail to the picture
she was composing in her mind. 'And the oranges and the
bananas grow there on trees and there are all classes of fruit
and flowers with all the colours of the rainbow in them?'

'Yes,' he said simply, for he was remembering his own picture. 'It is very beau-ti-ful, good lady. Very beau-ti-ful.'

'And the women,' Granny went on, 'do they wear long silk
frocks melting down to the ground? And the men, are the men
dressed in claret velvet and black shoes with silver buckles?'

He spread his hands and smiled.

'And the women, strolling about in the sun under the
orange-trees and the sun taking lights out of their hair and the
gallant men raising their feathered hats to them and stepping
off the roads to let them pass ... in the sun ... in the Punjab
... in the Garden of Eden ...' She was away from us as she
spoke, leaving us in the draughty, flagged-floor kitchen, listening to the wind ripping up the ocean below us and trying
the weaker parts of the thatched roof. The packman's eyes were
closed and his head nodded.

'The Garden of Eden,' said Granny again. 'Where the
ground isn't treacherous with bits of streams and the land so

rocky that even weeds won't settle in it. And you have God's
sun in that Punjab place and there is singing and the playing
of musical instruments and the children ... aye, the children ...' The first drops of a shower came down the chimney
and sizzled in the fire.

'Christ!' she said, springing to her feet. 'What class of dotter-
ing fools of men am I talking to? Up you get, you clowns you,
and let me get at the washing-up.'

The packman woke with a start and made for his case.

'And where are you going?' she shouted to him. 'Christ,
man, a badger wouldn't face out on a night like this!'

He stopped in the middle of the floor.

'Well?' she said. 'Don't look at me as if you expected a
beating. You'll sleep here tonight. There – across the front of
the fire. Like a cat,' she ended off with a shout of laughter.

The packman laughed too.

'Now, Mr Sing My Heart's Delight, get out of my road until
me and my wee man here gets cleared up.'

By the time we had the dishes finished and fresh peat spread
before the fire for the morning, it was bedtime. Granny and I
slept together in the bed in the corner, a huge iron bed whose
side was always warm from the hearth. She lay next to the wall
and I on the outside. Now we retreated to the shadowy end of
the room and undressed. Then, with a skip and a jump, we
were in bed together before the packman had time to be embarrassed.

Granny peeped across me. 'Blow out the lamp, Mr Sing My
Heart's Delight, and then place yourself on the floor there.
You'll find a mat at the door if you want it.'

'Good night, good lady,' he said. 'Very good lady.'

'Good night, Mr Sing My Heart's Delight,' she replied.

He got the mat and stretched himself out before the red
and white embers. Outside, the rain lashed against the roof and,
inside, the three of us were as cosy as pet hens.

It was a fine morning, a fresh, blustering day that kept the
clouds moving past and dried the path that led from the house
to the main road. The packman was young and bright and
his case seemed lighter too because he swung it easily by his
side as he stood at the door, nodding his head and smiling

happily as Granny directed him towards the parishes where he would have the best chance to sell his wares.

'And now,' she said in conclusion, 'God's speed and may the road rise with you.'

'To pay you I have no money, good lady,' said the packman, 'and my worthless goods I would not offer you because ...'

'Off with you, man. Off with you. There'll be rain before dinnertime and you should have eight miles behind you by then.' The packman still hesitated. He kept smiling and bowing and swinging his case as if he were a shy girl.

'Christ, Mr Sing My Heart's Delight, if you don't soon go, it's here you'll be for dinner and you ate it last night!'

The packman put his case on the ground and looked at his left hand. Then, drawing off the ring with those long, delicate fingers of his, he held it forward towards her. 'For you,' he said, in a very formal voice. 'Please accept from me in ... in grateful.'

Even as it lay on his hand, the stone turned a dozen colours. Granny was embarrassed. It had been so long since she had been offered a present that she did not know how to accept it. She hung her head and muttered churlishly, 'No. No. No,' and backed away from the gift.

'But please, good lady. Please,' the packman insisted. 'From a Punjab gentleman to a Donegal lady. A present. Please.'

When she did not come forward to accept it, he moved towards her and caught her hand in his. He chose the third finger of the left hand and slipped the ring on it. 'Thank you, good lady,' he said.

Then he lifted his case, bowed to us again and turned towards the barren waste and the main road. The wind was behind him and carried him quickly away.

Neither of us moved until we had lost him behind the hillock at the bend of the road. I turned to go round to the side of the house: it was time to let the hens out and milk the cow. But Granny did not move. She stood looking towards the road with her arm and hand still held as the packman had left them.

'Come on, Granny,' I said irritably. 'The cow will think we're dead.'

She looked strangely at me and then away from me and

across the bogs and the road and up towards the mountains which almost surrounded her.

'Come on, Granny,' I said, tugging at her overall. 'Come on. Come on.'

She allowed me to pull her; and as I led her towards the byre, I heard her saying to herself, 'I'm thinking the rain will get him this side of Crolly Bridge and the claret breeches and the buckled shoes will be destroyed on him. Please God it will make a good day of it. Please God it will.'

Gold Watch

JOHN McGAHERN

It was in Grafton Street we met, aimlessly strolling on one of the lazy lovely Saturday mornings in spring, the week of work over, the weekend still as fresh as the bunch of anemones that seemed the only purchase in her cane shopping basket.

'What a lovely surprise,' I said, and was about to take her hand when a man with an armload of parcels parted us as she was shifting the basket to her other hand, and we withdrew from the pushing crowds into the comparative quiet of Harry Street. We had not met since we had graduated in the same law class from University College five years before. I had heard she'd become engaged to the medical student she used to knock around with, and had gone into private practice down the country, perhaps waiting for him to graduate.

'Are you up for the weekend or on holiday or what?' I asked.

'No. I work here now.' She named a big firm that specialized in tax law. 'I felt I needed a change.'

She was wearing a beautiful oatmeal-coloured suit, the narrow skirt slit from the knee. The long gold hair of her student days was drawn tightly into a neat bun at the back.

'You look different but as beautiful as ever,' I said. 'I thought you'd be married by now.'

'And do you still go home every summer?' she countered, perhaps out of confusion.

'It doesn't seem as if I'll ever break that bad habit.'

We had coffee in Bewley's – the scent of the roasting beans blowing through the vents out on to Grafton becoming forever mixed through the memory of that morning – and we went on to spend the whole idle day together until she laughingly and firmly returned my first hesitant kiss; and it was she who silenced my even more fumbled offer of marriage several weeks later. 'No,' she said, 'I don't want to be married, but we can move in together and see how it goes. If it doesn't turn out well, we can split and there'll be no bitterness.'

And it was she who found the flat in Hume Street, on the top floor of one of those old Georgian houses in off the Green, within walking distance of both our places of work. There was extraordinary peace and loveliness in our first weeks together that I will always link with those high-ceilinged rooms – the eager rush of excitement I felt as I left the office at the end of the day; the lingering in the streets to buy some offering of flowers or fruit or wine or a bowl, and once one copper pan; the rushing up the stairs to call her name; the emptiness of those rooms when I'd find she hadn't got home yet.

'Why are we so happy?' I would ask.

'Don't worry it,' she always said, and with a touch sealed my lips.

Early summer, we drove down one weekend to the small town in Kilkenny where she had grown up, and in separate rooms we slept above her father's bakery. That Sunday, a whole stream of relatives – aunts, cousins, two uncles, with trains of children – arrived at the house. Word had gone out, and they had plainly come to look me over. This brought the tension between herself and her schoolteacher mother into open quarrel late that evening after dinner. Her father sat with me in the front room, cautiously kind, sipping whiskey as we measured each careful cliché, listening to the quarrel grow and rise and crack in the far-off kitchen. I had found the sense of comfort and space charming at first, but by Monday morning I, too, was beginning to find the small town claustrophobic.

'Unfortunately, the best part of these visits is always the leaving,' she said as we drove away. 'After a while on your own, you're lured into thinking that the next time will some-how be different, but it never is.'

'Wait – wait until you see my place,' I said. 'At least, your crowd made an effort. And your father is a nice man.'

'And yet you keep going back to the old place?'

'That's true. I'm afraid it's just something in my own nature that I have to face. It's just easier for me to go back than to cut. That way, I don't feel any guilt. I don't feel anything.'

I knew myself too well. There was more caution than any love or charity in my habitual going home. It was unattractive and it had been learned in the bitter school of my ungiving father. I would fall into no guilt, and I was already fast outwearing him. For a time, it seemed, I could outstare the one eye of nature. I had even waited for love, if love this was; for it was happiness such as I had never known.

'You see, I waited long enough for you,' I said as we drove away from her Kilkenny town. 'I hope I can keep you now.'

'If it wasn't me, it would be some other. My mother will never understand that. You might as well say I waited long enough for you.'

'You might as well say that, too.'

The visit we made to my father, not long after, quickly turned to disaster far worse than I had at the very worst envisaged. I saw him watch us as I got out of the car to open the iron gate under the yew, but instead of coming out to the road to greet us he withdrew into the shadows of the hallway. It was my stepmother, Rose, who came out to the car when we had both got out and were opening the small garden gate. We had to follow her smiles and trills of speech all the way into the kitchen to find my father, who was seated in the cane chair, and he did not rise to take our hands.

After a lunch that was silent in spite of several shuttlecocks of speech Rose tried to keep in the air, he said, as he took his hat from the sill, 'I want to ask you about these walnuts.' And I followed him out into the fields. The mock orange was in blossom, and it was where the mock orange stood out from the clump of egg bushes that he turned suddenly and said, 'What age is your intended? She looks well on her way to forty.'

'She's the same age as I am,' I said blankly. I could hardly think, caught between the shock and pure amazement.

'I don't believe it,' he said.

'You don't have to, but we were in the same class at university.' I turned away.

Walking with her in the same field close to the mock orange late that evening, I said, 'Do you know what my father said to me?'

'No,' she said happily. 'But from what I've seen I don't think anything will surprise me.'

'We were walking just here,' I began, and repeated what he'd said. When I saw her go still and pale, I knew I should not have spoken.

'Close to forty,' she repeated. 'I have to get out of this place.'

'I'm sorry for telling you, but it's so blatantly untrue that I didn't think you'd take it seriously. If anything, you're too beautiful.'

'I just want to get out of this place.'

'Stay this one night,' I begged. 'It's late now. We'd have to stay in a hotel. It'd be making it into too big a production. You don't ever have to come back again, if you don't want to, but stay the night. It'll be easier.'

'I'll not want to come back,' she said as she agreed to see out this one night.

'But why do you think he said it?' I asked her later when we were both quiet, sitting on a wall at the end of the Big Meadow, watching the shadows of the evening deepen between the beeches, putting off the time when we'd have to go into the house, not unlike two grown children.

'Is there any doubt? Out of simple hatred. There's no living with that kind of hatred.'

'We'll leave first thing in the morning,' I promised.

'And why did you,' she asked, teasing my throat with a blade of rye, 'say I was, if anything, too beautiful?'

'Because it's true. It makes you public, and it's harder to live naturally. You live in too many eyes – in envy or confusion or even simple admiration, it's all the same. It makes it harder to live luckily.'

'But it gives you many advantages.'

'If you make use of those advantages, you're drawn in even deeper. And of course I'm afraid it'll attract people who'll try to steal you from me.'

'That won't happen.' She laughed. She'd recovered all her natural good spirits. 'And now I suppose we better go in and face the ogre. We have to do it sooner or later, and it's getting chilly.'

My father tried to be very charming at dinner that night, but there was a false heartiness to it that made it clear that it grew out of no well-meaning. He felt he'd lost ground, and was now trying to recover it far too quickly. Using silence and politeness like a single weapon, we refused to be drawn in; and, when pressed to stay the next morning, we said unequivocally that we had to be back. Except for one summer when I went to work in England, the summer my father married Rose, I had always gone home to help at the hay; and after I entered the Civil Service I was able to arrange holidays so that they fell around haytime. At home they had come to depend on me, and I liked the work. My father had never forgiven me for taking my chance to go to university. He had wanted me to stay and work the land. I had always fought his need to turn my refusal into betrayal. And by going home each summer I felt I was affirming that the great betrayal was not mine but nature's own.

I had arranged my holiday to fall at haytime that year, as I had all the years before I met her, but since he'd turned to me at the mock orange I was no longer sure I had to go. I was no longer free, since in everything but name our life together seemed to be growing into marriage. It might even make him happy for a time to call it my betrayal.

'I don't know what to do,' I confessed to her a week before I was due to take my holiday. 'They've come to depend on me for the hay. Everything else they can manage themselves. I know they'll expect me.'

'What do you want to do?'

'I suppose I'd prefer to go home – that's if you don't mind.'

'Why do you prefer?'

'I like working at the hay. You come back to the city feeling fit and well.'

'Is that the real reason?'

'No. It's something that might even be called sinister. I've gone home for so long that I'd like to see it through. I don't want to be blamed for finishing it, though it'll finish soon, with or without me. But this way I don't have to think about it.'

'Maybe it would be kinder, then, to do just that, and take the blame.'

'It probably would be kinder, but kindness died between us so long ago that it doesn't enter into it.'

'So there was some kindness?'

'When I was younger.' I had to smile. 'He looked on it as weakness. I suspect he couldn't deal with it. Anyhow, it always redoubled his fury. He was kind, too, in fits, when he was feeling good about things. That was even more unacceptable. And that thing from the Old Bible is true. After enough suffering, a kind of iron enters the soul. It's very far from commendable, but now I do want to see it through.'

'Well, then, go,' she said.

We had pasta and two bottles of red wine at the flat the evening before I was to leave for the hay, and with talking we were almost late for our usual walk in the Green. We liked to walk there every good evening before turning home for the night.

The bells were fairly clamouring from all corners, rooting vagrants and lovers from the shrubbery, as we passed through a half-closed gate. Two women at the pond's edge were hurriedly feeding the ducks bread from a plastic bag. We crossed the bridge where the Japanese cherry leaned, down among the empty benches round the paths and flowerbeds within their low railings. The deckchairs had been gathered in, the sprinklers turned off. There was about the Green always at this hour some of the melancholy of the beach at the close of holiday. The gate we had entered was already locked. The attendant was rattling an enormous bunch of keys at the one through which we had to leave.

'You know,' she said, 'I'd like to be married before long. I hadn't thought it would make much difference to me, but, oddly, now I want to be married.'

'I hope it's to me,' I said.

'You haven't asked me.' I could feel her laughter as she held my arm close.

'I'm asking now.' I made a flourish of removing a non-existent hat. 'Will you marry me?'

'I will.'

'When?'

'Before the year is out.'

'Would you like to go for a drink to celebrate, then?'

'I always like any excuse to celebrate.' She was biting her lip. 'Where will you take me?'

'The Shelbourne. It's our local, and it'll be quiet.'

I thought of the aggressive boot thrown after the bridal car, the marbles suddenly rattling in the hubcaps of the honey-moon car, their metal smeared with oil so that the thrown confetti would stick, the legs of the comic pyjamas hilariously sewn up. We would avoid all that. We had promised one another the simplest wedding.

'We live in a lucky time,' she said and raised her glass, her calm grey intelligent eyes shining. 'We wouldn't have been allowed to do it this way even a decade ago. Will you tell your father that we're to be married?'

'I don't know. Probably not unless it comes up. And you?'

'I better. As it is, Mother will probably be furious that it is not going to be a big splash.'

'I'm so grateful for this time together. That we were able to drift into marriage without that drowning plunge when you see your whole life in the flash. What will you do while I'm away?'

'I'll pine,' she said, and laughed. 'I might even try to decorate the flat out of simple desperation. There's a play at the Abbey that I want to see. There are some good restaurants in the city if I get too depressed. And, in the meantime, have a wonderful time with your father and poor Rose in the nine-teenth century at the bloody hay.'

'Oh, for the Lord's sake,' I said as I paid the bill. Outside, she was still laughing so provocatively that I drew her towards me.

*

The next morning, on the train home, I heard the weather forecast from a transistor far down the carriage. A prolonged spell of good weather was promised. Meadows were being mowed all along the line, and I saw men testing handfuls of hay in the breeze as they waited for the sun to burn the dew off the fallen swards. It was weather people prayed for.

I walked the three miles from the station. Meadows were down all along the road, some already saved, in stacked bales. The scent of cut grass was everywhere. As I drew close to the stone house in its trees, I could hardly wait to see if the Big Meadow, beyond the row of beech trees, was down. When I'd lived here, I'd felt this same excitement as the train rattled across the bridges into the city or when I approached the first sight of the ocean. Now that I lived in a city on the sea, the excitement had been gradually transferred home.

As I turned in at the gate, I could tell by the emptiness beyond the beeches that the Big Meadow had been cut. At the house, Rose and my father were waiting in a high state.

'Everything's ready for you,' Rose said as she shook my hand, and through the window I saw my old clothes outside in the sun, draped across the back of a chair.

'As soon as you get a bite, you can jump in your old duds,' my father said. 'I knocked the Big Meadow yesterday. All's ready for go.'

Rose had washed my old clothes before hanging them outside to air. When I changed into them, they were still warm from the sun, and they had that lovely clean feel that worn clothes after washing have. Within an hour, we were working the machines.

The machines had taken much of the uncertainty and slavery from hay-making, but there was still the anxiety of rain. Each cloud that drifted into the blue above us we watched as apprehensively across the sky as if it were an enemy ship, and we seemed as tired at the end of every day as we were before we had the machines, eating late in silence, waking from a listless watching of the television only when the weather forecast showed; and afterwards it was an effort to drag feet to our rooms, where the beds lit with moonlight showed like heaven and sleep was as instant as it was dreamless.

It was into the stupor of such an evening that the gold watch fell. We were slumped in front of the television set. Rose, who had been working outside in the front garden, came in and put the tea kettle on the ring, and started to take folded sheets from the linen closet. Without warning, the gold watch spilled out on to the floor. She'd pulled it from the closet with one of the sheets. The pale face was upward in the poor light. I bent to pick it up. The glass had not broken. 'It's lucky it no longer goes,' Rose said under her breath.

'Well, if it did, you'd soon take good care of that,' my father said.

'It just pulled out with the sheets,' Rose said. 'I was running into it everywhere round the house, and I put it in with the sheets so that it'd be out of the way.'

'I'm sure you had it well planned. Give us this day our daily crash. Tell me this: Would you sleep at night if you didn't manage to smash or break something during the day?' He'd been frightened out of a light sleep. He was intent on avenging his fright.

'Why did the watch stop?' I asked. I turned the cold gold in my hand. 'Elgin' was the one word on the white face. The delicate hands were of blue steel. All through my childhood, it had shone.

'Can there be two reasons why it stopped?' His anger veered towards me now. 'It stopped because it got broke.'

'Why can't it be fixed?' I ignored the anger.

'Poor Taylor in the town doesn't take in watches any more,' Rose said. 'And the last time it stopped we sent it to Sligo. Sligo even sent it to Dublin, but it was sent back. A part that holds the balance wheel is broke. What they told us is, they've stopped making parts for those watches. They have to be specially handmade. They said that the quality of the gold wasn't high enough to justify that expense. That it was only gold-plated. I don't suppose it'll ever go again. I put it in with the sheets to have it out of the way. I was running into it everywhere.'

'Well, if it wasn't fixed before, you must certainly have fixed it for good and forever this time,' my father said. He would not let go. His hand trembled on the arm of the rocking chair – the same hand that would draw out the gold watch long ago as the first strokes of the Angelus came to us over the heather and pale wheaten sedge of Gloria Bog: 'Twenty minutes late, no more than usual ... One of these years, Jimmy Lynch will startle himself and the whole countryside by ringing the Angelus at exactly twelve ... Only in Ireland is there right time and wrong time. In other countries there is just time.' We would stand and stretch our backs, aching from scattering the turf, and wait for him to lift his straw hat.

Waiting with him under the yew, suitcases round our feet, we would look for the bus that took us each year to the sea at Strandhill after the hay was in and the turf home, and to quiet us he'd take out the watch and let it lie in his open palm, where we'd follow the small second hand low down on the face endlessly circling until the bus came into sight at the top of Doherty's Hill. How clearly everything sang now, set free by the distance of the years; with what heaviness the actual scenes and days had weighed.

'If the watch isn't going to be fixed, then, I might as well have it,' I said. I was amazed at the calm sound of my own words. The watch had come to him from his father. Through all the long years of childhood, I had assumed that one day he would pass it on to me. Then I would possess its power. Once, in a generous fit, he'd even promised it to me, but he did not keep that promise. Unfairly, perhaps, I expected him to give it to me when I graduated, when I passed into the Civil Service, when I won my first promotion, but he did not. I had forgotten about it until it had fallen out of the folded sheets.

I saw a look pass between my father and my stepmother before he said, 'What good would it be to you?'

'No good,' I said. 'Just a keepsake. I'll get you a good new watch in its place. I often see watches in the duty-free airports.' My work often took me outside the country.

'I don't need a watch,' he said, and he pulled himself up from his chair.

Rose cast me a furtive look – much the same look that had passed a few moments before between her and my father. 'Maybe your father wants to keep the watch,' it pleaded, but I ignored it.

'Didn't the watch once belong to your father?' I asked, but the only answer he made was to turn and yawn before starting the slow, exaggerated shuffle towards his room.

To my delight, when the train pulled into Amiens Street Station, I saw her outside the ticket barrier, in the same tweed suit she'd worn the Saturday morning we met in Grafton Street. I could tell that she'd been to the hairdresser, but there were specks of white paint on her hands.

'Did you tell them that we're to be married?' she asked as we left the station.

'No,' I said.

'Why not?'

'It never came up. And you, did you write home?'

'No. In fact, I drove down last weekend and told them.'

'How did they take it?'

'They seemed glad. You seem to have made a good impression.' She smiled. 'As I guessed, Mother is quite annoyed that it's not going to be a big do.'

'You won't change our plans because of that?'

'Of course not. She's not much given to change herself, except to changing other people so that they fit in with her ideas.'

'This fell my way at last,' I said, and I showed her the silent watch. 'I've always wanted it. If we believed in signs, it would seem life is falling into our hands at last.'

'And not before our time, I think I can risk adding.'

We were married in October by a Franciscan priest in their church on the quays, with two vergers as witnesses, and we drank far too much wine at the lunch afterwards in a new restaurant that had opened in Lincoln Court. Staggering home in the late afternoon, I saw some people on our street smile at my attempt to lift her across the threshold. We did not even hear the bells closing the Green.

It was dark when we woke, and she said, 'I have something

for you,' taking a small, wrapped package from the bedside
table.

'You know we promised not to give presents,' I said.

'I know, but this is different. Open it. Anyhow, you said
you didn't believe in signs.'

It was the gold watch. I held it to my ear. It was running
perfectly. The small second hand was circling endlessly low
down on the face. The blue hands pointed past midnight.

'Did it cost much?' I asked.

'No. Very little, but that's not your business.'

'I thought the parts had to be specially made.'

'That wasn't true. They probably never even asked.'

'You shouldn't have bothered.'

'Now I'm hoping to see you wear it,' she said, laughing.

I did not wear it. I left it on the mantel. The gold and white
face and delicate blue hands looked very beautiful to me on the
white marble. It gave me a curious pleasure mixed with guilt
to wind it and watch it run; and the following spring, coming
from a conference in Ottawa, I bought an expensive modern
wristwatch in the duty-free shop of Montreal Airport. It was
guaranteed for five years, and was shockproof, dustproof, waterproof.

'What do you think of it?' I asked her when I returned to
Dublin. 'I bought it for my father.'

'Well, it's no beauty,' she said, 'but my mother would
certainly approve of it. It's what she'd describe as "serviceable".'

'It was expensive enough.'

'It looks expensive. You'll take it when you go down for the
hay?'

'It'll probably be my last summer with them at the hay,' I
said apologetically. 'Won't you change your mind and come
down with me?'

She shook her head. 'He'd probably say I look fifty now.' She
was as strong-willed as the schoolteacher mother she disliked,
and I did not press. She was with child and looked calm and
lovely.

'What'll they do about the hay when they no longer have
you to help them?' she asked.

'What does anybody do? Stop. Do without me. Get it done by contract. They have plenty of money. It'll just be the end of something that has gone on for a very long time.'

'That it certainly has.'

I came by train at the same time in July as I'd come every summer, the excitement I'd always felt tainted with melancholy that it would probably be the last summer I would come. I had not even a wish to see it to its natural end any more. I had come because it seemed less violent to come than to stay away, and I had the good new modern watch to hand over in place of the old gold. The night before, at dinner, we had talked about buying a house with a garden out near the strand in Sandymount. Any melancholy I was feeling lasted only until I came in sight of the house. All the meadows had been cut and saved, the bales stacked in groups of five or six and roofed with green grass. The Big Meadow, beyond the beeches, was completely clean, the bales having been taken in. Though I had come intending to make it my last summer at the hay, I now felt a keen outrage that it had been ended without me. Rose and my father were nowhere to be seen.

'What happened?' I asked when I found them at last.

'The winter feeding got too much for us,' my father said, as if it were a matter of little concern. 'We decided to let the meadows. Gillespie took them. He cut early – two weeks ago.'

'Why didn't you tell me?'

My father and Rose exchanged looks, and my father spoke as if he were delivering a prepared statement. 'We didn't like to. And we thought you'd want to come, hay or no hay. It's more normal to come for a rest instead of to kill yourself at the old hay. And indeed there's plenty else for you to do if you have a mind to do it. I've taken up the garden again myself.'

'I've brought these,' I said, and I handed Rose a box of chocolates and a bottle of scent, and gave my father the watch.

'What's this for?' He had always disliked receiving presents.

'It's the watch I told you I'd get in place of the old watch.'

'I don't need a watch.'

'I got it anyhow. What do you think of it?'

'It's ugly,' he said, turning it over.

'It was expensive enough.' I named the price. 'And that was duty-free.'

'They must have seen you coming, then.'

'No. It's guaranteed for five years. It's dustproof, shock-proof, waterproof.'

'The old gold watch – do you still have that?' he asked after a time.

'Of course.'

'Did you ever get it working?'

'No,' I lied. 'But it's sort of nice to have.'

'That doesn't make much sense to me.'

'Well, you'll find that the new watch is working well, any-way.'

'What use have I for time here any more?' he said. But I saw him start to wind and examine the new watch, and he was wearing it at breakfast the next morning. He seemed to want it to be seen as he buttered toast and reached across for milk and sugar.

'What did you want to get up so early for?' he said to me. 'You should have lain in and taken a good rest when you had the chance.'

'What will you be doing today?' I asked.

'Not much. A bit of fooling around. I might get spray ready for the potatoes.'

'It'd be an ideal day for hay,' I said, looking out the win-dow on the fields. The morning was as blue and cool as the plums still touched with dew down by the hayshed. There was white spider webbing over the grass. I took a book and headed towards the shelter of the beeches edging the Big Meadow, for, when the sun eventually beat through, the day would be un-comfortably hot.

It was a poor attempt at reading. Halfway down each page, I'd find I had lost every thread and was staring blankly at the words. I thought at first that the trees and green and those few wisps of cloud, hazy and calm in the emerging blue, brought the tension of past exams and summers too close to the book I held in my hand, but then I found myself stirring uncomfortably in my suit – missing my old loose clothes, the smell of diesel in the meadow, the blades of grass shivering as they fell, the long teeth of the raker kicking the hay into rows, all the jangle and bustle and busyness of the meadows.

Suddenly I heard the clear blows of a hammer on stone. My father was sledging stones that had fallen from the archway where once the workmen's bell had hung. Some of the stones were quite beautiful, and there seemed no point in breaking them up. I moved closer, taking care to stay hidden in the shade of the beeches.

As the sledge rose, the watch glittered on my father's wrist. I followed it down, saw the shudder that ran through his arms as the metal met the stone. A watch was always removed from the wrist before such violent work. I waited. In this heat he could not keep up such work for long. He brought the sledge down again and again, the watch glittering, the shock shuddering through his arm. When he stopped, before he wiped the sweat away, he put the watch to his ear and listened intently. What I'd guessed was certain now. From the irritable way he threw the sledge aside, it was clear that the watch was still running.

That afternoon, I helped him fill the tar barrel with water for spraying the potatoes, though he made it known that he didn't want help. In an old piece of sacking he poured the small blue pebbles needed to make the spray, and he tied the sacking into a bag. By morning the pebbles would have dissolved in the water. When he put the bag of blue stone into the barrel to steep, he thrust the watch deep into the water before my eyes.

'I'm going back to Dublin tomorrow,' I said.

'I thought you were coming for two weeks,' he said. 'You always stayed two weeks before.'

'There's no need for me now.'

'It's your holidays now. You're as well off here as by the sea. It's as much of a change and far cheaper.'

'I meant to tell you before, and should have but didn't. I am married now.'

'Tell me more news,' he said, with an attempt at cool surprise, but I saw by his eyes that he already knew. 'It's a bit late in the day for formal announcements, never mind invitations. I suppose we weren't important enough to be invited.'

'There was no one at the wedding but ourselves. We invited no one – neither her people nor mine.'

'Well, I suppose it was cheaper that way,' he agreed sarcastically.

'When will you spray?'

'I'll spray tomorrow,' he said. And we left the blue stone to steep in the barrel of water.

With relief, I noticed he was no longer wearing the watch, but the feeling of unease was so great in the house that after dinner I went outside. It was a perfect moonlit night, the empty fields and beech trees and walls in clear yellow outline. The night seemed so full of serenity that it brought the very ache of longing for all of life to reflect its moonlit calm. Yet I knew too well such calm neither was nor could be, but was a dream of death.

I went idly towards the orchard, and as I passed the tar barrel I saw a thin fishing line hanging from a part of the low yew branch down into the water. I seemed to hear the ticking even before the wristwatch came up tied to the end of the line. What dismayed me was that I felt no surprise.

I felt the bag that we'd left to steep earlier in the water The blue stone had all melted down. It was a barrel of pure poison, ready for spraying.

I listened to the ticking of the watch on the end of the line in silence before letting it drop back into the barrel. The poison had already eaten into the casing of the watch. The shining rim and back were no longer smooth. It could hardly run much past morning.

The night was so still that the shadows of the beeches did not waver on the moonlit grass but seemed fixed like a leaf in rock. On the white marble, the gold watch must now be lying face upward in this same light, silent or running. The ticking of the watch down in the barrel was so completely muffled by the spray that only by imagination could it be heard. A bird moved in a high branch, but afterwards the silence was so deep it began to hurt, and the longing grew for the bird or anything to stir again.

I stood in that moonlit silence, as if waiting for some word or truth, but none came, none ever came; and I grew amused at that part of myself that still expected something, standing like a fool out there in all that moonlit silence, when only what *was* increased or diminished as it changed, became only what is, becoming again what *was* even faster than the small second hand endlessly circling in the poison.

Suddenly the lights in the house went out. Rose had gone to join my father in bed. Before going in this last night to my room, I drew the watch up again out of the barrel by the line and listened to it tick, now purely amused by the expectation it renewed that if I continued to listen to the ticking some word or truth might come. And when I finally lowered the watch back down into the poison, I lowered it so carefully that no ripple or splash disturbed the quiet, and time, hardly surprisingly, was still running; time that did not have to run to any conclusion.

A Cut above the Rest

VAL MULKERNS

I SUPPOSE in a way you could say I am my mother's justi-
fication, being the one who made it into the overdraft belt,
those parts of inner or scenic outer suburbia where the mere
lack of cash doesn't matter, has never mattered. I think often
of her careful stage-management of my future, and I can't
help smiling because I never really got away. No matter how
rich I have ever temporarily felt, I can't spend money on, let's
say, the trimmings of a meal. I can buy wine but never the
best cut of smoked salmon for a starter: I buy salmon tails
and bury them in what is known as good presentation. I buy
slightly flawed best bed-linen at annual sales but I can never
splurge on, say, really beautiful bath-towels or cut flowers.

I think poor, as a wealthy Jew whose father pushed a scrap-
cart said to me once. And this is strange, because the rule of our
house at home was that we thought rich. That was what set us
apart from our neighbours in the ugly northside terrace which
was near enough and similar enough to the municipal housing
estate to be frequently confused with it. In fact the ambition
of many of our neighbours was to be housed by the local
authority for even less than what seem, in retrospect, the
modest private rentals of those days when only the rich bought
their own houses. Most people rented houses big or small, and
it was the ambition of my mother to rent a bigger house in a
more acceptable district, which would land us in debt but do
us justice.

All the arguments I can ever remember between my happy
parents were about this. My father said that living in a stable
didn't make you a horse and that this was a mixed district

anyway. What about the Carters? The Carters, like ourselves, didn't quite belong. Mr Carter worked in advertising and Mrs Carter gave piano lessons. It was not the sort of house from which you got the smell of coddle or the sounds of a drunken brawl on a Saturday night. They even had two Victorian urns filled with geraniums on either side of the tiny hall door. The urns were a nuisance because you had to edge in sideways between them, and if Mrs Carter had had a baby and therefore a pram, the whole thing would have become impossible. But like ourselves (once my small brother grew a bit), there was no baby in that house. They had two small boys like ours and they had Annette who was my friend for a while. The other houses in the street were seldom without a pram in the hall and a raft of children tearing the garden to shreds or spilling over into the street with their games.

I had music lessons from Mrs Carter and I also practised there because, as my mother said, she hadn't yet found exactly the right piano for us. Exactly the right piano for us was, I presume, a second-hand one costing about a fiver. A good new piano cost about forty pounds then, but it was no further away from us in terms of attainability than a fiver. Fivers were needed for a new suit for my father when his position as a salesman would have been jeopardized by more mending. Fivers were needed to pay school fees and electricity bills and sometimes to give a really splendid present to my aunt Harriet – like a wireless set, for instance, which my father got (as he could get most things except pianos) at 'the right price'. So long as she could give the odd splendid present to her elder sister, my mother never felt inferior and therefore unhappy. It didn't matter that Harriet's presents to us were always of a much more modest nature. In fact that made it even better. And some day, my mother promised, some day she would find the right sort of piano for us.

What about Mrs Stapleton, my father said. Oh yes, Mrs Stapleton. She was elderly and sad and Protestant but she had once had a son. He was a poet, and the glory of his career filled the walls of the little house. He had not only been a poet but he had been connected with the Abbey Theatre at

one time, much more firmly connected than my father who
had merely played there once or twice. Roderic Stapleton, the
son's name was, and now nothing is remembered of his fame.
Poetry anthologies come and go with never a mention of him.
If my father were alive he would be quietly triumphant. He
always claimed the man was only a rhymester like himself, but
more successful. More confusing to all but the very alert. He
used the language of the Twilight, the language Yeats copied
from Ernest Dowson before giving it an Irish accent. Roderic
Stapleton was very fashionable at one time because the master
poet had publicly given him his blessing. He was a kind of
Crown Prince, good-looking, charming, a drunk and a gambler
like my uncle Dan, but a successful drunk, a successful poet,
even a very successful producer at the Abbey Theatre. His
lopsided grin and the hairstyle he copied from Yeats appealed
for admiration and indulgence from three dozen photographs on
his mother's wall. Playbills were framed and hung too, also
Roderic's conferring photograph in 1919 at Trinity, also his
Rugby cap. Well, that wasn't framed, but it hung with a
touchingly boyish air of waiting till tomorrow morning on the
wooden rack in his room, which was preserved as a sort of
childhood museum, rocking-horse and all.

Mrs Stapleton, poor soul, was all very well, my mother conceded, but we mustn't lose any opportunity to look for a better
house. Meanwhile she happily painted and polished and contrived until our abode resembled nothing so much as a glittering doll's house. There was of course, she kept reminding us,
the house in Drumcondra, and that might be ours one day.

Of course, the house in Drumcondra. It was a recurring
dream of my mother's to own it because, however rundown
it might have become since the death of my grandmother, it
was unequivocally middle-class. It was one of a terrace of
polychrome brick, set well back from the road with bay windows and tiled pathways and ornate boot-scrapers and railings
shaped like the ace of spades. Its Nottingham lace curtains
were held back by polished metal bands, and in the porch hung
a huge old gas lantern which at Christmas used to be garlanded
with ivy. It stood not far from the Bishop's Palace, but a bit

nearer to the Tolka Cottages whose elder children used to wheel out the red-brick babies in their prams or help in the house during spring cleaning. If they proved reliable, they were taken on as cook-housekeeper and 'trained' – that is, given practically no money while doing all the dirty work until some unspecified period had passed when they were judged to be 'trained'. In the early days of her marriage, my mother told me, my grandmother had found her a girl from the cottages who had cycled around by Goose Green every morning to help in our house, but it hadn't lasted long. Her name was Maisie Clancy, and reading between the carefully edited lines my mother gave me, I gather she had told my grandmother that our house wasn't much of a cut above the Tolka Cottages, and she'd sooner work near her own place, thank you. In the end my mother was fortunate the girl left, because soon afterwards she found Nanny Sheeran, but that is another story.

At the time I'm speaking of, the family in Drumcondra had dwindled to four souls locked together in what remained of a large-family interdependence. The two elder brothers of my mother were in America, one a dentist and the other an auctioneer. The next girl was married to a sheep-farmer in Australia. The youngest brother, Dan (a barrister who never held a brief), had moved in his merry young wife from Wexford who lived in perpetual mocking conflict with the remaining unmarried sister, my aunt Evelyn, until she, poor soul, was put into a home. I am not sure at this far remove whether she was always mentally retarded or not, or whether subnormality was attributed to her by that family because she used to go out with British Auxiliaries during the Troubles – actually be seen with them gossiping and giggling under the trees along Lower Drumcondra Road. Once she had even gone to the Volta with a sergeant from Swansea, and after this Harriet, the eldest, was detailed by my grandmother to watch Evelyn closely and report any sign of a recurrence. It was even said that the hussy had broken her mother's heart, because soon after this my grandmother apparently took to her bed with arthritis never to rise again. Harriet had left her job as a book-keeper in Lloyd, Armstrong & Frazer's to look after the invalid, and vowed she would never marry while her mother was alive. I remember seeing my grandmother dead at last like a marble statue on the high brass bed in her red bedroom, surrounded by six tall candles. Her face was cold and hard like marble when I was lifted up to kiss it, and Aunt Harriet said this was because her soul was in heaven. The only other thing I remember about this was my grandfather standing with his hard hat twisting in his hands at the open doorway, from which Harriet tried to hunt him on the grounds that he would only upset himself. Gentle old man though he was, he pushed her roughly aside and made for the white-draped bed, where he knelt down after kissing the corpse and stayed with bent head until my mother came to take him away.

After that he came often to our house for tea, and I think it was he who put it into my mother's head that the house in Drumcondra might one day be hers. Apart from Dan she was the youngest of that family and so had no possible claim on the house. But my grandfather had always liked her best. When he retired from the *Freeman's Journal* and began to spend most of every day tinkering with the two old cars in his coach-house, it was my mother who used to spend most time out there with him – she was twelve or so then, and she used to sit in the old Model T with him (which he hoped to re-vitalize with spare parts from the other old car) and read him her poetry. One piece written on old jotter paper I still have – a ballad about bold Robert Emmett and his love Sarah Curran. It was probably the nearest my grandfather ever came to the fight for Irish freedom (apart from interviewing revolutionaries for his newspaper), but his house was always open to men on the run and it is said Michael Collins had once hidden in one of the old cars out in the back until a house-to-house search for him was over.

That house in a way was my house. I passed it every day cycling along the Drumcondra Road to school, to the same school where my mother and all my aunts had gone before me. I often stopped at the house for a drink of milk on my way home from school if the day was hot. I often took shelter there from a shower in winter. Some of the girls in school thought I lived there, and I didn't correct them. Katy from Wexford, Dan's wife, was a slattern, but always welcoming. Under her direction the house went steadily downhill. She had been cured of cleaning for ever as a result of one holocaust soon after she arrived as Dan's bride. That orgy of spring cleaning had ended in a bonfire out in the back garden in which had perished my grandfather's press-cutting book from his days on the New York *Herald Tribune*, all the letters he had ever written to my grandmother, and the entire family stock of baby curls, milk teeth and First Communion photographs. Now she never even bothered to use the sunshade, and so the paint blistered and peeled on the green hall door. The door brasses which had once glistened under the old lantern grew green and mildewy. Soon even the stained-glass panels became so thick with dust you could hardly make out the delicate tulip pattern from inside. Dust gathered too on the plush curtains in the hall and built up in the corners of the old red and blue carpet. A smell of tomcats and sour dishwater came up the four quarry-stone steps from the kitchen, and I didn't wonder that my grandfather hardly ever emerged from the coach-house at the bottom of the garden.

I suppose he must have come in to eat and sleep, but I always had to hunt him out in the garden to say hello. He would ask me about old Mother Mary Thomas in Eccles Street and tell me what a merry young girl she had been when he was a boy. He would tell me again about the time he and some other Belvedere boys had taken part in an operetta at the Convent, or about trick-cycling in the Phoenix Park on Sunday mornings when he was a boy, or about when he interviewed the Fenian James Stephens for his newspaper in New York, or about the old days in the *Freeman's Journal* when he would battle to prevent a single word being printed against the Chief, the great Charles Stewart Parnell: sometimes he recounted these battles with his editor in detail. Or he would tell me about the first meal my grandmother had ever cooked for him when they were five years married and the girl in the kitchen ran off with a soldier who was killed in the Boer War, whereupon she came back to cook for them until she married again.

Her name was Nancy and she cooked the most melting bacon
and cabbage you'd taste in a day's walk. I think my grandfather must often have been hungry, but he would never hear
a word spoken against the Wexford wife by my mother or
anybody else. Maybe she *had* no taste for housework or cooking but she was a good wee girl, Katy, and she had a lot to put
up with from The Gentleman. That was what he called my
uncle Dan, The Gentleman. And it was a poor family, he
said, that couldn't support one gentleman.

He'd sit by the fire at home, eating buttered scones, and
play with my two young brothers, while encouraging my
mother in her dreams of owning his house. Old blue eyes lively
in the brick-red face, he would say that The Gentleman would
not be left unprovided for, but that Fanny, my mother, was
the girl to bring the old house back to life again, the way it
used to be in her mother's day, God be good to her. Later,
when he would drive away in the rattling old car to his spectral
house where he might often have to help Katy lug the drunken
Gentleman up to bed, my mother would sit up late over the
fire with my father, dreaming of when we would all live happily
in her old home again, and of the parties we would be able
to give. Half asleep in the 'return' room whose wall above my
bed was open to the staircase, I would listen to her giggling
and plotting and planning, and sometimes hear the futile
admonition of my father: 'But Fanny, my dear, think of the
upkeep, only think of what that house would cost us to run.'

Once, on an April Sunday morning I shall never forget, he
had taken me to see his own old home which was very
different. It was in Phibsboro, one of a square of identical
small houses fronting directly on to the pavement and built
towards the end of the last century for the employees of the
Great Southern & Western Railway Co. He stood taller by far
now than the little blue hall door of Number 16, and the sun
shone on his flaming red hair with its matching bushy eyebrows. He looked proudly down at me, like a farmer showing
off a particularly fine field of grain. Because it was Sunday
morning, a cluster of little girls in First Communion frocks
were giggling around us, wondering what we were doing there.

He chaffed them and pulled the long black hair of one of them.

'You'd be Tommy Byrne's girl, wouldn't you?'

The child giggled and nodded her head, and I felt extremely embarrassed as they all turned to gaze at me. 'I'd know you out of him in a dozen,' my father said, pleased. 'Tommy and I were boys at Knutsford together,' he explained to me as another might say, 'We were up together at Oxford.'

Before opening the door, the woman of Number 16 took a look through the parted curtains of the little front window. Her expression was not friendly, but my father gave her the full treatment in his big splendid voice.

'Bartholomew J. Mullens, Madam, at your service. Forgive me the disturbance at this hour of the morning, but I wanted to show the little girl here the house where her old father grew up when all the world was young. Bliss was it in that dawn to be alive – but I don't need to tell you that.' He smiled and shook her warmly by the reluctantly offered hand, and asked to whom he had the honour of speaking. She was Mrs Noonan, she said, and my father gave a theatrical shout of joy, to the renewed giggles of all the little girls.

'Not Mrs *Andy* Noonan, by all that's wonderful?' and the loud booming of his name brought the woman's husband out beside her into the tiny square place where coats hung on pegs behind them and a red lamp burned to the Sacred Heart.

'Andy, my dear fellow, after all these years!' said my father, and Mr Noonan shouted, 'Mullser, by God!' in great delight. We were escorted into the kitchen, where there was a smell of bubbling bacon and a floury table under the window where Mrs Noonan had been baking. The reunion ended as I knew it would, with the vanishing of the two old friends in the direction of Doyle's Corner, and Mrs Noonan made tea for me, which I didn't know how to refuse although the steamy heat of the little place made me queasy. She said Bernadette and Mollie and the four boys would be delighted to meet me when they got back from Mass, and when I'd somehow accounted for the tea I plucked up courage to ask her if I could look over my father's old house. She seemed surprised, and indicated the small scullery off the room where we were

which had a door presumably leading to the back. I thanked
her and went through the tiny, dark, cave-like scullery into the
sunlight of about three square yards of concrete. A door
painted red presumably indicated the lavatory – it was open
to the air above and below. Apart from two pots of geraniums,
a dustbin, a galvanized bucket, a water tap and a tiger tomcat
who wasn't friendly, there was nothing to see. The low walls
indicated identical concrete yards belonging to the houses
next door. Compared to this, our own undistinguished garden
(which at least had a tiny summer-house, an old tool-shed,
several shrubs and a sycamore tree) was a paradise in which
one could sit and read on summer days. It would be difficult to
sit out here. I looked up at what was presumably the tiny
square window of a bedroom (my father's?) above the kitchen,
but there were no other windows – was there in fact only one
bedroom which went through from front to back, and was
possibly partitioned in the middle?

Back again in the house, I noticed the small flight of steps
that looked really more like a ladder, leading up from the
kitchen into the upper storey, but there was suddenly a sort
of understanding between Mrs Noonan and myself that what
was beyond was none of my business. After my interminable
and rather embarrassing session with the Noonan boys and
girls, my father and his friend came back merrily from their
potations and my father issued a cordial invitation to the whole
family to visit us soon. He produced his card, struck out the
Gas Company's address in D'Olier Street and substituted our
own, before making his florid farewells.

On the way home I sulked because I had been abandoned,
but my father didn't even notice, so cheerful was he. Finally
curiosity overcame me and I asked him about the upstairs
regions. He verified the absence of a bathroom and the fact
that the single bedroom was partitioned. Where, I asked, did
all the children sleep? Half the partitioned room upstairs would
be occupied, he said, by the girls, since there were four of
them, and the other half by the parents. The two boys probably had camp- or chair-beds which only made their appearance at night in the kitchen. If there were more boys than

girls, then the girls would probably have the camp-beds, as had happened in his own family. He painted a jolly picture of Saturday night scrubbing sessions in the scullery, when his mother would fill the old hip-bath with hot water and allow each grown child ten minutes to conduct his ablutions with Lifebuoy soap. The little ones – all in America now – were bathed in front of the open fire in the kitchen itself, and dried off in the warmth of the flames.

When I told my mother later of the visit, she was amused and (there is no other word) tender. 'He took me to see his family for the first time the week before we were married, and I don't think I was ever in a happier house,' she said. She was no snob, my mother. She just had a highly developed sense of the fitness of things.

After the Carters went away to a new house in Monkstown and old Mrs Stapleton was found dead one morning in her bed, we were more islanded than ever. Boys and girls my own age left school and found work in Scott's jam factory or started to serve their time to their father's trade. I had no local friends who didn't regard me as a freak because I still went to school dressed in a black and white blazer and a crested beret. All my schoolfriends seemed to live miles away, in Clonskea or Rathgar or even in Dalkey. They travelled by train or car to school and occasionally I visited them for tea. My mother always insisted I invite them back in return, and she usually turned out a spread that was far superior to anything I was given to eat in their houses. But their mothers could afford to be casual. They had big, warm, tiled kitchens down flights of steps from the hall and in them were fridges and washing machines and larders and (in a few cases) even servants. They telephoned their order to the butcher or the grocer every day, and their houses were so big that an extra child or two would hardly be noticed.

The girl I envied most had a carpeted room of her own overlooking a long lawn that sloped down to the sea. When you looked out from her old mahogany desk in the bay window, you could see the Hill of Howth across the bay, and nearby on the lawn directly below were a sundial and a stone Cupid rather foolishly holding a bird-bath on his head. Fruit trees lined the red brick walls and there was a long curving rosebed. It was more orderly and more beautiful by far than my grand-father's garden could have been even in its heyday. Sometimes when a dense daytime fog blotted out everything beyond our tiny front garden, I daydreamed at my window, persuading myself that beyond the dripping privet hedge there was a long informal lawn with beech trees and soaring elms.

Sometimes I think my mother ceased to believe in the old fairy-tale of one day owning her father's house, and these seemed to me the bad days. I didn't know that she was ill. I would come home from school to find her staring at nothing through the kitchen window, hands idle in her lap, some silly pro-gramme blaring from the BBC. In the beginning when she had at last acquired the precious piano, the time Mrs Stapleton's things were auctioned, she often played it when her scouring and polishing were finished. Not any more. Nobody except myself ever touched the piano now. The music lessons at school were continued only because I could never bring myself to tell her what a bore they were.

This day, anyhow, I had something to show her which I believed would cheer her up. I was feeling friendlier towards her than I had felt for weeks, being at that time going through the stage when I often hated my mother for my father's continuing delight in her company, for all the times he didn't even hear what I was saying because he thought she was waiting to speak. I felt at times he was unduly concerned about her altogether, making appointments with a specialist in Fitzwilliam Square when what he needed was a new pair of shoes for himself. Anyhow, this day was just before the Christ-mas holidays and I had a thick shiny copy of the College Annual which contained my first appearance in print – a painfully twee piece of sub-Wodehousian humour of which I was extraordinarily proud. 'Look on page 17,' I said casually to my mother. 'You may be surprised.' 'Later, Emily,' she said. 'I have so many things to do.' But she went on staring out through the window, merely moving one hand to prevent the bulky volume from slipping off her lap. Disgusted, I went up to my room, leaving her to Henry Hall's Dance Orchestra and 'The Way You Look Tonight'. She had never behaved so insufferably before.

Later on, of course, when my father and the boys came home, there was great hilarity and my mother was pleased as Punch. She'd always known I'd do something to prove I was a cut above the rest, even if my piano playing hadn't ever amounted to much. She bit her lip and giggled as though she were a girl again, and she shot a triumphant look across the table at my father who was almost as delighted as she was. He went off to open one of the bottles of sherry he had hidden away for Christmas, and we all had a glass to celebrate. I think it was the last time I ever heard my mother laugh. I know it was the last time I heard them making love in the bedroom next to mine. The war in Europe was three months old that Christmas, I remember.

Long before that war was over, my grandfather, my wild uncle Dan and my mother were all dead. But it had nothing to do with the war, with the 'Emergency' as Mr DeValera preferred to call it. 'The Gentleman' Dan, that grown-up spoiled baby, had been riding for a fall all his life, so people said. When he got it, however, it was self-inflicted, a fall indeed. He was found one April morning on the pavement where he had thrown himself from an attic room in Holles Street, just opposite the National Maternity Hospital. A young nurse on her way to work almost tripped over him, and it was to that hospital he was ironically carried when there seemed to be some life left in him. But he died a few moments after his arrival, and in the mortuary he was surrounded by the small bodies of stillborn babies. There was an inquest, and it was said by my aunt Harriet that it would kill his father.

But my grandfather lived on even after Katy went back to Wexford to marry the farmer she had foolishly abandoned for Dan. After she had gone, the house in Drumcondra almost visibly crumbled. She had done nothing to maintain it except laugh and welcome anybody who knocked at the door, and when there was nobody to answer I used to go around by the back lane on my way home from school and call to my grandfather to let me in.

He still spent all his days messing with the cars in the old coach-house at the end of the wild garden. The tiny petrol ration had given new scope to his tinkering. He had converted one of the cars to run on wood-gas, generated in a contraption like an old-fashioned iron stove clamped to the back bumper, and he was using the remains of the other car to try and develop an improved version. Whenever I visited him, I would end by dragging him up to the house from his arduous and messy labours on the pretext of needing a glass of milk after my hard day at school, but usually there was no milk. I would make us a cup of tea on the 'glimmer' and open a tin of condensed milk if I could find one. Sometimes, if I'd had a few pence, I would produce a couple of sticky buns bought on my way past the Boston Bakery down the road, and my grandfather would make murmuring sounds of approval as he used to long ago over hot buttered scones by the fire at home, and he would suck his tea through the fiery moustache. Always I would try to persuade him to come home with me for a meal because my parents were always so delighted to see him, however bad the wartime shortages might be. About twice a week or so he would come, roping my bike on to the old dicky seat behind and rattling slowly and smokily around by Goose Green and Philipsburgh Avenue, the way I had dreamily cycled that morning with my eyes on the distant Sugarloaves. In the summer he sometimes took my young brothers out to Dolly-mount or Malahide, and sometimes my mother went too. I was usually too busy with homework, but once or twice at weekends we all went.

And then one day just before we broke up for the summer holidays, there was no answer when I called again and again from the back lane. The big lime tree that hung over the wall was heavy with bees, and there was no other sound except a distant whirr of lawnmowers. I knew he was dead and I knew where I would find him. Climbing up along the branches of the lime tree with whatever foothold I could contrive in the wall, I was quite certain I knew where I would find him. And I was right. He lay face downwards under the crank of the old Ford, which had probably kicked harder than he had anticipated. I lifted one of the oily chubby hands – the sort of hands you could never believe had supported his family by wielding a pen – and it fell like a stone from my own hand. He was already cold, and because I couldn't think what else to do I covered him with an old plaid rug from the car and went cycling home to tell my mother.

We went down to the public callbox and phoned my father at work and he phoned the police, and then we went by taxi to Drumcondra. My mother never stopped crying. I wanted to tell her, 'Now you'll have what he always wanted you to have and you and I will make the house beautiful again,' but I didn't dare. I was past crying myself.

A few days after the funeral, my mother was summoned to the solicitor's office and came back looking stunned. All that evening she lay on the old couch with her face to the wall, and that is more or less how I see her for the remainder of her life, which was only six months anyway. Her death certificate said Carcinoma, but I think she would have died anyhow because our fine future had been indefinitely postponed.

There was my grandfather's will all right, dated ten years previously, leaving her the house and everything else he possessed, but an enormous mortgage had been taken out to cover Dan's debts. Even after the sale of the house, the slate would never be wiped clean, but with any luck we would not be responsible, the solicitor believed.

'It's not fair,' my mother said, her speckled blue eyes swimming in tears.

'It's not a fair world, love,' said my father, 'but it's not the end of the world either. We'll have a lot of good times yet.'

But he knew what I knew, that the good times were all gone. For the foreseeable future, at any rate.

That Dark Accomplice

JOHN MONTAGUE

THE boys disliked him intensely, with his dark intolerant head, his way of walking as though contemptuous of stone and earth, they being merely the material on which he drew the unmistakable lines of his purpose and direction. 'No nonsense' the proud tilt of that head seemed to say from the start, and recognizing their master, as boys in a bulk nearly always do, they could still resent his mastery, as puppies resent sullenly the hand that makes them smart under the switch. Dislike? Was it anything as definite? Rather a vague resentment that forced its way towards expression through the long greyness of that Ulster winter term. Had you halted one of them, a shamefaced lad only broken to longers, dawdling by the ball-alley or kicking the scuffed grass of the Senior Ring slope with unpolished, slackly tied shoes, and asked him point blank 'Why?' he would have been startled and lost, with nothing to say for himself except to mutter rebelliously that the new Dean was 'a brute'.

Which seemed to mean, in fact, only that the new Dean knew how to handle them too, too well, and strode the dormitories punctually in the cold mornings as the electric buzzers clattered harshly against the wall, his high voice giving strength to the hated Latin greeting, 'Benedicamus Domino', the flexible cane twitching at his soutane's edge.

'Up, you sluggards! Little boys should be early birds. Come now, Johnson, don't fester in the bedclothes.' The cane rattled along the rails of the bed, flicked against thin legs dancing at a line of washbasins. 'Come now, boys, all together now – "Deo Gratias"!' Dodging on bare soles over scrubbed board, or tumbling from warm bedclothes, the boys mustered a weak, scattered reply: 'Deo Gratias.' O! he could handle them, reducing their boyish pride to little more than a scamper out of the way of a stick.

It wasn't only the cold mornings that gave them reason for hatred, but the hundred other deliberately irritating ways in which he proved his authority. Naturally an independent, high-spirited man, he had spent his early priesthood in England where he quickly gained a reputation as a successful missioner and preacher. Then, one day, he found himself transferred from the pulpit and placed among schoolboys, unable to relax his trained arrogance, his emphatic rhetorical gestures, and too far from boyhood to appreciate its special gauche tenderness. Even his speech seemed alien, brusque and clear-cut, the exact opposite of the slurred speech of the boys and the other local priests, snuffling over Greek texts in Ulster accents and making pawky jokes that endeared them to successive generations of pupils. 'Corny', 'Chappie', 'Dusty'; those were nicknames that testified to familiarity, even love, but all they could think to call him, reaching out vainly for some image to equal their dislike, was 'Death's Head' or 'Hatchet'. 'He's a brute', and with that recognition, humanity, for them, dropped from his shoulders; he became someone who struck, and must in turn be struck, the problem being where or when or with what concerted violence.

In one small incident or another, he came to sense their hatred, but remained unperturbed; indeed, he seemed almost amused by it, as though waiting to pounce with joy on the first reflex of insubordination. It became his custom to speak to them on every possible occasion, after prayers, in the still moment before Grace, from his dais in the study-hall above their sullen heads. His vibrant tones rebuked, lectured, played with them, sent them running out with a kindly general pat of dismissal. Under the substance of his words, the breaking of some minor rule, the loss of rosary beads in the grounds, or the 'slovenly disgusting' habit of sticking hands to the wrist into tattered pockets, ran a nervous note of triumph that seemed to recognize the silent war declared against him, even to defy it.

'Try it, you little fools,' it seemed to say. 'I'll soon show you how to handle a pack of grimy schoolboys.' Yet steadily they sensed in ₁him, somewhere and not explicit, a weakness, a febrile excess of emotion that might, for all his outward show and insistence, leave him helpless in some extraordinary situation.

One Friday evening, Benediction ending with the Divine Praises and the restless chink of the thurible in an altar server's hand, four boys, older than the rest, left the school chapel early, tiptoeing down the aisle with lowered heads and out on to the yard between the lavatory and the disused air-raid shelters. They stood, rubbing their thighs nervously, looking across at the lit glass of the chapel windows, all opaque save one where a Virgin's dark-blue head curved tenderly over the slight cube of the Child's body.

'Much time left?' asked one.

'A few minutes.'

'Maybe we've time for a fag. I'm nearly dead for the want of one,' said the third, gesturing towards the lavatory door.

The boys generally smoked in the damp lavatory, twenty yards or so from the back of the sacristy, passing the butts under the wooden partitions or pretending to stand at the urinal where the tepid water gushed and leaked. At a moment's notice the hot end would hiss into the water, or turn alive against the palm as the hurrying Dean peered and prodded under the doors, or turned out the pockets of malingerers. 'Pah, this place reeks of smoke, stinks of it.' The cane would grate across the glass in the top half of a lavatory door, while inside a frightened boy cowered among white tiles, a cigarette dead under his foot, braces dangling down his back.

'Better not. He'll be here any minute now, and we're to give the word to start.'

'Shush! There's the first touch of the Adoremus.'

Inside the chapel, the congregation of boys rose for the last hymn, singing loudly and unevenly, and then subsided into their seats. Some craned rudely around to watch the priests rising from their prie-dieus: old Father Keane was, as usual, the last to leave, lifting his lame leg outwards and shuffling towards the door. Others prayed with averted heads, making a cage of their hands. On the high-altar the server dowsed the last candlelight and the nave of the chapel was heavy with incense and smoke from the fuming wicks. Restless with the thought of some strange excitement, the boys waited as the head-prefect went over to lock back the swinging doors. Then they came in a rush.

Supper always followed Friday Benediction, the refectory only thirty feet away, with rickety wooden stairs up to it, the space between like a platform on to which the boys poured. This evening they were unusually silent; the four boys who had been waiting outside the chapel now appeared a little way apart, up the corridor, lounging with their backsides against the wall, eyes alert. At the far end they saw the Dean approaching, a tall figure with billowing soutane, carrying himself proudly as if bearing the Sacrament. 'Right, boys, let him have it!' they called. Turning their faces to the wall, everyone booed, dragging air into distended mouths, and forcing it out through tightened twisted lips. Boo-o-o-o.

Half-way down the hall he stopped, head flinching backwards as though from a sudden blow across the mouth. Watching intently, Tony Johnson, one of the four ringleaders, cried in excited confirmation: 'We have him, he's yellow.' The long harsh sound became stronger, gathering into itself all the suppressed vindictiveness of months and seeming to fill the area around the chapel door with the palpable presence of hatred.

Then, regaining confidence, he began to walk forward, but his eyes shielded slightly, his body in the exaggerated posture of a man under stress. The crowd opened before him. As the last students, timid boys with Holy Water damp on their foreheads, came pushing their way through the chapel door, having deliberately lingered to escape any possible punishment, he reached the foot of the stairs, and sprang into the refectory, two steps at a time. There was a moment of doubt and delay; the booing subsided; there were whispers of 'What'll we do now?' The bigger boys gave the lead, climbing after him into

the barn-like refectory, filing according to age and class among
the oil-clothed tables, with their regular mounds of loaf bread,
white damp plates with a print of butter on each, and exactly
arranged rows of chairs. There was the usual silence for Grace,
all facing towards the end of the hall, where, directly over the
Dean's bent head, the crucifix hung like a twisted root on the
yellow wall. 'Bless us, O Lord, and these thy gifts ...' the
voice was steady but the hands perhaps a little too tightly
joined. Chairs scraped on the linoleum as the boys settled into
their places.

Any ordinary evening, after the hush of Grace, conversation
broke out immediately, almost like an explosion. Now there
was silence, dead, utter silence, as though someone had given a
signal, or everyone been struck dumb. The white-aproned
country maids, grinning good-naturedly as they carted the big
blue and red teapots to each table, looked around with surprise,
hearing nothing but the rattle of knives, the chink of cups, the
bodily shifting necessary in the sharing-out of the tiers of white
sliced bread; in the space above the moving hands and heads
and the white cloth of the table covers, the air seemed to
thicken with expectancy, as though every breath was being
held too long, and the damp walls sweated.

A quarter of an hour passed without break. The meal was
nearly over and the Dean had done nothing yet, fidgeting
slightly before the dais, playing with the sleeves of his soutane,
brushing them, looking at the chalk-smeared elbows. At the
Senior tables the boys kept glowering around anxiously, hoping
that he would do or say something, while the little boys shifted
on their seats with half-frightened excitement. He gave no
hint of his feelings, however, appearing to turn the incident
slowly over in his mind, meditating some unusual form of
retaliation.

The boys began to feel uneasy; perhaps, after all, their
action had been too hasty, presenting him only with a new
cause for amusement? The unnatural atmosphere of silence,
in a place which usually resounded with laughter and squabbling
voices, strained their nerves to a jagged pitch. Perhaps indeed
their action had been foolish, a glancing ugly blow that left

him unharmed and put them even more at his mercy than
before. The very silence they had created cut them off from
further action, and his acceptance of it seemed to say with a
shrug: 'All right, if that's the way you want it, then all the
better for me. You can keep your silence to the crack of doom
for all I care. You're only depriving yourselves.'

Suddenly, every startled eye upon him, the Dean began to
walk up and down between the tables, his rubber soles squealing
softly on the linoleum. Slowly at first, a thinking pace, with
the head down; and then, as resolution formed, more swiftly.
The nervous lengthy stride, parallel to the listening tables, now
had its usual impulsive rhythm, the rhythm of a man whose
mind was made up, who was confident he could master the
situation. As he took a corner with almost theatrical swiftness
and firmness, the soutane belling out like a skirt round his
ankles, someone tittered. His head went up, with a sharp
decisive movement. Far down, at one of the Junior tables, a
boy sniggered helplessly into his teacup.

'You down there, O'Rourke. Was that you?'

He came hurrying towards the boy, now blubbering with
fear and hysterical laughter. 'Was it you, I say? Have you no
manners at all, man? Can't you speak up?'

'Yes, Father.'

'So it was!' Arms folded, he stood at the edge of the table.
'That's a pretty thing for a boy of your age to be at – sniggering behind backs like a schoolgirl. It's a pity we can't get you
something better to do than that, isn't it?'

'Yes, Father.'

'Well, I know something that'll fit you better than sniggering.
Do you see that book up there?' – he pointed towards the
dais for reading during meals, usual only during Lent. 'You
can go up there and keep us all edified with *The Lives of the
Saints*.'

'Yes, Father.'

'I suppose you can read' – the voice came down low and
sarcastic – 'and you all want to keep silence anyway, so here's
something to keep your little minds busy.'

The boy rose and scuttled towards the reading dais, the whole school watching him with stunned curiosity, while he searched eagerly for support in every face. Propped up high over all the wondering heads, a minute sulky figure, his ears red at the edges as though the flesh had been smartly slapped, his hands frantically turning the leaves, while a leaflet fell, swirling, to the floor:

'Hurry up, man, don't be so clumsy. You've got an audience, you know. We're all dying to hear you.'

'Where, Father?'

'Anywhere. We're waiting.'

' "The life of the saintly Vicaire d'Arcueil teaches us this lesson: that the true way of sanctity lies in an infinite gentleness and patience with all human follies, all human wickedness. We must expel from our rebellious hearts every taint of self before we can hope to see God. As a seminarian, he was ridiculed for his ignorance of Latin, his peasant clumsiness. As a sanctified priest, he was mocked by his parishioners, who found him naive ..." '

The Dean was enjoying his part now, playing it to perfection, almost a Mephistopheles in dark deliberate position, mouth tilted and sardonic, foot tip-tapping restlessly as he leaned back at an angle against the food-presses, under the crucifix. A kind of grim contentment arched his eyebrows; he seemed to savour every mispronunciation with intense interest, gloating over every slur and stutter – and there were many, the boy on the reading dais stopping and starting, squirming and shifting – till he could no longer contain his great mirth.

'Good Lord, man, higher.'

' "And yet for the forty years of his ministry, he moved through the parish of Arcueil like a ministering angel ..." '

'Louder, boy, louder. Is that the best you can do? Is there a stone in your throat, or were you never taught to read?'

'Please, Father, there are too many big words,' the boy wailed, his fingers hot and fumbling the pages, his timid eyes pleading for release. O'Rourke was an awkward lout at any time, the kind of boy who, through sheer lack of even the most ordinary schoolboy cunning, was always caught out in mischief, or found himself left behind to bear the blame after his more cute companions had skipped aside. And yet nothing pleased him more than to be thought daring and impudent, scuttling around the edge of a crowd with a vehement conspiratorial air or trying to catch the limelight in class by loud words and laughs. Knowing his victim of old, the Dean now played him˜ with all the nervous mockery he could command, goading the boy till he stammered like an idiot.

'Open your mouth, man. Wider!'

' "This humble man had learnt the ways of charity, that sweet radiance of the Christian soul which is our best weapon against evil. Conceit, egotism, pride, all the diverse and unsuspected ways of selfishness were alien to him; as though by dint of prayer he had driven that dark accomplice forever from his bosom ..." '

'Booosom. Is that the best you can do?' the Dean intoned down his nose, making the word sound broad as a snore. Driven past all enduring, O'Rourke collapsed into a flood of tears, weeping with great ugly shudders, as though the breath was tearing out the softer part of his throat. The Dean looked stunned; a faintly comic amazement made his mouth gape open like a fish. From every corner of the refectory, low but insistent, a growing undertone to the boy's abandoned sobbing, came again the sound of booing.

'Leave him alone,' someone called, 'leave him alone.'

He pulled himself up as though trying to escape the accusing sound, as though suddenly very weary.

'Boys,' he began uncertainly, striving to get away into some kind of speech that might right the balance, administer remorse. 'Boys, you have done something this day which I had not expected of you and which I will not forget for a long time to come. I have tried to keep silent, to pass the matter off as a joke, but if you are not careful it will go too far, and I will be compelled to put the whole matter in other hands.'

'Boys,' groaned a wag sepulchrally, from a corner. The whole school laughed madly, beating the spoons against the cups, the plates against the wood, jangling the gross enamel teapots. Above the tintinnabulation, his voice strove to be heard, no longer exact and peremptory, but high and nervous, falteringly demanding an audience.

'You are too young perhaps to know what duty means. You

do not know how hard it has been for me to play this unpleasant role of Dean. But since it is my duty, I have tried to
do it well, though it is the last thing I would have chosen for
myself. I'm not good-tempered, perhaps – I may have seemed
unduly harsh to you – and I may have made mistakes – but I
have tried to be conscientious. Do you think I like to be shut
up with schoolboys day after day, watching their every whim . . .'

At first they listened, struck by a note of sincerity in his
voice; then, ceasing to understand, recognized only the familiar
smoothness, the intellectual fibre of the words that was so
hateful to them. As they began again their systematic inter-
ruption, he lost all self-control and began to rail blindly.

'You have chosen to show your hatred for me in the only way
you know – that of booing. It is entirely typical. But I'm not
afraid to face it, I can tell you. I can take it. You might have
scared someone else with your Nazi hysterics, but I can take it.'

His own image, no longer proud and disdainful, but crushed
and reduced, returned to him openly from every grinning,
gesticulating face. Seized by something like the impersonal
frenzy of the hunting pack, no longer single ordinary boys,
hiding their hatred behind barred fingers, they rocked back
and forward in moaning laughter, hooting and cawing and
quacking.

'I can take it, boys,' squeaked someone in a high feminine
voice.

The Dean's face flushed and for a moment he seemed to
resist the temptation to lift the cane and plough madly among
the tables, striking everyone indiscriminately. But he would
have had to flail half the school and the big boys might easily
have struck back, made reckless by their hatred and conscious
of their advantage in numbers. The dangerous aloofness which
had been his power was now swept away from him; he was no
longer a priest or a person in authority, but merely someone
who had humbled and hurt another past enduring.

Almost crying, he tried to raise his voice above the noise:
'Do you know what you have done? Is there no limit for you at
all? Boo me if you like, it makes no difference now. But tonight
you have booed me, a priest, before the very chapel door. You

didn't think of that, did you? No one can forgive you for that, neither I nor anyone else.'

There was a sudden silence. He had played his last, best, and forgotten card, facing their monstrous grinning abandon with his outraged cloth. This was an appeal none of the boys had anticipated, a transference of their insult to the person of Christ himself. And in a moment they knew it was false, that he had only thought of it as a weapon to protect his injured egotism.

'You might have chosen some more suitable place for your hoodlum demonstrations. Has education taught you nothing better than that?' Refreshed, he felt the silence, guessed that his words had shocked them back to their senses, restored his shrunken image. 'Imagine, for a group of boys from good Catholic homes . . .'

At one of the three Senior tables, someone belched: a deliberate vulgar sound. The school shrieked with merriment. The sound was repeated on thick burbling lips, from every table in the hall. The Dean stumbled in his words as though shot; he fumbled and lost the thread of his argument and then let his head slip into his hands, seeking darkness in the warm shelter of his palms.

The head-prefect rose hurriedly and said Grace. The Dean did not look up, though it was normally he who announced the end of a meal.

'We give thee thanks, O Almighty God . . .'

Quietly and in perfect order the boys filed out between the tables. The winter mist had filled the corners of the large refectory windows, making them look like show cases. Going out, one or two looked closely at the Dean, without sympathy but with a detached curiosity. He was weeping silently. He looked like a man either drunk or sick, his back humped and his shoulders slack as though props had been taken away and the cloth sagged without support. 'Go away,' he said, without raising his head. 'Can't you go away!' The last clumped down the stairs, leaving the Dean alone, except for the boy on the dais who had stopped whimpering to watch him. 'Go away,' he said, sensing somebody still near. O'Rourke rose and scuttled towards the door.

Outside the evening was cold, softly growing darker, the ball-alleys a great grey bulk without separate outline. In the town below, the lights were coming on, vague points against the winter mist. The damp air was threatening; another night of rain would drown the playing fields and turn the slopes into a sea of mud. Already, around the Senior Ring, moist drops hung like grain from the naked branches.

The boys scattered with wild and joyous cries.

Let the Old Cry

JOHN JORDAN

THE shadows under Marguerite's eyes deepened, her face grew paler. She no longer bothered to apply the little bloom of rouge which she wore when I first met her. She walked more slowly, her shoulders hunched, and developed a way of hungrily caressing her throat with her ringless left hand. I lost touch with her.

Then one foxy Autumn day I met Melda, met her hobbling along Abbey Street, her glass beads quarrelling on her pleated blouse. I of course asked after Marguerite, and she told me that she had taken to hermitage and sat up late in her attic reading the sermons of John Donne. That she had taken to drinking brandy instead of gin, and that she, Melda, thought Marguerite was not long for this world. 'No more than myself,' said Melda, 'I'm seventy-three, you know, and very tired.'

But she did not look tired as I stood beside her in the greying light of Abbey Street: she looked like some legendary bird, with her piled-up head of snow and her wiry body flexing and straining in a black velvet suit.

'Imagine reading old Donne – though of course he wasn't *that* old – that's a bad sign. We used to read him in our last year at College, over cups of cocoa. Poor Marguerite. I know she hasn't been to Mass for ages. No more than myself.'

This seemed to amuse her and she tossed her high white head and went on: 'My landlady says I'll surely die howling. I've never been able to understand how people on the verge of death can be expected to howl. It's altogether too much. Don't you agree?'

And she hopped and bobbed and for days afterwards I

seemed to hear the jangle of beads and my dreams were troubled by a snow-polled bird.

Melda herself may or may not have howled. But Father Conlon, who was fussing around when I called at the house, said that her last moments were most edifying. 'Most,' he said, rubbing and blowing at his hands, for it was cold and the windows of Melda's room were like monstrous diamonds. The garden path was filigreed with frost and from the trees hung silver fronds. The landlady, Mrs McGurl, who had laid Melda out, said she had always suspected that Melda was a saint. She said that she had gone like a baby, whatever that meant.

'Did she say anything before she died?' I asked.

'Oh, only to ring up a few friends, yourself and that lady she calls Marguerite and some man. I forget his name now. So I phoned and when I came back I could see she was sinking. Thank God she'd had Father Conlon here last night.'

'And the funeral arrangements?'

'Oh, she gave me full instructions,' said Father Conlon. 'She was a most methodical lady. Was all prepared.'

'And she said nothing else?'

'Ah, poor soul, she was considerate to the end,' said Mrs McGurl. 'The very last thing she said was that it was altogether too much. As if I wasn't doing my Christian duty.'

'God will reward you a thousandfold, Mrs McGurl,' said Father Conlon. 'The corporal works of mercy are a great thing.'

The bell rang and Mrs McGurl showed in Marguerite. She went at once to where Melda lay stiff under an unsuitable crimson eiderdown. She almost knocked over a candle. I could not decide whether or not she was drunk. She kissed Melda's cheeks, touched her piled snow, knelt down and cried, her head, still raven, on the crimson cover. I touched her shoulder and she twisted away and spat, 'You've no right to be here. You're too young. Let the old cry for the old. They can do it much better.'

'Now, my dear lady ...' began Father Conlon.

The bell rang again. Marguerite whimpered. Father Conlon breathed heavily. I feared he was going to suggest a decade of the Rosary. There was a scuffling noise at the door and Marguerite sprang up almost.

'Keep them out,' she said. 'If it's her relatives, she wouldn't want them. They pestered her all her life. All her life and she was seventy-three.'

The door opened and a little old man came ahead of Mrs McGurl. He wore flannels and a tweed jacket and his eyes were swimming. The smell of whiskey bombed the room. He stood still when he saw Marguerite. He groped in the air with his left hand, then raised it till it was plucking his Adam's apple. He came forward unsteadily, he ignored the corpse and all the time stared at Marguerite. He began to whisper something and Marguerite looked at him, her tears for Melda still damp on her cheeks.

'Marguerite,' said the little man. 'My Marguerite, my little flower,' and he held out his arms and Marguerite came to him slowly and kissed him on the forehead.

'You have grown very old, Harry,' she said. 'So have I. And our darling Melda is gone. We are the last.'

Without looking around, she led him from the room and I was left alone with the corpse and Father Conlon.

'I have to be going now,' said Father Conlon.

'Yes.'

I watched over her till Mrs McGurl came back.

'You'd think they'd have the decency to say a prayer,' she said.

She was a large woman with cold eyes and a red nose. That is all I remember of her. I left her standing by the long narrow bed looking down on the thing under the crimson cover, her corporal work of mercy.

All of that winter was very cold and no one saw Marguerite. One day I saw a little old man crossing O'Connell Bridge. He was drunk, obviously, and stopped occasionally to lean against the parapet. Sleet was falling but the old man didn't seem to notice it settling on his bare head. I stopped beside him and watched him as he gazed down the river which before Butt Bridge was fading into a gloaming of rain and sleet. I thought of him standing in Melda's room, of his cindery voice as he whispered, 'Marguerite, my Marguerite, my little flower,' of the crimson eiderdown and Melda's snow-topped skull. Marguerite

had told me to let the old cry for the old. I had no business to
be hovering about this old man as he stared down the black
river into the swirl of grey. But I could not bring myself to
move.

He turned around and brushed past me and I had a clear
view of his profile. I realized suddenly that he must be a
brother, or at least a cousin, of Melda's. But he was surely
not one of the relatives who had pestered Melda all her life?
If he were a brother, he must be a black sheep. But Melda
herself ... what was the female for black sheep? A black ewe
perhaps? When last I saw her living, she was surely more akin
to a white blackbird.

I still stood watching him as he maundered across the road,
and at that moment I realized that some day I might be a
writer.

On the bridge in the blistering sleet I began to dream of a
new world born, or rather an old one, the old world in which
Marguerite and Melda and her brother were all young and
comely, a world that blossomed and withered before even I
was born. In that world friendships were made which were
to last because they had leisure to grow and mature and gather
up richness enough to withstand the pollution of lust or envy.
I wondered if ever I could weep for a friend as Marguerite
wept for Melda. I remembered Marguerite's tales of Berlin in
the twenties, and the glee in her voice as she said, 'Ah, we
had good times in Berlin.' She talked too of Vienna and Paris
and all the crochets in her face seemed to smooth out until for
a moment or so she was young and fresh and fragrant.

By this time, the little old man had disappeared and I became
conscious of the sleet melting on my ears and trickling down
the side of my neck. All I wanted to do was to find Marguerite
and take her hands and try to tell her how I felt. I walked
down the street to Grady's Hotel, that for so long had been
Marguerite's court, where the young and silly, the old and
crapulous, came and gave chat to her. So many times had I
seen her there surrounded by the dandruff of the intelligentsia,
blowing out clouds of Gauloise smoke from her thin pink lips,
giving counsel and encouragement or delicate dissuasion to her

acolytes. Someone had once told me that in her heyday she had been known as The Smile, and one could well believe that as she watched the antics of some saddening young man across the road from the Gate or listened to the pretensions of some self-styled, rarely practising poet.

But today, of course, she was not there. I ordered a drink and said to the barman, 'Hello, Larry. Has Miss O'Flynn been in lately?' Larry turned his head away, coughed and said in a stage whisper, 'Well, as a matter of fact she *was* in the other night.' Then after another cough, and in a louder stage whisper, 'We sent her home in a taxi.'

There were only two other customers. I had never seen them before. One was a big braying woman with dappled hair, the other was a ferret of a man with skin like crumpled toilet paper. I did not like them. They had stopped talking when I mentioned the name 'O'Flynn'. And now the man slunk up and said, 'Excuse me, but are you a friend of Miss O'Flynn?'

'Yes.'

'Well, so are we. My friend Gertie and I. We had the pleasure of a drink with Miss O'Flynn the other evening. A lovely lady.'

'I see.'

'Won't you join us?' He looked at Gertie who nodded her head insanely.

'I'm afraid I have to be going.'

'Oh, but just one.'

Some strange half-glance from the barman decided me.

'All right.'

'Oh, good-o.'

At the least they were a point of contact with Marguerite. To this day I do not know whether or not I was right to join this disagreeable couple, whom as soon as I sat down I saw to be half drunk.

The man, whose name was impossibly Norbert, said: 'Poor Gertie here is having trouble with her teeth.'

'Some of the most famous women in history had bad teeth,' said Gertie complacently.

'Is that so?'

'Oh yes, I read it in a book.'

'Miss O'Flynn has lovely teeth,' said Norbert.

'She'd want to be careful,' said Gertie.

'Why?'

'Oh, when Norrie and me were putting her into the taxi, she fell.'

'Yes,' said Norbert. 'She had a little accident. Oh nothing serious I'd say. She's a lovely lady.'

Suddenly I wanted to cry. Disgust and weariness rather than sadness had me by the sockets. I pictured Marguerite drunk, her still-raven hair dishevelled, her lipstick smeared, her stockings torn, a raddled old piece who couldn't hold her drink being helped into a taxi by these terrible people. I pictured worse things. I finished my drink and left.

'We'll tell Miss O'Flynn we met you,' Norbert had spouted out. 'She's sure to be in.'

Later that night I gazed across the table at my girl. 'Let the old cry for the old,' I said.

There was only bewilderment in her nut-brown eyes.

The Bracelet

TOM MACINTYRE

'MY God,' Aunty May said, 'when I think of that Roma Downes.'

She was home from the States again. Every second summer she came meaning to stay a couple of months, but after a few weeks she'd suddenly pack and take a taxi to Dublin and fly straight back to Hartford. This country, she'd say, looking out at the rain pissing down, this country is for the mushrooms.

'When I *thinkovit*,' she repeated, nursing the cup of black coffee which was all she ever took in the mornings, sipping.

We were having breakfast together. The rest of the house had slept late.

'Yesterday?'

She'd been in Dublin yesterday.

'Yesterday' – she looked across at me – 'is right.'

I didn't say anything. She'd go on. Her small brown face shiny with cream, curlers beetling her hair that was auburn this time. Wisps of red touched the blue of her eyes.

'I went into Stinson's' – she put down the coffee-cup, tightened the belt of her white dressing-gown, lit a cigarette – 'to get the Beleek ...'

The store smelled of – exquisite things. She loved handling the stuff, the glaze and the colours and the flower-decorations on the baskets. How in God's name do they do it? The place was full of English. Madam? ... Madam? ... She picked the items carefully, listing her promises, then lost her head – the baskets – and went thirty dollars over her limit. So what, the place would get you –

'May!'

And there was Roma Downes. Swimming out of one of the big glass cases. Like a young rainbow trout. Or something.

'Roma, hi!' They shook hands. 'Well, how're *you* doing?' Wasn't she supposed to be in London? Model? Secretary?

'Great! You're home, May – for long?'

Roma thin-as-a-bootlace. Hair *bouffant*, face this month's *Vogue* – nearly. Still. That coat. And the shoes.

'Couple of months.' She scribbled the cheque; what age was Roma, nineteen? 'And how's Mother?'

'Mammy's marvellous.' Prancing on the long legs. 'Just back from the West. A fortnight over there.'

'You tell her I'll call by some of these days, won't you?' Not a bad-looking girl. Except for the nose. 'Been rushing like mad since I got back, visiting, never had a second.'

'Sure. You're getting Beleek?'

'Can't resist it.'

' 'S beautiful. Love to have some. Sometime.'

They watched the man at the counter pack a magnificent creamer. The one for Lois. Roma murmured admiration but she could sense the lack of interest, their connection taking to the air, a thin smoke now, and beginning to nip –

'So – And what are you up to for the summer?' They went to it again. 'Take a vacation yet?'

'No' – bubbling of a sudden – 'Continent, with the boy-friend next month' – casual as you please, then qualifying – 'Of course there's four in the party. Another pair.'

'Well, great,' she managed. 'Good for you. France, I suppose? Italy? You'll adore Florence. I was –'

'Sorry, May' – Roma was off –'there's Pauline.' A blonde in slacks put her head in the door, chirped. 'Have to fly. See you. I'll tell Mammy. Bye!'

It was when Roma turned to wave from the door that she spotted the bracelet.

'Good-bye, Roma' – she worked up a smile that laddered instantly – 'See you.'

The crowd reached for the two, grabbed, shunted them away.

'Your parcel, madam.'

'My bracelet –'

'Madam?'

Well, of all the nerve –

'Would madam care to –'

The Beleek.

'Oh –'

From behind his eyes the man watched her.

'May I have it shipped to Hartford?'

'Certainly, madam.'

She gave him the address, paid the extra, and left.

'Wearing my damn bracelet,' Aunty May said, 'that I loaned her mother two years ago to wear at Tim Leonard's wedding.'

She took a long sip of the coffee. They were moving about upstairs. Flicking the windows, the day's first shower blew into the garden.

'Eighteen-carat gold,' she said, 'I got it in Rome when I went for the Marian Year with Dot and Lois.'

She switched her eyes to the window, irritably searching. Green light spewed from the grass.

'It was a charm bracelet. You saw it? You remember it?'

I nodded. Vaguely, I did.

'And will you tell me,' she asked loudly, 'why people can't give these things back?'

'No manners' – I fumbled.

'Is right. I was adding things to it,' she said. 'All the time. It had St Peter's. And the Eiffel Tower.'

'Can't you –'

'I tell you I nearly got weak,' she said.

'Can't you get it back? Won't she –'

'Standing there chatting me,' she said, 'and my gold bracelet sitting on her arm.'

Her voice starting to ravel. Steps on the stairs, and my mother coming down the hall. She entered – 'Good morning.' In the best of humour. Or prepared to be. I'd go.

'And what d'ye think,' Aunty May cried – for me, no pause – 'your mother had to say when I told her of Roma, and the boyfriend and the Continent?'

By the door, my mother stood motionless.

'She said' – opposite me the small brown face smirked to mimic – ' "Oh, what matter. They've no sense at that age." '

'But that' – Aunty May rose and flung back her chair: she was a rod inside the white dressing-gown, and she picked up her cigarettes, stuck them in her pocket, never taking her eyes off me – 'that wasn't what they told us. Hurry home and bolt the doors was the line then. Mirrors to the wall, bend your knees and pray. Lies' – her voice splitting open – 'And I wouldn't mind but they knew, they shaped the lie, and don't,' said Aunty May, her eyes wet and her mouth bright and her words a low terrible stitching, 'don't let them ever give that lie to you.'

She left and went straight up to her bedroom. Door-bang.

'Never mind her,' my mother said. 'Poor thing's just upset.'

That afternoon there was sun for a change, but sun chased by cloud. From early on, Aunty May was out in the garden. Towards evening I happened to glimpse her from an upstairs window. She'd fallen asleep over a magazine. Wearing a pink bathing-suit, she lay on her stomach, the white dressing-gown thrown for a rug. Sunglasses, netted pile of hair, white shoulders and arms and thin white waist, and thighs and calves white but veined, she lay, small, gathered, in the centre of the garden. A loose fear beginning to slide and spread, I watched until my taut breath blinded the glass.

The Creature

EDNA O'BRIEN

SHE was always referred to as The Creature by the townspeople, the dressmaker for whom she did buttonholing, the sacristan, who used to search for her in the pews on the dark winter evenings before locking up, and even the little girl Sally, for whom she wrote out the words of a famine song. Life had treated her rottenly, yet she never complained but always had a ready smile, so that her face with its round rosy cheeks was more like something you could eat or lick; she reminded me of nothing so much as an apple fritter.

I used to encounter her on her way from devotions or from Mass, or having a stroll, and when we passed she smiled, but she never spoke, probably for fear of intruding. I was doing a temporary teaching job in a little town in the west of Ireland and soon came to know that she lived in a tiny house facing a garage that was also the town's undertaker. The first time I visited her, we sat in the parlour and looked out on the crooked lettering on the door. There seemed to be no one in attendance at the station. A man helped himself to petrol. Nor was there any little muslin curtain to obscure the world, because, as she kept repeating, she had washed it that very day and what a shame. She gave me a glass of rhubarb wine, and we shared the same chair, which was really a wooden seat with a latticed wooden back, that she had got from a rubbish heap and had varnished herself. After varnishing, she had dragged a nail over the wood to give a sort of mottled effect, and you could see where her hand had shaken, because the lines were wavery.

I had come from another part of the country; in fact, I had

come to get over a love affair, and since I must have emanated
some sort of sadness she was very much at home with me and
called me 'dearest' when we met and when we were taking
leave of one another. After correcting the exercises from school,
filling in my diary, and going for a walk, I would knock on
her door and then sit with her in the little room almost devoid
of furniture – devoid even of a plant or a picture – and oftener
than not I would be given a glass of rhubarb wine and sometimes a slice of porter cake. She lived alone and had done so
for seventeen years. She was a widow and had two children.
Her daughter was in Canada; the son lived about four miles
away. She had not set eyes on him for the seventeen years – not
since his wife had slung her out – and the children that she
had seen as babies were big now, and, as she heard, marvellously handsome. She had a pension and once a year made a
journey to the southern end of the country, where her relatives
lived in a cottage looking out over the Atlantic.

Her husband had been killed two years after their marriage,
shot in the back of a lorry, in an incident that was later
described by the British Forces as regrettable. She had had
to conceal the fact of his death and the manner of his death
from her own mother, since her mother had lost a son about
the same time, also in combat, and on the very day of her
husband's funeral, when the chapel bells were ringing and
re-ringing, she had to pretend it was for a travelling man, a
tinker, who had died suddenly. She got to the funeral at the
very last minute on the pretext that she was going to see the
priest.

She and her husband had lived with her mother. She reared
her children in the old farmhouse, eventually told her mother
that she, too, was a widow, and as women together they
worked and toiled and looked after the stock and milked and
churned and kept a sow to whom she gave the name of Bessie.
Each year the bonhams would become pets of hers, and follow
her along the road to Mass or wherever and to them, too,
she gave pretty names. A migrant workman helped in the
summer months, and in the autumn he would kill the pig for
their winter meat. The killing of the pig always made her sad,

and she reckoned she could hear those roars – each successive roar – over the years, and she would dwell on that, and then tell how a particular naughty pig stole into the house one time and lapped up the bowls of cream and then lay down on the floor, snoring and belching like a drunken man. The workman slept downstairs on the settle bed, got drunk on Saturdays, and was the cause of an accident; when he was teaching her son to shoot at targets, the boy shot off three of his own fingers. Otherwise, her life had passed without incident.

When her children came home from school, she cleared half the table for them to do their exercises – she was an untidy woman – then every night she made blancmange for them, before sending them to bed. She used to colour it red or brown or green as the case may be, and she marvelled at these colouring essences almost as much as the children themselves did. She knitted two sweaters each year for them – two identical sweaters of bawneen wool – and she was indeed the proud mother when her son was allowed to serve at Mass.

Her finances suffered a dreadful setback when her entire stock contracted foot-and-mouth disease, and to add to her grief she had to see the animals that she so loved die and be buried around the farm, wherever they happened to stagger down. Her lands were disinfected and empty for over a year, and yet she scraped enough to send her son to boarding school and felt lucky in that she got a reduction of the fees because of her reduced circumstances. The parish priest had intervened on her behalf. He admired her and used to joke her on account of the novelettes she so cravenly read. Her children left, her mother died, and she went through a phase of not wanting to see anyone – not even a neighbour – and she reckoned that was her Garden of Gethsemane. She contracted shingles, and one night, dipping into the well for a bucket of water, she looked first at the stars then down at the water and thought how much simpler it would be if she were to drown. Then she remembered being put into the well for sport one time by her brother, and another time having a bucket of water douched over her by a jealous sister, and the memory of the shock of these two experiences and a plea to God made her draw back from the well and hurry up through the nettle garden to the kitchen, where the dog and the fire, at least, awaited her. She went down on her knees and prayed for the strength to press on.

Imagine her joy when, after years of wandering, her son returned from the city, announced that he would become a farmer, and that he was getting engaged to a local girl who worked in the city as a chiropodist. Her gift to them was a patchwork quilt and a special border of cornflowers she planted outside the window, because the bride-to-be was more than proud of her violet-blue eyes and referred to them in one way or another whenever she got the chance. The Creature thought how nice it would be to have a border of complementary flowers outside the window, and how fitting, even though *she* preferred wallflowers, both for their smell and their softness. When the young couple came home from the honeymoon, she was down on her knees weeding the bed of flowers, and, looking up at the young bride in her veiled hat, she thought, an oil painting was no lovelier or no more sumptuous. In secret, she hoped that her daughter-in-law might pare her corns after they had become intimate friends.

Soon, she took to going out to the cowshed to let the young couple be alone, because even by going upstairs she could overhear. It was a small house, and the bedrooms were directly above the kitchen. They quarrelled constantly. The first time she heard angry words she prayed that it be just a lovers' quarrel, but such spiteful things were said that she shuddered and remembered her own dead partner and how they had never exchanged a cross word between them. That night she dreamed she was looking for him, and though others knew of his whereabouts they would not guide her. It was not long before she realized that her daughter-in-law was cursed with a sour and grudging nature. A woman who automatically bickered over everything – the price of eggs, the best potato plants to put down, even the fields that should be pasture and those that should be reserved for tillage. The women got on well enough during the day, but rows were inevitable at night when the son came in and, as always, The Creature went out to the cowshed or down the road while things transpired. Up in her bedroom, she put little swabs of cotton wool in her ears to hide whatever sounds might be forthcoming. The birth of their first child did everything to exacerbate the young woman's nerves, and after three days the milk went dry in her breasts. The son called his mother out to the shed, lit a cigarette for himself, and told her that unless she signed the farm and the house over to him he would have no peace from his young barging wife.

This The Creature did soon after, and within three months she was packing her few belongings and walking away from the house where she had lived for fifty-eight of her sixty years. All she took was her clothing, her Aladdin lamp, and a tapestry denoting ships on a hemp-coloured sea. It was an heirloom. She found lodgings in the town and was the subject of much curiosity, then ridicule, because of having given her farm over to her son and daughter-in-law. Her son defected on the weekly payments he was supposed to make, but though she took the matter to her solicitor, on the appointed day she did not appear in court and as it happened spent the entire night in the chapel, hiding in the confessional.

Hearing the tale over the months, and how The Creature had settled down and made a soup most days, was saving for an electric blanket, and much preferred winter to summer, I decided to make the acquaintance of her son, unbeknownst to his wife. One evening I followed him to the field where he was driving a tractor. I found a sullen, middle-aged man, who did not condescend to look at me but proceeded to roll his own cigarette. I recognized him chiefly by the three missing fingers and wondered pointlessly what they had done with them on that dreadful day. He was in the long field where she used to go twice daily with buckets of separated milk, to feed the suckling calves. The house was to be seen behind some trees, and either because of secrecy or nervousness he got off the tractor, crossed over and stood beneath a tree, his back balanced against the knobbled trunk. It was a little hawthorn and, somewhat superstitious, I hesitated to stand under it. Its flowers gave a certain dreaminess to that otherwise forlorn place. There is something gruesome about ploughed earth, maybe because it suggests the grave.

He seemed to know me and he looked, I thought distastefully, at my patent boots and my tweed cape. He said there was nothing he could do, that the past was the past, and that his mother had made her own life in the town. You would think she had prospered or remarried, his tone was so caustic when he spoke of 'her own life'. Perhaps he had relied on her to die. I said how dearly she still held him in her thoughts, and he said that she always had a soft heart and if there was one thing in life he hated it was the sodden handkerchief.

With much hedging, he agreed to visit her, and we arranged an afternoon at the end of that week. He called after me to keep it to myself, and I realized that he did not want his wife to know. All I knew about his wife was that she had grown withdrawn, that she had had improvements made on the place – larger windows and a bathroom installed – and that they were never seen together, not even on Christmas morning at chapel.

By the time I called on The Creature that eventful day, it was long after school, and, as usual, she had left the key in the front door for me. I found her dozing in the armchair, very near the stove, her book still in one hand and the fingers of the other hand fidgeting as if she were engaged in some work. Her beautiful embroidered shawl was in a heap on the floor, and the first thing she did when she wakened was to retrieve it and dust it down. I could see that she had come out in some sort of heat rash, and her face resembled nothing so much as a frog's, with her little raisin eyes submerged between pink swollen lids.

At first she was speechless; she just kept shaking her head. But eventually she said that life was a crucible, life was a crucible. I tried consoling her, not knowing what exactly I had to console her about. She pointed to the back door and said things were kiboshed from the very moment he stepped over that threshold. It seems he came up the back garden and found her putting the finishing touches to her hair. Taken by surprise, she reverted to her long-lost state of excitement and could say nothing that made sense. 'I thought it was a thief,' she said to me, still staring at the back door, with her cane hanging from a nail there.

When she realized who he was, without giving him time to catch breath, she plied both food and the drink on him, and I could see that he had eaten nothing, because the ox tongue in its mould of jelly was still on the table, untouched. A little whiskey bottle lay on its side, empty. She told me how he'd aged and that when she put her hand up to his grey hairs he backed away from her as if she'd given him an electric shock. He who hated the soft heart and the sodden handkerchief must have hated that touch. She asked for photos of his family, but he had brought none. All he told her was that his daughter was learning to be a mannequin, and she put her foot in it further by saying there was no need to gild the lily. He had newspapers in the soles of his shoes to keep out the damp, and she took off those damp shoes and tried polishing them. I could see how it all had been, with her jumping up and down trying to please him but in fact just making him edgy. 'They were drying on the range,' she said, 'when he picked them up and put them on.' He was gone before she could put a shine on them, and the worst thing was that he had made no promise concerning the future. When she asked 'Will I see you?' he had said 'Perhaps,' and she told me that if there was one word in the English vocabulary that scalded her, it was the word 'perhaps'.

'I did the wrong thing,' I said, and, though she didn't nod, I knew that she also was thinking it – that secretly she would consider me from then on a meddler. All at once I remembered the little hawthorn tree, the bare ploughed field, his heart as black and unawakened as the man I had come away to forget, and there was released in me, too, a gigantic and useless sorrow. Whereas for twenty years she had lived on that last high tightrope of hope, it had been taken away from her, leaving her without anyone, without anything, and I wished that I had never punished myself by applying to be a sub in that stagnant, godforsaken little place.

Such Good Friends

ITA DALY

ALTHOUGH it all happened over two years ago, I still cannot think about Edith without pain. My husband tells me I am being silly and that I should have got over it long ago. He says my attitude is one of self-indulgence and dramatization and that it is typical of me to over-react in this way. I have told no one but Anthony, and I think that this is a measure of the hurt I suffered, not to be able even to mention it to anyone else. I don't think I am over-reacting – though I admit that I have a tendency to get very excited when I discover a new friend or a potential friend. This may sound as if I am wallowing in permanent adolescence, but even if this were so, the knowledge still wouldn't stop me being overcome with joy if I should meet someone whom I felt to be truly sympathetic.

It may be that I feel like this because I have had so few real friends in my life. I do not say this with any suggestion of self-pity; I am aware that such affinity of spirit is a very rare commodity and so, when there is a possibility of finding it, why, there is every reason to be excited. And it is something I have only ever found with members of my own sex.

Not that I have ever had any shortage of men friends. I have a certain bold physical appearance which seems to attract them, and before I was married, I always had four or five men hovering around, waiting to take me out. I don't deny this gave me a satisfaction – it was sexually stimulating and very good for one's ego – but I have never felt the possibility of a really close relationship with any of these men. Even Anthony, to whom I have been married for five years, and of whom I am genuinely fond, even he spends half the time not knowing what I am talking about, and, indeed, I am the same with him. Men on the whole are unsubtle creatures. You feed them, bed them, and bolster their egos, and they are quite content. They demand nothing more from a relationship, and for them physical intimacy is the only kind that matters. They don't seem to feel a need for this inner communion, they are happy to jog along as long as their bodies are at ease. I do not bare my soul to men. I tried to once with Anthony in the early days of our marriage, and, poor dear, he became upset and was convinced that I must be pregnant. Pregnant women are known to suffer from all sorts of strange whims.

You may by now think that I do not like men, but you would be quite wrong. I do like them and I am sure that living with one must be so much easier than living with a member of one's own sex. They are easy to please, and easy to deceive, and it is on the whole therapeutic to spend one's days and nights with someone who sees life as an uncomplicated game of golf, with the odd rough moments in the bunker. All I point out are their limitations, and I do so knowing that these views may be nothing more than an eccentricity on my part.

However, to return to Edith. I first met her during a bomb scare when that spate of bomb scares was going on, a little over two years ago. Before my marriage I had been studying law. I passed my first two exams and then I left to get married. About a year later I decided I would try to get a job as a solicitor's clerk, for I found I was bored doing nothing all day long and I thought it might be a good idea to keep my hand in, so to speak. It would make it easier if I ever decided to go back to College and attempt to qualify.

The firm where I got my job had its offices on the top floor of an old house in Westmoreland Street. The offices had a Dickensian air of shabbiness and dust, although I knew the firm to be a thriving one. It consisted of Mr Kelly Senior, Mr Kelly Junior, and Mr Brown. Along with five typists and myself of course. Mr Brown was a down-trodden man of the people, who was particularly grateful to Mr Kelly Senior for having lifted him from the lowly status of clerk to the heights of a fully fledged solicitor. He spent his days trotting round after the boss, wringing his

hands and looking worried, and, as far as I could see, making a
general nuisance of himself. Mr Kelly *père et fils* were tall dour
Knights of Columbanus. They had crafty grey eyes in emaciated
grey faces and they always dressed in clerical grey three-piece
suits. One day, Mr Kelly *fils* caused quite a sensation when he
ventured in wearing a yellow striped shirt, but this break with
tradition must not have met with approval, for next day, and
thereafter, he was back to the regulation policeman's blue.

The typists in the office were nice girls. I had little to do with
them, as I had my own room, and only saw one of them when
I had any work to give her. In the beginning, as I was the only
other female in the office, I did try joining them for morning
coffee. However, it was not a success. They were not at their
ease, and neither was I. I didn't know what to say to them, and
they were obviously waiting for me to leave until they could
resume their chatter of boyfriends and dances and pop music.
There was only about six years' difference in our ages, yet I felt
like another generation. It was because of this lack of contact
that I hardly noticed Edith's existence, although she had been in
the office nearly six weeks. That was, until the day of the bomb
scare.

We were cursed with bomb scares that winter and particularly
irritated by this one, the third in the same week. We filed out
of the building, silently, as people were doing on either side of
us. The novelty had worn off, and these regular sorties into the
winter afternoons were beginning to get under people's skin. It
was bitterly cold, and I thought I might as well go and have
a drink. It seemed more sensible than standing around in the
raw air, making smalltalk. I crossed over the bridge and turned
down towards a little pub that I had discovered on such a
previous occasion. I sat sipping a hot whiskey, enjoying the
muggy warmth, when I happened to glance across at the girl
sitting opposite me. She looked familiar in some vague way, and,
just as I was wondering if she were from the office, she caught
my glance and smiled back at me. Yes, now I remembered, she
was one of the typists alright, and now that she had seen me I
felt obliged to go over and join her. I hadn't wanted to – I had
been looking forward to a nice quiet little drink without the

effort of conversation. But I couldn't be so obviously rude. 'You're with Kelly and Brown,' I began, sitting down beside her.

Her smile was diffident, almost frightened.

'Yes, that's right. And you're Mrs Herbert. I know because the other girls told me – I haven't been long there myself. My name is Edith Duggan,' she added and held out her hand, rather formally I thought. We sat side by side, both of us ill-at-ease. I was wondering what I could talk about, and then I saw, lying open in front of her, a copy of *The Great Gatsby*. Good – at least this could be a common theme.

'Please call me Helen,' I said. 'Any friend of Gatsby's is a friend of mine. Do you like Scott Fitzgerald?'

'Oh I love him, I think he's great. He's marvellous.'

Her whole face lit up, and it was then I realized what a good-looking girl she was. As I have mentioned before, I have a certain showy attractiveness myself. I know I am not basically good-looking, and I depend heavily for effect on my skilful use of paints. But I have red hair and green eyes, and with a bold make-up I am very much the sort of woman that men stop to look at in the street. I could see now that Edith was not at all like this. She was small and slight, with a tiny face half hidden under a heavy weight of dark brown hair. You would pass her by and not look at her, but if you did stop to take a second look you would realize that her features, though small, were exquisitely proportioned, that her skin had a translucent sheen and that her eyes – her eyes were deep and soft and tranquil. I was the one getting all the barman's looks, but I could see at a glance that Edith was much the finer of us. She was such a charming girl too, shy and low-spoken, yet with none of the gaucherie and bluster that so often accompany shyness.

But though I was pleased by her good looks and her charm, it was not these that excited me. What excited me was a realization that here was someone to whom I could speak. Right from the beginning, from my remark about Fitzgerald, I think we both were aware that we were instantly communicating. We talked that day, long into the afternoon, and the more we talked the more we found we wanted to say. It was not only that we shared values and views and interests, but there was a recognition, on both our parts I thought, of an inner identification, a oneness. I knew that I would never have to pretend to Edith, that she would always understand what I was trying to say. I knew that a bond and a sympathy had been established between us and that I could look forward with joy to the times that we would talk and laugh and cry together. I had found a friend.

Do women love their husbands, I sometimes wonder? Do I love Anthony? I know that I like him, that I am grateful to him, that I feel the constant desire to protect him. But love? How can you love somebody you are so apart from? We live together comfortably, but so distinctly. Anthony wants it so, although if I told him this he would be incredulous. I have come to realize as I lie in bed at night, or at the first light of dawn, with his supple body, racked by pleasure, lying in my arms, that Anthony is undergoing his most profound experience. His body shudders, and his isolation is complete. Sometimes I am amazed by the exclusivity of his passion, although I know well that this sort of pleasure is something you cannot share. I know, for I am no stranger to pleasure myself: I have felt a tingling in the loins, a heat in the bowels. But I have always kept a weather eye out and asked – is there nothing more? Anthony's capitulation to his body is so complete, and his gratitude to me afterwards so overwhelming, that I know that, for him, this is where we touch, this is where he reaches me. And I am left in the cold outside.

But not once I had met Edith. Anthony should have been grateful to Edith, for with her coming I stopped harassing him. He didn't have to watch me in the evenings, sitting bleakly in our elegant drawing-room, upsetting his innocent enjoyment of the evening papers. I didn't suddenly snap at him for no reason, or complain of being bored, or depressed, or lonely. Edith became my source of pleasure. Soon we were having lunch together every day, and I would drive her home in the evenings after work. She soon confessed to me that she had been unhappy in the office before she met me, for the other girls were as unwilling to accept her as they had been me, although in both instances, to be fair, I think it was a sensible recognition on the

typists' part of our essential difference. We just had nothing to
share with them.

For a start, she was older than they were. She had been a
third-year philosophy student at the University, she told me.
A most successful student, apparently, who had hoped to pursue
an academic career. She had been working away quite happily,
looking forward to her finals, when one day her mother, who had
gone quite innocently in search of matches, had found a packet
of contraceptive pills in Edith's handbag. It was not, Edith told
me, the implication that she was sleeping with a man or men
that had so shocked her parents. It was the deliberateness of
the act. Young girls did from time to time fall from grace, and
it was wrong and they should be punished accordingly. But that
anyone, particularly a daughter whom they had reared so carefully, could arm herself with these pills beforehand – that sort
of calculation denoted a wickedness and evil of a far more
serious order. She was thrown out of the house that very evening
and told never to darken the door again.

'The thing I regret most,' Edith said, 'was hurting them.
You cannot expect them to understand, the way they were
brought up themselves. It's natural that they'd react like that.
But I do love them, and I really didn't want to cause them pain.
They'll come round, I'm sure. I'll just have to give them a few
months, and then everything will be alright I hope. I'll just have
to be a lot more careful. But I do miss them, you know – particularly Mammy.'

I had known Edith about six weeks when she introduced me
to Delcan. She had mentioned him several times, and I gathered
that they intended to get married as soon as Declan qualified.
He was an engineering student. What a surprise I got the first
time I saw him. I couldn't understand, and never did understand afterwards, how someone of Edith's delicacy and intelligence could fall in love with such a slob. And he *was* a slob,
a lumbering six-foot-two, with a red face and a slack mouth and
a good-humoured, apparently unlimited, amount of self-
confidence. The night I met him, he had come round after
work to collect Edith, and she asked me to stay and have a
drink with them. He took us to a rather draughty, gloomy pub,

and having bought our drinks, sat opposite me and fixed me
with a disapproving eye.

'What,' he asked, 'do you think of the situation in South
Africa?'

I later discovered that, being a swimming champion all
through his school days and most of his college days, Declan
had come late to the world of ideas. But not at all abashed by
his late start, he was now determined, it appeared, to make up
for lost time. I found his zeal rather wearying, I must admit,
and I resented the off-hand way he dismissed Edith's comments.
I wondered what would happen when he discovered Women's
Lib. With a bit of luck he might offer to liberate Edith by refusing to marry her.

In the meantime I realized that Edith would not take kindly
to any criticism I might voice and that I had better be careful
to simulate some sort of enthusiasm. So next day when she
asked me what I thought, I told her I found him very interesting,
and that I'd like them both to come to dinner soon and meet
Anthony. We decided on the next night, and I said I'd come
and collect them as Declan didn't have a car. I planned my
dinner carefully and told Anthony to provide an exceptional
claret – it was a special occasion. At these times, I'm pleased to
be married to a wine merchant, for Anthony can produce the
most miraculous bottles, guaranteed to revive any social disaster.
I did want Edith to be happy, to like my home and my dinner
and my husband. I didn't want to impress her – I knew anyway
that the trappings of wealth would leave her unmoved – but I
wanted to offer her something, to share whatever I had with
her. I was afraid she might be bored.

But I needn't have worried. The evening was a tremendous
success and Anthony and Declan seemed to take to one another
straight away. Anthony is a most tolerant man, and cannot
understand my own violent reactions towards people. I don't
think he notices them very much. Once he has had a good meal
and with a decent cigar in his hand, he is prepared to listen to
all kinds of nonsense all night long. I was amused that evening
at the interest he seemed to be showing in Declan's lengthy
monologues, nodding his head intelligently and throwing in a

'Really – how interesting' every now and again. Afterwards he told me he thought Declan a 'rather solemn but quite decent chap'.

I blessed his tolerance that night, for I thought it might provide a solution to a problem I saw looming. I had no interest in being lectured to by Declan, and on the other hand, if I saw as much of Edith as I wanted to, if I could take her to films, concerts, even perhaps on holiday, then I knew Declan would begin to resent me and feel perhaps that I was monopolizing Edith. But if I could manage to arrange these foursomes, then Anthony would keep Declan happy, and I would have Edith to myself.

And how happy I was at this prospect. The more I saw of Edith, the more I admired and loved her. She had a quietness and repose about her which I found particularly attractive – I am such a strident person myself. I always look for the limelight and though I have tried to cure myself of this fault, I know I am as bad as ever. But Edith actually preferred to listen. And when she listened, you knew that she was actually considering what you were saying, and not simply waiting for an opportunity to get in herself. I talked a lot to Edith, more, I think, than I have ever talked to anyone in my life. The pleasure I got from our conversation was enormous. The world suddenly seemed to be full of things and people and ideas to discuss. I asked for no other stimulant than the excitement generated by our talk, and I looked forward to our meetings with a sense of exhilaration. I loved to buy things for her, too. I have always liked giving people gifts, but through being married to Anthony my sense of pleasure had become dulled. Mind you, I don't think it was Anthony, most men would be the same. You can buy a man only a certain number of shirts, and after that – what is there? But with Edith the possibilities were endless. She dressed quite badly – I don't think she ever thought about the way she looked. But I, who saw all the possibilities of her beauty, felt like a creator when I thought of dressing her. A scarf to bring out the purity of her skin, a chiffon blouse to emphasize that fragile line of her neck – the changes I could make in her appearance. Of course I had to be careful not to offend her, as I

knew that one so sensitive might be made to feel uncomfortable
by all these gifts. So sometimes I would pretend that I had
bought something for myself and it didn't fit and she would be
doing me a favour by taking it. Or I would accept a pound for a
leather bag which had cost me fifteen, saying that I had picked
it up cheaply but that the colour wasn't right.

Creating this new Edith reawoke all my interest in clothes
and make-up. I seemed to have been dressing myself and putting
on my face for so long that I felt I could do it in my sleep, and
I had some time ago grown bored with myself. Besides, presenting my rather obvious persona to the world was a straight-
forward task, and the subtleties which I used in dressing Edith
would have been lost on me. And as Edith saw her new self
emerging, she grew interested too. I wondered how this would
affect her attitude towards Declan. As she began to realize what
a beautiful girl she was, might not she also realize what a slob
Declan was, and get rid of him? Not that I thought very much
about Declan any more. He was by now busy preparing for his
final examinations and when he did have time to go out with
Edith he seemed quite happy for them to come and have dinner
with us, or at Anthony's club. Anthony had even interested
him in wine, and as they sat sniffing their glasses and delicately
tasting, we sat giggling over ours, having quaffed too much of
the stuff in a most unconnoisseur-like fashion. Edith and I
both agreed that we knew little about wine, but knew what we
liked. Sometimes, when Declan was studying, I'd go round to
Edith's flat for supper, and we'd get through a bottle of plonk,
enjoying it just as much as any rare Burgundy. This formed a
bond between us and gave us a nice comfortable sense of vul-
garity, of which Declan would have disapproved for intellectual
reasons and Anthony for social.

I was happy. It is a state you have to be in to recognize. Before
I met Edith, it had never occurred to me that I was unhappy. I
knew that I was bored a lot of the time and often lonely. I felt
that something was missing from my life, and various well-
meaning girl friends had told me from time to time that what
I wanted was a baby. Instinctively I knew, however, that this was
not so. I have always rebelled at the idea of becoming a mother;

I could never see myself, baby at breast, looking out placidly at the world. Now I knew that my reservations had been right: I would probably have made a very bad mother, and I would not have fulfilled myself. All I needed all that time was a friend. A real friend.

But it seems to be a rule of life that, having achieved a measure of happiness, clouds begin to float across one's Eden. I don't know when things started going wrong with Edith and myself, for my state of happiness had begun to blur my perceptions, and I wasn't as conscious as I should have been of all Edith's reactions. Then little by little I noticed changes in her. She started to make excuses about not coming out to the house with me. When I'd ask her to go to a concert or lecture, she'd say no thank you, she was doing something else. She grew irritable too, and would cut me off short when I'd begin to talk about something. Then she took to avoiding me in the office, or so it seemed to me, and she started bringing sandwiches in at lunchtime, saying that she had no time to go out to lunch as she was doing extra work for Mr Kelly.

When I was certain that I had not been imagining Edith's attitude, when I could no longer fool myself that everything was as it had been, I grew very upset. What upset me most, I think, was that I could not offer an explanation for her behaviour. I knew I was not the most tactful person in the world, but I had felt that Edith and I were so close that there was no need for pretence; and anyway I couldn't remember having said anything so awful that she would stop wanting to see me because of it.

One afternoon I became so worried that I burst into tears in the office. Mr Kelly Junior was with me at the time, and I think I frightened the poor man out of his wits, for he told me that I looked tired and to go home at once and not to bother coming in the next day, which was Friday. That weekend I did a lot of thinking. Away from the office I grew calm, and I began to think that things would sort themselves out if I could remain calm. Maybe I had been seeing too much of Edith and, if I left her alone for a while, she would probably recover her equilibrium and everything would be alright again.

When I returned to the office, I stuck to my resolution. I remained perfectly friendly towards Edith, but I stopped asking her to come places with me, and I began to have my lunch half an hour earlier than the rest of the office. It was so difficult, this calm indifference, but I knew it was the only way. Then one morning as I was taking my coat off, one of the typists rushed into my room.

'Isn't it awful; have you heard?' she said.

'No, what is it, what's happened?'

'Edith Duggan's mother was killed last night. Run over by a bus as she was crossing the road. She died instantly. Edith, the poor thing, went to bits, I believe. They couldn't get her to stop crying.'

God, how awful. I felt quite sick. What must Edith be feeling? I knew she had loved her mother, and that she should have been killed before they sould be reconciled ... The guilt she must be feeling, added to the pain. I must go to her, I knew. I put my coat back on and got her home address from one of the girls, and left without even telling Mr Kelly where I was going.

The house was a shabby semi-detached with a few sad flowers struggling for life in the patch of green outside. A man I took to be Edith's father answered the door. He showed me into the little front room and there I saw Edith, sitting white-faced and stiff, staring at nothing. She looked up and gave me a wintry smile.

'Edith, what can I say –' I began, but she interrupted me with a shake of her head.

'I know. It's alright really. I understand. It was good of you to come.'

The words sounded so small and distant in that front parlour.

'Oh, Edith, my poor, poor Edith.' I ran towards her and put my arms around her, kissing her, kissing her to comfort her. Suddenly she tore at my arms and flung herself from me. She ran behind the sofa and stood there, trembling.

'Get out of here,' she shouted. 'Leave me alone. Go away you – you monster.'

I tried to say something, but she began to scream some incoherent phrases about the girls in the office and how stupid she'd been and how could I have come there then. I could still hear the screams as I made my way down the path.

She didn't come back to the office. Anthony suggested that she had probably been reconciled with her father and was now staying at home to mind the family. I worried about her, for it seemed to me that the shock of her mother's death must have unhinged her mind. How else could I explain the dreadful things she shouted that day in her front room?

Then about a month later, as I was walking down Grafton Street one afternoon, I saw her coming towards me. She saw me too, and as we drew level I put out my hand. She looked at me, directly into my eyes, with a cold hostility.

'Hello, Helen,' she said, and she sounded quite calm. 'I'm glad I've met you like this. You see, I want you to realize that I meant what I said that day. I wasn't hysterical or anything like that. I do not wish to see you, ever again.' Then she stepped aside and walked on down towards O'Connell Street.

I felt my stomach heave as she walked away. I felt I could never get home, that I would have to stand there, in Grafton Street, rooted to the spot in horror. I twisted and turned, like an animal in a cage, not wanting to face the fact that Edith's shouted obscenities were the result of no temporary derangement. When I did get home and told Anthony, he refused to discuss it. He said that the only thing to do was to put the whole business out of my mind, forget about it completely. But how could I forget? How can I shrug off the pain and the pleasure, as if it had never happened? I can find no way of doing that, no way of wiping out the profound sense of loss I am left with. You see, we were such good friends, Edith and I. Such good friends.

Sand

NEIL JORDAN

THE donkey's hooves were like his sister's fingernails, long and pointed. Except for the ends, which were splintered and rough, not fine and hard.

He was sitting on it, trying to make it move. He could feel its spine against the bone between his legs. He could feel its flanks, like two soft sweaty cushions against each knee and thigh.

He dug his heel into one of the flanks and it shifted a few feet.

'Stop kicking up sand,' his sister said. She had that annoyed tone in her voice.

'Will you come for a swim if I stop,' he asked.

'Oh just stop, would you.'

'No,' he said.

He kicked at the donkey again, though he dreaded his sister's tongue. When she spoke she seemed to know so much that he didn't. It was like her suntan lotion; like her habit of lying by the sea with her eyes closed, on their towel. He felt that somewhere he knew as much as she, but when he came to say it he could never find the words.

'If you kick more sand at me –'

'Alright,' he said. 'Alright.'

He put his hands on the donkey's neck and wondered how he could get down with some dignity, some of her dignity. He looked at the dark blue of the sea and the light blue of the sky, thinking about this. Then he heard something far away behind him. A shout. He turned on the donkey, saw someone running across the burrows, arms waving.

He clambered down quickly, without dignity. He thought of tinkers. He knew most donkeys belonged to tinkers. He looked at this donkey and it was as impassive as ever, its hooves curling out of the white sand.

The figure came nearer, running with a peculiar adult single-mindedness. It wasn't an adult however, it was a boy, not much older than him. The boy had run beyond the rim of the grass now and was kicking up sand. He was totally naked. He held a boot in one hand with which every now and then he covered his genitals.

But mostly he couldn't cover them, his arms flailing as he ran. And the boy saw the naked figure, smaller than him, but stronger and much browner, jogging to a halt. He saw the open mouth panting and the eyes, wary as his were, but older and angrier than his could ever have been. The brown nakedness stopping at the waist becoming grey-white nakedness. The boot stationary now in front of the patch of hair.

'That's my donkey. Leave hold of it.'

He did so immediately. Not because he was afraid, which he was, but because he would have done anything those eyes asked. He looked at the shoe and it didn't quite hide that curl of angry hair and that sex. He looked at his sister. She was looking the other way, blushing, arched rigid in her blue swimsuit.

'I'll give you that the next time.'

A small bony fist hovered before his face. Behind it were the eyes, young as his, but with clusters of ancient wrinkles round the edges.

'Okay,' he said. He tried not to sound defeated. And the tinker turned and pulled the donkey after him by the thin hair on its neck.

'Really,' his sister said.

And now he blushed. The tinker was on the burrows now, pulling the donkey by the hair on its neck. His buttocks swung as he walked, two white patches against the brown of his thin body.

He felt blamed for that nakedness. He felt he could hate his sister, for blaming him.

'Really,' she said. 'Some people.'

He felt the words were false, picked up from grown-ups. Her body was arched forward now towards her drawn-up knees, her arms were placed across her knees and her chin was resting on her arms. Her eyelids were lowered, not quite closed, but sealing him off. He wanted to say sorry, but her eyes lay between him and his words. Then he did hate her. He hated her in a very basic way, he felt he would tear her apart, the way one tears the many wrappings off the parcel in the pass-the-parcel game, to see what's inside. He didn't know whether he'd hate what would be inside.

'Jean –' he began, but she turned on her stomach, away from him, exposing her long back to the sun.

He heard a shout behind him and he turned, glad to escape her. He saw the tinker waving his hands some distance down in the burrows, shouting something he couldn't hear. There was something urgent about him, flailing hands against the sky. So he walked, even though he was afraid, leaving his sister with her cheek resting on her linked hands.

As he walked the tinker grew bigger and the flailing gradually stopped. There was the hot feel of the sand under his bare feet, then the feel of grass, whistling by his calves. Then the boy was in front of him, arms on his hips, waiting for him to approach. He was wearing men's trousers now, sizes too big for him.

'You want a go on the donkey?'

He nodded dumbly.

'I'll give you half an hour with the donkey for half an hour with your sister.'

The boy began to laugh at the thought, his sister and the donkey, an even swop. The tinker began to laugh too and that made the boy laugh louder, huge laughs that went right through his body and stretched his stomach-muscles tight. The tinker's laugh was softer, more knowledgeable. The boy heard this and stopped, and looked into the blue eyes which wrinkled in some complicity and kept laughing. Then the boy began to laugh again, loving his laughter, the way he sometimes laughed when adults were laughing. The joke had changed into another joke, a joke he didn't understand, but that made it all the more funny.

Then the tinker stopped suddenly. He cupped his hands together to make a stirrup and held them out.

'Here.'

The hands were grimy and lined, skin flaking off them. The boy felt compliant. He was opening a box to let the winds out. He knew and he didn't know. He placed his left foot in the stirrup of flaking hands and swung on to the donkey, and the tinker's foot kicked the donkey and the donkey ran.

He was holding its neck, fearful and exhilarated. It was running like he didn't know donkeys could run, with rapid thumps of hoof off the grass, with its spine, hard as a gate, crashing off his groin. He pressed his head against its neck and could hear its breathing, angry and sullen, thumping with its hooves. His knees clutched the swollen belly and his hands, gripping each other under the neck, were wet and slimy with saliva from the open jaw. His eyes were closed and he saw in the black behind his eyelids something even blacker emerging, whorling and retreating again.

Then it stopped. He slid over its head and fell to the ground. He fell flat out, his cheek against the burrows' grass and heard his sister screaming, a clear scream, clear as silver.

The donkey's head was hanging and its sides were heaving. Between its legs a black erection dangled, heaving with its sides. The scream still echoed in the boy's mind. Clear and silver, speaking to him, like the reflection of sun on sea-water. He ran.

He ran faster than the donkey. He saw the green burrows, then the white sand, then the clear blue of his sister's swimsuit, then a browned tanned back. The sand was kicking up in clumps around him as he threw himself on that back.

He felt the naked shoulders under his hand. Then he felt the shoulders twisting and a hard body pushing him downwards, something hot, hard against his stomach. Both of their fists were hitting the other's face until he was hit hard, once and twice, and they both, as if by mutual decision, went quiet. He lay until he became conscious of the other's hot hard groin, then squirmed away. He looked up at his sister. Her head was in one hand and the other hand was covering the bare skin above her swimsuit. He heard a rustle of sand and heard the tinker boy getting up.

'I thought we'd made a swop.' There was a spot of blood on his wizened mouth. He bent forward as if to strike again but changed his hand's direction just as rapidly and scratched the hair behind his ear. The boy started. He grinned.

'I'd only put it through you,' he said. Then he hitched up his falling trousers and walked towards the grass.

When he got there he turned.

'That's the last you'll see of my donkey,' he said. Then he chuckled with infinite sarcasm. 'Unless you've got another sister.' And he turned again and walked through the grass towards the donkey.

She was crying, great breathful sobs.

'You won't –' he asked.

'I will,' she said. 'I'll tell it all –'

The boy knew, however, that she would be ashamed. He picked up her towel and her suntan lotion and began to walk. He had forgotten about his hate. He was thinking of the donkey and the tinker's flaking palms and his sister's breasts. After a while he turned.

'Stop crying, will you. Nothing happened, did it.'

His hands were wet with the donkey's saliva and to the saliva a fine film of sand was clinging. When he moved his fingers it rustled, whispered, sang.

Red Jelly

EITHNE STRONG

MOLLY tells me today about the room. She got the thing all
fixed for me so I can move in straight away. So when I get home
I tell them. It's more or less as I expected from them, only
maybe not so bad. The worst was over already I suppose when
there was that show-down the first night, that night I said it's
either Sucker or me. Anyway, when I tell them, my father's
face tightens and all the little lines on it get a bit deeper. I
don't like looking at either of them although on principle I
stare at them just to let them see it's costing *me* nothing. SHE
doesn't say anything at all, only she has that ridiculous look
that comes over her when she's feeling sorry for herself: what
did I do to deserve this, life's so painful, ogodgivemethestrength
look. Max painted a picture of it once – shiny reds, all different
kinds of bloody sweat reds in a sort of huge egg shape and he
said,

'That's HER in agony.'

And I said,

'It looks sort of like red jelly.'

'Right,' he said, 'yes. That's what we'll call it – RED
JELLY – *an agony*.'

He's keeping it for his exhibition in the spring. Walter says
he'll buy it to hang, title and all, in his Bistro and I said it'll
put the people off eating if they have to sit under that. But
Walter has it that you should always play up your bad point,
make a big thing of it, communicate to people the idea of your
belief in yourself. He needs a bit of that since he took on the
Bistro and as the food in the place is hardly likely to improve
– not with *his* wife's dab hand – maybe his notion about the

picture is not so bad. Then he thought a bit and said he might change the name, make it maybe *Mélange Rouge* – he digs this French antic – and Max said he could once he'd bought it. Max is holding out for a tenner; Walter has offered him five but Max said he'd had more than a tenner's worth of trouble in our house to get all those shades of agony. I mean all the brats and everything.

As I'm telling them about the room S H E ' S crying, no noise of course. That silent suffering effort. But I despise her for it. Too far late in the day now for crying, as I told her the first time we had the row about the carry-on. I don't know what she expects – that I'm going to smile and grin and fair weather to her trucking around with that Sucker. My father is another kind of fool giving fancy names to what they are up to, himself, herself and the Sucker and blazes knows who else. It's all an excuse for whoring. I'm staying around no more. So I tell them about the room.

I say it stubborn and angry so they'll get no ideas about stopping me, not that I think they will – they want me willing, it seems, or not at all – but just in case. There's not much they can really do. That first night I threatened to tell everywhere about it all if they made any fuss about me clearing out. I'll say though S H E was able for me over that. She said:

'Go ahead. Do your worst. Shout it from the housetops if you want to – you jolly well know, Maryjane, I won't be bullied by that sort of tantrum. We are living our life the best we can : I've never not done anything, anything at all, for you I could. Full well you know it. You have been an – an adored child in this house.'

I didn't go for all that soft bit.

'You can do more,' I shout. 'I don't want that filthy Sucker nosing around here. I've copped on, make no mistake. Either that stops or I get out.'

'It's up to yourself now,' she says, 'it's blackmail what you're doing. You know your standing with us, I don't have to prove anything to you about it. In seventeen years you certainly know it.'

She was looking at me with that fierce kind of look, her eyes all drawn together and this groove between her eyebrows, and although she was red she didn't look like jelly I must say. I know what she meant too, 'tis just I can't stand this mucking around: she's my – my – my mother isn't she? The thought of a thing like the Sucker ... God it makes me just heave vomit P U K E. Inside out.

That was all the time we had the first row. But although I know she means what she says and that she'll stick to it to the last, she – they – won't do anything much about stopping me.

'It's up to you,' she had said. '*You* are separating *your*self from us. This is your home. You feel what you are feeling and I don't know that's it's helping you anyway to grow up more by letting that feeling dominate over what we believe to be – right.'

So pie, oh my so holy pie!

I tell them a friend will be sharing the room with me. I don't, naturally enough, breathe a word about Molly, that she's moving in with me only because she has to leave the place she and Walter have been sleeping in – his wife will be back soon and he won't be able to stay away from home every night. That's the thing about the parents that's so disgusting: so *pie* about it all as if it's something special they are doing; holy of holies. No such thing as calling a spade. I'd rather any day the lark Molly and Walter are up to. They certainly are not making any grand act out of it. Makes me want to throw up: all that high-pie talk.

I have to get my stuff moved in. Although he must hate to like cancer, my father says he'll do it. Then he is working when I am ready to shift so S H E does it. They are handy still for this kind of thing, there's that sloppy obliging streak that you see at the most peculiar times – this is a peculiar time. Anyway it all – the obligingness, the slop – goes with the high-pie.

'Omygod,' she says as we go up past the dustbins on the first landing. It is a very close heavy sort of a day. The smells don't get any better as we go further on up to the door of the room that is to be mine. I have to knock to get the key from the tenant opposite. He's hairy, I mean about two yards of hair, and not exactly clean. She doesn't say it any more but I can hear her thinking 'omygod' all the time. What's *she* so choosy about? The mess at home is a fright most of the time although she's always saying 'omygod' about that too. Her face is red from crying. She's been at it fit to make me retch all the time she was driving me to the place. What she meant to be that silent suffering. No sound much except an odd snort. Maybe it was giving her some soppy satisfaction but if it was supposed to stir me up, I was like a stone.

The room smells of sour dish-cloths and dead air. She goes to the window but does nothing about opening it. She hates bad smells but it is my room and she isn't going to interfere. She is learning the hard way. Outside the glass there are clogged gutters and broken black slates and a filthy backyard belonging to the dump opposite, all nicely in view. I know it looks bad and I am glad. At home my room looked out on trees and a bit of a river and grass and all that. It is her fault I am here. 'Nympho' I had shouted at her the night it came to a show-down.

After she had put down the stuff she was carrying, she went away and I didn't watch her going. Before all this whatever, I nearly always kissed her if I were going anywhere. Even in the crazy rush for the bus to school in town. And we'd say 'God bless'. It's a kind of thing they say all the time in the family like 'hello' or 'good-bye'. No more of that sop now.

I'm earning for myself and I won't have to touch them for anything – well maybe some things here and there if I just absolutely have to. They certainly owe it to me – it's too easy if my clearing-out means there is that bit more to spend on the rest of the pack. But I'd really rather not have to ask for anything. I'm off their hands young, that's one thing. Their own fault it is if they have to struggle and scrape: who asked them to have all that lot that wasn't exactly pleading to be born? I know *I* never asked it and now that I'm there I'm mucked up already at seventeen. A good job they did on me surely. Well they'll see. I'll drag their name maybe. Serve them.

Max comes in to paint up the place a bit. Not much, for we have hardly anything to spend on it but he had a few odd pots left from the time he was painting up his own studio in the summer. He has it nearly finished when I come in from work and then he stays on. Molly doesn't come till next week to halve the rent for me. But I'm O.K. for now, for the first week anyway, with the few extra quid my father gave me. He said he'd give me nothing, not that I asked him: he was just saying it to let me know he was giving no helping finances to what I was doing. Bullying, he said. Maybe so. But they know. Either a change from them or I stay away. In the end he gives me these few quid. He's always soft to us about money, struggling and all. S H E never has any. I've already decided I'll never be like that, waiting in hope for money. I'll take it where it will come from. I think anyway.

The room looks fairly all right now and we put *red* see-through paper in the lower part of the window to rich the view. Today though it makes me think of red jelly.

Now that Molly is here the place seems very cramped. S H E was forever ticking me off for keeping my room at home in a mess. She'd sometimes go through it all when I was out and make it tidy, hanging up my clothes, taking away the dirty ones and fixing it all up. When I'd see it that way, for a few days I might maybe keep it straight. Then I'd let it all slide. It was too much effort and I'd often be down in the dumps with the noise of the brats that you couldn't get away from and the rotten lot of homework and worrying about what was wrong with the way I looked. There are a lot of things I'd like different with the way I look although S H E was always saying I was lovely. Of course coming from her it meant nothing. Couldn't take any notice of that. I was in no way convinced. For Max to say it would be altogether another story. But he doesn't say it, nothing like that, only snide bits. I often cry about the things he says that way. It only matters coming from a guy, really, the praise bit. Bitches will *always* chew you up behind your back however smaamy to your face. Myself I don't much see the point of the praise bit from one woman to another so I say nothing to their face. I don't see the point. I often *think* they look great of course, but mostly the real good-lookers are stinkers. There's nothing can be done about bitchiness.

Now S H E wouldn't ever do the chewing-up bit I *know* – about me, that is. But she says the nice things because I'm H E R child, taking the credit to herself, you see. That's how it used to be anyway. Maybe she just gets some consolation from the drag thinking her bunch is just great. It wouldn't be surprising in a way. I mean forcing the consolation part. Give her due, she'd never hurt my feelings that way. It is the other carry-on, the Sucker thing and that being with her a matter of principle – *principle* mind you – as she put it the night I slammed cards on the table. I said me or the Sucker, which is it to be? So I'm here in this room and that was the answer. I wouldn't be here if . . .

I think I'll go up to Walter's Bistro for a drink.

Molly is untidy. Even I am better at sorting things out. And I'm cleaner. At least I scrubbed down all the old sink and draining board with disinfectant and I put down rat-poison. There were two rats in the dustbins the other night. Molly doesn't care. And I only buy stuff that won't go bad. I don't like bad smells either. But I was glad of the smell that day when S H E first came. Just to lay the whole misery on.

Walter came back with Molly the other night and he stayed on and on – till morning. So Max stayed too. It was a crush, four to the bed.

I think I'll go for a drink up to the Bistro.

I'm back at home today. I was out this way anyway on a job for my manager and it was handy to drop in to use the phone here. Calls to do with the job. I said to H E R I'd leave money for the calls – keeping up the independence bit, but she'll forget or I can pretend I forgot although I kind of meant it when I said it.

S H E is looking a bit of a wreck I must say. She wears every-thing out to the last possible, I mean acres of darns and patches up the leg. Shoes like boats. Clean of course, but the patchwork – God the clothes! I wouldn't be seen dead! She can look about passable sometimes. Going out, say. Only she must be finding it a stretch these days to keep looking anything. She hasn't much clothes and there's always this mess everywhere that she fusses so much about cleaning up. Don't slop; don't spill; pick up this, that and the other; keep the place decent, I can't do it all – HELP ME. That's the way she goes on, always struggling, cleaning, giving out about messes. All the fault of those grotty brats.

Christ I get mad when I'm trying to phone and they all start off a racket. Now that I'm not living here any more I don't want to screech and yell at them the way I used to, I don't want to let them see I'd be bothered, you know. But they drive me crazy and I can't hear a word on the phone and so I give a *small* roar at them. Not *too* much off my dignity. Will you P L E A S E keep quiet, and then when they take no notice I put the phone down and give them a few belts. Stephen is the worst. He goes yah yah yah back at me and runs away outside so I know I don't have a hope about catching him and I leave it at that. Anyway I think I've got rid of him, but I've no sooner started on the phone again when back he's in to make more racket with the rest. This time I don't pretend to notice until he is right up to me and then I grab him by the hair and give him what he's looking for. Then of course he goes screeching off to H E R where she's trucking round in the base-ment trying to fix up some of the grot. She comes up the stairs all red in the face.

'Maryjane,' she says, 'if you come back here you take us as you find us. We are as we always were. You were the same at his age. I'm not saying he's right but don't take it on your-self to wallop him like that. You come and tell me about him. I'll stop him.'

Don't make me laugh. Stop him. She will like fun. He's grinning now from one ear to the other. She says prim and posh as she always is when she's ticking off,

'Stephen, have manners. Don't you know when a person is on the telephone – I'm always telling you all when a person is on the phone ... to be ... to be quiet.'

He's still grinning away and she takes him by the shoulder
and rattles the daylights out of him. It's not hitting, you see,
and so it's all right to do it – that's the way she thinks. He
sees she's getting mad and pretends to try to straighten his
face, but the whole business now is too funny for him. Back
comes the grin. He's mocking her and it really gets her. Anyone
mocking her always get her. I know she's hard put not to strike
him but for one thing it wouldn't do in front of me. She's
supposed to be showing me how to handle the situation. She
suddenly spreads out her arms and sweeps them all out the
door and locks it. They stay for a bit looking back in through
the glass sniggering and not too sure whether to start off again,
but they have seen her wild before now and it seems they
decide they've gone far enough. She comes back to me very
stiff.

'You can go ahead with your calls. I daresay we are still
some convenience. Handy not to have to pay in a box outside.'

She gives me a stare and I stare her back and she goes off
down, her eyes red as well as her face by this. She looks a sight.
If the boyfriend saw her now. But come to think of it she
wouldn't be too put out – in all the years he must have seen
her a sight many a time. She used to say to me when I'd be
crying over the way I looked or over something Max had said
about it, 'Ah child, if he only likes the way you look 'tis a
poor story.' It was never any comfort, for what *is* there to like
in me? I wish someone did like whatever it might be; it's such
a drag always having to think about glamming up.

As luck would have it while I'm still here busy with phoning
the doorbell goes and it's the Sucker at the other side of the
glass. Harvey is really his name but I always call him the
Sucker. He can't work his key for she has of course locked the
door that time. I never could stand the way he has been
hanging around her for years. You could say I don't exactly
love him. And the hanging around was bad but on top of it
he'd try to jam up to us kids. Especially myself and Peg, us
two being the older ones. Trying to put himself in our good
books, trying to have us believe he was what he wasn't – kind-
hearted. As far as Peg and me and him were concerned there

was no trust lost. He has a stinking temper really. One of those poisonous polite-spoken smaamies, every so often making a sad hand out of a poor joke for our nothing-doing benefit.

Well I let him in. I'm pretty sure he knows the latest on me – he's always in on the big news and my move-out is B I G – but I couldn't care less what he knows. Force of habit he sets his head in that pompous way – mock-jolly-good-fellow pompous it's meant to be – and it's the way he used to try out on me when I was a kid about a century ago. And now suddenly, it seems to strike him what he's doing and that he's on to the wrong tack, for he starts the poisonous polite bit:

'And how are *you*, Maryjane?'

He cares damn all. Anyway I don't answer him. Just stare at him with the phone to my ear. The brats come bursting back in – I never locked the door the second time – and they start prancing around Harvey the Sucker. I see him trying the buttery bit, but he is hard put to to keep the smooth for they are galloping over his suede shoes and you can see he's dead afraid they'll mark them. He starts trying to be frolicsome, doing a bit of a dance, pretending to be enjoying their carry-on but it's killing him. I know I stand a chance to make them behave after what has just happened with Stephen and my mother but I'm not all that pushed now any more. I've really finished the phoning so their blasted noise doesn't bother me all that much and I'm getting a kick out of watching Harvey's fix.

'Children, children, please,' says the Sucker. The temper could be warming up there. Stephen falls over the young brat and bashes his own ear on something sharp and, true to form, he starts yelling like a stuck pig.

'You see I warned you' – Harvey's voice is like a preacher's and you can see he is glad to be able to say it. He's pulling Stephen up off the floor and rubbing his ear the way S H E might rub the bottom of the ninety-ninth saucepan – there are about a hundred dirty for washing-up every day. I'm not exactly grief-stricken for Stephen. Pity he didn't fall so as to hit his two ears.

S H E comes up the stairs wondering about the new fuss.

'Hello,' she says to Harvey and she was red again, but this time it's a blush for Sucker. She starts simpering although Lord knows she's had to do with the Sucker long enough to give over that jazz. She simpers in that put-on way with some people trying to take their mind off the wreck. The idea is they'll be so charmed by the sweet sweetness they'll overlook the jungle. She hopes. But it's a losing game, no one is fooled and anyway why use it on the Sucker? He must know the worst by now.

'Please excuse the chaos' – she had no other tune to start with. She dreams it, and when people stay the night and come down to the breakfast wilderness she begins the day with 'please excuse the chaos'.

'I don't see it' is what he mostly says. A stinking hypocrite. He knows I see through him and that is why he always goes out of his way to do the earnest sincere bit with me. I get the message that he doesn't exactly love me either.

'Would you like a cup of something?' She'll always ask him that, knowing well enough she's only going to get more bogged if she starts making a cup of anything with the swarm around. She isn't asking me though. I'm dying for a cuppa as it so happens. And anyway, just to let her see I'm a free agent whatever about the Sucker being around and all that, I follow the troop down the stairs. As they go down he has an arm across her shoulders. What does he see in her? She's gone off so much. Since the last baby she's a real drag.

Down below, with me there, the style is cramped. The two of them make *nice* conversation while I just hump against the wall and watch. The rabble are pelting things around the floor and the Sucker gets tangled up in roller skates that come flying at his ankles. He's worrying about his shoes again. The oil off the skates is his trouble. Sure enough the trendy suede has a streak, a lovely, dirty, greasy smudge.

'Oh Patricia, what shall I do?'

He is in real agony. Like a helpless baby. 'What shall I do', mind you. Take off your sock and pee in your shoe, that's what I've a mind to call. The thought of calling that out to him just *now*, sets me off laughing. The kids see me and start off too.

They think I'm laughing *with* them, but damn their eyes the whole bunch make me *puke*. The only reason I'm down here is to be a nuisance, just to be a nuisance in the way of a cuppa. I can always go on in to Walter at the Bistro if I'm not getting one here. Or maybe he'd stretch to a small brandy. I could, actually, even pay for it. But I'll have to bum a few bob at the club tonight.

Harvey's hanging around with the smudged shoe in his hand and she's dabbing away with some stuff out of a bottle and a piece that she's torn off the baby's napkin – not hard to do, that, the napkins are in ribbons this long day. Even those she makes last. Mending them. Mending *napkins!*

The kettle is steaming away like mad, but they're too busy with the shoe to do anything so I saunter over towards the stove, but then I think I won't bother. Serve her right if the bottom burns out: she's bound to have put on only a small drop, seeing I wasn't included.

The young brat is sitting on the floor beside the stove, dabbling in a pool of milk that's probably been lying there since the last lot for the baby boiled over. Anyway there's always some pool of milk by the stove because of the dip in the lino. 'Twas a yawk of a country yob (S H E has a soft spot for country yobs) put it down for her and he hadn't a clue. All lumps and bumps all over the floor that was uneven in the first place anyhow. He told her he was putting boards down to even it out for her. He put boards down all right, trudging in and out between the old shed that had fallen down and the kitchen. He used every sort of a board out of that old shed, all bits and pieces, so that you can imagine the floor was a real glory after him.

I'm watching that brat washing his filthy paws in the slop of milk and then he begins to pick at the lino, breaking it back in little pieces from the leg of the stove. Then he starts to squawk:

'Yuoooo mammeee, eeuch, eeuch, look at 'gusting spiders.'

'Yes,' she says, not really listening, and she half turns round and tells him, 'Now you naughty little boy, stop that dabbling. Omygod Harvey the mess gets me down.'

It's the first real thing she has said since he came. I mean
there is no simpering now and no *nice* air. She really means
that bit about it getting her down. She takes a full turn around
and with the piece of napkin she's been using on the shoe she
stoops to mop up the milk. Then she gives a shriek and her
face gets red as red and she clutches herself away from the
stove and squeezes her eyes up.

'What is it daaarling?' He loves the drama bit always.
'Daarling whatever is it?'

'Omygod don't even look at them the revolting things.' She's
still clutching herself and squeezing her face up. She is a proper
sight.

But he looks anyway.

'Oh Gawd.' He is horror-struck and his pulpit voice is all
tragic in the drama of it.

The mob gathers round and they are all shrieking and gab-
bling and doing a jig around the stove. I push a bit closer to
have a dekko. In the hole where the lino is picked away there's
about a trillion maggots; they all look as if they're standing
on one end and waving the other end up at us. There they are,
about a couple of trillion maggots like nothing I've ever seen
before in my life, different from blue-bottle ones, all standing
on their heads and waving their one leg at us. It makes your
back shrivel and your ankles give.

'They're from the milk,' says S H E when she gets around to
saying anything. 'It's always getting boiled over. I'm always
telling you all not to let the milk boil over.'

She's glaring at Stephen and the N E X T O N E – the two
of them are always making slops on the stove. Give her due
she's not the only slopper, but they all grew out of her. They
didn't have to be there at all, did they? She has only herself
to blame.

'There's a special sort of fly,' she goes on flapping around,
'I've been seeing them all over the kitchen lately a lot and
I've been wondering – so that's what they've been up to. Omy-
god.'

She says herself 'tis a free world. Multiplication. Everybody's
twistin'.

Stephen takes down the toasting fork that's never used except to grow cobwebs and he starts poking back the lino. The more he pokes the more maggots. Then there is this awful sudden smell, but that's only the kettle burnt black.

Harvey the Sucker has gone far back to the middle of the kitchen and he's bending over from the stomach in the direction of the stove. It's the big sympathy stance, making out he's tied up in her trouble, safe distance and all, but the way he's standing, it looks like he's ready to throw up any minute and is trying for his chance to make off in a way least likely to rile her. Maybe, though, she is glad enough for him to clear off at the moment: this, on top of, or under, all the other mess is hardly the memory of her he'll most treasure. Anyhow, for now he's yabbering away,

'Patricia I – I – don't quite see what use I can be at this moment; in fact though, even if I did, I have to be at that meeting I was telling you about, in five minutes. So – so – if you'll excuse me –'

He was backing to the door waving his body at her from the waist up. His face was a sight. A mixture of a Sucker agony and a Sucker smile. He showed her his front and back teeth in the sympathy effort.

'Oh of course, Harvey, of course. Forgive me if I don't come up.'

That's the way they always go on, so fecking polite to make you vomit.

Now for some real business. There are all the little grey slugs waving away at her, the little pets, not to be given the go-by.

'Godogod,' she starts off, 'you'll all have to go out. I can't tackle this with all of you crowding around me. Get away from me, right away and let me at it.'

But no one budges and she roars GET BACK ALL OF YOU FOR THE LORD'S SAKE. So they move a bit. About an inch.

'Now this is one instance when you'll get a good wallop, I'm warning you. Even though I don't believe in walloping I'm no saint, and I'm stretched to the limit.'

She turns on Stephen and the N E X T O N E, her hand lifted ready for it – she'd not touch the small ones I'll say.

'Get out, Stephen, d'you hear? And take them all with you. Lift up that child,' she says to the N E X T O N E, meaning for her to take the small one who picked the hole, 'and keep him outside till I say not.'

Stephen sees she means business but his love of the maggots, the dear little creatures, makes him brave.

'Ah Ma,' he says – he says 'Ma' sometimes and mostly it gets her goat, but this time she doesn't notice – 'I'll keep them all back over there,' he points to the far corner, 'I promise, if you'll let us stay.'

'Did anyone – don't C A L L me Ma –' (she noticed all right) 'ever have such a family? Morbid little brutes. Other mothers get far more result – they belt and wallop all the time – I'm far too soft with you all, far too soft.' But she has put her hand down, so she's not going to wallop, it seems. And she's looking sideways at the squirming multiplication. She can't face it square yet. Maybe she doesn't know which way she'd best turn.

'You can stay, but don't budge out of that corner.' She hooshes them all into the corner, where they start pinching and kicking just to keep in form. 'Oh God I need help. I N E E D help. So will you lot help me by just staying quiet? It's not too much to ask is it and it's the most help I can expect, I suppose.'

All the time I am standing there she acts as if I amn't around. I wish she might just chance asking me something so I could refuse or be lousy someway.

First she makes this ton of strong, boiling Jeyes' fluid stuff and pours a flood of it over the maggots. There's that army of them the odd kick's left in them even after that. She keeps clapping her hand up to her nose and mouth as if she's afraid to breathe. Then she gets these miles of newspaper – she always keeps the things for lighting fires 'and you never know how they'll be handy'. Now she knows like she never knew before – nor me either. She hauls out this old galvanized bath full of holes and starts wadding paperfuls of maggots and Jeyes into it. She's nearly dying for the want of breath and keeps going over to the window for a fresh gulp. She's not breathing while she does each separate bit of wadding. Every go she uses about twenty layers of paper as a kind of a scoop. Now if 'twere me I'd just get the mallet and shovel from the old shed and pound the lot to hell, rotten boards and all, and then shovel the whole mess into the bath. But she has no head like that. All fluster and squeam. Still 'tis hardly the job you'd exactly pick, especially with the crowd in the corner laughing their silly nuts off.

They are reasonable enough apart from that, I'll say, but if it goes on too long they are likely to break out. They can't stand anything for long and this looks like it could go on till kingdom come.

My father is due home soon for his meal. Appetizing welcome.

Ah well I'll go on up and out. There's just time to stop off at the Bistro. Imagine *tea* after that.

'See you,' I kind of call.

But she doesn't answer even a syllable. It's just about possible she didn't hear me. Maybe she's forgotten I'm there. I didn't exactly put my helpful presence forward since the maggot racket. Ah well ...

Still it's her own fault. Who asked them to have all the brats? Now with only me and Peg, with only me ... Peg's gone anyway, couldn't wait to spring the joint –

Well if it isn't the Sucker rushing against me back down to her. I hear him inside the kitchen.

'Patricia, I've rung them up to say I'm not coming. Look, I'll fix it up for you. Hang on, take it easy – there must be something in the shed – hang on.'

He gallops off out to the back, suede shoes and all, and he's back in a minute with a shovel and a bucket of sand. I never thought of the sand.

I'll have to go now, no time even for Walter's. Maybe Max might run to some brandy later.

And it's my father coming up the front steps.

'*Maryjane*, you're *back!*' and he stands looking at me all lines and puzzles in his face, and then he puts the kiss on my forehead.

But I'm not back.

I'm not so sure I like R E D J E L L Y as a name for what Max painted. I don't know if I even *like* that picture. In fact it's a lousy picture.

Secrets

BERNARD McLAVERTY

HE had been called to be there at the end. His great-aunt
Mary had been dying for some days now and the house was
full of relatives. He had just left his girlfriend's home – they
had been studying for 'A' levels together – and had come back
to the house to find all the lights spilling on to the lawn and a
sense of purpose which had been absent from the last few days.

He knelt at the bedroom door to join in the prayers. His
knees were on the wooden threshold and he edged them forward on to the carpet. They had tried to wrap her fingers
around a crucifix but they kept loosening. She lay low on the
pillow and her face seemed to have shrunk by half since he
had gone out earlier in the night. Her white hair was damped
and pushed back from her forehead. She twisted her head from
side to side, her eyes closed. The prayers chorused on, trying
to cover the sound she was making deep in her throat. Someone said about her teeth and his mother leaned over her and
said, 'That's the pet', and took her dentures from her mouth.
The lower half of her face seemed to collapse. She half opened
her eyes but could not raise her eyelids enough and showed
only crescents of white.

'Hail Mary full of grace ...' the prayers went on. He closed
his hands over his face so that he would not have to look
but smelt the trace of his girlfriend's handcream from his
hands. The noise, deep and guttural, that his aunt was making
became intolerable to him. It was as if she were drowning. She
had lost all the dignity he knew her to have. He got up from
the floor and stepped between the others who were kneeling
and went into her sitting-room off the same landing.

He was trembling with anger or sorrow, he didn't know

which. He sat in the brightness of her big sitting-room at the oval table and waited for something to happen. On the table was a cut-glass vase of irises, dying because she had been in bed for over a week. He sat staring at them. They were withering from the tips inward, scrolling themselves delicately, brown and neat. Clearing up after themselves. He stared at them for a long time until he heard the sounds of women weeping from the next room.

His aunt had been small – her head on a level with his when she sat at her table – and she seemed to get smaller each year. Her skin fresh, her hair white and waved and always well washed. She wore no jewelry except a cameo ring on the third finger of her right hand and, around her neck, a gold locket on a chain. The white classical profile on the ring was almost worn through and had become translucent and indistinct. The boy had noticed the ring when she had read to him as a child. In the beginning fairy tales, then as he got older extracts from famous novels, *Lorna Doone, Persuasion, Wuthering Heights* and her favourite extract, because she read it so often, Pip's meeting with Miss Havisham from *Great Expectations*. She would sit with him on her knee, her arms around him and holding the page flat with her hand. When he was bored he would interrupt her and ask about the ring. He loved hearing her tell of how her grandmother had given it to her as a brooch and she had had a ring made from it. He would try to count back to see how old it was. Had her grandmother got it from *her* grandmother? And if so, what had she turned it into? She would nod her head from side to side and say, 'How would I know a thing like that?' keeping her place in the closed book with her finger.

'Don't be so inquisitive,' she'd say. 'Let's see what happens next in the story.'

One day she was sitting copying figures into a long narrow book with a dip pen when he came into her room. She didn't look up, but when he asked her a question she just said, 'Mm?' and went on writing. The vase of irises on the oval table vibrated slightly as she wrote.

'What is it?' She wiped the nib on blotting-paper and looked up at him over her reading glasses.

'I've started collecting stamps and Mamma says you might have some.'

'Does she now –?'

She got up from the table and went to the tall walnut bureau-bookcase standing in the alcove. From a shelf of the bookcase she took a small wallet of keys and selected one for the lock. There was a harsh metal shearing sound as she pulled the desk flap down. The writing area was covered with green leather which had dog-eared at the corners. The inner part was divided into pigeon-holes, all bulging with papers. Some of them, envelopes, were gathered in batches nipped at the waist with elastic bands. There were postcards and bills and cash-books. She pointed to the postcards.

'You may have the stamps on those,' she said. 'But don't tear them. Steam them off.'

She went back to the oval table and continued writing. He sat on the arm of the chair, looking through the picture postcards – torchlight processions at Lourdes, brown photographs of town centres, dull black and whites of beaches backed by faded hotels. Then he turned them over and began to sort the stamps. Spanish with a bald man, French with a rooster, German with funny jerky print, some Italian with what looked like a chimney-sweep's bundle and a hatchet.

'These are great,' he said. 'I haven't got any of them.'

'Just be careful how you take them off.'

'Can I take them downstairs?'

'Is your mother there?'

'Yes.'

'Then perhaps it's best if you bring the kettle up here.'

He went down to the kitchen. His mother was in the morning-room polishing silver. He took the kettle and the flex upstairs. Except for the dipping and scratching of his aunt's pen the room was silent. It was at the back of the house overlooking the orchard, and the sound of traffic from the main road was distant and muted. A tiny rattle began as the kettle warmed up, then it bubbled and steam gushed quietly from its spout. The cards began to curl slightly in the jet of steam, but she didn't seem to be watching. The stamps peeled moistly off and he put them in a saucer of water to flatten them.

'Who is Brother Benignus?' he asked. She seemed not to hear. He asked again and she looked over her glasses.

'He was a friend.'

His flourishing signature appeared again and again. Sometimes Bro. Benignus, sometimes Benignus and once Iggy.

'Is he alive?'

'No, he's dead now. Watch the kettle doesn't run dry.'

When he had all the stamps off, he put the postcards together and replaced them in the pigeon-hole. He reached over towards the letters but before his hand touched them his aunt's voice, harsh for once, warned.

'A-a-a,' she moved her pen from side to side. 'Do-not-touch,' she said and smiled. 'Anything else, yes! That section, no!' She resumed her writing.

The boy went through some other papers and found some photographs. One was a beautiful girl. It was very old-fashioned but he could see that she was beautiful. The picture was a pale brown oval set on a white square of card. The edges of the oval were misty. The girl in the photograph was young and had dark, dark hair scraped severely back and tied like a knotted rope on the top of her head – high, arched eyebrows, her nose straight and thin; her mouth slightly smiling, yet not smiling, the way a mouth is after smiling. Her eyes looked out at him, dark and knowing and beautiful.

'Who is that?' he asked.

'Why? What do you think of her?'

'She's all right.'

'Do you think she is beautiful?' The boy nodded.

'That's me,' she said. The boy was glad he had pleased her in return for the stamps.

Other photographs were there, not posed ones like Aunt Mary's but Brownie snaps of laughing groups of girls in bucket hats like German helmets and coats to their ankles. They seemed tiny faces covered in clothes. There was a photograph of a young man smoking a cigarette, his hair combed one way by the wind against a background of sea.

'Who is that in the uniform?' the boy asked.

'He's a soldier,' she answered without looking up.

'Oh,' said the boy. 'But who is he?'

'He was a friend of mine before you were born,' she said; then added, 'Do I smell something cooking? Take your stamps and off you go. That's the boy.'

The boy looked at the back of the picture of the man and saw in black spidery ink 'John, Aug '15 Ballintoye'.

'I thought maybe it was Brother Benignus,' he said. She looked at him not answering.

'Was your friend killed in the war?'

At first she said no, but then she changed her mind.

'Perhaps he was,' she said, then smiled. 'You are far too inquisitive. Put it to use and go and see what is for tea. Your mother will need the kettle.' She came over to the bureau and helped tidy the photographs away. Then she locked it and put the keys on the shelf.

'Will you bring me up my tray?'

The boy nodded and left.

It was a Sunday evening, bright and summery. He was doing his homework and his mother was sitting on the carpet in one of her periodic fits of tidying out the drawers of the mahogany sideboard. On one side of her was a heap of paper scraps torn in quarters and bits of rubbish, on the other the useful items that had to be kept. The boy heard the bottom stair creak under Aunt Mary's light footstep. She knocked and put her head round the door and said that she was walking to Devotions. She was dressed in her good coat and hat and was just easing her fingers into her second glove. The boy saw her stop and pat her hair into place before the mirror in the hallway. His mother stretched over and slammed the door shut. It vibrated, then he heard the deeper sound of the outside door closing and her first few steps on the gravelled driveway. He sat for a long time wondering if he would have time or not. Devotions could take anything from twenty minutes to three quarters of an hour, depending on who was saying it.

Ten minutes must have passed, then the boy left his homework and went upstairs and into his aunt's sitting-room. He stood in front of the bureau wondering, then he reached for the keys. He tried several before he got the right one. The desk flap screeched as he pulled it down. He pretended to look at the postcards again in case there were any stamps he had missed. Then he put them away and reached for the bundle of letters. The elastic band was thick and old, brittle almost, and when he took it off its track remained on the wad of letters. He carefully opened one and took out the letter and unfolded it, frail, khaki-coloured.

My dearest Mary [it began] I am so tired I can hardly write to you. I have spent what seems like all day censoring letters (there is a howitzer about 100 yds away firing every 2 minutes) The letters are heart-rending in their attempt to express what they cannot. Some of the men are illiterate, others almost so. I know that they feel as much as we do, yet they do not have the words to express it. That is your job in the schoolroom, to give us generations who can read and write well. They have ...

The boy's eye skipped down the page and over the next. He read the last paragraph.

Mary, I love you as much as ever – more so that we cannot be together. I do not know which is worse, the hurt of this war or being separated from you. Give all my love to Brendan and all at home.

It was signed, scribbled with what he took to be John. He folded the paper carefully into its original creases and put it in the envelope. He opened another.

My love, it is thinking of you that keeps me sane. When I get a moment I open my memories of you as if I were reading. Your long dark hair – I always imagine you wearing the blouse with the tiny roses, the white one that opened down the back – your eyes that said so much without words, the way you lowered your head when I said anything that embarrassed you, and the clean nape of your neck.

The day I think about most was the day we climbed the head at Ballycastle. In a hollow, out of the wind, the air full of pollen and the sound of insects, the grass warm and dry and you lying beside me, your hair undone, between me and the sun. You remember that that was where I first kissed you and the look of disbelief in your eyes that made me laugh afterwards.

It makes me laugh now to see myself savouring these memories standing alone up to my thighs in muck. It is everywhere, two, three feet deep. To walk ten yards leaves you quite breathless.

I haven't time to write more today, so I leave you with my feet in the clay and my head in the clouds. I love you, John.

He did not bother to put the letter back into the envelope but opened another.

My dearest, I am so cold that I find it difficult to keep my hand steady enough to write. You remember when we swam, the last two fingers of your hand went the colour and texture of candles with the cold. Well that is how I am all over. It is almost four days since I had any real sensation in my feet or legs. Everything is frozen. The ground is like steel.

Forgive me telling you this but I feel I have to say it to someone. The worst thing is the dead. They sit or lie frozen in the position they died. You can distinguish them from the living because their faces are the colour of slate. God help us when the thaw comes ... This war is beginning to have an effect on me. I have lost all sense of feeling. The only emotion I have experienced lately is one of anger. Sheer white trembling anger. I have no pity or sorrow for the dead and injured. I thank God it is not me but I am enraged that it had to be them. If I live through this experience I will be a different person.

The only thing that remains constant is my love for you.

Today a man died beside me. A piece of shrapnel had pierced his neck as we were moving under fire. I pulled him into a crater and stayed with him until he died. I watched him choke and then drown in his blood.

I am full of anger which has no direction.

He sorted through the pile and read half of some, all of others. The sun had fallen low in the sky and shone directly into the room on to the pages he was reading, making the paper glare. He selected a letter from the back of the pile and shaded it with his hand as he read.

Dearest Mary, I am writing this to you from my hospital bed. I hope that you were not too worried about not hearing from me. I have been here, so they tell me, for two weeks, and it took another two weeks before I could bring myself to write this letter.

I have been thinking a lot as I lie here about the war and about myself and about you. I do not know how to say this but I feel deeply that I must do something, must sacrifice something to make up for the horror of the past year. In some strange way Christ has spoken to me through the carnage ...

Suddenly the boy heard the creak of the stair and he frantically tried to slip the letter back into its envelope but it crumpled and would not fit. He bundled them all together. He could hear his aunt's familiar puffing on the short stairs to her room. He spread the elastic band wide with his fingers. It snapped and the letters scattered. He pushed them into their pigeon-hole and quickly closed the desk flap. The brass screeched loudly and clicked shut. At that moment his aunt came into the room.

'What are you doing boy?' she snapped.

'Nothing.' He stood with the keys in his hand. She walked to the bureau and opened it. The letters sprung out in an untidy heap.

'You have been reading my letters,' she said quietly. Her mouth was tight with the words and her eyes blazed. The boy could say nothing. She struck him across the side of the face.

'Get out,' she said. 'Get out of my room.'

The boy, the side of his face stinging and red, put the keys on the table on his way out. When he reached the door she called to him. He stopped, his hand on the handle.

'You are dirt,' she hissed, 'and always will be dirt. I shall remember this till the day I die.'

Even though it was a warm evening, there was a fire in the large fireplace. His mother had asked him to light it so that she could clear out Aunt Mary's stuff. The room could then be his study, she said. She came in and seeing him at the table said, 'I hope I'm not disturbing you.'

'No.'

She took the keys from her pocket, opened the bureau and began burning papers and cards. She glanced quickly at each one before she flicked it on to the fire.

'Who was Brother Benignus?' he asked.

His mother stopped sorting and said, 'I don't know. Your aunt kept herself very much to herself. She got books from him through the post occasionally. That much I do know.'

She went on burning the cards. They built into strata, glowing red and black. Now and again she broke up the pile with the poker, sending showers of sparks up the chimney. He saw her come to the letters. She took off the elastic band and put it to one side with the useful things and began dealing the envelopes into the fire. She opened one and read quickly through it, then threw it on top of the burning pile.

'Mama,' he said.

'Yes?'

'Did Aunt Mary say anything about me?'

'What do you mean?'

'Before she died – did she say anything?'

'Not that I know of – the poor thing was too far gone to speak, God rest her.' She went on burning, lifting the corners of the letters with the poker to let the flames underneath them.

When he felt a hardness in his throat, he put his head down on his books. Tears came into his eyes for the first time since she had died, and he cried silently into the crook of his arm for the woman who had been his maiden aunt, his teller of tales, that she might forgive him.

Dear Parents, I'm Working for the EEC!

GILLMAN NOONAN

Pensionskuhhaltung.

Peter had been going great guns, and now this word. The more he looked at it the more it seemed to stretch away in front of him like a sticky thread of thought, defying his efforts to wrap it up nice and tidy in a few words of his own language. Yet for the past hour he had been able to identify fully with that word. Indeed all morning he had seen himself as an utterly malleable length of human tissue capable of being laid flat in a folder or wrapped around the telephone with no perceptible discomfort to the psyche. Some mental linchpin had snapped and he was floundering in a maze of words that were all the more infuriating because they retained a certain surface familiarity. Like this one.

Pensionskuhhaltung.

He should know it but his mind was a blank. Lighting a cigarette he paced the office. It wasn't an office at all but a cubicle among many others in this building adjacent to the main E E C complex on the Rond-Point Schuman. Worse still, it was one that connected two open-plan sections, so people were continually passing through. In his first weeks he had often smiled at the passers-through, particularly at the young women, apologizing for them for distracting him from his job of keeping the Common Market translating its business smoothly. By now he had cultivated a bleak stare over his glasses, a rictus of deliberate vacuity that finally intimidated even his heartiest colleagues. All except Vachy whom nothing could intimidate. After two years of cubicle life, Vachy was the only one who was still real for him. She was an enormous Belgian who was always pregnant and whose specialty was cattle. She knew everything about cattle; hence the name she was eventually given though no one could remember by whom. In Peter's first weeks when none of the dictionaries seemed to help, it was Vachy who had stood patiently by as he stumbled after his documentary herds, guiding them from German through the fence of her own language into English. Making a game of it he would say, *'Mutterkuh?'*, feasting his eyes on her magnificent breasts. *'Vache allaitand,'* she would sigh. 'In English?' 'Suckler, I believe.' At which they would burst out laughing. Yes, Vachy would know but she wasn't in today. Peter sat down again.

Pensionskuhhaltung.

Blank. That often happened after hours of translating. Going great and then the word cat would become as bizarre as an unfinished run in Scrabble. For two hours the smooth flow of the State Secretary's views on how to save the semi-viable farmer in sub-alpine Bavaria, and then the skein of gum that wrapped itself around the eyes oozed into the ears, dangled the State Secretary like a puppet uttering nonsense rhymes. *One other alternative would be ...*

Pensionskuhhaltung.

Period. No elaboration out of which could be gleaned some satisfactory explanation. No nothing. It had been a fairly easy text up to this point. Peter had been translating away even while his mind wandered, even while he worried about Jenny and Ted. Now impasse.

Pension was a pension or guest house. Was the State Secretary suggesting to the Bavarian Farmers' Union that cows should be kept in boarding houses? Or that rural pensions should take in ruminants in the off season?

He could probably type in anything and no one would be the wiser. The Secretary's speech was now ten months old, and it was unlikely that anyone would read it. Except Bewell, of course. Bewell, who spent his days waiting to pounce on other people's mistakes, would come running to him with an enormous smirk to tell him what a blunder he had made. But usually Peter never even saw again, corrected or uncorrected, what went into his out-tray. His work disappeared into the honey-comb of the EEC, possibly to be checked vaguely by some-one but most likely to be duplicated and fed further into the channels of documentary afterbirth, eventually to be dumped by someone of supreme common sense and forgotten. This was cattle time and Peter thought a lot about that animal's several stomachs. Then the EEC building at Schuman took on the aspect of an enormous ruminant that even at night continued to rumble and burp with months of undigested fodder, causing the cleaning women to look up and wonder.

Pensionskuhhaltung.

'Moo,' he said to no one in particular but nothing happened. He could consult with Bewell of course, but at the present time Peter had a genuine hate-relationship with that expert. Not only did Bewell consider all Irishmen to be mad and thus re-grettably at odds with the efficiency of such a vast institution as the EEC, but just then he was living with Peter while he looked for a more suitable flat; and he had moved in only be-cause he knew that Jenny had moved out of Peter's life into that of a rich Belgian businessman called van Pee, for God's sake. Even if Peter had possessed seven stomachs at that moment, all of them would have violently rebelled at the thought of asking Mr Bewell.

Pensionskuhhaltung.

The world right now was a pretty grey place for Peter. Two years previously he had come to Brussels with Jenny. Between them they had £100 in capital and lots of enthusiasm. They had made the break from wearisome teaching jobs and felt great. On the spot, it hadn't taken Peter long to land a job with the EEC as a translator. 'Dear parents,' he wrote home full of joy, 'I'm working for the EEC!' Then Jenny, who found a job with an American company, chanced on a lovely little flat in the rue de Dublin, and there they had lived for a whole year in great harmony. They had gone on weekends to Amsterdam and Paris and thought that Brussels was a great place, a city that paid you well and didn't kill you.

The strain had only begun to tell in the past few months. They had found less and less to say to each other. Both had

begun to realize that for all the good money they were in a
rut, Jenny with a purely functional secretarial job, he with a
seemingly endless herd of documentary animals that always
seemed to be going astray. No sooner had he nicely tucked
them away under some new EEC policy on agrarian structures
when, a week or a month later, they would be milling about on
the road again, lowing for yet another expert drover to smack
them on in some direction. His interest in cattle or indeed in
the problems of the EEC had by now sunk to below zero. On
the way to work in the mornings he had begun to think a lot
about the mountains of produce of which the European con-
sumer, a not exactly emaciated creature, seemed to need millions of tons to survive. In the flat he had worked off his depression in silence, and it had finally come as no surprise when
Jenny told him she was leaving. They had become people
standing in silence at the tram station not knowing which
direction to take. What Jenny hoped to achieve with van Pee,
for God's sake – Peter saw him once with her: thirtyish, sporty,
'cultured' – he hardly dared imagine. Perhaps he was an excellent fellow and a great companion. Peter didn't trust his judgement any more in such matters. That he himself seemed to
have become a hollow man at the age of twenty-eight was sufficient food for thought.

A far more acute problem at present was Ted. Since Ted, as
a young student, had been in Paris during the 1968 riots, he
had never looked back as a revolutionary, anarchist, misan-
thrope, freak – you name it. He was ejected from Trinity for
'Un-Irish Activities', but came in then for a small legacy
which he used to open a bar in Ibiza. This he proceeded to
drink dry himself, ably supported by a colony of hippies. Then
he worked in Switzerland for a while on the q.t. in a hotel –
under the foreign worker *plafond* at the time he shouldn't have
been there – until he was finally discovered and uncere-
moniously ousted from that country. After various wanderings
he gravitated to Brussels, where he lived with Peter and Jenny
for a few months before teaming up with Doris, a skinny
French girl with frizzy hair and wild eyes. Peter thought Doris
was the dippiest creature he had ever met and a good match

for Ted. He gave Ted about three months to survive before becoming *persona non grata* in Belgium, but in some perverse way Ted had hung on, earning his bread with this and that and learning French at an enormous rate. Doris would have been an incentive of course. Hardly speaking a word of English herself, her French patois was a challenge to any master of the language.

Again in some perverse way Ted's political activities – centred somewhere in the back streets of Louvain – never seemed to get him into trouble. It was when Peter was beginning to think that Ted had blown himself out after all and was coming around to a less militant way of thinking that the thing with the dogs started, and that was proving to be vastly more dangerous now because it involved theft and, worse still, Peter himself.

Peter thought he could pinpoint the origin of the malaise. One day Ted had arrived in his cubicle and, while glaring at the administrative fodder passing in and out and sniffing the air as though it contained some noxious gas, had told of the woman and her dog. She had been a typically well-dressed woman of middle age sitting on a park bench and holding in her hand a chihuahua no bigger than a rat and wearing a knitted pullover. After a while she had allowed the dog to run around, and the first thing he did was his ah-ah on the clean flags. *'Il a déposé ses crottes sur le trottoir,'* said Ted with relish. From then on, whenever Ted spoke about the dogs he lapsed into French as though that language alone could do justice to the scene.

Under normal circumstances the dog's lack of decorum wouldn't have been very grave, but apparently it happened to be a day when the other well-dressed representatives of the bourgeoisie sitting around had seemed to take exception, so much so that they all stared at the woman until, unnerved finally, she had got up and with a piece of cardboard or something removed the *crottes*. Not only that: whether or not it was that the bourgies hadn't expected her to go to such lengths to expiate the crime, they at any rate continued to stare at her until, unnerved still further, she had taken a Kleenex out of her bag, gathered her chihuahua into her fist and actually wiped its bottom.

Ted had been so stunned by the whole affair he had apparently sat there for a whole hour in the cold in utter paralysis. Then he had begun to laugh, so berserkly that people were making a wide detour around him. The incident related, all went well for a few weeks until Ted began to call around more and more often and talk of dogs, especially those of the Brussels variety which, though possibly similar to the dogs of many other cities in *coupe* and *toilettage*, had taken on for him a fascination of absolute intensity. It was then that Peter noticed the change in Ted's face when he launched into the subject of animals wearing *manteaux*, *imperméables* and even *souliers*. The skin grew taut and pale around the nose and the mouth widened in a leer that became almost a snarl.

Then one day Ted telephoned and said he had overheard one bourgie woman advising another concerning the pup she intended to buy: '*Assurez-vous, madame, de la présence des deux testicules!*' He had repeated this several times on the phone, going off into hysterical laughter that sent shivers down Peter's spine. He had tried to reason with Ted saying, you know, what the hell, let them have their fun, is it any different from your mother's six cats and so on, but he soon realized that Ted wasn't listening to a word he was saying any more. He was hooked. The *salon du chien*, the *toilettage* of Brussels' dogs, had come to symbolize for him all that was wrong in the world.

Shortly afterwards the thieving started and this soon reached alarming proportions. Ted would apparently haunt the *salons* and then stalk the women who appeared with freshly tailored dogs until an opportunity arose to whip the animal's tackle. A dog tied up outside a supermarket was easy prey. Slipping a *manteau* off a poodle's back in a crowded tram was a more difficult operation, but Ted and Doris had perfected their technique. While Doris engaged the woman in conversation Ted got to work with nimble fingers.

As time went on, Peter found himself functioning most unwillingly as a kind of copy-taker receiving the details of each

theft. By now he was afraid to pick up the phone in case it
was Ted giving through the facts of the latest scoop *en style
télégraphique*. In a deadpan voice he would announce: '*Manteau, vert, caniche, nom Prince, taille 50 cm, modèle Lorenzo.
Au revoir!*' An hour or a day later it would be: '*Allo, allo!
Imperméable, tartan, pékinois, nom Pou-pou, chienne, taille
naine, modèle Paul St Jean, au revoir!*'

Peter's own dangerous involvement dated from the night he
found two *imperméables* and a tiny *pull à col roulé* stuffed into
his letter box. Jenny was furious. It was about the time she had
begun to have drinks and meals with van Pee, and that gentleman would certainly not approve. There was danger for all
concerned because the rash of thieving had become news. The
police, the dog tailors, had been alerted. A Brussels columnist
had written facetiously:

Gardez la culotte de votre chien!

Police and *couturiers pour chiens* are baffled by a wave of dog-
accessory thefts presently sweeping through Brussels. Quicker than
it takes a terrier to shake his tail he is being *dénudé* of his trousers.

Detectives are working on the theory that it is a prank, but the
possibility exists that a person with a *cerveau brûlé* is at large in
our city. People are advised not to leave their dogs unguarded outside shops or business premises, or if they are obliged to do so
they should undress them before entering. Any information concerning persons behaving suspiciously in the proximity of *chiens
bien habillés* should contact the police. *A noter:* Accessories of all
breeds are being stolen, but those of smaller dogs such as poodles,
chihuahuas and pekingese are favoured targets of the cunning thief
or thieves. Those who own a *griffon bruxellois* should be especially
on their guard.

It would all be such fun if it weren't so lamentably serious.
You just cannot go around stealing things, even such hideous
symbols of social degeneracy as dogs' raincoats and leggings.
Nor can you jeopardize your friend's clean record with the
police by stuffing the stolen objects into his letter box.

'Problems?' said Bewell, romping through the cubicle.

'Oh, no. Just thinking.'

'Don't buy anything on your way home this evening. I'm making a stew.' He poked his head around the door again and said, beaming, 'An Irish stew!'

Peter almost threw the dictionary after him. Both had begun to behave like arthritic old women in the flat. Jenny's lingering presence was unsettling. Peter realized from listening to Bewell talk about her that he was a bit in love with her himself. They seemed to vie with each other tidying and cleaning as though Jenny, whose sense of order was highly developed, were about to walk in on them at any moment.

Pensionskuhhaltung.

It occurred to him now what it meant, or must mean, but it was too late. A whole herd of cows had broken into the pension demanding rooms. One pounded up the stairs spattering her shit all over the carpet, bumped open the door of a honey-mooning couple's bedroom and stood looking at them where they lay in shock and disarray on the bed, long gobs of saliva dropping from its sorrowful mouth. The brave husband franti-cally grabbed the quilt, sprang over the animal's back and, standing naked and beautifully poised on the landing, feinted and goaded, shouting: 'Vacha! Vacha!'

Downstairs another cow was arguing with the landlady, say-ing: 'What'cha mean you've no room? Six of us could fit into this stall alone, couldn't we, girls?' All the other cows said: 'Mooo.'

Peter reached for the phone and dialled Vachy's home num-ber. She was there, suckling her latest.

'*Mon petit chou*, are you not feeling well?' she asked after he had babbled on for a while about animals prancing around in his brain, dogs' tailors and Bewell.

'No, Vachy,' he said, calming himself with a cigarette. 'I'm not feeling well. I've been sitting here for an hour wondering why I'm sitting here at all. Vachy, I see nothing but a blank in front of me. I'll be twenty-nine next month and I've lost my faith in everything, in happiness, in the future, in the Common Market. I feel it's a bloated belly and I'm one of a billion ticks feeding on it.'

'*Écoute*, Peter ...'

'But, Vachy, I *have* lost my faith!'

'In me too?'

'No, Vachy, you're about all I have now.'

'*Alors*, that is something, is it not?'

'Yes, but Vachy, you're married and you're having babies all the time and you cannot concern yourself with me.'

'I am here for you now, am I not?'

'Yes, and I really appreciate that.'

'Now, you must not take things too seriously. We cannot change things very much. *C'est le cours des choses humaines*, is it not?'

'I know, but Bewell ...'

'Just forget Bewell!'

'And Ted ...'

'Forget Ted!'

'I can't! He keeps ringing me up. Twice already today he has rung and said, "*Auto da fé*, five o'clock!" I'm scared he's going to do something really bad this time.'

'How many things did he steal today?'

'I don't know about today, but yesterday he had his *coup suprême* when he stole a *chandail* from a police inspector's wife!'

Vachy roared with laughter. She must have bobbled the teat out of the infant's mouth because it began to scream.

'You come to me tonight, eh?' she said. 'I am making *crêpes*. You like my *crêpes*, don't you?'

'Of course, Vachy. You know I treasure them. But I don't know if it's pancakes I need right now.'

'You come and we'll talk,' she replied in her motherly way and hung up.

Peter closed his eyes, propped his forehead against his hands and tried to keep out the lowing babble. Now two enormous cows in Bavarian dirndls were sitting cross-legged on a bed licking ice-cream, their udders hanging down obscenely. '*Kuh!*' said one, '*die Pension ist ganz grosse Klasse, was?*' '*Prima*,' said the other, reaching for her Kleenex. '*Und gar nicht so teuer, was?*' '*Das Essen scheint mir auch wirklich wiederkäuerlich zu sein.*' '*Moo, es geht.*' They finished their ice-cream and, burping and rumbling, settled back to have it all over again.

Outside on the landing the young husband lay gored and dying. 'Water!' he gasped. His bride and the cow, shaved now and rosy-smooth like an enormous skinned rabbit, were lying on the bed fondling, while downstairs in a back room two young heifers from near Blessington were sharing a bucket of Guinness. 'Jasus, Consolata,' said one, 'I'm full of gas.' 'It's the porter, Penelope,' said the other, licking the froth off her nose. 'The Belgians fill a very flat bucket.' 'We should never have left Blessington,' sighed Consolata. 'It was the money,' said her friend. 'We were hornswoggled into it.' Consolata leaned over heavily on her haunch and farted. 'Oh, moo, sweet Taurus, I'm full of gas.' 'Everything is full of gas here,' sniffed Penelope. 'Especially the bulls. Did ya see that Frenchie gaping at us over the gate a while back? Prime beef and no balls, I'd say. To think that our fine, lean-haunched, cultured young Irish bullocks is going to turn out like that fella.' 'We should have kept far away from the Market,' moaned Consolata. 'Now it's a fate accomplee.' 'Watch the language now, girl,' said Penelope, 'or the fucking landlady will have us out on our udders ...'

The phone rang.

'I'm not going to answer,' said Peter.

But it rang and rang. He lifted the receiver.

'*Auto da fé*, five o'clock!' Click.

Peter got up and began to circle the table, placing his feet with great care to avoid certain cracks and patterns on the floor. They were all going mad. Ted had cracked, Bewell was mad in the way utterly rational and humourless Englishmen were mad, Vachy was mad to be having babies who would go mad later themselves, that pretty new girl passing through the cubicle was mad. 'Mooo,' he said to her and she smiled. She probably thought it was Irish for hallo.

A young man appeared on the roundabout below carrying a suitcase, an easel and an object in the shape of a large cone. It was Ted. Peter's first impulse was to fling open the window – he was only on the third floor – and shout to him. But suddenly he knew that anything he did would not matter now. The phone rang. It would be Doris.

'*Auto da fé*,' she cried. '*Il commence à l'instant!*'

'I know,' said Peter, and replaced the receiver.

It was after five. Behind him as he stood at the window many people were leaving the office. He saw them emerge on to the open space, heading for their cars or the tram station. Ted had set up his easel, deposited the suitcase and the other object, and was quite slowly and deliberately undressing. Peter spotted Doris running across the street from the direction of the garage where she had gone to phone. Ted was down to his briefs. A few people were already standing around, a little distance away. One little old lady wasn't quite sure whether to continue on her way and ignore the spectacle, but when she saw Ted slipping off his last dark red vestige of clothing she stood rooted to the spot, her umbrella pointing in front of her as though drawn to the naked body by a magnetic force beyond her control.

Ted opened the suitcase and took from it what Peter immediately recognized as a lot of dogs' clothes strapped together. This he slipped over his head like an enormous poncho. There were other things, collars and bells, which he attached to his arms or tied around his neck. Before he reached for the cone, which was of course a loudhailer, a large crowd had gathered around him. Peter opened the window. Above the noise of the traffic Ted's voice was barely audible. He was singing in chanson style, and while he sang he walked mincingly up and down, wiggling his bottom.

> '*Je suis la coqueluche des fem-mes*
> I'm never tailored quite the sa-me ...'

Then he began to address the crowd. Snatches were intelligible to Peter whenever he turned in his direction.

'*Je suis de haute lignée.* Wouldn't you know it, madame? *Ce n'est pas la coupe continentale* ... That's just a lot of *crottes. Moi, j'ai la coupe capitaliste!* And underneath my lovely shift (here he opened the flaps of his poncho) *la coupe socialiste! Voilà!* An international prick! *Le vrai socialiste! Il est beau, non?* You like to shake hands with a real socialist, mesdemoiselles?' (and here he offered himself to a group of young girls who fled from him).

A police siren wailed somewhere behind the E E C building. The people were now standing two and three deep. The easel had toppled over and was trampled on. The police car turned into the roundabout. Ted's voice rose to a scream.

'*Et si vous voulez vous assurer de la présence des deux testicules ... Voilà!*' (Again he allowed the flaps to swing open) 'I am the greatest! *Je suis conforme au standard, au votre standard, mesdames et messieurs!* I am unbelievably full of exclusive dog shit ...'

The three burly policemen didn't manage to catch him at once. He darted in and out among the people, spinning them around, moving towards Doris who flung herself viciously at one policeman only to be bowled aside like a skittle. But it was only a question of time before they dragged him off. A few seconds later the crowd, many shaking their heads, dispersed.

When Peter went down several minutes later, Doris was walking around in a circle, her head bent. She had wanted to be arrested too. Now she was reliving the whole scene, finding words for it to tell her friends and make of it a legend. On the ground was a muddied blow-up of starving Africans. Underneath, beside a painted poodle wearing an elaborate outfit, Ted had written in large letters '*LA VIE DU CHIEN!*' The police had taken away the easel and everything else.

Approaching the girl, Peter said, 'Doris?' She looked at him but her eyes were unfocused. Whatever world she was seeing, he had no part of it. All at once he envied her, as he envied Ted his madness which was the kind of sanity the world needed. But how pitiful it was! The people had laughed, shaking their heads. Had any even seen the picture?

Utter emptiness took possession of Peter. Where should he go? Certainly not to the flat and Bewell's stew. Vachy's pancakes had lost their attraction. It was not talk he wanted. He had a sudden desperate longing for Jenny, for the time when he delayed touching her white nakedness and she waited, waited, smiling at him. But Jenny too was gone from him. They all, Ted and Doris included, seemed to belong to some definite dimension of thought. Only he was the true outsider because he was neither in nor out. Looking up at the huge shining starfish of the E E C, along the row of deserted offices, he saw a man silhouetted at a window. Was he thinking the same? He would hardly say. The in-and-outers were taciturn people.

At the door of the Drum Peter hesitated. A beer would be nice. But he should really go and find out what had happened to Ted. Perhaps he would need money. Yes, he had money to give! A murmur of talk came from the warm within. He opened the door a crack and saw some of his colleagues standing at the bar. The pretty girl was with them. Yes, inside was good. He poked his head in and was greeted boisterously. But he only smiled and closed the door again.

Standing in the dark hallway, he wondered vaguely what he should do with the soiled and crumpled poster he still held in his hand.

Acknowledgements

For permission to reprint the stories specified we are indebted to: The Ulster Council of the Gaelic League for 'The Cards of the Gambler', translated by Benedict Kiely from *The Stories of Johnny Shemisin*: The Talbot Press Ltd for 'St Brigid's Flood' by Stephen Gwynn: John Farquharson Ltd for 'Lisheen Races, Second-Hand' from *The Experiences of an Irish R. M.* by Somerville and Ross (Longman Ltd): Jonathan Cape Ltd for 'The Tent'and 'The Conger Eel' from *The Short Stories of Liam O'Flaherty* by Liam O'Flaherty: Sean O'Faolain and A. P. Watt Ltd for 'Lovers of the Lake' from *Selected Stories* by Sean O'Faolain (Jonathan Cape Ltd): A. D. Peters Ltd for 'The Luceys' from *Travellers Samples and Other Stories* by Frank O'Connor (Macmillan London Ltd): Jonathan Cape Ltd and the Estate of Elizabeth Bowen for 'The Cat Jumps' from *The Cat Jumps and Other Stories* by Elizabeth Bowen: Constable Ltd for 'A Memory' from *A Memory and Other Stories* by Mary Lavin: Michael McLaverty for his story 'The Game Cock' from *The Game Cock and Other Stories* (Jonathan Cape Ltd): The Poolbeg Press Ltd for 'The American Apple' from *The More We Are Together* by Seamus de Faoite: Julia O'Faolain and A. P. Watt Ltd for 'First Conjugation' from *Melancholy Baby and Other Stories* by Julia O'Faolain (Constable Ltd): Mrs Katherine Kavanagh for 'Fairyland' from *The Green Fool* by Patrick Kavanagh (MacGibbon & Kee Ltd): The Talbot Press Ltd for 'They Also Serve' by Mervyn Wall: A. D. Peters Ltd for 'A Meeting in Middle Age' from *The Day We Got Drunk on Cake* by William Trevor (The Bodley Head Ltd): Richard Scott Simon Ltd for 'Desert Island' by Terence de Vere White from *Winter's Tales from Ireland* (Gill & Macmillan Ltd): Granada Publishing Ltd for 'Meles Vulgaris' from *At Night All Cats are Grey* by Patrick Boyle: Bryan MacMahon and A. P. Watt Ltd for 'Ballintierna in the Morning' from *The Lion Tamer and Other Stories* by Bryan MacMahon: John Calder Ltd for 'Lebensraum' from *Felo de Se* by Aidan Higgins: Michael J. Murphy for his story 'The Return of the Boy': A. D. Peters Ltd for 'The Eagles and the Trumpets' from *The Trusting and the Maimed* by James Plunkett (Hutchinson Ltd): Curtis Brown Ltd for 'Mr Sing My Heart's Delight' from *A Saucer of Larks* by Brian Friel (Gollancz Ltd): John McGahern for 'Gold Watch'. Copyright © John McGahern. Originally published in the *New Yorker*, 1980: A. D. Peters Ltd for 'A Cut above the Rest' from *Antiquities* by Val Mulkerns (André Deutsch Ltd): A. D. Peters Ltd for 'That Dark

Accomplice' from *Death of a Chieftain and Other Stories* by John Montague (MacGibbon & Kee): John Jordan for his story 'Let the Old Cry' (The Irish Press Ltd): A. D. Peters Ltd for 'The Bracelet' from *Dance the Dance* by Tom Macintyre (Faber & Faber Ltd): Weidenfeld & Nicolson Ltd for 'That Creature' from *A Scandalous Woman and Other Stories* by Edna O'Brien: The Poolbeg Press Ltd for 'Such Good Friends' from *The Lady with the Red Shoes* by Ita Daly: Neil Jordan and Anthony Sheil Associates Ltd for 'Sand' from *A Night in Tunisia and Other Stories* by Neil Jordan: Mrs Eithne Strong for her story 'Red Jelly' from *Winter's Tales from Ireland No. 2* (Gill & Macmillan): The Blackstaff Press Ltd for 'Secrets' from *Secrets and Other Stories* by Bernard MacLaverty: Gillman Noonan and Anthony Sheil Ltd for 'Dear Parents, I'm Working for the EEC!' from *A Sexual Relationship and Other Stories* (Poolbeg Press Ltd).

He just wanted a decent book to read ...

Not too much to ask, is it? It was in 1935 when Allen Lane, Managing Director of Bodley Head Publishers, stood on a platform at Exeter railway station looking for something good to read on his journey back to London. His choice was limited to popular magazines and poor-quality paperbacks – the same choice faced every day by the vast majority of readers, few of whom could afford hardbacks. Lane's disappointment and subsequent anger at the range of books generally available led him to found a company – and change the world.

'We believed in the existence in this country of a vast reading public for intelligent books at a low price, and staked everything on it'
Sir Allen Lane, 1902–1970, founder of Penguin Books

The quality paperback had arrived – and not just in bookshops. Lane was adamant that his Penguins should appear in chain stores and tobacconists, and should cost no more than a packet of cigarettes.

Reading habits (and cigarette prices) have changed since 1935, but Penguin still believes in publishing the best books for everybody to enjoy. We still believe that good design costs no more than bad design, and we still believe that quality books published passionately and responsibly make the world a better place.

So wherever you see the little bird – whether it's on a piece of prize-winning literary fiction or a celebrity autobiography, political tour de force or historical masterpiece, a serial-killer thriller, reference book, world classic or a piece of pure escapism – you can bet that it represents the very best that the genre has to offer.

Whatever you like to read – trust Penguin.